Bedded for His Pleasure

HEIDI RICE
KATE HARDY
TRISH WYLIE

D1099655

Published in Great Britain 2013
by Mills & Boon, an imprint of Harlequin (UK) Limited,
Eton House, 18-24 Paradise Road, Richmond, Surrey TW9 1SR

BEDDED FOR HIS PLEASURE
© by Harlequin Enterprises II B.V./S.à.r.l 2013

Bedded by a Bad Boy, In the Gardener's Bed and *The Return of the Rebel* were first published in Great Britain by Harlequin (UK) Limited.

Bedded by a Bad Boy © Heidi Rice 2007
In the Gardener's Bed © Pamela Brooks 2007
The Return of the Rebel © Trish Wylie 2007

ISBN: 978 0 263 90561 8
ebook ISBN: 978 1 472 00134 4

05-0813

Harlequin (UK) policy is to use papers that are natural, renewable and recyclable products and made from wood grown in sustainable forests. The logging and manufacturing processes conform to the legal environmental regulations of the country of origin.

Printed and bound in Spain
by Blackprint CPI, Barcelona

BEDDED BY
A BAD BOY

BY
HEIDI RICE

Heidi Rice was born and bred and still lives in London. She has two boys who love to bicker, a wonderful husband who, luckily for everyone, has loads of patience, and a supportive and ever-growing British/French/Irish/American family. As much as Heidi adores the 'Big Smoke', she also loves America, and every two years or so she and her best friend leave hubby and kids behind and *Thelma and Louise* it across the States for a couple of weeks (although they always leave out the driving off a cliff bit). She's been a film buff since her early teens, and a romance junkie for almost as long. She indulged her first love by being a film reviewer for ten years. Then a few years ago she decided to spice up her life by writing romance. Discovering the fantastic sisterhood of romance writers (both published and unpublished) in Britain and America made it a wild and wonderful journey to her first Mills & Boon® novel. This was Heidi's first book! Heidi loves to hear from readers; you can e-mail her at heidi@heidi-rice.com or visit her website, www.heidi-rice.com.

To my best mate, Catri, for all those Navajo
frybread moments. May we have many more.
And to my husband, Rob, for helping make
my dream come true.

I hope yours does, too.

CHAPTER ONE

'WHOEVER he is, he's completely naked,' Jessie Connor said as quietly as possible. Not easy with the heat flaring in her cheeks and her heartbeat pounding like a sledgehammer in her ears.

The most magnificent male specimen she had ever seen stood less than fifteen yards away. Stark naked. Thank goodness, he had his back to her, or her heart would have stopped beating altogether.

Dark tangles of wet hair flowed down to touch broad shoulders. Roped with muscle, his bronzed skin glistened in the afternoon sunlight as water dripped off his powerful physique and onto the white stone tiles of the pool patio. Oh, my.

Jessie edged back. She could feel the warm, weathered wood of her sister Ali's Long Island home through the thin cotton of her blue sundress, but it was nothing compared to the heat throbbing low in her belly.

'Who is he? Do you recognise him?' Ali hissed next to her ear.

Jessie stared at her sister, huddled beside her behind the house. She took in Ali's worried frown and her round figure, distended in pregnancy. 'Well, I can't be absolutely positive from this angle, but I don't think I know him.'

'Move over, I'm taking a look.' Elbowing Jessie aside, Ali

peered round the corner. After getting what Jessie considered more than a necessary eyeful for a married woman, Ali shuffled back. Her face had turned a vivid shade of scarlet. 'Wow, that bum's almost as gorgeous as Linc's.'

Jessie decided to ignore Ali's extremely inappropriate comment about her husband. 'Yes, but did you recognise it?'

'Of course not, I'm a married woman.'

'Now she remembers,' Jessie muttered.

'We've got to get out of here and call Linc.'

'Don't be daft. We can tackle him ourselves.'

Ali's eyebrows shot up. 'We most certainly cannot. I'm nearly eight months pregnant and he's enormous. Did you see those shoulders?'

'Yes, I did. Among other things.'

'You can't go out there. This is America. He could have a gun.'

'I'd like to know where he's got that hidden,' Jessie replied, her indignation rising. 'He's trespassing and I intend to tell him so. How dare he just come in and use the pool as if he owned the place?' Jessie glanced down at her sister's rounded belly. 'You better stay here.' She looked at her watch. 'Linc's due back with Emmy any minute.'

'What if he attacks you?' Ali's furious whisper sounded desperate.

'Don't worry, I've got a plan.'

Ali's brows set in a grim line. 'I don't think I want to hear this.'

'It worked a treat for Bruce Willis in *Die Hard 2*.'

'Oh, for goodness' sake!'

'Shh.' Jessie pressed a finger to her lips. 'He may be built but he's probably not deaf.' Taking a steadying breath, she leaned back around the corner and took another peek at their trespasser.

Jessie's teeth tugged on her bottom lip. Ali was probably right. They shouldn't approach him. But ever since they had returned from her sister's hospital appointment and spotted the powerful black motorcycle sitting in the driveway, the sizzle of adrenaline had been surging through Jessie's veins.

Impulsiveness was her worse trait. Hadn't Toby, her stuffy ex-fiancé, told her as much the whole two years they'd been going out? 'If only you were as reckless in bed as you are out of it,' he'd shouted at her during their final titanic row six months ago.

Jessie squinted as the sun sparkled off the surface of the pool. She watched as the stranger towelled himself dry with an old T-shirt. The familiar anger at Toby's insults flashed through her. Well, Toby could take his opinion and shove it in a place where the sun didn't shine. She wasn't reckless—or frigid, for that matter—it had just taken her a while to realise that Toby Collins wasn't the Mr Right she'd spent her whole life looking for. He hadn't needed her the way she'd thought he had. While she'd been dreaming of making a home, having children, building a family together, Toby had been fantasising about having a wildcat in bed and a mouse out of it. It still infuriated her that it had taken her two long years to figure it out.

The trespasser pulled a pair of jeans over his long legs. Jessie ignored the quick stab of disappointment as his beautiful bum disappeared behind faded denim.

Men! Jessie clenched her teeth. She simply was not going to let this arrogant stranger get away with his outrageous behaviour.

She toed off her sandals, her mind made up. 'Right, I'm off,' she whispered to Ali. 'You better go back to the car and call Linc.'

'Don't... Jess...'

Neatly sidestepping her sister's grabbing fingers, Jessie crept out from behind the safety of the building. Time to teach their trespasser a lesson.

Monroe Latimer fastened the threadbare jeans and stuck his hands into the pockets to straighten them. The tips of his fingers touched the old letter he'd been carrying around for over a year. He pulled out the heavily creased envelope. A drop of water slapped onto the paper, smudging the Key West address of his old parole officer, Jerry Myers. He raked the dripping hair off his forehead. Sighing, he wondered for about the hundredth time what had made him keep the damn thing for so long. And what had possessed him to take that exit off the interstate when he'd spotted the sign to the Hamptons this morning.

Curiosity. Monroe shook his head—just the sort of impulse he was usually smart enough to avoid. He pulled the letter out of its envelope and scanned the contents, though he knew them by heart.

Dear Monroe,

You don't know me, but my name's Alison Latimer and I'm your sister-in-law. I'm married to your older brother Lincoln. Linc's been trying to track you down for a long time now. I'm sending this letter to Jerry Myers, in the hope he will pass it on to you.

Linc and I have been married for five years. We're based in London, but we spend July to September every year in our summer house on Oceanside Drive, East Hampton, Long Island.

Please, Monroe, come and visit us. Linc and I would love you to stay for a while. From what Jerry tells me, Linc's the only family you have left. I know you haven't seen Linc in over twenty years, but he never stopped looking for you.

Family is important, Monroe.

Please come. Love Ali

Good thing the first line of the return address had been rubbed off the back of the letter months ago. He might have been dumb enough to go knocking on his brother's door, if he'd had the right house number. Of course, the minute he got to Oceanside Drive, he knew he shouldn't have come. Guys like him only came to neighbourhoods like this one if they were doing yard work.

Monroe crumpled up the letter, shoved it back in his pocket. At least now he could throw it away. He'd seen the way his brother and sister-in-law lived. No way was he ever going to follow up on their invitation. He didn't belong here. He had his Harley, his battered box of oil paints, spare clothes and a bedroll, and he had himself. That was all he needed; that was all he was ever going to need.

Alison Latimer was wrong. Family wasn't important. Not to him. He'd been free to do what he pleased, when he pleased, for the last fourteen years and that was the way he intended to keep it. Family was just another kind of prison and he'd had enough of that to last him a lifetime.

He pushed away the familiar bitterness. He could hear the rustle of a sea breeze through the flowerbed by the pool. Angling his head, he caught the fresh perfume of sweet summer blooms mixed with the chemical scent of chlorine—and grinned. Well, hell, at least he'd gotten a swim in a ritzy pool in one of the most beautiful homes he'd ever seen.

He'd been turning the Harley around, ready to head back to the interstate, when his artist's eye had spotted the wood and glass structure rising out of the sand dunes. Situated on its own at the end of the chunk of land that jutted out into the Atlantic Ocean, the modern structure had seemed to beckon him. Like all the other houses in the area, the grounds were surrounded by deer fencing and a high privet hedge, but Monroe had spotted the edge of the pool, winking at him in the sunlight as the bike had purred over the rise and down into the driveway. He'd been grimy and dog-tired, had been on the bike since daybreak in Maryland and he still had another few hours to go until he hit New York. The place was hidden from the road. He'd pressed the door buzzer to make sure no one was home and a quick check of the security system had told him it wasn't armed. So he'd boosted himself over the main gate and enjoyed the luxury of an afternoon swim. The thrill he recalled so well from his childhood of doing something forbidden on a lazy summer afternoon had been a nice fringe benefit.

Better hit the road now, though. The owners could return any minute and call the cops. With his record, it wouldn't go easy on him if he got caught trespassing. Time to move on.

Keeping her breathing slow and steady, Jessie tiptoed across the patio. She stopped dead when her trespasser shoved whatever it was he'd been staring at back into his pocket. When he didn't turn around, but reached for his T-shirt, she let go of the breath caught in her throat.

Humming some tuneless melody, he sat down on the sun-drenched tiles, rubbed his feet with the T-shirt and picked up a sock.

Sticking her two fingers out, Jessie shoved the points between his shoulder blades and shouted out in her most authoritative voice, 'Don't move. I have a gun.'

He stopped humming, his back went rigid and he dropped his sock.

'Okay, don't get excited.' His voice was gruff and tight with annoyance. He sounded American, but there was something else about his accent she couldn't quite place.

'Put your hands up, but don't turn around.'

His skin felt warm, but the muscles beneath were hard as rock, flexing under her fingers as he raised his arms. Up close, he looked a lot more dangerous. Jessie spotted a faded tattoo across his left bicep. Ridged white scar lines criss-crossed the tanned skin of his back. But then she noticed something else. Despite the impressive muscles across his shoulders and upper arms, he didn't have an ounce of fat on him. He was so lean, she could make out his ribs. A Goliath who didn't eat properly? How odd.

'Listen, put the gun down and I'll get out of here. No harm, no foul.'

He started to turn. She prodded her fingers harder into his spine. 'Don't turn around, I said.'

'Easy.' He didn't sound scared, just really pissed off. Maybe this hadn't been such a great idea after all. 'I'm putting my hands down,' he ground out. 'I've been on the bike all day and I'm beat.' He lowered his arms.

The seconds ticked by interminably.

'So what do we do now?' he asked.

Jessie's heart hammered against her rib-cage and sweat pooled between her breasts. Hell, she hadn't thought this far ahead. Where was Linc? Her fingers were starting to hurt.

'Where you from? You sound English?' he said.

'I think where you're from is probably a more pertinent question,' Jessie shot back. No arrogant trespasser was going to charm her.

He leaned forward. Jessie's heart jolted in her chest. 'What are you doing?'

'Grabbing my socks. Any objections?' The response was measured, calm and condescending.

Jessie bristled. 'Fine, but next time ask permission.' Just as she issued the order her tightly clamped fingers twitched.

The trespasser's back tensed and his head swung round. Oops!

'Damn it!'

Jessie jumped back, yelping, as her prey shot up and grabbed her in one quick, furious movement.

'Let me go,' she shrieked, struggling to pull her arms free as his large hands clamped on them like manacles.

'The finger routine. I got to hand it to you, I never thought I'd fall for that one.'

Striking blue eyes stared daggers at her out of a face that would have done Michelangelo proud. The man was quite simply beautiful. Jessie gulped, momentarily transfixed, taking in the high, slashing cheekbones, the rakish stubble on his chin and the daredevil scar across his left eyebrow. Adonis or not, his face was as hard as granite. He looked ready to murder someone and, from the way his fingers dug into her arms, she knew exactly who it was.

Her heart rate shot up to warp speed. Don't pass out, you silly cow. This is no time to panic. Twisting, Jessie kicked out with her bare foot and connected with his shin.

'Ow! Stop that, you little…' he yelled, yanking her towards him and wrapping his arms around her.

'Let me go. You—you trespasser.' With her face pressed against the soft, curling hair on his chest, the demand came out on a muffled squeak. The smell of fresh, wet male was overpowering. She lifted her knee, intending to stamp on his foot, but before she could make contact he tensed and shot backwards.

'Watch out!'

His hands let go. Jessie turned, poised to bolt for freedom, but he grabbed her from behind. Strong arms banded under her breasts, he lifted her off the ground as if she weighed nothing at all. She kicked, frantically, but he was holding her so close, so tight, she couldn't get any leverage.

Okay, now was the perfect time to panic.

'My sister's in the house with a shotgun,' she squealed.

'Yeah, right.' His arms tightened, cutting off more of her air supply. 'You're a danger to society, you know that?'

The buzzing in Jessie's ears became deafening. She was going to faint. His whole body was wrapped around her. His size, his strength, overwhelmed her. Why hadn't she listened to Ali? How the hell did she always get into these situations? And how was she going to get out of this one?

The whisper of his breathing against her ear made her shudder.

What would Bruce do now? Think, woman, think. 'I'm warning you,' she said, through gritted teeth. 'If you don't let me go, I'll hurt you, a lot.'

Monroe's lips twitched. Having gotten over the humiliation of falling for his captive's harebrained stunt, he had to admire her gall. The threat was ridiculous. She was close to a foot shorter than him and slender, too, despite the impressive curves he could feel pressed against his forearms. 'You're a real firecracker, aren't you?'

She must have heard the admiration in his voice, because she went very still. He loosened his arms a little. He should probably let her go and get the hell out of here, but she felt good in his arms, round and soft in all the right places. He wasn't going to hurt her, but he figured she deserved a little payback. After all, she'd scared the hell out of him.

'So how exactly are you going to hurt me?' He purred the words in her ear.

'You don't frighten me, you complete sod.'

'Sod, huh?' He grinned; her clipped, precise accent made

her sound like the lady of the manor addressing one of her peasants. It made him think of all those summers he'd spent in London as a kid with his English grandmother. It was one of the very few good memories from his childhood. He grinned. 'You are English, I'd know that accent anywhere. Hell, I'm half English myself. Kind of.'

'Isn't that flipping lovely for you?'

Funny, but she didn't remind him of prim and proper Granny Lacey one bit.

'Tut-tut.' He inhaled the heady scent from her wildly curling hair. 'And my sweet little granny always used to say English manners were the best in the world.'

'I'll give you manners,' she snarled, wriggling some more.

He laughed, really starting to enjoy himself. She was rigid in his arms, but he could feel her chest heaving with fury. He could imagine that pretty face of hers, glowing with temper. High cheekbones, smooth peach-toned skin, the sprinkle of freckles across her pert little nose, and those large, expressive sea-green eyes. He'd only glimpsed her face for a moment, but it had made a hell of an impression. She struggled again, and the firm swell of her butt pressed against his naked belly through the clingy little dress she had on.

The strong surge of arousal surprised him. He tightened his arms. She smelled good, too. 'You know, you're cute.' He smiled, nuzzling her hair. 'When you're not trying to kill me.'

'You are so going to die,' she snapped back.

'Get your hands off her!'

Monroe's head jerked up.

A man with a savage scowl on his face marched across the patio towards them. The little girl skipping along beside him didn't make him look any less threatening. Monroe registered the heavily pregnant woman behind them, but kept his gaze focused on the big guy.

The situation didn't seem quite so funny any more.

'Damn it.' Monroe let go of Miss Firecracker. She turned, glared at him, her green eyes sparking with fury, and then dashed over to the pregnant lady.

'Who are you and what the hell are you doing on my property?' the man bellowed.

Monroe held up his hands and tried to think fast. The guy was maybe an inch over his own six feet two and well built, but the tailored pants and pricey designer polo shirt he wore made him look rich and cultured. Monroe figured he could take him. But he couldn't swing at the guy when he had a kid beside him. And he didn't want to add assault to a trespassing charge if the cops arrived. Which left diplomacy as his only option.

'I just took a swim in your pool. I thought the place was empty.'

'Well, it's not.' The big guy ground the words out, his ice-blue eyes blazing with temper. 'Stay with Jessie, Emmy,' he said as he pushed the little girl behind him.

Monroe spotted Miss Firecracker take hold of the child's hand. The redhead was still glaring at him—and starting to look very self-satisfied.

The guy pushed the sleeves of his polo shirt up forearms that were ridged with muscle. 'I'm going to teach this idiot a lesson.'

A sick feeling in his gut, Monroe realised he'd have to take the punch. He closed his eyes, braced for the pain.

Then the pregnant lady shouted, 'Stop, Linc, stop!'

When nothing happened, Monroe risked opening one eye. The woman had a hold of the man's arm but she was staring right at him. 'Who are you?' she asked softly.

'Nobody, ma'am. All I took was a swim.' If only he could just deck the guy and get out of here.

'You're Monroe.' She said the words so quietly, Monroe wasn't sure he'd heard her right.

'What the hell is going on?' Mr Furious shouted back, still busting to take a swing at him.

'Linc, he's your brother. Can't you see the resemblance?'

Oh, hell. It hit Monroe just who these people were. He tried to swallow past the boulder in his throat, but his mouth had gone bone-dry. All he'd wanted was a quick swim and now look what he'd done.

'Monroe?' The big guy looked as if he'd taken a punch to the gut. Monroe knew how he felt.

He hadn't seen that face since he was ten years old, but now that he looked at it properly, Monroe recognised it all right. The guy had the same clear blue eyes as he did. And that mouth, that chin—didn't he see virtually the same ones in the mirror every time he remembered to shave?

'I should split,' Monroe mumbled.

Every one of them—his brother, the pregnant lady, who he figured must be his brother's wife, even the little girl and the woman with the flaming hair—was staring at him as if he'd grown two heads.

'I never thought I'd see you again.' His brother's voice was thready, his eyes shadowed.

'It's no big deal. It's a mistake. I shouldn't have used your pool.' Boy, was that the truth.

'I don't give a damn about the pool,' his brother said weakly.

'I need to go.' Monroe glanced at Miss Firecracker. She wasn't looking smug any more. Her face had gone stoplight-red to match that rioting hair.

His brother's wife stepped forward. 'You can't go, Monroe.' Her deep green eyes were steady on his. 'You and Linc have a lot of catching up to do. We want you to stay for a while. That's why we invited you.'

She seemed as if she meant it. Monroe felt honour-bound to set her straight. He didn't belong here; couldn't she see that? 'Look, ma'am, it's nice of you to ask me—' he huffed out a breath '—but I'm going to get on my way.'

He heard his brother curse, but his wife just shook her head, sadly. 'You're Linc's brother. You're family, Monroe. We want little Emily here to get to know you. You're her uncle.'

Monroe's gaze flicked to the little girl who was whispering furiously to Miss Firecracker and gazing at him in that penetrating way only kids could pull off.

He wasn't her uncle. He wasn't anyone's family.

'I'm Ali, by the way, Linc's wife,' the pregnant woman continued. 'That's our daughter Emmy and my sister Jessie.'

Monroe gave a stiff nod, the little girl waved back at him and said, 'Hi,' but the redhead just continued to stare at him. She didn't look anywhere near as welcoming as her sister.

'We've got five bedrooms in this place, Monroe,' his sister-in-law said as her fingers settled on his arm. 'Surely you can stay for a while and get to know us all.' The determination on her face told him there was no way she was going to let him bolt. The sinking sensation in his stomach dipped lower.

'I'm not staying in your home.' On that, he was firm.

'There's an apartment above the garage that will give you privacy.'

Monroe wondered if his sister-in-law had been a steamroller in a former life.

'Linc, why don't you take your brother into the house? Get him a beer, and then you can show him where he'll be staying.'

'Sure. Grab your stuff, Roe.'

The nickname reverberated in Monroe's mind, no one had called him that in close to twenty years.

'I think we both deserve a beer,' Linc said as he gave him a rueful smile. The crooked twist of his lips stabbed at Monroe's memory again.

'Hold on.' He hadn't agreed to anything, had he? But as he

tried to form a protest, his sister-in-law picked up his T-shirt and shoved it on top of the boots in his arms.

'Hell,' Monroe grumbled as the brother he'd never intended to see again led him into his home.

Jessie gaped at her would-be trespasser as he padded past her, carrying his boots and T-shirt with a bewildered look on his face. If she could just get her jaw off the floor, she might be able to speak.

Linc had a brother? She'd had no idea.

'Can you believe that?' Ali's face beamed. 'I wrote that letter to his old probation officer over a year ago on an off chance. I can't believe he's finally here.'

'His probation officer!' Jessie choked out the words. 'So he really is a criminal!'

'Don't sound so shocked. He was little more than a child when he went to jail. From what Jerry Myers told me, he's been clean as a whistle for the last fourteen years.'

Jessie didn't believe it. Did law-abiding citizens sneak into other people's houses and use their pools? Did they manhandle women they didn't even know? She didn't think so.

'By the way—' Ali sent her a saucy smile '—you guys looked like you were having fun when we arrived.'

Jessie stiffened. 'I thought he was a trespasser or worse. I wasn't having fun. I was trying to get away from him.'

'I see.' Ali looked doubtful. 'So that would explain why he was whispering sweet nothings in your ear, then, would it?'

Jessie's cheeks flamed. 'Actually, he was being rude and obnoxious.' She glared at her sister. 'He was having a ball trying to scare me to death.'

'It serves you right for haring off to confront him in the first place.'

'What?'

Ali waved away Jessie's indignant shout. 'Come on. We better get in there and make sure Linc doesn't let him get away.'

'I'm not going in there,' Jessie snapped back. 'I never want to see That Man again.'

'Jess, you can't avoid Monroe. If Linc and I have our way, he'll be here for a while.'

What was wrong with her sister? Couldn't she see the guy was trouble with a capital T? 'I think you and Linc are insane for inviting him, Ali. You don't even know him.'

The twinkle in Ali's eyes dimmed. 'I'm sorry I teased you. I shouldn't have. What happened by the pool was probably a bit of a shock.'

'I'll say.' At last, Ali was seeing sense.

'But you're going to have to apologise to Monroe about it.'

'You can't be serious.' Was her sister insane? 'I'm not apologising to him. He was trespassing.'

'No, he wasn't,' Ali replied softly. 'We invited him, remember?'

'But that's not the point.'

'Look, Jess. I can't explain this thing with Linc and Monroe to you properly. It's complicated. It has to do with their childhood.'

'Really?' A kernel of curiosity pierced Jessie's anger.

Jessie knew there was something wrong with Linc's family—the only person he'd ever mentioned was his British grandmother who'd died years ago. From the little Jessie knew, he'd spent his summers with her as a child, but he never spoke about the American side of his family and neither did Ali. But still, having met That Man, she wasn't convinced Linc needed to get to know him again. The guy had 'deadbeat' written all over him.

'I can't tell you about it, Jess. Linc wouldn't want me to.' Ali paused, seemed to struggle to find the right words. 'Since we had Emmy, it's been important to Linc to find his brother. He may not be able to have a relationship with Monroe. But the fact that he's here is important. Linc needs to make sure he's okay.'

Jessie looked at her sister and thought she understood.

Ali and Linc were such fantastic parents, they just naturally wanted to watch over everyone. It was the thing she admired most about them. Their devotion to Emmy and to each other had made her yearn for a home and a family of her own.

Jessie didn't think for a minute that the man who had been taking a dip in their pool needed anyone to watch over him. She could see, though, she wasn't going to be able to convince her sister of that. She heaved a sigh of frustration. 'If it's that important, I won't get involved.'

'Jess, you are involved. You're here and so is he. Couldn't you make peace with him? I don't want him to feel uncomfortable. It's taken us years to find him and get him here. I want Linc and him to have a chance.'

Put like that, what choice did Jessie have? Ali and Linc had done so much for her. They'd comforted her when she'd broken up with Toby. She was sure they'd only invited her to stay with them this summer because they'd been worried about her. She could never refuse them anything.

'Oh, all right.' But she'd be keeping her eye on Linc's bad-boy brother. No one took advantage of her family.

'Great.' Ali's eyes warmed. 'Once Linc has helped Monroe settle into the garage apartment, why don't you go over there with some clean sheets and towels? Show him there are no hard feelings, then you could invite him back to the house for dinner.'

Jessie groaned as her sister waddled off towards the house.

Flipping fantastic! How exactly had she gone from being Bruce Willis in *Die Hard 2* to the welcoming committee from *The Stepford Wives*?

CHAPTER TWO

'NICE place you got here,' Monroe said to Linc as they walked through the lush landscaped gardens towards the garage. Talk about an understatement, Monroe thought. A spread like this must have cost well into the millions.

There had to be at least two acres of grounds. They came to the large three-car garage, nestled at the end of the estate. Monroe was glad to see the two-storey building was a good distance from the main house, constructed in the same wood and glass.

Monroe knew his brother had done well for himself, built his own computer software company up from scratch. Monroe had picked up on a few magazine articles over the years about the Latimer Corporation and its successes. Still, he'd never given any thought to what that meant. His brother was a stranger, so why would he? But now his brother's wealth was staring him right in the face, he could see Linc and he weren't just strangers. They were from different worlds.

'It does the job,' Linc replied mildly.

Linc led the way round the side of the building. Monroe followed his brother up the outside steps.

'Your wife's English, right?' Maybe a bit of polite conversation would help ease the knot in his gut.

'Ali, yeah. We live in London most of the year, her family's there. But we vacation every summer in Long Island. We'll be here through September.'

'Right,' Monroe grunted. No way would he be here that long. Hearing the affection in his brother's voice as he talked about his family had made the knot in Monroe's gut tighten.

Linc opened the door to the apartment and flicked on the main light switch. Recessed spotlights illuminated the spacious, airy room. With a new kitchen and breakfast bar on one side and a comfortable, expensively furnished living area on the other, the room looked clean, modern and barely used.

'It's only two rooms and a bath,' Linc said.

Two rooms or not, it was the most luxurious accommodation Monroe had seen let alone stayed in for a very long time.

'It's a good thing we had it fixed up over the winter,' Linc said, opening the French doors at the end of the room that led onto a small balcony. 'Or we wouldn't have had a place to offer you.'

Monroe frowned. He needed to put the brakes on, before Linc got the wrong idea. 'It's nice of you to offer. But I don't know if I'll be staying more than a night. I've got stuff to do in New York and I don't have a lot of dough at the moment.'

It wasn't the truth. He'd worked like a dog the last six months so he could afford to spend a few clear months painting. He had stacks of sketches stuffed in his duffel bag that he wanted to get on canvas. He'd had a vague offer to tend bar that came with a room in Brooklyn where he'd been hoping to settle while he got it done.

Painting was Monroe Latimer's secret passion. Ever since he'd taken one of the art classes they'd offered during his second stretch inside, painting had been his lifeline. In those early days, it had been an escape from the ugliness and the sheer boredom of life in a cage. After he'd got out, it was the thing that had kept him centred, kept him sane. He always gave the pictures away or simply burned them when he had to move on. The process was the only thing that mattered to him. Making the oils work for him and putting the visions in his head onto canvas. He didn't need family and possessions. He could put up with the drudgery of dead-end jobs and enjoy his rootless existence, if every six months or so he got the chance to stop and create.

He wasn't about to tell his brother any of that, though. After all, he didn't know the guy.

'Monroe, if you're short right now, surely it'd be good to crash here for a while.'

Monroe stiffened. Pride was the one thing he never compromised.

The irony of the situation, though, didn't escape him.

When he'd been sixteen and desperate, after his first stretch in juvie, he'd been prepared to do anything to survive. Mooching off his rich brother back then wouldn't have bothered him; in fact, he would probably have enjoyed screwing the guy over. But in all of the years since, Monroe Latimer had learned a lot about self-control and a whole lot more about self-respect. He'd sworn to himself after that second stretch that he would never go back to that horror again. To do that, he'd stayed clean, and he'd learned to rely on nobody but himself.

'I'm not a freeloader.' Monroe forced the words out, trying to quell his annoyance.

Linc sighed, his voice weary. 'I know that, but you are family.'

'I'm not family.' Monroe watched his brother frown at the words. Tough. He needed to get this straight once and for all. 'We weren't that close as kids, but even if we had been, that was a million years ago. You're not obligated to me any more than I am to you. We're strangers.'

'All right, stop.' Linc held up his hand. 'I understand what you're saying, Roe,' he said slowly. 'Like you say, we're strangers. Don't you think I don't know that?'

'Then why the hell did you invite me?'

'Why did you come?'

The quick rejoinder had Monroe stumbling to a halt. Why the hell had he come? 'I don't know. Just curious, I guess.'

'Well, maybe that's enough for now.' Linc walked across the living area. 'Let me at least show you the rest of the place, before you run out on us.'

Monroe was thinking he should do just that when Linc flung open the door to the apartment's bedroom and his mind went blank.

The wall of glass at the far side of the room flooded it with mid-afternoon light. He could see the pool patio across the gardens, and the ocean beyond. Surf tumbled onto shore on an empty beach of white sand. The view was stunning, but it wasn't that which made his blood slow, his heart thud against his chest. With its walls painted pristine white and only a bed and a small chest for furniture, the room was so bright and airy, he'd never seen a better place to paint. Always before, he'd had to be satisfied with dingy rented rooms or, one memorable summer, a broken-down trailer next to a car dump in Virginia. He'd never had a studio before, had never thought he wanted one, but, seeing the play of sunlight across one wall, he wanted this one.

'You like it?' Linc's question interrupted his thoughts.

'Yeah, I do.' Monroe couldn't disguise the leap of joy in his voice. He refused to let his doubts surface. Couldn't he have this one thing, just for a little while? He'd pay his way; he'd make sure of it. 'Looks like you've got a house guest for a while.'

'Great.' Linc smiled back at him.

'But what I said about being a freeloader still goes.' Monroe walked to the glass and peered down at the garden below. 'You got anyone to do your yard work?'

Linc frowned as he stood beside him, looked down, too. 'No, the old guy who used to do it's having trouble with his arthritis. I figured I'd hire a local kid to keep it under control till Dan gets back on his feet.'

'No need.' Monroe took his eyes away from the window. 'While I'm here, I'll handle it. Looks like the lawn could use a cut. You got a mower in the garage?'

'Yes, but…' Linc's eyes narrowed. 'Monroe, I don't want you doing the yard work. It isn't necessary.'

'It is to me.'

Linc didn't look pleased. 'Fine. I guess I don't have a problem with you cutting the grass every once in a while.'

Monroe figured there were probably a lot of jobs needed doing about the place. From what he'd seen so far, the house and gardens were huge and, oddly for rich folks, they didn't seem to have much hired help. He reckoned if he devoted his mornings to helping out around the place, it'd go some way to paying his brother back for the opportunity to paint in this glorious room.

Jessie replayed her humiliating encounter with Monroe in her head for the thousandth time as she strolled over to the garage apartment, her arms loaded down with fresh linens.

By organising an outing to the local ice cream parlour with Emmy, she'd managed to delay her next encounter with That Man for a good three hours. Unfortunately, out of sight had not meant out of her mind. Of course, Emmy's endless chatter about her 'cool new uncle' over the hot fudge sundaes hadn't helped. But it was the memory of his naked chest pressed against her back that kept slamming back into her thoughts every ten seconds or so. Not to mention all the daft things she'd said and done before that.

Her palms dampened on the white cotton sheets as she mounted the steps to his door. Oh, this was ridiculous. He was just a guy, and a supremely irritating one at that, if their first meeting was anything to go by. She'd promised Ali that she would apologise and that was going to be hard enough, but she absolutely was not going to dissolve in a puddle at his feet as she had almost done by the pool.

Telling the butterflies in her stomach to go away, Jessie tapped on the door. No answer. She raised her fist to knock again when it swung open.

'Oh!' The sight of the tanned naked chest in front of her, glistening with sweat, had her gaping in shock.

'Hey, it's the bad cop. Jessie, right?'

Jessie's eyes shot up to his face. His hair, she noticed, was a dark, burnished blond when it was dry, streaked with gold. With a red and white bandanna tied round his forehead, his tanned, angular face and that thin scar across his brow, he looked like some beautiful Apache sun god, she thought in amazement. Then she spotted the glint of amusement in his riveting blue eyes.

'Don't you ever wear a shirt?' she snapped.

He grinned, sending some really annoying dimples into his cheeks. 'Not when it's hot and I'm doing manual labour.'

'Or when you're pinching a swim in someone else's pool.' The snide remark was out before she could stop it. There was something about the sight of those perfect pectoral muscles, or maybe it was the tantalising sprinkling of chest hair across them, that just seemed to bring out her inner bitch.

'Well…' The cool amusement in his voice made her bristle '…I figure swimming in your clothes is kind of dumb.'

At that precise moment, Jessie recalled exactly what he had—or rather had not—been wearing when she'd first spotted him and her traitorous skin flushed with colour.

* * *

Monroe watched the vivid pink flood her cheeks and grinned some more. No doubt about it, the woman was seriously cute. That mass of curly red hair, which was tied back but hardly tamed, and those round sea-green eyes. With the peaches-and-cream skin and high cheekbones, her face was made up of enchanting contrasts. He glanced down at her slim, shapely legs, showcased by the short skirt of her sundress. Her top half was hidden behind the pile of linens she carried, but he could still remember the feel of her lush breasts pressed against his forearm. She certainly came in one enticing little package.

Jessie hadn't missed the quick but thorough once-over. The flash of warmth and appreciation she'd seen in his eyes wasn't doing a thing for the burning in her cheeks. How humiliating. 'What are you grinning at?'

'Just admiring the scenery.'

Jessie sent him what she hoped was a withering glance. Unperturbed, he leaned forward and plucked the sheets out of her arms.

'Come on in.' He bumped open the door with his butt and strolled into the room.

Jessie stepped gingerly across the threshold. Calm down, woman, and don't show him how much he unnerves you. She was trying to think of a neutral comment when she spotted the bed frame leaning against the far wall. 'What are you doing to the furniture?'

He dumped the sheets on the sofa. 'No need to get ants in your pants. I'm not stealing it.'

Jessie could see the stiff set of his shoulders and suddenly felt ashamed of herself.

She'd promised Ali she'd make peace with him, instead

she'd been nasty as soon as he'd opened the door. 'I didn't think you were stealing it,' she said quietly.

'You sure about that?' She heard the humour in his voice, but it didn't quite reach his eyes as he studied her.

She swallowed. 'Of course I am. I was just curious. Is there something wrong with the bed frame?' The intense look in his eyes was making her jumpy again.

He shrugged. 'No, I'm just moving it in here. I've got plans for the other room.'

'Well, that solves that mystery.' She brushed her hands down her dress. 'You're obviously busy. I'll leave you to it.'

'Hey, hold up.' He walked up to her, blocking her exit. 'You're not still pissed about what happened by the pool, are you?'

Of course she was. 'Of course I'm not.'

'You are, aren't you?' That slow, infuriating grin spread across his face, shooting those irresistible dimples back into his cheeks. 'You've got that fired-up look in your eyes.' He flicked a finger at her ponytail. 'Suits you—goes with the hair.'

He was laughing at her again. How infuriating. Jessie put on her best queen-to-serf voice. 'Thank you very much. I don't think I've ever had such an original compliment.'

She tried to walk past him, but he simply reached out and took hold of her upper arm. The warmth of his hard, callused fingers was such a surprise, she yelped.

'Don't panic.' Despite the quiet tone, he continued to hold her in place.

'Let go!' Her voice came out in a breathless rush. He stood so close she could smell him, the musty, but not unpleasant, scent of fresh male sweat.

He dropped his hand, then held the palm up as if in surrender. 'No harm done. I just figured I should say sorry, for earlier.'

The contrite words would be more convincing, Jessie thought, if his eyes weren't dancing with amusement.

She took a quick step back. She really, really wanted to wipe that smile off his face. Tell him he was an overbearing oaf who needed to learn some manners. But she couldn't. His words had reminded her of her promise to Ali.

She was supposed to be apologising to him, not the other way round. Because she couldn't bear to see him laugh at her when she did it, she looked down at her feet. 'That's okay. I guess I was quite rude to you, too.'

She mumbled the words, but when he didn't say anything she was forced to look up. He wasn't smiling any more. In fact, he looked astonished. 'Are you kidding me?'

'No, I'm not.' Jessie bit back her annoyance. Why was he making this so difficult? 'My sister pointed out that, since you were invited here, you were the wronged party, so I should apologise to you.'

'Is that right?' He tucked his hands into the back pockets of his jeans; his lips twitched. 'So it was big sis that put you up to this. She make you come over with the linens, too?'

Irritated by his perception, Jessie kept her tone even. 'I'm trying to give you a simple and sincere apology. What exactly is your problem?'

'Simple, yeah. Sincere?' He considered the question for a moment. 'I don't think so.'

Jessie glared at him. Sod diplomacy. 'You really are insufferable, aren't you?'

He laughed then, the gesture making his handsome face relax in a way that was ludicrously appealing. Jessie glared at him some more, determined not to notice it.

'Like I said, Red. You're cute when you're mad.'

Jessie's belly tightened at the hot look in his eyes and the gruff way he said the new nickname. 'I'm leaving. I did my best,' she said as she stalked over to the door.

She could hear him laughing harder as she wrenched the

door open. She was just about to slam it behind her, though, when she remembered something else.

Turning back, she was dismayed to see he'd followed her. Gripping the door, he leaned against it and grinned down at her. 'What is it, Red? You got something else to apologise for?'

Ignoring the teasing glint in his eyes, Jessie stepped back onto the landing. 'Believe me, that's the only apology you'll ever get out of me.'

'Now that's a shame, when you're so good at it.'

For a deadbeat, he certainly had an answer for everything.

'My sister wanted to invite you to dinner this evening at the house.' She spat the words out. 'About seven o'clock. I'm sure you can find your own way there.'

Duty done, Jessie stomped off down the stairs. Just as she reached the bottom he called after her. 'Hey, Red. You gonna be there?'

She looked back over her shoulder. 'Of course I am.'

He let his gaze drift down to her butt and back. 'Be sure and tell your sister I'll be there, then. I wouldn't want to miss telling her all about that sweet apology you gave me.'

As Jessie stormed off she could hear his deep rumbling laugh all the way past the garage.

CHAPTER THREE

'DID you and Monroe get everything settled, then?' Ali asked as she placed a large plate of cold cuts on the dining table.

'Umm-hmm.' Jessie dropped her head and concentrated on chopping the tomatoes. 'I made my peace with him as requested.' And if he said anything different, she would see to it personally that he suffered.

'And you apologised, for what happened by the pool?'

Jessie suppressed the tug of guilt and dumped the last of the tomatoes into the salad.

'Yes, Ali.' Jessie gave an impatient sigh. 'I apologised to him.' Even though it had nearly killed her.

'And a real nice apology it was, too.'

Both sisters turned to see Monroe standing at the door.

In a newer pair of jeans and a faded blue T-shirt with a Harley Davidson logo, he looked as neat and presentable as Jessie had ever seen him. But as he sauntered into the room with that long, tawny-blond hair, the day-old stubble on his chin and a devil-may-care glint in his eyes, he didn't exactly look safe.

'It's got to be one of the sweetest apologies I've ever had.' He winked at Jessie as he said it and she felt herself flush.

He was laying it on thick to embarrass her. The rat.

'Monroe, I'm so glad you came.' Ali greeted him with a warm smile.

'You're welcome, ma'am.'

'Take a seat and Jess'll get you a drink. I'll just go and get Linc. He's reading Emmy a bedtime story.'

As Ali bustled out of the room Jessie busied herself putting the last of the food on the table. She pretended not to notice as Monroe folded his long frame into the chair opposite.

'A beer would be great, Red.' He said the nickname in a murmur that was deliberately familiar. Jessie looked up. He was watching her, confident and amused. 'Cute dress.' He tilted his head to one side, took a good long look. 'Fits you just right.'

Jessie felt her pulse skid into overdrive. She wasn't sure why she'd decided to change into the figure-hugging silk dress for dinner, but it certainly hadn't been to see that flare of heat in his eyes.

'I'll get your beer.' She walked stiffly to the fridge. The low, masculine chuckle from behind her made her jaws tighten. Where were Linc and Ali? If she had to spend much longer alone with him, she'd dump the beer on his head.

Jessie didn't miss the teasing heat in Monroe's gaze when she plunked the glass of beer in front of him. Lounging in the chair, his lean, muscular physique looked magnificent. Her pulse thudded against her neck. Why did all the best-looking men have the most aggravating personalities?

'Thanks, Red.' He picked up the glass; one brow lifted as he eyed the huge foam head. 'Looks like you need a little practice with your bar-tending skills, though.'

She smiled sweetly at him. 'I'm sorry to say I don't have the time. I'm too busy making obsequious apologies to people who don't deserve them.'

He barked out a laugh just as Linc and Ali walked into the room.

'Monroe, good to see you.' Linc held out a hand. 'I hope Jessie's making you feel at home.'

'She certainly is,' Monroe said smoothly as he stood up and shook his brother's hand.

As they all settled down to eat, Jessie couldn't resist sticking her tongue out at him from behind her sister's back. He winked back, making her regret the childish gesture. She'd ignore him, she thought, as she picked up her knife and fork. Now, if only she could swallow, too.

Monroe thought the dinner would be stiff and formal, but he found it surprisingly easy to talk to his brother and sister-in-law. He hadn't eaten since a stale bagel that morning in an interstate truck stop, so the mouth-watering selection of salads and cold cuts also went down well.

He'd expected lots of probing questions about what the hell he'd been doing all this time while his brother had made a staggering success of his life. Instead Linc and Ali kept their inquiries discreet and when he didn't elaborate they seemed more than happy to take up the slack, telling him funny stories about their family and how they'd first met.

Monroe hadn't missed the intimate looks that passed from husband to wife during the telling. He also noticed the way his brother never seemed to miss an opportunity to touch his wife.

The gentle, possessive hand resting on the small of her back when she sat down to eat. The way his fingers stroked her arm when she passed him the salad bowl. The love between them was so tangible, Monroe was touched despite his determination to remain aloof.

Monroe liked watching people. It helped him create the pictures he painted. But while he could see the love between Linc and his wife, he was more interested in the reaction of Ali's sister. He had seen the shadow of longing in Jessie's eyes.

When Linc and Ali left the table to get the dessert, Monroe kept his eyes on Jessie. She watched the couple walk over to the large open kitchen together, the yearning in her eyes obvious when Linc pulled his wife into a fleeting embrace behind the breakfast bar. What was Jessie thinking, he wondered, with that romantic look in her eyes?

She turned suddenly, and caught him studying her.

'Will you stop staring at me? It happens to be flipping rude.'

It was the first time she'd spoken to him directly since handing him his beer. The exasperation in her voice made him smile.

'So's swearing at the table, Red, but you don't hear me complaining.'

Would she never be able to get the last word with this man? Jessie thought as her teeth ground together.

To her surprise, the dinner hadn't been as excruciating as she thought it would be. For an ex-con and obvious reprobate he could be charming when he wanted to be. Although she noticed he'd been cleverly evasive whenever Ali or Linc had asked him about his life. He just said he'd been 'on the move.' Well, okay, she didn't exactly have a spectacular career at the moment, but she did have goals, objectives. At the very least, she did a bit more than just travel around on a motorbike.

She'd also caught him staring at her several times during the meal. That last probing look, when she'd been daydreaming about having a marriage like Linc and Ali's, had really unsettled her. The strange sense of envy she felt was one of her most shameful secrets.

'Flipping is hardly a swear word,' she whispered, so Linc and Ali wouldn't overhear them. 'It's just an expression.'

'Red, anything's a swear word when you say it with that look in your eye.'

She choked down her pithy response when Ali appeared with a huge lemon pie.

'I hope you've still got some room left, Monroe,' Ai said, placing the pie on the table.

Monroe leaned back and patted his flat belly. 'I might just have a little.'

The pie was served as soon as Linc arrived with a gallon of ice cream. Avoiding Monroe's gaze, which seemed to be fixed on her yet again, Jessie gave Linc her sweetest smile. 'I thought I'd go into town tomorrow and beg the people at the Cranford Art Gallery for the Saturday job they've been advertising. Could I borrow the BMW?'

'Sorry, Jess.' Linc scooped some more ice cream onto his plate. 'It's making a weird noise. I'm planning to get the guy at the shop to take a look at it.'

'I'll give it a look.'

Linc stopped eating at Monroe's casual comment. 'There's no need.'

Monroe forked up another generous piece of pie, sent his brother a level look. 'Sure there is.'

Jessie could see Linc was on the verge of refusing again, when Ali touched his arm, silencing him. Ali beamed a smile at Monroe. 'That's great, Monroe. It'll save us the trouble of having to call the mechanic.'

Jessie wondered at the sudden tension in the room between the two men. It was also odd that Monroe had made the offer. After all, wasn't he supposed to be a deadbeat? She shrugged the thought aside; it made no difference to her what he was. She turned to Ali. 'Are you using the people carrier tomorrow?'

Ali nodded. 'Linc and I promised Emmy we'd go to the funfair at Pleasance Beach. Maybe we could drop you off in town and then pick you up later. Did you have a particular time in mind?'

'It's okay. That'll take you miles out of your way.' Jessie couldn't help feeling a little crestfallen. She'd wanted to get to the gallery tomorrow. She needed to find a job.

'You can catch a ride with me on the Harley,' Monroe said. 'I've got to go into town and pick up some groceries. I've got a spare helmet.'

Jessie stared at him. Surely he couldn't be serious. 'No, really, it's no problem. I'll go in another day.'

'Don't be silly, Jessie,' Ali piped up. 'If Monroe's offering you should—'

'I couldn't possibly trouble him like that,' Jessie interrupted her sister and aimed a telling look at Monroe. His lips curved slowly. Why did she suddenly feel like a mouse being stalked by a tomcat?

'No trouble. No trouble at all.' He stood up, smiled at Ali. 'Thanks again for the dinner. It was delicious.'

'You're welcome.' Ali beamed at him as Linc rose and offered to see him out.

Just as he got to the door, Monroe turned and gave Jessie another of those winks that made her pulse scramble.

'See you in the morning, Red. Better put on some pants, though.' His gaze crept down and then back up, making her face heat. 'That little bit of a dress won't wear too well on the Harley.'

Jessie scowled as his tall frame strolled out the door ahead of Linc. How annoying that he'd gone and got the last word in again.

CHAPTER FOUR

THE next day dawned bright and clear, the sluggish heat kept at bay by a cool breeze off the Atlantic.

Jessie got up with Emmy, made a quick breakfast of cereal and toast for them both, and then handed her over to Linc and Ali. From the flushed look on her sister's face after the lie-in Jessie had promised the couple, it looked as if they hadn't been doing much sleeping.

Jessie ignored the stab of envy as she went upstairs to have her shower. Her sister had a fabulous marriage to a fabulous man. When Jessie had been a bridesmaid at their wedding, she'd known that theirs was the ideal marriage—full of passion but grounded in a deep, abiding love. It was the sort of marriage Jessie wanted for herself.

So far, though, things hadn't quite worked out that way.

It had taken her two long years and one broken engagement to realise Toby was about as far from her ideal mate as it was possible to get. She had thought he loved her, when the only person he really loved was himself.

She'd tried so hard to persuade herself that Toby was 'the one.' When he'd asked her to marry him, she'd been swept up in the romance of the moment. But the minute she'd said yes, a little voice in her head had started telling her to run like mad in the opposite direction. She'd been naïve and immature; she could see that now. The huge sense of relief when they had finally gone their separate ways had made Jessie determined never to make that mistake again. However glad she'd been to see the back of Toby, the relationship had left her with the depressing thought that she might never find what Ali had.

Heck, at twenty-six she'd never had halfway decent sex, let alone great sex. When Toby had accused her of being frigid, she'd had to accept that he might well be right. He'd never once stirred the passion in her that Linc so obviously stirred in Ali. She hadn't so much as kissed a guy since she'd hurled Toby's engagement ring at him six long months ago. Worse than that, she hadn't even wanted to.

Determined not to let the creeping sense of despair take hold, Jessie wrapped the towel around her and walked to the closet. After careful consideration, she picked out a chic but simple shift dress with large sunflowers on it. She needed to look hip and stylish if she was going to persuade the art gallery to take her on as a Saturday assistant. Cranford might be a small seaside town, but it was no backwater. A tourist Mecca for the Hamptons' super-rich and aspirational summer residents, the gallery and its clientele would be as sophisticated as any you'd find in Uptown Manhattan.

Jessie had promised Ali that she'd help out with Emmy until the family went back to London in September. But she hoped to get a Saturday job to earn some much-needed money in the meantime. Linc had insisted on paying all her expenses to get her over here, but Jessie didn't want him giving her spending money as well. He'd already tried to give her a credit card, which she'd flatly refused, but in the end she'd persuaded him to help her get a temporary working visa. Also, a job in an art gallery was just up her street. She loved art, and, while she'd accepted she didn't have the talent to be an artist herself, she had always hoped to whittle out a career in the art world. She'd spent six long months drifting since the breakup with Toby. It was time to get her life back on track. Ali handled her life calmly and competently, Jessie thought. If she wanted what Ali had, she needed to start doing the same.

At that thought, the memory of Monroe Latimer watching her in the dining room the night before, his pure blue eyes alight with amusement, blasted into her brain and wouldn't get out again. Jessie frowned. He might have the goods in the looks department, but luckily for her she was not a shallow person. It hadn't taken her long to see he was a long way short of her ideal mate in every other department. Flirtatious, arrogant and dangerously attractive, he could make any woman lose sight of what was really important. And for Jessie that was the long haul, not the quick flash-fire of sexual attraction.

Remembering Monroe's parting comment about the proper bike attire with not a little irritation, Jessie slipped into the dress and then pulled on a pair of jeans. She'd just have to take them off when she got to town. After dabbing on some lipstick, Jessie slipped a pair of yellow slingback sandals into her bag and tugged on her sneakers. She tied her hair into a ruthless ponytail and checked herself in the room's full-length cheval mirror.

Yep, she looked preposterous.

At least her daft get-up should stop Monroe staring at her in that disconcerting way. She wasn't looking forward to riding on his bike. Despite all his shortcomings, she had the uncomfortable feeling that being pressed up against that muscular back for the ten-mile ride into town might stir feelings she didn't want stirred. Quite why she was more sexually aware of him than she had ever been of any other man didn't bear thinking about.

* * *

'Damn it!' Monroe pulled his hand out from under the car's hood and watched the blood seep out of the shallow scrape.

'Did you hurt yourself?'

Turning at the voice, Monroe watched Jessie walk across the garage towards him. She should have looked ridiculous with denim on under the floating, flowery dress, but she didn't. She looked chic and summery. His eyes dipped to her cleavage, demurely displayed above the dress's scoop neck. Sucking the blood from his knuckle, he took in every detail.

'I certainly hope it's not fatal?' The sharp note in her voice suggested she hoped exactly the opposite. He grinned as his gaze lifted back up to her face.

Pulling a bandanna out of his back pocket, he leaned against the car's hood. 'You know, Red,' he said as he wrapped the cloth round his hand, 'that figure of yours would look great in just about anything.' And even better out of anything, Monroe thought, enjoying the way her eyes narrowed in irritation.

Trying to ignore the way her pulse was racing, Jessie fingered her bag strap and glared at him. 'While your fashion advice is certainly invaluable, I can see you're busy. Maybe I should come back later.' Or not at all, she added silently, already feeling unpleasantly flustered.

'No need.' He pushed up from the car's hood. 'I'll go clean up and then we can head out.' He walked towards her, forcing her to tilt her head back. 'It'd be a shame not to, Red. Now that you're all dolled up.'

She watched him mount the steps to his apartment. He made it sound as if she'd dressed up especially for him. The conceited jerk.

Monroe took less than ten minutes, but Jessie was just about to walk off, her heart rate still hitching uncomfortably, when he reappeared. He had a fresh white T-shirt on, the same worn jeans, a small plaster on his hand and a motorbike helmet slung over his arm.

'This is for you.' He handed her the helmet. 'The bike's out front.' As she turned to walk ahead of him she felt his palm on the small of her back. The minimal contact made her jump.

'Easy, Red.' He lifted his hand. 'Just being polite.'

Jessie didn't think so, from the mischievous twinkle in his eyes, but didn't trust herself to speak. When they reached the bike, she fumbled for a moment trying to put her helmet on, before he lifted it out of her hands.

He did a circular motion with his finger. 'Turn around.'

She did as he asked, grabbing her hair when he deftly removed the band holding it in a ponytail. 'What are you doing?' she demanded as his fingers combed through her hair.

He put his hands on her shoulders and turned her to face him. 'It'll be more comfortable like that, with the helmet on.'

He rewarded her scowl with another heart-thumping smile as he placed the helmet on her head and fastened the strap. The light brush of his fingers seemed to burn the soft skin under her chin. This was going to be a nightmare. She hadn't even got on the bike yet and already she felt as if she were about to explode.

Unhooking his own helmet from the handlebar, he put it on and then climbed onto the enormous machine. 'Hop on, Red.'

It took several attempts before she managed to clamber up behind him. She had to push her feet hard on the footrests and grasp the back of the seat to stop from sliding against him. She was grateful for the jeans now, because her dress had ridden right up to her waist.

'I'm ready,' she said, feeling like an idiot.

Instead of starting the machine, he took his hands off the handlebars, pulled off his helmet and turned round. 'You ever ride a motorcycle before, Red?'

'Well, no, not exactly.' She didn't like that smug look in his eyes.

'First rule, hold on tight.'

'I am holding on tight.' Her knuckles ached, she was gripping the seat so hard.

He shook his head. 'Not onto the bike, sweetheart—onto me.'

'Why can't I just hold onto the bike?' She could hear the whine in her voice, but couldn't help it. She didn't want to hold onto him.

'Because when we hit a curve, you're going to have to lean with me.' His lips quirked. What was so amusing? 'Wouldn't want you falling off.'

He was talking to her as if she were an imbecile. 'Fine. I'll hold onto you.'

He grinned, the dimples winking in his cheeks, before he turned and put his helmet back on. To her utter shock, he reached behind, put two large hands on her thighs and dragged her towards him. Before she could blink, she was snuggled against him, her legs spread wide to accommodate his denim-clad butt.

'Now, put your arms round my waist.'

She didn't want to, but what choice did she have? She wrapped her arms round him, tried to ignore the feel of his hard, flat stomach beneath her palms. His back felt firm and warm against the thin silk of her dress. He pushed back to kick the bike into life. The powerful vibrations of the machine rumbled up through her thighs, making Jessie painfully aware of all the places where their bodies touched. The very core of her started to throb. How humiliating. His shoulder shifted as he gripped the clutch and her nipples hardened. Worried that he might be able to feel them, she wriggled back, but his hand simply came round again and pulled her back.

'Stay put, Red, and hold on.'

As soon as he shouted the words at her, the big black machine started to roar up the small hill. Although it was probably only going ten miles per hour up the drive, Jessie tightened her grip on him, grateful for the solid, sure feel of him in front of her. As the breeze caught the ends of her hair beneath the helmet she pressed into his back.

By the time they hit the main coastal road, Jessie couldn't have cared less if she were naked behind him. The exhilarating feeling of speed and freedom as the scenery whizzed by around them and the wind whipping at her arms and face was fantastic. She loved roller-coaster rides but this was better. Every time they leaned into a bend, her stomach leapt up into her throat and she gripped onto his waist even tighter. He felt wonderful, warm and strong and unyielding. She could smell the clean scent of his cotton T-shirt and the subtle hint of soap and motor oil. The hard, sculpted muscles of his butt rubbed against her centre every time he moved his foot on the gears and her nipples were so hard now she was sure they were boring a hole in his back.

Despite the intimacy, the devastating effect he was having on her physically, she sighed when they drove into the main thoroughfare of town, disappointed that the ride was over so quickly. He slowed the bike down to a gentle purr as he drove through the wide, tree-lined main street of the picturesque seaside town, finally pulling to a stop in front of the grocery store.

Jessie took a moment before peeling herself off him and leaning back. He tugged off his helmet, and a huge grin split his face as he turned round. 'What did you think?'

'It's fantastic!' Her voice was muffled by the helmet but giddy with pleasure.

'You liked it, huh?'

She nodded, grinning back at him. As she tried to undo the helmet strap with shaking fingers, he brushed her hands aside and did the job for her, lifting it off her head. 'You're a real biker chick now, Red.'

The feel of her lush body wrapped around him had made Monroe's jeans uncomfortably tight, but he couldn't help smiling at the look of pure pleasure on her face. Seeing a small mark on her forehead, he rubbed it softly with his thumb. 'Looks like you could do with a better helmet, though.'

'Don't worry about that. It felt wonderful. Everything felt wonderful. It was so exciting. No wonder you've spent all those years riding around on your motorbike.'

There was no censure in her words, none of the disdain that she had shown him last night, only joy and enthusiasm. With her emerald eyes sparkling, her hair curling wildly and the pink glow of pleasure flushing her cheeks, she looked gorgeous.

He wanted to kiss her so badly it hurt.

Stunned by the sudden reckless urge, Monroe swung back round and concentrated on attaching the helmet to the handlebars.

'You better climb down first,' he muttered.

Jessie stared at his back as she hopped off the Harley. What had happened? One minute he'd been smiling at her, enjoying the moment with her, and then, all of a sudden, he'd as good as dismissed her.

She adjusted her bag as he lifted his leg over the bike.

'Thanks for the ride. It was…' She babbled to a halt, seeing the intensity in his eyes as he turned to her. She wetted her lips with the tip of her tongue and his gaze shot down to her mouth. 'It was really fun.' The words came out on a feeble whisper. What was going on here? Why was he staring at her mouth like that? She felt light-headed and she didn't know why.

'You're welcome, Red.' The nickname sounded anything but

casual. 'See that diner?' He nodded across the street. 'I'll hang out there when I'm finished till you're ready to head back.'

The instant thrill at the thought of being back on the bike with him was followed by uncertainty. Maybe she'd enjoyed the ride too much.

'I might be a while.'

'Take all the time you need. I'm in no hurry.'

As Jessie walked away from him she was sure she could feel his eyes following her all the way down the street.

After an hour of trying to sell herself to Mrs Belinda Bennett, the proprietor of the Cranford Art Gallery, Jessie was frazzled. She'd chewed off most of her lipstick during the interview, but the hard sell had been worth it. Mrs Bennett had agreed to give her the job of Saturday sales assistant on a trial basis.

Feeling worn out but enthusiastic, Jessie forgot to feel nervous as she wandered into the small coffee house Monroe had indicated. She spotted him immediately, lounging in a booth opposite the door. He looked relaxed and gorgeous with a few sacks of shopping on the seat opposite.

'Hi.' She waved. 'I hope you haven't been here long.'

He slid out of the booth as she walked up to it. 'Not long. I was about to order pancakes.' His gaze took a leisurely journey down to her feet, now encased in the flattering yellow slingbacks, and then came back up again. Jessie's nerves came back full force when he smiled. 'It looks even better without the denim,' he said.

'Thanks.' Her voice quivered annoyingly as she slipped into the booth.

'Move over,' he said.

She'd expected him to lift up the bags opposite and sit there, but instead he pushed onto the bench seat beside her, nudging her with his hips. When he leant back and put his long, muscled forearm on the seat behind her, she realised she was totally boxed in.

'So how did it go—you get the job?'

'Yes, I start on Saturday.'

'Hey, way to go.' He patted her shoulder. 'How about we order pancakes and coffee to celebrate?'

'That would be lovely, thanks.'

He seemed genuinely pleased for her, so she tried not to notice the way his long, firm thigh was touching her leg. The thin silk of her dress did nothing to protect her against the warm pressure.

As he ordered two short stacks with coffee for them, Jessie noticed the way the teenage waitress blushed profusely. Did he have that potent effect on every woman he met?

'Looks like you've been busy, too.' She nodded at his purchases, spotting the logo of the town's expensive art supply shop. 'What did you get at Melville's?'

'Sketching charcoal, a couple of brushes, stuff like that.'

'Do you paint, then?'

'Sure, a little.'

'Really? That's wonderful. Are you any good?'

He took his arm away from behind her, looked away. 'I don't know and I don't really give a damn.'

The statement was abrupt and rude, and so out of keeping with his usual easygoing manner, Jessie felt instantly contrite. Somehow she'd insulted him.

'I'm sorry.' She touched his arm. 'I only asked because I love art and I'm absolutely useless at it myself.'

He glanced down at her fingers, gave a stiff jerk of his shoulders. 'No harm done.'

'Here you go, folks, two short stacks straight up.' The teenager beamed at Monroe as she placed the pancakes and mugs of coffee in front of them.

'This looks great, Shelby.' He smiled at the girl, reading the name off the blue tag on her uniform. Jessie watched the waitress flush again before she rushed off.

'What sort of things do you paint?' Jessie asked quietly as Monroe concentrated on drowning his plate in syrup.

He didn't reply. She waited as he swallowed a generous helping of pancakes and syrup. He nodded towards her plate. 'You not hungry?'

'I was just wondering about what you paint,' she repeated, feeling a little foolish now but determined to get an answer out of him.

'I haven't done any yet.'

'Yes, but, when you have, what will you paint?'

'They don't taste as good cold, you know,' he said, looking at her plate again.

Jessie remained silent. He wasn't meeting her eyes. Why was he being so evasive? But as she watched him take a sip from his coffee it occurred to her. He was shy about his artwork. It seemed so unlikely, but it was the only answer that made sense. The thought made him seem vulnerable, all of a sudden, maybe even a little bit sweet.

She waited. Finally, he stopped eating, turned to her. 'Look, it's no big deal, all right? It's just a dumb hobby.'

'I'm still curious what sort of painting you do. I mean, is it abstract, expressionism, more traditional like portraiture, landscapes? I'm really interested in art. Looking at it, appreciating it, visiting art galleries—those are a few of my dumb hobbies.'

He let out a breath, put down his fork. He *was* shy. He looked almost as uncomfortable now as when Ali had identified him at the pool the day before.

'It's mostly people, landscapes, any stuff that catches my eye and I want to put it on canvas. But you won't see any of it in an art gallery, that's for sure.' He eyed her plate again. 'If you don't want them, I'll eat them.'

'Okay, okay, I'll eat them.' Jessie picked up the maple syrup and swirled it over her stack, feeling ridiculously pleased that she'd managed to get him to talk about his artwork. After finishing a mouthful, she smiled at him, her mouth sticky. 'Mmm, these are delicious.'

Licking her lips, she caught the quick flick of his eyes down to her mouth. Her belly tightened. Okay, so maybe sweet wasn't quite the right word for him.

Having insisted on paying for their pancakes and leaving what Jessie thought was an excessive tip for the smitten Shelby, Monroe guided her out of the coffee shop.

Given that he lived on a shoestring and had very few possessions, she thought it odd that he was so generous with his money. She began to feel a little ashamed about what she'd said to Ali yesterday. He might be poor, but he was no deadbeat.

She had watched his hands while they ate. Long, thin fingers and wide palms—they were really beautiful. He had an artist's hands. She wondered again about what sort of things he painted. He'd neatly steered the conversation away from his artwork after she'd started eating and she'd let him, even though the subject intrigued her enormously. Not just because she loved art, but because his unwillingness to speak about it had made him seem a lot less cocksure and confident.

She could feel the pressure on the small of her back from his palm as he steered her out of the diner. She couldn't ignore the warmth in her middle at the contact. He still made her nervous. Men as good-looking as he was would always make her feel a little inadequate. Then there was that aura of wildness and danger about him that was unlike anyone she had ever known before. But she had to admit that he was starting to fascinate her.

They walked across the street in silence, but as they reached the bike Jessie remembered her bare legs. 'Would you mind waiting a minute while I go and put my jeans back on?'

He glanced at her legs. 'Sure. Seems like a shame, though.'

She was busy quelling the little flutter of excitement at his words when she spotted a familiar face coming out of the grocery store. 'Oh, no.'

Monroe gave her a quizzical look as he opened the saddlebags on the back of the Harley. 'What's the problem?'

'It's Bradley Dexter. I don't want him to spot me,' Jessie whispered as she ducked behind Monroe.

Bradley Dexter III was the son of Linc and Ali's nearest neighbour. Pampered and idle, he thought his red sports car was an extension of his personality and had turned out to be as persistent as a woodworm after Jessie had met him on the beach a few weeks before. She might be hard up, but she was not *that* hard up.

Jessie realised she was too late to avoid another annoying encounter, though, when the well-muscled young man in the surfer's standard uniform of board shorts and vest-top walked up to them. 'Hiya, Jessie. How'ya doing?'

Monroe heard the sigh from behind him before Jessie appeared at his side.

'Hello, Bradley.'

'We've got a beach party going tonight at the Sunspot. You wanna come along?' The guy's eyes dipped down Jessie's frame in a way Monroe didn't like one bit. 'You could wear that bitching little bikini I saw you in last week.'

Monroe thought he could hear Jessie's teeth grinding together. 'That's nice of you, Bradley, but I think I'm busy.' She touched Monroe's arm. 'This is Monroe, by the way. Monroe Latimer—he's Linc's brother.'

Bradley gave Monroe an absent glance. 'Sure, nice to meet you, dude. I guess you could come, too. But I get first dibs on the babe here.' He winked at Jessie, the hunger in his eyes unmistakable. Seeing Jessie blush and stiffen, Monroe felt his anger rise.

He put a firm hand on Jessie's hip and pulled her to his side. Ignoring her quick intake of breath, he gave Bradley a sharp stare.

'I don't think so, dude.' He had the surfer's attention now. 'I don't share.'

Bradley stepped back, his Adam's apple bobbing. 'Sure, man, no problem.' He gave Jessie a nervous wave, his gaze fixed on Monroe. 'See ya 'round, Jess,' he said and scurried off.

'What was that about?' Jessie shrugged off Monroe's arm.

'I was getting rid of Bradley the wolf for you.'

'I don't need your protection, thank you.'

Miserably embarrassed, Jessie stepped past Monroe but was pulled up short when he put his hands on her hips, tugged her into his arms. 'He's looking back,' he whispered in her ear as he nuzzled her neck. Shock waves shot through her whole system. 'Let's show him we mean business.'

'What?'

Jessie had no chance to react. No chance to register his intent. Strong fingers combed through her hair, angled her head slightly and then his lips were on hers. The move was so smooth, so fluid, Jessie could only gasp before his mouth covered hers.

The contact was electric. His mouth was firm and commanding on hers, his tongue exploring and then retreating in a clever rhythm that robbed her of thought. He kept one hand on her head, anchoring her to him, while the other swept down, moulding her curves before settling firmly on her bottom and pulling her even closer.

The rough feel of his jeans against her legs, the strong, solid feel of his chest against her breasts were so unyielding she felt as if she were being smothered. Her response though was unstoppable. Her mouth opened wider as her tongue tangled with his. He lifted his head for a moment and her breath gushed out, but then his lips were back on hers again. His teeth bit into her bottom lip. She began to pant, feeling dazed, delirious.

Then, suddenly, it was over.

'There.' His voice sounded dim because of the blood pounding in her ears. 'That ought to convince him.'

Jessie blinked up at him, her face flooding with heat as she registered the words through the fog of arousal. It was as if she'd been doused with ice water. She shoved him, her arms still shaking from need. 'You bastard.'

He held onto her arm. 'What's wrong, Red?'

She was so angry she could have spat at him. He was smiling at her, as if it had all been a game. The terrible tug of need and desire still throbbing in her belly only made her feel more humiliated. 'You had no right…' Her voice shook. 'You had no right to do that.'

Monroe could see the sheen of moisture in her eyes and hated himself for it. He wanted to taste her again. God, he wanted to strip her naked and bury himself inside her. Her response to the simple kiss had been electrifying. He was hard as a rock and throbbing painfully in his jeans. It was a major struggle to keep the carefree smile on his face. 'I was just trying to help you out with Bradley. What's the big deal?'

It was a lie. He'd wanted to kiss her ever since he'd laid eyes on her. That he'd been unable to resist her wasn't something he wanted to admit, though, even to himself.

'I didn't ask for your help.' Jessie's words came out on a

broken sob. Desperate not to let him see her break, she struggled out of his grasp.

'No harm done. It was just a little kiss.'

He made it sound like nothing at all. It would only make her seem like an idiot if she let him see how much more it had meant to her. Biting her lip to keep the tears back, Jessie gripped the strap of her bag with unsteady fingers. She had to get away from him.

He tucked a finger under her chin, his eyes clouded with concern. 'Hey, I'm sorry.'

Was that pity in his eyes? Jessie pushed his hand away, forced her eyes to go flat and remote. 'It's okay, Monroe.' She'd made enough of a spectacle of herself already. 'Like you said, it was nothing.' She whirled away from him.

As Jessie walked towards the public restrooms she kept her head high, her back ramrod straight, but couldn't stop the silent tears of humiliation rolling down her cheeks.

The journey back to the house was agony for both of them.

As Jessie clung onto the back of the bike, refusing to hold onto Monroe, she felt none of the thrill from the earlier journey into town.

All she could think about was the kiss they'd shared. It had been like no other kiss she'd ever had before. She'd made love before with less excitement.

Why had she responded to him like that?

It was mortifying and, what was worse, it had meant less than nothing to him. 'What's the big deal?' —that was what he'd said. He must have kissed loads of women before her and she hadn't measured up very well. He hadn't even insisted that she hold onto him on the ride back as he'd done on the way there. She felt angry with him and humiliated, but worse, much worse, was the feeling of rejection that she couldn't seem to shake no matter how hard she tried. Why should she care what a womanising ex-con thought of her? But the problem was she did care.

Monroe wanted to kick himself for his stupidity. Why the hell had he kissed her? Now he knew what she tasted like, what she felt like in his arms, he was going to have a hell of a time keeping his hands off her.

He had to keep his hands off her.

He slept with women for mutual pleasure, for kicks, but it could never mean anything deeper than that. He never got involved with anyone who might mean more to him. That was the way he lived; that was the way he had to live. Free and easy. No commitments, no ties.

The way she'd looked at him after the kiss, the shattered horror in her eyes had touched a place inside him he'd never even admitted existed. The woman was bad news all round. He was going to have to keep well clear of her. But how the hell was he going to do that, when he wanted her so damn much?

CHAPTER FIVE

'Jess?'

'Over here, Al.' Jessie poked her head round the kitchen counter as her sister waddled into view.

'Do you think you could get Emmy for me? I'm so tired.'

Seeing the exhaustion on her sister's face, Jessie dashed over and took her arm. 'Sit down, for goodness' sake.' She guided Ali towards the sofa. 'Where is Emmy? I thought she was with Linc.'

'He's working today, some crisis at the New York office.' Ali settled into the cushions and gave a hefty sigh. 'Emmy's been camped over at Monroe's all morning.'

Jessie frowned. 'But I thought she went over to see him yesterday.'

'And the day before that.' Ali paused to rub her back. 'She's been helping him fix the BMW. You wouldn't believe the state of her clothes when she got back yesterday. I was worried Monroe might be getting tired of having her hanging around. But I think he was actually pleased to see her this morning.' She smiled, her eyes warm. 'Anyway, I thought maybe you could go rescue him, as lunch is nearly ready.'

'Um.' Jessie felt trapped.

She'd been avoiding Monroe for over a week. If the humiliating memory of their kiss wasn't bad enough, the fact that she'd been reliving it in her dreams every night had made it all seem so much worse. She still wasn't ready to see him again. But Ali looked shattered. She couldn't very well refuse such a simple request.

Jessie arranged the sandwiches she'd made on the table, tried to steady her breathing. 'I'll go get her in a minute, Al.'

'Why don't you ask Monroe if he wants to come over for the barbecue tonight?' Ali said from the sofa. 'I haven't been able to tempt him with any of my invitations so far, but maybe the promise of a medium-rare steak will do the trick.'

Jessie's cheeks coloured. She'd rather gnaw off her own foot than ask Monroe over for the family's evening barbecue. All she needed was his smouldering looks over the charcoal to put her right off her own steak.

She rustled up a sweet smile for Ali as she slipped on her sandals. 'Will do.'

It was an effort for Jessie not to curse out loud as she marched across the lawn to the garage apartment. She was just pondering how she could get away with not giving him Ali's dinner invitation when she heard the delighted peal of Emmy's laughter, followed by a gruff masculine chuckle.

Rounding the side of the garage, she spotted Monroe's long jeans-clad legs sticking out from under the car. All she could see of Emmy were two pink sneakers wiggling furiously.

Should she be shocked or amazed that he actually had her five-year-old niece doubling as a car mechanic?

There was a loud clanging sound.

'Hey, hold on there, kid.'

'Sorry. Did I break it?' Emmy's feet went still.

Monroe's reply wasn't annoyed, just amused. 'Nah. It's tougher than that, but just remember what I said.'

'Treat the car with respect and it'll respect you back.' Emmy said the words as if reciting holy scripture.

'You got it. You want to finish it?'

'Can I?'

Jessie frowned at the adoring tone of her niece's voice. Did every single female within a ten-mile radius have to fall at his feet?

'Go for it.' She heard Emmy's childish grunt before Monroe's deep voice continued. 'That's it, kid. You're a great mechanic. Why don't you haul out? I'll be right behind you.'

Jessie stepped back as Emmy crawled out from under the car.

'Oh, Aunt Jessie, Aunt Jessie.' Emmy leapt in the air. Her face, which was smudged with what could only be axle grease, glowed with excitement. 'I did a lube job. It was way cool. Uncle Roe showed me, he let me do it all by myself.'

'That's wonderful, Emmy.' Jessie tried to sound enthusiastic but couldn't help wincing at the huge oil stain all over her niece's favourite Barbie T-shirt. 'We better go get you washed up before lunch.'

'Do I have to go?' Emmy's chin hit her chest. 'Uncle Roe said I could have peanut butter and jelly sandwiches with him today.'

Jessie was just wondering how to deal with that request when the man himself slid out from under the car and got to his feet. Her heart thudded in her chest at the sight of him, tall and lean in ragged denim and faded cotton. She could feel her face getting hot at the long look he gave her and wanted to scream.

'Hi, Red.' There was that stupid nickname again. The heat in her face increased.

'Hello, Monroe.'

Jessie was grateful when Emmy tugged on his jeans, distracting him.

'Jessie says I've got to go now, but I want to have lunch with you.'

He kneeled down, gave the little girl a serious look as she rested her hands on his shoulders. 'Don't sweat it. We can do that another time.'

Jessie saw Emmy had left grubby fingerprints all over him, but Monroe didn't seem to notice as he held onto the little girl and stood up. The shadow of emotion crossed his face. For a moment he seemed lost in thought, but then his eyes focused on Jessie and he gave her a slow smile that made her feel unpleasantly warm.

'We'll go clean up,' he said. 'You want to come up and grab a drink?'

The statement sounded casual, but they both knew it was an olive branch.

Jessie wanted to stay mad at him; the memory of the kiss they'd shared still loomed large between them. But having seen the tender, thoughtful way he handled Emmy and the beaming grin on her niece's face as she clung to his neck, she just couldn't do it.

'That would be nice, thanks.'

As he turned to heft the little girl up the stairs to his apartment, Jessie wondered at this new, nurturing side of him she never would have expected. She followed them up the steps, trying to stop her eyes from straying to the very nice male butt displayed in front of her in worn denim.

Entering the apartment, Monroe let Emmy scramble down out of his arms. 'You know where the soap is, kid.'

'Yes, Uncle Roe.' She shot him an impish grin and scampered off to the bathroom.

Monroe felt an answering squeeze on his heart. He didn't have any experience with kids, but Linc's daughter had really gotten to him in the last few days.

He wasn't supposed to be making any attachments. He was

just passing through. But when the little girl had hugged him round the neck a few minutes ago and settled so easily into his arms, the trust and adoration in her eyes had made his heart hurt in a way that couldn't be good

Of course, the sight of Emmy's auntie, looking gorgeous and irritated, hadn't exactly made the emotional punch any easier to deal with.

Jessie had been avoiding him for the last week or so, ever since that incendiary kiss of theirs in town, and he'd been more than happy to let her.

The woman was a major complication—one he definitely didn't need. Over the last few days, his mind had strayed to thoughts of her without warning. The minute he'd seen her again, he'd had to admit he'd missed her. The woman looked good enough to eat and, now he knew what she tasted like, it was hard to resist taking another bite.

He heard her step into the apartment and close the door, but concentrated on washing his hands and pouring himself a long, cold glass of water.

If Emmy's sweet, uncomplicated affection was getting to him, it was nothing compared to the effect the kid's auntie was having on him. And one thing was for sure, his thoughts in that direction were a lot more dangerous. He turned, appreciating the way her hips moved as she walked into the room.

'Emmy's certainly taken a shine to you,' she murmured.

'I've taken a shine to her, too. She's a great kid.' He raised his glass. 'Do you want a glass of water? It's all I've got.'

'That would be nice.'

'No problem.' He pulled another glass from the cabinet above the sink and filled it. 'Here you go.'

She took the glass, her hand trembling as their fingers touched.

Her eyes met his and he watched as the heat crept into her

cheeks. Yep, it was going to be near on impossible to keep his hands off her now.

Jessie took a hasty gulp of water and spluttered as the cold liquid hit the back of her throat.

'You okay there, Red?' His voice was low and intimate.

He put his hand on her back and rubbed. She was positive she could feel the calluses on his fingers through the thin cotton of her dress and she shivered. Get a grip, woman.

'I'm finished, Uncle Roe.'

The little girl skipped back into the room, unaware of the tension that sizzled between the two adults.

'All clean?' Monroe said the words to Emmy but kept his eyes on Jessie.

'Yes, look.' Emmy held up her hands for Monroe's inspection. Jessie released the breath she'd been holding as he turned to look at the little girl.

'Good job.'

Emmy ran up and grabbed hold of his leg. 'Can I come back tomorrow? Can I? Can I?'

He ruffled the little girl's curly brown hair. 'Sure, if you want to and your mom says it's okay.'

'We better be going, Emmy.' Jessie reached for her niece's hand, but the little girl continued to cling onto her uncle. 'Lunch is already on the table.'

'Okay.' Emmy let go reluctantly and put her hand in Jessie's.

'I'll see you tomorrow, kid.' Hearing the affection in Monroe's voice, seeing the warm way he rested his hand on Emmy's shoulder, Jessie felt a sharp surge of guilt.

She had no right to keep this man from bonding with his family.

So what if she couldn't stop blushing every time she saw him? So what if she couldn't seem to forget that kiss? From what she could gather, Linc and Ali and Emmy were the only family Monroe Latimer had. Not giving him Ali's dinner invitation suddenly seemed both cowardly and selfish.

'Ali wondered if you'd like to come over for dinner tonight,' Jessie blurted out. She saw surprise flash in his eyes, but he said nothing. 'We're having a barbecue. Linc's doing steaks…' Her voice trailed off when Monroe remained silent.

'Come, come, come.' Emmy jumped up and down as she sang the words. Jessie was grateful that her niece had picked up the ball, but could see Monroe was still hesitating.

'I don't know.' He sounded oddly unsure of himself.

'We'd all love to have you there,' Jessie said, surprised to realise she meant it.

His gaze intensified. 'You would, huh?'

'We would, we would, we would,' Emmy sang again. He gave her a quick grin before he looked back at Jessie.

'I guess it'd be my pleasure, then. I can't say no to two pretty ladies.'

Emmy giggled and then shouted, 'Yippee,' punching the air with her small fist.

Jessie felt the same leap of joy, despite the ball of heat that seemed to have lodged beneath her breastbone.

'I'll tell Ali.' Jessie gave Monroe a shaky smile as she pulled Emmy towards the door.

'Bye-bye.' Emmy waved.

'See you tonight, kid. You, too, Red.'

Jessie glanced back. He was leaning against the kitchen counter. He looked relaxed again and amused, his thumbs hooked into his jeans and a ridiculously charming smile on his face. Jessie felt the fire blaze inside her. Unable to trust her voice, she gave him a quick nod as she hauled Emmy out the door.

* * *

No question about it, Monroe thought wryly as he watched Jessie close the apartment door. The woman was dangerous.

He strolled across the apartment to the French doors and watched as Jessie and Emmy made their way up to the house. Emmy was skipping ahead, while Jessie walked behind, looking lush and unbearably sexy in the tight little polka-dot number.

Dangerous or not, she was becoming damn near irresistible. She looked gorgeous, and he loved the way she blushed so easily. But it wasn't just her appearance or her obvious reaction to him that made her so appealing.

He also liked her as a person. She was full of spirit and fire and feisty as hell.

Maybe they could have a little fun together after all. She was a grown woman who certainly knew her own mind and didn't mind speaking it. She was obviously unattached and in need of a little romance or she wouldn't have kissed him the way she had in front of the grocery store. He'd already made it clear that he was just passing through, so there was no need for her to get the wrong idea.

He leaned against the glass as Emmy and Jessie disappeared from view. Maybe he'd test the waters tonight, see how she responded to the suggestion. His lips curved as he thought about what he and Jessie could do to amuse each other over the next month or so.

CHAPTER SIX

'GET a grip, woman!' Jessie stalked over to her wardrobe.

The cerise linen dress she shoved back in was the fourth outfit she'd tried on in less than twenty minutes. Staring into the snarl of colours and fabrics, she resisted the urge to stamp her foot.

What on earth was the matter with her?

Why did she care what Monroe thought of her outfit anyway? Determined not to waste any more time on a decision that should have taken her ten seconds, she grabbed the first thing that came to hand.

You could never go wrong with the old little black dress, she thought as she slipped the slinky Lycra sheath over her head.

She examined herself in the wardrobe's full-length mirror, caught her bottom lip between her teeth. Was the outfit maybe a little too sexy for an evening barbecue with her family? She could picture Monroe's lazy smile. The hot look in his eyes.

Stop it, you silly cow. The LBD was fine; he probably wouldn't even notice that the material clung a little too closely to every curve.

She never should have invited him. She'd known this was going to happen. She slammed the wardrobe door and slipped on a pair of simple red pumps. She pulled a matching silk scarf from the array in her dresser and tied it loosely round her neck.

She might have guessed she would blow this completely out of proportion.

She didn't know what it was about Monroe, but whenever she was near him she was so brutally aware of him she couldn't seem to think about anything else but the feel of his lips on hers. His long, strong body pressed against her. It was ridiculous—they'd only shared one kiss and he'd made it quite clear that, for him at least, it had just been play-acting. But her flustered response when their fingers had touched over the water glass that afternoon went to show she could not be trusted to keep her cool around him.

She was a grown woman. She did not have crushes. She'd just never been kissed like that before and she still needed a bit more time to settle.

The way she was feeling at the moment, twenty-five years probably wouldn't be long enough.

Jessie stepped out into the hallway and closed the door to her room. Relax and breathe, she told herself as she walked stiffly down the stairs.

Jessie was both relieved and disappointed when she walked out onto the terrace and saw that Monroe wasn't there yet.

The night was balmy and warm and the smell of jasmine hung in the air like a rich woman's perfume. The fairy lights Linc had rigged up over the barbecue winked in the dusk and reflected off the surface of the pool like cheeky little water nymphs.

The fluttering in her stomach calmed as she strolled round the water to the grill. As Linc lorded it over the flames with a pair of barbecue tongs, the mouth-watering scent of cooking meat surrounded him.

Looking up, he caught sight of her and smiled. 'Hey, good-looking.'

The tightness in Jessie's chest eased, the familiarity of

family making her feel safe and secure. 'That should be my line, shouldn't it?' She gave Linc a light kiss on the cheek. 'As in what you got cookin'?'

'About a half a cow,' Linc joked. 'I hope you're hungry.'

Where once the teasing admiration in her brother-in-law's eyes would have had Jessie blushing profusely, now she simply felt a warm, comfortable feeling settle in.

'Stop flirting with my sister and watch what you're doing,' Ali called out from behind them. 'I don't want burnt cow again, thank you very much.'

Jessie turned to see her sister flopped in a large armchair. Emmy giggled, glancing up from the jigsaw she was piecing together by her mother's feet.

'Stop your belly-aching, woman,' Linc replied, giving Jessie a conspiratorial wink.

Jessie grinned back at him, then sat down in the chair next to her sister. 'Still feeling exhausted?'

Ali adjusted herself in her seat and huffed. 'No, not really, I just have this devilish urge to make Linc's life hell at the moment.' The twinkle in her eyes was positively wicked. 'After all, he's the one responsible for this.' Ali laid her palms heavily on the impressive mound of her belly.

'The way I heard it,' Jessie leant in and whispered to her sister, 'he wasn't the only one there.'

Ali laughed and gave her a light slap on the arm. 'Hey, you're supposed to be on my side. And by the way, while we're talking about sisterly solidarity,' she continued, giving Jessie's figure a quick appraisal, 'it would help if you didn't look like a supermodel while I look like a beached whale.'

'Thanks, I think,' Jessie replied.

'Mummy, when's Uncle Monroe going to be here?' Emmy's sleepy enquiry made Jessie's pulse spike.

'Soon, honey,' Ali replied, her voice relaxed. 'What time did you tell him, Jess?'

'I don't remember. But he can see the pool terrace from his bedroom window, he must know we're out here.'

'Good point,' Ali remarked, eyeing her sister thoughtfully. 'You know, it's funny,' Ali continued, her voice suspiciously light, 'but I've noticed it's only your invitations that he accepts.'

Jessie's head swung round, the gaze that had strayed up to Monroe's apartment window focused on her sister again. 'What are you trying to say?'

'Nothing. Just that he's quite a hunk, isn't he?'

'I…I guess so,' Jessie sputtered, seeing the sharp look on her sister's face. She tensed. This was what she'd been afraid of. Did her sister think she was developing some sort of ridiculous crush on Monroe?

Ali touched Jessie's arm, her voice softened. 'I happen to know from experience, Jess, that the Latimer men are hard to resist.'

'I don't know what you mean.'

'All I'm saying is, if you need to talk, I'm here.' Ali smiled, patting her rounded belly. 'In fact, I'm anchored to the spot.'

Linc had started piling the steaks onto a large serving plate when Jessie spotted Monroe's tall figure strolling towards them in the darkening twilight.

Emmy scrambled out of her lap. 'Uncle Roe!' The little girl dashed across the lawn towards him, her drowsiness forgotten in a spurt of excitement.

Jessie watched as Monroe swung his niece up in his arms.

'Emmy's certainly fallen for him,' Ali murmured next to her. Jessie didn't dare turn round, worried her face had the same adoring look on it that Emmy's did.

* * *

Monroe hefted Emmy easily into his arms, enjoying her sleepy commentary on the 'hours and hours and hours' she'd been waiting for him. She clung to his neck, her light breath on his cheek making him feel good and at the same time strangely uneasy.

He'd watched the little group on the pool terrace from his apartment window for nearly half an hour before coming over. He'd almost decided not to come at all.

He hadn't been able to hear what they were saying, but they looked from where he'd been standing like a unit, a family. His brother's family, he'd thought, and the sharp sense of envy had stunned him. He didn't want this sort of life, this sort of commitment, so why did their comfortable companionship tug at some place deep inside him?

He'd accepted Jessie's invitation earlier because he enjoyed watching her. He'd told himself it was a nice healthy dose of lust that had dragged him out tonight.

But now, with Emmy's little fingers clinging onto his neck, the comforting warmth in Ali's eyes as she greeted him, the friendly handshake Linc gave him as he walked up to the grill, he realised that it wasn't only lust. The feeling of warmth, of need, scared him.

'Just in time.' Linc's voice was easy, confident. Why did Monroe feel so out of his element?

'Jess,' Linc said, 'grab Monroe a beer from the cooler— looks like he's got his hands full.'

Monroe's eyes settled on Jessie as she handed him an icy bottle. He shifted Emmy in his arms to take it. 'Thanks, Red.'

She gave him a quick nod then looked away, but he'd seen the flash of awareness and what looked like worry in her face. He couldn't take his eyes off her as she took the steaks from Linc and placed them on the long glass table laid out on the patio.

Her hair seemed to be made of flame tonight, tumbling

down her back in wild, lustrous waves. The simple little black number she had on should have been demure but it showcased the curves beneath in a way that was damn near indecent. Aware that Linc might be watching him, Monroe took a long pull of his beer and dragged his eyes away.

'We might as well get settled,' Linc said quietly.

Emmy laid her head on Monroe's shoulder. The little girl went still and heavy in his arms as Linc and Ali and Jessie put the last of the food on the table. The feel of Emmy's body relaxing against his made the ache in his heart sharpen.

Linc placed a hand on his daughter's back. 'Come on, Emmy. You can sit in my lap while we eat.'

'I want to stay with Monroe,' Emmy's tired voice whispered against Monroe's neck.

'It's okay, Linc. She's no trouble,' he found himself saying.

'You sure? It's not that easy slicing steak with a sleeping child in your arms.'

Monroe simply nodded. He didn't know why he wanted to keep the child with him. He just knew he did.

Jessie watched as Monroe struggled to finish his food. Emmy was sound asleep in his lap. Linc and Ali had started clearing the table. The meal had gone quickly, Linc and Ali keeping the conversation light and undemanding. Monroe had been surprisingly subdued.

Something had changed about him. The cocksure, devil-may-care confidence that seemed so much a part of him was gone tonight. The same vulnerability she'd glimpsed in the diner was back tonight. Why did he seem wary and unsure of himself?

'I feel stuffed.' Ali sighed and leaned back in her chair.

Linc gave her belly a reassuring rub. 'That's because you are, honey.'

Ali swatted his hand. 'Not funny, Latimer.'

Linc laughed and hauled her out of her chair. 'Come on, I'll take the plates in and you can put your feet up on the sofa.' Putting an arm round his wife, Linc smiled at Jessie and Monroe. 'You want me to take Emmy, Monroe?'

'She's out like a light. I can hold her a while longer.'

'Thanks.'

Jessie stacked all the plates except Monroe's and handed them to Linc.

As Linc and Ali walked off across the lawn, Jessie settled back into her seat and watched Monroe. The pungent aroma of the dying charcoal was overlaid with the rich scent of summer blooms and the crisp smell of the sea. She could hear the gentle hum of the surf on the beach, and the soft murmur of Emmy's childish snores.

It occurred to Jessie that for some reason during the evening her nerves had simply dissolved. The night had settled around them, comforting yet also intimate, but she didn't feel nervous about being left alone with Monroe. Maybe it was the two glasses of wine she'd had, she thought, as she took another sip. Or more likely it was the sight of him with the little girl curled in his arms. Tonight, for the first time, he didn't scare her.

When his knife clattered onto the plate again, Jessie took pity on him. 'Do you want me to cut it for you?'

He looked up, his brow creasing. 'Yeah, thanks, I'm starving.'

Leaning over, Jessie began slicing the meat on his plate.

'I feel like a first-grader.' His voice whispered close to her ear, making the soft skin of her nape tingle. But unlike before, when the giddy awareness had made her feel vulnerable and irritated, she enjoyed the warmth that seemed to spread up her neck.

'I could take her in.' She pushed his plate back to him. 'She probably ought to go to bed now anyway.'

'No need.' He adjusted the little girl in his lap, forking up a mouthful of the newly-cut meat as Emmy's head nestled against his broad shoulder. He chewed and swallowed. 'It's kind of nice to hold her when she's not talking a mile a minute.' He looked a little shocked at his own admission, making Jessie's lips curve.

'What's so funny?' The prickle of annoyance in his tone made Jessie's smile widen.

'You are. You're cute.'

He frowned at that, putting down his fork. 'Hey, that's my line.'

'Not any more, it's not.' Jessie nodded at Emmy. 'She's totally besotted with you, you know.'

'She's a good kid.' He sounded confused, making Jessie wonder.

'She's also a very good judge of character.'

Monroe blinked at the statement. The soft words sounded almost like an endearment. He studied Jessie in the flickering light. He'd planned to come on to her tonight. An opportunity like this, with her as good as flirting with him, should have been just what he was looking for.

He wanted to kiss her in the worst way. But something was holding him back. And it wasn't only the sleeping child in his lap.

He didn't only want to feast on those sweet lips of hers, he realised with a jolt. He wanted to bask in the approval he saw in her eyes. He wanted her to care for him. That was the problem. He felt the stab of guilt at the thought. He'd intended to seduce her, not make her fall for him. That would never work.

'She doesn't know me.' The words came out harsher than he'd intended. 'And neither do you, Red.'

* * *

The abrupt statement might have put Jessie off, but as he said it she could see the panic in his eyes. He wasn't angry. Not really. He was scared. But why?

'Does it frighten you, Monroe, to have people care about you?'

She knew she'd struck a nerve when he stiffened. Annoyance swirled in his eyes. 'What the hell does that—' The angry words cut off when Emmy stirred.

He rocked her gently, until the child settled again. When he looked back at Jessie, she could see he'd been careful to settle himself as well.

The slow, easy smile that she knew so well spread across his face. But for the first time she realised it was nothing more than a diversionary tactic. A defence. The lazy grin his way of distancing himself.

'Don't get the wrong idea, Red.' His tone was low and intimate, making the familiar shiver run up her spine. 'I won't mind a bit if you want to get up close and personal with me. In fact, I'm counting on it.'

He was teasing her again, but it didn't make her bristle as it once had, because she could see the usual twinkle hadn't reached his eyes. Enjoying her newfound power, Jessie raised a coquettish eyebrow and looked him straight in the eye.

'That's quite a challenge, Monroe. I'd be careful if I were you. I might take you up on it.'

She could see she'd surprised him when his eyes widened, but the surge of heat that followed made her breath catch. He was looking at her now as if he wanted to devour her. Suddenly the giddy fluttering in her belly, the heat in her cheeks from an hour before were back with a vengeance.

He might be cute, but she'd be a fool to think he wasn't still dangerous.

'Jess, you want to grab the rest of the plates while I put

Emmy to bed?' Linc's voice came to Jessie through the blood pounding in her ears. She forced her eyes away from Monroe to see her brother-in-law walking round the pool towards them both. She let out an audible breath.

Saved, she thought, and in the nick of time.

Jessie sat at the vanity table in her room and slathered moisturiser on her face. As had become a habit over the last week, her gaze strayed out her bedroom window, across the dark expanse of the gardens to Monroe's garage apartment. As always, his windows were a beacon of light in the night. She glanced at the clock on the mantelpiece. Nearly midnight again. Did the man never sleep?

She closed the curtains, shrugged into the simple satin shift she wore to sleep in and turned the switch by the door. The air conditioner subsided to a quiet hum. She walked across the room and sank into the huge double bed. As she pulled the thin sheet over herself she couldn't stop thinking about the apartment across the way and the man inside it.

He still made her nervous. After all, no matter what she did, she just couldn't forget that kiss. But despite that, tonight, and maybe even before that, her opinion of him had changed. She knew now there was a lot more to him than his staggering good looks and his industrial-strength sex appeal.

Over the past week and a half Jessie had let go of her suspicion that he had arrived on Linc's doorstep to sponge off his rich brother.

Monroe had spent every morning since he'd been there either tuning up the cars or working on the garden. He'd fixed the lawnmower and, after ten days of his tender loving care, the grass was at last green again and the flowerbeds were starting to perk up, too. And all this, even though Linc had told him again at supper that he was a guest and should act like one. Monroe had simply shrugged and said that he liked helping out.

He disappeared every afternoon, and apart from tonight had refused all of Ali's invitations to come to supper. Jessie wondered what he was doing right now. Maybe he was in bed, too. The thought sent a shaft of heat straight to her core.

Get a hold of yourself. She was acting like a woman with a serious problem. But Ali was right, he was a hunk, and right at the moment he seemed to be focused on her. She began to think about the other things she knew about him, and then shot upright in bed.

He wasn't in bed, now. He was painting. Of course, that was what he had to be doing.

If she hadn't been distracted by that kiss and her newfound feelings for him she would have remembered their conversation in the diner sooner.

Throwing off the covers, Jessie paced to the room's *en suite* bathroom and ran herself a glass of water. What did he paint? Whether or not he had any talent, he was certainly dedicated. He was at it every afternoon and most of the night.

Draining the glass, Jessie rinsed it out and walked back across the deep pile carpet to the bedroom window. She peeked out of the curtains. She felt silly, like an over-eager schoolgirl, fantasising about her first major crush and spying on him in the middle of the night. But she couldn't help it. This intriguing new turn of events only made him all the more irresistible.

His lights were still on.

She was dying to see what he was doing. After all, art was her passion, too.

When she'd left college, she'd kidded herself for a whole year that she was destined to take the art world by storm.

After a series of rejections, though, from a string of different galleries, she'd had to admit that, although she was passionate about art, her talent—like her portfolio—had been woefully inadequate.

It wasn't that she was dreadful; she just wasn't ever going to be great. Being able to see her own inadequacies had been her curse, she'd thought this spring, when she'd finally given up her job as a layout designer in a tiny print shop in Soho.

She'd been miserable doing the mundane, boring designs for pamphlets. Not only did it waste what little design talent she had, it was also a million miles from the beauty and elegance that she'd once hoped to embrace.

When Ali and Linc had asked her to come out to America for the summer and help out with Emmy while Ali awaited the birth of her second child, she'd jumped at the chance. It would be a chance to forget about her miserable failure with Toby as well as her pathetic attempt to start a career as a designer. Linc had also arranged a working visa, so she could 'keep her options open,' as he put it.

Being with Ali's family had lifted her spirits and now that she had her new job at the little gallery in Cranford, she finally felt as if she weren't spinning her wheels any more. She was starting afresh at last. Time to get a new master plan. Maybe this was where her talent lay—in the appreciation of art.

Jessie let the curtain fall back down. But how the heck was she going to make a life's work out of it if she had an artist living in the same house as her—or as good as—and it had taken her over a week to figure it out? Okay, so she had been slightly distracted by other things where Monroe was concerned, but really. It was totally pathetic.

Whipping the sheet back and climbing into bed, Jessie was struck by the sight of Monroe that evening when he had said goodbye to her. That cocky grin back in place.

Well, okay, so Monroe had a pretty devastating effect on

her, but she ought to be able to ask the guy to let her have a look at his work. Fluffing up her pillow, she plopped her head down on it. She would march over to his apartment tomorrow when she got back from work and demand to see what he was painting. How hard could it be?

CHAPTER SEVEN

'MONROE, we need to talk.' Linc's face was set, his voice firm.

'Yeah, what about?' Monroe raised an eyebrow. He didn't like it. They were standing in the kitchen of the main house. It was Saturday morning and, after the unsettling feelings stirred at last night's barbecue, the last thing he needed now was a brother-to-brother chat.

'Here.' Reaching into the fridge, Linc took out two frosty Pepsis and handed one across the breakfast bar. 'Take this and sit down.'

Monroe hooked a leg over the stool and opened his soda. He took a long drag, he'd been repairing the deer fencing most of the morning and his mouth felt as if he'd been chewing sand.

'What's the problem?' Monroe was glad to hear the easy confidence back in his voice.

Jessie had spooked him pretty bad the night before with that crack about him being scared of people caring. He'd spent the night painting—and thinking hard about what she'd said. It had taken a while for him to sort it out—too damn long, in fact—but everything was cool now.

Why should Jessie's comment bother him? She didn't know him. Nobody did. By the early hours of the morning, he'd managed to dismiss what she'd said and think about what had happened after.

Jessie had made it pretty clear she might be interested in a little fun. Given that, and the fact that she turned him inside out with lust, it was going to be impossible for him to ignore her for much longer. But fun was all it would be. Simple and uncomplicated. He could give her a good time. He just had to make sure she understood fun was all it would be.

'I want you to stop mowing the lawn.' The sharp tone of Linc's voice brought Monroe back to the matter at hand. Linc took a sip of his Pepsi, the movement jerky and tense. 'And tuning the damn cars, and working so hard around the place, for heaven's sake.'

'The BMW needed a tune.' Monroe kept his tone casual. 'I can't believe you'd treat such a beautiful machine with such little respect.'

Linc slammed his can down, knocking over one of the framed snapshots perched at the end of the breakfast bar. 'The damn car's never run better in years. That's not the point and you know it. You're a guest here. I don't want you working to pay your way.'

Monroe took another sip, watched his brother over the rim. 'I'm not a freeloader, Linc. I told you that from the get-go. Either you accept the work or I'm out of here.'

'Hell.' Linc drank down the last of the small can, crushed it in one hand and flung it in the trash.

Hearing the resignation in his brother's voice, Monroe relaxed as he put his own soda down. As far as he was concerned, the matter was settled. He reached for the photo that had fallen over. Flipping it upright, he studied the picture inside.

It was a wedding shot, but not the stiff formal type. Ali looked sexy and happy in a full-length white dress while Linc stood behind her. He was wearing a black tux, but the tie was gone, the top few buttons of his dress shirt were undone and his arms were wrapped around his bride's midriff. The smile on his face was relaxed and proud. The rest of the wedding party was arranged around them, all grinning or laughing at the camera.

'Nice shot,' Monroe said as he stared at the snapshot, ashamed at the familiar tug of envy.

Linc leaned across to take a look. 'Ali's dad took it. It was a great day.'

Monroe could hear the bone-deep contentment in his brother's voice and struggled not to feel jealous. He absolutely refused to go there again.

It was then he spotted the vivacious figure in a clingy fire-engine-red dress at the far left of the picture. The bold colour should have clashed with the mass of dark red hair, but instead it displayed the young woman's soft, translucent skin and luscious curves to perfection. Before he could stop himself, Monroe ran his thumb gently down the image.

'Jess is a real stunner, isn't she?' Linc murmured.

'What?' Monroe looked up to find his brother watching him. 'I guess so.' He put the photo back where it belonged. He could see the frown on Linc's face and knew why it was there. 'No need to worry, bro. I know she's out of my league.'

Linc frowned. 'What makes you think that?' he asked quietly.

Monroe lifted an eyebrow. 'Oh, come on.' He shrugged, tried to sound indifferent. 'Even I can see that girl's got commitment tattooed across her forehead in block letters and you and I both know I can barely spell the word.'

Linc's eyes narrowed. 'Why can't you spell it, Monroe?'

Monroe drained the last of his soda and glared at his brother. 'I don't know, Linc.' He couldn't keep the bitter edge of sarcasm out of his voice. 'Maybe because I was in juvie when I should have been graduating high school.'

Monroe stood up, his face rigid. Angry that his brother had made him lose the comfortable distance he'd struggled so long for the night before. Angrier still that he'd been forced to lie to Linc. Jessie might be out of his league, but he was going after her anyway.

Linc looked at him coolly for a moment before speaking. 'What's so scary about commitment, Monroe?'

Monroe's jaw tensed, his brother's words too damn reminiscent of what Jessie had said to him the night before. Didn't any of these people get it? His thoughts and feelings were his business and nobody else's.

'I'm not scared of commitment,' he snarled, and then stopped. Calm down. Keep it cool. Don't let him see he's rattled you. 'I'm just not interested in it.'

'Jess is, so you should be careful there, Roe,' Linc said evenly. 'You could hurt her.'

'I'm not going to hurt her.' To hell with keeping it cool. 'And anyway, it's none of your damn business.'

Sending the empty soda can sailing into the trash, Monroe stalked out of the kitchen.

Linc watched as his brother stormed off across the lawn towards the garage apartment, temper evident in each long, angry stride. He shook his head slowly, and smiled. 'That's where you're wrong,' he said gently. 'We're family, Roe. And that makes it my business whether you like it or not.'

'Hey, Monroe.'

Monroe caught Ali's shouted greeting over the roar of the lawnmower and switched off the powerful machine.

He struggled for patience as she walked towards him. He didn't want company. It had taken him most of the morning to calm down after his run-in with Linc.

As he watched her approach his eyes skidded down her figure. It had been dark last night and he hadn't got a good look at her. But now in the noon sun, her belly looked enormous in the stretchy little summer dress. Embarrassed that he found the sight beautiful, he looked away. He concentrated on pulling the bandanna out of his back pocket and wiping his brow.

Drawing level with the riding mower, Ali sighed and rubbed her back. 'You're just the man I needed to talk to.'

Monroe dismounted slowly. 'You got me.'

His glance seemed to flit to her abdomen again of its own accord.

Ali smiled. 'Don't panic, Monroe. I'm not due for at least another few weeks.'

Monroe felt his stomach pitch. 'You're gonna get bigger?'

She laughed. 'Probably, but don't worry. I won't pop.'

Monroe spent some time tucking his bandanna into his back pocket before looking at her. He could see the smile in her eyes and relaxed enough to smile back at her.

She didn't just look big. She looked gorgeous. Her sister Jessie would look the same when she had kids. He ruthlessly suppressed the thought. It wasn't something he was ever going to see.

'Anyway, enough about me and the bump,' Ali remarked. 'I wanted to thank you for all the work you've been doing around here. The people carrier drives like a dream now and the gardens look fantastic.'

'You're welcome.' His shoulders tensed. 'Linc hasn't sent you over to tell me to stop, has he?'

'No.' She looked surprised. 'Did he have words with you about it, then?'

'Yeah.' It annoyed him to realise it was still needling him.

'I thought he might,' Ali said slowly, a considering look in her eyes. 'Linc's a little hung up about money. He thinks because he's got heaps of it, nobody else should pay for anything. He's generous to a fault,' Ali continued, the calm understanding in her face making Monroe feel edgy. 'But he doesn't always stop to consider the importance of pride and self-respect. Especially to people who've had to earn it the hard way.'

Monroe was speechless. How the hell did she know that about him? They'd only met a week or so ago.

'Anyway—' Ali's voice was light, but the look in her eyes as she registered his reaction was anything but '—I didn't come to talk to you about Linc and his many shortcomings.'

Monroe tried to shake off his uneasiness. 'Right.'

'Linc's got a problem at the New York office, so we've decided to base ourselves at the penthouse for a few weeks. We're leaving tomorrow evening.'

'No sweat.' Did that include Jessie? he wondered.

'The thing is, it's Emmy's sixth birthday next Tuesday.'

Monroe gave a quick grin, recalling Emmy's endless chatter on the subject. 'She might just have mentioned that a couple of times.'

'I'll bet she has.' Ali grinned back. 'We thought it might be nice, before we head off to Manhattan, if we had a little surprise birthday party for her tomorrow afternoon.'

'Sounds like a plan.' Monroe refused to feel the little stab of pain as it occurred to him why Ali was telling him all this. 'You want me to make myself scarce. It's not a problem.'

'What? No!' Ali grabbed his arm. Her eyes, Monroe saw with amazement, were wide with shock. 'Monroe, for goodness' sake! I came staggering all the way out here—and, believe me, walking three hundred yards with a belly this size is no mean feat—to make sure you didn't make yourself scarce tomorrow. I want you there. Emmy would be devastated if you didn't turn up. We all would be.'

Now it was his turn to be amazed. He could see by the earnest look in her eyes that she was absolutely serious. 'Are you sure about this?'

'Monroe, I'm warning you, if you don't show up, I'm going to—' She broke off, grabbed her belly. 'Oh!'

Monroe felt the blood drain out of his face. 'What's wrong, Ali? Is it the kid?' He reached for her, but Ali only grinned when she got her breath back.

'No, no. It's okay.' She kept hold of his hand, pulled it towards her. 'The baby gave me the most almighty kick. Here, press down and you can feel it, too.'

She placed her hands over his and pushed his palm firmly into the stretchy cotton fabric. Monroe was about to draw back, miserably embarrassed, when he felt two quick jabs.

'Damn!' His heart jumped into his throat.

'Isn't it great? This one's a real slugger. Emmy used to just lie there all day. I guess she made up for it, though, when she got out.'

Lost in happy memories, Ali didn't look at him until he dragged his palm away.

Her face sobered instantly. 'Monroe, are you okay?'

'Yeah.' He felt sick with regret and a terrible longing that he thought he'd buried years before. 'It's just…it's pretty mind-blowing, isn't it?' That much was at least the truth. 'I need to get back to this. I'll see you later.'

Ali watched as Monroe climbed back onto the ride-on mower. Why was he avoiding her eyes? And why had he looked so shattered, so desperate, a moment ago? 'Don't forget, I want to see you at the house tomorrow, around about noon,' she said.

'Sure.' He gave her a vague nod as he pulled the bandanna out of his back pocket and tied it round his forehead.

'And I better warn you, I won't accept any excuses.' Her

parting words were lost in the roar of the engine. Ali could see the grim concentration on his face as he drove off.

What had happened to him? And what did it have to do with the baby?

CHAPTER EIGHT

As Jessie wrote out her third delivery slip of the day, she saw the Cranford Art Gallery's owner, Mrs Bennett, approach.

'Well done, my dear,' she said. 'I can't remember the last time we sold three canvases in the space of a couple of hours.' It was the first time Jessie had seen Mrs Bennett really smile. The gesture made her look younger and even a little carefree.

Jessie found herself smiling back. 'Thank you, Mrs Bennett.'

'You know, you're a natural at this.'

'I think I've been lucky with the sales,' Jessie said, cautiously.

'I'm not talking about the sales,' Mrs Bennett said. 'Although, that is a nice side benefit. No, I mean, you know about art. You've got a good eye, my dear.'

Jessie found her chest swelling at the appreciation in her employer's gaze. She'd been distracted since last night, thinking about Monroe and his artwork. Wondering if she even had the right to ask to see it. Would she really know if it was any good or not? But Mrs Bennett's praise gave her a newfound confidence. Maybe her idea that she could make a career out of her appreciation of art wasn't that ridiculous after all. 'Thank you, that means a lot to me,' she said.

'I'm glad.' Mrs Bennett leant forward. 'Actually, my coming over to speak to you wasn't entirely altruistic.'

'It wasn't?'

'Ellen Arthur just rang to say she's sprained her ankle.'

'That's dreadful.' Jessie knew the other woman was the gallery's chief sales assistant and part-time curator.

'It's not all that serious, but Ellen won't be in for the next two weeks and I need someone to cover for her in the mornings. I wondered if you could come in?'

'I'd love to,' Jessie answered instinctively, then remembered her conversation with Ali that morning. 'Oh, but I can't—I'm supposed to be going to New York with my sister and her family tomorrow.' After all, she'd come to America this summer to help out Ali and Linc. 'But I suppose I could speak to my sister about it.'

'Why don't you call her, dear, and find out if she needs you there?' Mrs Bennett sounded undaunted. 'I'll pay you Ellen's hourly rate and it will be a good opportunity for you to look at the rest of our stock. I need some advice about what to hang now you've managed to sell ten paintings in the space of two weekends.'

It wasn't until after she had confirmed with Ali it would be okay for her to stay in the Hamptons that it occurred to Jessie what else Mrs Bennett's impromptu job offer would mean. She'd be spending a fortnight alone with Monroe. Okay, so he'd be in his garage apartment and she'd be in the house, but she had as good as issued an ultimatum to him yesterday evening at dinner. What would she do if he decided to take her up on it? That the thought was exciting as well as terrifying could not be a good sign.

Jessie was debating that fact when Mrs Bennett strolled into the gallery's tiny office.

'Is it all settled, then?' she said.

'Yes, I'm okay to stay.'

'Excellent. Now, you're needed out on the floor—a very attractive young man's just strolled in. Either he's penniless or he's the first beatnik I've seen in twenty years, but, either way, it's never wise to ignore a customer.'

Jessie was walking out into the exhibition space, contemplating what the next two weeks alone with Monroe could mean, when her mouth dropped open.

Monroe Latimer was standing staring at one of the gallery's largest seascapes. His hands were tucked into the back pockets of ragged jeans, his head tilted to one side as he studied the work. He didn't just look attractive. He looked mouthwatering—and ridiculously out of place in Mrs Bennett's ritzy little art gallery. That combination of cute and dangerous could well be her undoing, Jessie decided as every nerve ending in her body stood to attention.

Taking a deep steadying breath she walked over to him. Challenge or no challenge, they were going to be the next best thing to room-mates for two whole weeks and she had to learn to deal with him. She also had the little matter of his artwork to work on, too. The perfect opening had just presented itself and she wasn't going to be a coward and ignore it.

'So, what do you think of it?'

As Monroe turned and saw Jessie standing behind him, his first thought was he'd made a big mistake. In the businesslike silk suit, her wild hair pinned up, she looked ridiculously prim and pretty. The urge to tug the pins out, feel the gilded flaming mass fall through his fingers, was almost uncontrollable.

He'd been offkilter, out of sorts the whole day, thanks to Linc and then Ali and even the unborn baby. It seemed the whole damn family was working against him, forcing him into a place he didn't want to be. It made him feel trapped, but much, much worse, it made him feel wanted. He didn't like it.

He didn't know what impulse had sent him into town to see Jessie.

Somehow, the thought of seeing her had buoyed his spirits. Even when she'd messed with his emotions the night before, the tug of arousal had been there. That, at least, was familiar territory. Something he understood. But standing here looking at her he wasn't so sure. He wasn't in control here, either.

It had to do with that look in her eyes he had seen the night before. The same look he could see in them now. Awareness. Yes. Desire. Yes. But where before there had been irritation and annoyance, now there was understanding. It made him very uneasy. Unfortunately, that still didn't stop him from wanting to drag her into his arms and muss up that pretty hairdo.

'Monroe?'

He'd been staring at her blankly for almost a minute, looking dazed. It was so unlike the cool, confident guy she knew. It worried her. She could see then what she'd seen yesterday evening; the confusion in his eyes.

'Right, the painting, sure.' He gave it a quick glance. 'It's too flat.'

She looked past him at it and saw he was exactly right. The oils had been expertly applied but failed to capture the churning magnificence of the sea in full storm mode. 'Gosh, you're right, it's rather cheesy, isn't it?' Jessie turned back to him. 'Monroe, you're staring at me again. What's wrong?'

'Nothing, nothing at—' He stopped, seemed to collect himself. 'I've been invited to a six-year-old's birthday party.'

Jessie grinned. 'You're going to come?'

'Ali didn't give me a choice.' He sounded a little annoyed, she thought, and grinned some more.

'We don't call her the stormtrooper for nothing.'

'It's just that—' he pinned her with his eyes '—I don't know what to get Emmy. For a present, I mean.'

'You don't have to get her anything, Monroe.'

His gaze sharpened. 'Yeah, I do.'

It occurred to Jessie, even if he was down to his last dollar, he would get Emmy a present. And she had once accused him of being a deadbeat. How wrong could a person be?

'There's a lovely little toy shop on Main Street,' she said, feeling guilty, desperate to make amends. 'You're bound to find something perfect in there.'

He gave a furtive glance round, took a step closer. 'No way am I going in there alone.' The words came out on a strained whisper.

'Let me get this straight,' Jessie said, enjoying the look of horror in his eyes. 'A big, bad guy like you is scared of going into a toy shop?'

'Right down to my toes.' He gave a mock shudder. 'When do you get off here?'

Jessie looked at the clock on the gallery's wall. 'In about half an hour.'

'Great, I'll meet you over at the diner. Don't even think about skipping out on me. I'll hunt you down.'

Jessie couldn't imagine why the threat excited her. 'Okay, but you'll owe me.'

'No sweat.' Monroe tapped his finger on her nose. 'See you later, Red.' He sauntered out of the shop.

Jessie grinned, already anticipating an afternoon of toy shopping with the most intriguing, desirable man she'd ever met.

She'd revised her opinion somewhat, ninety frustrating minutes later.

'What is this? A severed head?' Monroe grumbled.

Jessie grabbed the hair and styling doll out of his hands and put it carefully back on the shelf. 'Shh. It's a hair-dressing kit. What about these dolls? She loves them.'

'What the hell?' He stared at the gaudy toys a moment. 'I'm not buying a little kid a doll that looks like a hooker.'

Jessie tried to quell her irritation. After all, it was touching that he would want to get Emmy something really special— but also that he would worry that he might get it wrong. She wondered if he knew how hard he'd fallen for the little girl.

'Don't worry, Monroe.' She laid a hand on his arm. 'We'll get the right gift, even if it takes us all afternoon.'

He dragged his fingers through his hair. 'Thanks. It's important.'

'Yes, it is.' She never would have guessed how important until now.

Jessie studied the row of fussy little boutique shops across the street as they left the toy shop. Her eyes lighted on something at the end of the road, nestled between a cookware emporium and an expensive leatherwear shop. It made a slow smile spread across her face.

'I've just had a fantastic idea.' She grabbed Monroe's hand and pulled him across the street.

'You're a smart lady.' Monroe tucked the small toolbox under his arm. Full of handy little car maintenance accessories, it was just what any budding mechanic could wish for.

'Now all you need is a card and some wrapping paper and you're all set.'

'Great.' The relief in his voice made her smile. 'I owe you big time, Red. How about we grab a beer down by the marina? My treat.'

'That would be lovely.' She looped her arm in his, feeling more relaxed and comfortable around him than she ever had

before. His arm felt solid and warm against hers, the hair on
it soft and yet very masculine. The awareness between them
was still there, but, having seen him agonise over Emmy's
present for over an hour, she didn't find it nearly so threatening. Now would be a good time to bring up the request that
had been nagging at her for nearly twenty-four hours.
'Actually, I wanted to ask you a favour, too.'

'Sure. What is it?' He pulled his arm out of hers and rested
his hand on the small of her back. Hefting the toolbox under
one arm, he drew her close to his side, guiding her through the
Saturday shoppers on the raised clapboard sidewalk. His palm
seemed to sizzle through the thin silk of her work suit, the possessiveness of his gesture making her feel light-headed.

'I'll tell you when we get to the marina.' Maybe she needed
a little Dutch courage after all, Jessie thought.

'Okay, shoot. What was the favour?'

As they settled on the deck of the waterfront bar, two icy
beers on the small table between them, Monroe waited for her
answer. What could she possibly want from him?

Jessie took a sip of her drink. 'I'd like to see what you've
been painting for the last week and a half.'

He paused, the bottle of beer halfway to his lips. 'How do
you know about that?' He put the beer back on the table.

'You mentioned it. When we were in the diner that time.
Is it supposed to be a secret, then?'

'No.' He picked up a few peanuts from the little dish on
the table, cracked them in his palm and then studied them as
he removed the shells. 'It's not a secret.'

It wasn't, not really, but he didn't know if he wanted her
to see his work. Which was weird. He'd never been bothered
about anyone looking at it before. He didn't paint for anyone
but himself. He didn't have to justify or prove himself to

anyone. But he couldn't help feeling that her opinion would matter to him. What if she hated his stuff? What if she thought it was trash? And why the hell did he care what she thought?

She tilted her head to one side, watching him as he popped the peanuts into his mouth, chewed. 'I only wondered because you've never mentioned it,' she said. 'To Linc or Ali, I mean.'

He swallowed, stretched his legs out under the table, and tried to look relaxed. 'Why would I? It's not important.'

Jessie knew he wasn't telling the truth. His artwork was important to him. He'd been working at it all afternoon and well into the night, every day since he'd arrived.

'All right.' She lingered on the words, could already see the refusal in his eyes. 'If it's not important, you won't mind me seeing them, will you?'

He lifted his bottle again, took a long drag of his beer. 'There's nothing much finished yet.'

He was lying again; she was sure of it. But why? 'Could I look at them when you have?'

He shrugged. 'I guess so, but, like I said, it's no big deal.'

'I'd still love to see them.'

He hitched his shoulders, but the movement was stiff, dismissive.

Jessie turned away and stared at Cranford's famous Tall Ship, standing alone in the bay like the proud sentinel of a bygone era.

He'd been deliberately offhand and evasive about his artwork. He didn't want her to see it and the realisation hurt. She thought in the last few days they'd become friends, a little. Yet, it was obvious that he didn't trust her. Not to look at his work anyway. Which must be a very big deal if he would guard it so carefully. Sighing quietly as a small flock of seagulls nearby flew off in a rush, she forced herself to let the hurt go.

She was overreacting, as usual. She liked the easy camaraderie they'd established. If he wasn't ready to show her his work yet, she'd just have to wait.

Turning back, she was discomfited to see him watching her, his beer bottle empty now, the peanuts in the bowl gone.

She plastered a smile on her face. 'Are you coming over for dinner tonight?'

Monroe's brow furrowed. 'Nah, I'll wait for the big birthday bash tomorrow. I don't want to outstay my welcome.' He drained the bottle, pushed his chair back and got up. 'It's getting late. You ought to get back.'

As they paid the bill and left the bustling marina, the sun starting to dip towards the horizon, Jessie wanted to tell Monroe that he couldn't possibly outstay his welcome. That he was family, and family was always welcome.

But she didn't say it. She knew he would reject the personal comment.

As Jessie watched him ride off alone on his Harley and she climbed into the BMW she'd borrowed from Linc that morning, for the first time it occurred to Jessie how lonely Monroe's life was.

He had no one.

How could he survive without family, without any real friends? And was that really the way he wanted it?

She began to wonder as she drove home along the coastal road; was he really as indifferent as he pretended to be? Maybe it wasn't that he didn't want her to see his work. Maybe it wasn't that he didn't want to come over to the house for dinner that night. Maybe he was simply scared to open himself up to something he'd never really known. Family. Approval. Love.

CHAPTER NINE

'HE LOOKS like he's outnumbered. Think I should rescue him?' Linc's voice in her ear made Jessie jump. She'd been lost in thought watching Monroe organise a game of tag with five little girls all clinging to his legs.

Once Ali had strong-armed him into organising the party games, Jessie had watched him starting to enjoy himself. Emmy and her little friends obviously adored him. He was a natural with kids and yet from what he'd said yesterday at the marina it was clear he wanted to keep the family at arm's length. Couldn't he see that they could make his life so much richer?

'You know,' Linc continued, 'I think he's beginning to regret his way with the ladies.' He laughed, the sound low and relaxed as they watched Monroe pick Emmy up and turn her on her head. The chorus of squeals that followed made Jessie wince.

'Ali sent me to tell you the food's ready.' Linc glanced down at Jessie. 'Could you corral the kids over to the pool? I've got a surprise for Monroe, too. I'm going to go get it. So make sure he doesn't run off.'

'I'll make sure he's there.' Jessie's eyes followed Linc as he left the room. A surprise for Monroe. That sounded intriguing. She clapped her hands over her head but still had to shout to be heard. 'Emmy, kids. Tea's ready out by the pool. Last one there's a rotten egg.'

As the little girls ran off in a flurry of frills and shrieks, Monroe collapsed on the rug.

'Hell, they're like a swarm of locusts,' he groaned.

Jessie smiled down at him. 'You survived.'

'Just about, but it was a close call.' He looked up at her, his arms propping up his long, lean body as he lay back. 'Ali forgot to mention they operate in a pack, like ravenous wolves.'

Jessie laughed, but stopped abruptly when warm, strong fingers gripped her ankle. She gasped when a quick pull had her stumbling on top of him.

'That's better.' His hand shot out and before she knew it she was on top of him, his arms banded around her back, in the middle of the living room floor.

'What do you think you're doing?' She wanted to sound indignant but the heat in his eyes was making her pulse leap like a scared rabbit.

'What I've wanted to do since the last time we did this.' He turned over, taking her with him. Her back was on the floor, his body pressed on top of hers and his lips hot on her mouth before she could blink.

The sudden rush of heat and intensity shocked her. She struggled for a moment, then went still, letting him explore her mouth with his. The flames licking at her belly, making her centre throb, were so shocking and so sudden she couldn't seem to find the will to stop him, or herself. She could feel every inch of him, but most of all his lips. Wet and wonderful on hers. Then he pushed his tongue into her mouth. She gasped and the kiss went deeper, so much deeper it scared her. She struggled against him, pushed him back.

'We have to stop.' Her voice panted out on a breathy sob. 'We're at a children's party.'

He cursed then and moved off her.

She scrambled up. 'I can't believe we did that.'

Her face was so hot it burned. He sat up, draped his arm over one knee and stared up at her. He gave his head a rueful shake. 'Seeing as I've been planning it for over a week, I guess it lacked a bit of finesse.'

'What do you mean planning it?' Why did she suddenly feel totally out of her depth?

He stood up and rested his hands on her hips. She tried to step back, but he held her in place. 'We need to talk, Red.'

Monroe couldn't believe he'd blown it so badly. But, hell, he'd been watching her for the whole afternoon in that sunny yellow dress. Seeing the way it fitted so demurely, giving a tantalising glimpse of the curves beneath—and he'd wanted to kiss her again ever since that afternoon by the grocery store.

He wasn't a man used to denying his instincts. Damn it, he wasn't a man who usually had to.

So when she'd grinned down at him a moment before, her red hair rioting round her face, that bright, friendly look in her eyes, instinct had taken over. Seeing the way she was staring at him now, flushed but wary, he could have kicked himself.

'What do you want to talk about?' Her voice was tremulous, unsure.

'I want to talk about us.'

'But…' she hesitated '…there is no us.'

'There will be. Don't tell me you don't know it.'

Jessie scrambled about for something coherent to say. She could still feel the pressure of his lips on hers, the solid weight of his body covering her own. And the way he was watching her was making her legs shake and the heat in her belly feel like an inferno. She couldn't seem to get a single coherent thought into her head.

'We can't talk about it now. We have to go cut the cake with Emmy.' She knew it sounded ridiculous, but she couldn't think of anything else to say.

He stroked a finger down her cheek, and then tucked it under her chin, forcing her gaze up to his. 'Sure, Red, but afterwards we talk.'

The bustle and noise of a children's party in full swing helped to calm Jessie's nerves as she stepped out onto the pool terrace.

Five little girls stuffed down biscuits and sweets and chattered away as if their lives depended on it. Linc was pouring out soda into plastic cups like a pro and Ali was busy sticking candles into the cake they had baked that morning.

Monroe gave her hand a quick squeeze, making her heart skip another beat, before walking over to Emmy. Jessie watched as he stroked the little girl's head, leant down to whisper something into her ear. Emmy giggled and handed him a cake off her plate.

'Jessie, great, grab this, will you?' Ali huffed out a breath and handed her the cake—a huge chocolate structure that was supposed to be a fairy-tale castle but looked more like a mound of newly-turned earth. 'Are you okay, Jess? You look a little flushed.'

'I'm fine.' Jessie tried to sound offhand, but as Ali bent down to light the candles, Jessie met Monroe's gaze over her sister's head.

His eyes were intent on hers as he bit slowly into the pink-frosted fairy cake Emmy had handed him. Jessie's heart pounded heavily in her chest. What exactly had she unleashed here?

After a rousing chorus of Happy Birthday and much merriment as Emmy tried three times to blow out her candles,

Monroe sauntered back towards Jessie. She couldn't seem to draw her eyes away from him as he came to stand beside her. He flashed her that dimple-cheeked grin but said nothing. She was searching her mind for something to say to him, when Linc's voice boomed out from the other side of the terrace. Thank God, it took Monroe's eyes off her as he turned to listen.

'Now, folks, before we start digging into this—' Linc glanced down at the cake '—very interesting-looking cake—' Ali jabbed her husband in the ribs, making him laugh '—I've got an announcement to make. It so happens Emmy's not the only person in the Latimer household with a birthday this month.'

As Linc reached under the table and drew out a large brightly-wrapped package, Jessie felt Monroe go very still beside her. She turned to look at him. His jaw had gone rigid.

'Turns out—' Linc walked towards Monroe with the package in his arms, smiling '—her uncle's birthday was last Wednesday.' He offered the present to Monroe. 'Better late than never. Happy Birthday, Roe.'

Jessie could hear Emmy and her little friends applauding and doing a spontaneous chorus of Happy Birthday. Ali and the other adults were clapping, Linc was still smiling.

But something was wrong. Monroe made no move to take the gift. He stared down at it, then back at Linc. Embarrassed for both men, Jessie nudged him. 'Take it, Monroe.'

He glanced round at her then. He looked dazed.

'Roe, it's okay,' Linc said softly. Jessie saw his smile fade as he lowered the present.

Ali came up behind her husband and rested her palm on his back.

Monroe still said nothing, still made no move to accept the gift.

Jessie could feel the hollowness inside her. Linc had been

so eager, so pleased about the surprise he had planned. It was awful to see him look so dejected. Why didn't Monroe just take the present? Why was he hurting his brother's feelings like this?

She gave Monroe's arm another nudge. 'Take it, Monroe. It's for you.'

Jolted out of whatever trance he seemed to be in, Monroe slowly took the gift out of his brother's hands. But he didn't look at Linc, Jessie saw, her temper rising, he just continued to stare at the prettily-wrapped present.

'I…' Monroe cleared his throat. His Adam's apple jerked, tension snapped in the air around him, tension and something else Jessie couldn't explain. 'I've got to go.'

With a quick nod to Linc, he slung the present under his arm and strode past the dismayed party-goers. He disappeared across the lawn, without looking back once.

Jessie stood dumbstruck. She heard Linc sigh and speak quietly to Ali. 'Hell, that went well.'

Jessie watched Ali rub her husband's back. 'It was the right thing to do, Linc.'

'I don't know,' Linc murmured. 'It was too soon.'

Jessie could see the thin glaze of tears in her sister's eyes as she shook her head, the look of desolation in her brother-in-law's. What were they talking about?

'I can't believe you're being so nice about this,' Jessie said. 'That was rude.'

Both Linc and Ali stared at her. It was as if they'd only just seen her. Jessie's temper and her confusion spiked up another notch. 'I'm going to go and tell him so,' she said. But as she tried to march past them both Ali stopped her.

'Jessie, don't go over there now. Monroe needs time.'

'I don't give a toss what he needs,' Jessie hissed.

Linc had walked off to talk to the other adults, obviously to try and smooth things over. Watching him, Jessie felt her anguish increase at the shoddy way this good, strong man had been treated by his own brother.

'Monroe was totally out of order, Ali. He didn't even say thank you.'

'There are things going on here you don't understand, Jess. This is between Linc and Monroe. You mustn't interfere.'

Jessie bit down on her lip, trying to shore up her temper. What didn't she understand?

'Come on.' Ali gave her a weak smile. 'We need to sort out the party bags. And don't forget Emmy's still got all her presents to open. Will you help me?'

Jessie nodded, but couldn't bring herself to smile back at her sister.

The fact that she didn't understand, that she didn't know what was going on, didn't make her feel any better about what had just happened. It only made her feel angry and insecure. She had come to like Monroe in the last week or so, had come to think she knew him a little. He'd been right when he'd said there was something between them. But it wasn't just passion she felt for him. She had come to care about him. A lot, if she was honest with herself.

The cavalier way he had treated Linc proved to her that she didn't really know him at all. It seemed she had come to care about a man, desire a man, who was a complete stranger. And that frightened her.

Jessie's unhappiness increased as the party bags were handed out and Emmy's presents were opened. The little girl was thrilled with the mechanic's kit Monroe had given her, but threw a small fit when her mother told her she'd have to wait to thank her uncle. Emmy's reaction made Jessie's anger towards Monroe grow. Why had he skulked off like that, without even a thought for Emmy? After spending so long picking out her present yesterday, why hadn't he at least stayed to see it opened? It showed a careless, callous disregard for the little girl's feelings that couldn't be excused.

Finally the last of Emmy's friends and their parents had left the house.

Jessie gritted her teeth and set about tidying up the mess from the party while the rest of the household packed for their trip to New York. By the time she'd finished an hour later, the room was spotless and she'd managed to work up a pretty good head of steam. Monroe had not appeared to apologise.

Jessie helped load up Linc and Ali's people carrier. She mentioned to Ali again that someone should go and talk to Monroe, but Ali simply shook her head as she climbed into the car.

'Let it go, Jess. Don't worry about him.'

It had been on the tip of Jessie's tongue to say she wasn't worried, not about Monroe anyway. But she stopped herself. Ali looked tired, Linc was clearly subdued and they needed to get on their way if they were going to get into the city before midnight.

The minute the car was out of sight, Jessie closed the property's gates and scowled at the garage apartment.

If Ali and Linc were worried about hurting Monroe's feelings—she snorted; as if the man had any feelings—she certainly wasn't. She stalked across the lawn, righteous indignation wrapped around her like a cloak.

She could hear the music blaring from his apartment as she crossed the lawn. Rock music was howling at a decibel level that could make your ears bleed, masking the sound of the cool sea breeze rustling the flowers and tall grass.

It was just another sign of his thoughtlessness. There was no point in knocking, so she marched on in, sailing through on a wave of anger. She shouted his name at the top of her lungs.

And then shouted it two more times before the music shut off.

Her eardrums were still throbbing in time to the rebel chant when Monroe strolled into the room. His chest and feet were bare, his T-shirt hooked through the belt loop of his jeans. Flecks of paint stood out against the dark hair that curled lightly across his chest. The easy grin she had come to expect was gone. His face was hard, his eyes flat and expressionless. He looked savage and intimidating.

'How long have you been here?'

'Long enough.' Jessie clung onto her anger, ignoring the weakness she felt at the sight of him. 'Linc and Ali and Emmy have left, by the way. Just in case you're interested.'

He gave her a dismissive nod. 'If there's nothing else, I'm busy here. I don't have time to chit-chat.'

Jessie sucked in a breath. How dare he talk to her like that?

'You don't say.' She marched up to him, stabbed a finger into his chest. 'You should have come and said goodbye. You should have apologised to Linc. You hurt him.'

Something flashed into his eyes at the mention of his brother's name. But then his face went hard again. He grabbed onto her finger, held it away from him, but his voice remained calm. 'You don't want to be around me right now. I'm not feeling civilised.'

She heard the menace in his words and pulled her finger free. She didn't know this man at all. He looked dangerous. He was breathing heavily as if he'd been running, the firm bronzed skin of his chest glistened with sweat, but his eyes were so remote it was frightening.

She took a step back. 'What happened by the pool? Why was it so hard for you to take the gift?'

Suddenly, she wanted desperately to know, to understand. Where was the man she'd come to care for?

'Just because we've shared a few hot kisses…' he gave her a slow, deliberate once-over '…just because I'd like to see you naked, doesn't mean you're my shrink.'

He was trying to upset her. With a flash of insight she saw that he wanted her to run. 'Why are you being deliberately cruel? It's not like you.'

'You don't know what I'm like.'

Something swirled into his eyes as he turned away. Unhappiness? Pain? Was he hurting, too?

'Monroe, what is it?' She walked up behind him. He stood in front of the window, the muscles of his back and shoulders rigid.

'I'm warning you, Jessie. You need to get out of here.'

He didn't look round. She studied the thin white scars that marred the smooth, bronzed skin. Reaching up, she hesitated a moment and then stroked her fingers down his spine.

He shot round. 'Don't touch me.'

She could see his eyes clearly now. Desperation and confusion burned in the blue depths.

'Tell me. What is it? Why was it so hard for you to take Linc's present?'

'I didn't know how.' He shouted the words, fisted his hands in frustration and thrust them into his pockets. 'I've never been given a birthday gift before in my whole damn life.'

CHAPTER TEN

ANGER at himself churned like molten lava in Monroe's gut. Anger and a desire that he was struggling real hard to ignore.

He'd been raw, ragged with emotions he'd never felt before ever since Linc had handed him the birthday gift two hours ago. And guilt was right slam-bang at the top of the list.

He'd played them all, like an orchestra. He'd done a few odd jobs, befriended the little girl and managed to con them all into thinking he was a good guy—Emmy, Linc, Ali and most of all, Jessie.

Since he'd got out of prison, Monroe's life had been nomadic. It was the way he liked it. Women had come and gone, friendships had been shallow and fleeting. He didn't want it to be any different.

But when Linc had held the present out to him, the sparkly wrapping paper glinting in the sunshine, all those foolish old feelings of wanting to have a place to belong had come flooding back. He'd realised in a rush that they'd all accepted him into their home, into their hearts. The yearning that had gripped him at the thought, the desperate need to be accepted, had stunned him. But worse had been the knowledge that he could never have a place here.

Because he wasn't a good guy, not really.

He was a user. He used people and moved on. That way he didn't have to be bothered by anyone but himself.

He'd taken Linc's gift in a daze of confusion and pain. He'd stormed back to the apartment, turned up the stereo to blast level and painted like a madman. But the storm of emotions had continued to churn inside him. And when Jessie had shown up, the only thing he could think was he had to make her run before he took something he could never give back.

She was beautiful, fresh, impulsive and honest. No wonder he wanted her so badly; she was all the things he wasn't.

Looking down at her, seeing the concern in her eyes as she absorbed what he'd said about the present, he wanted to take her so badly, claim her so badly, it hurt.

'Why did you never have a birthday gift before?' she asked gently.

He could hear the compassion and it crucified him. He shrugged. 'I don't live like that. All neat and pretty.'

He turned, stared blankly out the window at the gathering dusk, the darkening red of sunset mirroring his own shadowed thoughts. He couldn't look at her and tell her the truth. 'I do what I want, when I want. I don't have a family. I don't need one. Nobody's going to tie me down. That's the way I like it.'

Jessie could hear the defiance, the desperation in his words. She had been right, was all she could think. He was lonely and he was scared.

No wonder he hadn't been able to take Linc's present. It had meant something to him he didn't understand. It meant love and trust and affection. All things he'd spent most of his life without. He was always so sure of himself, so cocky. But beneath that was a good, caring man who needed things that he seemed determined to deny himself.

Jessie had a huge well of love inside her that she wanted to give to someone. And here was a man who needed it. She wouldn't ask herself why Monroe denied love, denied family. It was enough for now to know he needed her and she needed him.

She'd been falling in love all along—and now she knew why.

He was the one she'd been waiting for. He was everything she'd ever wanted, standing there before her. So handsome, so vulnerable and so confused. Taking the next step now was all that mattered. The rest of it would sort itself out in time.

'Everybody needs family, Monroe,' she said softly.

He swung around, his eyes fixed on hers. 'Damn it. Don't you get it? I used you. I saw something I wanted, so I went after it.' His voice was rough with self-loathing. 'You heard what I said when I jumped you at the party. I've been planning this all along. Getting you to like me. Getting you to trust me. It was all just a damn game so I could get you into bed.'

She laughed, the mix of arousal and excitement making her light-headed. He wanted her. 'If that was the plan, you seem to be mucking it up a bit now.'

'What?' His mouth dropped open.

She stepped forward, drew her hands up his chest, wrapped her fingers around his neck. He smelt wonderful—linseed oil, turpentine and the musky smell of man. He felt even better. The hard, rigid muscles of his chest quivered against her breasts, as if he were a racehorse, ready to leap out of a starting gate. She had the power. For the first time, she was the one in control.

'You know, Monroe.' Her voice came out on a soft purr; she heard him swallow. 'It was really nice of you to do all the work, up to this point.' She caressed the back of his neck, threading her fingers through the soft hair of his nape.

He shuddered.

'But it looks like I'm going to have to take over now,' she said.

He pulled her into his arms, forcing her hard against him. 'You're playing with dynamite, Red. I'm no saint.' Slowly, he drew his palms up her sides, his thumbs caressing the swell of her breasts through the linen of her dress. 'If you keep on going the way you are, I'm going to have you and to hell with the consequences.'

She drew in a sharp breath at the harsh demand on his face. The fire in his eyes made her knees go to jelly, but she kept her voice steady. 'Promises, promises.'

The teasing words were barely out before his lips cut her off. He feasted on her mouth, thrusting his tongue in as his hands came up to fist in her hair. She began to shake, her breath gushing out when he lifted his head.

'Are you sure about this?' he rasped in her ear, his voice low and barely controlled. 'You've got to be sure.' His lips skidded up her neck as he spoke.

'I'm positive,' she murmured.

His lips covered hers again. His tongue probed, demanding entry. Her mouth opened, allowing him to explore her, to devastate her.

He stopped, rested his forehead on hers. 'I want to look at you, Red.'

His fingers came up in a brief caress, then he tugged the straps off her shoulders, pushed the dress down to her waist. She pulled her arms free.

Nudging the lacy cup of her bra down, he bent his head to watch as he exposed her breast. Fire flared in her belly, flooding between her thighs. His lips, hot and insatiable, closed over the swollen peak, suckled strongly. Her breath caught as the arrow of lust shot down to her centre.

Fumbling, he released the clasp, pulled the bra off. He stood back, holding her away from him. She flushed as his eyes devoured her body, naked from the waist.

'You're beautiful, Red,' he murmured. He cupped the ripe breast in callused palms, rubbed his thumbs over the engorged nipples. She went lax under his stroking hands. The heat was so intense now, she felt she might faint.

He pulled the dress down the rest of the way, taking her hand as she stepped free on teetering legs. He hooked his finger in the thin cotton of her panties and ripped them off. She gasped, totally exposed before him, drifting beyond pleasure to panic.

Lifting her limp body high in his arms, he stalked to the sofa, laid her down. She watched him, dazed and unsure, as he stripped off his jeans. He seemed savage, overwhelming all of a sudden. What had she done?

The muscles of his chest heaved from his staggered breathing. His arousal jutted out. He looked magnificent, like a powerful male animal.

She wanted to cover herself, but seemed powerless to do anything, enthralled by the sight of him as he knelt beside her. He stroked his fingers across her belly, making her jump as he reached lower and gently probed the folds of her sex. She could feel how wet she was as his thumb glided over the nub he exposed. She shuddered violently and cried out.

'I'm sorry, Red. I can't wait.' He lay on top of her, his weight making her sink into the soft cushions. He grasped her hips, his eyes harsh on her face, and she felt trapped beneath him. Still she was dazed, detached, as he positioned himself, probed and then thrust within. She cried out, the shocking fullness and discomfort hurling her out of the strange trance and slamming her hard into reality.

She grabbed at his shoulders, pushed frantically. 'Stop it. It hurts,' she cried out.

He reared back.

She could see the surprise and confusion in his eyes and the rigid control as his arms tensed at her sides.

'What's wrong?' He pulled out of her, cupped her face in unsteady hands. She could see the bitter regret in his face and she shattered—the pent-up emotions of long years of inadequacy and denial bursting out.

'I can't do this. I'm no good at it.' She began to shake, raw with humiliation. The misery engulfed her. Why had she thought that with him it might work? For a while, as they'd kissed and caressed it had been so wonderful. She'd been spun up in a whirlwind of passion and excitement. But then, it had been dragged away. She'd failed, as always.

He held her gently, drawing her into his arms, settling her close.

'Shh. Don't cry. I rushed you. I went too damn fast. It's my fault.'

'It's not.' She snuffled, determined to tell him the truth. 'I'm rubbish at this. I've been told I'm frigid.'

She wanted to get up, get away. But his arms tightened around her, holding her in place.

'Please, I have to go.' She could hear the pathetic whimper in her voice and despised herself for it.

She couldn't look at him. Couldn't bear to see the disappointment in his eyes, or, worse, the pity. But then he tucked his finger under her chin, forced her face up to his.

'Don't go, Red.' There was no pity, just concern. He touched his lips to hers, the kiss so gentle it was like a whisper. 'Who's the dumb bastard who said you were frigid?'

'Toby. His name was Toby Collins.'

'Toby, huh?' He pushed the hair from her brow, brushed it back carefully as he met her eyes. Then his own went hard with anger. 'I'd like to get Toby Collins and string him up by his nuts.'

'Oh!' What else was there to say?

He looked so fierce and forbidding she almost felt sorry

for her former fiancé. If Toby hadn't been on the other side of the Atlantic, his nuts would surely be in grave danger.

Monroe drew her closer. 'But seeing as Toby and his pea-sized nuts aren't here right now, we're gonna have to undo the damage he did instead.'

'What do you mean?' she asked, wary of the determination in his voice.

'You're not frigid. And we're going to prove it.'

She tensed in his arms, painfully aware of his nakedness and her own.

'I don't…' She paused. 'That's really not necessary.'

'Oh, yeah, it is.' He dipped his head, took her lips in a slow, tender kiss.

The low throbbing in her belly seemed to come from nowhere. But she drew back, flushed but horribly unsure of herself. 'I don't think I can, Monroe.'

He trailed a finger down across her breast, watching it intently as he circled the peak.

'You can do it.' He glanced up, dazzled her with that easy, confident grin she knew so well. 'If you're treated with the proper care and attention.'

His fingertip toyed with her nipple. A breath she hadn't realised she'd been holding gushed out. She glanced down at him hard against her thigh. Her breath caught in her throat; he was still fully aroused and he looked enormous.

His grin spread as her shocked gaze met his. 'We were so close before. We're going to take it real slow and easy this time and do it right.'

He levered himself up, got off the couch and pulled her up with him. Dumping the two large cushions onto the floor, he knelt on them and then tugged her down beside him. 'Lie down.'

She did as she was told, confused and wary, feeling hideously exposed, like an offering on a sacrificial altar, as he lay down next to her.

'Don't look so worried.' He kissed her. 'The only rules are, you don't think and you don't touch. All right?'

'Okay.'

Slowly, carefully, he began to stroke his fingers down the length of her. He seemed to take for ever. At first, she felt foolish, inadequate, but when his touch swept the underside of her breast, she shuddered. His fingers trailed down her arms next, catching the soft skin inside her elbow, and she gasped. Then he found the sensitive place behind her knee as he drew her legs up.

Her centre throbbed, insistent and intense. He followed his hands with his lips and when she tried all she could think of was where he would go next. Anticipation, then delight. The process was slow, delicious torture as his tongue delved and dipped, stroked and slid across her heated flesh.

She had to touch him. But when his lips closed over her nipple and she tried to grab his head, he pulled back. Capturing her wrists in one hand, he held them above her head. 'No touching. Remember?'

'Please, I want to feel you, too.' The words came out on a sob as she strained against him, but he simply shook his head and held her in place.

It seemed he caressed her breasts for ever. Lathing the sensitive tips and then blowing softly, making them pucker fiercely before his appreciative gaze. Making her writhe against his controlling hands.

She panted, all thoughts flown from her head but the unbearable heat, the intense pleasure at her core. Her heart raced so fast, it would surely explode. The burning between her thighs was so intense she couldn't draw breath. He released her wrists to circle the soft skin of her inner thighs. At last, he was going to touch her there, where she needed him most. But still his fingers teased, stroking the soft curls at the juncture. Finally, he probed within. The touch was barely there, but her sigh choked out on a sob. Then he stroked again, pushing the folds back, watching her face. His eyes held hers as she sobbed again. She was clinging to the edge of a desperate precipice. He was there now, right at the heart of the heat, making it burn.

'I… Please, don't stop.' She didn't know what she was begging for, but saw his slow grin, the blaze of desire in his eyes.

'Let it go, Red.'

He purred the words as she shot over the edge. Everything inside her released, crashed down and then exploded into a million tiny, glittering pieces. She could hear herself, a thousand miles away, cry out on a shattered moan.

'Come on, baby, we're not through yet.'

She was still shivering, dazed by the aftermath of passion as he reared above her. He held her legs apart and settled between them. Angling her hips up with firm hands, he probed at her entrance and then pushed his rigid sex within in one long, slow, shocking thrust.

The fullness was unbearable. She felt stretched, impaled. But where before there had been pain, now there was only the sure, unstoppable rush of pleasure. She sobbed as passion slammed back into her full force, like a runaway train, hard and fast and out of control.

'Look at me, Red. I want to see you do it again.' His voice was low, thick with desire. Her eyes fixed on his face. He looked so gorgeous at that moment. The inferno built inside her with each powerful thrust.

She soared over this time, falling free as they shouted out their release together.

CHAPTER ELEVEN

'Wow!' Jessie stroked Monroe's back. She loved the solid feel of him on top of her, his ragged breathing echoing her own.

He grunted and lifted himself up on his elbows. 'Am I crushing you?'

'Yes.' She sighed, enjoying the flushed look on his face. She'd done that to him, she thought, and welcomed the rush of female power. 'But don't go.' She hugged him. 'I like it.'

He smiled, but eased away. Turning on his side, he tugged her to him with one arm. The cushions had fallen apart in their frenzy, leaving them in a dip between the two. He tucked a tendril of her flyaway hair behind her ear. 'You're looking kinda smug, Red.'

'I am?' She laughed, the sound girlish. His eyes flared with arousal. 'That was...' She paused. How should she say this, without sounding ridiculous? 'That was unbelievable. I mean, I never... I never had the foggiest...' She stumbled to a halt, realising his grin had widened. She was making an idiot of herself.

He stroked a finger slowly across her midriff. The feel of it, warm and lazy, made her shiver. 'The foggiest?' He chuckled. 'Is that your cute English way of saying this was your first time?'

'No, of course not. I'm not a virgin. Don't be ridiculous. I'm twenty-six years old.' She wanted to sound indignant, but it was hard with his fingers trailing down to the red curls at her core.

'But that was your first orgasm, right?' Now who sounded smug?

'Okay, yes, it was.' She felt foolish, now, foolish but unbearably needy as his fingers stopped circling and he looked at her.

Pride, fierce and possessive, blazed in his eyes. 'Well, it sure as hell won't be your last.' He patted her bottom. 'You can bet on that.' His lips quirked as he started to rise.

She reached for him. 'Don't go.'

'Don't worry, I'll be back.' He knelt beside her. 'You know, Red, you make one hell of a picture.'

She crossed her arms over her chest, feeling shy, but he drew her hands away. He kissed both her palms in turn. The gesture was so gentle, so loving, it made her heart swell.

He stood up. 'I'll go get something to clean you up.'

As he headed for the bathroom, his words registered. She felt it then, the stickiness between her thighs. She bolted upright.

'Monroe.' He turned, naked and beautiful, and looked back at her. 'I…' Her face burned. 'We didn't use a condom.'

Monroe could see the fear in Jessie's eyes. Walking back, he squatted beside her, touched the side of her face.

'Don't panic, Red. I don't have any nasty diseases, I swear. This is the first time I haven't been properly dressed for the party since I was fourteen.' It occurred to him that he hadn't even thought about using a condom.

'I didn't even think of that.' Jessie's face went an even brighter shade of red. 'I've never done it before without protection either. You know, in case you were worried about me.'

He drew his finger slowly down her cheek, his lips curved.

'That's good,' he said, feeling the swell of pride and possessiveness.

How could she be so untouched and so arousing at the same time? He realised he was starting to stir again. He stood up and reached for the jockeys still tucked into his jeans. He didn't want to scare her. But as he took a step back towards the bathroom she got up and touched his arm.

'Monroe, it's not just, well…' she swallowed audibly '…it's not just communicable diseases. I'm not on the pill. I could get pregnant.'

Jessie was so embarrassed she wanted to die on the spot. One minute she'd been the flame-haired seductress she'd always wanted to be and the next a silly schoolgirl. Why hadn't she told him she wasn't on the pill? She was such a complete idiot.

He went very still and stared at her for what seemed like an eternity. Was he annoyed? she wondered. But he didn't look annoyed. It was strange, but for a moment she thought he looked sad. Then he simply shook his head.

'Come here.' Holding her hand, he threw one of the cushions back onto the sofa, sat on it and pulled her into his lap. Tugging the throw rug off the back, he wrapped it carefully around her. 'When's your next period due?' he asked in a quiet voice.

'Not for a while. I finished one less than a week ago.'

'I don't think there's much reason to worry, then. You only usually get pregnant in the middle of your cycle.' He pulled the throw rug to one side, laid a warm palm on her belly and rubbed slowly. When he looked up, his smile was warm, but she could still see that faraway look in his eyes. 'We'll make sure we use protection from now on. Okay?'

She chewed her lip. 'You're not annoyed with me—for not saying something sooner, I mean?'

He lifted his hand, held her chin and kissed her. His lips were light and tender on hers. 'I should have asked and I didn't. I guess we're both guilty of getting carried away.' He lifted her off his lap. He leaned down and gave her a gentle kiss on the forehead and then a long, slow kiss on the lips.

He was so gentle she felt herself getting aroused again. She could see from his boxers that he was aroused, too. She pulled him towards her.

'Don't tempt me, Red.'

'Oh, Monroe.' She put her palm on his cheek.

He put his hand over hers, drew it down. 'We can wait till tomorrow for the next round. Anyhow, I need to get some condoms, remember?'

Although Monroe was desperate for her, no way was he going to take her to bed again so soon. He'd seen the heart-melting look in her eyes after they'd made love. Didn't doubt that she probably thought she was falling in love with him. She was young and naïve and unbearably sweet. A romantic to the core. He was older, much more cynical and had never had a romantic moment in his life. Thank heaven.

He knew that great sex, no, *fantastic* sex, was all he could give her. So they'd keep things light and simple and they'd both have a good time. He felt okay with it, knowing that he could give her something she'd never had before. That first orgasm was just the start, for both of them. He wouldn't think about the future because they didn't have one.

'I better get dressed.' Jessie stood up, struggling with the throw. Why did she suddenly feel as if there was a distance between them that hadn't been there before? 'I should go.'

'No, you don't.' He swung her up into his arms.

She grabbed for his shoulders and the throw fell away, exposing her to the waist.

'What are you doing?' She tried to cling on and pull the throw back up.

'Forget about that.' He tightened his arms. 'I want you naked in my bed tonight.' He sniffed at her hair. 'God, you smell fantastic. No way you're going anywhere tonight.'

She was clinging onto his neck now, his chest hair brushing unbearably against the swollen, sensitive peaks of her breasts. 'But I thought we weren't going to do it again.'

He laughed, the sound rough and rueful. 'Red, you've got so much to learn.' He wiggled his brows, lasciviously. 'Wouldn't you know it? I guess I'm gonna have to teach you.'

He didn't sound remotely put out about it.

Kicking the throw rug away, he sauntered through into the bedroom with her. Bumping the door closed, he whirled her round into the room.

Jessie saw the bed first, a large mattress on the floor, the bed sheets strewn across it, but as he knelt down to dump her on it her head fell back and she caught a glimpse of the blaze of colours over his shoulder.

'Oh, my goodness, Monroe.' She scrambled out of his arms and rushed over to the canvases stacked against the wall.

They were strong, bold, striking images. People's faces, some tender, some touching, others unbearably sad and strong. Stunning landscapes of vibrancy and life. Ugly urban places that had a haunting beauty. Each one of his subjects leapt off the canvas in its own distinct way. His use of colour, of light, of contrast was vivid and demanding, as if he had drawn the emotion out with the paint. She turned back to him, tears forming in her eyes. He stood next to the mattress, watching her, his eyes carefully blank.

'That bad, huh?'

'Monroe.' Walking to him, she placed her palms on his cheeks, searched his face. 'They're incredible. You have an amazing talent.'

'You like them?'

'Are you joking? I don't like them. I love them. They're phenomenal.' She turned, ran back, picked up a small square canvas of a woman and a girl, standing by a gas pump. The girl, who looked little more than a child, was heavily pregnant. Her eyes shone with bitterness and defiance. The paint strokes were rough, the fierce strength elemental on the girl's face.

As she studied it Jessie felt her own emotions well up inside her. 'You've captured her so perfectly. Who was she?'

'Hey.' Walking up behind her, he scooped the tear off Jessie's cheek, laid a hand on her shoulder. 'Don't cry, Jess. The guy responsible stuck by her and so did her mom. She did okay.'

Jessie put the canvas back against the wall, turned to him. 'I'm not crying because of her. She looks tough enough to wrestle an ox. I'm crying because of your art, Monroe. It's so exquisite.'

He looked taken aback. 'You like them that much?'

Monroe pulled her into his arms, the surge of pride inside him so huge it was choking him. No one had ever said something to him that could have meant more. This was better than when she'd had her first orgasm in his arms and that had been pretty damned overwhelming.

'It's only a hobby,' he said, inhaling the fresh, flowery scent of her hair.

She drew back. 'Don't lie.' She took another long look at his paintings. When she turned back, her eyes were full of wonder. His knees felt shaky.

'That's not a hobby,' she said softly. 'That's a passion.'

CHAPTER TWELVE

'JESSIE, dear, your young man's outside.'

Jessie's stomach did a little flip as Mrs Bennett walked into the gallery's tiny office. The leap of joy was something she'd got used to in the last few days.

'He's only a few minutes early,' her boss continued as she put the sales invoices down on Jessie's desk. 'You can go now if you like.'

'Thank you, Mrs Bennett.' Jessie tapped the shutdown button on the desktop computer, grabbed her bag from under the desk and ran out.

Monroe stood outside the gallery's main doors. He looked tall and slightly tense through the glass. Her young man. Wasn't that the most wonderful phrase in the whole wide world?

They'd been together now for four whole days and she felt as if her heart were going to burst in her chest at the sight of him. Had she ever been happier in her life?

The sex, of course, was fabulous. The man made love like a god. She'd never experienced anything like it before. Toby had always treated foreplay like a chore. Maybe that was why she'd never been able to relax, enjoy it. Monroe seemed to know instinctively what to do to make her forget everything except the touch, the feel of him.

But it wasn't Monroe's lovemaking skills that had dazzled her, had lifted her onto a cloud of such intense pleasure and contentment. It was the companionship. They made love every morning and then they would have breakfast in his apartment before he took her to work on the Harley. He'd be waiting outside to pick her up when she got off at noon and then they'd drive like mad things straight back to the apartment and make long, lazy love together all afternoon and most of the evening.

And yesterday, he'd brought her flowers, for goodness' sake. A small bunch of wildflowers he'd said he'd spotted on the way in to town. His obvious embarrassment, when he'd thrust them at her, the delicate blooms wilting in the heat, had only made the gesture more wonderful. It was so romantic.

Thinking about their tempestuous lovemaking by the pool afterwards made Jessie's heartbeat throb heavily and the flush hit her cheeks as she pushed open the door of the gallery.

'Monroe!' She flung her hands around his neck, making him almost drop the grocery sack in his arms.

'Watch it, Red. This is our lunch.'

She pressed her lips to his. 'I'm too happy to see you to care about food.'

The grin spread slowly across his face. 'Is that right?' He slung the sack under his arm, put one hand around her waist and pulled her closer. 'Let's do that again.'

The kiss was long and heated this time. 'Mmm.' He licked his lips. 'Damn it, there you go tempting me again. You'll make me forget.'

'Forget what?'

'Come on. The Harley's round the back.' He gripped her hand, pulled her behind him down the small alleyway that led to the customer car park.

'Are we going home?' She certainly hoped so.

'No way.' He shot her a quick grin, but carried on walking, forcing Jessie to jog to keep up with his long strides. 'You'll just end up jumping me again.'

'Yes, please.'

'Who knew you sweet little English girls could be so damned insatiable?'

'Well, really.' Jessie laughed. 'Who knew you Yankee guys would get knackered so quickly?'

'Knackered!' He stopped in front of the Harley, dumped the grocery sack on the bike seat and put his hands on her hips. He placed a light kiss on her lips, his eyes challenging. 'You wanna bet on that?'

'I certainly do.' She drew her arms up, threaded her fingers through the soft, shaggy gold-streaked hair that she adored. 'Still think you can handle me?'

His hands slid around to her bottom, massaging the flesh through the thin fabric of the cotton trouser suit she wore. 'If it's a matter of my Yankee honour.' He dipped his head, took her lips in a hot, demanding kiss.

She drew back, breathless. 'You win, Yankee boy.'

He gave her bottom one more quick squeeze and then let her go. 'Hell, I guess that means I don't get to ravish you, right?'

'You can't have it both ways, buster,' she said, lifting a coquettish eyebrow.

He sighed, pulled her helmet out of the bike's saddlebags and handed it to her. 'Mount up. We're going on a picnic.'

The streets of Cranford were clogged with tourists. Monroe had to ease the bike down Main Street, threading through the crowds of people heading to the town's beach. The old-fashioned clapboard sidewalks were overflowing, spilling tourists into the road like so much flotsam. The midday sun was a killer, scorching bare flesh and making children cranky and unmanageable.

Monroe didn't mind the delay a bit. He could feel Jessie's arms tight around his waist, her thighs pressed against his hips. As much as he would have loved to head straight home, he forced himself not to.

He'd gorged on her the last four days. But it seemed the more of her he had, the more he needed. The way she responded to him was like a fire in his blood, making him want more all the time, making him take more. He knew he'd exhausted her last night—and himself.

He'd slept like a log.

Ever since prison he'd had trouble getting to sleep. Not any more, it seemed. With her in his arms, snuggled against him in the darkness, the stir of passion still flowing through him, he'd drifted off like a baby.

He'd decided on the way to town that this afternoon was going to be different. He was going to prove he could keep his hands off her.

He'd stopped by the grocery store on his way into the gallery and picked up some stuff for lunch. He knew of a nice little spot at Montauk Point that shouldn't be too crowded, but there would be enough people about to stop him getting any ideas. Not that he needed them there, of course; he could keep his hands off her if he had to.

As the bike finally cruised past the town limits he revved his hand on the throttle. As they shot down Sunrise Highway, he couldn't ignore the thrill that surged through him as Jessie's arms tightened around his waist.

Jessie could see the lighthouse, tall and solitary at the end of the point, as the sea breeze whipped at her face. She clung onto Monroe as the bike angled down to the left, along a narrow strip of path that led to a small spray of sand hugging the Point's leeward side. A few tourists had been milling about up top, but once Monroe brought the bike to a stop at the edge of the sand she couldn't see anyone.

Could Monroe have found anywhere more romantic for their picnic? Maybe missing their afternoon lovemaking session wouldn't be so terrible after all.

He took her hand as they walked onto the sand. The bracken bushes provided some handy shade from the noon sun as he spread a thin blanket on the ground, and dropped the brown paper sack onto it.

Jessie took off her jacket, the lacy camisole beneath fluttered in the breeze and cooled her heated flesh. Sitting down, she toed off her sandals and reached for the bag.

'I certainly hope we've got something more inspired than sandwiches in here,' she said. 'I'm starving.'

'You know what?' He sank down onto the blanket next to her and grabbed the grocery sack. 'She who doesn't buy doesn't get to belly-ache about what's in the bag.'

'What are those—Latimer house rules?' Jessie's lips curved as she watched him pull an assortment of ready-made salads and a large foil bag out of the sack.

'Yeah,' he said as he brought out a chilled bottle of wine with a flourish. 'Now who's griping?'

'Not me,' she replied.

He up-ended the sack and paper plates, plastic cups, napkins, forks and a bottle opener dropped onto the blanket.

'You thought of everything. I'm impressed.' Jessie tried to sound contrite but was enjoying the moment too much. He looked so pleased with himself. Like a little boy who'd just got straight As for the first time.

As he concentrated on opening the wine, Jessie leant forward on her knees and placed her hands on his shoulder. When his head came up, she put her lips on his. The kiss was a whisper, full of the love blossoming inside her.

He dropped the wine, fisted his fingers in her hair. Dragging her mouth across his, he plundered. The kiss shot to scorching, but only for a moment. When he released her, his face was dark with arousal, and something else, something she wasn't sure of.

He scooped up the bottle of wine. 'Don't get carried away, Red. We haven't tasted it yet.'

Jessie forced herself to ignore the stab of regret. Why hadn't he carried on kissing her? Don't be a ninny. Of course he didn't want to take things any further—they were on a public beach. Anyone might see them. But she couldn't quite shake the feeling that he had withdrawn for some other reason.

She turned round on the blanket, stared out at the waves gently lapping against the shore. She could hear the screech of seagulls overhead, see the tip of the lighthouse in the distance over the long grass and bracken that edged the bluff.

'Here you go, Red.' He nudged her arm. She turned and took the plastic cup. He tapped it with his own. 'Here's to sand in your potato salad.'

Jessie forced her lips to curve. 'Here's to guys who know how to pack a picnic.'

Monroe took a long gulp of the light, fresh white wine. It tasted pretty good, but did nothing to calm the fire inside him.

She had wanted to continue the embrace, had looked disappointed when he'd pulled his mouth away. That fact and the memory of her warm and willing in his arms was making the need claw in his gut like an angry dog. He screwed the plastic glass down into the sand and started pulling the wrapper off the plates.

He'd brought her here to have a nice sensible lunch, not climb all over her again as soon as they got here. He refused to feel bad about it. Even though the confusion in her eyes and the surge of blood to his groin made it damn near impossible not to drag her across his lap right now and…

Jessie opened the salads, searched for something to say as she arranged them on the blanket. 'Ali called the gallery today.'

'How are they doing?'

'Ali's exhausted. I don't think she's left the penthouse much.'

'The heat's a bitch in Manhattan in August.' Monroe ladled some potato salad onto her plate, then his.

'Emmy's having a great time, though. Linc took her to the Bronx Zoo yesterday.' Jessie laughed, remembering the conversation with her sister that morning. 'She said Linc was so shattered when they got back he could hardly string together a coherent sentence.'

Monroe chuckled. 'I bet Emmy was still chattering away like a little magpie. The poor guy.' Tearing open the foil sack, he put a piece of fried chicken on Jessie's plate. 'Did you say anything to Ali about us?'

Jessie glanced up, watched him lick his fingers. 'No, I didn't.' Was that relief she saw flash in his eyes? No, she was being silly, paranoid. 'Ali wouldn't be all that surprised, though.'

'Why?'

Jessie wished she hadn't blurted that out. How did she explain the statement without sounding pathetic?

'It's just…' She looked down at her plate, concentrated on forking up the potato salad. 'I used to have a pretty massive crush on Linc when they were first married.'

'You're kidding me?'

She looked up. He put his fork down on his plate. He was watching her, his expression unreadable.

'It's silly really. It was just a stupid schoolgirl's fantasy.'

He dumped the plate down on the blanket. 'What kind of schoolgirl's fantasy, exactly?'

'Not that kind of fantasy, you numbskull.' Was he jealous? It was so ridiculous it was almost sweet. If she hadn't felt like a complete fool for bringing up this whole business, she might have been flattered. 'It took me a while to realise it, but it wasn't Linc I fancied. Well, not much anyway. It was what he represented.'

'And what was that?' Monroe didn't even know why he was asking the question. He didn't want the answer.

Jessie huffed out a breath, put her own plate down. 'He adored Ali. It was obvious whenever they were together that they adored each other. And then, about a month after they announced they were getting married, they told us that Ali was expecting a baby.' Jessie picked up her fork, toyed with her food. 'Of course, it was wonderful news. We were all so excited.'

Monroe wasn't convinced. He could see the misery in her eyes at the memory. 'You sure about that?'

'A part of me was,' she said, so quietly he almost couldn't hear her over the churn of the sea. 'But a part of me was pea-green with envy.'

'Because she was having Linc's kid?' He really didn't want to hear the answer to this one.

'No,' she said.

The knot of tension in his shoulders released.

'Because she had this perfect life,' Jessie continued. 'Marriage to a gorgeous man who worshipped her. When Emmy arrived, a beautiful daughter.' Jessie shook her head, her eyes downcast. 'I was a stupid, selfish, silly little girl who wanted what she had without having to work for it.'

'Red.' He reached out, stroked his hand down her arm. 'Don't be so damn hard on yourself. You were only a kid at the time.'

'I was old enough to know better. And I didn't really get over it until after Toby.'

'Toby.' Monroe felt his shoulders tighten again. 'The dumb bastard who couldn't give you an orgasm?'

Jessie laughed, breaking the tension at last. 'Yes, that would be Toby.'

'How long were you guys together?' Funny, but he didn't feel nearly as threatened by her relationship with her ex-boyfriend as he did by her teenage crush on his brother.

'Two years.' She sighed, picked up her plate again. 'Two very long years.'

'Two years without an orgasm. No wonder they felt long. You'd have to be some kind of a nun not to be mad about that.'

'If I had known what I was missing, I'd have walked out on him in about two seconds.' Jessie started to laugh.

Monroe smiled back at her. No, he didn't feel remotely threatened by Toby the jerk.

'But then again,' Jessie said, sobering, 'Toby's abilities in bed weren't why I agreed to marry him.'

'You were going to marry the guy? What the hell for?'

Jessie gave a small smile. 'Well, because he asked me, for one thing. And because he told me he wanted to have children, make a home. For a while there, I persuaded myself he was my dream come true.'

Monroe felt the mouthful of potato salad he'd eaten turn over in his stomach. 'That's your dream? A home, kids?'

Jessie frowned. He looked stunned. No, not stunned, he looked horrified. Just for a moment, before he looked away.

'Well, yes. Sort of. But not right now.'

Was he scared she was going to ask him to marry her or something? While it was lowering to know the question might put that devastated look in his eyes, even she wasn't that much of a romantic fool. They'd only been together for four days, for goodness' sake.

'Monroe, you don't have to look so worried. I'm not picking out the bridesmaids' dresses yet. I learned my lesson with Toby. If I do settle down, it'll be when the time's right with the right person.' She was not going to make a fool of herself over that fantasy again.

He lifted up the wine. 'Put up your glass, Red.'

She lifted the plastic cup, trying to figure out what she could see in his eyes as he splashed some more wine into it.

'Let's drink to dreams, then.' He put down the bottle, picked up his own cup and shot her that heart-breaking grin. 'And not letting them get in the way of good sex.'

Jessie smiled, tapped her cup to his. 'Now that, I can drink to.'

Monroe swallowed the wine, but it tasted like acid on his tongue. Why the hell did he care that he could never be her dream man? That he could never make her dreams come true. He wasn't in the business of dreaming. Reality was hard enough.

CHAPTER THIRTEEN

'FLIP over. I've been fantasising about putting sunscreen on that back since we got here.'

Jessie smiled at the low rumble of Monroe's voice. Lying on the small stretch of private beach next to Linc and Ali's property, she could feel the familiar warmth that had nothing to do with the early-morning sunshine.

She sat up, dipped her sunglasses off her nose and shot Monroe a flirty look. 'You're too late. I plastered myself in cream before we came out.'

'And this would be relevant how, exactly?'

Seeing the mischievous twinkle in his eye, she giggled. The sound was light and girlish, just how she felt. 'Okay, you've persuaded me.'

Pulling the cream out of her bag, she threw it to him and turned over on the towel they'd arranged on the sand.

She could hear the rhythmic churn of the Atlantic behind them, but there was no other noise. Apart from the occasional jogger, the beach—reserved for use by the four houses on the promontory—was as good as deserted on a Sunday morning.

It was their last day alone together before Ali, Linc and Emmy returned from New York. As much as she wanted to see her family again, Jessie couldn't help feeling sad that the intimacy would soon be broken. The two weeks since she and Monroe had first made love had drifted past in a romantic haze.

They'd settled into a routine that had meant sunny, sexy afternoons and hot, insatiable nights. After their picnic at Montauk Point they had got in the habit of going for motorcycle rides most days once she finished work at noon. Discovering parts of Long Island she had never seen before. They had romantic dinners by the pool most evenings. Sharing companionship and passion over seared tuna and white wine when she cooked and steak and beer when it was his turn. He touched her in ways she'd never been touched before, drove her to ecstasy and beyond. And every night she fell asleep, exhausted, content, her love swelling stronger in her chest with each passing day.

She adored watching him paint most of all, both proud and in awe of his talent. Had woken up only last Sunday to find him sketching her naked while she slept. She'd been horrified at first, but once he'd plied her with kisses, caresses and a shattering orgasm, she'd sat for him most of the afternoon and evening.

She'd asked him about his art. Why didn't he let Mrs Bennett take a look at the paintings? Didn't he know how good they were? Didn't he want to pursue his art as a career?

But he hadn't really answered any of her questions.

If she was being honest with herself, she had begun to feel a little uneasy about his unwillingness to talk about that or anything else more personal.

Ever since that first picnic he had been careful to keep everything light, relaxed. He hadn't asked her any more questions about her dreams, about her plans, her past or her future, and whenever she tried to ask him any about his own he brushed them off. Jessie had let him, scared to break the feeling of contentment, of unity, that cocooned them.

Propping her head on her hands, Jessie watched a lone

woman stroll past in the distance, an energetic young puppy jumping at her heels.

Jessie closed her eyes, willed the doubts away. What was wrong with her? She was being silly. She and Monroe were in the first flush of their relationship and she should just lie back and enjoy it. All those big, serious questions could wait for another time.

The warm sun lotion sprayed onto her back and she stretched like a contented cat.

'Heck, this stuff's like house paint,' Monroe remarked from behind her.

'Factor fifty-five, otherwise I become one big freckle.'

His lips buzzed her shoulder blades. 'I like the freckles.' His hands began to massage the heavy cream in. She could feel the large, callused palms on her skin. She pictured his beautiful hands as she'd seen them late last night, stroking her into a frenzy. His hands, she decided, were the first thing that she'd fallen in love with.

Maybe she should tell him tonight how she felt? It was probably a record for her to have kept it a secret for this long. She'd already promised herself she wouldn't be hurt if he didn't tell her he loved her back, straight away. Didn't men always take longer to figure it out?

'You like that?' he said. She could hear the seductive smile in his words.

'I certainly do,' she murmured. 'Even though it's completely unnecessary.'

'Well, now,' he said, running his fingers under the strap of her bikini top. 'That's what you think.' Deftly, he unhooked the clasp.

'What do you think you're doing?' Turning sharply, Jessie grabbed her top and held it to her breasts.

His knowing grin turned devilish as his eyes flicked down

to her bosom. 'I thought, seeing as you're European, you might find that unnecessary.'

'I'm not that European,' she replied tartly as she rehooked the bikini top. 'And neither are the families that live around here.'

He shrugged, keeping his eyes trained on her bikini top. 'You can't blame a guy for trying.'

'No, I suppose not.' She grinned back at him. 'Here.' She whipped the bottle of sun lotion off the sand, did a quick twirling movement with her finger. 'I think it's my turn.'

His lips quirked, before he turned over and stretched out on the towel. 'You know what? That was the other thing I was fantasising about,' he said wryly. 'Except in my dreams you were a lot more European.'

She laughed, pouring a generous dose of the heavy cream into her palms. She studied the lean, hard expanse of his back. The muscles had bunched up under his shoulder blades where he was resting his head on his arms. Spreading the liquid across the warm, tanned skin, she heard him give a low moan. She began to dig her fingers into the firm, smooth planes of sinew and muscle. He felt wonderful, she thought, and imagined what she was going to do with him that evening.

'You're too good at this.' He groaned. 'Don't forget this is a public beach, Red.'

She was having trouble doing just that, when the familiar ridges across his shoulder blades rippled beneath her fingertips. In the bright sunlight, the thin white scars stood out more prominently than ever.

'Did you get these in prison?' The question popped out before she'd thought about it. She regretted it instantly when his shoulders tensed. Her hands went still.

His past was one of the subjects they never talked about. From the little she knew about it, she guessed it was something he didn't want to be reminded of, so she had tried hard not to pry.

'No,' he said finally.

'I'm sorry, Monroe. I shouldn't have asked that.'

He rolled over, studied her.

She sat back on her haunches. What had she done? 'I really am sorry, Monroe. I didn't mean to bring back bad memories.'

Seeing the stricken look in her eyes, Monroe reached out, took her hand in his. 'Don't look so scared, Red. You're curious. You're entitled to ask.'

'I didn't mean to. It just sort of slipped out.'

She hadn't asked, he thought, although he knew she was curious. By not asking, she had given him her unconditional trust. And he hadn't done the same for her.

He'd told himself over and over that keeping things light, keeping things easy, was how it had to be—especially after their conversation at Montauk Point. He couldn't be her dream man, he didn't want to be, so there was no use pretending that they had anything more here than great sex and a good friendship.

But in the last two weeks he'd been more settled than he'd ever been in his life. He didn't know how it had happened, but gradually the restlessness that had been a part of him for so long had disappeared.

He'd fed off Jessie's compassion and her generosity, had basked in her approval and had revelled in the passion they'd shared. But underneath it all had been the tug of guilt and the knowledge that, when it ended, leaving her was going to be harder than he could ever have imagined.

He could see, with the worry swirling in her eyes, that the reasons why he had deflected her questions weren't so clear-cut any more.

Had he kept silent because he didn't want her getting any

wrong ideas about where this relationship was headed or because he was scared? Scared that once she knew all the sordid details of his life she wouldn't look at him with the same adoration, the same affection any more?

Should he stay silent, let the moment pass, or should he give her something back? Didn't he owe her that much?

He sat up slowly. 'I didn't get the scars in prison. My mother used a belt on us when we were kids.'

She blinked, stiffened. 'That's terrible.' The tear that spilled onto her cheek shocked him, and touched him in a way he would never have expected.

'Don't cry. It was a long time ago. It doesn't matter now.'

'Your own mother scarred you. Of course it matters.' She sniffed, wiping the moisture away with an impatient hand.

'She hated us. She had her reasons,' he said.

'What reasons could she possibly have for doing that to a child?'

The vehemence in her tone made him feel oddly comforted. 'Do you really want to know? It's ancient history.'

'Yes, I do.' Her eyes were fixed on his face. 'But only if you want to talk about it.'

Drawing a leg up, he rested an arm on his knee and studied the undulating sand and the insistent drift of the sea beyond.

Could he talk about it? Did he want to?

It was weird. He'd never felt compelled to talk about it before, but, oddly, with her he did.

He couldn't give her a future, he knew that, but would it be so terrible for him to give her a little of his past?

Jessie waited, watching his profile, her emotions a confusing mix of anger—at the boy he had been, the horrors he had suffered—and anticipation. She so desperately wanted to know more about him. Was he finally going to talk to her about himself?

It seemed like an eternity, but eventually he turned back to her. 'The night before she had me arrested, my mother told me why she hated us. Me and Linc.'

'She had you arrested?' Jessie couldn't disguise the horror in her voice.

He shrugged, as if it weren't important. 'Yeah. Corruption of a minor, that's what I did time for in juvie. The girl was fifteen. I was just sixteen, so technically they were right. She was hot and she was as eager as me. I didn't stop to ask for ID.'

He picked up one of the small pebbles nestled by his feet, skimmed it absently across the sand. She noticed the ridged skin on his back and had to force the next question out.

'What happened when your mother found out?'

'One of her friends from the country club saw us together.' His shoulders hitched as he turned back to her. 'When I got home that night she was wired on the prescription drugs she popped like candy. She tried to go for me with the belt. Kept shouting at me, saying all this really ugly stuff. It didn't take much to wrestle the belt away from her. She told me then about what it had been like for her with my old man. How I was just the same.' He shook his head slowly, his breath coming out on a long sigh. 'First time I ever saw her cry.'

Jessie could hear the pity in his voice, but couldn't begin to share it, for a woman who had terrorised and despised her own children. 'What did she tell you?'

He looked at her, his eyes shadowed. 'That he'd raped her, repeatedly. That he'd wanted sons and even when she'd had several miscarriages, even after she'd begged him not to get her pregnant again, he'd forced himself on her. Forced her to have us.'

Jessie recoiled at the horror of it. What should have been a proclamation of love had become for Monroe's parents a proof of hate. Could it really be so?

'Did you believe her?'

He nodded. 'My old man was in his late fifties when she met him. She was seventeen, just off the plane from London, keen to find the American Dream. He was from one of Newport's richest families. She held out till she got his ring on her finger, then I guess she found out that it wasn't just sex he wanted.'

'What was your father like?' Jessie tried to keep her voice steady, not to let her disgust for the man who had sired him show.

He shrugged. 'I didn't know him. He died when I was still a kid. We didn't see him much. My mother sent us back to stay with our grandmother in Britain every summer.' He shrugged. 'When we had to be with her, we lived on his Rhode Island estate, but he had several other properties.' He looked up and gave her a hard look. 'He died of a heart attack. He was busy balling an eighteen-year-old showgirl in Vegas when it hit.'

He picked up a fistful of sand, watched it run through his fingers. 'He wasn't interested in us. Linc and I, we knew that, we were just a means to carry on the family name. But we never understood why our mother hated us. Her own mother, our granny, she was strict, but she wasn't twisted like her; she never once raised a hand to us like our mother did. After a while, I just kind of accepted it, but I know it screwed up Linc real bad. She beat on him the worst, because he would stand up to her.' He shook his head slowly. 'I guess the more he did that, the more it reminded her of the old man.'

'She hit Linc, too?'

'You don't know about that?'

'No. Linc and Ali have never spoken about his mother or father.'

He pondered that for a minute.

'Did you tell Linc,' she asked, 'what your mother told you?'

'No, he was long gone by then. He left when he was

twelve and I was only ten. Our grandmother had died that summer. I guess he couldn't stand knowing we'd be stuck with her all the time.'

'You mean, until this summer, you hadn't seen Linc since you were children?'

He shrugged. 'Not since the day he ran off.'

Suddenly, so much became clear to Jessie. These men had been trying to forge a relationship after over twenty years apart, after the abject horror of their childhood, and she'd nearly messed it all up. 'I'm so sorry I behaved like such a silly cow when you arrived, Monroe.'

'Red.' He brushed a finger down her cheek, smiled. 'As far as I'm concerned, you were feisty and gorgeous and you felt great wriggling around in my arms, so there's no need to apologise.'

The blush became more intense as she thought of their first meeting. 'Will you tell me about prison, Monroe?'

She wanted to know about the boy he had been—and how he had become the man she loved.

Monroe huffed out a breath. He had to do this. She had the right to know what he'd come from, how ugly it was.

'The first stretch was okay.' He couldn't even remember the green kid he'd been then. 'It was only six months in juvie.' He'd been wild and angry, he realised now, but determined to see it through and get out. 'I behaved myself, didn't attract too much attention. I was more bored than anything.'

The experience in juvie had made him think doing time wasn't so bad. It was three square meals a day and they didn't shout at you or beat you simply for existing.

'Ali said you did two terms?'

'Yeah, the second stretch was...' He paused. 'It was different.'

'How?' She said the words on a fragile whisper.

Monroe's gaze lifted to hers. Could he tell her? Would she despise him, for what had happened, for what he had let them do to him?

He took a slow breath. 'It was real time. After juvie I skipped parole, took to the streets. A year later, I was picked up in Buffalo after a bar fight. One of the local barflies went after me with a broken bottle. I defended myself and hit him back but then loads of others piled in. Glass and fists were flying everywhere. A guy got hurt bad that night. I wasn't from around there and I had a record, so it was me who ended up doing a stretch in the local pen. One of the meanest pens in the whole state of New York I found out after I'd been there less than a day.'

He could still remember the horror of that night, could still remember the fear afterwards, during two years of tests to make sure he was healthy. Looking at her, he could see the compassion, the understanding in her eyes. Maybe she wouldn't judge him, maybe she would understand.

'I had a pretty face. I was seventeen, cocky and stupid with it. I thought I knew the score.'

Jessie could see the shadow of bitterness in his eyes and felt her heart race in sympathy.

'They cornered me in the shower on the first night,' he continued, his voice low and thick with tension. 'Two of them. I fought back at the start, but what was the point? It was two against one and I didn't stand a chance.'

The tears slid down Jessie's cheeks. How had he survived?

He stared down at his feet in the sand. His words came out on a low murmur. 'They held me down, took turns.'

Leaning forward, she pressed herself against him, wrapped her arms around him and held on tight. She could feel the solid beat of his heart against her ear as she rested her head against the warm skin of his back. He didn't say anything, but slowly she felt his shoulders relax. He put his hand on top of hers.

After a long time, she let go, moved round, knelt in front of him. She gripped his face in her hands, made him look at her.

'You survived, Monroe. That's all that matters.' She could see the shadow of humiliation in his eyes, fought to control her anger at what he had been forced to endure, at what he was still enduring. 'Don't ever feel ashamed.'

'You don't think I'm less of a man?'

Where the hell had that question come from? he wondered. He'd never known the doubt was inside him until he'd asked her.

She flashed a seductive smile at him through the veil of tears. 'Monroe. I don't think I could cope with you if you were any more of a man.'

He brought his arms round her then, held her close, sank into the comfort and support she offered. He'd told her the worst of it and she hadn't been disgusted. She hadn't judged him as he had so often judged himself.

'Did it happen more than once?' she asked quietly.

'No, that was it. I got beat up a few more times after that, but mostly I kept to myself.' He folded his legs, settled her onto his lap, but kept his arms around her. And thought about how much he was going to miss her when he had to let her go.

As they walked back towards the garage apartment, the noon sun heating the grass beneath Jessie's feet, she considered what Monroe had told her of his past.

He'd been through so much, as a child and as an adult. Yet the only person he really seemed to blame was himself. She could feel the rough skin of his palm as he held her hand. He'd worked so hard, in dead-end jobs, yet he had such great talent as an artist but didn't want to promote it. Now she understood why—because he lacked the confidence.

She loved him. It wasn't just a silly girlish dream. It couldn't be. She understood him now. This was more than she'd ever felt for Toby.

She had planned to tell him how she felt tonight, but now she wasn't so sure. Maybe she shouldn't rush him, put pressure on him. He'd told her things she was sure he'd never told anyone else. He'd shared so much with her and that should be enough for now. She squeezed his hand as they mounted the apartment steps together.

'You all right?' he asked. The slight frown on his face made it clear he wasn't sure. The thought made her heart ache for him. How could such a strong, admirable man be so unsure of himself?

'Yes, I'm wonderful.' She glanced away. The heaviness of the conversation was making him uneasy. She needed to change the subject. 'It'll be nice to see Ali and Linc and Emmy again tomorrow, but I think we're going to miss the privacy.'

He pushed the apartment door open, held it as she went in ahead of him. 'I guess.'

'We may have a few awkward moments with Emmy when she comes skipping over in the morning to play mechanic with you.'

'About that…' He stopped dead beside her, the strain clear in his voice. 'We probably shouldn't say anything yet.'

'Why not?' Jessie felt the flutter of uneasiness in her stomach.

Monroe dumped their towels on the sofa. He took his time walking into the kitchenette and getting himself a glass of water.

'You want one?' He held the glass up.

Jessie shook her head. 'Why don't you want us to say anything to Linc and Ali?'

He put the glass down with a solid plop on the breakfast

bar, looked at her for the first time since they'd entered the apartment.

'Is there something wrong, Monroe?'

When he didn't answer straight away, she felt a lump start to form in her throat. What exactly was going on?

'No.' Her relief at his words was tempered by the look of regret she could see in his eyes.

Reaching across the breakfast bar, he took her hand, pulled her around beside him. Putting his palms on her cheeks, he lifted her face to his.

'I can't let you go, Jessie. Not yet.'

She didn't know what to make of the statement. 'Why would you have to?'

He gave her a light kiss. 'Let's just keep it private for now, okay?' His voice was low, possessive. 'I want it to be just the two of us. I don't want to share you with anyone, Red. Not even Linc and Ali.'

'But, Monroe, how can we keep it a secret? If we're sleeping together?'

'Come over in the evenings, after they've gone to bed.'

She stepped back, a cold feeling in the pit of her stomach. 'That seems a bit sneaky.'

'It's not sneaky.' He snagged her hand, before she could take another step away. 'Listen, Jess.' He rubbed her palm absently with his thumb. 'Linc as good as told me to keep my hands off you.'

'Wha-at?' The shock came first. She pulled her hand out of his. 'I don't believe it. When?'

'The morning after the barbecue. I guess he could see I was interested. He was just protecting you.'

Shock was followed by indignation. 'But that's…' She spluttered to a halt, words failed her. 'But it's none of his business.'

'Sure it is. He's your brother-in-law.'

'Exactly, he's my brother-in-law, not my keeper. How dare he? I've got a good mind to give him a kick up the bum when he gets back.'

Monroe grinned at her indignation, making her more angry.

'What on earth are you smiling about? It's not funny.'

'Oh, yeah, it is.' He held onto her hand as she reeled away. 'I didn't tell you so I could see you kick my brother's butt.' He paused a moment, humour sparking in his eyes. 'Though that would be kinda fun.'

'Why did you tell me, then?'

He pulled her close, held her still when she struggled.

'Linc doesn't want me to touch you and I don't want him to know that I have.' He loosened his grip so she could see his face.

'But that's so Neanderthal of you both.'

His lips tilted. He didn't look remotely offended at the suggestion. 'I guess it's a guy thing. It's just… Linc and me are on shaky ground. I screwed up pretty bad with the birthday present.'

She sobered, remembering the painful incident at Emmy's party. 'Don't feel bad about that, Monroe. Linc understood. I'm sure he did.'

His hands stroked up her arms. 'He feels protective of you. I don't want to hit him with this…situation yet. Could we let it ride for now?'

She didn't want to let it ride. She wanted everyone to know how she felt about Monroe. That she was head over heels in love with him. But if she couldn't even bring herself to tell Monroe yet, how could she tell anyone else?

But still Jessie hesitated.

It was worse than sneaky not to tell everyone about their relationship. It was dishonest. But what could she do, seeing the insecurity in his eyes? He was worried about his relationship with his brother and, however misguided his suggestion might be, she couldn't stand in the way of him building a better bond with Linc. The two of them had been robbed of that in their childhood. She would not be the one to put a spanner in the works now.

'Okay, Monroe, I won't say anything, but just for a little while.'

Monroe pulled her into his arms, so she couldn't see the sadness in his eyes. 'Thanks, Red,' he said, knowing a little while was all they had.

CHAPTER FOURTEEN

'So, what have you and Monroe been getting up to while we've been away?'

Jessie's fingers stopped dead on the garment she was busy folding into Ali's dresser drawer. 'Sorry, what did you say?' She could feel the heat creeping up her neck as she stared down at the newly washed T-shirt.

'Hmm,' Ali murmured from the soft leather armchair by the master bedroom's French doors. 'From the fantastic shade of red you're going, I'd say it's quite a lot.'

Jessie turned slowly to face her sister. She was trapped. That was the problem with having red hair and fair skin. She couldn't keep a secret from Ali if her life depended on it.

'Don't look so mortified, Jess. You've been here two weeks alone together and it was obvious the night of the barbecue there was an attraction there. I'm not all that shocked you guys went for it.'

Jessie stared at her sister, keeping her feelings a secret now seemed pointless. 'Actually, it's a little more than just sex.'

Ali studied her sister for a moment, then her eyes widened. 'My goodness.' She hauled herself out of the chair, waddled over to Jessie. 'You're in love with him.'

The depth of emotion in Ali's eyes made Jessie's own begin to water. 'Yes, I think I am.'

'How does Monroe feel?'

Jessie looked down as she closed the dresser drawer. 'We haven't talked about it.'

'Why not?'

'I don't want to pressure him.'

'But, Jess, you have a right to know how he feels, don't you?'

'He cares about me. I know he does.' He had made love to her so carefully, so tenderly the night before, it had to be true.

'What's the problem, then?' Concern tinged Ali's words. 'You don't look happy, Jess.'

'I…' Jessie paused, feeling guilty. She'd already broken the promise she'd made to Monroe. 'He didn't want you and Linc to know about us.'

'Why?'

It was such a simple question. Why did she find it so hard to answer? 'He says it's because Linc warned him off. Told him not to touch me.'

'That's ridiculous. Linc wouldn't say that.' Ali sounded so sure, Jessie's confusion increased.

'I know,' Jessie replied softly. 'After I thought about it for a while I came to the same conclusion. I mean, I know Linc can be a bit overprotective, but I'm sure Monroe got the wrong end of the stick somehow.'

'There's a very simple way to sort this out.' Ali headed for the bedroom door. 'We'll go and ask Linc what he said.'

'No.' Jessie caught up with her sister, held her arm. 'You can't ask him. I don't want Linc to know about this.'

Her sister stared back at her for a moment. 'I can't believe you and Monroe think you'll be able to keep it a secret. It took me about ten seconds to figure it out after we got back this morning.'

'Yes, well.' Jessie could feel the heat in her cheeks again but soldiered on. 'I don't think Linc's quite as astute as you are. He didn't spot a thing.' It had been almost comical, the way Monroe had been so careful not to touch her or look at her when the family's car had pulled up in the drive that morning.

'Linc was nervous,' Ali said. 'After what happened at Emmy's party. I told him to ring Monroe and talk to him while we were in New York. But he wouldn't do it. You know what men are like. They'd rather saw off their own tongues than talk about their feelings. But he's desperate to make things right with Monroe.'

'Monroe wants to sort it out as well, Ali.' Jessie pleaded with her sister. This she understood. 'That's why I don't think we should tell Linc about Monroe and me right now. They've got so much baggage to get through already. This will just cloud the whole thing. And anyway, we've only been an item for two weeks.'

'But you're in love with him, Jess.'

'I know, but it's still new. They've waited over twenty years to become brothers again. I don't want to make it more difficult.'

Ali plopped down on the bed, her eyes clouded. 'Did Monroe talk to you about their family, then?'

'Yes, he told me about their mother. What she did to them. What happened to him in prison. He's had such a tough life, Ali. He's had to overcome things I couldn't even imagine.'

Ali watched her for a long moment, then patted the bed beside her. 'Sit down, Jess.'

Jessie perched on the bed. She could see the worry and regret in Ali's face.

'All right, Jess,' she said. 'I won't tell Linc about you two.'

Jessie let out an unsteady breath.

'But I still think you're wrong about this.'

'Why? I—'

'I know you're doing it for all the right reasons,' Ali interrupted her. 'You're warm and you're giving and I think you've been waiting a long time to have someone to love.'

'Do you think I'm being a romantic fool?'

'No, I don't, Jess.' Ali's words were heartfelt. 'I don't think you're a fool at all. But,' she continued, 'Monroe is a very complicated man. He's not going to be an easy man to love.'

'I know that. But, Ali, he really needs me. And I think he's worth the effort.' How could she explain to her sister how special he was? 'He's such a wonderful person in so many ways. He's tender and caring and so careful with me. He's also fun and exciting and… Well, you already know how gorgeous he is. And, Ali, he has the most amazing talent. He paints, portraits, landscapes. In oil, mostly. But, Ali, he's got this incredible way of putting the emotion there on the canvas. I wish you could see his work. But he's sort of shy about it.' Jessie's heart felt as if it were going to beat right out of her chest. It was so wonderful to be able to talk to someone at last about how she felt.

Ali put her arms around Jessie, gave her a tight hug. 'I'm glad for you, Jessie. And Monroe. He's a lucky man, but I've got one word of warning.'

Jessie stilled her features, the concern in Ali's eyes stemming her euphoria. 'I'm listening.'

'By not telling Monroe how you feel about him. By not telling Linc about the two of you because Monroe has asked you not to. You're putting his needs above your own, Jess.'

'I know, but it feels right at the moment.'

'Fine, but it can't go on for ever. What you need is just as important as what he needs. Remember that.'

'Hey, you want a hand with that?'

Monroe looked up from the lawnmower to see his brother walking towards him across the freshly mown grass. He wiped his forearm across his brow as he stood up.

'All finished,' he said. 'I'm just gonna haul these clippings over to the garage. The garbage truck will get them tomorrow.'

Drawing level, Linc grabbed one of the sacks. 'Let me take one.'

Monroe bent to tie up the other. They walked in silence across the lawn with the cumbersome garbage bags in their arms. Monroe waited for his brother to speak. He could feel the sweat trickling down his back. It was a hot day; the mid-afternoon heat was a killer. He should have waited until evening to mow the lawn, but he'd been antsy ever since his brother and his family had got back from New York.

'Why didn't you come over for lunch? Ali was expecting you.' Linc's voice was neutral.

Monroe threw his bag into the large trash receptacle in the garage. 'Couldn't. Got caught up doing the lawn.'

Linc dumped his own bag into the bin. He slammed the lid down and then whipped around to face Monroe. 'That's bull.' He didn't sound neutral any more; he sounded good and pissed. 'Nobody asked you to do the damn lawn.'

Monroe's own temper spiked. 'I told you I'm not a damn freeloader—'

Linc held up a hand. 'Can it. I'm not arguing about that again.'

'I'm not the one who brought it up again.' Monroe bit the words out.

Linc dragged a hand through his hair, huffed out a breath. He didn't look angry any more, just miserable. 'Hell, Roe, why don't you come out and say it?'

'Say what?' Monroe felt a trickle of guilt.

'I screwed up. I know that,' Linc replied. 'I shouldn't have tried to give you the gift at Emmy's party. It was too soon. You weren't ready.'

'It's not that,' Monroe said, the trickle now a bitter torrent.

'You don't have to pretend with me, Roe. I know we don't know each other. But we were brothers once. I wanted you to remember. I was pushing you. I shouldn't have.'

Seeing the torment in his brother's face, hearing it in his voice, Monroe knew he couldn't hold out any longer.

'I do remember.' He watched Linc's eyes jerk to his, saw the rush of emotion in them. 'I remember you always gave me birthday cards. Some of the ugliest drawings I've ever seen in my life.'

Linc shrugged. 'I was never much of an artist.' His gaze was intent on Monroe's.

'I remember when I was ten.' Monroe's voice cracked a little, he cleared his throat. 'The last one you ever gave me. You said it was the Silver Surfer. Looked more like an icebox with wings.'

'Hey, I thought that was one of my best.'

'It meant something, Linc.'

Linc nodded, but didn't say anything.

Monroe swallowed, forced himself to continue. 'When you gave me that gift by the pool, it brought it all back. How it was when you were there, what it was like afterwards, when you weren't.'

Linc sighed. 'Hell, I didn't mean to bring all that back, Roe. I'm sorry.'

'Don't be an ass.' Monroe's words were sharp, angry. 'It's always there. So what? It doesn't mean a damn thing any more. You took me by surprise, that's all. The duffel bag's great, by the way. Just what I needed.' Seeing the pleasure in his brother's face, Monroe realised he should have said something much sooner. 'Thanks. It's the best birthday present I've ever had.'

Linc put his hand on Monroe's shoulder, squeezed and then let go. 'Not better than the Silver Surfer card, surely?' His voice was thick with emotion.

Monroe grinned. 'You got me there—maybe not quite that good. But pretty damn close.'

Ali's words of advice were still ringing in Jessie's ears when she tiptoed through the garden that evening. It was nearly midnight. The grass was cool under her bare feet as she skirted the Cape Myrtle trees, their branches bending under the weight of their summer blooms. She'd waited until the house was quiet before coming out. She could see the lights from Monroe's apartment blazing as always in the darkness, beckoning her back to him. The smell of lavender scented the sea air, making her smile with the romance of the moment.

She would tell him tonight. Ali was right. Monroe should know how she felt. Her love wasn't some burden that he would have to bear, after all. It was a joy, a gift. He could take it or refuse it or put it to one side and think about it. But whatever happened, she wanted him to know about it.

She remembered the difficulty he had had in accepting Linc's gift. The symbolism seemed so clear to her now. That was why she'd been afraid to tell him. Because she knew he wouldn't know how to respond, what to say. It seemed cowardly to her now. She felt so happy, so confident. He was the right man for her. He might be unsure of himself but he didn't have to be unsure of her.

She glanced up at his apartment window and saw his tall, lean figure standing next to the glass. He was watching her from the window. Her heart leapt into her throat. Her lover was waiting for her. She gave a quick, delighted wave, picked up the hem of her skirt and ran round the side of the building to join him.

As Monroe watched Jessie disappear from view, the weight of the guilt he'd been carrying around all day got heavier still.

She had looked eager and so beautiful, the reddening twilight shining off that mass of fiery hair.

Bewitched, that was what he was. She'd cast some sorceress's spell over him. He was so desperate to hold her again, his hands fisted at his sides. It was getting harder and harder for him to contemplate letting her go.

When he'd bumped into her that afternoon and she had whispered that she was coming over tonight, he should have told her no, made some excuse. But he hadn't been able to. Not while he could smell that fresh scent of hers; not while she'd been looking at him with that combination of desire and trust that drove him insane.

So he'd told her to come, that he would be waiting. But as he heard her feet, light on the steps up to the apartment, as he turned and watched her step into the room, he knew that tonight he would have to start the process of drawing away from her. He would have to start putting the brakes on. He would have to let her see that there was no future for them.

'Monroe, don't look so forbidding. I'm positive nobody heard me.' Jessie ran across the room and clung onto his strong frame.

He hesitated for a moment, then his arms came round her, and he hugged her to him. She could feel the rough stubble against her forehead where he'd forgotten to shave again that morning. She could smell the wonderful musky scent of him that made her knees tremble.

'I missed you,' he said.

Jessie's heart stuttered at his words. Could he possibly have said anything more wonderful? 'Me, too.'

He pulled her dress off her shoulders, pushed her bra straps down.

'I can't wait. Is that okay?' That he should ask, the need and arousal thick in his voice, made her heartbeat skip again.

'That's good, because neither can I.' She laughed as he lifted her into his arms.

He carried her into the bedroom and in seconds they were both naked. There was little foreplay tonight, for none was needed. She was so giddy with the feel, the smell of him, that when he touched her core for the first time she was already slick and ready.

His tongue thrust inside her mouth as his fingers probed gently, stretching her and then retreating, stroking the swollen nub and making her cry out.

The heat was engulfing her, so suddenly, so shockingly. It was as if she couldn't breathe. She clawed the firm skin of his back as he pulled the condom onto his rampant sex. She gasped as he thrust inside her, filling her unbearably.

His hands tugged on her knees, forcing her legs wider still until he was buried deep. It felt like more, so much more this time.

The intense pleasure built to fever pitch as he moved in and out, the rhythm matched by her small, helpless cries. She was reaching now, trying to cling to the top; each vicious thrust seemed to take him further inside her, force her further over that edge. She cried out as she exploded over the top, shaking, shuddering, and dissolving into that wonderful oblivion. He sped up, thrusting hard, filling her to bursting. He gripped her hips, his eyes hot on hers, and she felt herself build again. So fast, so hard. The raw shock and arousal seemed to clog her throat, burn her to her core.

'Oh, no, not again,' she cried, on a pant of need and disbelief. The pleasure was so intense it was almost pain. He exploded inside her and shouted out as she shot over that last impossible crest and fell with him.

* * *

They lay panting together. Jessie watched the curtains billow beside the bed, the light breeze cooling her heated flesh. She was awed at how quickly the pleasure had overwhelmed her.

She propped herself up on his chest, looked down into his face and brushed the strands of hair back from his forehead. The satisfaction welled up inside her as she felt the moisture on his brow.

'I expect you already know this by now, Monroe. But I'm hopelessly in love with you.'

He tensed, but his eyes opened and fixed on hers. She didn't know what she'd expected to see, but the one thing she hadn't expected was regret. It was only there for a moment before his usual grin took over, but it was there for long enough to make the chill go right through her.

'You are, huh?' His voice was low, seductive.

'Yes, I am.' Now was not the time to back down, she decided. Maybe she'd been wrong. He didn't look regretful now. In fact, he looked cocky, his devilish grin dazzling her.

'That's sweet, Red.' His hands stroked up her back. Then he pulled her down on top of him, tucked her head beneath his chin.

She could hear the solid beat of his heart, feel the soft sprinkle of his chest hair beneath her cheek as the silence stretched out between them.

She wanted to know if he loved her, too. The question almost spilled out, but she stopped herself, biting down hard on her lip. The sea-scented air breezed through the open French doors, making her shiver.

'You cold?' he asked.

'No, I'm fine.' The words came out sounding stiff.

'Here.' He leant down and pulled the sheet up to cover them both. After tucking it around her, he settled her back into his arms, her head pillowed on his shoulder. 'That better?'

'Yes, thanks.'

Still she waited. Was he really going to say nothing more to her? She listened to the faint hum of the sea beyond the gardens. Could hear the murmur of his breathing. His arms were warm and strong around her. She could feel the gentle rise and fall of his chest beneath her cheek. Lifting her head, she looked up at the planes of his face in the shadows.

He was asleep.

Reaching, she caressed his cheek with one unsteady finger. She would not feel bad about this. She would not. Just because he hadn't declared his undying love, it didn't mean that he didn't love her. Her teeth tugged on her lip; her body trembled. She would not let the tears fall. She was not going to be a ninny.

She groped in the darkness for that feeling of euphoria, of contentment that had assailed her earlier in the afternoon when she had spoken to Ali. The glow of romance when she had looked up that night and seen him waiting for her. The exhilaration when they had been making love just a few minutes ago.

But the joy, the pleasure, refused to come. In its place was a feeling of uncertainty, of confusion, of rejection and, worse, that miserable feeling of foolishness she'd suffered so many times before in her life when she'd charged head first into something, letting all her defences down, only to discover that it hadn't been what she'd thought it had been after all.

CHAPTER FIFTEEN

'HELL!' Monroe shouted, shattering the quiet in the garage apartment.

The afternoon light was flooding through the French doors. The intoxicating scent of turpentine, sea salt and fresh grass swirled in the air.

It should have been the perfect time to paint, but he'd been trying to get this picture of Jessie on canvas for three hours and it wouldn't come. He'd never had this problem before.

Cursing under his breath, he dumped the useless paintbrush back into the mug of turpentine and braced his arms against the table top. He could feel the burning tension in his neck and shoulders. He'd hardly slept at all last night.

He picked up the washcloth, began to rub his hands, and then threw it down again, cursing more vehemently.

It was no good. He couldn't fool himself any longer. He should never have touched her. He could still see the confusion in her eyes when she'd told him she loved him the night before and he'd said nothing.

She hadn't asked him to say the words back to her, had let him hold her afterwards as if it were okay. But he knew he'd hurt her.

He'd pretended to be asleep, unable to face her, unsure

what to say. And in the darkness he'd felt her tremble beside him. It had been like having a knife thrust into his chest, knowing she was crying over him.

She'd been so quiet this morning, seemed so fragile, he had forced himself not to touch her before she'd left.

He should have been glad. Maybe she had begun to see that what they had didn't stand a chance.

But he couldn't seem to get past what had happened last night. He wanted to make things right, even though he knew he couldn't.

And he missed her. Not being able to hold her this morning, not being able to bury himself inside her had put him on edge all day.

He pulled off his T-shirt and dumped it in the laundry basket he kept under the painting table. Picking up the washcloth again, he cleaned his hands and tried to ignore the grim thought that had haunted him since yesterday. If he was honest, it had haunted him ever since he'd first taken Jessie to bed.

What if he was falling in love with her, too?

He hung the washcloth over the table's edge, shook his head. What on earth was wrong with him? Of course, he wasn't in love with her. Any more than she really was with him. She was sweet and innocent and they'd both had the best sex of their lives together. That would dazzle anyone. But she couldn't love him; no one could.

He picked up one of the oils he'd been using, screwed on the cap.

He slammed it into the box.

He couldn't let her go, not yet. The muscles in his back went rigid at the thought of it, with panic and more than a little pain.

There were still lots of things he needed to get done here, he tried to reason with himself. He couldn't be around her every day, see her every day and not want her, not want to take her to bed.

But there was one thing he could do, he thought grimly, and he needed to start now. He had to distance himself. So when he moved on, they would both be able to handle it.

He finished putting away the paints.

He needed to see her, to talk to her. He couldn't wait until tonight to get this settled. She should be back from the shopping trip with Linc and Emmy she'd mentioned that morning. He could stroll on over to the house. If he could just get her on her own for a moment.

He walked into the bathroom, stripped off his stained work jeans and stepped into the shower.

As the cold water hit him full in the face, he gasped. But once the water had heated up and he began to soap his tired, aching body, the tension inside him finally began to ease.

All he needed was to talk to her, maybe hold her a little, make love to her again. Everything could be as it was before. He couldn't tell her he loved her. Serious wasn't for them. But they could still enjoy each other for a little while longer.

Ali leaned back on her heels and felt every single muscle and sinew in her lower back scream in protest. She dropped the small garden fork clenched in her fist and tried to massage the pain away.

What had she been thinking trying to weed the flowerbeds while she was over eight months pregnant? She'd had some vague idea that it would help her forget the throbbing ache that had been pummeling her back all morning, but it hadn't helped a bit.

She was just trying to figure out how she was going to get up off her knees without a tow truck when Monroe strolled into view round the side of the house.

'Thank you, God,' she gasped.

* * *

Monroe spotted his sister-in-law immediately, her dress speckled with mud and her face contorted in pain. His heart skidded to a halt and then started beating in double time as he raced over and knelt beside her.

'Ali, what are you doing?'

'Digging my way to China. What does it look like?'

Okay, so she wasn't in the mood for kidding about. He took her arm and saw her wince as he eased her to her feet. Now he wasn't either.

'What was Linc thinking?' he ground out. 'Letting you loose on the garden when you're about to have his baby?'

'Oh, shut up,' Ali huffed. 'I put up with enough macho rubbish from him this morning before he left.'

'I see,' Monroe said carefully. 'So I guess the trip to China wasn't Linc's idea?'

Ali shot him a withering look, but her fingers tightened on his arm as she tried to straighten.

'Can you walk?' he asked.

'Of course, I can walk. I'm not an invalid.' The crankiness in her tone didn't dim the pain and frustration he could see in her eyes. It was starting to scare him.

'I don't know what makes men think that women lose all their faculties the minute they become pregnant,' she snapped.

The statement would have had more heat if she hadn't then groaned and clutched her back. 'Ow-w-w!'

'Forget this.' Monroe bent down and picked her up.

'Put me down. You'll do your back in. I weigh a ton.'

She certainly wasn't light. But he had no intention of putting her down as he marched across the pool terrace and into the house.

'Where's your bedroom?' he asked as he walked across the living room.

'You are not carrying me up the stairs. I can… Ah-h-h!'

He felt it then, the way her belly clutched hard and rigid against his forearm. She started to pant, tears sliding down her cheeks as she squeezed her eyes shut, gritted her teeth against the pain.

'Damn it, you're having a contraction!' His arms shook. She was in agony. What should he do?

The contraction seemed to last for an eternity before she opened her eyes and looked at him.

'Don't you dare drop me!' she said weakly.

'I won't drop you.' He'd cut his arm off first, he realised, before he'd cause this woman a moment of additional suffering.

He started up the stairs, carrying her as carefully as if she were made out of spun glass. But it made no difference. When they reached the landing another contraction seized her. She gripped his neck hard, the groan long and low, before she started to pant desperately again. He waited for it to pass before taking her into the first bedroom he came to. By his calculation, the pains were less than two minutes apart and lasting at least forty seconds. He had worked on a cattle ranch one murderous spring pulling calves so he knew it was not a good sign.

Neat and tidy and with no personal possessions in it, the room they entered looked like a guest room. He laid her on the bed, but she grabbed his arm as he straightened.

'Please, don't go.'

'I'm not going anywhere.' It surprised him to realise he didn't want to leave her. He gripped her hand as the next pain assailed her, rubbed her back until it passed.

He stroked her hair back from her brow. 'I'm going to go and get the phone to call Linc and the doctor. Okay?'

She nodded, meekly. 'There's a hands-free phone in our bedroom next door.'

He ran into the next room, grabbed the phone and ran

straight back with it. He sat next to Ali on the bed and held onto her hand as he dialled Linc's cell phone.

'Linc, you need to get home. Your wife's about to have your kid.'

There was a crash on the other end of the line and then he heard Linc's voice. 'Is she okay? How is she?'

He could hear the panic in his brother's voice. Monroe fought to keep his own cool and even. 'She's doing fine.' He gave Ali a quick wink. 'She's a pro at this. But she wants you and Jessie here now. I'm calling the doctor as soon as I hang up, so just concentrate on getting your butt back here.'

Ali panted her way through another contraction as soon as he hung up.

'They're so strong, Monroe.' She gasped. 'I can't believe how strong they are.'

'I think we need to get the doc here,' he said as he began dialling the obstetrician's number that Ali reeled off, clearly knowing it by heart.

Reassured that the paramedics were on their way, he put the phone down. Ali was clutching the covers, her face set in grim lines of agony as she panted off another contraction. He gathered her into his arms and let her cling onto him. The helpless cries of pain she made until it subsided tore at his heart.

He eased back, looked into her face. 'How are you doing?'

She shook her head, tears trembling on her eyelids. 'I'm so scared. I've never done this before without pain relief. It hurts so much.'

He took her face gently in his hands. 'Ali, you're doing great. The medical crew will be here any minute, I promise. Just hold onto me and yell all you want. Okay?'

She nodded. He could see the pain swirl into her eyes again as her fingers dug into his arms. 'Here's another one,' she groaned.

She cried out in pain. Monroe heard a loud crash as the door slammed downstairs.

Monroe figured Linc must have flown up the stairs, because he burst through the door less than three seconds later.

'Ali, Ali, are you all right, honey?' Linc dashed across the room, his face whiter than the bed sheets. Ali shook her head, still panting, crying and holding onto Monroe.

As Jessie ran into the bedroom behind Linc she saw her sister cocooned in Monroe's arms. He held her gently as Ali's fingers fisted on his upper arms in a viselike grip and she screamed. At last, the cry of pain and anguish dimmed and Ali collapsed against him. He stroked her back, speaking softly into her ear. 'Linc's here, now, Ali. He's going to take over.'

She nodded weakly as Monroe pulled back carefully and stood up. He continued to hold Ali until Linc had taken his place on the bed.

'The paramedics arrived just after us,' Linc said softly to his wife as she huddled in his arms, exhausted. 'They're coming right up.'

Jessie blinked away the tears of emotion gathering in her eyes as Monroe walked across the shadowed room towards her.

He looked shattered, she thought. His eyes were swirling with an emotion so intense, so naked, it stunned her. She could see the vicious bruises already forming on the tanned skin of his arms where Ali's fingers had gripped.

'Where's Emmy?' he asked softly.

'We left her at Jill's house over the road, she's keeping her for the night.'

He nodded as he leaned past her to open the door.

She could hear the heavy tread of the paramedics coming up the stairs with their equipment.

'I'll see you later.' He glanced back briefly at Ali on the bed. 'You look after her,' he said.

He slipped out of the door, held it open as the medical team rushed into the room. And then he was gone.

CHAPTER SIXTEEN

HUGGING her newborn nephew in her arms, Jessie stared out the windows of Ali's bedroom at the garage apartment across the lawn.

Something was wrong with Monroe. But she had no idea what and no idea how to fix it.

It was almost three weeks since little Ethan Monroe Latimer's tumultuous birth, and Jessie felt as if she had been in the middle of an emotional hurricane. Being flung in hundreds of different confusing and conflicting directions. The wonder of her nephew's birth had been tempered by the fear that Monroe was drawing away from her and the rest of his family and she didn't know why.

The house had been a hive of activity since Ethan was born, but Jessie had welcomed the chaos. By concentrating on everything that had to be done, she'd managed to keep her worries about Monroe at the back of her mind. But she couldn't do that any longer. She had to face it. Something was very wrong.

'Is he asleep yet?'

Jessie turned at the sound of Ali's sleepy voice from the bed. She pulled the tiny bundle back from her shoulder and looked at his scrunched-up little face. 'Yes, he's out like a light.'

'You can put him in the Moses basket. He should sleep

now for a good few hours.' Giving a huge yawn, Ali stretched and sat up.

Jessie kissed the soft fuzz on her nephew's head. She inhaled the sweet scent of baby before tucking him into the basket by the window. 'He's so gorgeous. I don't know how you can stop yourself from cuddling him constantly.'

As she said it Jessie caught sight of the garage apartment again through the window. The heavy feeling that had settled on her in the past few weeks came back full force. Monroe was never far from her mind.

'How are things going with Monroe?' Ali said softly.

Jessie looked at her sister. It seemed she hadn't lost her ability to read minds.

'We've hardly seen him since the birth, Jess,' Ali continued. 'Is something the matter?'

Jessie nodded slowly. Maybe talking about it would help. 'I think there may be.'

'Did you guys have a row?'

Jessie sighed. 'No, but in a way that's the problem. Something's wrong, but he won't talk about it.' She sat down on Ali's bed. 'It's really weird. But I think it has something to do with the baby?' And me, she thought, silently.

'How do you mean?'

Jessie frowned. 'I really don't know. But ever since the birth, Monroe's been—' She paused, trying to describe it. 'He's been sad, somehow, and withdrawn. And he's made all sorts of stupid excuses not to come over here. Not to see the baby.'

'I know. Linc's noticed it, too. He's pretty hurt about it, actually.' Ali shifted on the bed, the dismay plain on her face. 'Linc felt they were really starting to get somewhere as brothers. But now he says Monroe's shutting him out. And he's doing it with Emmy, too. She was crying yesterday because she said Monroe wouldn't let her help with the cars.'

Jessie bit her lip, feeling her throat close at Ali's words. 'I think he's going to leave, Al. It's like he's just waiting.' There, she'd finally said it. Her deepest fear. The thing she hadn't even been able to admit to herself. The dread flooded through her. She felt the first tear slide down her cheek.

'Oh, Jessie.' Ali reached over and wrapped her arms around her.

Snuffling loudly, Jessie pulled back, wiped the tears away impatiently. 'We still make love, every night. He's so tender, so careful with me, Al. But...' Jessie raised watery eyes to her sister '...I've told him I love him now, I don't know how many times. But he's never said it back, Ali. Not once. And every time I say it, I feel him pull away that little bit more.' She sniffed again, determined not to let any more tears fall. 'But I can't seem to stop myself.'

'It's nothing you've done.' Ali's voice was heavy. 'You've been honest with him. You've told him how you feel.'

'I think he needs me but he doesn't want to.'

Ali stroked her sister's hair. 'I doubt it's as simple as that, Jessie.'

'Maybe it's not, but, whatever the problem is, he refuses to talk about it.'

'Shall I tell you what I told Linc?'

Jessie straightened, nodded.

'I told him to give Monroe space.'

Jessie's brow creased. 'How do you mean?'

'Well, for starters, you should stop going over there every night.'

Jessie felt her heart sink. 'I've been an idiot, haven't I? He doesn't need me at all. It's just the sex.'

'No, that's not what I meant.' Ali grabbed Jessie's hand, holding her down when she tried to rise. 'I don't think that, Jess. He does need you. I think he needs you much more than he knows. But he has to admit it to himself, before he'll ever admit it to you. As long as you keep doing everything his way, he's not having to confront his own feelings.'

Jessie got up slowly, walked over to the bedroom window. She studied the garage apartment. He was in there now, she thought, painting. Waiting for her to come over tonight.

How hard would it be not to go to him, to deny herself what little joy they might have left? But what if Ali was right? What if, by not going, she could make him see what he was really pushing away?

She looked back at her sister. 'You're right. I know you are. But, Ali…' Jessie could feel the heat in her cheeks but forced herself to say it '…the sex is so wonderful. I never knew it could be like that before Monroe. I'm really going to miss it.'

'If he's anything like his brother, I know just what you mean.' Ali's eyes took on a wicked gleam. 'Linc and I haven't been able to do it for over a month. I'm ready to tear his clothes off now every time I see him.'

'Just listen to us.' Jessie smiled for what felt like the first time in weeks. 'We sound like a couple of nymphomaniacs.'

'Good sex happens to be essential to a happy life. Don't knock it.' Ali sobered, her voice going soft. 'But it sounds like you and Monroe already have that bit sorted. It's all the complicated stuff that needs figuring out now.'

'I still don't understand why you can't come over tonight.' Monroe struggled to keep the desperation out of his voice.

'I told you. I promised Linc and Ali I'd babysit so they can have a bit of privacy tonight. It's been weeks now since Ethan was born and they're…' Jessie paused '…they're ready to have a bit of alone time.'

Monroe's temper spiked. 'I get it. So because my brother

wants to have his way with his wife, we have to do without.'
He threw the paintbrush down that had been clenched in his fist.

'I'm sure we'll survive for one night.' Jessie didn't sound exactly devastated at the prospect, which bothered Monroe a lot more than he wanted to admit.

She turned to leave.

'Hold up.' He snagged her wrist, pulled her round. 'Where are you going now?'

'Out.' She hesitated. 'Just out.' He watched her teeth tug on her bottom lip. 'With Emmy. I'm taking Emmy down to the beach.'

He drew his hands up her arms. Stroked his thumbs across the sensitive skin inside her elbows. 'You sure you've got to go right away?'

'Yes. Yes, I have.'

He let his thumbs drift across her breasts, lightly circled the nipples. He felt her shivered response, saw her eyes flare with desire. He grinned. That was more like it. 'Can't you stay a little while?'

He reached up to caress her shoulders. Then slipped his fingers beneath the thin cotton straps holding up the vest-top she was wearing over a denim skirt. 'We could maybe, make up for tonight, before you go.'

He bent to nibble her neck. He knew she loved to be kissed there. Her head fell back, giving him better access. She gave a breathy moan and he hardened in his jeans. She smelt gorgeous, the light flowery scent she used making his nostrils flare as he reached down. He pulled up her skirt, slipped his hands under the lacy panties she wore. He massaged the soft skin of her butt with his fingers. He wanted her, now.

'Stop it.' Suddenly, she was pushing him away.

He watched astonished as she pulled her panties frantically back into place, smoothed her skirt down.

'I said, I've got to go.'

'What the hell's going on here?' He tried to snag her arm again but she raised her hand.

'Don't touch me, Monroe. We're not having a quick shag just because you're feeling hard done by.'

He scowled, the heat rising in his cheeks. 'What's this really about?'

She blinked at the shouted words. But then she skewered him with a look he could only describe as dangerous. 'You tell me. Monroe, what is this all about?'

He cocked an eyebrow, feeling angry and humiliated and more than a little desperate. Something had changed. Something important. He knew she'd wanted to make love as much as he had a moment ago. He knew her responses now almost as well as he knew his own. He knew how to make her want him, how to make her beg. It was the one thing he could give her. It had made her fall in love with him. But he'd persuaded himself over the last few weeks that, at least, he could give her something back. He could show her how he felt with his body even if he could never say it to her in words.

Why didn't she want it any more?

'I don't know what you're talking about,' he choked out. It was a feeble response, but it was all he had.

'You know what I think, Monroe?' She put her hands on her hips, her back ramrod straight and her eyes blazing. 'I think you're using sex as a substitute for communication.'

'What?'

'You heard me. Until you're willing to talk to me properly, I'm going to be too busy to have sex with you.'

She walked out of the bedroom. He caught up with her as she flung open the door to the apartment. Grabbing her arm, he hauled her round to face him.

'What is this—some kind of game?'

'No.' She yanked her arm free. 'It's not a game.'

'You want me as much as I want you, Red.' The bitterness, the desperation in his voice surprised him, but not as much as the anguish that flashed into her eyes.

'Yes, I want you.' Her voice broke on the words. 'You're absolutely right about that. But what I want a lot more is to know what the hell's going on in your head. And until you're willing to talk about it, the sex isn't enough. No matter how great it is.'

He stood there in shock. Horrified and dumbfounded as she turned and walked out of the apartment. She slammed the door behind her and he could hear her feet rattling down the stairs outside. But all he could do was stare at the polished oak of the door.

He wanted to stop her. To tell her he was falling in love, too, and it scared him to death. Because he could never give her what she dreamed of. He could never give her a happy family, stability, all the things that Linc and Ali had.

He walked slowly across the apartment. Standing at the window that looked out over the lawn, he watched her slender figure cross the grass. She was running, her shoes held in her hands, her hair fluttering in the light breeze. She was running away from him and he couldn't stop her. She wanted things, needed things he couldn't possibly give her. He closed the curtains, throwing the apartment into gloom as he shut out the light.

She'd been right; he'd been trying to hold her with sex.

He'd been devastated after the baby's birth. Had wanted to howl with frustration and anguish when Linc had told him that they were naming the child Ethan Monroe Latimer, after him. Because he couldn't have a relationship with this baby, any more than he could have a relationship with Emmy, or his brother, or Ali, or even Jessie. Not really. And the birth had finally made him realise it.

What if he gave up the rootless existence that had sustained him? The lifetime of roaming that now seemed so shallow and pointless? What if he stayed in touch with them all, became part of their family? He knew the answer only too well. He'd end up some bitter, lonely old man, watching their family from the outside, knowing he could never have what they had. Eventually the love he felt for them would be swallowed up by the envy.

So how had he consoled himself? By keeping Jessie close to him, by binding her to him every night, driving them both into sexual oblivion and hoping that it would halt her questions.

He'd started creating the distance he needed to create with Linc and little Emmy and Ali, but it had been too painful to do that and lose Jessie, too. So he'd used her again. Like some consolation prize.

He sat down heavily on the couch, stroked his hand slowly across the cushions where they first made love. So this was it, then. Either he had to tell her the truth or let her go.

He didn't have a choice. Not really. Not if he was going to survive with even a small piece of his pride—and his heart—intact.

CHAPTER SEVENTEEN

THE next week was torture for Jessie. Every night she had to steel herself not to creep out of bed and go to Monroe. He was like a drug and she a drug addict going through the worst kind of withdrawal symptoms.

Every night without fail the dreams would come. Powerfully erotic, devastatingly arousing. She would wake up covered in sweat, her nipples painfully erect, the throbbing in her sex so intense she could feel the heat flooding between her thighs. She'd actually taken to having cold showers in the middle of the night. Which made her feel ridiculous. And the lack of sleep had made her tired and irritable, added to which, for some odd reason, her breasts had become unbearably tender.

But worse than the exhaustion—and the knife-edge of unfulfilled passion—was the loneliness. She missed him, his teasing, his companionship, and his friendship.

She hadn't been back to the garage apartment since she'd issued her ultimatum and he hadn't come up to the house.

Each day Jessie became more convinced that Monroe would soon be gone. She checked the driveway each morning to see if the Harley was still there. Scared that he might leave during the night without a word to any of them.

172   BEDDED BY A BAD BOY

But, really, how much worse could it be? She felt as if she'd lost him already and it was almost more than she could bear.

A week after the whole nightmare had started, she was sitting by the pool with Ali. The baby was sleeping in the Moses basket in the shade beside their sun loungers. Linc had taken Emmy to the beach.

'Jess, you've been looking miserable all week. I take it Monroe's still being a complete baboon with you, too,' Ali said, leaning over the basket to check on the baby.

Jess shook her head, not sure she could talk about what was happening and not burst into tears. 'I haven't spoken to him since last Sunday.'

Ali looked up, shocked. 'But that's a week ago.'

'I know. Has he said anything to Linc—about his plans, I mean?'

'No. They're barely speaking to each other.' Ali sat back on her lounger. 'He was out yesterday morning pruning the privet hedge. I went over there to give him a piece of my mind about the whole situation. Linc's upset, Emmy's being completely horrible, as you know. Which is partly because of the new baby, I'm sure, but the situation with Monroe hasn't helped. I was pretty mad with him. I mean, he still hasn't come over to see Ethan yet. I was going to give him some serious grief about his behaviour towards the whole family.'

Jessie had seen him out there too, but had hidden in her room, clinging onto the small scrap of pride she had left. 'What did he say?'

Ali looked a little sheepish, then sighed. 'I couldn't bring myself to say anything in the end.'

'Why not?' Jessie was amazed. It was unlike Ali to back down from a confrontation, especially when the happiness of her family was at stake.

'He looks awful, Jess. If it's any consolation, I think he's suffering as much as the rest of us.'

'You do?' Maybe there was some small hope after all.

'I don't think he's been sleeping. He looks like he's lost weight. He was so tense I thought he was going to snap in two.'

Jessie could feel the rush of sympathy for him. Why was she torturing them both? She sat up, put her bare feet on the tile. 'Maybe I should go to him.'

Ali leant across, gripped her forearm. 'No, you shouldn't, Jess. He needs to work this out himself. He's like an angry bear licking his wounds right now. He's probably blaming you, me, Linc and everyone else for what he's going through. But once he figures it out, he'll come to you.'

'But what if he never figures it out, Ali? What if he just leaves?'

'That's a chance you'll have to take,' Ali said firmly. 'But I wouldn't give up hope yet.'

'Why not?'

'Well, for starters, while we were talking, his eyes kept straying up to your room.'

Jessie felt the bubble of hope swell inside her. 'Really?'

'Yes, really,' Ali replied, her voice rising with enthusiasm. 'And when I mentioned that Linc and I and the kids were heading back to London in ten days, he looked really worried. And then, you know what he asked me?'

Jessie shook her head, not quite as desolate as she had been.

'He asked me if you were going, too.'

Jessie woke up the next morning and for the first time in seven days didn't slip out the front door to check if Monroe's bike was still there. Maybe her dream wasn't completely dead after all. Maybe all this pain would actually be worth it. Maybe Monroe really did love her and he was going to tell her so soon.

It wasn't until after she'd shared breakfast with Linc and Emmy that something about the conversation the day before finally dawned on her.

The family was heading back to London in less than two weeks. She checked the wall calendar as she stacked the breakfast dishes into the dishwasher. Over the long lazy summer days, she'd completely lost track of the date. It was August twenty-seventh already.

Jessie finished clearing the kitchen and then rushed up to her bedroom and fished her diary out of the bedside table. She never could remember when her next period was due so she'd got in the habit of writing a small P next to the date each one started.

Flicking through the pages furiously, she got right back to July tenth before she found the little red P she was searching for. She stared at the date for a long time, then slowly counted the weeks forward. She'd made love to Monroe for the first time four days after that, on the night of Emmy's birthday party. And it was now the end of August. Jessie took a deep steadying breath, her heart pounding like a timpani drum in her chest. That was over six weeks ago.

She shook her head, tried to focus. This was ridiculous; she couldn't possibly be pregnant. They'd only done it that once without contraception. Monroe had been really careful to use a condom every time since; even in the throes of passion, he never forgot.

'Jess, I'm heading into town for some diapers. Is there anything you need?' Jessie's head shot up as she heard Linc's voice coming up the stairs.

'Wait a minute, Linc. I'll come with you.' Jessie shoved the diary back into the drawer and dashed to the closet, trying to ignore the flock of birds now swooping around in the pit of her stomach. She slipped on a pair of sandals, tied her hair back and began to plan how she was going to buy a pregnancy test at the chemist without Linc seeing her.

The stick was pink. A rich, lurid, candyfloss pink.

Jessie stared at the thin plastic strip in her hand. Dazed, her mind racing in a thousand different directions, she reached up and pulled the instruction leaflet off the top of the vanity. Had she read it wrong?

But she hadn't, and there was the proof in black and white—and pink.

She was pregnant.

Her fingers began to shake and she dropped the stick on the bathroom floor. It clattered, the noise deafening in the silence.

She was going to have Monroe's baby.

She looked down at her belly. Placing warm palms over it, she began to rock. What had they done? She loved him, desperately, passionately, unconditionally. And she loved this baby, too. The thought was so intense, so shocking, so sudden, that the tears started to flow down her cheeks.

But how would she tell him? What would he say? He wouldn't even talk to her about how he felt. He'd never even told her that he loved her. What if he didn't want children? What if the reason he hadn't come to see the baby was that he hated babies?

Jessie shook herself, pulled some tissues out of the dispenser on the vanity and blew her nose, wiped her eyes.

Don't be silly. He adored Emmy. He was great with kids. He didn't hate babies or children. Something else was going on there, she was sure of it. But they'd only known each other for two months, had only been going out for six weeks and for over a week now they'd been avoiding each other. Maybe they had a chance of sorting the whole mess out, but bringing a baby into the equation was bound to make it so much more complicated.

As she sat on the toilet seat in the brightly lit bathroom, the worries just kept flooding through her mind.

What were Monroe's plans? She didn't have any real clue. What if her worst fears were true and he was planning even now to get on his bike and go? A single comment to Ali about whether Jessie was going to London or not next week hardly constituted a commitment on his part. She hadn't let herself think about what would happen if he did leave. What she would do. Until now. Now she had to. She hugged her belly again. And murmured a promise to her baby.

'We'll tell Daddy tomorrow. But whatever he says, whatever he does, Mummy will love you. Mummy wants you.'

'So let me get this straight. You're pregnant and I'm supposed to be the daddy?'

Jessie recoiled at the harshness in Monroe's voice. She had expected the shock she'd seen in his face a moment before. But she hadn't expected what had followed. He'd said nothing for what seemed like ages. Then his eyes had gone dark and bitter and he'd hurled the accusatory words at her.

'Yes.' Her voice trembled.

It had taken her all morning to pluck up the courage to come over to the apartment and talk to him. She'd wanted desperately to tell Ali, to ask her advice, but had decided that Monroe had the right to know first.

She hadn't slept all night, the questions hurtling around in her brain like dodgem cars, crashing against each other but never finding anywhere to settle.

Would he be angry? Would he be happy?

It scared her to realise she just didn't know. They'd certainly never talked about family or the future together. But of all the scenarios that had gone through her head while she'd toyed with her breakfast and waited for Linc and Ali and the kids to head off to the beach, nothing had prepared her for the coldness she saw in his eyes now. He looked like a stranger. Not the man she knew, not the man she loved.

'I don't think so,' he said.

'What do you mean?' Jessie felt her stomach pitch and roll. What was he saying?

'You really want me to spell it out?' The words dripped with contempt.

'Yes, I think I do.' Her voice broke, her throat began to close, but she kept her back ramrod straight. This had to be some kind of misunderstanding, didn't it? Where was the warm, caring, vulnerable man who'd held her with such care over the past weeks, had made love to her with such passion? Why was he looking at her like that?

'I'm not the damn father. I can't be. If you're pregnant, it's someone else's kid.'

The words were brutal and ugly, but it was how he felt. Monroe could see the tears starting to leak out of her eyes, the stunned horror in her face, but he didn't care. Monroe Latimer was too busy chasing his own demons.

He'd been through hell. He'd tried to leave, a dozen times. Had even got to the stage of packing his duffel bag. But then, he had to unpack it again. Like a damn lovesick fool. And it was all her fault. In his misery, he'd persuaded himself that she'd tricked him into this. He didn't do commitment and this was why. It caused too much damn pain. When she'd walked through the door, he'd been so overjoyed to see her, it had made him feel pathetic.

Then she'd made her announcement.

For a moment there, he'd wanted to believe it was true. It

would have been the answer to all his dreams, all the things he'd wanted his whole life and never been able to have. But then the bitter truth had hit him.

It wasn't possible. It would have to be some kind of miracle. And Monroe Latimer was a man who didn't believe in miracles.

Either she was lying about the baby or she was lying about who the father was.

A longing, a yearning he'd thought he'd buried years ago had come slamming back to him. He could hate her for that alone.

The rage Monroe hadn't known still existed inside him rose up to choke him.

He wanted her gone now and he'd be as cruel as he had to be to get rid of her. The fact that the water flowing down her cheeks made him want to drag her into his arms only made him more mad. Even when she was conning him, lying to him, he still cared about her, he still wanted her. What kind of a fool did that make him?

'I don't know what you're saying, Monroe. But the baby's yours. I haven't…' Jessie could hardly say the words, to defend herself against a charge so cruel, so horrible. 'I haven't been with anyone else but you. You're the first person I've slept with in a long time.'

He laughed; the hollow sound hit her like a blow. 'You do that wounded look real well. You should be in Hollywood.'

'Please, Monroe.' She reached out, tried to touch his arm, but he flinched and pulled away. 'I'm not lying. Why would I lie?'

'You can plead and beg all you want. It won't change the facts.'

He didn't sound angry any more, just indifferent.

'What facts?' The sob rose in her throat; her voice hitched as she tried to control it. 'Why won't you believe me?'

He dipped his head, shook it slowly, before looking back at her. 'I can't have kids. I had to give a sperm sample to the cops when I was sixteen. My sperm count's so low it's non-existent.'

Jessie felt the blood drain out of her face, grasped shaking hands over her mouth. 'But that's not possible.'

'It's possible all right.' He seemed immune to her distress, his voice calm, his eyes remote. 'You can see how it gives us a little problem with your announcement.'

She lowered the hands from her face, but she couldn't stop the tears, the tremors raking her body.

He really didn't believe her.

It wasn't a mistake, a misunderstanding. She could tell him now that he was wrong about himself. That somehow they had conceived a child. But even if she begged him to believe her, even if she had paternity tests when the baby was born, the truth would never take away the contempt he felt for her now. He didn't trust her. He didn't know she would never lie about something like this. So what exactly would she be begging for? The love of a man who didn't care about her, didn't know her or understand her?

The full horror of the situation finally dawned on Jessie. She wiped the tears from her face with the back of her sleeve. She put a hand on her belly, trying to protect the life growing inside her from the cold contempt of its father.

'I have to go.' She would have to get away from here, she knew, as far away as she could. 'I can't believe I was so wrong about you.'

'I guess I'm not as dumb as I look.'

It wasn't what she meant, but she didn't correct him. She didn't care what he thought of her any more. She couldn't let herself care.

She turned and walked away, her legs shaking, but her

shoulders rigid. Once she had closed the apartment door, she ran down the stairs, her heart shattering inside her.

Monroe grabbed the coffee cup he had been drinking out of when Jessie arrived, and hurled it against the wall. He watched as the dark liquid dripped down the white paint.

He'd been fooling himself right from the start. He was madly, hopelessly in love with her. If not, why did her betrayal hurt so much now?

Jessie couldn't stop shaking as she stuffed clothes into a leather holdall. She had to get away before Ali and Linc got back with the children. She couldn't stand to see the pity in her sister's eyes, the fury in Linc's.

How could she have been so stupid?

She'd fallen in love with a man who didn't care about her at all. She'd foolishly thought that his tenderness, his care with her, the fun and laughter they had shared, the things he had told her about himself and his past had been the sign of deeper emotions.

It wasn't just her heart that had been broken, though. There was a life involved here. A new, unprotected life that she would be bringing into the world without a father.

As she picked up the phone to call a cab to the station Jessie dismissed the excuse that she hadn't chosen to get pregnant, that she hadn't planned this baby. She loved the life inside her, and she already felt totally responsible for it.

How would she explain to her child that its father didn't want it, didn't even believe it was his? That was the price her baby would pay for its mother's stupidity, its mother's naïve, romantic, ridiculously optimistic belief that she and Monroe had been meant for one another.

Going to Ali's bedroom, she located her sister's address book on the chest of drawers. She would have to talk to Ali soon, but she would not ask her for help with this. It felt as if her sister had spent all her life helping her deal with her mistakes. Well, maybe her affair with Monroe had been a mistake, but this baby wasn't a mistake and she was going to have to start making her life work for both of them.

She'd started something this summer at the Cranford Art Gallery. Mrs Bennett had told her only this week that she thought Jessie could have a career in the art world. In the haze of love and romance that she'd indulged in with Monroe she hadn't planned anything out, but now she would have to. She'd spoken to one of Ali's friends in New York last week who had mentioned a job in an art gallery in SoHo. Jessie had ignored it at the time, she hadn't thought she'd ever be moving to New York. Jessie took a deep breath. Her whole life had turned upside down in less than twenty-four hours.

She sobbed, quietly, unable to hold back the tears any longer as she jotted down Lizzie's address and telephone number. When she got to New York she'd contact her, see if the job was still available. Tearing off the page, she slipped the information in her bag then scribbled a note for Ali on the pad and left it on the dresser.

The loud beeping sound from the door buzzer made Jessie jump. Picking up her bag, she left the room and walked downstairs.

As the cab took off up Oceanside Drive, Jessie forced herself not to turn back and take one last look at the garage apartment. That wasn't where her future was any more. Despite the heavy weight of despair and humiliation, the sick feeling of fear, of devastation churning in her stomach, Jessie kept her eyes on the road ahead. She had a long way to go but she would get there in the end.

Monroe had destroyed her dreams, but he would never be able to crush her spirit.

CHAPTER EIGHTEEN

MONROE slashed the paint onto the canvas—the vivid red reflecting the violence bubbling inside him.

'Monroe, you in here?'

The shouted enquiry from the living room had Monroe dumping his brush in the turpentine. No doubt Jessie had gone running to Linc and Ali as soon as she'd left him. They would want him to go now, for sure. The fact that it hurt to know he would have to go only made him angrier. It took a titanic effort to plaster a cocky grin on his face as he walked into the apartment's living room and closed the bedroom door behind him.

'Yeah, what's happening?'

'I think you know what's happening.'

The sharp words and the heat in Linc's eyes made it clear he knew about Jessie. This was it, then, Monroe thought. The moment when his brother would cut him loose.

'I guess she went crying to you, then, did she?'

'If you're talking about Jessie—' Linc's voice was tight, brimming with annoyance '—no, she didn't. But she has run off to New York and, since you know why, you'd better tell me—and fast.'

Monroe shrugged. 'She says she's pregnant.'

Linc's brows shot up, before he exploded forward and grabbed Monroe's T-shirt. 'You got her pregnant? How the hell did that happen?'

He could see the fury in Linc's eyes, but it was nothing compared to the raw, bitter anger that was choking Monroe. Damn Jessie for making him have to tell his brother something he'd never wanted to tell anyone.

'Let go of me,' he snarled. Pushing Linc's hands away, he struggled back a step, his own breath heaving. 'It happened in the usual way, I guess.'

'You son of a—' Linc jumped on him again and would have landed the punch but Monroe blocked the blow. They struggled for a moment, before Monroe managed to grab his brother in a headlock.

'Let me finish,' he snapped. 'If she is pregnant, I'm not the one responsible.'

Wrestling free, Linc turned and fisted his hands in Monroe's shirt again. 'How do you figure that?'

'I can't have kids.' The words came out on a broken shout as Monroe tried to shove his brother away. 'When I went to juvie I had to give a sperm sample. The police doctor told me my sperm count is practically zero. I only shoot blanks. Now do you get it?'

Monroe could see his brother had got the message, when his fists released.

Monroe looked away, unable to bear what he thought might be his brother's pity. He paced across the room, stared out of the glass doors. The tumbling waves in the distance matched his own churning thoughts.

'Hell.'

Hearing the anguish in his brother's tone, Monroe turned round. Linc had collapsed onto the sofa. When he lifted his face, Monroe realised it wasn't pity he saw there but concern and compassion.

'So when Jessie told you about the pregnancy, you told her it wasn't yours?' he said.

Monroe jerked his shoulders, tried not to picture her stricken face. 'Yeah, because it's not mine, it can't be.'

'Monroe, have you ever had yourself tested since—to make sure, I mean?'

Monroe felt his face flush at the quietly spoken question. 'No, why would I?'

'If Jessie says she's pregnant, she is. And if she says you're the father, you are. She wouldn't lie about that.'

Linc seemed so certain, Monroe almost wanted to believe it, but he couldn't let himself go there again. 'I'm not the father.'

'Monroe, you're going to get tested. I'll find someone near here that'll do it. If you won't do it for yourself, for Jessie, you'll damn well do it for me.'

'Why are you making me do this?'

Monroe could see the anger and regret in his brother's eyes, but his mouth was set in a firm line. 'You'll do it, Roe— you owe this family at least that much.'

As Monroe watched his brother walk out the door he felt temper take over.

How had he been suckered into this? The result was just going to humiliate him more. He thought of Jessie again and cursed. How could he have been so foolish as to break his golden rule? Never get involved. Never make a commitment. Now he'd made one, not only to a woman who could turn him inside out, but also to a family he'd never wanted any part of.

CHAPTER NINETEEN

'DR CARTER WILL see you now, Mr Latimer.'

Monroe threw down the glossy magazine he'd been pretending to read for the last half hour. Clinging onto the anger that had helped keep the pain at bay, he stalked into Carter's plush private office.

He didn't want to be here. He'd been forced into this and he was mad about it. He'd had to spend the afternoon yesterday giving sperm samples. If that wasn't bad enough, now he had to go through the humiliating charade of getting the results. He already knew what Carter was going to say. Had known it for most of his life.

The plump, grey-haired physician looked up from the papers he was busy shuffling and pointed to the comfy leather armchair across from his wide maplewood desk. 'Good afternoon, Mr Latimer. Take a seat.'

'No, thanks.' Monroe didn't want to sit down. He wanted this over with, so he could take the good doctor's results and shove them down his dear brother's throat.

'Well, Mr Latimer.' Carter put the papers down and studied Monroe. 'I'll cut straight to the chase. There's no point in beating about the bush, after all.'

Did the man talk in nothing but clichés? Monroe thought bitterly. 'You do that, Doc.'

'Simply put, Mr Latimer,' Carter replied, 'your sperm count is perfectly normal. In fact, I'd place it in the high end of the range.'

Monroe felt his heart stop. 'What did you say?'

'That you're not infertile—far from it, in fact.' Carter smiled.

Monroe dropped into the armchair. He felt as if his legs had just been yanked out from under him. 'But that's not possible. I was tested, when I was sixteen. The prison doctor said I was infertile.'

'Well,' Carter continued, 'that may possibly have been true at the specific time your sperm count was taken.'

'How?' Monroe's heart was banging away in his chest now as if it were about to explode.

Carter folded his arms on the desk in front of him and happily went into lecture mode. 'Mr Latimer, there has been a great deal of research into male fertility in the last ten to fifteen years.' Carter paused for breath, and then gave Monroe a self-satisfied smile. 'One of the most fascinating discoveries, in my opinion at least, has been how much the male sperm count can fluctuate given certain circumstances. All sorts of factors can affect the count at any one time. If you'd recently had a high fever, say, or were particularly stressed at the time the sample was given, it could wipe out the count completely or lower it substantially. But it would recover remarkably quickly. It's often the case that—'

'Hold on a damn minute.' Monroe's mind simply wouldn't engage. 'How the hell do you know that's the case with me?'

Carter sighed heavily. 'Mr Latimer, as I told you, your samples yesterday showed a high volume of active sperm. Whatever the test showed in the past, your sperm now are more than capable of getting a woman pregnant.'

Monroe staggered out of the office in a daze. Carter had droned on for another twenty minutes but he hadn't heard a word of it. His mind kept reeling back to Jessie and the anguish on her face when he'd last seen her.

There hadn't been any other guys. If he'd been honest with himself he'd known that all along. He'd had to work harder to get her into bed than any woman he'd ever met. And she hadn't exactly been the most experienced woman he'd ever slept with. It was one of the things about her he'd found irresistible—that captivating combination of innocence and passion.

Pushing open the double doors of the clinic, he walked onto the sunny street outside. But he didn't see the snazzy cars flashing past in the high-end neighbourhood, the afternoon shoppers rushing to make their latest purchase. All he could see was Jessie's shattered eyes, her tear-soaked cheeks.

A young woman with a toddler barged past him. Pushed to one side, Monroe leaned against the outside wall of the clinic. His legs were too weak for him to stand unaided. He scraped the hair back from his brow with a shaky hand.

She hadn't lied to him. She was having his baby.

Then another thought struck him and his knees gave way beneath him. His back scraped down the hot brickwork, until he was crouched down on his haunches. He stared blindly out at the legs of the people milling past on the sidewalk on a hot, humid Friday afternoon.

Jessie Connor had given him something he thought he'd never be able to have.

He was going to be a father.

As Monroe drove the Harley over the rise and gazed down on Linc and Ali's house by the sea, the tumultuous combination of euphoria, guilt and despair churning in his gut was making him feel nauseous.

How was he ever going to repair the damage he'd done? Jessie would hate him now; for all he knew she might even have run off to have an abortion. He sure as hell wouldn't blame her.

He shook his head, cruised the Harley down towards the house. He couldn't think about that. If she'd got rid of the baby, he would be devastated, but he would deal with it.

What was more important, what he wanted most, he realised with stunning clarity, was to get her back.

How would he ever persuade her that he loved her, that he had fallen head first before they'd even slept together, before they'd ever even conceived their baby? The whole time he'd been trying to keep his distance, his heart had been lost. Maybe that was the real reason he'd reacted the way he had when she'd told him about the pregnancy. Because he was scared to death, not just because he wanted it so desperately to be his baby, but also because he had always felt inadequate where she was concerned.

Well, he was going to have to get over his self-pity and all his self-doubts now. He was going to have to fight for her and he didn't kid himself it was going to be easy. But then he didn't deserve it to be easy.

Parking the Harley in the garage, he switched off the engine. First of all, he needed to find out where she was. He had to face Linc and Ali, tell them the truth and then beg them to help him find Jessie. What if they didn't want to help him? Why would they? After what he'd done to Ali's little sister, they probably hated him now, too.

'Roe, what happened at Carter's office? We expected you back over an hour ago.'

Monroe looked up to see his brother standing by the garage door. He pulled off his helmet, stared at Linc, unable to find the words.

Linc saved him the trouble. 'So Carter told you what the rest of us already knew. Am I right?' Pushing away from the door, Linc walked towards him. Monroe couldn't see the expression on his face with the afternoon sun shining behind him, but he didn't doubt that what he would see was contempt. Attaching the helmet to the bike's handlebars, he climbed off, ready to face it.

'The baby's mine.'

Linc considered the statement for a moment. 'Is that bad?'

'What do you mean?'

Linc crossed his arms over his chest and gave Monroe a steady stare. 'What I'm asking, Monroe, is do you want to be the father?'

'Yeah.' This part at least was easy. 'Yeah. I do.' Monroe jerked a shoulder, stared down at his hands, his voice thick with a yearning that he'd spent so many years trying to hide. 'Ever since I was sixteen, I never thought I'd have a family. I convinced myself I didn't want one. I always kept on the move, never made any attachments. I figured family wasn't for me. Seeing you with your kids, though, Linc, it made me so envious. Feeling Ali's baby kick inside her, watching her go into labour.' He sighed, dragged unsteady fingers through his hair. 'It hurt, knowing I could never have that.'

Linc took the few steps to his brother and pulled him into his arms. He held him close for only a moment, but that brief manly hug pulled them together through all the years of their childhood and adult lives when they had been forced apart. At last they were brothers.

Linc stood back, gave Monroe's shoulders one last quick squeeze. 'So, I guess congratulations are in order.'

Monroe gave a harsh laugh. 'Yeah, although I don't deserve any of them. I screwed up big time.'

Linc nodded. 'I can't argue with you there, Roe. Question is, what do you intend to do about it?'

'I want her back, Linc. Not just because of the baby.'

Monroe ground his fists down into the pocket of his jeans. 'I'm not kidding myself. After the way I treated her, there may not even be a baby any more.'

'Don't sell her short again, or I'll have to get mad at you.' Linc put a hand on Monroe's shoulder. 'You realise you're going to have to do some serious explaining and probably more than your fair share of grovelling if you're going to fix this?'

Monroe didn't like the sound of that 'if' but said nothing.

'It's up to you now to get Jessie and your baby back, Roe.'

Monroe shrugged Linc's hand off. 'Do you think I don't want that?' He raked shaking fingers through his hair, despair settling on him like a lead weight. 'But I don't even know where to start. I don't even know where she is.'

'Ali does.'

Monroe's head jerked up.

'Jessie phoned last night to make sure we weren't worried about her.'

'Where is she?'

'I don't know. Jessie asked Ali not to tell me. I guess she figured I might tell you.'

Monroe's shoulders slumped. 'How am I gonna find out, then?'

'You'll have to ask Ali.'

'Are you kidding me? She won't tell me. It's a miracle you don't hate me, but she must after what I did to her sister.'

'Monroe.' Linc huffed out a breath. 'You are one stupid guy sometimes.' He gave Monroe a wry smile. 'Ali doesn't hate you. She wants to see you and Jessie work this out as much as I do.'

'Really?' Monroe felt the first stirrings of hope since he'd stumbled out of Dr Carter's office that afternoon. Maybe there was a small chance he might be able to pull this off.

* * *

'Where is she, Ali?'

'Monroe, Jessie told me in confidence,' Ali said softly, cradling her sleeping son in her arms. 'She didn't specifically tell me not to tell you, but I think that's only because she didn't think you'd care.'

'Damn it.' The baby flinched, making Monroe soften his voice. 'Sorry.' He touched the baby's head, and his heart stuttered at the soft, warm feeling before he stuffed his hand back in his pocket. 'I have to talk to her, Ali. I have to at least try.'

'I understand that.' Reaching up, Ali touched his arm. 'Sit down, Monroe.'

He plopped down on the sofa opposite her, his body rigid with tension.

'Is it just because of the baby that you want to contact Jessie?'

'No.' The denial came so quickly, so forcefully, he knew it was the truth. He paused, though, and stared at the hands clenched in his lap. 'No, it's not just because of the baby.'

How could he make Ali understand what he had done, if he didn't really understand himself?

'I love her, Ali. I think I knew that even before Carter told me the truth. I was just too scared to admit it. I've always known I didn't deserve her.'

He stood up, walked over to the window and stared out at the pool. The sight reminded him of the first time they'd met.

'Why do you think you don't deserve her?' Ali asked quietly from behind him.

The note of incredulity in her voice made Monroe shake his head as he turned back to her. 'Because I'm an ex-con. I've got no money and not a lot of prospects. The only thing I own is a Harley and the clothes on my back. And even if that meant nothing, even if we could get past all of that, I didn't think I would ever be able to offer her kids. I knew how much she wanted them. How much she wanted a family. She told me that was her dream.'

Ali sighed, adjusting the baby in her arms. 'You know what I think?'

He almost smiled, the clipped, precise note of irritation in her voice reminding him of Jessie.

'I think you're an idiot.'

'Thanks.' He did smile then, realising that he hadn't just found a brother in the last few months, he'd also found a sister.

Getting up, Ali tucked the baby carefully into its crib before walking back to Monroe. The look she gave him was more annoyed than sisterly, though.

'Firstly, you were little more than a child when you went to prison. Secondly, we know now that the baby-making thing isn't going to be a problem.' The look she gave him was direct enough to make his face heat. 'As for the no money and no prospects, we both know that's a load of rubbish, too.'

'How do you figure that?' Monroe raised his voice in exasperation. This was not the reaction he had expected.

'Jessie told me about your artwork.' He felt the flush deepen on his face as she continued. 'Jessie knows art, she's studied it and she's convinced you could have a career as an artist. So I think if you're worried about money and prospects, Linc has a friend called Carole Jackson who owns a very successful gallery in New York—you should contact her and let her take a look at the stuff you've been working on for the last two months.'

Monroe straightened. 'I'm not asking favours from one of Linc's friends.'

'Oh, don't get your knickers in a twist.' Ali waved her hand impatiently. 'I know how important pride is to you. But it's misplaced here. Carole's a tough lady and she has one of the best and most influential independent galleries in New

York. She's not going to agree to exhibit anything unless she thinks it's outstanding. The question here is, do you have the guts to try? Or are you going to spend the rest of your life hiding behind your insecurities?'

Annoyed and embarrassed at one and the same time, Monroe had to force himself not to pout. 'We're getting off the point here. I want to know where Jessie is. I didn't come here to get a lecture about my insecurities.'

'Well, tough, you happen to need one.' Ali's face lit up, as if she had been struck by divine inspiration. Then her eyes narrowed and she gave Monroe a look that he could only describe as sneaky. 'I tell you what, Monroe. These are my terms. You call Carole and get her to have a look at your work. Whatever she says, once she's seen it I'll let you know where Jessie is.'

Monroe blinked in astonishment. 'You're not serious?'

'Yes, I am,' came the sharp, no-nonsense retort. 'And another thing.'

'I don't want to hear this,' he muttered.

'Well, that's a shame, because you're going to. I think it's about time you started making something of your life, Monroe. You were forced to cope with some terrible things in your childhood and your adolescence. But I think you've spent enough time running away from them, don't you?'

He didn't bother to answer the rhetorical question, just fumed in stony silence.

'You're thirty-two years old.' Ali's voice was firm. 'And in about seven and a half months' time you're going to be a father to boot. When you see Jessie again, you'll need to offer her a bit more than a grovelling apology and a declaration of undying love.'

'Who said I was going to grovel?' His angry words were answered with a disdainful look.

'You'll need to show Jessie that you've changed. That you've got something to offer her and the baby. That you're running towards something now.'

'But what if this woman hates my stuff?' He snarled the words, but even he could hear the insecurity behind them.

'Do you think your work is any good, Monroe?'

He shrugged. 'I mostly get what I aim for.'

'Then that's all the answer you need, isn't it?'

Monroe was furious. He'd been cornered, but he could see from the determination in Ali's face that he wasn't going to be able to charm or bluff his way out of this one.

'Hell, okay, I'll call this Carole Jackson today. But whatever she says you'll tell me where Jessie is, right?'

'Of course I will. A deal's a deal.'

After watching her brother-in-law stalk out of the room, Ali walked over to the crib. Leaning down, she stroked an unsteady hand down her newborn son's downy cheek.

'I hope your auntie doesn't kill me for this, when your uncle turns up on her doorstep.'

CHAPTER TWENTY

JESSIE stepped out of the glass-fronted art gallery onto the bustling Prince Street sidewalk. She'd done it. She'd got the job. She should be overjoyed.

The assistant sales position was low-paying but Cullen's was a well-respected Manhattan gallery and the job had prospects with a capital P.

This was the sort of opportunity she wouldn't even have dreamt of when she'd left London to join Ali and her family in the Hamptons.

She ducked into the tiny coffee shop to get out of the sweltering hustle and bustle of lunchtime SoHo, ordered a herbal tea at the counter and then sat down at the only available booth. She needed to get in touch with Ali, who had been leaving messages demanding that she call her for the last few days. But she dumped her bag on the table and left the phone inside. Staring blankly out at the busy street through the café window, she absently rested her hand on her still-flat belly. She took the peppermint teabag out of the earthenware mug and sipped the steamy brew.

The joy wouldn't come.

Had Monroe destroyed this for her, too?

She couldn't stop the anger, the resentment and misery

from welling up inside her. With this new job, she was beginning the brilliant career she had always dreamed of. But after what had happened with Monroe, she wondered how long it would be before she'd find joy in anything again.

She finished the last of the tea, grateful that the usual nausea didn't come. Her hand rested again on her stomach and she glanced down.

When would she feel the baby kick for the first time?

The errant thought made her smile. Maybe it wouldn't be so long before she felt joy again after all. Despite the horror of what had happened with the baby's father, every time she thought about the baby her pulse jumped with excitement and anticipation.

She sighed. As usual she was getting ahead of herself. At the moment, the only sign of her pregnancy was incredibly tender breasts and the fact that for the last few days she'd been hideously sick every morning.

She blinked furiously as her eyes began to glaze over again. Grabbing her bag, she pulled out her tissues. It must be the pregnancy hormones. Her emotions were all over the place. Yes, she was ecstatic about the baby, but she was also dreading having to deal with its father.

Ali had called her two days ago to tell her Monroe had been tested and now knew the truth. He was the father.

Jessie blew her nose and stuffed her tissues back in her bag. All right, sooner or later she'd have to deal with him. As much as she hated to admit it, she knew he would want to have a part in the baby's life.

But that didn't mean he had to have a part in hers, she thought bitterly. She wasn't the romantic fool she'd been just a week ago—blinded by her optimism, her immaturity and her love from seeing him for what he really was. A hard man who'd been forced to make hard choices in his life. A man who would never trust and appreciate her, had probably never really trusted or appreciated anybody. Over the last few days, she had accepted the fact that a part of her heart would always be lost to him, but she couldn't risk her happiness—or her child's happiness—on a man who could never love her back.

Here she was thinking about him again when she should be out celebrating her new job, the new life she was about to embark on.

Reaching into her bag, Jessie pulled out her cell phone and started keying in a text message to Ali. Her eyes jerked up when someone slid into the booth opposite.

'Hello, Red.'

The phone slid out of her hand and thudded onto the Formica table.

Monroe had been following Jessie since she left Cullen's.

He'd caught the first train out of the Hamptons that morning, as soon as he'd gotten the call from Carole Jackson. He still couldn't quite believe the lady was planning a major debut show of his work in her ritzy uptown gallery.

He had checked into the room Jackson had booked him at the Waldorf that morning, feeling like a vagrant in his ragged denims and faded T-shirt. He'd put off the meeting with Carole and her staff until tomorrow, though. He had more important business to conduct in New York and it couldn't wait any longer.

He'd tracked down Jessie's whereabouts and raced down to SoHo, the nerves over what lay ahead nearly making him miss his stop on the subway.

He'd spotted Jessie leaving Cullen's. Seeing her again had made his heart pound like a jackhammer. But he hadn't had the guts to go up to her on the street. When she'd walked into the nearby coffee shop, it had seemed perfect. He could

confront her there. But when she'd slipped into the booth, still
he'd held back. Even after seven long days of going over everything in his head, he didn't know what the hell to say to her
to make it right. The creeping feeling in the back of his mind,
that she might have had an abortion, wouldn't go away. He
couldn't let that cloud things, but it did. He'd hate himself even
more if she had, because that would be his fault, too.

He tried to plaster a smile on his face. Look easy, don't look
desperate, was the only thing that kept going through his head
as he sat down opposite her.

'You look great, Red.'

The ice in Jessie's chest turned to fire.

'You bastard.' Grabbing her phone, she turned. She had to
get out of here.

He leant over and took her arm.

'Let go of me,' she snarled, trying to yank her arm free.

He didn't let go, but got up and slid onto the seat beside
her. 'Calm down, Red.'

She glared at him. Boxed in. 'Don't you tell me to calm
down, you…you…' she couldn't think of a word bad enough
'…you bastard.'

'All right, fine. Letting go.' Monroe lifted his hands,
looking defeated.

'Get out of my way.' She tried to push past him.

He didn't budge. 'Jess, we need to talk.'

'We do not need to talk,' she snapped. 'There is absolutely
nothing I want to say to you.'

'I figured that,' he said as he ploughed his fingers through
his hair. 'But there's something I've gotta say to you.'

She tried to push past him again. He held firm.

'I'm sorry, Red,' he said, touching her arm. 'You don't know
how sorry I am for what I said. About you, and about the baby.'

She felt herself weaken. Just for a moment. She could hear the torment in his voice, see the misery in his eyes. She could imagine how much he had suffered all those years, thinking he couldn't have a child. But then he reached up and ran his finger down her cheek. She jerked her head away, the gesture bringing back a rush of memories.

'Don't touch me.' She slapped his hand away. 'I don't want to hear that you're sorry,' she cried. 'I don't care that you're sorry.' A thought struck her and she felt as if she might break apart. 'You're only sorry now because you found out the baby's yours.'

He flinched.

'I'm right, aren't I?' she said. 'That's the reason you're here?'

'It's not the only reason.' He paused, seemed to think about it for a moment. 'But it is one of them.'

'I knew it.' Jessie's voice shook on the words.

'Is there still a baby, Jessie?'

Jessie could hear the anguish in his voice, see the fear in his eyes and the urge to hurt him as badly as he had hurt her overwhelmed her.

'No, there isn't.' The lie lay like lead on her tongue the minute she'd said it.

He cursed, closed his eyes and let his head fall back onto the high leatherette seat of the booth.

I don't care, Jessie told herself silently. I don't care if I've hurt him.

But then he turned and studied her. Instead of the bitterness, the anger she had expected, there was just a terrible sadness in his gaze. 'Jess. I'm sorry for that, too, then,' he said softly.

She would have told him the truth then, would have done anything to take the self-loathing out of his eyes, but the wave of nausea hit without warning.

'Oh, get out of my way.'

'What is it?' he said, lifting his head off the seat.

'Mo-o-ove!'

He jumped back. Jessie rushed past him, her hands clasped over her mouth.

She managed to make it to the kerb outside before her stomach heaved.

When the vomiting finally stopped, her legs started to wobble. She was about to collapse in a heap when strong arms wrapped around her waist and held her upright.

'I've got you, Red.'

He handed her some napkins. The shrill whistle in her ear made her jerk. A yellow cab screeched to a stop in front of her and she was lifted against his chest.

'What are you doing?' she said weakly. 'Leave me alone.'

'Not a chance.'

Monroe settled her on the cab seat before giving the driver quick instructions. Jessie wanted to rise, to get away, but her legs simply wouldn't do what she told them. He lifted her effortlessly into his lap as the car sped off into the midday traffic.

'I can sit on my own, thanks.'

She struggled, but he held her in place.

His lips curved slightly. 'Forget it, Red. We're going to have that talk.'

She stared at him in astonishment. 'What the heck are you smiling about?'

'So there's not still a baby, huh?' The light dancing in his deep blue eyes made it clear it was a rhetorical question.

'Well…' She'd made a fool of herself.

Okay, so she was glad he didn't look stricken any more. But he didn't have to look quite so ecstatic. That was just plain annoying.

'All right, there is still a baby. I lied.' She sounded huffy. She didn't care. 'I said that because I wanted you to suffer.'

Despite the catty remark, he grinned. 'Yeah, I figured that out while I was watching you decorate the sidewalk.'

Parting the jacket of her linen trouser suit, he stroked his palms over her midriff, stared down at it. She could see the fierce pride and joy in his face, struggled hard not to be moved by it.

'How big is he in there—d'you know?' he said.

'Who says it's a he?'

'You think it's a girl?' It was as if he hadn't heard the sneer in her words. 'That'd be so cool.' His gaze stayed on her belly; his hands felt warm through the thin fabric of the pink silk camisole.

Without saying anything, she pushed his hands away and wriggled off his lap. He didn't stop her as she shifted as far away from him as she could get. Turning her back to him, she stared out of the cab window.

She didn't want to see the joy in his face, didn't want to see his intense happiness at the baby. It might make her forget what he was really like. It might make her forget what he'd put her through.

Monroe let her go, his euphoria fading. Yeah, there was still a baby, the best gift anyone had ever given him, could ever give him. But he wanted so much more. He wanted Jessie, too. And the problems between them were far from solved.

'Jess, I can say I'm sorry for the rest of my life. But it won't ever undo what I said. It can't ever take away the wrong I did you. I know that.'

When she turned, he saw the sheen of tears in her eyes and felt his heart clutch at the sight.

'Just tell me one thing,' she whispered. 'Did you really think I'd slept with someone else?'

He shook his head. 'No.' About that he could be honest. 'Not when I thought it through. I just…' He stopped. How could he make her understand? 'I never thought I could have kids, Jess. I'd spent my whole life convincing myself I didn't want them. When you told me, I wanted so bad for it to be true.'

'Why didn't you believe me, then?'

What did he say to that?

The cab came to a stop and the driver opened his grill. 'We're here, buddy.' Monroe slapped a twenty into his palm and guided Jessie out.

'Why have you brought me here?' Jessie said, gaping at the ornate art-deco frontage on the landmark hotel.

'I'm staying here.'

'You are?' She looked stunned.

He shrugged. 'Yeah, the gallery's paying for it.'

'What gallery?'

He didn't want to go into all that now. This was more important.

'It's a long story.' He took her elbow, guided her towards the stairs. 'I've got a suite. I can order in room service. If you want, you know. If you're hungry now. We can talk.'

She pulled back, looking confused and wary. 'You don't have to explain anything to me, Monroe. Not really.'

Monroe didn't like that look of resignation, or the note of finality in her voice.

'Yeah, I do.' Of that he was certain, but how to do it was a whole other question.

She clutched her hands together, stared down at them. 'I won't keep the baby from you,' she said, and looked up. 'You can still be a part of its life. I wouldn't keep your child from you. I know how much it means to you.'

He let her run down before he spoke.

'Hell, Red. I know that. But the baby's not what this is about.'

'Of course it is, Monroe,' she said reasonably. 'But the point is, now you know you can have kids, this won't be the only baby. You can have other kids, they don't have to be with me.'

Looking at her on the steps of the Waldorf, wringing her hands and trying to be fair to a man that had as good as flayed her alive, Monroe knew he would never want anything again the way he wanted her.

'We can talk about visitation rights once the baby's born,' she continued in a murmur, 'but until then, I don't want to—'

'Jessie, stop being so damn noble for a minute and let me say what I need to say.'

Okay, so that wasn't exactly diplomatic, he thought as he saw her stiffen. But he was feeling raw at the prospect of what he was going to have to do next. Grovelling, he realised, didn't even come close.

'Don't you dare shout at me,' she shouted back at him.

He wanted to grab her and carry her into the hotel, but figured that wasn't going to work either. 'Jess,' he sighed. 'Will you please just come upstairs?'

She stared at him for what seemed like forever. When she spoke her voice was quiet, her eyes wary. 'I'll come on one condition.'

'Sure. What is it?'

'You promise not to touch me.'

He felt the sharp stab of pain and regret, but nodded.

Silence suited her fine, Jessie thought as Monroe picked up his key card at the reception desk and directed her to one of the dark-panelled lifts in the foyer. He was careful not to put his hand on the small of her back as he had always done before, she noticed, and was grateful. Seeing him again had been enough of a jolt to her system without him touching her. The fact that her hormones had responded as they always did to his hard, leanly muscled frame and that magnificent face just made her feel twice as vulnerable.

Why did he have to look so flipping gorgeous?

She tried hard to recall the cruel things he had said to her, the sneer on his face when he'd told her the baby wasn't his, but as the lift glided smoothly up to his floor she could see no trace of it on his face. He looked tense and nervous, tapping the key card against his thigh as he studied the elevator's indicator lights. He hadn't so much as glanced at her since she'd agreed to come to his room. That cool, confident charm that had always been a part of him was gone.

He led her down to the end of the wide hallway and slipped the key card into ornately carved double doors with a panel on them that read 'The Ambassador Suite.'

Jessie gaped as she stepped into a huge, lushly carpeted sitting area ahead of him. Three long mullioned windows across the room showcased the New York skyline in all its glory.

Monroe dumped the card on a small table next to one of the two large leather sofas that dominated the room. 'Have a seat.' He gestured to the sofa. 'You want a drink?'

'Water's fine.' She sat down stiffly and tried to quell her curiosity. Where had he got the money for this place, and what was that he'd said about a gallery?

None of your business, she thought ruthlessly as he turned from the minibar with a pricey bottle of Scottish mineral water and a glass in his hand.

Passing the drink to her, he sat down on the sofa opposite. He watched as she gulped the water down. She drank in silence, determined not to be the first one to speak. But when she slapped the glass down on the coffee table and he still hadn't spoken she'd had about enough of the tension snapping in the air. 'I thought you had something to say. If you don't, I'll go.'

She went to get up, but stopped when he shook his head and held up a hand.

'Don't go, Jess. I…' He stood up, paced to the window and back. He didn't just look nervous, she realised as he sat back down. He looked scared.

'I have stuff I need to tell you. But it's stuff I never told anyone before and I don't know how to say it.' He sounded like an idiot, Monroe thought grimly. 'I wanted to explain, about what happened. You know, when you told me about the baby. Why I lost it.'

'You already explained that, Monroe.' Her voice was curt, dismissive. Frightening him even more.

'No, I didn't, not properly.'

Her eyes widened, but she didn't reply.

He wanted to touch her, to pull her into his arms and bury his face in her hair. He wanted to make the horrible memory of what he'd said and done just go away. But he knew he couldn't. Seeing the anguish in her eyes only made him remember the ugly scene more clearly. She was probably re-membering it, too. He had to make it right, even if it meant exposing himself to the kind of heartache he'd struggled so hard his whole life to avoid.

No way could he look at her while he did it, though. He walked back over to the window, plunging his fists deep into his pockets. 'Before you told me you were pregnant, I'd already decided I had to let you go. And it was killing me.'

'What do you mean, you'd decided?' He could hear the anger in her voice. 'But I thought you…'

Monroe swung round, but she'd gone silent, and very still. Beneath the bright light of temper in her eyes, Monroe could see the dark flush of embarrassment, humiliation.

The guilt swamped him.

She'd opened herself up to him, had been honest and forth-right about her feelings, while he'd been secretive and cowardly, hoarding his emotions like a miser scared to let go of his loot.

He forced himself to walk back across the room, sit beside her. She straightened, but didn't move away.

'Jess, I can't keep saying I'm sorry. What I want to do is tell you the truth.' He reached for her hands, held on when she tried to tug them out of his grasp.

'You said you wouldn't touch me. You promised.' Her voice quivered.

He stroked the limp palms with his thumbs and looked into her eyes. 'Don't cry, Red. I can't stand it.'

'I'm not crying.' She sniffed as the first tear fell.

'I love you so much, Red.' There, at last, he'd said it.

'What?' She pulled her hands out of his, brushed at her eyes.

'It scared me to death,' he said. 'That's why I let you say it and I never said it back.'

'You can't say this now, Monroe. I won't let you.' He had to admire the steel in her eyes. 'I don't believe you.'

He touched his forehead to hers briefly. 'I know you don't, Jess. And I don't blame you. But it's the truth, I swear.'

Somehow Jessie found the strength to stand up, to step away from him. 'If you loved me you never would have said those things to me.' Her voice hitched. How dared he tell her this now, when it was too late? 'If you loved me, Monroe, why did you never ever say it to me?' Just thinking about how he had rejected her in so many subtle ways brought the anger back. 'I told you how I felt and I waited like an idiot for you to say it back, but you never did. It was always, "Sure, baby," or, "That's nice," or some other lame response. You made my feelings seem silly and immature.'

He stood up. She took another step back.

'I didn't say it because I couldn't,' he said quietly.

'Why couldn't you?' She could feel the tears running down her cheeks now, but she didn't stop to brush them away. Why should she feel ashamed of them?

'Jess, no one had ever loved me before the way you did. My mother hated my guts, Linc cared about me, but there was always so much guilt and responsibility between us. No woman I'd ever slept with had meant much more to me than a good lay. I treated them nice when I was with them, but I never missed them when I moved on. With you, right from the start, it was different. The way you turned me on. The way you responded to me. Your honesty, your openness. You never held anything back. You told me you loved me and I was…' he paused '…I was stunned. I knew I didn't deserve you and knowing I couldn't keep you was destroying me. If I'd have told you how I felt, it would have just made it harder to let you go.'

'If you couldn't tell me you loved me—if you knew there was no future—why did you still make love to me?'

He stopped dead, and his faced flushed.

'Every time we made love, Monroe, you were pulling me in deeper. You must have known that.'

'I did, I guess. I figured it was something I could give you back.'

Could it get any more humiliating than this? she thought. 'So now you're saying I was some kind of mercy lay.'

'Jess.' He tried to grab her arm but she spun away. 'I couldn't keep my hands off you. You weren't a mercy lay, it was the best sex I'd ever had in my life. When I figured out the reason why, that I was in love with you, it only made it worse. Because I knew it was going to hurt us both when I had to let you go.'

Jessie frowned. 'Why do you keep saying that? Why would you have to let me go? What are you talking about?'

His face was rigid with frustration. 'Isn't it obvious? What the hell could I offer you? I was an ex-con, no fixed abode. Living off my brother's charity like some damn deadbeat. Your dream is to have kids, a family, a home. All I could give you was good sex.'

'Whoa! Hang on just a minute.' She held up her hand. He actually believed what he was saying, she could see it in his eyes, beneath the anger, the frustration. 'You're serious about this?'

He sank his fists back into his pockets, his voice sharp and annoyed. 'Of course I am.'

She couldn't believe it. He'd rejected her, had put them both through hell, had even convinced himself the baby wasn't his, out of some twisted sense of gallantry.

He really did love her. She could see it behind the temper and embarrassment. She felt the heavy, dragging weight that had been lodged in her chest for days begin to lift.

Her lips quirked, relief warring with disbelief.

His eyes darkened. 'What's so funny?'

'You are, Monroe. You mean to say that because you went to prison all those years ago you thought you weren't good enough for me?'

'Well, yeah.' It suddenly sounded dumb to Monroe, too.

She stepped up to him, placed warm hands on his cheeks. 'Monroe, you complete fool.'

Annoyed or not, humiliated or not, he wasn't going to miss the opportunity to touch her at last. He put his hands on her hips and pulled her closer. 'So, do you believe that I love you now?'

She smiled into his eyes, but only said, 'Hmm.' He went to wrap his arms around her, but she slipped away, leaving him empty-handed again.

She pointed a finger at him when he tried to follow her. 'Don't come any closer, Monroe,' she said. 'I want to get something straight here.'

Monroe didn't like that considering look in her eyes, or the fact that she'd been close enough to smell and now she was gone again.

'So you mean to tell me *you* decided you weren't good enough for me?' she said.

'Yeah, that's right.' He wasn't sure where this was leading, but he had a feeling he wasn't going to like it.

'And *you* also decided that you were going to let me go.'

He nodded, warily.

'And then, when I told you I was pregnant, you panicked. You accused me of cheating because—' she paused for effect '—let's face it, it was easier to jump to that conclusion than to have to actually deal with all those messy emotions that you didn't want to deal with.'

At this point, he decided, it was probably best to keep his mouth shut.

Jessie walked up to him and poked him hard in the chest. He stumbled back, shocked to see the satisfaction in her face when he did.

'And, although when you thought about it you knew I hadn't slept with someone else,' she continued, the glint of steel in her eyes making him very nervous, 'it still took Linc to persuade you to go and get checked out.'

'Okay, so I was an idiot.' What the hell else did she want from him?

'You weren't just an idiot, Monroe. You were a coward.'

He bristled, but looked her square in the eyes and nodded. 'Yeah. I was.' He took her arm in a firm grip and pulled her back to him. The tantalising scent of summer flowers made him ache. 'Jess, just tell me, do you still love me, despite all that?' He couldn't wait any longer to know for sure.

She stared at him for a long time. 'You know, I'm not sure if it was really love in the first place.'

* * *

It seemed a lifetime ago, Jessie thought as she watched Monroe's face fall.

The eager, impulsive, stupidly romantic girl she'd been but a week before was gone. In her place was a woman, with a woman's heart, a woman's love and a new life growing inside her.

He dropped her arm. He looked bewildered and hurt, but Jessie knew she had to see this through, for both of them. She hadn't been fair to him, either. She could see that now. She'd put him on a pedestal, when he was just a man—a man who'd been through hell and had all the insecurities to show for it. She hadn't seen him for what he was. Funny, now she did, she loved him so much more.

'I idolised you,' she said, thinking back. 'You were gorgeous, cooler than cool with that Harley and that easy, devil-may-care charm. And you were incredible in bed. You gave me an orgasm.' The heat throbbed low in her belly at the memory.

'Hey, I gave you a lot more than just one,' he said—rather testily, she thought.

'But it wasn't really love. It was infatuation. I can see that now.'

'Well, thanks a bunch.' He sounded angry but she could see the pain in his eyes. 'I've bared my damn soul and now you're telling me you don't love me.'

'Now, now, don't get all surly.' It was cruel to tease him, but she couldn't help it. Maybe she wanted him to suffer, just a little bit. 'Even though it suits you.'

'What, you think this is funny?' Okay, so he was shooting past surly straight to furious.

'No, what I'm saying is, I didn't love you then, because I didn't know you. You were some ridiculous white knight, to me. A romantic dream I could never have. Of course, that all came tumbling down when you told me you thought I'd cheated on you.'

He groaned. 'Please, can we forget about that?' He slid his hands round her waist, looked relieved when she didn't pull away.

'I'm sorry, Monroe, but that one's going to get thrown at you every time we have a row. And I'm telling you now that every time it does I'm going to love you more.'

His eyes flared with hope. 'What did you say?'

'I said, I'll love you even more, Monroe.' She ran her hands up his back, felt the tension ease out of his shoulders. 'Because I'll know that you're not a white knight, or some super cool dude who's too damn gorgeous for me. I'll know that you're really surly and unsure of yourself and, like most men, don't know a damn thing about how to express your feelings. You've got just as many hang-ups—actually you've got a lot more hang-ups than I have. And a chip on your shoulder the size of a Californian redwood.'

'Hold on a minute.'

She grabbed hold of his hair and kissed him hard on the lips before he could say anything else.

'But you know what?' she said.

'What?' He looked really confused now.

Jessie felt the love inside her swell to impossible proportions.

'You're mine. With all your problems and daft ideas about yourself. We're going to have this baby and it's going to be loved and cherished by both of us and when it drives us nuts—and it will—we'll know how to deal with it. Because we learnt the hard way, having to deal with each other.'

'You think?' The cocksure grin she knew so well spread across his face, making her blood heat. 'So, let me get this straight,' he said. 'You're saying you do love me, now?'

'Uh-huh.'

'No, I don't think so.' He hugged her tight, lifted her off the ground. 'Uh-huh won't do it. You've got to say it.'

'Oh, all right, if you insist.' She wanted to sound miffed, but the lilt in her voice, the joy leaping in her breast, made it impossible. 'But only if I get another orgasm—and soon.'

'You got it.' He grinned, put strong hands on her butt and pulled her against him so she could feel the hot, hard length of his arousal through his jeans. 'Now say it, Red.'

'I love you to bits, you big oaf.'

'Okay, that's it.' He swung her up into his arms, and strode across the room heading for the bedroom door with her high in his arms. 'One orgasm coming right up.'

She laughed, clung onto his neck and covered his lips with hers.

EPILOGUE

'WILL you sit down? You're nearly six months pregnant, woman.'

'My point exactly, darling. I'm pregnant, not an invalid.' Jessie grinned at Monroe's annoyed expression. 'I think the hormones must be messing with my brain cells. But I'm actually finding that Lord and Master routine of yours quite a turn on.'

Monroe put his hands around her waist, caressed the soft swell of her belly. Arousal dimmed the annoyance in his eyes. 'I'm warning you, Mrs Latimer.' He pulled her to him, dropped his voice to a whisper. 'If you don't do as you're told, you're gonna pay.'

Jessie wedged her hands against his chest. 'Don't you dare kiss me here, Monroe. It'll end up in the morning papers.'

She peered over his shoulder at the beautiful people that thronged around them, resplendent in their Christmas finery. The clink of champagne glasses and animated conversation, mostly being conducted in loud New York accents, echoed off the art gallery's bare brick walls. Even though they were discreetly tucked away in a corner, she could see their little embrace had already attracted attention.

She eased Monroe back. 'Stop pestering me and go and

do some more schmoozing. You're the star attraction to-night, remember.'

It was the opening of Monroe's second show at Carole Jackson's elegant New York gallery. Even on Christmas Eve, with the traffic a misery outside and the weather even worse, the space was crammed with the art world's movers and shakers.

Monroe gave a frustrated sigh. He kept his arm around her waist as he turned to survey the crowd. 'I guess I can give it another twenty minutes. But that's it. I hate these things.'

Jessie smiled. Four months as the darling of the Manhattan art scene and Monroe Latimer was still embarrassed by his own success.

She could still remember that first dizzying showing when she'd still been plagued by morning sickness and had been sporting a shiny new ring on her wedding finger.

Carole Jackson had got the press salivating beforehand, by feeding them stories about the handsome bad boy who was about to conquer New York. How Monroe had hated that. But over the next month, with his face plastered over every art magazine in the country, even Monroe had to admit that some of the agony had been worth it.

Since then his painting and his celebrity had gone through the stratosphere. His work was hanging in the homes of Hollywood stars, European princes and even on the walls of the White House. Only the day before, they'd been out doing some last-minute Christmas shopping at Bloomingdales and Monroe had been asked for his autograph three times. He'd cringed with embarrassment every time.

'I'm afraid it's all part of the package, honey,' Jessie said, the pride in her voice helping it rise above the noise of the chattering crowd.

Monroe gave her waist a quick squeeze. 'Okay, I'll go

butter them up some more, but only if you promise to get off your feet for ten minutes.'

'Stop being such an old woman,' she said mutinously. 'I feel fine.'

He lifted his head. 'There's Linc and Ali. Great—they can keep an eye on you.'

Jessie followed his gaze to see her sister and brother-in-law weaving their way towards them.

Easy kisses and warm greetings were exchanged. Linc got to Jessie first, giving her a kiss on the cheek. 'Jess, you look gorgeous. How are you feeling?'

Jessie patted her protruding stomach, which was prominently displayed in the strapless velvet evening dress she was wearing. 'Wonderful. Now if you could just explain that to your brother.'

'She's been on her feet all day,' Monroe grumbled. 'What with her job at Cullen's and now this.' Monroe shot Jessie an exasperated look. 'She needs to sit down.'

'For goodness' sake, Monroe,' Jessie replied. 'I'm perfectly healthy. I feel absolutely fine. Will you stop obsessing about it?'

Jessie would have said more, but Linc slung an arm around Monroe's shoulder. 'Come on, little brother. Let's go get a beer, and I'll explain the fine art of how not to annoy a pregnant lady.' Winking at Jessie, he drew Monroe away.

Jessie watched as the two men pushed their way to the bar, Monroe fending off the throng of reporters, dignitaries and art lovers who kept trying to waylay him.

'I love the way Linc says that as if he's some kind of expert.' Ali threaded her arm through Jessie's. 'He never stopped trying to wrap me in cotton wool during both my pregnancies.'

Jessie grinned; she could just imagine. 'Well, Monroe

needs any help he can get. He's still moaning on about how I don't need to work and why don't I give up the job at Cullen's now that he's doing so well. I think he expects me to sit at home all day and stare at the ceiling. Just to be on the safe side.'

Ali laughed, then rubbed her hand over Jessie's bump. 'It's only because he's completely besotted with you—and the baby. I think it's sweet.'

Searching the room for Monroe, Jessie smiled when she spotted him, looking gorgeous and irritated as a reporter gesticulated madly in front of him.

'You got your dream, then, Jessie?' Ali said quietly beside her.

Jessie thought back to the summer and all the dreams she'd spun when she'd first fallen in love with Monroe.

'Not exactly,' she said eventually. 'My dreams didn't include stretch marks, or enormous boobs.' Ali started to laugh. 'Or puking my guts up for three months solid.'

Ali wiped a tear of mirth from her cheek. 'I'll bet Monroe hasn't complained about the boobs once.'

Both sisters laughed.

It was another hour before Monroe managed to muscle Jessie towards the gallery's front doors. As he grabbed his wife's coat from the hat-check girl, he was feeling agitated, annoyed and more than a little sexually frustrated. He'd been trying to figure out all evening how that sexy dress stayed up.

He grinned as he held the door open for his wife. The surprise he had planned should get things rolling in the right direction at last. Not too much longer to wait before he got his answer.

A cold blast of winter air hit Monroe as he stepped through the gallery's stately glass doors. He tucked Jessie's coat around her shoulders, grabbed her hand and pulled her out onto the sidewalk. Cab horns blasted and the frigid wind whipped down the street, stirring the grey sludge that had been pristine white snow only that morning. Emmy would be thrilled, he thought, if they got snow in Long Island for Christmas Day.

He was relieved to see the long, sedate black limo waiting at the kerb for them. The chauffeur jumped out and rushed round to open the back door, blowing his hands to warm them.

Jessie's teeth chattered beside him. 'It's freezing.' She looked confused as he took her hand and pulled her towards the open door of the limo. 'What are you doing, Monroe?'

'We're not going home tonight,' Monroe said. He could see she was about to protest, so he lifted her up in his arms. 'I've got an early Christmas present for you, Red.'

Jessie clung onto his neck. 'Put me down, you mad man. You'll fall on your bum. The pavement's covered in ice.'

He carried her into the luxurious interior of the limo without a single slip.

'How long are you going to live in Manhattan, sweetheart, before you realise we don't have pavements here, we have sidewalks?' He settled her onto his lap as the chauffeur slammed the door.

'What on earth is this all about, Monroe?' she said eventually.

'Nothing,' he said, wrapping his arms around her waist. 'Just taking my wife out on a date.' He loved the sound of those words; 'my wife.' He still hadn't gotten out of the habit of saying them as often as was humanly possible.

He leaned across and pressed a small button on the console in the door.

The chauffeur's black screen slid back. 'Yes, sir?'

'Take us to the Waldorf, buddy. But we don't want to get there for at least an hour. And keep the screen closed.'

'No problem, sir,' the man replied.

The screen slid silently shut and the car pulled out. The colourful lights and chaotic sounds that were Manhattan at Christmas whirled past outside as Monroe settled into the warm, seductive darkness. The smell of leather and his wife's perfume filled the air. The familiar flowery scent never failed to make his blood heat. He stroked his hands up the soft velvet that clung to her curves. She shivered as he kissed the sensitive skin at her nape. It was incredible the way she responded to him.

Their tongues danced in a well-remembered rhythm. His demanding, insistent, hers giving, seeking, until they were both panting.

Finally, he lifted his head. His deep blue eyes were dark with desire and intent on hers as he twisted her in his lap.

Fisting his hands in her hair, he brought his lips to hers. When they were a whisper apart, he paused, grinned. 'You know, Red. I may never have been your dream guy. But you sure are my dream girl.'

To hell with the dream guy, Jessie thought as she sank into the hot, passionate kiss, the heat throbbing in her core at the promise of what was to come. The real one's much better.

IN THE
GARDENER'S BED

BY
KATE HARDY

Kate Hardy lives in Norwich, in the east of England, with her husband, two young children, one bouncy spaniel, and too many books to count! When she's not busy writing romance or researching local history she helps out at her children's schools. She also loves cooking—spot the recipes sneaked into her books! (They're also on her website, along with extracts and stories behind the books.) Writing for Mills & Boon has been a dream come true for Kate—something she wanted to do ever since she was twelve. She's been writing Medical Romance™ for nearly five years now, and also writes for Riva™. She says it's the best of both worlds, because she gets to learn lots of new things when she's researching the background to a book: add a touch of passion, drama and danger, a new gorgeous hero every time, and it's the perfect job!

Kate's always delighted to hear from readers, so do drop in to her website at www.katehardy.com.

For Julie C and Diane, with love—
and thanks for the techie help…

CHAPTER ONE

SO MUCH for the paperless office, Amanda thought as she hefted the two enormous briefcases off the tube. But this was probably giving her arms as much of a workout as she'd have got at the gym. And she didn't have time for the gym tonight anyway; if she wanted to get these schedules signed off, she needed to get home, grab a ready meal from the freezer, and eat it while she worked on the files.

The moment she walked in to the flat and sniffed the air, she knew she didn't stand much chance. Dee was clearly entertaining this evening. And her flatmate's friends, being an arty lot, were *loud*. With the amount of red wine that was bound to be consumed tonight, she'd need to add another item to her mental to-do list: *insert earplugs*.

'Hey, Mand! I was beginning to wonder if you were planning to sleep at the office tonight,' Dee teased, coming out of the kitchen.

'No.' Though perhaps she should've done—at least then she could've avoided having to be nice to people she knew didn't really like her. Dee was a sweetheart, but Amanda knew only too well that she didn't fit in with the rest of Dee's crowd. She was too quiet, too serious, not someone who made the room sparkle with her witty conversation. 'Sorry, I didn't realise you had people round tonight.' She gave Dee an apologetic smile. 'Let me nuke something in the microwave and I'll be out of your way in less than ten minutes.'

'No, no and no,' Dee said.

Amanda frowned. 'What?'

'No, I don't have anyone coming round. No, you're not eating your usual rubbish—you're having a decent meal, for once. And, no, you're not holing up in your room all evening with a pile of work.' Dee ticked the points off on her fingers. 'Especially not on a Friday night.'

Amanda stared at her flatmate. 'You've cooked for me?' They'd agreed the ground rules ages ago: they shared all the chores except cooking. Half the time Amanda ate out, and she was a hopeless cook, so she didn't think it fair to subject her flatmate to burnt offerings.

Then she had a nasty thought. 'Dee, is this your way of telling me that you're going to move out with Josh and I'm going to need a new flatmate?'

'Don't be so paranoid!' Dee smiled. 'It's nothing.'

It didn't feel like 'nothing'. It didn't look like it, either, from the expression on Dee's face.

'I just thought you deserved a treat. You've had a rubbish couple of weeks and you work too hard,' Dee said.

That was a sore point. Amanda was still stinging from last week's appraisal, and right now she could do without the work–life balance lecture she normally got from Dee.

'So I'm cooking you dinner tonight to give you a break. A girly chat'll do you good.'

Amanda wasn't so sure about that. She'd never been much good at girly chats. Numbers and percentages were so much easier to deal with than people were.

'I've made us Cajun chicken with sweet potato mash, green beans and roasted peppers,' Dee tempted.

It sounded almost as good as it smelled, and Amanda knew

from experience that it would taste even better—Dee's cooking was legendary.

'Oh, and panna cotta with raspberries. Home-made.'

Pudding to die for—Amanda's big weakness. 'OK, I'm sold,' she said with a smile. 'But you've gone to a lot of trouble, Dee. It hasn't made you late with a deadline or anything, has it?'

'No-o.'

Was it her imagination, or did Dee sound slightly guilty?

She found out, the second after she'd taken the first delectable bite.

'I, um, need a favour,' Dee said, wriggling on her seat. 'The thing is, you know I want to work in TV, produce programmes?'

Amanda nodded.

'You know my friend is a PA to a TV producer—well, she talked to her boss about one of my ideas. He says if I can give him some kind of pilot tape to back up my treatment, he might be able to get me a break of some sort.'

'That's brilliant news.' Though Amanda still didn't see why Dee needed her to do a favour. 'So what's it all about?'

Dee filled their wine glasses. 'I'm pitching a series called *Lifeswap*. About two people with opposite lifestyles spending a week with each other and learning from each other's lives.'

Reality TV. Just the kind of thing Amanda loathed. 'Sounds interesting,' she said politely, not wanting to hurt her friend.

'And you'd be perfect for the pilot.'

'*Me?*' Amanda frowned. 'How do you make that out?'

'City girl, works hard in high finance, never gets time to smell the roses.' Dee spread her hands. 'You're an extreme case.'

'*Case?*' She wasn't anyone's case, thank you very much!

Dee ignored Amanda's indignation. 'You'd be great to pair with someone else who does actually take time to smell the roses.'

'I don't *need* to smell the roses.' Amanda folded her arms. So this was the favour—Dee wanted her to be in the pilot.

Swap lives with someone who was her complete opposite. 'You can't seriously want me to swap places with someone who spends all day in a beauty salon or messing about on a games console.'

Dee laughed. 'You'd go bananas in seconds! No, it's sort of…' She frowned, as if thinking about the best way to put it. 'Think of it as job enrichment. What different businesses can learn from each other.'

'It's a great idea, Dee—for someone else,' Amanda said. 'I don't need job enrichment. I'm perfectly happy as I am.'

'No, you're not. It's been over a week since your appraisal and you're still brooding about it.'

'Of course I'm not,' Amanda lied.

'You said your boss told you they want you to be more flexible. Doing this pilot would prove just how flexible you are,' Dee said, 'because you'll be able to show that you can do someone else's job for a week. A job in a totally different area than yours. Which means you can bring your skills to it to improve the other person's life, and learn some new ones that you can take back to your job and wave in your boss's face.'

'Maybe.' Right now, Amanda wasn't sure anything would convince her boss. Her face didn't fit—it was as simple as that.

'I think this'd work really well. You're photogenic, you have a clear voice with no obvious accent, and you're a complete professional at everything you do. That's why I'm asking you.'

'Flannelling me, more like.' Amanda laughed wryly. 'I'm no supermodel. And I've never done any acting in my life. I wouldn't know where to start.'

'This isn't acting. It's reality TV, so all you have to do is be yourself,' Dee reminded her. 'This could be good for both of us, Mand. You get to showcase your talents and prove to your boss that you're ready for promotion to the next level.

And I make a superb pilot and get my chance to prove I can do the job. We both win. You're doing me a favour, yes—but you'd get something back from it, too.' She gave Amanda a mischievous smile. 'And I could make sure that whoever you swap lives with is a great cook and would make you panna cotta or some kind of lemony pudding every single day.'

Amanda raised an eyebrow. 'If I want panna cotta, I can buy it at the deli on the way home.'

'The deli's normally shut by the time *you* leave work,' Dee pointed out. 'And this would be home-made.'

Home-made food…And Dee had been talking opposites. 'You're not thinking of making me be a chef for a week, are you?' Amanda asked, horrified at the idea of being stuck in a hot kitchen with some temperamental chef who'd rant and rave at her.

Dee chuckled. 'I don't think anyone could teach you to cook in a *year*, let alone a week!'

'And I don't want to learn, either. Food's just fuel.' Amanda made a dismissive gesture with her hand. 'I'm not wasting time in the kitchen—'

'That you could spend working,' Dee said, rolling her eyes. 'Yeah, yeah. I've heard that a million times and I still don't agree with you.'

'So we agree to disagree.' Amanda leaned back in her chair. 'Have you got someone in mind?'

'I'm working on him. *It*,' Dee corrected herself swiftly.

'Him?' Amanda felt her eyes narrowing. Oh, no. 'This isn't some elaborate set-up for a blind date, is it?'

'No, no, no.' Dee crossed her splayed hands rapidly in the air. 'I'm not fixing you up with anyone.'

Ha. That made a change. 'Good. Because I'm perfectly happy being single. If I want to be the youngest partner ever in the firm, I don't have time for distractions,' Amanda reminded her flatmate. Especially as it seemed she was going to have to work twice as hard to prove herself worthy; it still rankled that the bloke in the office who'd failed his exams when she'd got distinctions had been promoted ahead of her. His face fitted, but she had to work twice as hard to make up for the fact that hers didn't.

'I was just thinking about you swapping lives with a bloke— showing the difference between the sexes, that sort of thing.'

'And he's going to be my complete opposite.'

'*Relax.* You just have different lifestyles.'

It sounded as if Dee really did have someone in mind. 'What does he do?'

'Not finance.' Dee sighed. 'Look, I know you're an *über*-planner, and it's probably driving you mad that I'm not giving you the full details, but until I've got both of you to agree to do the pilot I can't give you a proper brief.'

Both of you. So it was definitely someone Dee knew. One of her arty mates, then. 'Musician? Painter? Photographer?' Amanda guessed.

'I'll tell you as soon as I can. Just trust me on this,' Dee said firmly. 'Think of it as an opportunity to be flexible.'

Back to her appraisal again. 'Hmm. How long are we talking about, exactly?'

'Two weeks. You shadow this person for a week, and the person shadows you. You film some of the things that happen and talk to the camera about what you've learned from each other.'

'If I do it—and I mean *if*—I'd have to clear the shadowing side with my boss. And there'd have to be something built in about client confidentiality,' Amanda said thoughtfully. 'I'd probably need to take some leave to do my side of the shadowing.'

'You've got loads of time in lieu stacked up that you never take—and you didn't take all your holiday entitlement last year,' Dee pointed out. 'They owe you. Mand, it'll be fun. Trust me. All you have to do is keep a video diary for a week and analyse the situation at the end, work out which bits of your life would make the other person's better and which bits of theirs would be good for you. What have you got to lose?'

Amanda didn't have an answer for that. She ate another spoonful of panna cotta and thought about it. 'I'll talk to my boss on Monday. If it's okay with work, I'll do it.'

'You,' Dee said, 'are a complete star.'

'And how's my best brother?' Fliss asked as she opened the front door.

'Your only brother,' Will corrected with a smile. 'And usually you insist on calling me your baby brother.' Though nowadays he was more likely to look after Fliss than the other way round.

'You're still my best brother.' Fliss hugged him. 'Thanks for coming round. I know your schedule's a bit mad right now.'

He ruffled her hair. 'That's this time of year for you. A never-ending round of sowing, potting, weeding…'

'And you love every second of it. Watching new life spring forth, caring for your plants, working a little magic in people's lives to change the space they hated into the space they'd always dreamed of.'

He grinned. 'You've finally learned my spiel, then.'

'Not spiel. It's how you are.' She smiled back. 'I appreciate it that you've shoehorned me in.'

'Hey. I've always got time for you. You know that.' Family was important. It was just a pity that their parents didn't feel the same way. He pushed the thought aside. 'So, what was so desperately important that you needed to see me rather than talk over the phone?'

'Come and sit down.' Fliss led the way into her kitchen, where the pile of exercise books told Will he'd found his sister halfway through marking her class's homework, and switched the kettle on.

'There isn't anything wrong with the baby?' Sudden fear for his sister clenched in his gut.

'No.' She smiled at him. 'Nothing like that. And Cal and I still want you to be godfather. I just need a bit of a favour, that's all. And I thought it'd be easier to explain face to face than over the phone.'

'What sort of favour?' Will asked, shepherding her into a chair and taking over the tea-making. 'Something to do with the school's sensory garden?' He'd helped them plan a workable layout, earlier in the spring—plants with textures and scent and colour. 'If you want me to come and do another session on the lifecycle of plants and plant some sunflower seeds with the kids, give me a list of dates and I'll fit one of them in for you.'

'No-o. The favour's not exactly for me.'

He frowned. 'Who, then?'

'Dee.'

'She's doing some article about gardening and health and wants some quotes? Sure.' He'd given Dee 'expert' comments before now. 'Tell her to email me with what she wants and the deadline.'

'It's a bit more complicated than that.'

He brought two mugs of tea over to the kitchen table and set one in front of her. 'Hit me with it, then, sis.'

'She needs you to swap lives with someone.'

'She what?'

Fliss pulled a face. 'Stop looking at me as if I've got two heads.'

'Strictly speaking, you have,' Will said, gesturing to her bump.

She flapped a hand at him. 'Be serious, for once. This is important. It's my best friend's big chance to break into TV. If Dee can put together a pilot of her idea, she's found someone who might be interested.' Fliss looked animated. 'The idea is, two people with opposite lifestyles swap over for a week and see what they can learn from each other.'

'So you want me to leave my clients in the hands of someone who doesn't even know how or when to water a plant, let alone understand soil types or putting the right plant in the right aspect?' Will shook his head. 'Sorry, Fliss. I like Dee a lot—but I'm not putting my business on the line for her.' He'd spent too long building it up.

'She's not going to take over from you—just shadow you for a week. Do what you do, under your direction,' Fliss explained.

'*She?*' His eyes narrowed.

'Well, you need to be opposites—that's why it's going to be called *Lifeswap*. You'll be perfect: country boy and city chick.'

Will laughed. 'Small problem. Last time I looked, I lived in a city.' Though his laughter was hollow. City chick? No, thanks. He'd spent too many years of his life already with a woman who was so wedded to her career, she'd stuck her children into boarding school at the first opportunity—and palmed them off on to any relative who'd have them in the holidays. Thank God for Martin, their father's elder brother.

'We could get round that for the film, if you stayed at Martin and Helen's holiday cottage in the middle of the Fens and did some work for the garden centre. It'd be good publicity for you.'

He reached out and ruffled his sister's hair. 'Fliss, it's sweet of you to think of me, but I'm doing fine. I don't need publicity. I've got a six-month waiting list of people wanting me to give their gardens a makeover. And, yes, I know I could expand the business and take on some staff, but I like being hands on. I like seeing my clients personally—I like being the one who gives them that corner of magic in their life.'

'You're a control freak,' Fliss grumbled.

'No, I'm not. But people come to me because they want *me* to design their garden. It wouldn't be fair to palm them off on someone else. And if I expand, I'll spend half my life shuffling paperwork and the only plants I'll see will be stuck in pots in my office. Stuck in one place, like me.' He grimaced. 'No, thanks.'

Fliss took a sip of tea. 'See. You're opposites. She's wedded to her office. You're wedded to the outdoors.'

Wedded. He didn't like the sound of that word. Or the gleam in his sister's eye. 'Fliss, this isn't one of your hare-brained schemes to set me up with someone, is it?' His sister, being happily married and pregnant, wanted him to feel just as settled and was for ever introducing him to potential Misses Right. It drove him crazy because she refused to see that, right now, his career took up all his time. 'Because if it is, let me tell you yet *again* that I'm not ready to settle down with any-one. If and when I decide that I am, I'm quite capable of choosing Miss Right for myself.'

Fliss gave him a wicked grin. 'The last six have been… um…'

'*Not* Miss Right. Which I knew when I dated them. It was for fun, not for ever, and they knew from the start I wasn't planning to settle down with them.' He coughed. 'And if you're going to mention Nina, don't. Even you didn't see that one coming—and my solicitor's letter sorted it out.'

'But you haven't dated anyone since. You've let her get to you and ruin your life.'

Will laughed. 'Stop fussing. My life isn't ruined at all. I just haven't met anyone lately who interests me enough to want to date them. And if this is your idea of setting me up with someone, then you'll just have to explain to her that you made a mistake, because your little brother is a grown-up who knows his own mind.'

'Point taken. And this isn't a set-up—this really is for Dee's pilot programme.' Fliss sighed. 'Look, if you don't want to do it for your business, you could do it for Martin's.

You know he's struggling to compete with the garden-centre chains.'

'I put as much business as I can his way,' Will reminded her. 'My clients like the unusual plants he grows.'

But it wasn't enough, and they both knew it.

'Publicity like this would be good for him,' Fliss said gently.

'Yes. And I know how much I owe him,' Will said, equally softly. 'Not just for all the school holidays when the parents dumped us on him. He's taught me so much about plants. And he backed me all the way when I decided to study horticulture—even gave me somewhere to live.'

Not that their parents had actually thrown Will out. He just hadn't been able to live with the constant comments about how there was no money in gardening and the City was crying out for high flyers—people who were expected to get straight As at A-level and had been offered an unconditional place at Oxford. 'And he recommended me to customers at the garden centre when I started up on my own. Doing this would be—well—my chance to pay some of that back.'

'Your decision, bro.' Fliss held up her hands. 'As you said, you're a big boy now. And you have the right to say no.'

He smiled at her. 'I'm glad you realise that. But okay, I'll do it. Assuming the holiday cottage is available.'

'I've already checked. It's available in a fortnight's time.'

'And if Martin's happy for me to do this,' he warned. 'You might be interfering in his plans.'

Fliss grinned. 'No, I'm not. And of course he'll say yes to his favourite nephew. Not to mention the fact that it's a brilliant excuse for Helen to make him take a week's holiday.'

Will ignored her. 'And *if*,' he emphasised, 'my clients give permission.'

She smiled. 'Nobody ever says no to you, Will.'

Not quite true. The two people he'd always wanted to say

'yes' had usually said 'not now'…but there never *had* been a time for 'now'. He looked at his sister, unsmiling for once. 'So, what do you know about this woman I'm supposed to be swapping lives with?'

'Lives in London. Accountant. Knows nothing about plants.' Fliss ticked off the points on her fingers.

Accountant? Ouch. Still, it could've been worse—it could've been banking. Though something in his sister's expression tipped him off. 'Do you actually know her, Fliss?'

She winced. 'Sort of.'

'And?'

'Let's just leave it that she's your opposite, Will.'

He shook his head. 'I've got a bad feeling about this. Look, I can ask around and see if anyone else could help Dee.'

'But then Martin would lose out,' Fliss put in quietly. 'Which isn't fair.'

Will stared at her. 'That's manipulative, Fliss. Worthy of our mother.' That was the biggest insult he could throw at her.

Fliss ignored the barb. 'Dee's desperate to get this right, Will. She needs a real flora-and-fauna guy, someone who knows birdsong and wildlife and the countryside.'

He sighed. 'I'm an *urban* landscape gardener. My clients all live in a city. So do I.'

'But you know about birdsong and wildlife and the countryside. Look, you got the highest mark in the history of your degree course. You know exactly what you're doing.' Fliss rolled her eyes. 'And you'd be perfect on screen.'

'I'm not looking to be a TV gardener,' he warned.

'It might,' Fliss pointed out, 'force our dear parents into acknowledging what you do for a living. They might even admit that you're a raging success and you made the right choice in turning down that place at Oxford.'

He shrugged. 'I don't need their approbation. I already know I made the right choice.'

'And you're fast becoming one of the best-respected names in the business,' Fliss said. 'But look at you. Tall, dark and handsome—and I'm not just biased because I'm your big sister. You'd look great on the pilot, you're laid back and unflappable, and you've got a lovely voice.'

'So, if this woman's my opposite, from your description, that'd make her short, blonde, ugly, uptight and with a voice like a foghorn?' he asked.

'She's short, blonde and pretty, actually,' Fliss corrected. 'But you're warm. She's ice. You connect with people. She's in an ivory tower.'

'And I'm meant to learn something from her?' Will asked with a raised eyebrow. 'Like what?'

'Well, you're a bit too soft-hearted and—oh!' She clapped a hand over her mouth.

He laughed. 'Maybe I should start toughening up right now, then. By saying no,' he teased.

'Please, Will. Dee deserves this chance. And it'll do Martin some good, too.'

He sighed. 'All right. I'll look at my schedule, see what I can rearrange, and sweet-talk my clients. But I'm doing this for Martin. And if this woman turns out to be the woman from hell…'

'You'll be fine,' Fliss said. 'You're good with people.' She patted her bump. 'Bambino, it should go on record that you have the best uncle in the world.'

'Only because I had a good role model. Uncle-wise, anyway.' Their parents were role models for how *not* to bring up your kids, and he knew Fliss thought the same.

'You're a star.' Fliss smiled at him. 'Thanks. You won't regret it. And it's only for two weeks.'

'Fourteen days. Three hundred and thirty-six hours.' He grimaced. 'Twenty thousand—'

'Stop, stop, stop,' Fliss said, holding up both hands. 'I

can't calculate that quickly in my head. Are you *sure* you're not a secret banker?'

'Very funny.' Not. No way in hell would he work in high finance. He didn't *like* the people from that world. The way they appreciated the price of everything and the value of nothing. He tried for lightness. 'Don't let the parents hear you say that.'

But the bitterness must have sounded in his voice, because Fliss shook her head. 'Hey. They're way past pressuring you. You stood up to them over ten years ago and you did the right thing.'

'Yeah.' He sighed. Even if this woman turned out to be an utter pain, he'd make sure the pilot programme was good. For Martin's sake, and Fliss's. 'Give me Dee's number, then. I'll ring her and tell her I'll do it.'

CHAPTER TWO

THE MIDDLE of nowhere. That was the only way to describe where Will Daynes lived.

Amanda groaned inwardly as she parked outside the little cottage. If anything, this was worse than the village where she'd grown up. At least there *had* been a village, even if it had been a tiny place with a school, a pub and a post office-cum-village shop. Here, there was nothing round the cottage at all. Just the Fens, stretching out for miles and miles. Flat, featureless fields.

And this was where she was supposed to spend the next seven days. Shadowing a garden centre manager. Right now, she wasn't sure if she'd last seven hours in a place like this, let alone seven days! Some people thought the country was a place for lovely days out—pretty scenery and birds singing and what have you. Amanda knew better. The country meant being lonely—never fitting in, with nowhere to go and nothing to do. No wonder her mother had become so distant and bad tempered, being stuck there. The country was a *trap*.

Then she remembered. *Flexibility*. She wasn't going to give up before she'd even started. Though what on earth Dee thought she could possibly learn from a backwater like this...

She climbed out of the car, marched over to the front door and rang the bell.

No reply.

She frowned. She knew Will was expecting her. So why wasn't he here to meet her? Unless he'd had to deal with some sort of crisis at the garden centre—wherever that was—and hadn't been able to get in touch with her. Maybe he'd called Dee. Though surely Dee would've texted her to let her know he was going to be late?

She rang the doorbell again. Still no reply.

Impatiently, she grabbed her mobile phone. No texts. She punched the speed-dial number for home.

'Hel-lo.' Dee sounded distracted.

'Dee, it's Amanda.'

'Hello? Hello? Is anyone there?'

'It's *Amanda*!' she yelled.

'Oh, sorry! You sound really faint. Is everything all right?'

'No. Nobody's here.' And it made her want to stamp her foot in frustration. 'Have you heard anything from Will Daynes?'

'No. But don't worry. He knows you're coming. Unless you're early?'

'Ten minutes,' Amanda was forced to admit. Because she was never late for anything. Ever.

'That'll be it, then. Chill. He'll be there when he said he would be. Enjoy your week.'

Amanda wished she could be as sure as Dee sounded. But Will hadn't given her any of the kind of details she'd given him. He hadn't sent her a photograph or contact details, so she had no idea what he looked like or how to get in touch with him, except via Dee. He'd given her no idea about what she'd be expected to wear, or the sort of schedule they'd have for the week. And as for confidentiality agreements…

Well. At least he'd returned *her* agreement. Signed in a bold, spiky script. And he'd sent her a hastily scribbled set of directions to the cottage on a scrap of paper. Ha. If he'd given her the postcode of the cottage, she could've used SatNav. As it was, she'd had to rely on him. He hadn't even given her enough information for her to pinpoint the place on a map.

To be fair, his directions had been perfect. But it still niggled her that she'd given him a decent brief and he'd given her not the faintest clue. She hated being in a situation where she couldn't plan ahead. What kind of a man was Will Daynes, anyway?

But there was nothing she could do about it, and no point in wasting time. She opened the boot and fished out the little video camera Dee had lent her. 'Day one,' she said. 'I've arrived. Nobody's in. And I've never seen a place so empty. It's bleak in the summer, so I hate to think what it'd be like in the winter. I don't know about taking time to smell the roses—there *are* no roses, here. Just endless flat fields and huge skies.'

She panned a shot of the fenlands, to show the viewers what she meant. *Keep a video diary*, Dee had said. *Be honest. It doesn't matter if you use loads of tape; I'd rather have too much than too little, so I can edit everything down.* 'I don't think I'm going to learn anything from this lifeswap week. Other than that London's definitely the right place for me.' And that Will clearly didn't bother preparing and planning things. Not that she was going to be rude about him right now. She'd reserve judgement until she actually met him.

'This place is such a backwater,' she said, leaning against the car with her eyes closed, 'and I want to go home.'

'Given up before you've even started?' a quiet, slightly posh voice asked.

Amanda shrieked and nearly dropped the camera. Just in time, she rescued it and switched it off. 'Oh, my God! Where did *you* come from?' she demanded.

He pointed to the battered-looking estate car parked behind hers—the car she hadn't even heard pull up behind her—and gave her a faint smile. 'Amanda Neave, I presume.'

'Yes. And you must be William Daynes.'

'Will,' he corrected.

True to form, he was her complete opposite even in that, preferring the short form of his first name.

She took the time to study him, and then wished she hadn't when she felt a weird twinge in the region of her heart.

How corny was that?

But Will Daynes was a heartthrob. No wonder Dee had wanted him for her pilot. Female viewers would just melt at their first glimpse of him. Tall, with fair skin—very fair, considering he must spend a good deal of his time outdoors—and very dark hair. Curly—messy, even—and a bit too long; obviously the owner of the garden centre Will managed wasn't a stickler for appearances, then. Broad shoulders and a firm chest hugged by a black T-shirt, and long, long legs encased in denim so faded and soft it made her want to reach out and touch. She only just stifled the impulse.

And then there were his eyes.

They were most stunning light green colour; no, on second thoughts, they weren't so much green as gold. Grey. Silvery. A strange, unearthly mixture of colours. Incredible. Beautiful.

Or maybe these wide-open spaces were getting to her.

'And this is Sunny.' A brown-and-white springer spaniel sat at his heels, eyeing Amanda curiously, but clearly having no intention of moving without her master's permission.

Dee hadn't said anything about a dog.

Amanda had spent the last twenty-four years avoiding dogs. Oh, lord. Why hadn't Dee warned her? Or why hadn't she thought of it for herself? Of *course* a country boy would have a dog. More than one, perhaps.

How was she going to cope if he had three or four?

'Hello, Sunny.' Involuntarily, she took the tiniest step backwards.

And he clearly noticed, because he said quietly, 'She won't hurt you.'

What a first impression she'd made. He'd overheard what she'd said about this place. And now she'd flinched away from his dog. He'd have her pegged as a complete coward who ran away from things. Which wasn't how she was, at all.

'Just stretch your hand out and let her sniff you. She won't bite. Though she might lick you.' He ruffled the dog's fur. 'I think she'd probably lick a burglar to death—wouldn't you, girl? She's Sunny by name and sunny by nature.'

Gingerly, Amanda stretched out her hand. At a nod from Will, the dog stepped forward, sniffed Amanda's fingers and gave her an experimental lick that took all of Amanda's backbone not to snatch her hand away. And then the dog sat politely, thumped her tail against the ground once, and looked expectantly at Amanda.

'She's waiting for you to stroke the top of her head,' Will said.

Flexibility, Amanda reminded herself inwardly, and tried it.

'Oh! Her fur's really soft.' She'd expected something that felt rough and wiry, whereas Sunny's fur was more like that of an old-fashioned, well-loved teddy bear.

Sunny's tail thumped again; and Will was still wearing that enigmatic smile. Mona Lisa had nothing on him. Amanda hated the fact that she hadn't worked him out. She was good at judging people quickly. With Will Daynes, she didn't even know where to start.

'Come in,' he said. 'Where are your things?'

'I'll manage,' she said, lifting her chin.

'I'm sure you can,' he said drily, 'but I was brought up to look after my guests.'

And she was a guest. For a week. In his house. In his life.

Without another word, she opened the boot of her car. She let him take her single suitcase and followed him and the dog into the house.

He led her up the stairs. 'Your room,' he said, opening

the door and setting her suitcase next to the bed. A double, she noticed.

'If you want to freshen up, the bathroom's there.' He indicated a door at the end of the corridor. 'There are a couple of fresh towels in your room; if you need any more, they're here, in the airing cupboard.'

The remaining door, she assumed, belonged to his room.

'I'll be in the kitchen when you're ready.' He gave her another of those faint smiles, and left.

Amanda blew out a breath and sat down on the bed. Home for the next week. Though this didn't really feel like a home. Everything was neutral. Pastel. There was a painting on the wall—a watercolour of a garden—but it, too, was neutral. Nothing like what she'd expected from a gardener's house.

Though what *had* she expected? Will had given her nothing to go on, and Dee had refused to give her much more information other than that he was a 'good sort'. Hmm. As his opposite, did that make her a 'bad sort'?

She pushed the thought away. She really needed to talk to Will and find out what was going to happen this week.

She unpacked her things swiftly, made a swift detour to the bathroom—another neat, neutral room—and splashed her face with water, then headed downstairs.

Kitchen, he'd said.

She followed her nose. Something smelled *gorgeous*.

Will was stirring something in a pan on the cooker. 'Lunch,' he said, pouring a bright green soup into two white bowls and setting them on the scrubbed pine table. 'Help yourself to bread and cheese.' There was a loaf sitting on a wooden board next to a bread-knife, a white shallow dish of butter, another white dish containing tomatoes and a plate with a large hunk of cheese.

Rustic. But more fuss than she'd have made; on Saturday

she normally grabbed a slice of toast for lunch, if she bothered
with anything at all.

'Thanks.' She gave him an awkward smile and slid into one
of the chairs. At the first taste of the soup, she felt her eyes
widen. 'This is lovely. Where did you buy it?'

He lifted an eyebrow. 'The mint's from my garden and the
courgettes were from the farmer's market.'

It took a moment to sink in. 'You *made* this?'

He shrugged. 'Just before breakfast. So it's had time to let
the flavours develop.'

Dee hadn't been joking, then, when she'd said she'd find
Amanda someone who cooked.

'It's, um, very nice.' And what an idiot he must think her.
'Are the tomatoes from your garden, too?'

He shook his head. 'Farmers' market. Mine aren't quite
ready yet.'

Right then, Amanda wished she'd boned up on gardening.
Read a few books. *Why* hadn't she prepared properly? She'd
never be this slack with a new client. She always read up on
the company's background, and made sure she knew about
their competitors and their aims and what have you, so she
could have an informed discussion right from the start. With
Will, she'd done nothing. And she was already regretting it.
'I, um, don't know a lot about gardening,' she muttered.

'Isn't that the whole point of this lifeswap thing?' he asked.

'I suppose so.' How was it that she was putting her foot
deeper and deeper into her mouth? In the city, she never had
this problem. She always had the answers. Never said stupid
things. Out here…

Out here, she was beginning to think she was a different person.

Amanda Neave wasn't anything like Will had expected. Small,
blonde and pretty, according to Fliss. And an ice maiden. Up-

tight. At first glance, Fliss was spot on—even Amanda's eyes were an icy shade of blue. And she was pristine down to the last detail. He'd just bet she'd never walked through a garden in bare feet or muddy wellies. Her shoes would always be perfectly polished, her clothes without a wrinkle, her hair groomed into that sleek bob, her nails manicured.

Ha. She was a typical city girl who, from her biography on the company website, seemed ambitious with a razor-sharp mind and a very definite goal. He'd been absolutely spot on, preparing himself to deal with someone like his mother. Though there was one surprising difference. His mother wouldn't have been nervous about a dog—she'd have seen Sunny as a nuisance who ought to be kept out of sight. At least Amanda hadn't told him to get rid of the dog.

Yet.

He watched her through lowered lids. Amanda Neave also had the most beautiful mouth he'd ever seen. And it was just as well they were here in Martin's holiday cottage rather than in his own home. Because, although Will had two spare rooms, he could imagine carrying her up the stairs to his room. To his bed. The thought sent a ripple of desire down his spine.

Desire he had no intention of acting on. He was doing this as a favour to his family and Dee—Amanda Neave was definitely the wrong sort of person for him to get involved with. His opposite. Undomesticated, business-oriented, the sort who'd put her career before everything else. He knew her type. And he also knew a hell of a lot better than to get involved with her—the sort of woman who had a calculator instead of a heart.

He tried not to let his hostility show. Telling Amanda what he thought of her kind wouldn't exactly be good for Dee's pilot. 'Help yourself to bread and what have you. So, how do you know Dee, then?' he asked.

'She's my flatmate.'

That surprised him. Why would someone as laid back and relaxed as Dee share a flat with a control freak? Amanda was definitely a control freak: the dossier she'd sent him via Dee proved that. The business confidentiality thing he could appreciate, given her job—but the schedules and timetables she'd given him were rigid and inflexible. No way was he letting Amanda push him into providing the same sort of information for her. That wasn't how he worked. And this week, just to emphasise the differences between them for Dee's pilot, he'd push that lack of structure to its extreme.

'What about you?' she asked.

He shrugged. 'She's my sister's best friend.'

For a second, shock registered on her face. 'Fliss Harrison's your sister?'

'Mmm. She mentioned that she knew you.'

He'd never seen a face shutter so quickly. Fliss clearly hadn't liked Amanda much and it was entirely mutual, but Amanda was obviously too polite to say so—and didn't want to hear what Fliss had had to say about her, either.

'So, what are the plans for this week?'

He hid a smile. Her abrupt change of topic was a clear attempt to get things back under control. *Her* control. Well, this was his week. Which meant it wasn't going to be regimented—at all. In fact, he was going to push her right to her limits.

'Depends on the weather,' he drawled.

'On the weather?' There was a gratifying squeak in her voice before she got herself back under control. 'But I thought you were a garden centre manager?'

Uh-oh. He'd slipped up already. 'Sort of. I'm only at the centre for some of the time.' So far, so true. 'I have more of a specialist role.' It just happened to be for himself, not for Martin.

'Doing what?'

Best to stick to the whole truth, this time. 'I design gardens.'

'You mean decking and water features and what have you?'

She'd obviously caught some TV gardening programmes. He grimaced. 'Personally, I'm not into catwalk gardening.'

She frowned. 'Catwalk?'

'Fashionable stuff,' he explained. 'Fashions change. And that leaves my client stuck with something that maybe he doesn't really like. Designing a garden's more than just digging holes, plonking in a few shrubs and sculptures or what have you and hoping for the best.'

'Oh?'

There was the faintest tinge of disbelief in the word, and Will felt his hackles rise. She was definitely from his parents' world; she even had the same attitude as they did towards gardening. That it wasn't really a valid career—that it was something you only did if you weren't bright enough to go into finance or computing or law or medicine.

And it annoyed him intensely that she'd managed to get the same reaction from him that they did. Getting him on the defensive within seconds. He didn't *need* to defend himself. Not to her. And yet the words came out anyway, crisp and haughty, and he hated it the way he'd let her make him sound. 'On the kind of garden makeovers you see on TV, they use mature plants so there aren't any gaps to be filled. Mature plants are expensive. If you take the average person's budget, the plants they can afford will be a lot smaller, so it'll take time for the garden to grow into the design.'

'I see.'

No, she didn't. And he needed to make her understand. 'It depends on the kind of soil and the aspect of the space—that means the light and the shape of the area. And, most importantly, it depends on the client's lifestyle and how they want to use the space. A design only works if it fits the client's needs properly. It's part experience, part experiment and part instinct.'

She looked at him. 'So what sort of garden would you design for me?'

'I don't know you well enough to answer that properly.'
He'd need to talk to her, fill in the mental questionnaire he
went through when discussing a garden with a new client.
'But I'd hazard a guess that you'd prefer a low-maintenance
garden with an automatic watering system that you don't
have to think about. Something formal, maybe slightly mini-
malist, that wouldn't be disturbed by kids and pets.' He'd just
bet that if her flat had a garden, Amanda never set foot in it,
because she would always be at the office. 'And all the flowers
would be white,' he added before he could stop himself. Cool
and glacial. Just like Amanda herself.

She didn't seem to take offence. 'Are you seeing any clients this week?'

'Maybe.'

'Scared I might frighten them off?' She raised an eyebrow.
'That's why you didn't send me an agenda for the week.'

'Partly,' he admitted. He'd wanted to see what she was
like, first.

'I'm always polite to clients. There's no point in being otherwise. And if you don't listen to what they want, you won't
do a good job because you won't be meeting their needs.' She
cut herself a piece of bread. 'Which is what you said about
making a good design for a garden. Maybe we're not so far
apart, after all.'

He raised an eyebrow. 'I doubt it. For a start, I don't organise my time down to the last second.'

'So you could be wasting time. Maybe that's what Dee
thinks you'll learn from me. Organisation.'

Was she trying to rattle him? Lord, she sounded exactly
like his parents. He'd just bet she did her filing several times
a day. 'Who says I'm not organised?' He wasn't tidy, true, but
he knew exactly where everything was. 'Besides, creative
jobs need thinking time.'

'Planning time,' she corrected. 'And there's a point where

you have to start acting on those plans, or you'll just drift and fall behind your schedule.'

She was wasted in the civilian world, he thought; with that efficiency and precision, she should've been something military. She'd make a great field marshal. Crisp and incisive.

Battling with her was probably going to be a mistake. But it was either that or... No, he couldn't possibly start liking her. She was meant to be his opposite. The sort he detested. That funny little feeling in his stomach...he'd probably just drunk too much coffee today. It wasn't desire. He couldn't want her.

'You're forgetting something. It's not possible to control the weather. If it's blowing a gale, you don't sow seeds outdoors.'

'I might not know a lot about gardening, but even *I* know you wouldn't plant seeds outside in the middle of winter.'

Was that the hint of a smile? No. She was absolutely serious. Too serious. Though he couldn't help wondering what Amanda would look like if she smiled. Ha. It was probably a good idea that he didn't find out. Because that beautiful mouth, once curved, might be impossible to resist. Okay, he might despise her world and everything she stood for, but he couldn't stay in denial for ever. The physical attraction was there.

He also couldn't deny that lust wasn't a decent basis for a relationship. He could never, ever, have a relationship with a woman like Amanda Neave—someone who didn't understand his world, didn't want to understand his world and would expect him to give up his dreams for a 'proper' job. 'Winter's not the only time when it's blowy. March is a good time to sow outdoors. Think of March winds and April showers,' he said.

'Then you have contingency plans.'

'Does everything have to be planned?' he asked. 'The best gardens start out as an experiment. They change. Adapt. It takes *years* to make the right garden for you. And even then it might not be the right garden a year later—your circumstances might have changed.'

'So you adapt the plan,' she said firmly.

'Are you ever spontaneous?' he asked. 'Or is everything rigidly fixed?'

For a second, he thought he saw her flinch. But she rallied. 'I can be flexible.'

He doubted it. But maybe that was what Dee thought she'd learn from him. The art of adapting.

Ha. Who were they trying to kid? Amanda wouldn't adapt. She'd expect his world to adapt to her, instead. This lifeswap thing was going to be a nightmare.

Especially because his heart was trying to overrule his head, to drop in sneaky suggestions. Like wondering how soft her mouth was. Or whether those ice-blue eyes would go all soft and dreamy when she'd just been kissed. And—

No. Absolutely no. He wasn't going to fantasise about Amanda Neave. He'd get through the next thirteen and a half days, and everything would be fine.

CHAPTER THREE

'YOU COOKED lunch. Washing up's the least I can do.' It was the deal Amanda had with Dee, on the rare occasions they ate together. Trading skills. And Amanda hated to be beholden to anyone in any way.

Will shook his head. 'Guests don't wash up. Sit down and finish your coffee.'

'I've finished my coffee.' She took a deep breath. 'And I'm not a guest, strictly speaking. I'm your shadow.'

'So you're intending to share the cooking with me to-night, then?'

Not in a million years. 'We could eat out,' she offered.

'We're meant to be opposites.' His eyes crinkled at the corners as he clearly realised the implications. 'You can't cook, can you?'

'I don't *need* to cook,' she said, aiming for loftiness.

He leaned against the sink, tipping his head on one side. 'No? Let me see. No cooking. So either you're one of these people who believe in eating only raw foods—in which case you would've refused to eat the soup at lunchtime—or you live on takeaways.'

'Neither.' She could feel herself blushing, and willed her-self to remain cool about this. There was nothing wrong with choosing not to cook, was there? Not everyone needed to be into this domestic bliss stuff. 'Supermarkets sell perfectly adequate cook-chill food.'

He snorted. 'Do they, hell. I don't know what they do to white sauce, but it turns slimy, and the rest of it doesn't taste much better.' He paused. 'So are you telling me you see food as fuel, and nothing else?'

She shrugged. 'What else is it?'

She wished she hadn't asked when he drawled, 'Pleasure.'

Oh, lord. The pictures that word conjured up. Pictures involving his hands stroking her skin. His mouth skimming the hollows of her throat. His body sliding over hers, bare skin against bare skin, teasing her until—

No. She grabbed the tea-towel and snapped, 'Don't you think we should get the washing up out of the way?'

'Do we have a time limit? Interesting. How many seconds per plate, do you think?'

He was laughing at her, the rat. She really, really wanted to throw something at him.

Except he'd probably throw something back. The nearest thing was that bowl of sudsy water. Which would turn her white blouse completely transparent and...

What on earth was wrong with her? Since when did she start having sexy fantasies about men she barely knew? She didn't have *time* for this sort of thing. Hadn't her mother always drilled it into her? *Don't let sex get in the way of your career.* No matter how attractive a man was, he wasn't worth losing her place in the line for promotion.

She lifted her chin, ignoring his comment. 'I was rather hoping that you'd give me a tour of the garden centre this afternoon—if you weren't planning to do any other work I could shadow, that is. And as it's two o'clock already, we really should be getting a move on.'

* * *

Bossy didn't even begin to describe this woman. And Will had never met anyone so driven by time. He was very, very tempted to remove all the clocks in the house—including commandeering her watch and her mobile phone and stowing them in a safe place—to see how she reacted. To see if he could get her to slow down and take time to see that there was more to life than being stuck in an office.

But he said nothing. He simply washed up and allowed her to dry the crockery and cutlery. Meticulously, of course. Then he put the things away.

'I'll drive you over to the garden centre, then,' he said, settling Sunny in her basket. 'And you can look after the house for us, honey.' He fondled the dog's ears. 'No chewing, okay?' He didn't think she would—but at three years old, Sunny still had enough puppy left in her to do something mischievous from time to time. And this was the first time they'd stayed in the cottage. Please, don't let her do something mad like chewing a chair, Will thought; the house needed to be spick and span by eleven o'clock next Saturday morning for the new lot of guests.

'I really thought you'd be working today. I mean, aren't Saturdays and Sundays the busiest days at garden centres?' Amanda asked.

'With the weekend gardeners coming in for supplies, you mean? Uh-huh. Though we're not like the big chains, selling garden furniture and barbecues and the like. We're a specialist nursery.'

'Specialist?'

'We couldn't compete with the big chains in terms of price. So we differentiate ourselves by service and by providing a different product: old-fashioned English roses and apple trees, cottage garden plants—'

'That makes good business sense,' she said.

Was it really possible to want to push someone into a deep,

muddy puddle and to kiss them senseless at the same time?

'I'm so glad you approve,' he said drily.

She flushed. 'I didn't mean to sound patronising. I'm sorry. I'm not very good at this.'

'Because you're used to being in an office. Driven by time.' He gave her a calculating look. 'Take off your watch.'

'What?'

'Take off your watch. Because it drives me crazy when you keep looking at it.'

Her flush deepened. 'I don't keep looking at my watch.'

'Maybe I should film you for five minutes, without you realising it, and make you watch the footage. Make you count for yourself how many times you check.'

For a moment, he thought she was going to make a smart comment; but she said nothing. Just took off her watch and stowed it in a compartment in her handbag. 'Anything else you'd like me to do?'

Kiss me.

He felt colour stain his own cheeks, then. What the hell was he thinking, letting his body rule his head? No way could anything happen between them. They were far too different.

Though all the same, he couldn't help wondering what her mouth would feel like beneath his. Or whether she'd kiss him back. Would the ice maiden melt and turn out to be warm and giving and—?

Hands off, he reminded himself. This is business. And he needed to prove to her that his business was just as important as hers.

'Hop in,' he said, ushering her to the car. He really, really hoped that the garden-centre staff would remember what he'd said in the team meeting this morning: while Martin was away, he was going to act as the manager for the week. He wouldn't be there all the time, and he'd have a shadow with him when he was in the office. If there were any problems while he was out at a client's, ring his mobile.

He wasn't expecting any major problems, though; most of the staff had worked with Martin since Will was a child, and the team gelled so well that the garden centre virtually ran itself. The admin side wouldn't do so well in Helen's absence—his aunt kept all the paperwork in order—but she'd taken pity on him and told him to leave anything that didn't need immediate attention.

The only thing that could go wrong was if someone forgot he was meant to be the manager and made some comment—because Amanda would pick up on it and ask questions. Just as well he was good at thinking on his feet.

For a moment, he was tempted to come clean and admit that he didn't live in the middle of nowhere and he hadn't worked at the garden centre since the year after he'd graduated. Whenever he did go to Daynes Nurseries, he spent his time choosing plants or sitting on the edge of his aunt's desk, eating her biscuits. But telling the truth would mean letting Dee down and letting his family down. He wasn't prepared to do that. When he made a promise, he kept it.

He climbed into the driver's side. 'One thing,' he said as he drove off, 'did you bring some more suitable clothes with you?'

'How do you mean?'

'Jeans, or something.'

'I always wear a suit to work.'

'For your job, that's fine. For mine, it's not practical. Do you actually *own* a pair of jeans, out of interest?'

Her face set. 'That's a personal question.'

'In other words, no.' He sighed. 'What did you think we'd do this week, sit in the office all day at the garden centre? You need clothes that can stand a bit of wear and tear. Something where it doesn't matter if you accidentally wipe mud on it. Something that won't crumple.'

He could hardly believe that she didn't own any jeans. And she was wearing a business suit today—on a Saturday, the weekend, when most people would wear something comfortable and casual. Was she always this buttoned up and formal?

Lord. She was going to find this week really tough. 'I can borrow some overalls from the garden centre for you,' he said, 'but… Oh, we'll sort that out later.'

Will lapsed into silence, and Amanda had plenty of time to study him. She noted that his hands were slightly rough, strong looking and yet fine at the same time. She also noted that his car was a complete mess—although her seat was clean, the back seat had a blanket on it covered in dog hair, and there was mud on the carpets as well as a pile of papers in the passenger footwell. For goodness' sake, hadn't he heard of a briefcase or even a cardboard folder to keep his papers together? Let alone a car vacuum cleaner…

Irritating, *irritating* man.

And it irritated her even more that her body wasn't agreeing. It was reacting to him. It wanted to move closer. Touch. Taste.

Absolutely not. She folded her arms to stop herself acting on temptation.

Ten minutes later, he turned into a gravelled driveway. She noticed the single-storey brick building bore a sign saying 'Daynes Nurseries'.

Then she remembered what he'd said earlier. 'I thought you were the manager here? Do you own it, too?' she asked.

'It's a family business,' he said, his face completely unreadable.

She followed him inside. There was a small area with a cash desk, but she couldn't see any of the gardening equipment, soft toys or plastic ornaments she'd expected to find in a garden centre. Just a coffee shop with watercolours lining the walls and a couple of display cases containing ceramics, a shelf with jars and a small notice about free-range eggs; the rest of the building appeared to lead to glasshouses.

He smiled and waved at the checkout staff, then shepherded her into an office. His, presumably—like his car, it was completely untidy with paperwork everywhere.

Odd, then, that his house was so neat.

There was more to Will Daynes than met the eye, she was sure, but she didn't have the chance to speculate further. 'There are some overalls in the bottom drawer,' he said. 'They should fit you—if they're a bit long, just roll the legs up a bit. You might as well change here.'

Change? What did he mean, change?

The question must have shown on her face because he said, 'Your suit's going to get a bit crumpled if you pull overalls on top of them.'

She hadn't thought of that. 'I…'

'Pull the blind. I'll get the overalls and stay outside the door until you're ready.' He gave her a sweet, sweet smile— a smile that told her he was enjoying her discomfiture—and closed the door behind him.

He thought she was going to chicken out? Ha. She'd show him. She pulled the blind, found the overalls, stripped off her suit, changed, rolled up the legs of the slightly-too-long overalls and was outside the door within a minute.

'Fast. Impressive.' He nodded, then glanced at her shoes. Her expensive, Italian designer shoes with kitten heels. 'They might get messy. What size shoe do you take?'

'Four.'

'We might have some wellies in your size. Otherwise you'll have to wear thick socks to make them fit.' He headed for a cupboard, rummaged inside. 'Ah. You're in luck.'

Green wellies, to go with her green overalls. She couldn't remember the last time she'd worn wellies, even as a child. Though at least these ones were new, still wrapped in a polythene bag. She really would've hated having to borrow some-one else's boots.

'Right. Tour, first.'

Her cue to film, she thought.

He took her through to the greenhouse area and talked her through the different groups of plants, telling her how they could be used to transform everything from a tiny patio to a huge formal garden. Amanda noticed how his eyes glittered with passion as he talked—the same passion she'd seen when he'd talked earlier about what designing a garden meant—and she could almost feel his enthusiasm sweeping her along.

Then he stooped down to show her a pale lilac flower that looked like a pastel-coloured gerbera. 'One of my favourites for borders,' he said.

The way his fingers gently caressed the petals made desire flicker down her spine. Would he touch her skin in the same way, treat her as if she were as delicate and rare and special? And the passion in his voice as he spoke about his plants—what would that passion be like, directed at a person rather than a plant? Directed at *her*?

Oh, lord. She couldn't start thinking like that about him. 'What is it?' she asked, hoping the heat she felt in her cheeks didn't actually show.

'*Dimorphotheca*—the rain daisy. You can use it as a weather forecaster. If it's open, it's going to be sunny all day. As soon as it closes, you'll know to bring the washing in.'

A functional plant. She liked the sound of that. And it was quite pretty, with its pale petals and strikingly dark middle.

Another wave from another green-overalled member of staff, which Will returned warmly. Hmm. Everyone here seemed pleased to see him; somehow Will Daynes made peo-ple smile. Something she wasn't aware of in her own job, probably because people were more focused on business.

She'd always thought that a good thing. Now, she wasn't

so sure. Why didn't people smile around her like that? She was good at her job and what she did stopped people from worrying. So why didn't they relax around her, the way they seemed to relax around Will? Why did she still have that same awkward feeling she'd had as a child—the feeling of never quite fitting in?

To distract herself, she asked, 'You really love your job, don't you?'

'Life's too short not to. I couldn't be anything else but a gardener.'

It felt like an obscure comment on her own lifestyle. There was nothing wrong with what she did. A muscle tightened in her jaw and she switched off the camera. 'I love my job, too. I like being able to take the worry from my clients, by making everything neat and tidy for them.'

'Uh-huh.' He was clearly doing his best to sound neutral, but she had the sneaking suspicion that she'd amused him. Probably the words 'neat and tidy'. Well, not everyone wanted to live in chaos.

'Um…excuse me?' A nervous-looking woman stood next to them. 'Sorry to interrupt, but I was wondering if you could help me when you've finished with your customer?'

Amanda suddenly realised the woman was asking *her*, not Will. Because of the green overalls, no doubt. 'I'm afraid I don't actually know much about plants, but I can find someone for you.' She looked at Will, hoping he'd direct the customer to the right place.

'I'm Will Daynes,' he said with a smile, offering his hand. 'Amanda's actually an office specialist, working with me on a project. But I can help with plants, if you like.'

The woman shifted from foot to foot. 'I've just moved—it's my first house and my first garden, and I don't even know where to start. All I do know is I just don't want this horrible, bare concrete square.'

Will's smile broadened. 'Actually, that's the best sort of starting point because if there's nothing there it means you can have exactly what *you* want. Tell me more about it.'

Amanda watched in amazement as Will chatted to the woman, drawing her out and making her feel so at home that she stopped shifting from foot to foot and talked to him about her dream garden. He didn't make a single note, but clearly took in every detail she told him, because he then took a small note-pad from the back pocket of his jeans and drew a quick map.

Then Amanda realised there had been a structure to the conversation. He'd found out the area's aspect, how much the woman wanted to spend, what she wanted from the area and her favourite colours. And he was actually sketching a design as he talked to her—a design based around pots and troughs, shrubs and bedding plants and herbs.

She followed him as he took the woman into the glasshouses, and showed her the sorts of plants he'd talked about and which ones she needed to start with. Then he told her how she could add to the garden over time, but one key shrub, some geraniums and some herbs would brighten it up until she'd had a chance to think more about the kind of plants she liked the look of. Finally he wrote down some instructions for her about how to look after the plants—when to water them, how much, what kind of feed they should have and how often.

'Thank you so much,' the woman said with a smile when Will found her a trolley, loaded the plants onto it and handed her the design sketch. 'My neighbour said Daynes was a good place to come. That they have time for you here—they don't just rush you into buying stuff you don't have a clue how to look after.'

Will smiled back. 'It's what we've always believed in.'

'I really appreciate it,' she said.

Time. Amanda went to glance at her watch, then remembered it was in her handbag. No way was she going to let him catch her looking at it. But how much time had Will spent with the customer? Surely it wasn't cost-productive use of his time, as the garden centre manager?

As if he'd guessed what she was thinking, he said, 'Time's relative. We have a satisfied customer who'll go and tell her friends about us. And word of mouth's the most effective kind of advertising.'

'Mmm.'

'There's a big difference,' he said softly, 'between value and worth. I could cost out the price of my time—but you can't put a price on the happiness that woman's going to get from her garden. And *that*'s important. It's why she came here.'

Amanda nodded slowly.

'So what *is* the time?' he asked.

She knew that he was teasing her, and decided to call his bluff. 'No idea.'

'Actually, I meant it.' He took out his mobile phone and glanced at the screen. 'Right. That'll do here for today. There's something we need to do.'

'What?'

'Go shopping.'

'Shopping? What for?'

'Essential supplies.'

Clearly he wasn't going to tell her any more than that. She had no choice but to go with him as he shepherded her back to the office, waited for her to remove the wellies and boiler suit and change back into her usual clothes, then drove her to Cambridge and parked in the car park next to a shopping mall.

'Why are we here?' she asked.

'Because your clothes are completely unsuitable for the job. You can't garden in a business suit,' he said.

'But—'

'No arguments. What size are you?' When she didn't reply, he said with a casual wave of his hand, 'Fine, I'll guess.'

'No, wait.' His legs were so long that she was having difficulty keeping up with his strides.

As if he realised, he slowed his pace. 'Size?' he asked again as he shepherded her into a shop. She told him. And then he rapidly picked out three pairs of jeans, four T-shirts and the most revolting sunhat she'd ever seen.

'Why—?' she began.

He almost seemed to know what she was thinking, because he cut in, 'Because if it's sunny, you'll need protecting from the sun—you have fair skin and without a hat you'll burn. This isn't trendy or sexy, I know, but it'll be effective. That's more important.'

Before she realised his intention, he'd paid for the clothes.

'I'll reimburse you,' she said.

He shook his head. 'This isn't the sort of thing you'd normally buy, is it?'

Even so, nobody bought her clothes. Or chose them for her. Part of her was annoyed at the implied slur on her competence, but part of her was charmed. Will Daynes was looking after her. Cherishing her. Making her feel…special.

She couldn't remember anyone ever making her feel this way before.

'And if it makes you feel any better, I'll claim it as a business expense. You're shadowing me. This is equipment you need.'

'Clothes don't count as a bus—' she began, and then subsided when Will gently laid a forefinger over her lips.

'It doesn't matter. And I'm not exactly poor. I can afford this, Amanda. Go with me on this one.'

Her mouth actually tingled where he touched her. A tingle that spread over her skin until her whole body was very, very aware of his. It felt as if every nerve end was whispering his name, wanting him to stroke her and tease her and build up the desire until her climax burst through. For one mad moment she almost sucked the tip of his finger into her mouth.

Almost.

She managed to keep hold of her common sense. Just. But she couldn't speak. Dared not speak, in case she said something completely inappropriate. Something needy.

So there was only one thing she could do. Nod acceptance.

CHAPTER FOUR

IT FELT weird, wearing jeans. Amanda hadn't done that since her student days. And even then she'd been more likely to wear smart trousers than scruffy jeans. Although she owned a pair of trainers, she only used them in the gym. The ones Will had made her try on and then bought before she could argue were half-running shoe, half-casual shoe. Nothing like what she would have chosen for herself. But she supposed they were practical for walking around in a garden.

And they were marginally better than green wellies.

'Ready?' Will asked.

'Mmm.' She finished fiddling with the camera so it had a good shot of the kitchen table: they'd agreed that the seed-planting would be a good piece of film for Dee to edit. Then she eyed the kitchen table. 'I didn't think you were going to cover it with mud. Isn't it a bit—well—unhygienic?'

'Firstly, this isn't mud, it's compost. Secondly, there's plastic sheeting on the table. Thirdly, I'll scrub it before dinner. And, fourthly, if you really want to do it on the floor instead…'

What was it about Will that made all these pictures flash into her head? Of herself lying flat on the terracotta floor and Will leaning over her, his mouth dipping to tease hers?

'Do it' did *not* mean 'have sex'. They were *working*. It was time she got a grip. She really, really hoped she didn't look as hot and bothered on the camera as she felt.

'...then you'll end up with chronic backache and I'll have absolutely no sympathy for you,' he finished.

'You know best,' she said—a little more crisply than she'd intended, but that picture in her head had rattled her. Big time.

'Right. Firstly, we need to get the compost in the right state for planting.' He slanted her a mischievous look. 'I would say like making pastry, when you make the mixture into fine breadcrumbs, but I doubt you make pastry.'

'I don't eat it, either. Too much saturated fat,' she shot back.

He didn't look in the slightest bit abashed. 'Okay. What we're doing here is putting air into the compost and making it easy for a root system to start growing through it.' He demonstrated the action.

'Shouldn't we be wearing gloves?' she asked.

'No. They decrease sensitivity.'

Was he deliberately making *double entendres*?

She dragged her mind back to the task in hand. As if anticipating her next comment, he added, 'You wash your hands thoroughly afterwards and use a brush on your nails.'

'Oh.'

'No lumps. We want this to be fine and smooth, almost like dry sand...or didn't you ever play in a sandpit as a kid?'

Her teeth gritted; Will was way too close to the bone. Her mother had hated going to the park so Amanda had never gone to play on the swings and dig in the sand. They'd lived too far away from the beach to go for impromptu trips on the weekend. Playing in the sand had been... Well, what you've never had, you shouldn't miss, she reminded herself. She ignored the question and concentrated on working the lumps out of the compost.

Will sighed and came to stand behind her chair. He was so

close that she could feel his body heat. 'You're leaning on the compost and squashing the air out. Try this.' To her shock, he took her hands, scooped up a mound of compost, then gently encouraged her to rub her palms lightly together.

'Remember, you're not trying to make it stick together. You're trying to get the lumps out,' he said, then returned to his own pile.

Amanda wished she wasn't wearing a T-shirt. Right now she could do with a really, really thick sweater. Or some armour-plating. Anything to hide the signs of her body's arousal before he noticed them.

This was crazy. She wasn't interested in Will Daynes. So why was her body reacting to him in this way? Why was her skin tingling where he'd touched her? Why could she still feel the warmth of his body against her back?

They worked in silence for a while, and then Will leaned over to inspect her compost. 'That's great. Well done. Next, we fill the pots.' He took two pots from the stack next to him. 'Don't squash the compost into it. Just let it fall in and end up in a mound. Then brush your hand lightly over the top.' He demonstrated with his pot. 'Your turn.'

Brush your hand lightly over the top...

Oh, lord. She really had to get her mind out of the gutter.

It bothered her, because she didn't usually fantasise about anyone. She never had time. There was always work, or something to focus on that would improve her mind.

And this was more like playing than work, which made her feel uncomfortable. A discomfort that grew when he demonstrated actually sowing the seed. She really *shouldn't* be having these kinds of thoughts. Watching his finger slide into the compost and wondering how it would feel sliding into her body instead...

It must be the country driving her crazy. She wasn't some

sort of sex maniac. Never had been. She was sensible and grounded and...

Her mouth went dry as her eyes met his. He knew what she was thinking. She was sure of it. And, worse, she had a feeling that he was imagining the same scene. His palms flattening against her thighs, stroking them apart. His fingers playing along her sex, teasing and inciting until she was wet and almost crazy with the need to feel him inside her. His mouth...

Oh-h-h.

Somehow she managed to plant the seed and water it.

And then Will made it worse.

'Label it so you know what it is—the plant's name, the date sown, and your initials.' He handed her a pencil and a piece of plastic that reminded her of an ice-lolly stick with a pointed end. 'If you rub the top half between your finger and thumb, you'll feel that one side's rougher than the other. That's the side that's easier to write on.'

All she had to do was slide the plastic between her fingers. It was a perfectly innocent act. And yet it felt somehow...sexual. A come-hither kind of gesture. As if she were suggesting to Will that her fingers could stroke him in the same way.

She really, really, had to stop this. Focus. Get it back to business. 'What's the plant name?' she asked.

'*Helianthus*. Sunflower.'

Thank God for that. If it'd been the sort of plant Georgia O'Keeffe had painted, all sexy unfurling petals just waiting for a man's touch...

She quivered. No, no, no. She couldn't possibly desire Will Daynes. He was so laid back he'd drive her mad with frustration.

But, oh, the thought of how he'd soothe that frustration...

They finished planting the sunflowers; then, as he'd promised, Will took the plastic covering outside, shook the last bits of loose compost into the back garden, and scrubbed the table.

Odd about the back garden, she thought. It didn't look like a garden expert's garden—it didn't even have a greenhouse. And it was nothing like the designs he'd done for the garden centre. Maybe it was a case of not having time to look after his own backyard because he was too busy sorting out other people's.

'Can I help with dinner?' she asked.

'No, you're fine. Though you could pour us both a glass of wine, if you like. There's a bottle in the fridge.' He busied himself at the hob while she located the corkscrew and two wine glasses.

'Thanks,' he said when she handed him a glass.

'So, why did you become a gardener?' she asked.

'Why did you become an accountant?' he parried.

'I was good at maths and economics, so it made sense to go into a career in finance.' Plus it meant she'd never again have to live in a tiny village where everyone knew your business and you didn't fit in—where you were always found wanting because you weren't like everyone else. Never again would she feel a burden, knowing that she was the reason her mother hadn't been able to have the high-flying career of her dreams, because, after a career break, everyone would be too far ahead for her to catch up so there was no point in trying. The city was anonymous, nobody judged you, and Amanda liked it that way.

'So it was a decision you made with your head, not your heart?'

'Heart doesn't come into it,' she lied. Her heart had told her to run from the country as fast as she could, find somewhere that she'd fit in. And she'd been good at figures. She'd been so sure a career in finance would be right for her...

She suppressed the thought that maybe it wasn't. Of course it was. Figures meant common sense and no difficult emotions. You knew where you were with figures.

He raised an eyebrow. 'So if you had no restrictions on you, what would you do?'

'Be an accountant.' Stick with the safety of figures and calculations. 'What about you?'

'What I do now,' he admitted. 'I'd hate to be stuck in an office all day, having interminable meetings with self-important people who waffle on about nothing. Having to be at certain places at certain times and account for every second of my time.' He grimaced.

'Don't you have to do that at the garden centre? Have meetings and appointments, I mean?' she asked.

'It's not all day, every day. I don't know how you stand it, being stuck indoors all the time and never breathing in fresh air, hearing the birds sing or feeling the sunlight on your skin.'

'Let me see. The choice is working indoors in a nice, quiet environment where the temperature's just how I like it and coffee's nearby—or having to do heavy physical work when it's hot and sticky, not being able to feel my feet because it's so cold outside, and being soaked to the skin because it's bucketing down,' she countered. 'I know which I'd pick.'

'Hmm.' He sprinkled something into the pan, stirred it a bit, threw some scraps to Sunny, and then dished the contents of the pan on to two plates.

She took a mouthful. The peppery taste of rocket merged with the sweetness of the bacon, the nuttiness of the pearl barley and the saltiness of the parmesan. 'It's very good.'

'And it virtually cooks itself.'

Right. But if he thought she was going to cook this for him when he shadowed her... No way. They'd be eating out.

'So,' he said when they'd cleared their plates and he'd fed the dog, 'I suppose you'll go and find yourself a quiet corner and tell the camera all the things that are wrong with my lifestyle.'

'I'll tell you now, to your face.' She picked up the camera

and switched it on. 'You want to know what's wrong with your lifestyle, Will? You have no sense of time. There's no order to your life—you value being spontaneous above everything else. You keep everything in your head.'

'And that's wrong *how*, precisely?' He folded his arms, looking at her with narrowed eyes. 'Flexibility's a business asset.'

That wretched word again. She shoved the thought aside. 'Yes, and if you can't be there for some reason, if you're called away urgently or you get the flu and you're in bed for a week—' bad choice of phrase; she had to swallow hard to suppress the thought of Will Daynes in bed for a week. In *her* bed for a week, all rumpled and sexy '—what does the rest of your team do?'

He shrugged. 'They're experienced enough to carry on. They know what they're doing.'

'But *how*, if you don't have anything planned? How do they know which client they need to be seeing, what stage the design is at, what materials you've already ordered, what still needs to be done?'

'They'll work it out.' He leaned back in his chair and spread his hands. 'It's a matter of trust.'

'Trust?'

'You have to trust people at some point, Amanda. Delegate. Let people use their initiative.'

Yeah, right. The last time she'd done that, there had been an unholy mess and she'd taken the flak for it. Nowadays, she checked everything herself.

'But you can't let yourself do that, can you? You need to be in control all the time. Look at your confidentiality agreement,' he said. 'Why did you feel you needed that?'

Wasn't it obvious? 'Because I deal with people's finances. Personal data. Most of what I do in my job is confidential.'

'I thought all company accounts had to be registered and visible for public inspection?'

'They are. But balance sheets and profit-and-loss accounts are only the end product.'

'I'm not with you.'

She sighed. 'Okay. Suppose you were going to bring in a new line of plants, and you were going to be the first people in the area to do it, maybe even the first in the country—that takes planning. And as your accountant I'd know about it.'

'How?'

'Because it'd be part of your budget and I'd have asked you what the money was earmarked for. If I gave those details to your competitor, so they could do exactly the same thing, but do it a month earlier, that would mean your advertising spend was wasted and your publicity would be out of date before you even started. It would have a knock-on effect on your business, too, because people who wanted those plants would visit your competitor instead of you, and maybe switch their entire business there.'

He was silent for a moment. 'I wouldn't divulge any details of your clients' business.'

She believed him. There was something solid and dependable and trustworthy about him. Will wasn't a man who'd lie or cheat. But… 'I can't take that risk,' she said softly. 'What about you? Why didn't you ask me to sign a confidentiality agreement?'

'I don't need one. As I said, you have to trust people at some point.'

She smiled wryly. 'You're so laid back, you're flatter than horizontal.'

He raised an eyebrow. 'So what's the alternative? Stress about things until I make myself ill?'

She made a noise of contempt. 'I don't stress about things.'

'No? You plan everything to the last detail.'

'There's nothing wrong with that.'

'And what if something changes? How do you cope with change?'

'I cope fine with change.'

His expression suggested that he thought otherwise. 'So what do you do to relax?' he asked.

'I go the gym on the way home.'

'And I bet you do a workout on your own.'

She stared at him. 'Meaning?'

'I can't see you working in a class. Letting someone else have control of what you do.'

'I'm not a control freak.'

'Aren't you? You gave me an itinerary about what we're going to do on your week. And I bet it's driven you crazy that I haven't done the same for you.'

'I think it's a little unprofessional, yes,' she said carefully.

He laughed. 'You need to learn to chill out, Amanda.'

'And you need to be more organised.'

'This,' he said softly, 'is going to be an interesting two weeks. And I'm going to teach you something you've maybe forgotten about.' He reached over and switched off the camera. 'Fun. And pleasure.'

She really wasn't sure whether that was a promise…or a threat.

CHAPTER FIVE

'SO WHAT do you normally do on a Saturday night?' Will asked when they'd finished washing up.

Amanda shrugged. 'Depends.'

'Would I be right in guessing "work"?' he asked.

She sighed. 'Don't give me a hard time about it. I get enough of that from Dee. Look, I know where I want my career to go, and I'm still at a level where that means putting in the hours to prove myself and get the experience I need. Is it so wrong to be committed to my job?'

'No. But there is such a thing as balance. And you're on my schedule, this week—so we're chilling out tonight.'

She looked slightly nervous. 'Please don't tell me that involves clubbing.'

He laughed and ruffled Sunny's fur. 'In the middle of the Fens? Hardly.'

'You're not that far from Cambridge.'

Fair point. Guilt twinged through him. She was closer than she thought, too—he often did go into the city. Because he lived there. Within a very short walking distance of the city centre, actually. Lying didn't come easily to him, but how could he tell her the truth without messing things up for Dee and Martin? 'I'm not a clubbing fan.' He much preferred the theatre and live music. 'We could watch a film, if you like.'

'At the cinema?'

'I was thinking more along the lines of watching a DVD here,' he said. 'We've already left Sunny on her own a fair bit today.' And if they went into the city, he'd probably leave the cinema on autopilot and end up outside his house with his front door key halfway towards the lock. Which would need a *lot* of explanations.

'Fair enough.' She coughed. 'Um, I meant to ask earlier. Is your girlfriend all right about this lifeswap thing and my staying here?'

He smiled. 'Are you asking me if I have a girlfriend, Amanda?'

'Only out of politeness.'

Politeness? Interesting that she was blushing, then. 'Since you're asking, I'm single.' He raised an eyebrow. 'And I'd guess you don't have time for a boyfriend.'

She lifted her chin. 'That's making assumptions.'

'But I'm right.' No question about it.

Her eyes narrowed. 'Don't be so smug.'

He pantomimed hurt. 'Smug? *Moi?*'

She didn't smile. 'Not that it's any of your business—I don't need a boyfriend.'

She'd already told him why, more or less. 'Because your career comes first.'

'Look, there's no law that says unless I'm going out with someone I'm an alien species.'

'You don't need to defend yourself to me,' he said softly. 'I understand.' Amanda was a lot like his mother—though he had a feeling she wouldn't make his mother's mistakes of settling down, having a family, then paying more attention to her career than her kids. Amanda would never have children in the first place.

'Is that why you're single?' she asked.

Because he was putting his career first, too? 'Sort of. I'm

not ready to settle down yet.' He'd dated a fair bit—but he'd kept things light, and made sure his girlfriends knew that the relationship was for fun rather than for ever. Except his last girlfriend had been convinced she could change his mind, and had taken it badly when she'd realised she couldn't. The break-up had been messy enough to make him avoid dating for the last six months. Not that he intended to discuss that with Amanda. He changed the subject. 'So. Want to choose a film?'

She glanced at the single bookcase in the room. 'From where?'

He followed her gaze. There were a few battered paperbacks on the shelves, but that was all. Not even his taste; these were blockbusters, holiday reading for the cottage's usual holidaymakers. Another mistake. He should've thought to bring some films with him.

Served him right for lying to her.

He pushed the guilt away. 'The local video-rental shop's got a reasonable choice.' At least, it used to have, in the years when he lived around here. He really hoped there was a DVD player in the cottage or he was going to have to come up with a believable excuse. Maybe he could claim the player was broken and they'd have to play the film on his laptop. 'I've had only one glass of wine and a decent meal to soak it up, so I'm below the limit. I'll drive us into the village.'

While Amanda went to freshen up, he had a quick scout round. To his relief, there was indeed a DVD player, and a membership card for the local video shop. Well, it was what he'd expect from his uncle and aunt: making sure that their guests had everything they wanted. Like the massive folder full of local information and the visitors' book, both of which he'd temporarily moved to his room to avoid awkward questions from Amanda.

He slid the card into his wallet, and had Sunny sitting ready in the car by the time Amanda came downstairs again.

She was back in her business suit, he noticed. Was she just not comfortable with anything casual—or did she too feel that weird pull of attraction between them, and this was her way of reminding him that this lifeswap thing was strictly business? Not that he was going to ask. He simply drove them into the village.

'Choose whatever you like,' he said when they walked into the shop.

'I don't mind.'

He grinned. 'So I can pick a really gory slashfest movie, then?'

Just for a moment, her mask slipped and he glimpsed horror in her eyes. Then she was back to being polite ice-maiden. 'Of course. It's your house,' she said.

On loan for a week. Guilt flooded through him again. 'I was teasing. What sort of thing do you like?'

'Really soppy, girly films.'

Her delivery was so deadpan that he almost fell for it. Then he laughed, pleased that she'd relaxed enough to tease him back. Maybe these couple of weeks were going to work out okay after all. '*Touché*. I deserved that.' He slid his arm round her shoulders, squeezing gently before releasing her again—and was shocked to realise that, actually, he didn't want to let her go.

He knew he'd be mad to give in to the urge—they could both do without the complications. His head knew that Amanda was wrong for him. She hated the country as much as he loathed her world, she didn't share the same interests and she was a workaholic who'd always put him second to her career, the way his parents had. But his heart wasn't listening. Now he'd touched her, he wanted to hold her again. Closer, this time. Close enough to feel her heartbeat against his. Close enough to find out for himself if her hair felt as silky as it looked. Close enough to brush his mouth against hers and tease her until she opened her mouth and really let him kiss her, hot and wet and deep and—

Oh, he really had to get a grip. And a long, freezing cold shower might be a good idea, too. 'So what sort of thing do you really like watching?' he asked. 'Comedy? Serious drama? A weepie? An action movie?'

In the end, they settled on a critically acclaimed drama that had just been released, and Will bought a large bag of popcorn.

'I'm surprised you approve of popcorn, being such a foodie,' she said when they got back to the cottage and he tipped the popcorn into a large bowl.

'Of course I approve of popcorn. It goes with a film, doesn't it? Like ice cream. But I like my popcorn salted—better still if it's freshly cooked and still warm.' He slanted her a look. 'Though the ice cream has to be good-quality vanilla, not the cheap and nasty stuff that tastes of powder.'

She rolled her eyes. 'You're such a food snob.'

'No. Unlike you, I believe that food is more than just fuel. Which I guess is something else we can explore in this life-swap thing,' he said. He settled in one corner of the sofa with the remote control, and patted the seat next to him. 'Come and sit down before I spill the popcorn everywhere.'

This was surreal. If someone had told Amanda she'd be watching a film and eating popcorn with a man she barely knew, on his sofa, with his dog stretched out on the floor at their feet, she'd have thought them crazy. She never just sat down and watched a film. There was always something to do, something new to learn that would give her that edge in business and make sure she never ended up in her mother's position, trapped in a world she hated. Why waste a couple of hours in front of the small screen?

And yet here she was, sitting on the sofa with Will, watching a film. Sunny was sprawled out on the floor, snoring happily. Amanda would normally have run a mile from this sort of situation, but somehow this felt…right.

'Help yourself,' he said, offering her the bowl. 'I'm perfectly capable of eating this all on my own—and you're too polite to stop me.'

Too polite? Hmm. He had a point. Maybe she was. She took a couple of pieces of popcorn, but she was aware of Will watching her. 'What?' she asked.

'I was just wondering…do you ever let go?'

'I don't need to,' she said quietly. 'And there's nothing wrong with being anchored. Stable.' She refused to let herself hear the word 'rigid'.

Will said nothing; it felt like a quiet criticism. She ignored it and settled down to watch the film. Every time she dipped her fingers into the bowl of popcorn, her fingers seemed to brush against his—the lightest, tiniest touch—and it felt as if every nerve in her body had been galvanised.

Weird.

This wasn't the sort of thing that happened to her. She was sensible, practical and efficient, not a dreamer. She was *not* going to start having fantasies about Will Daynes.

Yet she couldn't help giving him a sidelong glance—and blood scorched into her cheeks when she realised he was doing exactly the same. Glancing at her, those incredible eyes full of interest.

Was he wondering the same sort of thing that she was?

Just one tiny move. That'd be all it would take. All she had to do was let her lips part, tip her head back slightly in invitation, and he'd kiss her. She could see it in his eyes. And it would be one hell of a kiss. Enough to blow her mind and—

And she'd completely mess up this thing for Dee. She needed to remember why she was here. Not because Will had invited her here as his lover—because they were helping Dee with this project. This was business. She was going to count backwards from a hundred until her pulse slowed down again, and she'd keep some mental distance between them in the future.

When the film finished, even though she wasn't tired, Amanda yawned and placed her hand in front of her mouth. 'Sorry, Will. I'm shattered. Must be all the fresh air,' she fibbed.

'It usually makes people eat a lot and sleep a lot,' he said with a smile. 'See you in the morning. Sleep well.'

And what were his plans for tomorrow? She just about managed to stop herself asking. He clearly knew it, because there was the tiniest twinkle in his eyes. 'See you in the morning,' she echoed, and walked deliberately slowly. Just to prove she wasn't running scared of him.

In her room, she took up the camera and sat next to the window, where she could see the first few stars breaking through. Training the camera on her face, she began to speak, quietly yet precisely.

'I can't work him out. Will Daynes is passionate about what he does and he's a complete food snob—he's got high standards. And yet he drives around in a scruffy heap of a car and never seems to plan anything. I have no idea what such a strange mixture of a man could teach me, to make my work better. And I don't even know where to begin teaching him, because what he does is so far away from what I know, it's untrue. I know about planning and order. He does spontaneity and...well...untidiness. I think for a lifeswap thing to really work both people need to have more of a crossover in their lives. Will and I...we're just too opposite.'

She turned the machine off. What she didn't say out loud—and wasn't really happy about admitting to herself, even—was that Will Daynes was also the most intriguing, most attractive man she'd ever met. Worse, it wasn't just sex. There was something about him. And she was scared that if she got to know him better, she'd be halfway to falling in love with him. They were too different for it to end in anything but heartbreak. So it was better not to start anything.

She was going to be sensible about this. Absolutely sensible.

It took a long while for Amanda to fall asleep that night. Strange house, strange bed—and very, very strange sounds. There wasn't the quiet hum of traffic she was used to; here, the silence was broken every so often by a howl or a cry. Owls, foxes, bats… She shivered, despite the warmth of the night, and pulled the bedclothes tighter.

She only realised she'd fallen asleep when she blinked and the room was full of sunlight through the thin cotton curtains. She glanced at her bedside clock and gasped in horror. It was almost ten o'clock. She never slept this late. Ever.

Will must already be awake; she could smell coffee.

Proper coffee.

Just what she needed to get herself functioning again, back to normal efficiency.

She showered, washed her hair, dressed and was downstairs in fifteen minutes flat. Will was sitting at the kitchen table, drinking coffee and reading the paper. Sunny was beside him, her head on his knee; Will was absently scratching the top of her head. Her tail thumped once when she saw Amanda; the noise made Will look up.

'Morning.'

Oh, lord. That smile was amazing. Imagine waking up to

that every day… The idea sent a shiver through her. 'Morning,' she said, striving to sound cool and responsible and hoping she didn't sound as breathless as she felt.

The table was set for two, and it felt oddly domestic. As if she belonged. Which, of course, she didn't—she was a city girl through and through, and this was most definitely the middle of the country. A particularly *isolated* spot of the country. Worse even than the place where she'd grown up and been so miserable and lonely. You're just shadowing him for a week, she reminded herself. This isn't real.

He filled her mug from the cafétière and added a splash of milk—just how she liked it. Amanda was impressed that he'd remembered.

'Would you like a croissant? I picked some up from the baker's this morning.'

He'd left the house and she hadn't even heard his car? 'Thanks. I'm sorry for sleeping in so late.' She bit her lip. 'I must have forgotten to set my alarm.'

'Listen to your body,' he advised sagely. 'It's telling you something.'

She groaned. 'You're not going all New Age on me, are you?'

He laughed. 'No, but I did warn you that the air around here makes people sleep longer than usual. Relax. It's Sunday morning and we don't have to rush about.'

'Sunday's usually your day off?'

'Yes and no.'

Infuriating man. Why couldn't he give her a proper answer? If she asked him for a straight answer, he'd probably say 'Roman road' or something equally facetious. If it wasn't for the look on his face when he talked about a garden or food, she'd say Will Daynes wasn't capable of being serious about anything.

While the croissants were heating in the oven, he raided

the fridge for juice, and put butter and homemade jam on the table.

'Don't tell me—local farmers' market?' she asked.

'Don't get me started about food miles and carbon footprints and the importance of buying local produce in season. Fliss tells me I can be very, very boring.' He smiled at her. 'Let's just say this will be the best strawberry jam you'll ever taste.'

Three minutes later, she had to admit it. 'Gorgeous.'

When they'd demolished the plate of croissants, he said, 'Question for you. How many senses are there?'

She frowned. 'Five, obviously.'

'Which are?'

She wasn't quite sure where this was going, but she played along. 'Sight, hearing, touch, smell, taste.'

There was just the tiniest quirk of his lips. 'I'm surprised you didn't add "six, if you're gullible", with your views on New Age stuff.'

'Are you telling me now you're an old hippy?'

He laughed. 'No. The real question is, how many of your senses do you use in your job?'

She took a mouthful of coffee, hoping the caffeine would kick in soon because she really wasn't following this. 'I'm not with you.'

He picked up a camera very similar to the one Dee had lent her, and switched it on. 'How many of your senses do you use in your job?' he repeated patiently.

'Sight, obviously—I'm looking at figures. Hearing, if I'm listening to a client. Um…touch, as I'm touching the computer keyboard or turning pages in a file.'

He lifted his hand to stop her. 'Ah, no, there's a difference—you're pressing the keys, but you're not *touching* them.'

'That's illogical. Of course I'm touching them.'

'But you're doing it on autopilot. It's just a function. You're not registering the feel of the keyboard.'

She must have looked blank, because he asked, 'So are the keys on your computer smooth or slightly rough?'

She shook her head. 'No idea.'

'My point exactly.'

'That's trivial, Will. It's not *important* whether they're rough or smooth.'

'Yes, it is. The point I'm making is that you're not using all your senses. You don't notice texture.'

Lord, the way he said the word. It made her want to reach out and touch him. Explore the texture of his skin and find out if he felt as good as he looked.

'You also don't use smell or taste.'

Smell. He'd been close enough for her to smell his clean, personal scent earlier. And taste... Just how would Will Daynes taste? With difficulty, she dragged her eyes away from his mouth and her mind back to the point. *Business*. 'Not unless I'm doing an asset inspection or a stock-take and the stock happens to have some kind of scent. Tasting's not really on the agenda.'

'But your office has a scent. Whether it's dust—well, no, in your case no dust would dare to settle,' he corrected himself swiftly, 'or the scent of paper or ink or whatever plants grow in your office.'

She didn't think the plants in the office had a scent. There certainly weren't any on her desk. 'I don't *need* to smell or taste.'

'We'll prove that later,' he said, and switched off the camera again.

'I thought I was doing the filming, this week?' she asked.

'It's a two-way thing. Your impressions of my job—my impressions of how you'd cope with it.'

He'd already filmed his view of her—the way she had of him?

Part of her wanted to know what he'd said; and part of her thought it would be safer not to know.

'Next week, we swap over.' He topped up her coffee. 'Right, time for work.'

'We're going to the garden centre?' she guessed.

'No. I'm not there all the time. Today I'm working from home.' He walked over to one of the worktops, where she hadn't noticed a board leaning against the wall. He turned the board round to face her. 'What does this say to you?'

'It's a collection of pictures of gardens.' Completely haphazard. Some had ragged edges, as if they'd been ripped out of a magazine. Others looked like proper photographs.

'It's a mood board,' he explained. 'I ask my clients to look through magazines and newspapers and on the internet and collect pictures of gardens they like the look of.'

'So you make their gardens look like whatever they've seen in a magazine?'

He shook his head. 'I capture the mood—these are the sort of gardens that have the look and feel the client wants me to create for them.'

'What if the mood board is full of huge gardens, but they only have a tiny space?'

He smiled. 'Then we use clever planting to make a small space feel like a large one.' He rummaged in a cupboard and brought out a tray. 'Okay, imagine this is our small garden.' He grabbed items from the kitchen worktops and plonked them at random on the tray. 'How does it look?'

'An untidy mess,' she said without thinking.

'You are *such* a neat freak.' He laughed. 'Well, apart from untidy. What does the space look like?'

'Cluttered,' she said, 'and small.'

'Exactly.' He removed most of the items and arranged the others more carefully.

She couldn't help watching his hands, wondering how they'd feel on her skin. It drove her crazy.

'And now?'

He sounded completely businesslike—and she was grateful that these mad desires clearly didn't show on her face. She nodded. 'Less is more. I see.'

'And then there are gardens within gardens, for larger areas.'

'How does that work?'

'If they want the garden to do lots of different things, you can divide the space up. Have a place for the kids to play, an entertaining area, a formal garden and a place for just chilling out with a good book and a long, cold drink.' He smiled at her. 'Today, we're going to design a garden.'

'We?' But she knew nothing about gardening. Or design.

'You're shadowing me; the rules are, you're doing what I'm doing. Here's my report.' He handed her a plastic wallet filled with paper. 'If you can't read my handwriting, just yell and I'll translate.'

That wasn't a problem. His script was big and bold and spiky. An artist's handwriting, beautiful to look at and yet easy to read.

'And when you've read it, you can tell me what you think.'

'I don't know anything about gardens,' she reminded him.

'You know about analysing data, don't you? It's the same sort of skill—just different data, really.' He looked at her. 'Do you mind if I put some music on? I usually work to music.'

'Sure.' She preferred to work in silence, but she could tune it out. Unless he listened to really loud, intrusive stuff with a heavy bass.

'Thanks.' He took a laptop case out of a drawer in the kitchen, slid what looked like a very expensive piece of kit on to the kitchen table, and plugged an MP3 player into it. Soft piano music—something she didn't recognise, but actually rather liked—floated into the air.

'What's this?' she asked.

He gestured to the MP3 player. She glanced at the display, and was none the wiser. 'Fulham?'

'That's where the garden is.'

'Your playlist is called *Fulham*?' she asked in disbelief.

'My playlists are organised by gardens.' He fiddled with the player. 'Remember what I said about using all the senses? Sound helps to set the mood. Close your eyes and listen. What does this one make you think of?'

Classical guitar music, not quite flamenco, but getting that way. It made her think of hot afternoons under a Mediterranean sun. Lying in the grass in a field full of orange trees under a blue, blue sky. With Will propped on one elbow next to her, leaning over, his mouth about to—

Focus, she reminded herself. 'A Spanish garden?' she guessed.

'Near enough. A Mediterranean terrace,' he agreed. 'How about this? And keep your eyes closed, Amanda.'

Right now, she didn't dare open them. In case he was doing what she was just imagining, leaning over her with his mouth about to tease hers.

The sound of the Beach Boys floated into the air. She smiled. 'California. Palm trees and surf.'

'And what are they doing?'

'I don't know. Driving along the seafront? Finding waves or whatever it is surfers do?'

He laughed. 'Not in a garden.' He flicked to the next track in the playlist—an upbeat, summery, boppy track. 'This is for the same garden.'

'They're partying?' she guessed.

'More or less. This was a house with four kids aged nine to sixteen, and their friends came round a lot. So we're talking ball games, water fights, that sort of thing—we needed robust plants that could stand a ball being thrown into them, but which wouldn't end up with kids being covered in scratches or needing thorns taken out of their skin.'

In a weird way, this was starting to make sense.

'How about this one?'

Mellow, jazz-based music, a sultry-voiced female singer. Sunday-morning music. She suppressed the idea of waking up in Will's bed on a Sunday morning and making love to this record. 'A place to chill out,' she said. 'And nothing that needs a lot of looking after.'

He nodded. 'Well done. You're getting the hang of this. This was a rooftop garden in Docklands. A place to entertain on a Saturday night—and sleep off a hangover on Sunday morning.'

She wouldn't have a hangover, with Will. She wouldn't need to drink. His nearness was enough to make her dizzy.

'Go back to the first one,' she said. She listened for a while. 'It reminds me of raindrops.'

'It's Chopin's "Raindrop" prelude. Which means?'

'Water feature? Your client wants a fountain?' she guessed.

'Near enough. The garden backs on to the river.' He nodded to the file. 'Read, assimilate, and talk to me in twenty minutes.'

She felt the corner of her mouth quirk. '*You're* giving *me* a time limit?'

'Only because that's how you like working,' he shot back.

She read the file, glancing up at him every so often. He was clearly concentrating hard on whatever was on his laptop; his lips were very slightly parted and she could see the tip of his tongue caught between white, even teeth. In a faded black T-shirt and with that slightly too-long hair, plus the fact he clearly hadn't shaved that morning, he should've looked scruffy and a bit disreputable. Instead, he looked sexy as hell. Like a pirate. She could imagine him with a gold earring in one ear, and a red bandanna tied round his hair, and it made her knees weak. How easy it would be to reach across the small table and stroke his cheek, rub her thumb along his inviting lower lip, cup his chin and then touch her mouth to his…

Amanda was shocked to realise that she'd actually started to reach across towards him, and snatched her hand back. What on earth was wrong with her? She never got distracted like this at work. Several of her clients were good looking—probably more conventionally so than Will Daynes, because their hair was neater and they wore designer suits and shirts and ties—and she'd never once thought about kissing any of them.

It was just as well this lifeswap thing was only for two weeks. She could keep herself under control for two weeks, couldn't she?

Then she realised that Will was talking to her.

'Sorry. I missed what you said,' she admitted.

'Either that was the most boring file you've ever seen, or you're away with the fairies.' He laughed. 'And you don't have to be polite. Or answer that.'

'I was just surprised that your questions seemed to be—well—in a logical order.' Which was true. But it was also a million miles away from what she'd really been thinking about.

'If I don't ask, I don't find out what my clients need, and that means I can't give them what they want so I've failed in my job,' he said. 'Now, this is what we're working with.' He'd drawn a scale map, showing the aspect of the garden and its surroundings, and there were notes about the soil composition. The attention to detail surprised her—given Will's untidiness, she'd expected him to be a little more slapdash, taking the attitude that 'nearly there is good enough'. Instead, this was meticulous. Perfectionist. More the way she worked when she was detailing a client's systems.

Maybe they had more in common than she realised.

And clearly he knew his report by heart, because he talked her through building the garden, bouncing ideas off her and pointing out things on the mood board that he was going to adapt for the garden. He worked in pencil, she noticed, occasionally rubbing something out when a better idea occurred to him. And the end result was an incredibly detailed sketch.

'So there you have it. Your first garden,' he said with a smile.

It was hardly hers. 'You did most of it.'

'Teamwork, then.'

'I didn't exactly pull my weight,' she said.

'You did more than you think. You bounced some excellent ideas off me.' His smile broadened. 'But if you really want to do something for me…'

Down, girl, she warned her libido.

'…you can make us some lunch.'

CHAPTER SIX

'I DON'T cook,' Amanda warned Will.

'You don't have to cook salad. Well,' he corrected himself, 'not unless you're making a warm salad or you want to char the peppers first.'

'*Cold* salad I can do.'

'Okay.' His eyes were almost pure gold with mischief. 'The ingredients are in the fridge. I'll leave it up to you while I transfer some of these details to my computer.'

She opened Will's fridge and blinked. Nothing was in plastic boxes or bags, or shrink-wrapped: everything was in greaseproof paper or brown paper bags. A rummage in the salad drawer found her a lettuce with dirt still on it, wrapped in paper—a far cry from the bag of mixed leaves she was used to opening and tipping straight on to a plate. There was a red and an orange pepper, tomatoes in a brown paper bag, a cucumber that was clearly home-grown because it curved instead of being drainpipe-straight, and a brown paper bag of rocket.

Well, he'd set her a challenge—she had no intention of failing. Amanda didn't fail at anything, any more.

A bit of washing and chopping, and then she mixed the salad together in a large glass bowl. Will was a foodie, so she thought he'd expect something added on top.

Part of her wanted to give him the salad as it was—take it or leave it, because at the end of the day it was just fuel. But part of her wanted to please him. Wanted to make his eyes light up with pleasure. Wanted that sexy mouth to smile at her.

She poked about in the fridge and found a jar of olives and a hunk of parmesan. Although she spilled a bit of brine on the worktop, she managed to retrieve some of the olives from the jar and scattered them on top. The parmesan looked more like crumbled chunks than elegant thin slices, but it would do. There was a greaseproof packet filled with sliced ham, which she placed on a plate so they could help themselves.

'Lunch is ready when you are,' she said, looking over at Will.

And then she realised he'd been watching her. And he was smiling. Not quite the smile she'd had in mind. Was he laughing at her? She felt her eyes narrow.

His smile broadened. 'Don't scowl at me. It looks lovely. And I appreciate it even more because this isn't the sort of thing you normally do, is it?'

'No,' she admitted.

'Cooking's like gardening. You experiment. Try things out. If it doesn't work, it doesn't matter—you've learned something from it and know to try something different next time.'

She shook her head. 'It isn't like that in my job. You have to be accurate. There isn't any room for error—not unless you want to get a large fine for submitting false information.'

'That's a lot of pressure,' he observed.

She shrugged. 'I'm used to it.'

'Don't you ever think there might be something…more?' he asked softly.

'Like being stuck in a tiny village where everyone knows everyone else's business?' And where it was painfully obvious if you didn't fit in?

He didn't reply; he simply helped himself to the salad and started eating. 'Very nice,' he said. 'Thanks.'

She was fairly sure that he was feeding Sunny choice bits of ham under the table—but it was his house. It wasn't her place to tell him it wasn't hygienic.

'Did you sort your file?'

He nodded. 'We'll go and see the client tomorrow.'

'Don't you need to go to the garden centre?'

'I'm not there all the time,' he said, 'and the team's perfectly capable of getting on with what needs to be done.'

A level of trust she couldn't give her team. Not after the last time she'd trusted someone and then discovered, the day before the file was due in, that all the figures in a key section had been made up and she'd had to work through the night to fix it. She'd learned a lesson the hard way: as the senior on a job, she needed to spot-check her juniors' work.

'So, what's on the agenda for this afternoon?' she asked when they'd finished washing up.

Will glanced out of the window. 'Practical research, I think.'

She frowned. 'What's that?'

'Come and find out,' he invited. 'But you need to change first.'

Oh. So they were going to grub around in soil. She should've guessed that was what 'practical' meant.

'What you really need is a flowery dress and a straw hat,' he added, surprising her.

'Why?'

He shook his head. 'No matter. Jeans and a T-shirt will do fine. Remember the hat. And wear shoes you can walk in.'

Meaning the trainer-type things? Oh, wonderful.

By the time she'd changed, Sunny was settled in the back seat and Will had hooked up his MP3 player in the car. 'Today's a day for driving an open-topped car,' he said, sounding wistful.

'Your dream car?' she guessed.

He shook his head. 'I used to have one. It was way too small to fit much gardening equipment in the back. And, I…' He mumbled something into his hand.

'You what?'

'Got two speeding fines in the first week I had it,' he admitted, looking slightly rueful.

She could just imagine him in an open-topped sports car. Dark glasses, dressed completely in black, the wind ruffling his hair; just about any woman who saw him would melt into a puddle of hormones. And probably forget her fear about the fact he was driving way too fast. 'I see.'

'So I switched to a more, ahem, sedate model. One that suited a dog better, too.' He reached over to the back seat and ruffled Sunny's fur. 'Her mother, actually.'

'So you've had Sunny since she was born?'

He nodded. 'I still miss Sal—her mum—but Sunny's got the same sweet temperament. I can't work without a dog.'

Love me, love my dog. Yet another barrier between them. 'I suppose it goes with the territory. Being a countryman.'

'I suppose.' He shrugged. 'Want to choose some music?'

'Which garden do you suggest?'

He laughed. 'None. Try "Drive summer chill".'

It turned out to be slow, bluesy guitar music. Not the kind of stuff she was used to hearing on the radio on the rare occasions she switched it on.

As if guessing her thoughts, he said, 'I was brought up on Pink Floyd and Nick Drake by the original Sixties child.' His smile broadened. 'If you think I'm a hippy, you should meet him.'

'Your dad?'

For a moment, his face shuttered. Did that mean that his relationship with his parents was as strained as hers was with her own? 'Uncle,' he said.

His expression told her he didn't want to discuss it, so she let it be; she just listened to the music and watched their surroundings as he drove them into the city.

'Don't you need a permit to park here?' she asked, noticing a sign at the side of the road.

He stared at her in surprise for a moment, then seemed to shake himself. 'Good point. I always forget and I could do without a parking ticket.'

He parked in a nearby multi-storey car park, and sorted out Sunny's lead while Amanda got out of the car.

'So we're working in a garden in Cambridge?' she asked.

'No. Researching ideas,' he said.

Although she prided herself on her sense of direction, she would've been hopelessly lost in the maze of streets; Will seemed to know all the shortcuts and took her through narrow alleyways, past tiny cafés and second-hand bookshops, and finally through one of the colleges.

'This is the Backs,' he said. 'It's a bit touristy, but it's still beautiful. I thought we'd go on the river as it's the easiest way to see the gardens,' he said.

'Can't we walk?'

'Nope—the colleges own the river banks, so there's no public right of way.'

'What about Sunny? Will she be all right in a boat?'

The dog gave a soft woof, as if to reassure her.

'It's a punt, not a boat,' he said, and then his smile faded. 'Apart from the fact that she loves water, I'd never, *ever*, leave a dog locked in a parked car. People who do that should be locked up with the key thrown away for ever.'

There was a fierceness to his words that made her think this was personal. 'What happened?' she asked quietly.

'Let's just say that Sal's original owner was going to sue me for smashing his car window,' Will said, his voice soft and yet very, very dangerous at the same time.

So he'd rescued his first dog from an overheated car? Oh,

lord. 'I…I don't know what to say. I'm a bit nervous around dogs, but I'd never hurt one.'

Will regarded her for a moment, then nodded. 'I know. And I'd rather not talk about it, if you don't mind. Let's just leave it that justice was done and he won't be owning another animal. Ever. Let's go hire a punt.'

'You know how to paddle?'

'Pole,' he corrected with a smile. 'I've done it a few times.'

A few minutes later, she was seated in the middle of the flat-bottomed boat, with Will standing on the flat platform at the end of the boat, wielding a long pole.

'Just lie back and relax,' he said. 'Or are you as nervous about boats as you are about dogs?'

'I'm not a coward,' she said, lifting her chin.

'I didn't say you were.' He eyed her curiously. 'So why are you scared of dogs?'

'This enormous Alsatian came up to me when I was three. Snapped at me.' She rubbed her arm without thinking. 'The owner stopped it before it could take a second bite, but I've still got the scar.'

'I'm not surprised you're scared. The dog probably would've been bigger than you, at that age,' he said thoughtfully. 'Didn't your parents try to get you to stroke a puppy or an old, quiet dog, to take away your fear?'

'My parents weren't into pets.' A neighbour had brought them a puppy, but her mother had refused to keep it, citing Amanda's fear of dogs, but Amanda had overheard her mother complaining to her father that night about 'yet another tie'.

'Shame. I was lucky—Martin and Helen have always had at least two dogs and three cats.'

Again, no mention of his parents, she noticed. He sounded closer to his uncle and aunt.

He nodded at Sunny. 'She's great with kids. Though she does have a bad habit of stealing shoes.'

'I'll remember to keep mine out of the way.' Though, looking at the spaniel's huge brown eyes and soft mouth, she couldn't imagine Sunny actually chewing anything.

She glanced up at Will again. He'd taken off his shoes, she noticed, and was actually punting in bare feet. He reminded her more and more of a pirate.

And he had the sexiest feet she'd ever seen. Well shaped and clean and… 'Um—is that safe?' she asked, to cover her confusion.

He smiled. 'It's how I've done it since I was a student.'

'You were a student here?'

'No. I spent a lot of time around here in the holidays. Now, we're going from Silver Street Bridge down to the quayside at Magdalene and back again,' Will said. 'This first bridge is the Mathematical Bridge at Queens' College.' He laughed. 'Some of the tour guides will tell you that Isaac Newton built it—then the story goes that the Fellows and students took the bridge apart and couldn't put it back together, and that's why it looks so rickety and twisty.'

She turned round to glance at the bridge. 'So what's the truth?'

'Newton died over twenty years before it was built and he went to Trinity, not Clare. And think how big and heavy the pieces are.'

She studied it. 'Not easy to take apart.'

'It's built according to a mathematical analysis of the forces in it. Clever stuff.' His smile broadened as she turned to face him. 'I just think it looks pretty, especially in spring when all the crocuses are out. It's like a sheet of deepest purple covering the bank. It's lovely in winter, too, when the trees are draped in frost.'

He really adored this place: it was obvious in the way he talked about it and the look on his face. 'This is Clare. The Fellows' garden there is fantastic. Mind you, so is the one at Christ—that was Milton's favourite garden.'

Such a casual namedrop. She knew who Milton was, of course—she just hadn't studied him. She had a feeling that Will knew just about any fictional or poetical garden, and could quote accordingly. His deep, slightly posh voice would sound amazing, quoting poetry.

There was something decadent about leaning back against the cushions, watching Will propel the punt along—and she had to admit, he was good at it. Really good. She felt perfectly safe here.

Then she remembered her earlier vision of him as a pirate. He could be a pirate right now, taking her back to his ship…

No. To lighten the mood—and to stop her thinking about how even looking at Will made a little knot of lust tighten in her stomach—she asked, 'Ever thought about being a gondolier?'

He laughed. 'If you really want me to sing "*O Sole Mio…*" Actually, that's timely, because this is the Bridge of Sighs.'

'I thought the Bridge of Sighs was in Venice?'

'This one's built in the same style. That's how it got its name.'

'And you prefer the Cambridge one.'

He smiled. 'Yes. I love this city. Even though it's impossible to park and it's always full of students on bicycles. I love the fact the city's full of green spaces—and they don't let you walk on the grass in the colleges, so it *stays* green. I love the Botanical Garden, too. I might take you there later in the week.'

'Won't we be too busy working?'

'It counts as work. Background research,' he said. 'As does this.'

She scoffed. 'We're messing about on the river.'

'We're multi-tasking,' he corrected.

'Like how?'

'As you said, we're messing about on the river. Relaxing on a Sunday afternoon. But it's also educational,' he said. 'I brought you here to see the gardens, to look at how they work against the backdrop of the river. Which means that while you're lying there like a princess…'

He thought she was a spoiled brat? She glanced quickly at him. No, there was no censure in his expression. And this had been his idea, anyway. He was just teasing. That hot look in his eyes was her imagination, it was more of that stupid day-dream about him being a sexy pirate about to take her off to his lair and have his wicked way with her.

'What do you mean, princess?'

'Queen, even. "The barge she sat in, like a burnish'd throne…"' He gave her another of those hot looks, and her temperature went up a couple of degrees. What would it be like to lie back against the cushions with him leaning over her, that sensual mouth tracing over her skin until she forgot where and even who she was?

'You said this was a punt, not a barge.'

'Nicely corrected.'

There was a teasing glitter in his eyes; she just hoped he hadn't guessed why she'd said it—to stop herself leaping on him.

'Back to business. I brought you here so you can have a think about the garden we designed this morning,' he continued. 'Would you change any of it, now that you've seen what they can do here?'

She listened, fascinated, as he pointed out buildings of interest and features of the gardens he particularly liked, then told her about the narrow little streets in the town and the markets and the antiquarian bookshops and the offbeat museums.

'If you ever get fed up with gardening, you could be a tour guide,' she said, when they returned to the quay at Magdalene.

He laughed. 'I'll never get fed up with gardening. And I'd get bored, having to repeat myself over and over again. I like the challenge of the new.'

Was he warning her that he saw her as a challenge? Or was he warning her that she wouldn't be able to keep his attention for long enough?

He helped her out of the boat, and her arm tingled where he touched it. If he had this effect on her with such an impersonal touch, what on earth would it be like if he touched her more intimately? If he undid her shirt and stroked every inch of skin as he uncovered it. If he unclipped her bra and let her breasts spill into his hands. If he slid his hands under the hem of her skirt and smoothed her skin all the way up to the top of her thighs, and—

Oh, Lord. Slow, heavy desire throbbed through her at the thought.

And she really, really hoped he couldn't read her mind.

'Come on. I think Sunny could do with a walk—let's go out to Grantchester for afternoon tea,' he suggested.

'Where's Grantchester?' she asked.

'It's a village on the upper reaches of the river. Do you know the Rupert Brooke poem about lilacs being in bloom, the church clock standing at ten to three, and having honey for tea?'

She shook her head.

Softly, he quoted a few lines from the poem. And she was very glad they were leaning against the bridge, because her knees went decidedly weak. She'd been right in her earlier guess: Will could quote poetry about gardens from memory. And, with a gorgeous voice like his, Lord help her if he ever started quoting love poetry. She'd be a puddle of hormones within seconds.

'It sounds lovely,' she said, hoping the shivery feeling didn't show in her voice. 'Is it far?'

'No. A couple of miles, that's all.'

What she'd forgotten was that Will was used to walking a lot. She wasn't. Even though she worked out at the gym, she wasn't used to tramping down a country path. Forty minutes later, she felt hot and out of sorts—how was it possible to feel so sticky and fed up, when the cool clear water was running alongside them? Every so often she saw a punt glide past, and she wished she'd asked him to punt them up the river rather than walk all this way.

'Let's sit down a minute,' he said.

He'd noticed that she was struggling? Pride kicked in and she straightened her back. 'I'm all right.'

'Course you are. But I want to show you something. Well, not *show* exactly…but we need to sit still for this.' He sat on the bank, then lay back with his arms cushioning his head. Sunny nestled close to him.

For a second, Amanda actually thought about doing the same on his other side, resting her head against his shoulder and curving her arm round his waist and cuddling into him. And one of his arms would slide down to cradle her closer…

Then she pulled herself together and just sat on the bank next to him.

'Lie back,' he instructed, 'so you can see the sky. Look up through the trees.'

Sunlight slanted through the leaves and dappled the ground around them. It was a tiny piece of paradise, the air full of bird-song and the river running gently by them and the fields stretching out flatly to reveal a huge expanse of sky. A place where lovers had no doubt stopped to kiss, she thought. And when Will raised himself up on to one elbow, for a crazy moment she thought he was going to lean over, dip his head and brush his mouth against hers. Just as she'd imagined him doing under the Spanish orange trees he'd conjured into her mind.

Worse—she wanted him to. She really, really wanted him to kiss her. Here, in this perfect space. She could feel her lips parting and her eyes closing and…

'What can you hear?' he asked softly.

He wasn't going to kiss her. This was about the senses, not about sensual. A tiny shift in semantics, but one that made a huge difference.

And she was shocked to realise how disappointed she felt. 'Amanda?'

She swallowed hard. 'Birds singing.'

'Can you hear anything specific?'

She had no idea what she was supposed to be listening for. And she really didn't want him to guess what she'd just been thinking, so she grabbed the camera to put a barrier between them and started filming him. 'What should I be listening for?'

'Can you hear a bird singing something that sounds like "Did he do it? He-did-he-did-he-did?"' Will asked.

She paused, hoping that the camera was picking all this up. 'I think so.'

'That's a songthrush,' he said. 'And then there's the great tit—it sounds like a squeaky wheelbarrow.'

She listened, and heard the pause-and-squeak he'd told her about. 'Oh—yes!'

'Listen harder,' he said softly. 'Can you hear that little frrrrr sound, almost like a firework fizzing?'

She paused. 'Yes—just there.'

'That's a greenfinch,' he said.

'How do you know all this?' she asked.

'You listen for the sound and then you look around to see which bird made it.'

'I wouldn't even know where to start.'

'Just listen,' he said softly.

And amazingly, what she'd thought of as just background noise seemed to separate out—she could hear different songs. 'What's that one that sounds a bit like a bored lift attendant saying, "Going uuup, going uuup, going up now"?' she asked.

'Another blackbird.'

She stopped filming him. 'You know, you'd be a natural on TV.'

He shook his head. 'Not my thing. I like my life as it is.'

'You could teach people a lot.'

'I sometimes go into Fliss's school and do a workshop with the kids,' he said. 'It makes them think a bit about their environment. We plant sunflowers in the summer term, then harvest the seeds in the autumn term and make birdfeeders.'

She could see him doing that. Will Daynes would be brilliant with children; she could imagine him teaching children about plants and minibeasts and birds.

Shockingly, she could actually imagine him with children of his own. With a dark-haired girl and a little boy with her own colouring… The vision took her breath away. What on earth was wrong with her, imagining him with *her* children? For goodness' sake. Nothing was going on between them. And she most definitely wasn't planning to settle down and have children. That wasn't what she wanted. At all. She wasn't going to make the same mistake her mother had, ending up trapped in a cottage in the country with a child she didn't want.

'Ever thought about lecturing?' she asked.

'I'd be stuck indoors most of the time and I'd *loathe* it. I need to be outside,' he said simply. 'Though I do have links with one of the local colleges—some of their students do their work experience with me. They do a bit of casual work for me in the holidays or at weekends, too.'

No wonder he'd found it so easy to teach her about gardening. He'd done this countless times before.

And she was beginning to think that there was nothing at all she could teach him.

'Come on. I want a cup of tea. And some cake,' he said, getting to his feet in one lithe movement. He held out a hand to pull her up. Again, her skin tingled where he touched her. But he didn't seem in the slightest bit affected by the skin-to-skin contact, and no way was she going to let him know what it did to her. She didn't want him to think she was needy.

When they reached the village, he ordered them afternoon tea in a little café, and found them a chair underneath apple trees.

Tiny sandwiches were served along with gorgeous cake; Sunny, once she'd had her fill from a water bowl, lay between them, looking hopeful. On impulse, Amanda took the ham out of her sandwich. Will had said that Sunny was gentle, that she wouldn't snap or hurt her…and Amanda was charmed at how gentle the dog was when she took the ham from Amanda's fingers. And at how the dog licked her fingers, as if to say thank you.

'She's suckered you, then,' Will commented with a smile.

Amanda felt her eyes widen. 'Sorry. I should've asked you first.'

'No worries. Like all spaniels, she's incredibly greedy. A bit of ham won't do her any harm.' He ruffled his dog's fur. 'I'm glad she's helping you with your fear of dogs,' he added softly.

Yeah. That was one thing she'd be able to take back from this week—she wasn't scared any more.

Of dogs, that was. Because when they returned to the car she realised she hadn't looked at her watch once all day. Will had made her forget the importance of time. And that was a very, very dangerous thing.

CHAPTER SEVEN

WILL LAY back against the pillows, staring out of the window. The cottage wasn't overlooked, so he hadn't bothered closing the curtains at the window with a view on to the garden; he enjoyed watching the sky darken and the stars slowly wheeling round.

But tonight he wasn't seeing the constellations. The picture in his head was of Amanda, lying back against the grass in Grantchester Meadows earlier that afternoon, her eyes closed and her mouth very slightly parted. He'd been propped up on one elbow. How easy it would've been to lean over, dip his head and steal a kiss.

She had a beautiful mouth. A perfect rosebud. And he'd just bet she had no idea how tempting it was. Or how the soft cotton of her T-shirt had settled against her body, revealing curves he wanted to smooth with his palms and tease with his fingertips. He'd wanted to see her hair mussed by the grass, her mouth reddened with passion, her head tipped back in abandonment as he touched her, stroked her, teased her, and brought her nearer and nearer to the edge.

Or maybe she *had* guessed. Maybe that had been why she'd suddenly grabbed the camera and filmed him talking about birdsong.

He'd talked about one of the senses. Sound. But that hadn't

been the uppermost one in his mind. His fingertips had been tingling, yearning to touch her skin and find out just how soft it was. And his mouth had wanted to know exactly how she tasted. He'd wanted to breathe in her scent, hear the change in her voice and her breathing as her arousal grew. See her pupils dilate and the ice-blue of her eyes sharpen with desire.

He knew she didn't do relationships. Neither did he, right now. And a relationship with her was out of the question, any-way—he loathed her world, the people and the attitudes and the brittleness. But he was beginning to think that a short, mad affair might be the best way forward; if they could get the physical attraction out of the way, they'd be able to concen-trate on business.

Tomorrow, he'd find the right moment—and suggest it.

The next morning, Will woke to the smell of coffee. He glanced at the clock. It wasn't even seven yet. He had a nasty feeling that Amanda was one of these women who was at her desk be-fore eight in the morning and didn't leave until almost eight at night. He showered swiftly, dragged a comb through his hair, dressed at the speed of sound and came downstairs to find her sitting at the kitchen table, working on a laptop computer.

But just as he was about to make a rude comment about workaholics, he noticed that Sunny was sitting with her head on Amanda's knee, and Amanda was fondling the dog's ears with her left hand. And Amanda was actually dressed for his kind of work—in jeans and a T-shirt.

Was he in some kind of parallel universe? Amanda was a buttoned-up businesswoman who was afraid of dogs. But the woman sitting at the kitchen table was someone else. Some-one warmer. Softer.

Someone he could lose his heart to, if he wasn't careful.

His head knew that she was absolutely Miss Wrong. So why was he getting that warm feeling in the pit of his stomach every time he looked at her? Why did the ends of his fingers tingle with the need to touch her?

He became aware of a humming noise. 'What's that?' he asked.

'The washing machine. The weather forecast says it's going to be good today. Might as well put the washing out to dry before we go out—it'll save messing about with the dryer, later.'

His eyes narrowed. 'You've done the washing.'

She shrugged. 'There was enough to make a load.'

'My washing as well as yours?' The idea of her clothes tangling with his made him think about her limbs tangling with his. Very pleasurably. It was exactly what he'd dreamt about for what seemed like the whole of the previous night.

'And the towels. More efficient that way.'

The word broke the spell. No, he wasn't in a parallel universe. *Efficient*. That was Amanda all over. Efficient, organised—an ice maiden who was so far removed from her senses, it was untrue. He sat down and poured himself a mug of coffee from the cafétière; Sunny padded over to him and rubbed her nose against his knee.

'So what are you working on?' he asked.

'The client questionnaire. You know, you could save a lot of time by emailing your client a list of the questions you need to ask and getting them to start filling them out in advance.'

She was organising him. Putting a structure in place. He'd bet she'd even tried grouping the questions together in what she saw as a logical order—gleaned from the file on the design they'd worked on together the previous day, and the file he'd given her as bedtime reading. 'I hate to burst your bubble,' he said softly, 'but I've tried that already. And I've found that what they write on a questionnaire often isn't the same thing at all as what they really want. It's head stuff rather than heart stuff.'

'How do you mean?'

'They write down what they think they should have, not

what they really want. It's only when they're chatting to me and say that they'd really love such-and-such a feature but they know their garden's too small that I can show them how to scale things down or create the same kind of effect with different plants.'

'I see.'

He noticed the glimmer of disappointment the second before she masked it. And he couldn't help reaching out to squeeze her hand. Just briefly. Comforting her. Even though the touch of her skin made his whole hand tingle with awareness. 'Hey. It was a good thought. Though I thought accountants were all about—well—figures?'

'Business systems, too. Making things work efficiently so the client can concentrate on the important bits of their job instead of getting bogged down in paperwork.' She smiled wryly. 'I've worked with personal tax clients who just bring me a shoebox full of receipts to sort out at the end of the tax year. And they're panicking they might've lost something important.'

'Uh-huh.' He knew that feeling. It had happened to him, a couple of times. Filing had never been at the top of his agenda.

'So I've set up an easy system for them—a concertina file, where one pocket's for stationery and another's for travel, and so on. At the end of the month they just drop the contents of each pocket into an envelope, seal it and write the name of the month and the title of the pocket on the front, and that saves a lot of time sorting through. It means their accountancy bill's lower because we don't have to spend so much time sorting out the files, and they don't have to worry about whether they've lost anything. Just a tiny, tiny bit of organisation and it's so much less stressful for them.'

'It means your company loses out on billing hours,' he pointed out.

'But if I left things as they were, we wouldn't be giving the client the best-value service. And that's dishonest. Wrong.'

She might be bossy and a control freak, but she meant well. The last remnants of his irritation vanished, replaced by a twinge of guilt. Honesty was important to her. And he'd been lying to her. It was for the best of reasons, but it was still lying.

Maybe today he'd find a way of telling her the truth, without making a complete hash of it.

'So is there a schedule today?' she asked.

'We're seeing my client at ten to discuss the plan, then going out to see another client to start the groundwork for a design that's already been agreed.'

'Is Sunny coming with us?'

'Not today. If it's going to be hot, she'll find travelling miserable.' He fondled the dog's ears. 'But I promise I'll take you on a long walk in the Fens as soon as we get home,' he said softly to the dog.

When they'd sorted out the washing and he'd loaded his car with the tools he needed, they set off.

And although Will knew that Amanda didn't watch much television, he was quite prepared for the shock of recognition in her face when his first client opened the door to them—a high-profile actress in a long-running television series.

Will had said he was a garden designer. He hadn't told her the half of it! Landscaping consultant to the rich and famous, more like.

'Why didn't you warn me?' she asked when they were back in the car.

'What?'

'Your client. She's *famous*. I mean, even *I* know who she is, and I don't watch the show! I can't believe you didn't make me sign a confidentiality agreement.'

'No need. I trust you.'

'And if you wake up on Friday and see it splashed all over the gossip mags?'

He shrugged. 'I'll deal with it if it happens. Though I don't think it will.'

He trusted her that much?

Clearly he did, because after a quick sandwich in a nearby pub he drove them to St John's Wood and introduced her to the client whose garden they'd be working on that week. The woman's surname meant absolutely nothing to Amanda—but the framed photographs of her husband were definitely familiar. It was a face she'd seen on the news. A lot.

'This place belongs to a famous footballer!' she hissed when they were in the garden.

'And?'

Will seemed completely unperturbed. Not in the least bit starstruck.

'Are you *sure* you don't want me to sign a confidentiality thing?'

'Yup.' He smiled at her. 'Though you might want to stick this fork in me by the end of the day,' he added, handing it to her. 'This is London clay.'

'What's wrong with clay?'

He bent down and scooped up a handful. 'See how it rolls into a ball and keeps its shape? That means there aren't many air spaces and it doesn't drain well.'

'So it gets waterlogged?' she guessed.

'In winter, yes; and in summer it's rock hard. So what we have to do is dig in some good organic matter to improve the soil crumb and drainage. The good news is, it holds nutrients better than other types of soil. It's brilliant for roses—which is just as well, as they want a rose arbour here.' He gave her a sidelong look. 'We have one other teensy problem.'

The way he said it made her realise it was a big problem. 'What's that?'

He pulled a leaf from a plant and showed it to her. 'Ground elder. It spreads like crazy, it doesn't die off in the winter and the only way to get rid of it is to dig up every single tiny piece of root.' He handed her a pair of padded gloves. 'You'll need these. You're not used to digging, so if your hands start to feel at all sore I want you to stop. Don't be stubborn about it,' he warned, 'because blisters aren't pleasant. And you need to stop every fifteen minutes to have a drink of water.'

Will—the most laid-back, spontaneous man she'd ever met—was working to a schedule? She couldn't help asking in disbelief, 'You're actually planning in breaks?'

'Just making sure you don't dehydrate, as it's such a warm day. I don't want you overdoing things and getting ill.'

He was looking after her. As any boss would look after a team, she reminded herself. As she looked after her own team, by making sure they had a proper lunch break—even if she didn't—and were clear about their tasks and knew to come to her if they were stuck.

But with Will, things seemed *personal*. As if he really cared.

When he made Amanda stop for a drink, he also made her take off the gloves and show him her hands. 'Hmm,' he said. He ran his fingers very lightly over her palm at the base of her fingers—weirdly, it felt as if he was stroking her spine and it made her want to purr with pleasure.

'Does that hurt at all?' he asked.

'No.' Her voice sounded croaky, even to her own ears, and she really hoped he'd put it down to a dry throat—one caused by thirst, not desire.

'Good. The second you feel even the slightest twinge, I want you to stop.' His mouth compressed. 'This is hard work, especially in this sort of soil. It's too much to expect you to do. I'll find you something easier.'

He was offering her a cop-out? No way. She didn't want him thinking she couldn't cope with any challenge he threw her way. And this whole week was about flexibility, wasn't it? She lifted her chin. 'I'm shadowing you. So I'm doing what you're doing.'

'Remember, I'm used to this and I'm bigger than you are. This isn't a competition, Amanda,' he said softly. 'It's all about teamwork.'

Teamwork. Funny how that word made her insides glow.

'You're doing well—especially for a gardening rookie,' he said, and drained his glass of water.

She followed suit. 'Let's blitz the ground elder.'

She watched him surreptitiously as he dug. The way he moved was almost like a ballet dancer—graceful, sure and strong. It was just as well he hadn't taken his T-shirt off because, half-naked, he would be more than tempting.

No doubt their client thought so, too, because she kept popping down to see them. She hardly bothered speaking to Amanda, but Will got the full-wattage smile and the breathy little voice and the batted eyelashes—false ones, too, Amanda noted.

Surely he could see the woman was flirting with him? After all, who on earth wore designer high heels and floaty cocktail dresses and full make-up when they were just pottering about in the garden?

'What?' he asked when the client had sashayed back to the house.

'I didn't say a word.'

'You didn't have to. You look immensely disapproving.'

Amanda stared at him. 'Well, she's married.'

'Uh-huh.'

'She's *flirting* with you, Will.'

'And that's a problem?'

He didn't sound in the slightest bit bothered. Well, he was probably used to women falling at his feet. He probably flirted all the time—though he hadn't really flirted with Amanda.

Not that she was jealous.

At all.

She resolved to say nothing, and kept digging.

Then she became aware that Will's hand was resting on the shaft of her spade; she stopped and looked up at him.

'Just for the record, Amanda, I believe in fidelity. I'm single, but she's not. Flirting's harmless. I don't mind having a laugh with my clients. But if she actually propositioned me, it would be a different matter and I'd make sure I was never here on my own with her again,' he said softly. 'I'm here to do a job, and that's all: to make this a dream garden. If she's having Lady Chatterley fantasies to go with it, they'll just have to stay in her head, because I have absolutely no intention of acting them out for her.'

Amanda felt the colour flood into her cheeks. 'Oh.'

'And just to make sure we're clear on that…' He stripped off his gloves, cupped her face in both hands, and brushed his lips lightly against hers. Once, twice…

His mouth teased hers, nibbling gently at her lower lip until, with a sigh, she opened her mouth. And then the kiss deepened and her senses went into overload. She knew her eyes were closed, but she could see coloured lights and hear the birds singing. She could smell the sweet, loamy scent of freshly dug earth and feel the sun warming her skin. And Will's mouth tasted tangy, of cool lemon and warm man.

Just as unexpectedly as it had started, the kiss stopped.

'Why did you do that?' she asked, her voice a husky whisper.

'Because our client is standing at her French windows, watching us. Now she'll think you're not just shadowing me, you're involved with me as well, and that will put me off limits as far as she's concerned. She's not going to give me a blatant come-on in front of my girlfriend. My lover,' he added in a voice so husky it made her knees weak.

His eyes were the most peculiar colour. Almost like molten silver. Sexy as hell. And she was shocked to realise she wanted him to kiss her again. For one crazy moment she nearly reached up to pull his head back down to hers and demand a replay.

'Expect huffs from her for the rest of the day—but there won't be any more flirting. Okay?'

No. She didn't feel okay at all. Her head was spinning. *Will Daynes had just kissed her.* It had been the most spectacular kiss of her life—but from the coolness of his tone and the way he'd replaced his gloves and gone back to digging out the ground elder, it had meant nothing to him. Nothing at all. It had all been for show. To make the client think that Amanda was his lover.

His lover.

Of course she wasn't. But now the idea was in her head, it wouldn't go away. What would it be like to be Will's lover? To find out where he liked being touched, where he liked being kissed? To have him explore her with the same intensity and passion he gave to his other love, gardening?

Oh-h-h.

'Okay,' she lied, and resumed her battle with the weeds.

That kiss had definitely been a mistake, Will thought. He really shouldn't have done it. He'd annoyed his client—she'd been very terse with them both when she'd brought out a jug of cold drink—and he'd made Amanda wary of him. She'd avoided all eye contact ever since; she hadn't even looked at him when they'd stopped for a drink. So much for his earlier idea of suggesting a mad, short-lived affair. It was completely out of the question. There was no way she would consider it.

The kiss hadn't sated his desire for her either. It had made it a hundred times worse. Now he knew what it was like to kiss her, he wanted to do it again. And again, until neither of them could speak coherently.

Well, he'd just have to exercise a bit of self-control.

* * *

The journey from London to Cambridgeshire took a long, long time, Amanda thought. Will didn't bother making conversation; he just put some music on. Music that maybe relaxed him, but made her feel taut as a wire. It was music with a sensual beat—the sort of songs she could imagine in the background as they made love.

Not that she was going to make love with him.

She didn't do casual relationships, and she most definitely wasn't in the market for marriage and babies and having to put her career second. She'd seen what that had done to her mother. It wasn't going to be the same for her.

At last they were back at the cottage. Sunny bounced around the kitchen, clearly delighted to see him again, and Will made a huge fuss of her. Then, without actually making eye contact, he said to Amanda, 'The bathroom's all yours.'

Good. Maybe she could scrub this ridiculous desire away.

'What about you?'

'I'm used to digging. A shower'll do me fine. Don't rush— let the water soak the ache out of your muscles.'

And if it didn't, would he offer to knead the soreness out himself?

Uh. Bad thought. It was only one step from kneading her muscles to stroking her skin, and one step from stroking to caressing, and one step from caressing to—

She realised that he was talking again, and hoped he wasn't waiting for a response. She didn't have a clue what he'd just said.

'Take as long as you like,' he said. 'I'll cook dinner when you're ready—and in the meantime I'll take Sunny for a walk.'

A bath full of bubbles. She never lounged around like this; a shower was more efficient after a long day at work or a session at the gym. But it felt good to have the hot water melting away the strains of an afternoon's digging.

It would be even better if she could stop reliving the moment he'd kissed her. The feel of his mouth against hers. The way he'd coaxed her into kissing him back.

Maybe she should break her personal rule and suggest it. A mad, crazy, one-night stand to get this thing between them out of their systems, and then they could concentrate on Dee's project.

But if he turned her down…she'd never be able to face him again.

Annoyed with herself, she climbed out of the bath, dried herself, and dressed in clothes more within her comfort zone—a business suit. Just to remind herself that things between her and Will were strictly business.

She walked into the kitchen at the same time as he did.

'You look hot,' she said—then realised her words could be taken to mean something she hadn't intended. Not consciously, anyway.

'It's boiling outside. I could do with a long, cold drink,' he admitted. 'Join me?'

'I'll make it,' she said.

Funny how they'd slipped into a routine—she sorted the drinks while he cooked.

'Let's eat outside tonight,' he suggested.

Weird how it felt so intimate, she thought as she carried the cutlery and drinks through to the patio. The garden had only low fencing around it, and she could see the land stretching for miles around. Yet it felt as if they were in a tiny, tiny space.

It was probably her imagination. He'd kissed her, yes—but it had been for show, to get a message across to his client. It was not because he, Will Daynes, wanted to kiss her, Amanda Neave.

'This is very good,' she said after her first taste. Simple: grilled chicken and a warm pasta salad laced with a tomato, olive and basil sauce. Yet it tasted better than the food in most of the restaurants she ate at in London.

Will could've had a career as a chef, she mused. He didn't seem to have any cookery books around, so he clearly didn't make things from recipes. And yet he wasn't domesticated: it was just a question of being good at anything he tried. Will Daynes, she thought, was a bit like a wild flower. Sturdy, strong, and secure in his environment, but put him in the city and he'd droop. This was where he belonged. Not in her world.

'I love the huge skies out here,' he said. 'The way you can watch the sun set, and see the stars come out.'

'It's pretty,' she said, looking up at the clouds.

'A mackerel sky,' he said.

'Because it looks like the scales on a mackerel?' she guessed.

He nodded, looking pleased that she'd cottoned on so quickly. 'It means there's probably going to be some rain overnight.'

'The countryman's way of forecasting the weather?'

'Sure. Everyone knows the one about "red sky at night, shepherd's delight".' He gave her an easy smile. 'The saying that goes with this one is "mackerel sky, mackerel sky, never long wet and never long dry".'

'How do you *know* all this stuff?'

'Martin taught me some; and I read a lot as a kid.'

A sudden hardness in his expression warned her not to ask any more. She switched topic. 'Don't you find it lonely out here,' she asked, 'with these flat fields stretching out for miles and miles?'

'I couldn't live anywhere else but Cambridgeshire,' he said quietly. 'I like the empty spaces and wide skies.'

It was the opposite for her—she liked the busyness of London, where something was always happening, and although there were always people around they weren't endlessly inquisitive.

She and Will were complete opposites. And there could be no compromise. She couldn't settle out here; and he would never settle in London. They had no future together. So there was no point in starting something that would only end in tears.

She'd just have to keep her imagination on its usual tight rein.

CHAPTER EIGHT

TUESDAY STARTED off very similar to Monday—an early start and a drive to St John's Wood, but this time Sunny came with them and drowsed in a sunlit patch of grass while Will and Amanda worked on digging out the ground elder.

Despite her good intentions, Amanda couldn't stop thinking about the previous day and the way Will had kissed her. Worse, she couldn't stop wondering if he'd do it again…or suppress the disappointment when he didn't.

Halfway through the afternoon, Will's mobile phone rang. Although she tried not to listen to the conversation, she really couldn't help overhearing him. She was shocked to realise that he was talking figures. Prices and budgets and percentages. If she closed her eyes, she'd imagine she was listening to a man at a board meeting—a man wearing a dark suit, white shirt, silk tie and polished handmade shoes, with a set of figures and a laptop in front of him.

In real life, she was watching a man wearing faded, dusty jeans and an equally disreputable T-shirt, not to mention scruffy green wellies; instead of sitting on an executive chair in a board room, he was sprawled on a patch of grass and there weren't any papers in sight, let alone a computer.

And yet he was clearly more than holding his own in the

conversation. All the necessary figures were in his head—did he have some kind of photographic memory? she wondered.

If it wasn't for the fact it was obvious that Will knew about plants, she'd think she'd been had. Because right now he didn't sound a bit like the hick countryman who was supposed to be her opposite. He sounded like a man well used to dealing with her world.

He wouldn't lie to her, though. She'd only known him a couple of days, but she was a good judge of character. Will Daynes wasn't the deceitful type.

She continued attacking the ground elder. Then something hot and clawlike raked over her arm. 'Ow!'

'You all right?' Will asked.

'Yes,' she fibbed.

But the soreness on her arm got worse. And when she looked at the painful area, she saw raised pink bumps all over it.

'Nettle rash,' Will said, taking a look at it. 'You got too close to the stingers. Sorry, I should've warned you to steer clear.'

She brushed it aside. 'I'll be okay.'

'Don't be such a martyr.' He pulled a leaf from a nearby plant. 'Here. Let me rub this over it.'

'Herbal medicine, now?' Embarrassment made her sharp.

'It's a dock leaf. Rub it on your arm and it'll stop the pain and swelling and make the rash go down quicker.' He shrugged and put the leaf back on the ground. 'Up to you if you prefer to be a victim and suffer.'

She grimaced, aware she'd been rude to him. 'Sorry. I didn't mean to snap. I'm just not used to people making a fuss over me.' She picked up the dock leaf and rubbed it against her skin. Strangely, her skin began to feel cooler almost immediately. 'Thanks for the advice.'

'No worries. Nettle stings aren't pleasant.' He gave her a sidelong look. 'Want to know something really weird about nettles?'

He had that mischievous little-boy look about him that she was beginning to find distinctly appealing. 'Go on.'

'They grow about thirty centimetres taller in land that has bodies buried in it—that's why they're always huge in churchyards.'

'How do you *know* this stuff?' she asked. Then, without giving him time to answer, said, 'Don't tell me—your uncle, Martin?'

'That's the one.'

'He sounds nice.'

'He is.'

And Will wasn't giving away any more information, she noted. He was even cagier about his background than she was. Strange. Because surely parents would be proud of a son who was doing well in a job he loved?

Not that hers were proud of her. Her father was distant, and her mother... Well, she'd made no secret of the fact she resented the fact her daughter was doing what she hadn't been able to do. Even being a high flyer hadn't made Amanda fit into her family.

Sometimes, she wondered if she'd ever fit in anywhere. If she'd ever really belong.

She brushed the doubts away and continued digging. When she made partner, of course she'd belong. She'd have a place. And a car parking space with her name stamped all over it, to prove it.

Two sleepless nights hadn't done much for Will's equilibrium. Spending the Wednesday morning in the garden centre had made it worse, too. Sharing a desk—Martin's very untidy, messy desk—with Amanda, shuffling paperwork and looking at budgets and what-have-you. And all the time, he couldn't stop thinking about how he could sweep all the papers from it with one extravagant gesture, lift her on to the desktop and...

He was going crazy. There were dozens of reasons why he

shouldn't do anything of the kind. Number one, there wasn't a lock on the door and anyone could walk in at any time and catch them in a very compromising position. Number two, Amanda had been wary of him since he'd kissed her among the ground elder on Monday afternoon, so giving in to the urge to grab her right now would make her even warier. Number three, it wasn't his desk anyway, and his dog happened to be sitting underneath it.

The list could go on and on and on.

And since when was a pair of bright green overalls a sexy garment anyway?

Since Amanda Neave had been wearing it, he thought grimly. He needed some fresh air to get some sense into his head again. Or, better still, caffeine.

'I need coffee,' he muttered. 'Want one?'

'Thanks. That'd be nice.' As he reached the door, she said his name.

He paused and looked back at her. 'What?'

'Are you all right?' she asked.

No. Because I can't stop thinking about kissing you, he thought. 'Sure,' he fibbed. 'Why?'

'You don't seem, um, in a very good mood today.'

'Lack of…' Sleep. Sex. '…caffeine.'

The coffee didn't help much, because he could still smell her perfume.

By lunchtime Will had had enough. If he didn't get out of here, right now, he knew he'd do something stupid. Like grabbing Amanda and kissing her until he forgot where he was.

'We're going into town,' he announced abruptly.

'Bunking off?' Amanda asked.

'No. Look, all the admin's been sorted. We've looked at stock figures and budgets.' He took a deep breath. 'And I can't do more than half a day in the office without going stir-crazy.'

'You're going to find next week a bit tough, then,' she observed.

'About as tough as you find it wearing jeans instead of a business suit,' he snapped back.

She raised an eyebrow. 'You really *are* out of sorts.'

'Sorry,' he muttered. 'I shouldn't take it out on you.'

'No offence taken.'

No. Because the cool, poised ice maiden didn't seem to get rattled about anything. She planned her way round everything. And Will felt an overwhelming need to see her melt. No, more than melt—he wanted to turn her into a volcano. He wanted to see her let go. He wanted to release the passion he was sure lay locked underneath that cool façade.

Right now.

'Let's go,' he announced.

He called over at the reception area on their way out to say that he was contactable on his mobile if anything cropped up, drove back to the cottage to drop Sunny home, then drove Amanda into Cambridge. With an effort, he remembered to leave the car in a car park rather than in the space outside his house, then marched her into a patisserie and ordered two baguettes.

'Ordering for me, now?' she asked.

He gave her a look that said very plainly, don't argue; it seemed to work, because she subsided. And she didn't say a word when he dragged her into another bakery for Chelsea buns. He needed a sugar fix.

He needed something much sweeter, actually. But a sugar fix would have to do.

For now.

'Chelsea buns?' she asked as they left the shop.

'World famous for them for the last eighty-odd years,' he said. 'They do the best chocolate cake in the world, too.'

And then, at last, they were in the Botanical Garden. He

led Amanda over to the lakeside gardens and they sat down to eat their lunch, watching the birdlife and the dragonflies. Being in a garden usually soothed his soul, yet today the tension inside him wouldn't ease.

He lay back and closed his eyes. Right now he really needed his equilibrium back. He needed to get himself back under control.

And then he felt a hand stroke his hair back from his forehead.

Was he having some kind of physical hallucination, or had Amanda just…?

He opened his eyes to see her looking at him, her lower lip caught between her teeth.

'Amanda? Did you just…?' His voice faded at the embarrassment on her face—embarrassment, he guessed, at being caught acting completely out of character.

She flushed. 'Yes.'

'Why?'

She shook her head. 'I don't know. But I don't like it when you look sad. You're always smiling, always laid back. Today, you seem stressed. And I…' she sighed '…I don't know how to make you feel better. I'm not good at this sort of thing. I'm rubbish with people.'

Her eyes were a deep, intense blue—and filled with pain. Her words suddenly filtered into his consciousness. She felt bad because she didn't know how to make him smile…because she thought she wasn't good with people.

He sat up, curled his fingers round hers, and rubbed the pad of his thumb across the back of her hand. 'How do you mean, you're rubbish with people? You've been okay with me.'

She shook her head. 'I'm not like you, Will. People warm to you. They *like* you. You make their worlds light up. The staff at the garden centre, your customers, your clients— even when they're in a huff with you, you can still make them smile.' She looked bleak. 'Somehow, you seem to just charm them.'

He frowned. 'I don't set out to charm people.'

'You don't even have to try. It's inbuilt. I bet kids flock to you, and dogs and cats and…' Her voice actually sounded wobbly. She clearly knew it, because she closed her mouth and looked away from him.

'Hey.' He dropped her hand and put his arm round her, held her close. 'It's all right.'

She shrugged him away. 'Just ignore me. It must be PMT or something.'

No, it wasn't. She was being honest with him and letting him see a part of her she'd maybe never shown anyone else. And he wasn't going to let her hide it away again and bury the pain—like a splinter, it would fester and the feeling would get worse and worse. He took her hand again. 'You really think people don't like you?'

'I know they don't.' She didn't sound in the least bit self-pitying—typical Amanda, she was brisk and matter of fact about it. 'Even Dee…sometimes I think she just puts up with me because I don't give her any hassle, I'm never late paying my share of the rent and I don't leave the place in a mess like her last flatmate did.' When he continued to hold her, her words came out in a rush, as if they'd been walled up for years and years and years and finally the dam had burst. 'Her friends all think I'm too straight and boring. And even at work I don't really fit in. I bet you've never gone into work and heard people talking about a party at the weekend and then realised you were the only one who wasn't invited because you're not one of the crowd—you're not trendy or exciting to be with.'

His heart went out to her. She'd been rejected; and he'd just bet she'd done her best not to show how upset she was. The ice maiden, so cool and calm and collected. Except she was crying inside, where nobody could see.

'I'm sorry,' he said softly.

She lifted her chin in a clear attempt to be dismissive about it. 'I wouldn't have gone to the party anyway. I was busy.'

Working. That was obvious. 'But it still would've been nice to be invited.'

'I don't need pity. Not from you, not from anyone.' She took a deep breath. 'And if you tell anyone about this, I...I may just have to kill you.'

Brave words. A flip, throwaway phrase, an attempt at being funny—and it didn't work, because he could still hear the hurt in her voice. He stroked her face. 'I've got a better idea than that,' he said softly. 'Why don't you kiss me instead?'

Her eyes widened. 'What?'

'Kiss me,' he whispered. 'Let me kiss you back. Kiss you better.'

She shivered. 'We can't. We're in a public place.'

'Forty acres of garden. People come here to see the plants. They're not going to look at you and me. They're not going to notice one little kiss.' He scooped her up onto his lap to draw her closer. This was just where he wanted her. In his arms. 'If you'd been called Katharina instead of Amanda, I could've said, "Kiss me, Kate."'

Her eyes narrowed as she caught the reference. 'Are you saying I'm a shrew?'

He grinned. 'Ah, now I was banking on you not knowing your Shakespeare.' After all, she hadn't picked up on his reference to Cleopatra, in the punt.

'So now you think I'm ignorant.'

He saw the glimmer of hurt in her eyes before she masked it again, and he tightened his arms round her, not willing to let her wriggle off his lap. This was too important. 'No, I don't. But I do think maybe there's a valid point in this life-swap stuff. Maybe we can teach each other things. Fill in the gaps for each other.' He leaned forward and kissed the tip of her nose. 'I don't think people *dislike* you, Amanda. I think they're scared of you. You have very exacting standards—and they're terrified they won't match up to them.' He paused. 'Do you really want to know why I was in a bad mood this morning?'

She was silent. Wide-eyed. And Lord, he wanted to kiss her. Kiss all the hurt away and make her smile again.

'I'll tell you anyway. It's because I kissed you on Monday. And I haven't been able to stop thinking about it since. In my head, I know this is crazy. You belong in a city, and I couldn't stand being in that sort of cage; just as you don't like the wide open spaces around here. But that's my head talking.' She'd told him a secret. He'd tell her one in return. Even up the balance. 'If I'd listened to my head, ten years ago, I probably would've ended up doing the same sort of job that you do.'

She blinked in surprise. 'You would've been an accountant?'

'Or worked in finance of some sort,' he agreed. 'I turned down an unconditional offer to read PPE at Oxford.'

'Why didn't you apply for botany or something instead?'

It wasn't the reaction he'd expected. He'd been sure that she would've sided with his parents, and claimed he was completely crazy for turning down the offer. But Amanda had seen the point straight away: it was the wrong course for him. And the way she'd asked why… It didn't sound judgemental. She really wanted to know his reasons for applying for the PPE.

'Because in my heart, I knew it wasn't what I wanted,' he said softly. 'I didn't want to work in a lab or in research, which is probably what would've happened if I'd chosen botany. I wanted to work with plants, with people. Garden design. Making magic. I only applied to Oxford to—well, to stop my parents nagging. I never had any intention of going there because they didn't do the course I wanted. Yes, if I'd listened to my head, I probably could've been earning ten times my current annual salary by now…but I would also have been seriously miserable. I'd probably have ended up drinking too much or doing recreational drugs to block out the fact I'd made the wrong choice.'

'Drugs?' She looked wary.

He smiled wryly, guessing what she wanted to know. 'Don't worry, I don't do them. Never have. I don't even drink that much—the occasional beer, a couple of glasses of wine if I'm out for dinner somewhere, and that's about all. What I'm trying to say—very badly—is that I had to make a choice. Listen to my heart or listen to my head. And I made the right choice for me. Not everyone agrees with that.' His parents still didn't. 'But sometimes less is more. And sometimes your head's plain wrong. Sometimes it's better to listen to your heart instead.' He took her hand and placed it on his heart. 'What does this say to you?'

'I don't know.'

'Then I'll translate it for you.' His gaze was fixed very firmly on her mouth. 'Kiss me.'

'I…I don't do this sort of thing. I don't have casual affairs.'

He had, in the past. But he had a nasty feeling there would be nothing casual about this. Which was yet another reason why he shouldn't do it. But he couldn't help smoothing the pad of his thumb over her lower lip. 'My head's telling me to stop right now. But my heart's telling me that this is right. Kiss me, Amanda.' He tilted his head back in invitation, wanting her to make the move.

Slowly, so slowly that he could barely hold his impatience in check, she reached up, slid her hands round his neck, and touched her mouth to his. Almost shyly, at first—a kiss so sweet that it made his bones melt.

Even though he wanted to pull her closer, deepen the kiss and let this thing between them explode, he let her set the pace. It was a lovely gentle kiss that made him ache for more.

She pulled back, and he saw a single tear trickle down her cheek.

'Ah, honey. Don't cry.' He kissed the tear away. 'I'm not going to pressure you.'

'This isn't supposed to happen. It's meant to be business. You're messy and disorganised and—'

'And you're a control freak who's neat and tidy and has always got one eye on the clock. Let's throw away the rules and see what happens.' He stroked her hair away from her face. 'Just so you know…I'm not going to sign a confidentiality thing about what you told me.'

He saw the faintest, faintest hint of fear in her eyes.

'Because,' he continued, 'I want you to trust me. You don't *need* me to sign anything because I'm not going to tell anyone. It's just between you and me. Just as I know you're not going to tell anyone what I told you. And even though there's nothing I want more right now than to carry you home to my bed and make love with you until we're both dizzy, we're going to stand up and stroll through the gardens and look at structure and form and colour. Light and shade. I want you, Amanda, but I'm not going to push you.'

'No?'

He smiled. 'That's the thing about gardening. You learn to be patient. Wait until the time's right.' Gently, he lifted her off his lap. Stood up. Helped her to her feet. And refused to let her hand go.

'I thought you said you were patient?' she whispered.

He raised her hand to his mouth and kissed the backs of her fingers. 'To a degree. I'm not setting any time limits.' He kept his fingers twined through hers and began to walk through the gardens. 'To get your perfect bloom, you need to be patient. But you also need to be persistent. That's something I'm very, very good at.' He slanted her an intense look. 'And that, honey, is a promise.'

CHAPTER NINE

WILL KEPT his word. He didn't push Amanda; he didn't even try to kiss her again, that night. But over dinner, when he was talking about work and gardens, she could see in his eyes that he was thinking about kissing her, and remembering the heat that had flared between them that afternoon. The thought made her whole body tingle with anticipation.

There's nothing I want more right now than to carry you home to my bed.

Will the pirate, sweeping her off her feet.

Let's throw away the rules.

She wanted to. How she wanted to. But if she threw away the rules, and threw away the structure she'd built round her life…Fear seeped through her. What then? What if she fell so hard for Will that she'd never bounce back again when it was over?

Because it wouldn't last. It couldn't last. He'd said it himself. *You belong in a city, and I couldn't stand being in that sort of cage; just as you don't like the wide open spaces.*

There was no possible compromise.

Sometimes it's better to listen to your heart instead…my heart's telling me that this is right.

But supposing his heart was wrong?

She dared not take that risk.

* * *

On Thursday, too, he kept things light; they spent an hour at the garden centre, sorting out some admin, and then went to see another of Will's clients for an initial discussion. She filmed him and listened, fascinated, as Will skilfully drew out what the client really wanted from the space. How did he do that? How did he get people to open up to him in that way?

'And now it's the technical stuff,' he said with a smile. 'You'll like this, Amanda. It's structured.'

That stung. Did he really think she was so buttoned up?

Well. He was right. She *was*.

She pushed the hurt aside. 'So this might be good to film.'

'If you like. But you're going to do some of this with me. First, we'll test the soil type.'

'Chemicals?' she guessed.

'One of the tests involves a pH indicator, yes.' He fetched a cardboard box from the back of his car. 'Right. First we need a soil sample.' He took a metal pole with a pointed end from the box, took samples, then put a handful of soil into a glass jar which he filled with water and stirred.

'That's for the pH thing?' she asked.

'No, this is sediment so we can see the type. This one's the pH—different plants like different levels of acidity or alkalinity, though my gut feeling is that this is going to be neutral.'

'How do you know?'

'Take a handful of the sample and look at it,' he advised.

She did. 'And?'

'How does it feel?'

'Sticky.' Enlightenment dawned. 'It's clay?'

'We'll see from the sediment test—but I'd say so.' He added another sample to a small test tube that contained powder, added some water, put a stopper on the top and shook it up before placing it in a rack.

'Right—while those are settling we'll do the measurements.' He took another gadget from the box.

'What's that?'

'My new toy—an electronic measure. Obviously, it only works if there's a solid structure to bounce the rays off; if there isn't, it's back to a good old-fashioned tape measure.' He gave her a sidelong look and drawled, 'Want to play with me?'

She knew he was teasing her. But her body responded anyway, a tingling surge of desire starting at the base of her spine that ran right down to the ends of her fingers and toes. 'Boys and their toys,' she said sniffily.

His eyes went gold with mischief. 'I could *dare* you to play with me.'

So tempting. What would he do if she called his bluff and kissed him? Wrapped her arms round his neck, pressed her body close to his and nibbled his lower lip? Would he open his mouth, let her deepen the kiss? Would he take control? Would he incite her to take charge?

She folded her arms to stop herself acting on the urge. 'We have work to do.'

He smiled, but Amanda marvelled at the ease with which he switched from playfulness to seriousness, taking the measurements and noting them meticulously.

Then he took photographs.

She frowned. 'The files you gave me showed sketches. Going into the modern age now, are we?' she asked.

He laughed. 'No. I'll do the sketches later. This is an *aide-mémoire*—quicker than a sketch.' There was the most appealing dimple in his cheek as he added, 'Neater, too. Right—aspect, next.'

'And you test that how?'

'Sitting in a deckchair for the day with a long, cold drink and a good book.'

She blinked. 'You're joking.'

'Spend a day lazing around a garden and you can really see how the light changes,' he said. 'Though as we're doing this *efficiently*…' He produced another gadget from his box. 'It's west-facing.'

She was surprised that he actually needed to use a compass to tell that. Will probably knew how to navigate by starlight.

She tried to ignore the idea of being under the stars in Will's company. Just the two of them and a million pinpoints of light. 'West-facing's good?' she asked.

'South-facing's the best aspect for a garden,' he said, 'but this still gets a lot of light—afternoon and evening sun rather than morning.' He walked over to the jar and test tube. 'You see this water's cloudy and there's only a little bit of sediment at the bottom?'

It had been years since she'd done any chemistry or biology. 'Yes. Because you haven't left it long enough?'

'It'll still be like this in an hour, because this is clay soil and the particles take ages to settle. It confirms what you said: clay. Which usually means neutral pH, so we can grow virtually anything there—we could add a bit of lime to make it more alkaline, but if our client likes acid-loving plants we'll have to think about making a raised bed with different soil, or container gardening.'

We. Except her time shadowing him was almost over. When the lifeswap project had finished, she wouldn't see him again. She wouldn't see what he planned for the garden here; wouldn't see the actress's garden turn from the sketch on the page into the living colour of Will's vision; wouldn't see the rose arbour replacing all that ground elder in the footballer's garden.

And she was shocked by how sad that made her feel.

She shook the feeling aside and asked coolly, 'So what does the chemical test tell you?'

'It's bright green. That means neutral,' Will said. 'So that's fine. The client's going to do me a mood board over the next couple of weeks, and we can take it from there.'

'We' again. But there was no 'we'. No 'us', she thought.

They called in to a supermarket on the way home—at least, Will did. He informed her that she was staying put. Clearly he planned to cook her something nice as a surprise, as this was her last evening here. Still, at least it meant she could check her emails on her mobile phone and see how her team was getting on with the audit. On Saturday she'd be back in the office and could look over the files for herself.

'Tut. Sneaking in some of your own work. Is this allowed under the lifeswap rules?' a voice whispered in her ear.

She'd been concentrating so hard, she hadn't realised Will was back; his voice made her jump. 'Oh! Yes. Of course it is,' she said crossly, flicking out of the emails and turning off the phone. 'Look, you're going to want to check that things are going smoothly at the garden centre next week, aren't you?'

He didn't reply, just gave her a wry look, which she interpreted as meaning no.

He didn't let her help unpack things from the car, either—just shooed her upstairs to have a bath. 'And don't put your business suit on,' he added. 'No armour required, okay?'

On the contrary. Where Will Daynes was concerned, she needed all the armour she could get. But she did as he requested and wore the faded denims he'd bought her. Though, just to prove she wasn't a doormat, bowing to his every command, she wore a shirt rather than a T-shirt, rolling the sleeves up to her elbows.

When she returned downstairs, Will barred her way to the kitchen and handed her a glass of wine. 'Go and chill out in the garden.'

'Look, I know cooking's not my thing, but don't you want me to set the table or something?'

'Remember what we were saying earlier this week about the senses?'

Trust him to answer a question with a question. She sighed. 'Yes.'

'Indulge me,' he said, 'because I'm going to teach you about the importance of taste.'

She felt her eyes narrow. 'Does this have anything to do with the fact that I don't cook?'

He gave her the most mischievous grin. 'That might have a bit of a bearing on it, yes. I'm not sure I can cope with a week of pre-packaged food.'

She frowned. 'It's perfectly nutritious. You're making a fuss over nothing.'

'Am I?' His eyes glittered. 'Tell me that in a few minutes. Now off you go. If you see what I'm preparing, it's going to defeat the object.'

'Surely I'll smell dinner?'

He handed her a glass of wine. 'Not necessarily. Indulge me, Amanda. Go and sit outside in the garden.'

A few minutes later, he walked outside. 'Ready?'

She nodded.

'No, don't get up. We're going to eat out here tonight.' He smiled at her. 'Close your eyes.'

'Why?'

He sighed. 'Maybe I should make you wear a blindfold for this.'

A blindfold? Her cheeks scorched as a decadent image slid into her mind. Herself, naked except for a blindfold, lying back against silk sheets in a pirate's boudoir, and Will the pirate locking the door behind them so they wouldn't be disturbed…

That wine really must have gone to her head.

'Just close your eyes, Amanda. And no peeking.'

'Okay,' she whispered.

She heard the noise of something being placed on the cast-iron table—a plate or tray of some sort, she guessed.

'Keep your eyes closed,' Will reminded her. 'And trust me. Agreed?'

'Agreed.'

'Good.'

She felt something sliding against her lower lip.

'Eyes closed,' he insisted, just as she was about to open them. 'Tell me. How does it feel?'

'Cold. Smooth.'

'Open your mouth,' he said softly, and slid the morsel inside. 'Now eat it. Then describe it to me.'

She recognised the taste instantly. 'An olive.'

'And it tastes of?'

'Olive.'

He groaned. 'That olive was marinated in chilli and thyme, I'll have you know. Okay, so your sense of taste needs a bit of fine-tuning. Next.'

'Cool. Wet. Slippery.' Again, the taste was recognisable. 'A chunk of cucumber.'

'And this?'

'Soft.' She heard the murmur of frustration before he managed to mute it. Okay, she'd try and give him what he wanted. 'It's sweet and salty and a bit tart, all at the same time. It's obviously cheese, but I'm not sure which type.'

'Feta.'

'You're feeding me a Greek salad?' she guessed.

He laughed. 'No fooling you, is there? So what's missing?'

'Tomato?'

'Uh-huh. This time, I want you to describe the scent.'

She breathed in. 'It smells of…tomato.'

'This is a baby plum tomato off the vine. It smells gorgeous, like a greenhouse on a hot summer day.' He groaned. 'Don't you *ever* do flowery language?'

'You mean, like these wine buffs who talk about a hint of gooseberry and new-mown grass?'

He laughed. 'I think that's a perfect description of the sauvignon blanc you've just been drinking.' He fed her more bites of salad. 'Right. Scent again.'

She shook her head. 'Don't know this one.'

'What does it conjure up?'

'Something woody. A hillside in Greece.'

'Hallelujah. Finally she gets it.' He rubbed the morsel against her lips and her mouth parted.

'Mmm. Bread. A bit salty. And something else—a taste I don't know.'

'Rosemary bread. It's best warm, dipped in olive oil.'

'Can I open my eyes now and just eat this normally?'

'No. I'm enjoying myself.' He fed her delicate morsels of lemon-scented chicken, more bread and more Greek salad.

'I'm starting to feel a bit stupid,' she said, wriggling in her seat.

'You don't look it. But okay, this is the last one. I want a proper description. How does this feel?'

'Bumpy. Shiny—no, wait, something can't feel shiny, can it?'

'Shiny's fine.' There was laughter in his voice, but she knew he was laughing with her, not at her. 'Take a bite.'

It was the sweetest, juiciest strawberry she'd ever eaten—and she could feel a tiny rivulet of juice running down from the corner of her mouth. She was about to lick it away—but then Will beat her to it.

She opened her eyes. 'Will!'

'Hey. There's only so much temptation a man can stand.' He brushed his mouth against hers. 'You taste of strawberries. And I'm *hungry*, Amanda.'

'Then you should have eaten properly instead of feeding me like a baby,' she said, striving to sound cool and collected and the complete opposite of how she felt right now, gazing into the sexiest eyes she'd ever seen and so very close to the sexiest mouth that had ever taken hers.

'I wasn't feeding you like a baby, honey. I was feeding you like a lover,' he told her huskily.

Oh-h-h. Desire trickled between her shoulderblades.

One more kiss and she knew she'd say yes. This had to stop. 'This isn't a good idea, Will.'

'No?'

'We're too different. You don't belong in London, and I don't belong here.'

'We're more similar than you think,' he said softly. 'And it's not a question of *belonging*. I don't know where this is going to take us. I don't even know what I'm offering you. There's just something about you that tips me off balance.'

Yeah. She knew that feeling.

'When we were in Grantchester Meadows, and you were looking up at the sky, all soft and sweet with your face full of wonder as you really heard birdsong for the first time…I wanted to kiss you then.'

She'd wanted him to kiss her, too.

'And yesterday, in the Botanical Garden…' He pressed a kiss into her palm and folded her fingers over it. 'I want to kiss you now.' The lightest brush of his lips against the pulse beating in her wrist. 'I love how soft your skin is.' A trail of tiny butterfly kisses up to her inner elbow. 'How sweet you smell.' He nuzzled the sensitive spot in the curve of her neck. 'How sweet you taste,' he whispered.

She was nearly hyperventilating. Lord, his voice was so sexy. And the feel of his mouth against her skin was driving her wild.

'I want to kiss you, Amanda. Right here, right now.'

That was it. She closed her eyes again and tipped her head back, offering him her throat.

'But even more than that…' he took the tiniest, gentlest,

sexiest bite, just grazing his teeth against her skin, and she shuddered with need '…even more than that, I want you to kiss me back. Let go. Let go the way you didn't yesterday. Turn me to flames.'

She slid her hands into his hair, and nibbled at his lower lip; he opened his mouth, letting her deepen the kiss, and it suddenly became hot and wet and wild.

She wasn't aware of their mouths ever leaving each other's, but they must have done at some point because now her hands were gliding over bare skin and hard, well-defined muscles. Will's shoulders. Somehow, she must have stripped off his T-shirt. She couldn't even remember doing it.

And she was no longer buttoned up. He'd undone every single button on her shirt. Untucked the soft cotton from the waistband of her jeans. And he was nuzzling the vee between her breasts, slowly pulling the edge of her bra down to expose her nipples. The contrast between his dark hair and her fair skin sent a jolt through her.

And oh, Lord, as his mouth closed over one hard peak, she whimpered, 'Will!'

He lifted his head, his molten-silver gaze matching hers. 'What?'

'We—we can't do this. We're outside. In the garden.' Her breath hitched. 'Anyone can see us.'

'Not here,' he reassured her softly. 'We're at the back of the house. There's nobody in the fields. Just you and me and the wide open skies. But if you'd rather…' He got to his feet and scooped her up so she was forced to cling round his neck for balance. Her naked breasts rubbed against the hair on his naked chest and she'd never been so turned on in her entire life. 'I'll carry you indoors.' He punctuated each word with a kiss. 'To. My. Bed.'

The last vestiges of her common sense roared in her ears. 'Will—no.'

He froze. Then, with what was clearly a huge effort, he lowered her until her feet touched the floor, then restored order to her clothes. As he did up every single button, his fingers brushed against her skin; and his eyes were telling her that she could change her mind at any time. All she had to do was say 'yes'.

And she wanted to. How she wanted to.

But her head wouldn't let her make that kind of mistake.

Her legs still felt so weak, she needed to hold on to the chair for support. 'I'm sorry,' she whispered.

His face was completely unreadable. 'I'm not going to force you, Amanda. I'd never do that.' He dragged in a breath. 'But I warn you now, this thing between us isn't going away any time soon.'

She shook her head. 'It can't work between us.'

'You don't know that. Neither do I. We could be brave, give it a try. See where this takes us.'

Brave. That was the point. She was too scared. Too scared that she'd lose her heart to him and then he'd be like everyone else, deciding that her face didn't fit and she'd be left…empty. 'I can't,' she whispered. 'I just *can't.*'

He looked at her for a long, long moment. As if he were battling with himself, fighting the urge to ignore what she'd said and carry her off like a pirate. She saw a muscle tighten in his jaw.

And then he nodded. 'I'll respect your wishes.' He pulled his T-shirt on. 'I'll take Sunny for a walk to give us some breathing space.'

Enough to restore her equilibrium. His, too.

How she wished it could've been different. But it wouldn't work. It *couldn't* work. She needed to listen to her head. Even though her heart was telling her to grab him before he walked away, kiss him until they were both crazy with need, and just let it happen—she needed to listen to her head. Cool, calm, common sense. Keep things strictly business between them.

CHAPTER TEN

WILL WAS gone for an hour. And from the way he walked into the kitchen with damp, curly hair and Sunny drained a whole bowl of water before curling up on her bed, Amanda guessed that he'd been for a run rather than a walk to get rid of his frustration.

Frustration that she'd caused by calling a halt, when they were already half-naked. She'd led him on and made him stop. Guilt flickered through her. 'Will. I'm sorry,' she said again.

'Not a problem.' He shrugged. 'We'll both pretend it didn't happen.'

'Thanks.'

Though it was easier said than done. A lot, lot easier. She slept incredibly badly that night. Half a dozen times, she thought about climbing out of the double bed and knocking on Will's door. Saying yes.

Common sense stopped her. Just.

But the next morning, her eyes felt heavy and her head ached.

A hot shower didn't make her feel any better. In fact, she couldn't remember the last time she'd felt this miserable. This empty.

She should've said yes.

Even if it had been a one-night stand, it would've been worth it.

Too late, now.

'Morning,' Will said when she walked into the kitchen.

He didn't look too brilliant, either. There were dark smudges under his eyes, as if he'd slept as badly as she had last night.

'Morning,' she muttered.

He pushed a mug of coffee over to her, and topped up his own. 'So. Last day of you shadowing me.'

'Uh-huh.'

'Have you enjoyed your week in the country?' he asked.

Making polite conversation. Well. She could be equally polite. 'More than I expected to.'

'Good.' He looked at her, and for a moment that hungry pirate look was back. 'Will you have dinner with me before you go tonight?'

She shook her head. 'I need to get back to London. And you'll be busy catching up with whatever you need to sort out for next week.'

Was it his imagination, or had her cheeks turned very slightly pink? Was she scared that they'd take up where they'd left off last night—and that this time he wouldn't stop if she tried to call a halt?

Ah, hell. This mess was all his fault. He shouldn't have pushed her, last night. But the way her even white teeth had sunk into the strawberry, the way her beautiful mouth had smiled at him…he just hadn't been able to resist kissing her. Letting the heat rise between them.

'Yeah, you're right. I have things to do.' Such as getting the holiday cottage back to how it was supposed to be, then sorting his house out. He just hoped that his neighbour had remembered her promise to water his plants and he wasn't going to return to utter carnage on his patio.

'Um…there's one thing. About Sunny. When I agreed to do this lifeswap thing, I didn't realise you had a dog. And—well—my rental agreement says no pets,' she said.

'Not a problem. Fliss is looking after her for the week.' He smiled at her, pleased that she'd been worried about the dog. 'I imagine you have to catch the tube to work, and as dogs aren't allowed unless they're guide dogs, it'd mean leaving her in a strange place, which wouldn't be fair. At least she knows Fliss.'

They spent the rest of the day at the house in St John's Wood, tackling the ground elder again. Then there was lunch at a pub followed by more ground elder. And finally he drove them back to the Fens. The last time.

The music he was playing seemed to be giving her some sort of message—slow country-rock ballads with promises that the singer would be there for her, love her more than she'd ever been loved, that the future would be fine because they were together.

When he began to sing along with the music—and Lord, he had a gorgeous voice—she was even more sure that he was trying to tell her something.

But then her common sense kicked in. Will couldn't possibly give her promises like that. He was just singing along to songs he liked and had played often enough to know the words and the melody.

Back at the cottage, she packed her things swiftly. And saying goodbye to Will was awkward. 'Thanks for, um, teaching me about gardens,' she mumbled.

'Pleasure.' He was equally polite and formal. 'I'll see you on Sunday evening, then. And you can teach me…'

What? What the hell could she teach Will, whose life was chaotic, but it didn't matter because he was happy that way? How to be buttoned-up and avoid people?

Not in a million years.

She wished she'd suggested taking her car to St John's Wood as well, so she could've said goodbye to him at the garden, where it would've been quick and relatively painless. But she'd been too sleep-deprived this morning to think straight. 'See you Sunday,' she said, avoiding his eyes, and made her escape.

Will leaned against the doorjamb, watching Amanda drive away. Now there would be two days of space between them. More than enough time for her to rebuild every single wall. And next week he'd be in her world, on her schedule.

The kind of life his parents had planned for him.

The kind of life he'd promised himself he'd never have to lead.

Somehow he didn't think he'd last the week without breaking a few rules.

'Let's get this place tidy,' he told Sunny, 'and then we're going home.'

'So, how was it?' Dee asked.

Amanda shrugged. 'Fine.'

'Are you sure?' Dee looked worried. 'You've hardly said a word since you've been home. You had an early night last night—a *really* early night.'

'That's what all that fresh air and digging gardens does for you,' Amanda said.

'Well, you don't look rosy-cheeked and bushy-tailed or however you're supposed to look after a week in the country.'

She didn't feel it, either. 'Probably because I'm a city girl and smelling the roses gets pretty boring after a while.'

Dee bit her lip. 'Sorry. Was it really awful?'

Yes. Because I think I might have fallen in love with some-one who's so wrong for me, it's untrue. And because I can't stop thinking about him. And because I think I might have made a huge mistake in saying no. And because I know that saying yes would be an even bigger mistake. 'It was okay,' Amanda lied. 'I'm not sure what I can teach him, though.'

Dee coughed. 'Yeah. He pretty much makes his own de-cisions.'

'How well do you know him?' Amanda asked.

'Um…well, as you probably know by now, he's Fliss's brother. So I've known him since he was a spotty, gangly sixteen-year-old.' Dee smiled wryly. 'If anyone had told me then he'd turn out to be six foot two of gorgeous man, I'd have said they were mad. He was just Fliss's annoying kid brother back then. Actually, he's a lovely guy. He's got a big heart. But he has his own ideas about things. And he can be a bit stubborn.'

'I noticed.'

'Ouch.' Dee flinched. 'Look, you can call off this second week if you really hated each other that much.'

That was just the problem, Amanda thought. They hadn't hated each other. Far from it. 'I said I'd do this. I'm not going to let you down.'

She just hoped she wouldn't let herself down, either—by falling at Will Daynes's feet the second he walked into her flat.

'Rightio—you're off to Aunty Fliss's for the week,' Will in-formed Sunny.

The dog looked at the car, and then at Will as if to say, 'Please, can't we just stay here?'

He knew how she felt. The second he'd opened the door, she'd searched the entire house, sniffing every nook and cranny to make sure her home was still there exactly as she'd left it.

And he'd made a beeline for the kitchen-cum-conservatory, his favourite place. It had been built to his specifications, so the glass addition complemented the Victorian terrace: the place where his garden and his house merged.

The plants on his patio were still lush and green, to his relief; his neighbour had more than deserved the flowers and chocolates he'd picked up on his way home to say thank you. And then he'd had dinner on his own. A meal where he'd just gone through the motions of cooking and fed half of it to Sunny because he wasn't in the mood for eating: and he was shocked to realise that he actually missed Amanda.

How could she have got so deeply under his skin in six days?

And although he hated the idea of leaving home again so quickly, it wasn't so bad—even though he'd be in London—because he'd be with *her*.

'Oh, no. Please tell me you haven't,' Fliss said, the second she opened the front door to him.

'What?'

'You've got a moony look on your face. Please tell me you haven't fallen for the Ice Queen.'

Will frowned. 'She's not icy.'

Fliss sighed. 'Amanda Neave is about the worst possible woman you could fall for. Her career comes first, last and all the spaces in between—and I don't want to see you get hurt.'

The way he'd been hurt by their parents, who'd done exactly the same thing. 'I'm not going to get hurt.' Will folded his arms. 'And may I remind you that you asked me to do this lifeswap thing in the first place?'

'I know. And I'm beginning to wish I hadn't.' Fliss bit her lip. 'I really didn't think she'd be your type.'

'I don't *have* a type,' he said. 'I'm not that shallow. And this really isn't a problem.'

'Hmm.' Fliss clearly wasn't convinced, because she fussed over him during lunch. To the point where he ended up shepherding her into the kitchen and made her sit down.

'Right. Let's take this step by step. The age at which you're officially an adult—when you can drive and own a house and vote and get married without parental consent—is…?'

'Eighteen.'

'And my age is…?'

She sighed. 'Twenty-nine.'

'So logically, I've been an adult for…? Come on, Fliss, even you can do the maths,' he added with a teasing grin.

She glared at him. 'Eleven years. But you're still my baby brother.'

'And you really don't need to worry about me. Look at me, Fliss. I'm together and I'm happy. I have my own house and I have a job—my own business, if we're being pernickety, and it's doing fine. I don't do drugs and I stay on the right side of the law—well, apart from those two speeding tickets eight years ago, and I learned my lesson very quickly. I don't repeat my mistakes.'

Fliss reached out and ruffled his hair. 'I know. But I just don't want to see you get a broken heart from falling in love with someone who wouldn't be good for you.'

'I'm not in love with Amanda.' He was more than halfway there, but he was trying to be sensible about it. 'And even if I was, you don't know for definite that she'd be bad for me. Trust me to be the judge of that, hmm?' He smiled to take the edge from his words. 'You know, I'll be very, very glad when my niece or nephew appears and you can stop practising your parenting skills on me.'

Fliss's eyes filled with tears. 'I don't mean to be bossy. It's just…I love you.'

'And I love you, too, sis.' He gave her a hug. 'Now, stop worrying about me. I'm old enough and big enough to take care of myself. If I had a problem, you'd be the first one I'd come to. Okay?'

She nodded.

With the pad of his thumb, he brushed away the tear sliding down her cheek. 'Please stop crying, or Cal will have my guts for garters for upsetting his pregnant wife.'

'It's just hormones,' she sniffed.

On cue, Cal walked in, took one look at his wife and groaned. 'Oh, no. What did you do, Will? Tell her you loved her, or something?'

'Yeah.' Will wrinkled his nose. 'It was meant to stop her nagging. She was being bossy.'

'Part of the job description for a schoolmarm,' Cal teased, walking over to his wife and kissing her.

'I'd better ring for a taxi,' Will said, 'or I'll miss my train to London.'

'I'll drive you in to town,' Cal said. 'And you, honey, need to put your feet up in the meantime and *rest*,' he reminded his wife.

Fliss groaned. 'I'm perfectly all right, Cal.'

Will laughed. 'Dosed with your own medicine, sis.' He dropped to a crouch and made a fuss of Sunny. 'Look after her and make sure she behaves herself, okay?' He looked up at his sister. 'And I'm talking to her, not you. I know my dog'll be on her best behaviour.'

'Oh, *you*,' Fliss said, rolling her eyes.

But at least she was smiling again, he thought. 'See you when I get back from London.' He hugged his sister goodbye. 'And thanks for looking after Sunny for me.'

'It's the least I could do, considering I lumbered you with this in the first place.'

When Cal had dropped him in the city centre, Will headed for a certain florist he knew, then caught the train to London.

Two changes of Tube lines later and he was at the road leading to Amanda's flat.

This was it. He took a deep breath and rang the intercom.

A few moments later, he heard her say, 'Hello?'

The weird jolt in the region of his heart was unsettling. How could just the sound of her voice do that to him? He pulled himself together. 'Hi. It's Will.'

'Come up.'

He heard the buzzer go and pushed the door open.

Just as he'd expected, she was back in a business suit. The buttoned-up finance whiz, not the woman who'd started to turn to fire in his arms.

'Hello,' he said.

She didn't meet his eyes. 'I'll just get you a permit for your car, so you don't get a parking ticket.'

'No need. I know parking's at a premium in London, so I came by Tube.'

That made her look at him. 'So how are you going to get home?'

'Taxi from Cambridge train station.' Although he lived within walking distance of the train station, he'd left his car at Fliss's. 'Oh—these are for you.' He brought his hands from behind his back and gave her the flowers.

She stared at him, looking shocked; clearly she didn't receive flowers very often, he thought. 'You didn't need to do that,' she said; then recovered swiftly. 'Thank you. It's very kind.'

So cool and polite. He wanted the woman who'd kissed him back. Though it looked as if she was in hiding—and it was going to take a while to tempt her out.

He'd bought her flowers. Cool, elegant calla lilies. A huge sheaf of them, arranged professionally, and they must've cost him a small fortune. When had someone last given her flowers—let alone flowers that had been chosen personally?

'I'll put these in water, then show you to your room,' she said.

Over the last two days, she'd managed to gloss over the way he made her feel, almost to the point where she thought she could treat him like any other male of her acquaintance, a colleague or client. But now he was in her space and she realised how wrong she was.

Will Daynes simply radiated energy.

And sex.

And there was no way she was going to get any sleep tonight, knowing that his bed was only a few feet away from her own.

He'd followed her into the kitchen so she arranged the flowers carefully, not wanting Will to know how much it rattled her that he'd closed the space between them. 'Dee's away at a conference for the week, so you'll be staying in her room.' Without meeting his gaze, she showed him round the flat. 'Living room—well, obviously. Bathroom. Your room. I've put a fresh towel on the bed, but there are more in the airing cupboard.'

'Thank you.'

She eyed his suitcase. It didn't look that big. Then she looked at Will again. He was wearing faded jeans, a clean but old T-shirt, and trainers. No way could she take him into the office like this.

'You're not planning on going to the office dressed like that, are you?' she asked.

He gave her a lazy smile that made ripples of lust lick down her spine. 'What do you think?'

Oh, Lord. He *was*. Lust turned to dread. 'Will, it's Sunday evening and no shops are open!' She dragged in a breath. 'Okay. We'll just have to go in late tomorrow. We'll go in via Oxford Street and get you a suit on the way to the office.'

His smile broadened. 'You're panicking, aren't you?'

'Are you surprised? Look, you knew exactly what we were doing this week. I gave you a schedule. I thought you'd—'

'Dress appropriately?' he cut in, his eyes sparkling.

Then she realised that he was teasing her. 'That's unkind,' she said, glaring at him.

'I'm sorry. But you were being stuffy. I couldn't resist it.' He smiled at her. 'I'm not going to show you up, Amanda. I do own a suit. Though I'll probably need to borrow your iron tomorrow morning to get the creases out of my shirt.'

The thought of Will, bare-chested, ironing a shirt, made her heart miss a beat. It had been three days, and she still remembered exactly what his naked chest had looked like. Still remembered how his skin had felt against hers. Still—

Oh, she really had to get a grip. 'Can I get you a drink, while you put your things away?' she asked.

'Something cold would be lovely, thanks. Whatever you've got.'

For a moment, she thought he was going to reach out and touch her; she tensed, but then the moment was gone and he picked up his suitcase. 'See you in a minute.'

A whole evening. How on earth was she going to spend a *whole evening* with him? She almost cut herself when she sliced the lemon, because she wasn't paying attention to what she was doing—she was remembering the feel of Will's mouth against hers.

Well, this time she'd exercise some self-control. Five days, that was all—they'd agreed it would end on Friday afternoon at three. She could keep some distance between them for five days, surely?

But when she returned to the living room and handed Will his glass, her fingers brushed against his. It felt like pure electricity fizzing through her veins. It was the same for him, too; she could tell by the way his pupils dilated and his eyes changed colour from serious green to that sexy molten silver.

'What time do we leave for the office tomorrow?' he asked.

'I usually leave here at seven,' she said.

He sighed. 'I had a feeling it was going to be something like that.'

'Except on Wednesdays, when I leave at six and have an hour in the gym first.'

'And I have to go to the gym, too?'

She nodded. 'It's all part of the shadowing, isn't it?'

He raised an eyebrow. 'I can't remember when I last set foot in a gym. Oh, well.'

'I'm sure you won't have any problems. Your muscles are…' Her mouth dried.

'My muscles are?' he prompted.

'Never mind.'

'Too big? Too small?' He paused and said huskily, 'Just right?'

Oh, yes. They were just right. She dragged in a breath. 'You're used to physical exercise. From gardening, I mean, and taking Sunny for a walk.'

His mouth quirked. 'You're blushing, Amanda.'

'No, I'm not.' She folded her arms. Come on, come on—surely she could think of something neutral to say? She fell back on the old standby. 'So your degree was in horticulture. Which A-levels did you do?'

He smiled, as if knowing exactly why she'd asked. To keep the conversation cerebral instead of sensual. 'Maths, economics, biology and chemistry.'

She frowned. She'd expected the economics—after all, he'd applied to read PPE at Oxford—but she'd thought he'd studied English. 'How come you know so much Shakespeare and poetry, then?'

'I used to go out with an actress. I helped her learn her lines by reading the other parts for her. I think my favourite's *Antony and Cleopatra*. Sheer poetry. "Eternity was in our lips and eyes…"' He drew the tip of his tongue against his lower lip, and she couldn't help watching him, fascinated. 'Funny how I can't stop thinking of mouths when I'm with you,' he added softly.

'That's not fair. This is meant to be business.'

'Then I'll do you a deal.' His eyes glittered. 'Kiss me, and I'll shut up.'

She remembered the last time they'd kissed. They'd both become so carried away, they'd ended up being half-naked. Outside. Completely oblivious to everything and everyone. 'No deal.'

He grinned. 'So I don't have to shut up? Good.'

'That isn't what I meant, and you know it.'

'Are you afraid to kiss me?' he taunted.

'No.' *Yes.*

His smile vanished and he looked serious. 'For what it's worth, what happened on Thursday—that doesn't normally happen to me. I never forget where or who I am. And I don't think you do, either.'

'No,' she admitted. And she really hoped he hadn't heard that wobble in her voice. The shiver of pure desire.

'I can't stop thinking about it,' he said softly.

Neither could she. 'Well, you'll just have to,' she said, trying to sound as prim and proper as she could. 'It's not part of the lifeswap thing.'

'No.' But his eyes were saying something completely different.

It's going to happen.

Soon.

And neither of us will want to stop.

CHAPTER ELEVEN

AMANDA'S HAND was on the door to the bathroom when it opened abruptly and she almost pitched forward straight into Will, who was wearing nothing but a towel slung low over his hips, and his hair was still damp.

'Sorry,' she muttered. 'I didn't realise you were…'

Since when had she lost her ability to form a sentence?

She was really, really glad that her dressing gown was thick towelling—she'd be mortified if he could see how just the sight of his half-naked body had turned her on. With difficulty, she pulled herself together. 'I've left the iron and ironing board out for you in the living room.'

'Thanks.'

She showered and washed her hair; but she couldn't get the thought out of her head that, just a few moments before, Will's naked body had been in exactly the same place hers was right now. What would it be like to share a shower with—?

Don't even *think* about it, she warned herself.

But her head wasn't listening. It was creating pictures of Will ironing his shirt, naked to the waist, the muscles on his back flexing. And by the time she'd finished dressing and went into the kitchen to make breakfast, she was quivering.

'I made you some coffee,' he said, and handed her a mug.

'Thanks.' Please, please let the caffeine jolt some sense

back into her head. Because Will, dressed in a formal white shirt and silk tie, was unbelievably beautiful. How on earth was she going to be able to concentrate for the next week, with him working in the same room as her? How on earth was she going to be able to pay attention to a set of figures, when what she really wanted to do was rip his clothes off and—?

Focus, she reminded herself. They had fifteen minutes before they had to leave the house. 'Can I make you some toast?'

He chuckled. 'Does that count as cooking?'

'Even I can shove two bits of bread in a toaster. Or there's cereal, yoghurt, fruit…'

She wished she hadn't said that last word. Because it made her think of the way he'd fed her that strawberry and licked the juice from the corner of her mouth.

'Just help yourself to whatever you want,' she finished, hoping he hadn't noticed the sudden huskiness in her voice.

Will opted for toast. She didn't dare, knowing that the act of licking buttery fingers would only give her libido ideas. Fruit was worse still. Cereal, at least, was safe.

'So tell me about your job,' Will said, picking up the camera and zooming in on her.

'My job's auditing,' she said. 'Which is basically checking the client's systems to make sure everything's recorded properly, and that any stock or machinery or buildings are where they're supposed to be. So then we can be sure that the financial statements we make—the year-end accounts for a company—are accurate and complete.'

He smiled. 'That's the textbook definition. What does it mean in practice?'

'Anything from doing a stocktake in a walk-in freezer for a food company—where you learn that at minus forty degrees ink freezes so you have to use a pencil when ticking things off a schedule—through to checking that computer systems are handling stock in the right way. We're doing a manufacturing company this week, so we need to understand their production processes from start to finish—from the raw material coming in to the finished product you see on the shelves.' She shrugged. 'I suppose in your terms that'd be like seeing an overview of a garden, from the initial meeting with your client through to the last plant going in.'

'So you have people doing this for you, or you do it all yourself?'

'I prepare the testing plan and initial documents for the audit, and write up the final report,' she said. 'And I carry out the more complicated tests myself. But, yes, I have a team. And part of my job is to develop them and make sure any assignments I give them fit in with their training plan.'

'Who develops your career?'

'My boss,' she said. Not that it was being developed at the moment. The way things were going, she would be at a complete standstill until she could prove herself. 'Though I know where I want to be. Audit manager, head of department, then partner.' If she worked hard enough. Proved how flexible she was. Made her boss realise that she was an asset, not a liability. 'I'm doing an MBA from September.'

'You're taking a career break?'

She shook her head. 'I'm studying part time, a couple of evenings a week.'

'That's a tough schedule, doing an intensive course like that and a demanding full-time job at the same time,' he said softly. 'What about time for you?'

'The MBA *is* for me.' He didn't look convinced, and she sighed. 'Look, Will, it's what I want to do with my life. The only way to get there is to work hard.'

'And what about when you get where you want to be? What then?'

'Then I'll find a new challenge.'

He switched off the camera. 'What about getting married? Having kids? Or isn't that on the agenda?'

'It's not mandatory, Will.' She looked at him. 'What about you? Is it on your agenda?'

'Not at the moment. But if I meet someone and realise they're the one I want to grow old with…'

Amanda was shocked at the flash of jealousy. When this whole lifeswap thing was over, she and Will probably wouldn't see each other again. She didn't have any *right* to be jealous. But the idea of Will falling in love with someone…

…was probably the best thing for both of them, she told herself sternly. 'We'd better get going,' she said. 'I'll have a pile of mail in the office, not to mention a site visit to arrange.'

'You don't have a secretary?'

'Not until you make partner.' With a brass plate on her door and a plaque with her name on it in the car park.

As Will half-expected, Amanda insisted on doing the washing up and making the kitchen spotless before they left. He would've been quite happy just to stack the breakfast things next to the sink and deal with them after dinner. But this was her week, her rules.

The Tube was even worse than he'd expected. She'd said they would go in early to beat the rush hour. But already it was crowded—too cramped to talk. Not that you could hear a lot, exactly, over the noise of the train and the tinny sounds from people's headphones.

It was hot, sticky and smelly—and this was first thing in the morning. Will grimaced at the thought of what it was going to be like when they caught the Tube this evening, after people had spent a hot day at work and their deodorants had stopped functioning.

'You do this every single day?' he asked when they'd

finally left the tube station behind and were walking to the Amanda's office in the City.

'Unless I'm out at a client's where it'd be easier to go by car, yes.'

He grimaced. 'Don't you hate it—that feeling of being hemmed in, squashed together with all those people in the tiniest little space?'

'It's why I go in early. To avoid the rush.'

'You mean, that wasn't the rush?'

'No.' She frowned. 'Will, it's not that bad. You get used to it.'

Absolutely not. He'd never get used to this.

At the office reception, they paused to get Will a temporary pass for the week. Then he discovered that her office was on the eighth floor—and she always took the stairs.

'It's a good way of keeping fit,' she said, 'in between gym sessions.'

'Hmm.' Walking up and down a flight of stairs in a tower block or going to the gym. He'd much rather be walking along the riverbank or in the green spaces of Cambridge with his dog, or doing some serious digging.

Amanda's office turned out to be open plan. There were low dividers between the desks; Will presumed they were meant to act as soundproofing, as well as somewhere for people to pin notes and memos.

And he could've guessed which desk was hers. Even though she'd been away from it for a week and her in-tray was piled high, her desk was neat. There were a couple of notices pinned to the divider, but no photographs of family or cut-out cartoon strips or pictures of hunky actors. No flowers or plant on her desk. Nothing to give a clue about Amanda as a person, the sort of things she liked.

Which was part of the problem, he thought. In business, she cut to the chase. With anything personal, she was reserved, giving nothing away. It would make it very hard for someone to strike up a conversation with her. Where would they start? Talking about the weather?

'My desk,' she said, somewhat unnecessarily. 'It's up to you if you want to work here with me or use someone else's desk while they're out at a client's for the day.'

'I'm meant to do what you do. So your desk it is,' he said.

There was just the tiniest glitter in her eyes. Interesting. So she was nervous of him again—and even more so here, in her world. Was she worried that he'd make ripples?

'I need to introduce you to everyone. We'll start with my team—we have a team meeting scheduled for nine.'

He nodded. 'Does everyone know about the lifeswap thing?'

'Only my boss. Everyone else thinks you're shadowing me for a week. Management for a large potential client.'

He raised an eyebrow. 'So you're telling fibs.'

'No. You *are* management,' she pointed out. 'And the nursery could be a potential client.'

'Daynes is a small, personal, family business. Not the sort of place that employs London professionals with London prices.'

'Okay, so it's not the whole truth. But I don't want people—' She broke off abruptly.

'What? You're ashamed of me?'

She sighed. 'No. If you must know, I don't like being teased.'

She really thought her colleagues would tease her about this? Then again, this was the world of high finance. Any possible weakness in a team member would be mercilessly picked on. It'd be disguised as teasing, having a laugh—but there'd be an edge to it. He remembered Helen having a row with his parents about it once, asking them why they hadn't stepped in and warned some of their staff they were going too far and telling them to back off, before the secretary concerned had gone off on long-term sick leave with depression.

Nothing had changed in this world in the last fifteen years, then.

'Nobody's going to tease you about me,' he promised. And if they tried, they'd answer to him.

'I need to check my emails. The coffee machine's at the end of the room, if you want one.' She took a card from her wallet and handed it to him. 'Get whatever you want. It works in the snack machine, as well.'

Will got her a coffee as well; she murmured her thanks, but she was already clearly focused on her work. He watched her, fascinated as she worked through first the emails and then the paperwork in her top tray. He'd never seen anyone deal with a pile of papers so quickly: she opened the envelope, scanned the contents swiftly and either binned it, put it in one of three folders on her desk, or made a note on her electronic to-do list.

'So you only touch each piece of paper once,' he commented.

She frowned. 'That's common sense. If it's important, think about what needs to be done and by when and put it on your to-do list so you can prioritise your day's work; if it's not, delegate it or bin it.'

At three minutes to nine, Amanda shepherded him into the meeting room, set up at the head of the table with her laptop in front of her and an agenda placed neatly in front of Will and the other three places. The files she'd had on her desk were neatly stacked beside her.

At one minute to nine, three people filed in. So was everyone in this firm a stickler for time like Amanda? Was it because they were so focused on facts and figures, everything had to be precise? And would she drive her team as hard as she drove herself?

'Morning, team. This is Will Daynes. He's shadowing me

for a week,' she said. 'Will, this is Rhiannon, who's just done her final exams; Mark, who's halfway through; and Drew, who's been with us for a year.'

They all smiled politely at him and made some sort of greeting, which he returned with a heavy heart. He had a nasty feeling this week was going to be dull, dull, dull.

'Rhiannon, can you give me an update on last week?' Amanda asked. She made the odd note as her junior spoke, checked with all three if there had been any problems or if anything had come up where any of them felt they had a training need, then talked them through the week ahead.

Amanda didn't work on one job at a time, it seemed. There was one—like the manufacturing company—in planning, one in progress and one that needed to be written up. And he noted that she was careful to ask all three of her staff how their recent exams had gone—Rhiannon's final papers, Mark's Part Ones and Drew's graduate conversion course.

There was nothing he could teach her about organisation, planning and looking after staff, Will thought. She knew exactly what she was doing.

At least the meeting was short. Well, it would be—Amanda was in charge of the agenda and didn't like wasting time. By the end of it, everyone knew what they were doing and when.

Next up was a brief meeting with Amanda's boss. A man with very shiny shoes, a weak handshake, and long, thin arms and legs. A spider, Will thought, at the middle of the web, plotting and snaring. But Will managed to be polite and to crack the obvious jokes.

Then there was a quick tour of the department. Will noticed that Amanda was polite but brisk, wasting no time with personal chat. Nobody asked her how her week off had been, he noted. She'd told him she didn't fit in; now he could see why.

Or had she simply stopped making the effort to be sociable after a few rebuffs?

And then work. Going through files and cross-checking references. Will was bored to tears within half an hour.

'Who's responsible for the plants around here?' he asked.

'Internal landscape firm,' she said, still working through her files.

'They haven't been properly cared for. Some of them are in the wrong aspect and it looks to me as if the watering's been sloppy. When were they last fed?'

Amanda looked up from her desk. 'You hate this, don't you?'

He almost said yes—until he saw the look in her eyes. If he told her what he really thought, he had a feeling she'd take it personally. And it wasn't Amanda that was the problem— it was her lifestyle. 'I just noticed the plants.' He lowered his voice. 'Professional interest. Why aren't there any plants on your desk?'

'Because I'm rubbish with them,' she replied, her voice equally low.

'You need them to soak up radiation and what-have-you from your computer.'

She narrowed her eyes and gave the tiniest, impatient shake of her head. 'I'm fine. Stop fussing.'

Will managed to get through the next hour, thanks to two strong coffees. And then he needed some fresh air.

'Cabin'd, cribb'd, confin'd.' He grimaced into the video camera. 'Not bound to saucy doubts and fears, I admit. But I can't bear being stuck in an office like this. Nobody talks to each other here—they all talk *at* each other. Okay, so maybe in the garden centre they waste a few minutes yakking about whatever they saw on TV or read in the papers yesterday, but at least they talk to each other. At least there's teamwork. Here, it's all competition.'

* * *

Lunchtime was even worse. 'Aren't you having a break?' he asked.

Amanda stared at him as if he'd grown two heads. 'I've been away for a week, I've got an audit to plan and we're out at a client's tomorrow. I don't have *time* for a break, Will.'

'The way you work, you probably could do all that with your eyes closed.'

Bad choice of phrase. It reminded him too much of the evening when she'd closed her eyes and let him feed her, let him tempt her with tastes. When he'd kissed her properly, and she'd kissed him back. He dragged his thoughts back to the present with difficulty. 'What do you do for lunch?'

'Vending machine. In the corridor.'

'You're kidding.' Please, let her tell him she was kidding. 'You mean white bread that tastes like cardboard and a plasticky filling that's been stuck in a machine all day?'

She rolled her eyes. 'It's chilled and the packages are sealed. It's not going to make you ill.'

He wasn't so sure.

The afternoon dragged even more. For the first time in his life, Will found himself clock-watching. He couldn't remember ever being this bored. It wasn't that he couldn't do the tasks Amanda set him—he could—but they just didn't hold his interest. It felt like being on a treadmill, going on and on and on with no end or purpose in sight.

He noticed people leaving the office. Some went on the dot of five; others, clearly wanting to be seen to be keen, stayed until six. Amanda waited until ten to seven before calling it a day.

'Ever thought that maybe if you work fewer hours, you'll be fresher and work at a faster pace so you'll get the same amount of work done in a shorter time?' he asked.

She smiled. 'You're the one who was complaining about

the Tube this morning. If you really want to travel home in the middle of the rush hour…'

'Hmm.'

And then she made it worse by calling in at the supermarket on the way back to her flat. She put two TV dinners and a ready-prepared salad in the wire basket.

'You're not serious,' he said. She had to be teasing him. She wasn't really expecting him to eat that stuff…was she?

She raised an eyebrow. 'My week, my rules.'

Oh, Lord. He was *never* going to survive this week. 'Is it really that much effort to chop salad?' he asked.

'Yes. Stop being such a food snob.'

It tasted as bad as he'd expected, but he forced it down and nagged her into letting him do the washing up.

And, just when he thought she was going to relax, out came some textbooks.

'You're not surely going to work now?'

Another of those polite but distant smiles. 'I'm doing some preliminary stuff for my MBA.'

'Amanda, working at this pace really isn't good for you.'

'I'm fine. Stop nagging.' She frowned. 'Look, if you're bored, just flick through the channels on the telly or something.'

He picked up the camera and switched it on. 'I don't think you need to stop and smell the roses, Amanda,' he said quietly.

She didn't even look up from her book. 'Good.'

'I think,' he said softly, 'you need to stop and learn to *breathe*.'

CHAPTER TWELVE

To Will's relief, Tuesday was better. No horrible Tube journey, as they were driving out to visit a client and picking up Drew, the most junior member of the team, on the way. Amanda introduced them both to the finance manager, talked the client through what they were going to do, and then it was straight into the audit.

'So we're all working separately?' Will asked.

'As part of the team, but, yes, we've all got set tasks. I've written a brief for each one,' Amanda told him, 'so all you have to do is follow it through and write up what you do and the results of the investigations.' For a moment, there was a hint of mischief in her smile. 'Unless you don't think you're up to it? I could find you something easier.'

That little flicker of feeling heartened him; and it amused him that she'd chosen to throw his own words back at him. 'If you can dig up ground elder, I can do this,' he retorted, returning the smile.

'Good. Just come and see me if you've got any questions,' she said.

There was one in his head, but now wasn't the time or place to ask it. *When are you going to kiss me again?*

Being busy was good. The more so because she'd assigned him tasks where he had to talk to people and get them to show him different processes. And, better still, she let him persuade her to go out for lunch at the kind of pub he liked best—the sort that served really, really good food.

Though she kept the conversation focused very firmly on work, he noticed. 'How did it go, this morning?' she asked.

'No problem,' Will said with a smile.

'Okay.' Drew didn't sound convinced, and Amanda zeroed in on that.

'What's up?' she asked.

Drew grimaced. 'Those invoices you told me to look at— well, the woman who deals with them is a real dragon. She's bitten my head off every time I've asked—she won't do a thing to help.'

After a day and a half of Drew, Will had a pretty good idea why. 'Ever thought,' he asked, 'of putting yourself in her shoes?'

Drew frowned. 'How do you mean?'

'You're an auditor. That means you're checking what she does. Like anyone who has the auditors in, she's scared that maybe you'll find something wrong and she'll lose her job.'

Drew scoffed. 'That's ridiculous—though if she does do things wrong then maybe she shouldn't be doing the job.'

'That,' Will said in near disbelief, 'is the most callous thing I've ever heard. Does Amanda treat *you* like that?'

There was a slight stain of colour on the younger man's cheeks. 'Well, no.' He gave her a sidelong look. 'But she does check up on things more than any of the other seniors do.'

'Because the buck stops with me,' Amanda said. 'And rule number one is that you're *always* polite to clients. When it comes to losing jobs, consider this: if you upset the staff on an audit, they might complain about you. Complaints could mean our firm loses the job to someone else next year. If we lose a certain number of clients, we'll have to downsize. Try extrapolating that.'

Drew thought about it. 'You lose your job?' he asked.

Amanda smiled thinly. 'As would my team.'

Drew shook his head. 'They couldn't get rid of *me*. I'm on a training contract,' he said loftily.

'It doesn't make you safe. Think about it. And I'm going to add a course on interpersonal skills to your training plan.'

Drew gave her a speaking look. Will, just about keeping a lid on his impatience, said, 'You might find it helpful to lose the attitude. Amanda's interpersonal skills are fine.'

Drew scoffed. 'Yeah, well, you would say that.'

Amanda's cheeks flamed as she caught the implication.

Will said very softly, 'What goes around, comes around. If you treat other people with that kind of contempt, they'll have no respect for you. Would you want *your* juniors gossiping about you behind your back when you're audit senior?'

Drew shifted in his seat. 'Well, no.'

'Think about it,' Will advised sagely. 'And I'm going with you to see this woman, this afternoon. Watch and learn.'

Hang on, Amanda thought, *I'm* supposed to be teaching *Will* this week—and Drew's *my* responsibility. Will seemed to have taken over the teaching role. Though she had to admit he was better with people than she was. And the way he'd stood up for her against Drew's little snipes sent a warm glow through her whole body.

After lunch, Will did exactly what he'd said, and returned to Amanda alone.

'What happened?' she asked.

He shrugged. 'Drew is looking through the papers he wanted to see.'

The papers the woman apparently hadn't wanted to give him earlier. 'So what happened?'

'I asked for him,' Will explained. 'The poor woman was clearly run off her feet and didn't need the added irritation of having to sift through a pile of papers for someone who was swaggering around with a superiority complex. So I did a deal with her—I made her a cup of coffee and she showed me where the invoices were. I promised we wouldn't muddle up the order of the papers and we'd put everything back where we found them. And then I got Drew to talk me through exactly what I just did and why that approach worked better. He doesn't like me very much right now—and that's completely mutual, by the way—but I think his behaviour's going to improve.'

'Thanks, Will.' She smiled wryly at him. 'I find managing a team a bit tough sometimes.'

'With attitudes like that, I'm not surprised. Drew clearly believes that he's better than everyone else because he's been to university or got a job while his mates are still looking at their student loans and worrying. Whereas in the real world, that's not the case.' Will shrugged. 'He just needs the edges smoothed off him, and that'll happen, given time.'

'He was right about one thing, though,' she admitted. 'My own interpersonal skills aren't exactly brilliant.'

'You're more comfortable with figures than people, yes. But that's no excuse for the way he behaved to you.' Will raised an eyebrow. 'I still can't believe what you said to him in the pub. "Try extrapolating that." It's not the kind of word I'd expect to hear in everyday conversation.' He gestured to the audit schedules next to her. 'But then again, I can see the other words you're using here. Scrutinise…that's quite a threatening word,' he said thoughtfully.

'So are the alternatives: inspect, examine, analyse, check. And this is a formal business document—one that might have to stand up in a court of law—so don't suggest something like "give the purchase ledger the once-over."'

'As if I would.' His eyes twinkled. 'Okay, boss. Next task.'

The afternoon went by quickly, but, because they'd eaten out, Amanda decreed a sandwich would do for their evening

meal. It wasn't the kind of bread or ham Will was used to, but
he supposed he should consider himself lucky it wasn't one
of the vacuum-packed sandwiches they'd had for lunch the
day before.

She must have caught the distaste in his expression,
because she sighed. 'Will, you're being such a snob. Most
people eat sandwiches just like this.'

'I'm not being a snob. I'm just used to…' he knew he had
to be careful about the way he phrased it, because he didn't
want to hurt her '…less processed food,' he finished.

'My week, my rules,' she reminded him.

Amanda worked on her studies again that evening, while
Will sprawled on the sofa with a book and his MP3 player.
And at the end of the evening he delivered his verdict to the
camera. 'She's driven. Absolutely driven. Though I can't
work out *why*.'

Unless she was trying to avoid being too close to him, in
case last Thursday evening repeated itself? Not that he'd say
that on screen.

'She doesn't let people get close. Although I'm shadowing her, the barriers between us are growing thicker by the
minute. And I have no idea where to start breaking them
down.' He switched off the camera.

Actually, he did have one idea. But that was most definitely
not for sharing with anyone except Amanda. And if he got it
wrong, the barriers between them would not only be enormous, they'd also be covered in anti-climb paint.

The next morning, Will and Amanda left the flat an hour
earlier. The Tube was marginally better—either that, Will
thought, or he was already getting used to the squash.

'So this gym's near your office?' he asked.

She nodded. 'It means I can go on the way home—which

I normally do on Fridays—or do an early session and have enough time to cool down before work.'

The idea of being squashed into a hot, sticky train after a workout really didn't bear thinking about. Will was grateful that the gym was within walking distance of Amanda's office.

Amanda arranged a temporary pass for him as her guest.

'Do you go to a gym regularly, or should I book you an induction course in the weights room?' the receptionist asked.

No to both, Will thought. 'Are there any classes?' he asked. 'Circuit training or what-have-you?'

The receptionist checked the gym schedule. 'There's a spinning class in ten minutes.'

'Spinning?'

'A forty-five-minute static cycling workout to music,' she explained.

Bicycles were the main form of transport in Cambridge, though Will was more used to walking or punting. It had been a while since he'd done any cycling. 'I'll give it a go,' he said with a smile. 'Amanda, are you going to join me?'

'No. I have a routine.'

He grinned as they walked to the changing rooms. 'I was right, then—you're way too much of a control freak to take a class.'

She glowered at him and pushed open the door to the ladies' changing rooms.

Will got changed faster than she did and was waiting outside, leaning against the wall, when she emerged.

In knee-length clingy shorts and a close-fitting T-shirt that showed all her curves, she looked mouthwatering.

And he knew exactly how she tasted.

He shoved the thought to the back of his mind. If he started thinking about that kiss, he'd end up doing something stupid. Like pinning her to the wall and kissing her until they both forgot where they were—and the gossip machine would go into overdrive. Someone as private as Amanda would just hate being the subject of office gossip, especially because a slip-up from her would be so rare that it would be the top talking point in the office for days instead of blowing over quickly. And hadn't she already told him she hated being teased?

'That was an inflammatory comment earlier and I take it back,' he said.

'Apologies normally contain the S word,' she said, her voice crisp.

'Sorry,' he said, meaning it. 'But this class sounds like fun. Why not come and do it with me?'

He honestly hadn't meant to make an innuendo. But Amanda clearly took it that way, because she blushed. Really blushed. 'I have a personalised workout that suits me. As they say, if it ain't broke, why fix it?'

For a moment, he was tempted to goad her into it—make clucking noises or something. But Amanda wasn't the easily manipulated sort. And that blush had made him feel a hell of a lot better because now he knew for sure that he wasn't alone in these feelings. That maybe there was a chance. 'See you after class, then,' he said.

'Hey. You're forgetting something.'

'What?'

She handed him a bottle of water. 'Hydration.'

She'd brought a drink especially for him? The thought warmed him. 'Thanks.' He wanted to hug her, but her expression said 'keep off'. Clearly here, just as much as at work, she was this self-contained little island.

He picked a bike smack in the centre of the room, where he'd still be able to see the instructor but could also see people around him and maybe follow them if he got lost in the middle of a routine.

'Wow—we actually have a man in the class today,' a woman said, walking over to him and smiling. 'I'm the instructor.'

He smiled back. 'Will Daynes.'

'Is this your first spinning class?' At his 'yes', she talked him through how the resistance switch on the bike worked. 'Don't feel you have to compete with other people,' she warned. 'The only person who will see what your resistance level is will be you. So just do what's right for you—if it's too much, then turn the resistance down and don't try to be a hero about it.'

Will laughed. 'I know the sort of guy you mean. That's not how I work.'

'Good.' She gave him an approving look. 'We warm up first with some low resistance, and then do a "hill climb"—you turn up the resistance as you go, to make it feel as if you're climbing a hill. Some songs, you'll stand up and pedal for some counts and sit down for others.'

'Stand up on a bike? Won't it fall over?' Will asked.

'No, because a spinning bike has a heavier frame and flywheel,' she reassured him. 'At the end, we slow everything back down to normal and finish the cool-down routine with arm stretches and leg stretches. There aren't any brakes on the bike, so you'll have to slow your pedalling down to stop.'

'So how's a spinning class better for you than going for a ride on an ordinary bike?' he asked.

'In London? No traffic, for starters.' She laughed. 'And you can burn anything from five hundred to seven hundred calories in a class. Have you got a drink?'

'Yep.'

'Good. Enjoy the class.' She nodded at the towel beside his bike. 'And you'll need that afterwards.'

It was a much more intensive workout than he'd expected, but the adrenalin kicked in. Even though the music wasn't quite to his taste, the pounding dance track was perfect for keeping them all in rhythm. And after the cool-down, he noticed everyone used the towel placed next to the bike to wipe it down; he followed suit.

'Did you enjoy it?' the woman on the bike next to his asked.

'More than I expected,' he admitted. 'I definitely feel that I've done a workout. How about you?'

'It's brilliant. I've been coming for three months now,' another woman added, walking over to join them. 'So are you coming back?'

'I'm not sure,' Will said. 'I'm only in London for a week.'

'Pity,' the first woman said with a smile. 'Here on business?'

'Yes.'

'Nothing worse than being stuck in a hotel on your own at the end of the day,' the second woman said as they walked back towards the changing rooms. 'Look, there's a group of us going to the pub tonight. Why don't you come along?'

Give me strength, Amanda thought, coming from the weights room and overhearing the last bit. Will had been in the gym barely an hour and already there were women flocking round him. Asking him out, too.

She'd been pretty much ignoring him in the evenings, concentrating on her studies, so she wouldn't blame him for accepting the invitation. But there was a tight knot of disappointment in her stomach at the thought of being on her own.

Crazy. She liked her life the way it was. Will Daynes was way too spontaneous for her comfort. And it wasn't as if he was anything more than a business associate anyway. She shouldn't start feeling possessive about him. Or jealous.

'That's really sweet of you to ask,' Will said, 'but I'm not actually on my own. I'm with a colleague.'

The tall, statuesque brunette actually fluttered her eyelashes at him, Amanda noted with disgust. 'Bring him with you.'

'Her, actually,' Will corrected with a smile.

Uh-oh. She hadn't expected him to bring her into it. Was

he going to say yes for both of them? The idea of spending an entire evening in a noisy pub with a crowd of people she didn't even know—an evening when she could be preparing for her MBA course—was just hideous. He wouldn't do that to her…would he?

'I'm sorry, we've already promised to be somewhere tonight. But the offer's really appreciated—isn't it, Mands?' he asked, looking over at her and smiling.

Mands? That was a new one on her. And it was even worse than Dee's version of her name. She forced a smile to her face. 'Hi, Will. And, yes, you're right.' About one thing. 'The offer's appreciated.' The rest of it was a complete fabrication. Why had he lied? And if he could lie that convincingly…

No. She didn't want to start extrapolating that.

'Good workout, Mands?' he asked.

To her utter shock, Will slid his arm round her shoulders. And her brain turned to mush. What was the question? 'Mmm,' she said, hoping the response would cover the fact that she'd completely lost the plot.

'So are you up in London for the week, too?' one of the women asked.

She shook her head. 'I work round the corner.'

'I haven't seen you at any of the classes before,' the woman remarked.

'I, um, tend to use the weight room.'

'Uh-huh.'

Being the centre of attention was just…horrible, Amanda thought. The other women were clearly looking at her and wondering what on earth someone as charming and sophisticated as Will was doing with someone like her. Colleagues, they might have swallowed. But the way he'd draped that casual arm round her more or less said they were an item.

And nobody believed him.

Why did that hurt so much?

'We're going to be late for work,' she muttered to Will. 'I need a shower.'

His thumb caressed the back of her neck as he moved his arm away, sending a shiver down her spine. 'See you in a minute,' he said, giving her a slow, sexy smile that told everyone around them that he'd much rather be having the shower with her.

Lord, the *embarrassment* of people knowing that. And even when she turned the temperature of the water right down, it couldn't cool the heat in her face.

She was still hot and bothered when she'd dressed and walked out of the changing rooms to find Will already waiting for her.

'Okay?' he asked.

'Mmm,' she said, meaning *not on your life*.

When they'd left the gym, she said softly, 'You can't help yourself, can you?'

'What?'

'Flirting. In the gym.'

He blinked. 'I wasn't flirting. Those women were just being friendly.'

'To you, yes.' She hadn't actually meant flirting with *them*. She'd meant the way he'd flirted with her. The hand-and-eye stuff. The way he'd stroked the back of her neck.

He raised an eyebrow. 'Hmm. That sounds like jealousy.'

'Of course it isn't,' she said crossly.

Will rubbed his nose, and she knew exactly what he was thinking. Pinocchio. It goaded her into saying, 'You're meant to be shadowing me, not flirting.' The moment the words left her mouth, she regretted them. The last time she'd accused him of flirting, he'd kissed her. A covert glance at his face told her he remembered, too.

Oh, Lord, she had to get thoughts of kissing out of her head, or else she was going to go crazy.

'And don't call me "Mands",' she said.

'Why not?' Mischief was written all over his face. 'It's cute.'

'It's irritating,' she corrected. 'My name is Amanda.'

'*Amanda.*'

How did he manage to make the word sound like a caress sliding over her skin? She needed more than just coffee to kick-start her brain cells this morning before work. She needed something to keep her libido where it belonged.

Under control.

Another interminable day in the office. Will lasted half a morning before he snapped and started sorting out the plants.

Amanda didn't say anything, but there was a note on his place on her desk in her neat, precise handwriting when he returned. *What are you doing?*

Sorting out the plants. I told you on Monday, they're not being watered properly and they were in the wrong aspect. They'll grow now, he scribbled and shoved the note back to her.

You're supposed to be shadowing me.

He knew that. *Could you have stood by if I'd been doing something seriously wrong in accountancy terms?*

Probably not.

Exactly. QED.

She didn't reply. Just continued working.

He rather liked this little game. Private messages. What would she do if he wrote 'I want to kiss you'?

Probably run a mile.

But there was another way…He scribbled her another note. *Let's have lunch out today.* Before he got too stir crazy. *Find a park somewhere near.*

There isn't one, came the reply. *Anyway, it's too hot. The office is air conditioned.*

He should've expected that. Amanda wasn't the sort to play hooky and go to the park for a picnic lunch. She'd been horrified when he'd taken her to the Botanical Gardens for the afternoon.

Though she'd also kissed him…

He really ought to stop thinking about that, or he'd make a stupid mistake—and he didn't want her having to cover for him. But she was sitting so close to him, he could smell her perfume. So close that his knee could press against hers.

He'd deliberately agreed to sit at her desk with the aim of unsettling her, and making her aware of his presence. It looked as if he was hoist with his own petard.

Somehow he got through the rest of the morning, a vacuum-packed sandwich at their desk for lunch, and an interminable afternoon. But when Amanda dragged him over to the chiller cabinet in the supermarket, pointed to the TV dinners and asked him which one he'd like that evening, he lost it.

'That's it. We're breaking the rules.'

She frowned. 'How do you mean?'

'I know I'm meant to be shadowing you, but I can't eat this stuff. I'm cooking for you tonight.'

'But—'

'No arguments, Amanda. We're doing this one my way.' He took the wire basket from her, shepherded her round the shop, filled the basket with salmon and fresh vegetables, and paid before she had the chance to protest.

'I'll pay you back,' she said as he nudged her out of the door.

'Believe me, not having to eat the stuff you serve up is payment enough,' he said feelingly.

She must have realised he'd reached his limit, because she didn't argue once, all the way back to her flat.

'Now. Cookery lesson,' he said when they were in her kitchen. 'Turn on oven. Take one glass dish.' He suited his actions to the words. 'Tear off one big piece of foil. Put salmon in the middle. Put a tiny bit of butter on the top and a grind of black pepper. Fold foil like so. Put in oven.' He closed the oven door and leaned against the worktop with his arms folded. 'That's hardly any more work than preparing one of those vile ready meals—and you don't have unbiodegradable rubbish to dispose of, either.'

She frowned. 'Are you trying to make me feel guilty about carbon footprints and what-have-you?'

'No. I'm trying to get you to eat properly. You put this in the oven and leave it for thirty minutes—and you can do the same with a boneless chicken breast or a pork loin steak. Use lemon juice and herbs, or a bit of bottled marinade, if you want to ring the changes. Get an electric steamer and put your veg on at the same time, and they'll all be ready together.' He sighed, exasperated that she didn't see it. 'It's no more difficult than putting a plastic tray into the oven.'

Her jaw set. 'I don't have time.'

'Five minutes. That's all it takes.'

'I don't see the point of cooking.'

'Or eating? I thought I'd already taught you that food's more than fuel.'

Her pupils expanded; clearly she was remembering that lesson in taste in his back garden. 'That's in your world, Will.' She dragged in a breath. 'This is mine.'

A world where he didn't fit.

Somehow they'd have to find a place to compromise. Though right now he wasn't sure where.

CHAPTER THIRTEEN

'AH, AMANDA—just the woman I wanted.' Ed perched on the edge of her desk and smiled at her.

In other words, he was running late on an audit and wanted to borrow a couple of her juniors. She flapped her hand casually at him. 'Fine. I'll give you a note of their charge codes for your budget sheet.'

He laughed. 'I don't always want to borrow your juniors, you know.'

Oh, yes, he did. It was just about the only time he ever bothered with her.

'What can I do for you, then?' she asked, pinning her politest smile to her face.

'I wondered if you wanted to come out for a meal with us after work tonight. There's a few of us going for Chinese.'

She stared at him, not quite believing what she'd just heard. Since when did Ed ever include her in invitations to meals out? 'Chinese?'

'They do other stuff if you don't like Chinese,' he said quickly. 'Will said to check with you.'

So that was it. She ignored the tight little knot of hurt in her stomach. They wanted Will to go, and he'd probably said something about not going without her. It was exactly the same way that those women in the gym had invited him out for a drink and he'd made sure that the invite had included her. 'I—um—'

'You've had him to yourself every evening this week,' Ed pointed out, grinning.

'He's shadowing me.'

'At work, yes.' Ed's grin broadened. 'Outside…well…' He winked.

He thought she and Will were…? She lifted her chin. 'I don't know what you're implying, but we're just colleagues.'

'Oh, come *on*, Amanda. The rest of the women in the office have got the hots for him and you're spending all day, every day, with him. Don't tell me he hasn't managed to melt the ice in your veins yet.'

She knew he was trying to goad her into a reaction, and that made her just about capable of resisting the urge to slap him. 'My private life,' she said coolly, 'isn't up for discussion. I've already told you he's a colleague. If you want to make ridiculous speculations, I suggest you do it on your own time rather than the firm's. Now, if you don't mind, some of us have work to do.'

Ed shrugged and hauled himself off her desk. 'Suit yourself.'

'I will.' She made a show of concentrating on her work, but inside she was fuming. How come Ed always got away with it? He'd failed his exams twice, but he'd still been promoted to audit manager, whereas she'd passed hers with top marks and was still stuck exactly where she was.

And now he was spreading rumours about her.

'I'm glad that's a pencil and not a dagger.'

She looked up at the sound of his voice. 'Oh. Will.'

'You okay?' he asked.

'Fine.' If you didn't include wanting to murder someone. 'If you want to go for that Chinese meal tonight, that's fine. I'll give you my spare key.'

'Don't you want to go?'

'I have a meeting. Dinner with a client.'

He raised an eyebrow. 'That wasn't on the schedule.'

'Late amendment.'

'Sounds like an excuse.'

She sighed. 'You know as well as I do, I don't fit in.'

'And if you don't make the effort, how are you ever going to fit in?' he asked softly.

'Maybe,' she said, her fingers tightening round the pencil again, 'I don't want to. Maybe I'm perfectly fine as I am.'

'Hmm. Come with me.'

'Where?'

'Meeting room.' He unfolded her fingers from the pencil, took her hand and tugged her to her feet. Then he took a file from her desk.

'What's that for?'

'Discussion,' he said, ushering her over to the meeting room and closing the door behind them. He put the file on the desk, unopened. 'Right. Now you're going to tell me what's really wrong.'

'Nothing.'

'Okay. Let me put this another way. If I have a tree with scale and I don't do anything about it, it'll spread and feed on the sap until the leaves go yellow and the tree starts to die. If I treat the problem, I'll have a healthy tree.'

She frowned. 'And?'

'It's the same for you. Whatever's upsetting you, if you keep it to yourself, it's going to grow and grow and make you feel worse. Tell me what's wrong, and that's half the problem solved.'

She felt a muscle flicker in her jaw. 'I told you before, I hate people gossiping about me.'

'Who's gossiping?'

'Ed. He thinks you and I are...' Her voice faded. Said aloud, it would sound even more ridiculous.

'Maybe,' Will said, 'we should give him something to talk about.'

Before she had any idea what Will was going to do, he picked her up, set her on the edge of the table, slid one hand to the base of her spine to press her against him and the other at the nape of her neck, and kissed her.

Stars exploded in her head, and she slid her hands into his hair and kissed him back. The whole of London vanished— the whole of the world, even, because Amanda wasn't aware of anything else right at that moment except Will and the way his mouth was teasing a response from her.

When he broke the kiss, she was practically hyperventilating.

And then she remembered where they were. In the meeting room. Where anyone could've looked through the narrow glass pane in the door and seen them kissing.

Especially Ed.

The office grapevine would go crazy.

'We're in the *office*,' she hissed. 'I don't *do* this sort of thing at work.' She didn't exactly do it outside, either, but that was another matter.

Will ran the pad of his thumb along her lower lip, making her shiver with need. 'Neither do I. But I've been fantasising about this for a week.' His eyes glowed gold with desire. 'Sweeping everything off the desk and putting you in its place and kissing you.'

In her office, there was a clear desk policy, so he didn't need to sweep any papers aside. In his… 'It'd take you a week to *clear* your desk.'

He laughed. 'Ever heard of the volcano principle? If a piece of paper is important enough it'll make its way to the top of the pile.'

'More like it'll take you hours to find anything. All you

need to do is file a little tiny bit a day; then it won't build up and be an impossible task.'

'Stop trying to organise me.' He stopped her wriggling off the table by the simple means of resting his palms on her thighs. The thoughts that roused in her brain were enough to keep her absolutely still.

'There's nothing wrong with my filing system,' he said.

'Your filing system is the passenger footwell in your car,' she pointed out.

'And that's a problem how, exactly?'

Could he really not see it?

'Aren't you going to tell me?' he asked, stealing another kiss.

That kiss had leached away all coherent thought. She couldn't for the life of her remember the logical argument she had planned. She shook her head and smiled wryly. 'Will, you're impossible.'

'But you're smiling now.' He stroked her cheek. 'So I've achieved my objectives for the day.'

She frowned. 'What objectives?' Was kissing her some kind of objective? And then a seriously nasty thought wormed into her mind. Ed and his cronies were competing with each other to see who could play the field hardest—and they'd asked Will to go on this meal out. And Ed had made that crack about Will melting the ice in her veins. She didn't think Will was like them…but then again, she didn't understand the male bonding process at all. Just please, please don't say he had a bet with one of them about getting her into bed. Because, if that happened, she'd never live it down—and she'd never forgive him for betraying her.

'I'm just following your business principles and setting objectives, that's all,' he said.

Heat prickled at the back of her neck. Heat and adrenalin and the tiniest bit of fear. 'What objectives?' she asked again.

'Firstly, to make you smile. And, secondly, to kiss you—for long enough to make you kiss me back.'

She felt her face flame. He was right. That was exactly what she'd done. Forgotten where she was and kissed him back. 'Why did you want to kiss me?'

He looked at her in obvious disbelief. 'Do you really not know?'

'I wouldn't be asking, otherwise.'

He rolled his eyes. 'I want to kiss you, Amanda, because I'm attracted to you. Extremely attracted. And if you don't believe me…' He slid his hands under her buttocks and pulled her against him so she was left in absolutely no doubt about his arousal.

She'd thought her face had felt hot earlier. Now, her temperature had gone beyond scorching.

Clearly it showed, because he smiled. 'Do you know how sexy you look when you blush?'

With difficulty, she dragged her thoughts together. 'Will, I can't do this. We're in the office. And I have a client meeting in ten minutes.'

'Shame.' He leaned forward and whispered in her ear, 'Ten minutes isn't anywhere near long enough to do what I want to do with you.'

Oh, Lord. The ideas that he put into her head. She felt as if she were spiking a fever.

'I need much, *much* longer,' he drawled.

Oh-h-h.

She clung to the last shreds of coherence. She had a client meeting. Will had just kissed her stupid. And it probably showed. She couldn't walk out of here and face Ed and the others. 'I…I need to fix my lipstick.'

'You look lovely as you are.' He tucked a strand of hair behind her ear. 'Relax.'

That was just the problem. She couldn't. Didn't know *how*.

'I have to prepare for this meeting, Will. It's important.'

'Okay. This thing between us isn't going away. It can wait until later.' He held her gaze. 'And that's a promise, Amanda.'

Amanda actually had to force herself to concentrate during the client meeting. She certainly didn't dare meet Will's eye. Because she knew what she'd see there: a heat that would make a matching need rise in her own body.

She absolutely refused to set foot outside the office over lunch. Knowing Will, he'd checked out the nearest park on the Internet and was planning to whisk her off for a picnic or something. She didn't have *time* for that.

Ha. More like she was too scared, she admitted silently. The last time they'd been in a garden together, she'd ended up naked to the waist. She didn't think he'd go that far in a public place—but then again, the way he'd made her feel in the meeting room earlier that morning, she couldn't trust herself.

He made no comment and disappeared. But when he came back, he brought her a little box of strawberries. Ready-to-eat, hulled and washed strawberries. The fruit he'd teased her with that evening in his garden.

And she thought of it every time she ate one of the tiny, sweet fruits.

She was pretty sure he was thinking of it, too—because that hungry look was back in his eyes.

Dinner was murder. She had no idea what anyone was talking about, because Will was sitting opposite her. Will, who had the sexiest smile in the world. Will, whose eyes promised her that he was going to continue where he'd left off last time over the strawberries.

He didn't touch her. He didn't have to. It was the way he held her gaze as he bit into the dark chocolate thin that accompanied their coffee.

Tasting it the way he planned to taste her.

* * *

He still didn't touch her all the way to the Tube. But then he sat next to her, so close that his thigh rested against hers.

'So, beautiful lady, what now?'

She frowned. 'What did you call me?'

He smiled. 'You heard. Beautiful.'

Her frown deepened. 'But I'm not—I'm just ordinary.'

'No, you're not. Has nobody ever told you how cute you are?'

Cute? It wasn't a word anyone ever used around her.

The tip of his finger traced the curve of her eyebrows. 'Your eyes are the same colour as the Fenland sky in early spring,' he whispered. 'And your mouth's a perfect cupid's bow. When you smile, it makes your whole face light up. And it makes me want to do this.' He leaned over and kissed her very lightly on the lips, then pulled back far enough so she could see his eyes. See the sincerity.

'We've both been fighting it. Decided we're too different for it to work between us. But I've been thinking. Maybe we've got it wrong,' he said. 'Maybe it's more that our differences make us balanced. That we complement each other.'

Was he suggesting…? But no. It couldn't work out between them. He loathed the city and no way could she bury herself in a backwater. Even for Will. She'd seen what it had done to her mother—it would do the same to her.

As if he saw her doubts surfacing, Will leaned forward again, and drew a trail of kisses to her ear. 'I want to do more than just kiss you. A lot more. Because I know what it's like to be half-naked with you. And I really, really want to be completely naked with you.' He nuzzled the sensitive spot behind her ear. 'Just you and me and nothing in between,' he whispered.

'You're drunk,' she said shakily.

'Not on one glass of wine. And you didn't drink much, either. This isn't alcohol.' He nibbled her earlobe. 'This is pheromones. Much, much headier stuff.'

'Sex—' she could barely drag the word out '—is overrated.'

'Is it, now?' His eyes glittered. 'Then I dare you.'

She folded her arms. 'I don't take dares.'

'Live dangerously for once,' he said, his voice husky. 'I dare you to find out—with me.'

Could she? Should she?

'If you're worried about protection,' he added softly, 'don't be. I'll take care of you.'

Of course he'd carry condoms. A man as gorgeous as Will Daynes had women throwing themselves at him all the time. She'd seen the way every single female in the office had looked at him. Not to mention the gym, the pub, even the supermarket. Will turned heads.

As if he'd guessed her thoughts, he said, 'Just for the record, I'm picky. I don't sleep with all my girlfriends.'

'I'm not your girlfriend.'

He didn't deny it, she noticed. Well, she'd known for a while she wasn't girlfriend material. And it didn't bother her because she didn't need distracting from her career goals. She already had her life planned out the way she wanted it.

'Last week you were my shadow,' he said. 'This week, I'm yours.'

Okay. That summed up the situation very nicely.

'But tonight, I want you to be my lover.'

Could she? *Should* she?

'Say yes,' he murmured next to her ear.

His breath was warm against her skin; a shiver of longing rippled down her spine. *Live dangerously for once.*

'Yes,' she whispered.

He didn't say anything, but the hot look in his eyes told her everything she needed to know. She couldn't even remember getting off the Tube and walking back to her flat with him.

* * *

The second the door had closed behind them, he was kissing her. Really kissing her. The kind of kiss she'd only ever seen in a girly movie when Dee dragged her off to the cinema. Hot and wet and open-mouthed. Ripping each other's clothes off and not caring where the garments landed. Pressing each other against walls and doors. Urgent and needy and hot.

Will picked her up, carried her to her room, and kicked the door open, still kissing her. Stripped her of the last bits of lacy underwear. Got rid of his own clothes. And then they were skin to skin, belly to belly, thigh to thigh.

She couldn't remember ever wanting anything as much as she wanted Will, right here and right now. His teeth against her throat. His hands stroking her breasts and her belly and easing her thighs apart. The scorching desire in his eyes as he looked at her.

But as he nudged his thigh between hers, she froze.

Will stopped immediately. 'What's the matter, honey?' he asked.

Tell me what's wrong, and that's half the problem solved.

Maybe, maybe not. But this was something he really ought to know. 'I'm not very good at this,' she admitted, her voice cracking.

Will stroked her face and kissed her so gently, so tenderly that her heart swelled. 'It's not a competition. It's team-work,' he said.

'Teamwork?' she croaked.

'Uh-huh. You and I, we're on the same side. I want to find out how you like to be touched, what gives you pleasure, what makes you feel good.' He kissed her again. 'And I'm going to show you what I like, too.'

'I think I'm scared.'

She hadn't realised she'd spoken aloud until he told her huskily, 'There's no need. Because we're going to be very,

very good together.' He rubbed the tip of his nose against hers. 'Trust me on this. And I'm going to start by kissing you all over.'

By the time he'd finished, she was quivering. And more desperate than she'd ever have believed possible. 'I want you,' she said, her voice shaking.

'Good. Because I want you, too. So much that I think I'm going to die if I don't…' Slowly, slowly, he eased his body into hers.

Filling her, easing the ache—and when he started to move, she stared at him in wonder. She'd always thought sex was overrated, but this was nothing like anything she'd ever known. The way his thrusts stoked her desire, built it higher and higher; the way he brought her closer and closer to the edge, little by little and kiss by kiss and push by push. She could feel heat radiating from the soles of her feet all the way up to the top of her head—and then suddenly she was falling, falling right over the edge.

'Will!'

His mouth jammed over hers, and she felt the answering surge of his body within hers.

Some time later, he whispered, 'Did I hurt you, honey? I'm sorry.'

Then she realised her face was wet. 'No.' She scrubbed the tears away with the back of her wrist, not wanting him to think she was weak. 'No, you didn't hurt me.'

He caught her hand, kissed the back of it and then kissed her tears away. 'Tell me, Amanda.'

They'd shared too much for her to be anything but honest with him. 'I didn't know it could be like this.'

He nuzzled his cheek against hers. 'Neither did I.'

No way. She wasn't swallowing that one. A man as gorgeous as Will Daynes—one who managed to get women flocking round him within a few minutes of walking into a room—it wasn't possible that he'd never experienced something like that before. 'You've had plenty of girlfriends,' she said, her eyes narrowing.

'If you're asking, yes, I've dated and, yes, I've slept with my partners. But it's always been mutual and it's always been fun.' Then his eyes widened and he looked utterly shocked. 'Oh, my God. Have I just been completely insensitive? Are you telling me that was your first time?'

Her jaw set. 'I'm twenty-seven. I'm not *that* sad.'

He laughed, rolled over on to his back and pulled her into his arms so that her head was resting on his shoulder and his arm was curved round her waist. 'Honey, there's nothing sad about being a virgin at twenty-seven. It shows you value yourself—that you're choosy.' He kissed her shoulder. 'I'm sorry. I would have taken it a little slower if I'd realised.'

'I'm *not* a virgin,' she said through clenched teeth. 'I've slept with someone before.'

'And since then you've thought sex was overrated?'

Trust him to remember what she'd said to him on the Tube. And work out why. Embarrassed, she muttered, 'Yes.'

'Sounds to me as if he didn't take enough time.'

'How do you mean?'

'He didn't try to find out what made you feel good. So he wasn't doing it right.'

'So it wasn't me?' The words slipped out before she could stop them.

He tightened his arms round her. 'No, it most definitely wasn't you. Was that what he said?'

Oh, Lord. She'd forgotten how good Will was at reading people. Of course he'd work it out. She turned her face away, not wanting him to see the humiliation and hurt the memories dragged back.

'Look at me, Amanda.'

His voice was so gentle, so soft, she did so.

'He lied. It wasn't you.' He stroked her face. 'So here you

are, thinking that you don't fit anywhere and you're useless with people and no good at sex.'

'Don't pull your punches, do you?' He'd homed in on everything that was wrong in her life. Everything that was wrong with her.

'It's how you see yourself. Not the way I see you.' He kissed the tip of her nose. 'You fit me perfectly.'

'How? How, when we're so different?'

'Complementary.' Another kiss, at the corner of her mouth. 'It works. And you're not useless with people. You sparkled tonight, at dinner.'

Had she? She couldn't remember a thing about the evening. Except Will.

'When you let go, relax, people like being around you. Then they're not scared they'll fail to meet your standards,' he told her. 'You're clever and you're good company. Just relax, believe in yourself and they won't reject you.'

She felt the tears pooling in her eyes again. 'I hate this. I *never* cry.'

'Tears can be healing.' He kissed the other corner of her mouth. 'And then we have the third thing. This belief that you're no good at sex. Now, if that were true, neither of us would have climaxed. And I wouldn't have to go to the bathroom pretty shortly to deal with something.'

'Oh.' She hadn't thought of that.

'I'm not going to be long. And I'm not going to my own room tonight, either.' He brushed his mouth against hers. 'I'm coming back to you. Because I want to spend the entire night with you, Amanda. I want to hold you and fall asleep with you and wake with you in my arms.'

Even though she knew it was anatomically impossible, she could feel her heart melting.

'Hold that thought,' he whispered, brushing another kiss against her mouth. 'I won't be long.'

He was as good as his word. A couple of minutes later, he was spooned behind her, his arms wrapped round her and keeping her close to his body. She'd never felt more protected and warm and *loved* before.

Loved? No. He hadn't said the L-word. Will didn't love her. He was attracted to her, yes, and he'd been honest about it. He'd also been honest enough *not* to have told her that he loved her, just to get her into bed.

So tonight was a gift.

Tomorrow, the lifeswap would be over. Will would walk out of her life, go back to his world. And she'd go on with her plans—do her MBA, make partner, and prove to everyone in the firm that she belonged.

But tonight…tonight, he was hers. To have and to hold.

And as she drifted to sleep in his arms, she was smiling.

CHAPTER FOURTEEN

THE NEXT morning, Amanda woke to find Will sprawled across most of the bed. By contrast, she had most of the sheet she'd substituted for her duvet during the hot weather—there was only one corner of the sheet draped over Will's hips.

Naked, he was beautiful. His pectoral muscles were perfectly defined, his stomach was washboard flat and his thighs were strong. She could tell by his regular breathing that he was still asleep, and she couldn't resist sliding her hand under the sheet to stroke his hipbone.

A man to die for. A man who'd made love to her so thoroughly last night that the endorphins were still fizzing round her system this morning. And that sculptured body wasn't due to working out at the gym, it was from his lifestyle.

Her smile faded and she paused with her hand still resting on his hip. A lifestyle so far away from her own. This wasn't going to work, so she needed to end it now before she was in too deep. Before she got *really* hurt.

'Right a bit,' a sultry voice murmured in her ear.

She snatched her hand away, her face burning with embarrassment. 'How long have you been awake?'

'Long enough.'

'Why didn't you say anything?'

'Because I was enjoying myself.' He gave her a sidelong

look. 'I like it when you touch me, Amanda.' He propped himself up on one elbow and leaned over to kiss her lightly. 'Don't stop,' he whispered.

'I…we can't. I have to be in the office. And you hate the rush hour.'

'So we need to save some time? Hmmm.'

Before she guessed his intentions, he'd climbed out of bed, whipped the sheet away, scooped her into his arms and carried her into the bathroom.

'What are you doing?' she asked.

'Saving time.' He kissed her shoulder. 'We're going to have a shower together.'

Just as well he was carrying her, as the idea made her knees buckle.

'Why do you keep picking me up?' she asked.

'Because I can.' He laughed, and let her slide down his body until her feet touched the floor again. 'You're little and cute and it brings out the caveman in me.'

She hadn't seen him as a caveman—more as a pirate, dark and dangerous and incredibly desirable.

He switched on the shower, stepped inside, and beckoned to her.

When she didn't move, he shrugged, walked out of the shower—trailing water everywhere—and hauled her in with him.

'Will! We can't—'

'Yes, we can,' he cut in, and poured shower gel on to his palm. He gave her the sexiest smile she'd ever seen, then worked the gel into a lather, spun her round so her back was towards him, and stroked lather on to her skin. Stroked from the nape of her neck across her shoulders, then down to the base of her spine and fluttering up her sides.

Oh-h-h.

And then he turned her to face him again, lathering across

her collarbones and down her sides to her ribcage; he circled her navel, teasing and inciting her until she was near the point of begging him to touch her breasts.

As if he could read her mind, he did so, cupping them and rubbing the pads of his thumbs over her nipples.

'You're exquisite,' he breathed, 'and I think this is torturing me more than it's teasing you.' He dropped to his knees and worked on lathering her legs, working from her feet to her ankles to her calves to her knees. When he reached her thighs and stroked them apart, she was shivering with need. And when he touched the tip of his tongue to her sex, she nearly screamed.

He brought her nearer and nearer to the edge, until her hands were tangled in his hair and she was actually whimpering.

Then in one lithe movement he stood up, lifted her and supported her weight against the wall; the coldness of the tiles made her gasp and arch towards him so her body was pressed against his.

'Wrap your legs round my waist,' he told her huskily. 'It'll balance us better.'

And then he entered her.

Amanda wasn't prepared for how he made her feel. With the water streaming down over her and his body pushing into hers, it was astonishing, as if she were in the middle of a thunderstorm, with lightning flashing every time he pushed deep inside her and the thunder being the beating of her heart.

She cried out as her climax hit her. Will supported her weight, holding her close until the aftershocks had died away, then set her down on her feet.

Then it was her turn to wash him. Such an *intimate* task. But she enjoyed the feeling of his muscles beneath her fingers, exploring him and finding out where he was ticklish and what made him hiss with pleasure.

Just as she was about to return the favour—use her mouth to drive him as crazy as he'd driven her—he drew her to her feet.

'We,' he said huskily, 'are going to be late. And although I'd love to spend the entire day in bed with you, you'd hate me for it.'

'Hate you?' she asked, mystified.

'Because it'd mean throwing a sickie. Which I'd guess is very much against your principles.'

She closed her eyes. 'Yeah.'

'Hey...' he kissed her, slow and lingering '...we have time. Later.' He stroked her face. 'Have I told you how incredible you are?'

She couldn't speak.

'Feel.' He took her hand and placed it over his heart. 'You actually make my heart miss beats.'

'Now you're flannelling me.'

He shook his head. 'Honest truth. Race you to getting dressed.' He turned off the shower. 'Amanda.' His voice grew husky. '*Amazing.*'

She didn't feel quite so amazing when she'd finished dressing, walked into the kitchen and registered just how crumpled Will's suit was. Her own would have to go to the dry cleaner's, she thought wryly.

'Coffee,' he said, pushing the mug over towards her.

'Thanks. I, um, I'm sorry about your suit.'

'I'm not.' His eyes were still that sultry, sexy, storm-gold colour. 'And before you start panicking that people are going to notice, they won't.'

She wasn't so sure. Ed and his cronies were always the first to pick up the faintest hint of a scandal. They'd guess straight away that she and Will had had a mad affair.

'Don't worry,' he said. 'Everything's going to be fine.'

'How do you know that?'

'I just do.' He picked up her hand and kissed each finger in turn. 'You worry too much.'

All the same, she couldn't shift the uneasiness—despite the fact that Will held her hand all the way to the Tube station. It was already too much of a squash for them to get a seat next to each other, and Will, being Will, insisted that she should be the one to sit down.

'I'm taller than you are,' he reminded her. 'It's not such a stretch for me to hang on to the bar.'

She could hardly argue with that.

More and more people got onto the train, and in the end she could barely see Will. At their stop, he waited for her outside the train; they walked in near silence to her office.

For the first time ever, Amanda found that work actually dragged. The morning was full of time-consuming, annoyingly trivial things that needed to be sorted out. A phone call from Rhiannon meant that she'd be out at the client's tomorrow morning, sorting out some glitches in the audit. Yet, at the same time, the minutes seemed to rush by. The last few minutes before Will would be leaving London.

And then it was three o'clock.

The time they'd agreed to leave the office so Will wouldn't have too much of a nightmare journey back to Cambridge.

He hadn't actually packed yet. Because they'd been otherwise occupied that morning, Amanda thought with a flash of shame. But it only took him ten minutes—and half of that involved changing back into his scruffy jeans.

'So. The end of Dee's lifeswap project.'

'Was it as bad as you thought, in my world?'

'Put it this way, I wouldn't swap it for mine,' he admitted. 'Though there were some high points. One or two *really* spectacular ones.' He brushed his mouth against hers. 'Come home with me for the weekend, Amanda.'

It was tempting. So, so tempting.

A weekend of pottering around the garden and walking by the river on Sunday afternoon.

A weekend of Will's fabulous cooking.

A weekend of making love and exploring each other—a whole weekend with the sexy pirate who'd hauled her into the shower and made love to her until she'd forgotten the world.

So tempting.

But she didn't belong in the Fens, and she knew it. She was a city girl. If he tempted her there, she'd end up like her mother, bitter and resentful, and everything they'd shared would be like ashes in her mouth. 'I can't,' she whispered. 'I need to sort something out at a client's tomorrow.'

'So where do we go from here?' he asked softly.

Crunch time. She'd been thinking about it all day. Will and his…*we have time*. *Later*. Except that was then and this was the real world. 'I think it's best that we end it now. Before either of us gets hurt.'

He raised an eyebrow. 'Is that what you really want? Or are you just scared to take a risk?'

She didn't rise to the bait. 'We're too different. There isn't enough crossover between us for this to work.'

'Ever heard the saying "where there's a will there's a way"? I'm good at fixing things.'

She shook her head. 'I don't need fixing.'

'Okay. If you won't come home with me, I'll ring Fliss and ask her to take care of Sunny for a bit longer, change my train ticket, and stay with you for the weekend. The gardens can wait.'

He'd put her before his business? But it wasn't just his business, was it? 'That's not fair—and, anyway, Dee's due home tonight.' She dragged in a breath. Neither of them had said they loved each other. It was the right time to call a halt. Before she lost her heart completely. 'Will, a clean break's better.'

'So this is goodbye, not *au revoir*?'

She nodded. 'This is goodbye.'

He looked at her. 'The lady's not for turning, eh?' he asked wryly. 'Well—goodbye, then. Good luck with the MBA. And you deserve to make partner at a terrifyingly young age.'

'Good luck with the designing. And think about entering Chelsea. I think you'd be up for a gold.'

'Maybe.'

For a moment, she thought he was going to kiss her. Then he picked up his case and walked out of the door. Out of her life.

It was all over.

'I thought Will was supposed to teach you to slow down a bit?' Dee asked, almost a week later. 'If anything, you're working even harder.'

Hard enough not to miss him. That was the idea. She needed to work until she was too tired to think about him. Too tired to remember how it felt to sleep in his arms. Too tired to pick up the phone and call him and admit how much she wanted him. 'I'm fine,' Amanda lied. 'Busy time at work. Year ends, and all that.'

Dee scoffed. 'The tax year ends in April.'

'But a company's year end doesn't necessarily end in April. Some end in July. Anyway, I need to start preparing for my MBA.'

'You're heading for a breakdown, if you keep up this pace,' Dee warned.

'I'm fine,' Amanda insisted. Or she would be if she could get Will's face out of her head.

'So Fliss decided to bring in the big guns, hmm?' Will asked, giving his aunt a hug.

'Something like that. Will, she's worried about you. She says you're working like a demon.'

'Just making the most of the light evenings. The nights are starting to pull in already,' Will said.

'Hmmm. Even Sunny looks as if she's moping.' Helen made a fuss of the dog. 'It's this girl, isn't it? The one you did that lifeswap thing with.'

Will grimaced. 'Helen, you're the nearest I have to a mother—' a hell of a lot more so than his own was '—but I don't want to talk about it. Even to you.'

'Why don't you just go and see her? Talk to her?' Helen asked.

'Because she made it clear she isn't interested.' He placed a mug of coffee in front of her. 'And I'm not going to beg.'

Helen rolled her eyes. 'Male pride. Tell me—what use is it? You're clearly eating your heart out over her. Go and see her. What have you got to lose?'

Will shrugged. 'We're from different worlds. She'd hate it here and I can't live in London. I can't *breathe* in London.'

Helen frowned. 'She does know you live in Cambridge, doesn't she? You did come clean?'

He didn't answer; merely turned his own mug of coffee round and round on the table.

'Oh, Will. For someone so clever, you can be such a dope.' She reached over to ruffle his hair. 'I can understand the Fens aren't everyone's cup of tea. But if she's a city girl, she'd be able to settle here in Cambridge. There's a solution staring you right in the face. But if you're intent on doing this stupid male pride thing…'

'Helen, she's *driven*. Even more so than my parents. And I spent too much of my childhood coming second to their career. I don't want to come second to hers.'

'Who's to say you will?' Helen asked.

'She's studying for an MBA, part time. Between that and her job, she doesn't have any spare time.'

'And how long is this for—a couple of years?' At his nod, she smiled. 'What's a couple of years, in the whole of a lifetime?'

'I suppose,' Will said.

'Go and see her. Don't let your pride get in the way. If you want her, fight for her,' Helen advised.

'Mmm.'

'Before,' she said quietly, 'it's too late.'

It took Will four days to swallow his pride. He considered ringing Amanda first; then again, she was stubborn enough to refuse to see him. If he drove up and knocked on her front door, she'd have to talk to him.

The seeds they'd planted together had grown into sturdy little seedlings. He gathered up four of the pots she'd planted, placed them carefully in a box in the back of his car, then made a fuss of Sunny and checked that she had plenty of water. 'You can't come with me, this time,' he told the dog gently. 'She's not allowed to have dogs in her flat. But hopefully…' Hopefully she'd listen to him. Agree to give them a chance.

But when he knocked on the door, Dee answered.

'Hello! I didn't know you were coming tonight.'

'Just passing. How's the pilot tape?' he asked.

'I'm waiting to hear from Saskia's boss. Keep your fingers crossed for me.' She gave him a hug. 'You were a star. Thanks. I couldn't have done it without you.'

'No worries. Um, is Amanda in?'

Dee shook her head. 'Working.'

'What, at this time of night?' he asked, shocked. He'd been so sure she'd be home.

'Tell me about it. I think she's in the library, preparing something for her MBA.' Dee sighed. 'She works too hard. Like you said on the tape, she needs to learn to slow down and breathe, let alone smell the roses. I have no idea what time she's going to be back.'

Will shrugged. 'I brought her these—they're the ones she planted.' He handed the box to Dee.

'Look, can I get you a cup of coffee, or something?'

'No, it's okay. Thanks for the offer, but I was just passing. Really.'

'I could ring her mobile?' Dee offered.

Will shook his head. There was no point. Because finding her working at this time of night told him that this was what life would always be like with Amanda—he'd always come second to her career, just as he had to his parents'. Exactly as he'd told Helen. 'I can't really stay. I need to get home for Sunny.'

'Well, it was nice to see you. I'll give her the plants,' Dee said.

'Thanks.'

And he tried to ignore the regret seeping through him as he drove home. Amanda was right. It was never going to work.

So how come he felt as if his life had just turned monochrome?

When Amanda finally came in, an hour later, Dee was curled up with a magazine. 'Hey. I wondered if you were coming home tonight!'

'I told you I was going to be late,' Amanda reminded her.

'Will stopped by.'

'Will?' Amanda's spine tingled. She'd had no idea he was going to call in. He hadn't phoned her once since he'd left London. No text, no email, nothing. No contact whatsoever. And she'd told herself she was an idiot for hoping he'd ignore her words about a clean break. 'Why?'

'Just passing. He dropped off some plants—something about them being the seeds you'd planted?'

'Oh.' Amanda swallowed hard.

'He looked nearly as bad as you do,' Dee said thoughtfully. 'Dark shadows under his eyes. I've never seen him like that before.'

'He's probably busy at work,' Amanda said. If he was feeling as miserable and alone as she was, right now, then he should have called her. Or at least waited for her to get back tonight. The fact he hadn't waited…well, that told her everything. He wasn't prepared to wait. Loathed the city. He'd expect her to be the one to make all the compromises: and she couldn't bear the idea of feeling cut off and out of place, as she always had as a child.

'Hmmm,' Dee said. 'I think you're in denial. Both of you. Why don't you go and see him, Mand?'

'Because,' Amanda said crisply, 'there's no point. And if you'll excuse me, I'm going to have a bath.'

And this time, maybe, she wouldn't have flashbacks to the time Will had made love to her in the shower…

CHAPTER FIFTEEN

A FEW weeks later, Amanda was feeling decidedly out of sorts. Maybe it was some sort of summer flu, she thought. Except she didn't know of anyone else who was feeling as grim as this. Besides, she was almost never ill.

But when she couldn't even drink a cup of coffee at her desk, she began to wonder. Especially when she realised that her period was over a week late.

Stress, probably. Nothing more than that.

She couldn't be pregnant. When she and Will had made love, they'd definitely used protection.

But supposing…?

No. Of course not. The chances of contraception not working were pretty low.

Yet the idea wouldn't shift from her head. And she ended up going home via a supermarket she didn't normally use, to buy a test kit. It'd prove once and for all that this whole thing was in her head and she just had some sort of virus.

To Amanda's relief, Dee was out at a journalist's party— a party she'd tried hard to persuade her flatmate to go to, though it really wasn't Amanda's kind of thing at all—and she had the flat to herself. No questions to answer.

She read the instructions, did the test, and waited.

Two minutes, while the second hand ticked slowly, slowly round the dial.

She couldn't be pregnant.

Please don't let her be pregnant.

This really wasn't the right time to fall for a baby…

One blue line. So the test was working. Okay. Now let the other window stay blank.

Please.

Please, please, please.

Fifteen seconds to go.

Tick, tick, tick.

Please, please, pl—

She stared at the test in disbelief. It couldn't be. There had to be some sort of mistake.

But there were two blue lines.

She was pregnant.

It took Amanda a good ten minutes to walk into the kitchen again. She poured herself a glass of water and slumped into a chair. Pregnant. With Will's baby. What the hell was she going to do?

The obvious thing was to tell him. He had a right to know. But this was hardly something she could do on the phone. Supposing he was out? No way could she leave him a message like that on the answering machine. *Hi, Will. It's Amanda. By the way, I'm pregnant with your baby.*

She needed to tell him this face-to-face. Which meant going back to his world.

And then what?

She couldn't have a baby. Not when she was just about to start two years of intensive study. Not when she was at such a crucial point in her career—if she put everything on hold to have a baby, she'd be finished. Just like her mother had been. Everything she'd worked so hard for thrown away. She'd never get another chance—and her juniors would overtake her. She'd lose out. Have to work for people who'd worked for her. Take steps *backward*.

She couldn't do it.

And what made her think she'd be any good as a mother anyway? Not with the role model she'd had, growing up. Supposing Amanda had the baby and then discovered she disliked children as much as her mother did? She'd never really been around children. Not so much as held a baby, because none of her friends had children or wanted them.

Friends? Ha. Who was she trying to kid? She didn't really have friends. She had colleagues. Just like her mother had. And when they'd moved to the country, the bonds of acquaintanceship had snapped.

For the first time, Amanda began to understand how her mother had felt when Amanda had been a child. All these plans, a glittering career before her—and then everything juddering to a halt because of what some people called a 'happy accident'.

There hadn't been anything happy about Amanda's childhood.

Could she really make her own child go through that same misery, the same knowledge that she wasn't wanted and she'd ruined her mother's life?

And her mother was the last person she could discuss this with. There wouldn't be any sympathy, any understanding—just contempt and a demand to know how Amanda could have been so stupid, making exactly the same mistake her mother had done. Pregnant before she'd reached the top. A career break that would give everyone the chance to rush past her. Moving out to the country when the family budget hadn't been able to stretch back to London—and then being stuck because house prices in London had rocketed so much faster than the rest of the country that they couldn't afford to move back to the city.

Trapped.

And alone.

'What the hell am I going to do?' Amanda whispered.

There was one solution. One obvious solution.

But she was going to have to sleep on this one.

Luckily Amanda's colleagues were used to her being quiet in the office, so nobody made any comments over the next few days. Nobody noticed that she'd stopped drinking coffee, either; the summer had blossomed into a heatwave, so everyone was opting for chilled drinks. And Dee, who was finding it too sticky and airless to sleep properly at night, accepted Amanda's explanation that it was the same for her.

Night after night, Amanda lay awake and thought about it. Keep the baby—or stop everything now. It was her body, her choice…

Except it wasn't just her choice, was it?

Every time she thought about it, a little bit more of her said she couldn't go through with it. And as the week went by, she began to realise that she didn't have to follow her mother's path. She wasn't her mother. It didn't have to be the same for her. She wouldn't bring up her child in the same way.

She could have it all.

If she was brave enough.

And then at last it was Saturday morning. Amanda supposed she ought to call Will first, but then what would she say? 'I need to talk to you.' He'd ask why. And it wasn't a conversation she wanted to have on the phone. No, best just to turn up and tell him.

She left early and was parked outside the cottage at half past eight. Will's battered estate car wasn't there; another car was in its place. She frowned. Maybe he had friends staying and his car wasn't there because he was at the garden centre or at a client's.

There was only one way to find out.

She ignored the adrenalin prickling at the back of her neck, climbed out of the car and knocked on the door.

It was a while before the door opened and a man she didn't recognise leaned against the doorjamb. 'Can I help you?' he asked.

'I was looking for Will,' she said.

'Will?'

This must be the man's idea of a joke—pretending that he had no idea who Will was. Of *course* he knew. He was in Will's house, wasn't he?

'Will Daynes,' she said.

He shook his head and smiled ruefully at her. 'Sorry, love. I think you've got the wrong place.'

No, no, no. There had to be some mistake. She'd spent a whole week here. She hadn't got the wrong place—she *knew* she hadn't.

A woman came up behind him and slid her arms round his waist. 'Did I hear you say Daynes?' she asked.

Amanda felt sick. 'Yes.'

'Mr Daynes owns the cottage—he might be at the garden centre. We collected the key from him there last Saturday afternoon, remember, love?' she said to the man.

The words sank in: *collected the key from him.* 'You're on holiday here?' she asked.

The woman smiled. 'Some of our friends stayed here last year and recommended it to us. It's one of the nicest holiday cottages we've stayed in.'

Holiday cottage?

The full ramifications slammed into her. Will had lied to her. He'd made her believe this was his home and he'd *lied* to her.

'I'm sorry to have disturbed your holiday,' she said.

'You haven't disturbed us. We're packing to go home,' the woman said.

'It'll be a shame to leave here. It's a lovely part of the world and the kids adored it,' the man added.

Kids.

Oh, God. If Will had lied to her about where he lived, had he lied to her about being single, too? Was he married? Did he have children? Had she made the most stupid mistake of her life? Was she pregnant by a married man whose wife 'didn't understand him'?

'Are you all right, love?' the woman asked.

'Yes—it's this heat. Takes it out of you,' Amanda said swiftly.

'Can I get you a glass of water or something?' the woman asked, still looking concerned.

A complete stranger, and yet she'd been kind. It was enough to make Amanda want to cry.

Hormones. And she needed them back under control. Right now. 'No, no, I'm fine. Glad you enjoyed your holiday.' She forced a smile to her face and got back into the car.

The garden centre. When she'd arrived here on the Saturday morning, Will had said something about a staff meeting at the garden centre. Or had he lied about that, too?

She'd still tell him about the baby, because he had a right to know. But that was as far as it went. This baby was hers—they didn't need a lying, cheating rat like Will Daynes in their lives.

She drove to the garden centre, scrubbing the tears from her face with the back of her hand. She was *not* going to cry over Will Daynes. This was just her hormones going haywire, that was all.

The first person she saw in green overalls was a young lad she didn't remember from her visits to the garden centre. 'Excuse me, is Mr Daynes in, please?'

The young lad frowned. 'I'm not sure, I'll just check—who shall I tell him it is?'

'It's personal.' She shook her head. 'Never mind. I know

where his office is.' She stomped through the corridor and slammed the door open.

But the man sitting behind the desk wasn't Will. He was a good twenty years older than Will, though she could see a resemblance in those beautiful eyes and the shape of his face. And in the same second of realisation she heard barking.

A dog.

More than one dog.

Remembering the Alsatian from her childhood, she flinched back against the wall.

'You two, sit down and be quiet. Now,' the man ordered, and the two dogs slunk back to their position behind his desk, looking sheepish. Then he turned to Amanda. 'Can I help you?'

'I was looking for Will…' To her horror, she heard her voice quiver and felt tears welling up.

The man came round to her side of the desk and gently shepherded her into a chair. 'Sit down, love. You look all in. Wait there, and I'll get you a glass of water. The collies won't hurt you, though they might try to herd you on to a chair.'

He was joking about the latter.

She hoped.

He fixed them with a stern look. 'Charlie, Susie—*stay*.'

Before she could protest, he disappeared, and came back with a glass of water. 'I'm Martin Daynes, Will's uncle,' he said.

The one Will really liked. *The original Sixties child.* The one who'd given him his love of music. 'You own the garden centre?' she asked.

'Yes.'

'And the cottage?'

He winced. 'Um, yes.'

'I'm Amanda Neave,' she said quietly.

He nodded. 'I should've guessed.'

'Will *lied* to me.' She dragged in a breath. 'About everything.'

Martin sighed. 'Oh, love. I'm sorry. I knew this was a bad idea right from the start.'

'The lifeswap thing?' A tall, pretty woman walked into the room and held her hand out to Amanda. 'Hello. I'm Helen, Will's aunt.'

Amanda was too distraught to take Helen's hand. 'He lied to me,' she repeated.

'Not out of ill intentions. He's not like that.' Helen perched on the edge of Martin's desk. 'Will's very family oriented.'

Worse and worse. 'So he's married?' Amanda dug her nails into her palm.

'No. He's single,' Martin said. 'And he hasn't been seeing anyone since—*ow*.'

Helen had clearly poked him with a pen to shut him up. And before Amanda could ask what Martin meant, Helen said, 'He did the lifeswap thing to help his sister's best friend, because she needed a country boy for her project.'

A foil to the city chick. 'Dee. My flatmate,' Amanda said tonelessly.

Helen nodded. 'And also for me, so I could get Martin to take a week's break—you wouldn't believe how hard it is to persuade some people to take a holiday.' Then she put her hand over her mouth and her eyes widened. 'Whoops. Sorry, I wasn't being rude about you.'

'It's okay. I know what people think of me. Control freak, workaholic…Whatever.' Amanda lifted her chin. 'So Will isn't a garden designer?'

'Oh, he is,' Martin reassured her. 'And he's brilliant. But he likes to do things his way. Which is why he works for himself, not for me. He kept an eye on the place while we were away for the week, but he can't stand being stuck in an office.'

So he'd been truthful about that part.

'And he doesn't live in the Fens.' It was a statement rather than a question.

Helen frowned. 'He said he was going to come clean and tell you the truth about where he lived. Didn't he come and see you?'

Amanda nodded. And he'd brought her the sunflowers they'd planted together. 'I wasn't there.'

'You were working late,' Helen guessed. 'Stupid boy. Why didn't he wait for you to come home?' She rolled her eyes. 'Men! Mind you, in some respects I'm not surprised.'

'Why?' Amanda asked.

Helen shook her head. 'I think he should be the one to explain that. But if he doesn't, ask him about his parents.'

His parents? 'He didn't say much about them,' Amanda said. 'Though he talked about you both.'

Martin and Helen exchanged a glance.

'I did get the impression his parents weren't pleased he turned down an unconditional place at Oxford.'

'He told you about *that*?' Helen asked.

Amanda frowned. 'It's not something he talks about?'

'Almost never. The fact he told you…' Helen shook her head in exasperation. 'I could strangle him for being so dense. I think you two need to talk. Sooner, rather than later. He's not far away—he lives in Cambridge.'

No wonder he'd known so much about the city. And that explained why they'd seemed to recognise him in the bakery and why he'd parked in a side road instead of a public car park before she reminded him it was a permit-parking area.

The area for which he possessed a permit, she'd guess.

'I'm sorry I disturbed you,' Amanda said, standing up.

'You're not disturbing us—and you're not a nuisance, either, before you suggest it,' Helen said. Her eyes narrowed. 'You look as if you've been crying, love.'

Tears never seemed far from the surface at the moment. 'I'm all right,' Amanda said.

'No, you're not. I'll ring him and get him to drive over here,' Martin said.

Amanda shook her head. She really didn't want an audience when she spoke to Will—especially people who were as kind and concerned as Martin and Helen. What would they say if they knew they could be a great-aunt and great-uncle in a few months' time? 'I'll be fine.'

'Then why don't I drive you over to his place?' Martin suggested.

Helen laid her hand on his arm. 'I think Amanda might need to see Will on her own, love.'

Amanda felt her eyes widen. Surely Helen hadn't guessed? It was really early days—no way were there any physical signs.

But Martin was still frowning. 'You know what Cambridge is like. It's a nightmare to park.'

Helen fished a piece of paper out of the mess on Martin's desk and scribbled down an address and a rough map. 'It's really easy to find. Just park outside his house. And he can either sort out a permit or pay your parking ticket, whichever you prefer.'

'At the moment,' Amanda said, 'I think I want to strangle him for lying to me.'

'Hear him out,' Helen advised. 'He's a good man. And his heart's definitely in the right place.' She smiled. 'Good luck, love. It'll all work out. Just talk to him.'

Yeah. Though everything she'd planned to say…it had changed. Will hadn't been honest with her during the life-swap. How could she trust him to be honest with her now?

CHAPTER SIXTEEN

AMANDA DROVE to Cambridge, still with no idea about what she was going to say, how she was going to tell Will that she was pregnant with his baby. Since Martin and Helen's revelations, everything seemed to be topsy-turvy and she really didn't have a clue what she was doing any more.

She parked on the street and then walked down the road, counting up the numbers until she reached Will's house. Though even without the house number she could've guessed which one was his: a turn-of-the-century terraced house, painted cream, with original sash windows and a door painted a bright sky blue. There was a low brick wall around the pocket-handkerchief-sized front garden and a wrought-iron gate. The plants were a riot of colour, old-fashioned cottage garden plants like the ones he'd shown her at the nursery: delphiniums, foxgloves, love-in-a-mist and lavender, along with other plants she didn't recognise. And the little lilac-coloured rain daisies he'd told her were his favourite—right now they were wide open in honour of the heatwave.

The windows at the top were open, so it looked as if Will was home.

Feeling sick, she opened the gate and walked down the path. She stood there for two whole minutes before she nerved herself to use the polished brass knocker.

There was a soft woof, and then she saw a silhouette behind the frosted glass of the door. Her heart was beating so hard, so fast, she was sure the whole of Cambridge could hear it.

The door opened—and there he was. Will. Wearing only a pair of faded cut-off jeans, frayed round the edges. His hair was wild, he clearly hadn't shaved that morning, and he looked absolutely edible.

As well as very shocked to see her. Clearly his aunt and uncle hadn't called him to warn him she was on her way. She wasn't sure whether that was a good sign or a bad omen.

'Hello, Will,' she said, trying her best to sound cool and calm and collected—even though right now she was in turmoil. She wanted to scream at him for being a liar and making such a fool out of her, but at the same time her body was running riot and ignoring her mind. Remembering what it felt like to touch him. Remembering what it felt like to be touched by him. And how she wanted him to hold her.

'Amanda? What are you doing here?'

'We need to talk.'

He sucked in a breath. 'Oh, hell. You know.'

No way was she making this easy for him. Not after the way he'd lied to her. 'Know what?' she asked, wanting to hear him admit it.

'About the lifeswap thing. That I wasn't completely straight with you about it.' He raked a hand through his hair. 'This wasn't how things were meant to… Look, you'd better come in.'

The interior of the terraced house was nothing like the cottage in the Fens. This felt like *home*. The entrance hall was painted a deep sand colour, the stairs were stripped and varnished, and there was a gorgeous landscape picture hanging on the wall—the kind of painting she'd expected Will to own.

He bypassed the door at the front of the hall and ushered

her through to what was clearly the living room. 'Take a seat. I'll make us a drink.'

Again, the room seemed to fit him, warm and vibrant—not like the neutral, cool colours in the Fenland cottage. The walls were a rich red, and a sky-blue fringed silk rug was flung casually onto a stripped and varnished wooden floor. There were pictures clustered on the mantelpiece above the cast-iron fireplace—one of Sunny, one of Fliss in a wedding dress and Will looking amazing in top hat and tails, a couple of Martin and Helen, and one of Fliss in graduation robes with Will making bunny ears behind her head.

Family oriented. Exactly what Helen had said about him. Though there were no pictures of anyone who could be his parents, she noticed. Was he that estranged from them?

The cushions on one of the deep plush chairs appeared to be covered in dog hair—clearly Sunny's chair—and the book-shelves on either side of the chimney breast were crammed to bursting. Gardening books? Novels? Unable to resist browsing, she discovered an eclectic collection of poetry and novels and horticultural texts, all well thumbed. She'd known that Will was well read—this just confirmed it.

There was a pile of papers on the coffee table; the topmost one looked like a rough design for a garden. She was about to reach out for it when a soft nudge at the side of her knee made her jump: Sunny. Gingerly, she stroked the top of the spaniel's head; apparently satisfied, Sunny bounced on to the chair covered with dog hair and settled down with her nose on her paws.

Yes, this was definitely Will's home. Untidy—and comfortable.

For a second, she wondered what it would be like to call this place home. To come back from the city and see Will sketching a design or messing about with a mood board. To walk in and smell the scent of a good meal being cooked, with ingredients picked from their garden. To see their child playing ball in the garden with Sunny…

But this wasn't her home. She didn't fit Will's life. And she still hadn't told him about the baby.

She returned to her chair and waited; a moment later, Will came in with two mugs of coffee and handed one to her.

He'd pulled on a crumpled T-shirt, she noticed. Though he was still barefoot, like a pirate, and his hair was still a mess, curling everywhere in a way that made her want to run her fingers through it.

Coffee. Um. She really couldn't drink this. But without telling him why… She just hoped he'd think she was too hot for coffee, or something like that, and put the mug beside her on the floor.

Time for the reckoning. 'You lied to me, Will. About the cottage, about your job—about everything.'

He leaned back against the sofa and balanced the side of one foot on his knee. Though she wasn't fooled by his apparent calm; his face looked strained. Guilty. As if he regretted what he'd done.

But what did he regret? Lying to her or making love to her?

'I'm sorry, Amanda. I didn't do it to make you feel like a fool. It was to play up the differences between us for the lifeswap thing.'

'You still lied to me. You're not the honourable man I thought you were.' She felt her hands bunching into fists. 'I'm so *angry* with you, Will.' And confused. And miserable. And her hormones were running riot, now she'd seen him again. She didn't know whether she wanted to kill him or kiss him. Just as well she was sitting in a chair on the opposite side of the room rather than next to him on the sofa.

'If it makes you feel any better, I hate myself for lying to you, too. But what else could I have done?' His eyes were clear green, glittering with a mixture of guilt and pain. 'I never meant to hurt you, Amanda.'

'But you have.' He hadn't trusted her with the truth. So how could she trust him?

'And I'm sorry for that. Truly sorry.' He swallowed hard. 'I wanted to help Dee. She's my sister's best friend—practically family. And it was my chance to give something back to Martin. He and Helen brought me up.'

Helen had told her to ask him about his parents if he didn't tell her. It sounded as if this was the key to Will. But could she trust him enough to tell her the truth? 'Why?' she asked quietly. 'Are your parents…?' No, she couldn't ask him that. If his parents had been killed in an accident or something, asking him about it would rip his scars wide open.

As if he'd guessed what she'd been about to ask, he said, 'No, they're alive. Probably—' he glanced at his watch '—asleep. In Tokyo or New York or somewhere.'

'You don't know where they are?' Despite her difficult relationship with her own parents, she was shocked that he could be so isolated from his.

He shrugged. 'If I need to know, I can ask their secretary for a schedule.'

'So you're not on good terms with them, then?'

'Not on bad terms, either.'

She frowned. 'I'm not with you.'

'I don't really have a relationship with my parents,' he said. 'I don't see them very often. We've never been close.'

She could appreciate that one—it was how things were with her own parents. But *she*'d been a mistake. 'You're the youngest.' His parents must have planned to have at least one child—having two accidental pregnancies was pretty unlikely. 'And surely they were delighted to have a son and heir?'

He quickly disillusioned her. 'They couldn't wait to ship me off to boarding school. Martin and Helen couldn't have children, so they more or less claimed Fliss and me in the summer holidays.' He shrugged. 'Otherwise, my parents would've probably engaged a string of nannies or something to look after us. Which is pretty much what they did when we weren't old enough to go to boarding school.'

Why on earth didn't his parents have time for him?

The question must have been written all over her face because he said, 'They're merchant bankers. Rather high up in their respective companies. And they have a very, very, *very* busy schedule.'

Uh-oh. Finance. His parents came from her world. Probably worked the kind of long hours that she did. Suddenly, it fell into place—why Will loathed London so much. And why he hadn't waited for her. He'd thought she was in the same mould as his parents were and he'd always come second to her job, the way he'd come second to theirs. 'I'm sorry.'

'Not your fault.'

'So they expected you to follow in their footsteps.' Get a First at Oxford and follow them into finance. Pretty much what he'd said to her before—he could have ended up doing a job like hers. 'Except you followed in Martin's.'

He nodded. 'My first job was a holiday job in the garden centre. Martin taught me everything I know about plants. And he backed me when I decided to study horticulture. Encouraged me to follow my heart and do what I really loved. So doing the lifeswap thing for Dee was a way of paying him back. Getting him some publicity for the garden centre—publicity he needs.'

'Because he's a specialist and he's finding it hard to compete with the big chains?'

'Exactly.'

'So your garden design…'

'That bit was true. But it's for me, not for Martin, and it's full time. I've made enough of a name that I can pick and choose my clients.' He shrugged. 'Will Daynes, landscaper to the rich and famous.'

'A modern-day Capability Brown.'

He raised an eyebrow. 'Been reading up?'

He'd caught her out—and he knew it, because his eyes crinkled at the corners. 'I'd like to think my work will be remembered in the same way in years to come. Sometimes I think I've sold out—but on the other hand it pays me well enough so I can do smaller gardens for fun. Help people who have a dream, but who don't know where to start making it come true—and who can't afford to buy mature plants.'

'Like the woman with the tiny courtyard who came to the garden centre for advice.'

'Yup.' He paused. 'So now you know the truth.'

'All of it?' She needed to know. 'Did you lie to me in London?'

'Just to get you into bed?' He shook his head. 'Of course not. And I'm not in a relationship with anyone else.'

He wasn't in a relationship with her, either.

Except…

She had to tell him. Tell him *now*. 'As you've brought the subject up…I'm here because you need to know something.' She swallowed. Why was this so hard? It was the kind of news most people would consider 'good'. Though she wasn't his partner and he had issues with his parents, so having a child of his own might not be on his agenda.

Not that she was planning for him to be a big part of the baby's life. This was her mistake, and she'd deal with it.

'Amanda?' he prompted.

There was no easy way to tell him. Might as well just tell him straight. 'I'm pregnant.'

He stared at her. 'Pregnant?'

At least he hadn't asked her if it was his. One small mercy. 'Don't worry, I'm not expecting anything from you. I'm perfectly able to support a child by myself.'

'You're pregnant,' he repeated.

'I just thought you had a right to know. And it's not the kind of thing you can say on the phone or in an email.'

He shook his head as if trying to clear it. 'You're *pregnant*.'

He looked shell-shocked. Well, that made two of them. Though she'd had the best part of a week to get used to the idea.

Then his face changed. The strain vanished—replaced by a smile of sheer joy. 'You're pregnant,' he breathed in wonder. 'We're having a baby.'

'I'm having a baby,' she corrected.

'You're having *my* baby. Our baby.' The silver was back in his eyes. 'When?'

She hadn't exactly thought about that. 'I did a test earlier this week.'

'We're going to have a baby.'

'You're not listening to me, Will. This is *my* baby.'

The corner of his mouth quirked. 'You don't make a baby on your own, Amanda. It takes two. And in this case, that means you and me. Our baby. And I'm going to look after you.'

She shook her head. 'No way. That's what happened to my mother.'

Amanda's mother. She hadn't said much about her parents—but the little she had told him made Will think that hers were as bad as his. They hadn't tried to help her get over her fear of dogs. When she'd stung herself on those nettles, she'd admitted she wasn't used to people making a fuss over her. And if nobody had paid her much attention as a child…no wonder she was reserved with people now. Because nobody had ever taught her how to make friends. 'What happened to your mother?' he asked, his voice gentle.

'She got pregnant with me. She was meant to be a high flyer. Except…she had me.'

He frowned. 'There are such things as career breaks.'

'Not back then. And when I was old enough for her to go back to work, she was way behind everyone else. They'd all moved on.' Her face tightened. 'And we couldn't afford to move back to London anyway. So she was still trapped—trapped in a place she hated.'

Finally, he understood why she was driven. Because of her mother's disappointment. 'So you became a high flyer for her. To make it up to her.'

A muscle twitched in her face. 'Don't be ridiculous. I did it for me.'

Talk about in denial.

He'd just bet Amanda hated the country because she associated it with her mother being miserable and had convinced herself she'd feel the same. The middle of the Fens was probably too remote for her, admittedly, but Cambridge was another matter. Helen's words echoed in his ears: *There's a solution staring you right in the face.* Of course there was. Cambridge. A city with lots of green spaces and gardens. A place that would work for both of them.

'Have you told your mother about the baby?' Will asked.

Amanda shook her head. 'You're the only one who knows.'

And he could imagine how much it had cost her to tell him.

Ah, hell. He couldn't stay away from her any longer. He scooped her out of the chair, sat down in her place, and settled her on his lap.

'Will, what are you—?' she began.

'You've just told me that you're expecting my baby.' He placed one hand gently over her abdomen. 'Do you really think I'm going to stay on the other side of the room rather than be close to you?'

'I…' She shrugged.

'That's not who I am.' He took a deep breath. 'Look, the baby…this changes everything. This isn't just about you and me any more. We're going to have a baby. I had a rough childhood, apart from Martin and Helen. I don't think yours was much better. And that's not going to be the case for our baby.'

'My baby,' she said stubbornly.

'*Our* baby,' he insisted. 'And I'm even more stubborn than you are, so don't argue, Amanda. You'll lose.'

She said nothing, just glared at him.

Lord, he wanted to kiss that scowl away. But he knew they needed to sort this out properly first. Amanda needed to know things with her head before she could trust her heart. 'I know part of the problem is that you work in London and you thought I lived in the middle of nowhere. But it's not the real situation. I live in a city.'

'Cambridge isn't London.'

'No. Actually, it's the best of both worlds. I'll still have a decent garden and be able to hear birdsong in the morning, and you're in commuting distance of London.'

Her mouth thinned. 'So I'm going to be the one making all the compromises.'

'It's not a compromise. You'll still be doing the job you love, and I'll be doing mine. Actually, the more I think about it, you don't even have to commute. Your firm has a branch in Cambridge. What's to stop you getting a transfer and a partnership here?'

'With a baby?' She stared at him in seeming disbelief. '*And* I'm going to have to give up my MBA. How can I study when I'm having a baby?'

Was Amanda like her mother? Was she seeing a baby as an obstacle to her career rather than a tiny miracle that would enrich her life? 'Are you thinking about having a termination?' he asked, not sure he wanted to hear the answer.

'I don't know.' She dragged in a breath. 'Right now everything seems a mess and a muddle.'

'And you think your career plans have all gone down the plughole.'

'Of course they have.'

'Actually, they haven't.' He stroked her face. 'Think about it. You'll need to take some time off—even *you* can't make notes on a lecture while you're in labour—but there's no reason why you can't still do your MBA.'

'How?'

'You're not doing this on your own.' He tucked a tendril of hair behind her ear. 'This is my baby too. I'll be supporting you.'

'On weekends?'

He rolled his eyes. 'I have no intention of being a weekend father. I'm going to be a full-time father.'

She stared at him, eyes wide and full of fear. 'You're going to take me to court for custody?'

'For someone so clever, you can be completely clueless at times.' Pretty much what Helen had said to him: *For someone so clever, you can be such a dope.* He smiled at the memory. 'No. I'm going to live with you.'

She blinked. 'But I live in London. You live here.'

'That's easily solved. Move in with me.'

She shook her head in exasperation. 'As I said, you're expecting me to be the one who has to make all the compromises.'

Put like that, she had a point. Moving in with him was the perfect solution—but it would mean she'd have to give up her flat, change her job. 'Okay. Let's do this another way. I'll sell my house and we'll buy another one. Together.' At her narrowed eyes, he added quietly, 'In London.'

'But you *hate* London. You said you couldn't live anywhere else except the Fens.'

'Cambridgeshire,' he corrected. 'But you're absolutely right. I need to make compromises, too. So I'll learn to live in London.'

She swallowed. 'It won't work. I heard what you said on the tape about feeling trapped.'

'Cabin'd, cribb'd, confin'd?' He smiled. 'Forget it. I was being a bit melodramatic. Pretending I was Macbeth.'

'No, you weren't. You could barely sit still in the office. You kept fiddling with the plants and you were desperate to get out of the building and go for a walk in the nearest park.'

He tried to make a joke of it. 'Rats. Rumbled.'

'You'd feel as trapped in London as I would in the Fens. I grew up in the country, Will. I grew up with everyone watching every single thing I did. I grew up never quite fitting in because my mum was a city girl and didn't want to be part of the village. She never invited people back to our place and people got sick of being the ones doing all the hospitality, so the invitations stopped. I was a nuisance, to everyone. And I don't want to feel like that again.'

'You won't. Because you'll be with me. You fit with me, Amanda.' She'd been brave enough to come here and tell him about the baby. Maybe it was time he was brave enough to tell her something, too. 'I came to London because I missed you. I wanted you back in my life. And I'd rather be caged in London with you than free without you.'

She stared at him, frowning. 'Really?'

'Really.' There was a tiny, tiny spark of something in her face that gave him courage. 'So I'm going to say something to you now that I've never, ever said before to anyone.'

She looked worried.

He smiled. 'Hey, it's not that bad. Just that I love you.'

Her eyes narrowed. 'You didn't say that in London.'

'Would you have believed me?'

'Probably not,' she admitted.

'I love you, Amanda.' He paused. 'Will you marry me?'

If he'd said that to her in London…

But he hadn't.

He was only saying it now because she'd just told him she was pregnant. He didn't really want *her*. Just like her parents hadn't really wanted her.

'No.' The word was dragged from her. No. She couldn't marry someone who didn't want her. Couldn't chain herself to spending the rest of her life in the country, so far away from the world she'd worked so hard for, with someone who didn't really want her. Been there, done that, never again. Last time, she hadn't had a choice. This time, she did. And she wasn't going to do it.

'What do you mean, no?'

'I'm not going to marry you.'

He frowned. 'Why not?'

Did he really need it spelled out? 'This is the twenty-first century. You don't need to get married just because you're having a baby.'

'Ah.' He stroked her cheek and gave her the sweetest, sweetest smile she'd ever seen. 'You think I'm only asking you because of the baby.'

Her throat felt as if it were clogged with sand. Just as well, because otherwise she'd be crying an ocean. 'Well, aren't you?'

'No.'

He expected her to believe that?

As if she'd asked the question aloud, he said softly, 'I was in a relationship a few months back. Nina wanted to get serious; I didn't. When I tried to end it, things got messy. I ended up having to get my solicitor to send her a letter. It sorted things out, but I decided then I wasn't going to get burned like that again. I had a life I liked: my home, my dog, my family, my job. I thought I was fine. Keep all my relationships strictly for fun.' He paused. 'And then Miss Wrong walked into my life.'

'Miss Wrong.' That was exactly what he thought of her. She tried to wriggle off his lap, but he wouldn't let her; he kept his arms very firmly round her.

'Or so I thought when I met her. Miss Wrong. My complete opposite. Everything I thought I didn't want—someone from my parents' world, someone who was undomesticated and lived on junk food and wouldn't know a rare plant from a weed. Someone who was neat and tidy and bossed me about. I should've wanted to drop her in the Cam and send her back to London. Except there was something about her. Something that made me feel...different. Protective, even.'

What? That was utterly ridiculous. She could look after—

'Which was crazy,' he continued, as if reading her thoughts, 'because I knew she was more than capable of looking after herself. She's the most capable woman I've ever met. Clever and competent and...' he took her hand and pressed a kiss into her palm, then folded her fingers over it '...so damned sexy I could barely keep my hands off her. With my head, I knew it was completely wrong. But I couldn't help myself. I wanted her so badly.'

It had been the same for her. Unexpected, unwanted...and irresistible.

'Lust,' she said, striving to sound cool and collected.

'It wasn't lust,' he said, his voice utterly sincere. 'It was more than that. A lot more. She made me feel *whole*. Because her differences fill the empty spaces in me, just as my differences fill her empty spaces. I can cook; she can't. She's organised; I'm untidy. Apart, we both have something missing. Together...' He stroked her face tenderly. 'Together, we make a fabulous team.'

She remembered the last time he'd said that to her. The night they'd made love. *It's not a competition. It's teamwork.*

'And now we're going to make an even better team,' he said. 'You, me and our baby. Our family.' He brushed his mouth very lightly against hers. 'I love you, Amanda. My world's a better place with you in it. So how about it?'

She still couldn't say yes. Because it wasn't just him to think about, was it? 'Will, I'm not going to fit in. Your sister doesn't like me.'

'You're not marrying Fliss, you're marrying *me*. And I

think, once she actually gets to know you, she'll change her mind about you.'

How could he be so sure, when she wasn't? 'What about the rest of your family?'

He smiled. 'Helen and Martin sent you here. Doesn't that tell you anything?'

She thought about it for a moment. They wouldn't have told her where he lived if they'd disliked her on sight. Or if they thought he hadn't missed her. 'Oh.'

'Oh,' he mimicked, rubbing his nose against hers. 'Amanda, it's going to be fine. We'll have a new life. A better life. The best bits of yours and the best bits of mine. Teamwork. I want to marry you. Because you're *you*,' he emphasised, 'not because you're pregnant.'

How she wanted to believe him. But she couldn't. 'I...need time to think.'

He looked at her. 'Okay. You didn't drink your coffee. It's cold. I'll get you another one.'

'Will—thanks, but no. I can't face coffee right now,' she admitted.

'Then I'll get you something cold. Come into my kitchen.' He eased her to her feet, stood up, took her hand and led her through to the kitchen.

Wow.

Double wow.

Instead of the tiny little galley-style kitchen Amanda had expected, the room opened out into a high-ceilinged conservatory, and from there into the garden. Entranced, she let go of Will's hand and walked into the conservatory and looked out at the garden. There was an old-fashioned apple tree at the bottom, and a greenhouse and a vegetable patch—all looking incredibly neat and tidy. Next to the garden room was a shady patio with pots of bright red geraniums and herbs, and a table and chairs.

'I eat outside when I can,' he told her, handing her a glass of cold water with ice and a slice of lime.

Ha. Trust Will to go for the foodie option. Lime rather than lemon.

'It's gorgeous.' And he'd said he'd move to London. For her. He'd give all this up for her.

How could he bear to do it?

As if he knew what she was thinking, he said, 'It's just a house and a garden. We can make another one. All it takes is a bit of time and patience.'

'You'd really give this up and move to London for me?' she asked.

He smiled. 'In a heartbeat. Without you, this is all monochrome. Scentless, tasteless, no birdsong.'

He meant it. He really meant it. His eyes were green and clear with sincerity

And as she looked out at the garden, she realised what she wanted. A little girl, running around this garden with the dog. A little boy planting sunflowers with his daddy. Herself—complete with MBA—coming home from the office in Cambridge.

Home.

To Will.

Here.

Because this was where she belonged. Punting on the Cam on a Sunday afternoon and wandering hand in hand with her man through Grantchester Meadows. Making snowmen in the garden with their children in winter. And partner in a big accountancy firm. She could have it all. With Will.

'Teamwork.'

'Hmm?' He looked quizzically at her.

She repeated his words back at him. 'The best bits of your life and the best bits of mine.' She smiled. 'Don't give up the house, Will. It's perfect.'

'So are you saying…?' Hope bloomed in his face.

And then she knew he really meant it. He really wanted her.

'Is the offer still open? Of moving in with you?'

He smiled back. 'Yes, but there's a condition attached.'

'What condition?'

'Most people would call it a wedding ring.'

'You're supposed to go down on one knee and ask properly.'

'I already did.'

'Not on one knee.'

'Trying to organise me again?' he teased.

Her smile broadened. 'Better get used to it.'

'Oh, I can get used to it. As long as it's *wifely* nagging.'

She coughed. 'One knee, Will.'

He rolled his eyes. 'You'd better say yes this time.'

'One knee.'

He dropped to one knee and took her hand. 'Amanda Neave, I love you. Will you do me the honour of being my wife?'

'William Daynes…' Words she'd never thought she'd say. Words that almost hurt because they came from so deep inside her. And although it scared the hell of out her, she knew that Will was going to be worth all the risks. He'd hold her hand and never let her fall. Make their life a rose garden—and keep her safe from the thorns.

'I love you too.'

His hand tightened round hers, as if he knew how much that admission had cost her. And his voice was slightly cracked as he asked, 'Yes or no?'

She couldn't resist teasing him a little. 'I thought gardeners were supposed to be patient?'

'Ah, now, if we're playing dirty…' He sucked the tip of her index finger into his mouth, and desire sparkled through her.

'Uh. That's cheating.'

'Yeah. And I shouldn't have done that because I think I'm more uncomfortable than you are, right now,' he admitted ruefully.

Lord, his mouth was so sexy. And she wanted to feel it against hers, right now. Wanted to feel it all over her body. She shook her hand free, dropped to her knees, and cupped his face. Her big, bad pirate. The man with hands gentle enough to protect the most delicate flower.

All hers.

She brushed her mouth over his. 'Then I guess I'll have to do something about that.'

He groaned. 'You're killing me. Amanda, you're the love of my life. I'm going to go crazy if I don't get an answer. Will you marry me, be my wife and my lover and the one I want to be with for the rest of our days? Yes or no?'

She smiled. 'Yes.'

EPILOGUE

Just over two years later

'MUMMY!' THE little girl ran straight to Amanda, missed her footing and fell.

Before she hit the kitchen floor, Will scooped her up and handed her to her mother. Amanda wrapped her arms around her daughter and spun her round. 'Hello, darling. My beautiful girl.' Her little girl, with Will's unruly hair, her own blue eyes and the sweetest, sweetest smile.

'Boo-ful,' Lily said as Amanda set her down on her feet, and blew a kiss.

Will smiled at her. 'You, Mrs Daynes, have got post.'

She kissed him lingeringly as she took the envelope from him. 'Mmm.' Then she glanced at the franking. 'Ah. Results.'

'Want me to open it?' Will asked.

'No.' She took a deep breath. 'Well, if I bombed out, I can always resit.'

He grinned. 'No chance. You'll have passed with flying colours.'

She opened it and scanned the page. 'Oh.' She shrugged, and folded the paper again.

Will stared at her in shock. 'You're *kidding*. No way in hell could my genius wife have failed an exam.'

She handed the letter to Will, who unfolded it again, read it, whooped and spun her round. 'Fantastic. I knew you'd do it!'

'Mummy dance,' said Lily. 'Lily dance. Sunny dance.'

Amanda laughed, picked up her daughter and spun her round, while the spaniel bounced round them in a circle with one of Lily's shoes in her mouth. 'You know, Will, things come in threes.'

'Uh-huh?' Will was delving in the fridge for a bottle of champagne.

'I wouldn't open that *just* yet,' Amanda said.

'So what's the other news?'

'Patrick called me in to the office today.' She beamed at him. She loved the office in Cambridge. So different from London… Or maybe it was different because Will was in her life. She'd become audit manager virtually as soon as she'd transferred to the Cambridge branch—and she'd fitted in with the team right from the start.

'And?'

'Guess who the new head of department is, as of next Monday morning?'

Will whooped again. 'MBA and promotion on the same day? Forget champagne. We're having dinner out tonight.'

'Pizza,' Lily said gleefully.

Will groaned and ruffled her hair. 'You've inherited your mother's junk-food tendencies, young lady.'

'Ah, but her dad's a foodie, so it'll be posh pizza,' Amanda said with a grin. 'I take it you haven't done your filing today?'

Will rubbed a hand over his face. 'Been busy painting with Lily,' he muttered.

She could see that. There were bits of paper with blobs of paint on them all over the kitchen and the garden room. A painting set that Lily's godmother Dee—who was having a ball in her new job as a television producer—had brought down the previous weekend.

'It's my day off, Mands,' he protested, seeing her expression. 'I'm not doing any filing on my day off.'

'I think you should,' Amanda said. 'There might be something you need to look at in your in-tray.'

'I doubt it.'

'There really might be something you need to look at,' she repeated.

Will rolled his eyes. 'Oh, for goodness' sake. It can wait.'

'No, it can't.'

'Your mummy,' he told Lily, 'is a control freak.'

'Troll feek,' Lily repeated dutifully, and beamed at her mother.

Amanda laughed and rubbed the tip of her nose against Lily's. 'You'll pay for that later, Will. When I teach her to bat her eyelashes and give a gorgeous smile so Daddy buys her really, *really* expensive shoes.'

'Yeah, yeah,' Will retorted, but disappeared into his study.

Amanda set Lily back on her feet, folded her arms, tipped her head on one side and counted.

She got to thirty-two before she heard his sharp intake of breath. And it took him less than five seconds to get back to her, waving the envelope that contained the test stick. 'Absolutely positive?'

She laughed. 'That's what two blue lines usually means.'

The last time she'd seen a test stick with those two lines, she thought her world had fallen apart. This time…this time, it was joy right from the start. Because she'd swapped the worst bits of her life for the best bits of Will's.

'Teamwork,' she said softly.

'Yeah.' He held her close. 'Together, we're unbeatable. You, me, Lily, Sunny—and our bump-to-be.'

THE RETURN
OF THE REBEL

BY
TRISH WYLIE

Trish Wylie tried various careers before eventually fulfilling the dream of writing. Years spent working in the music industry, in promotions, and teaching little kids about ponies gave her plenty of opportunity to study life and the people around her. Which in Trish's opinion is a pretty good study course for writing! Living in Ireland, Trish balances her time between writing and horses. If you get to spend your days doing things you love then she thinks that's not doing too badly. You can contact her at www.trishwylie.com

For my good friend Shona—
proof-reader extraordinaire!

CHAPTER ONE

SHANNON HENNESSEY WAS just hitting that point in the morning when her coffee craving was kicking in, which meant, without her even checking her watch, that she knew it had to be almost eleven. Her craving tended to be an excellent timekeeper.

Then the front door opened with a familiar creak.

It wasn't an unusual sound, so at first she didn't even bother looking up. When she did, her usual bright smile in place for whatever familiar friendly face she might discover there, her heart stopped. *Seriously.* A miniature cardiac arrest. She even had to blink a couple of times to be sure she was seeing who she was seeing.

It just couldn't be *him!*

He stepped down into the foyer, his chin lifting, dark eyes locking with green.

And Shannon swallowed hard as inside her head she could suddenly hear—*Barry White.*

Yup, for no apparent reason—apart from the obvious one walking her way—she could hear Barry White singing in her head.

While Connor Flanaghan made a cursory examination of his surroundings with dark eyes before his gaze found hers again.

And Shannon's mouth went dry.

Oh, Lord. It was *Connor Flanaghan*.

'Hi.'

Oh, way to go with the witty opener, Shannon!

But in fairness what was she supposed to say? She wasn't prepared for this. Not now. Not here. Not when she finally had a hold of her life! After all, it was a seven-year-cycle thing, wasn't it? She'd promised herself that it was. And she was now due the good times!

Raising her hand in annoyance to tuck an errant corkscrew of long blonde hair behind an ear, she watched him walking across the room to her through narrowed eyes. How in the name of heaven did someone look that good after all this time? Couldn't he at least have aged badly? Grown a paunch? Had a receding hairline? *Anything—*

Anything at all that might have stopped the old, oh-so-familiar ache forming low in her abdomen, while a once-over-played memory appeared unbidden across the backs of her eyes. *Damn.* He'd just always been disgustingly irresistible, hadn't he?

And Barry sang in her head while a dark, impenetrable gaze remained fixed on his face as he got closer, somehow magically cementing her feet to the floor with just that silent look.

Oh, he was just too damn good-looking for his own good, wasn't he? As he got closer she recognized that look in his eyes that said he maybe knew something she didn't and was silently amused by it. Even the way he walked was full of the kind of arrogant self-confidence that came from more than just physical strength. Not that his six-foot-two, long-legged, broad-shouldered frame didn't move with more than a hint of finely tuned physical strength, but his confidence stemmed from more than that. *Yes, indeed-y.*

He probably knew that women all over the place had Barry White singing in their heads when he was around.

Less than a foot away from her, he stopped, a slow, oozing-sex-appeal smile forming on the sensual sweep of his mouth as his gaze dropped to read the message on her T-shirt.

Forcing Shannon to drop her chin for a second to check what message she was wearing that day. Of all the varying stupid things she had on T-shirts this one was at least a safer: 'Spelling Bee Runnor Up'. Lord alone knew what kind of a look she'd have earned for her favourite: '*Here I am. Now what are your other two wishes?*'

But even so, it still meant he was looking at her breasts—within two minutes of walking back into her life.

Barry was singing a little louder.

Shannon cleared her throat, waving a hand upwards to bring Connor's attention back to her eyes. 'My eyes are up here, Connor.'

He laughed, the very male sound low and deep as thick dark lashes rose, his brow furrowing with momentary curiosity. 'Sorry, do I know you?'

She sighed in resignation. The sparks in his dark eyes told her he knew rightly who she was. And he knew she knew.

They had too much history.

'Hello, Shannon.'

Man, but he still had it didn't he—that way of saying her name *just so?* And Barry could just shut up—she wasn't gonna get pulled back into the maze that was being fascinated by Connor Flanaghan. He could say her name that way as many damn times as he wanted. Shannon was *over him.*

The music stopped with a screech similar to a scratched record in her head. Ha! See—with age came control over one's raging hormones…

'What brings you to Galway?' She pinned a smile in place while her pulse continued ignoring her attempts at willing it into a slower pace.

Connor dragged his gaze from her face, looking around the room for a brief second before he locked eyes with her again, his deep baritone voice low and flat. 'I'm in Galway on business.' He paused. 'I own this place.'

Shannon laughed aloud, the sound wobbling a little nervously despite her best effort. 'No, you don't. Devenish Enterprises owns this building. I should know; it's on my lease. Nice try, though, funny guy.'

He'd always been one for a good wind-up.

Light sparkled briefly in his eyes. 'I *am* Devenish Enterprises.'

'No, you're not.'

'Yes, I am.'

'No, you're not.' Shannon shook her head in frustration as she realized how childish the level of conversation had become—she'd obviously been working with kids for too long. Any second now she'd no doubt feel the need to stick her tongue out at him. 'Frank McMahon is Devenish Enterprises. He's a big-shot millionaire property developer who owns buildings all over the country. Last I heard—you hadn't won the lottery.'

'Been checking up on me, have you?' He grinned the kind of devastating grin that had turned her knees to mush every darn time back in the day. But when she merely quirked a disbelieving brow at him, he glanced away, his voice lower as he asked, 'You still speak to Tess?'

Shannon ignored the first cheeky challenge and focused on the second question. 'Yes, we talk and e-mail from time to time—which is why I think she'd have mentioned it if your numbers came up or you suddenly made a fortune overnight. So, what are you *really* doing here? Honestly?'

It sure as hell wouldn't be because he'd been specifically looking for Shannon. Oh, no. She'd waited half her life just to have him notice her. And in the end she had taken fate into her own hands…

Yes, indeed-y, and look how karma had punished her for *that* one in the long term!

'You talk recently?' His gaze flickered briefly back to her face, searching intently, almost as if he was trying to read her mind, before he began to prowl around the large foyer, stopping to read some of the fliers on the notice-board before he looked back at her again.

Shannon had to take a moment to think about her answer. And not just because of the way he had casually leaned back against the table below the notice-board, folding his arms across his broad chest while he waited on her reply.

Silently she warned Barry to be quiet.

All right. Question. He had asked her a question. What was it again? Oh, yes. Tess. When had she last talked to her best friend of old? Erm…

She'd been so busy for months now getting settled in, putting down some roots for the first time in a long time while she got everything running smoothly and adjusted to her new surroundings, and, yes, she'd probably been so passionate about it that she'd blocked the rest of the world out. But had it really been so long since she'd spoken to her friend? With a frown, she realized—yes, it *had* been quite a while since she'd talked to her.

Something that would have to be rectified, sooner rather than later, now that Shannon had this new *visitor*.

Another thought crossed her mind. 'Has something bad happened I should know about?'

Maybe it was the genuinely concerned tone she voiced the question in, or maybe it was simply the question itself, but either way it changed something in Connor's steady gaze. So that, when he glanced away from her yet again, Shannon had to use her deep well of memories to read his familiar profile. What she saw worried her.

It was there in the tight line of his jaw, the lowered dark brows, in the way that he pursed his sensuous mouth into a thin line.

Something wasn't right here.

'Connor?' She forced herself not to allow her upper body to physically sway forwards in his general direction. Because seven years apart didn't give her any right to 'sway' anywhere near him. Not that that had stopped her before.

This 'sway' was just a reflex, nothing more. Those seven years had made plenty of changes to the person Shannon was now. Just because Connor Flanaghan had walked back into her line of vision didn't mean she would fall all over his feet again.

No matter how damn good he looked.

Had he changed his hair? She pursed her lips together while she studied it. It was shorter, hints of chestnut on the ends of the dark chocolate spikes that suggested he'd recently spent a lot of time in the sun. And he was pretty tanned too…

Shut-up-Barry!

Connor's broad shoulders lifted and fell, his chest expanding briefly as he inhaled. But instead of answering her, he unfolded his arms, pushing fluidly onto his feet before shoving his large hands deep into the pockets of his tailored trousers and glancing around the room again as he *prowled*.

And it was most definitely prowling. He had a way of moving that looked so effortless, all that restrained strength, all that silent self-control while he continued to take in his surroundings with observant eyes. He was practically predatory.

Every female hormone she possessed recognized and immediately reacted to that sheer alpha-male, leader-of-the-herd quality in him. It was positively compelling.

Shannon had to shake her head a little to clear her thoughts when he spoke again.

'So, you work here? Which one does that make you— Senior Citizens Aerobics, Potty about Pottery or Yummy Mummy Yoga?'

He'd got all that from a thirty-second glance at the noticeboard? Oh, he was *slick*.

'I lease the entire building. The bottom two floors I sublet to various groups, and I live on the third. If you're interested in any of the classes I can enrol you—' she couldn't help smiling at the glint of amusement in his eyes when he flashed a half-smile her way '—though if you're thinking of upping the rent and you're *really* the new owner of Devenish, we could just have a nice long chat about some upgrades to the plumbing and electricity instead. I have a list, as it happens…'

'As tempting as the Yummy Mummy Yoga might be, no, I don't need enrolling. I'm too busy at the minute. And we don't need to chat about the plumbing or the electricity, because the sale of this place was agreed two days ago.'

Shannon's breath caught. *'What?'*

Another shrug. And this time, despite the turn in the conversation, Shannon was suddenly struck by the way he was dressed. She had never seen Connor in a suit before, not that she could remember. Let alone in a suit that looked as if it had probably cost more than she paid in rent for the whole building per month. Suits like that one had to be made to measure, didn't they? The cut of the cloth highlighting the lean, muscled frame beneath to devastating perfection. Oh, no. That hadn't come off the peg, had it? Even if an off-the-peg one would still probably have looked just as good on him, or *off him.*

Shannon knew that, either way, he was a sensational specimen of manhood. She hadn't forgotten *anything.*

She swallowed hard.

But the suit was the first thing to persuade her that this might not be a wind-up—what he was saying might actually be true. Because the Connor she had known had been a jeans and T-shirt kind of a guy, the simplicity of the things he chose to wear only adding to his attraction back then. He hadn't had to dress to impress when he'd had an innate ability to sail through life on a combination of wit, charm and innately sexual good looks.

In a suit he was a very different male altogether. Not just appearing suave or businesslike as the suit no doubt intended, but *exuding* authority, especially on a man like Connor; he had the look of a man of power—a man in control. In fact, he really could pass as the owner of Devenish Enterprises if he wanted to, dressed like that.

If he really *was* the new owner, that would make him some kind of multimillionaire, wouldn't it?

But a man with so much money that it didn't matter to him who he trampled along the way? That wasn't the Connor Flanaghan she'd known once upon a time.

Either way, it made no difference. Whoever he was now, he wasn't the Connor she had loved, was he?

Yep, she'd sailed that ship. And it had gone down like the *Titanic*.

The thought brought a momentary sense of familiar grieflike loss into her heart. One she forced back down into its place but came out in the tight tone in her voice,

'So, you're suddenly a millionaire?'

Connor's mouth quirked. 'So it would seem.'

'Overnight?'

'It's been known to happen.'

She couldn't stop the snort of laughter that escaped., 'Yeah, sure it does. We're just tripping over millionaires in here right enough. It's a big problem for us. I can't tell you the number of Dior dresses I've been given.'

Connor sighed impatiently in response. 'It doesn't really matter how it happened, Shannon. I'm the new owner. And this place has just been sold. That's why I'm here.'

The repercussions of what he was saying began to sink into her addled mind, slowly, like water through the tiny cracks in a wall. 'Just like that? No warning? It's done and we're, what, forced to leave? *Ooh*—do we even get to pack or is this an eviction right now this minute? Do you have a nice white van outside?'

Still prowling the room, he ignored her sarcasm, answering in a businesslike tone that she had never heard from him before. 'I'm narrowing down the amount of properties on the company books, so—'

'Well, bully for you.'

He quirked a dark brow at her sharp interruption. 'Is there a problem?'

'Now, why would there be a problem?' She tilted her head to one side, the curled lock of blonde hair working loose again to bob against her cheek. 'I mean, you've just wandered in here and informed me that you're some big-shot property owner and I'm about to lose my home and my livelihood in one fell swoop. Why on earth would there be a problem with that?'

'Of course, we'll organize an alternative building for you.'

'That's big of you.'

He stopped prowling and aimed a small amused smile at her. 'Shannon. It's not that big a deal.'

Well, that was where he was wrong. It was *absolutely* a big deal. The Connor she had known might have taken the time to find that out before he wandered in with this life-changing decision already made—and it wasn't just Shannon's life either.

The building, the small community that had built up inside it, was everything to her. For the first time since her grand-mother had died and left her alone in the world, she'd had a place to call home; even a hodge-podge of eclectic family to surround her.

And now Mr Millionaire was here to take it from her? There was a certain cruel irony to that…

Shannon's chin rose in defiance. 'It's a big deal to me. The Connor Flanaghan I knew would have taken the time to find that out.'

Connor studied her with his dark eyes for what felt like for ever, while Shannon did her best to swallow back the wave of anger and resentment building inside her.

This was *so* not the way she had planned on it being if she ever saw him again. But, hey, at least she couldn't hear Barry White in her head any more. Every cloud, right?

'Why?'

'*Why?*' Was he *kidding?*

'Yes—why? Why is it a big deal?' With his gaze still locked on hers he took one large hand out of a pocket and waved it in an arc at his side. 'It's just some crumbly, old, and, in fairness, *incredibly* ugly building. And I have no problem with helping you find an alternative. I owe you that much at least.'

She'd been about to defend the classic Victorian Gothic exterior she loved so much before he'd added the last part.

'You *owe* me?' The colour drained from her face as her hands went cold. 'What does *that* mean?'

Another shrug. 'We knew each other. Because of our history I'm prepared to make some concessions.'

Shannon stood statue still and stared at him, her heart missing several beats in her chest while she fought to find the words to express her incredulity without giving anything away.

In the ensuing silence Connor's mouth quirked, another low chuckle of laughter escaping. 'What's *that* look for?'

Shannon shook her head, turning her back on him as she opened the large daily diary on the counter behind her and silently prayed that she had misinterpreted his meaning.

'Maybe you should just go out the door and come back in again and we'll try starting this conversation over because, *really,* this is a little too surreal right now. I haven't even had my second cup of coffee yet. I can never think straight 'til I've had my second cup of coffee. So go away, come back later, and we'll start with the weather and work our way up to the difficult stuff.'

The only noise in the room for a few minutes was the tapping of one end of Shannon's pen off the wooden surface while she waited for him to say something or leave. Leave being her personal preference.

And she needed that time. That brief break from just looking at him. In order to try and calm her thoughts, to push back the momentary sense of panic that she'd felt when he said he'd 'owed' her something because of their 'history'.

Maybe if she closed her eyes and tapped her heels together three times this little nightmare would just disappear? It might be worth a try…

She almost jumped out of her skin when he touched her.

If she hadn't been wearing a T-shirt then maybe he wouldn't have touched his heated fingers against her cool, bare skin. If she hadn't still been recovering from the shock of seeing him again and everything he had told her in the space of a few minutes, then maybe the heat of that touch on her cold skin wouldn't have felt like a bolt of pure electricity.

And then maybe she wouldn't have spun round and snatched her arm from his long fingers so fast that she knocked her elbow hard off the edge of the counter.

'Damn it!'

Rocking back from him she nursed her elbow, scowling at the sharp shard of pain working its way up into her shoulder while tears immediately stung in her eyes.

It really hurt! And it was all *his* fault!

She glared venomously at him.

Connor's mouth twitched as he reached out to her again. 'Let me see.'

Shannon sidestepped him. 'No. Go away, Connor.'

'I'm not going anywhere until you let me see your elbow.' He stepped in front of her again.

So, with a smirk she lifted her hand past her shoulder to point her aching elbow at him. 'Happy now? Or do you want to kiss it better?'

His dark eyes flamed briefly and Shannon gasped.

But when he attempted to reach for her arm again and she snatched it away again, this time with an accompanying grimace, he sighed loudly.

'When did you get to be so pigheaded?'

Shannon tilted her head, mouth pouting, batting her lashes at him. 'Oh, maybe around about the same time you became a big-shot multimillionaire?'

With all attempts at helping her rebuffed he finally refolded his arms across his broad chest, tilting his head *without* pouting or batting his lashes. He didn't need to do anything more than stare at her to get his point across. He was losing patience. Fast.

And his words confirmed it. 'Are you done with your little tantrum now?'

Shannon glared harder.

While he lifted his arm slightly, shrugging back the end of his sleeve to check his watch. ''Cos I have another meeting in a half hour, but I can wait a few more minutes for you to calm down if that'll help any.'

She opened her mouth to say how very sweet that was of him, only to have him step closer so that she was trapped between the counter and his large body.

Uh-oh.

When he spoke again, his voice was lower, deeper; it held a more determined edge. So that she was completely distracted from sarcasm and instead mesmerized by his sheer maleness. Had he been this overwhelming up close before? She didn't remember that part.

Barry White started singing in her head again.

'I could have just sent you a letter, Shannon. But when I

saw whose name was on the lease I decided to come and talk to you face to face, out of respect. This isn't personal, selling the building, it's just business. And I'll make sure there's a place for you to move to. I already told you that. There are plenty of other buildings in better places where you could run all these little things you do to amuse yourself.'

Shannon scowled, opening her mouth again, this time to discuss the meaning of the word 'patronizing' with him.

But Connor was on a roll. 'Believe it or not, I didn't come here to have a fight with you. I actually *wanted* to see you.'

Her eyes widened. 'Why?'

This smile was slow, smouldering, sensuous. And whatever else might have changed about him, Shannon recognized *that* smile. He was turning on the charm. *For her.* Seven years too late.

'I've always been curious why you left without saying goodbye. Don't you think that was a little rude of you?'

'You're here to tell me off for my manners after *seven years?* You've got to be *kidding* me!'

She watched as his eyes made an intensive study of her, from the top of her head, to each of her eyes, along her nose, finally resting on her lips. The lips she involuntarily swiped with the tip of her tongue before parting them to draw in several short gasps of air.

'I just thought that, considering what happened between us, you might have taken five minutes to say cheerio before you flew out of the country. It's what *I'd* have done.'

Shannon swallowed hard. 'After—*what*—happened?'

His gaze lifted, ever so slowly, locking with her wide-eyed stare as he leaned his head a little closer, his voice dropping to pillow-talk level. 'Was it that easy to forget? I always thought the first time was supposed to be an unforgettable experience?'

Her breath caught. *O-h-n-o!*

'You knew it was me?'

He chuckled, the dimples in his cheeks creasing. 'Of course I knew. You knew I knew. It was all part of the game that night. There's no way you could have thought that disguise *worked?*'

Well, actually…

Despite the ache in her elbow, Shannon lifted both arms, reaching her hands out to his chest to push hard, a wave of almost adolescent humiliation driving her to get as far away from him as possible.

'Get away from me.'

She was halfway across the room before he spoke again, a hint of humour still in his voice. 'We're not done discussing the building and where you're moving to.'

Shannon laughed sarcastically. 'Oh, we're done, believe me. And there's no discussion to be had about this building, because I have a long lease and I won't be moving anywhere.'

'The sale is already agreed. It'll take approximately six weeks to go through the solicitors. So you don't really have a choice. And the next owners might not be so considerate about where you end up—unless you have some history with one of them too.'

Son-of-a—

She swung round and advanced back to him with gritty determination. She wasn't some naïve teenage girl any more. And the sooner he realized that, the better.

'I have a choice all right. I'll fight you for this place if I have to, because it's not just a crumbly old ruin to me. But I don't expect you'd understand that any more than you understand how lower than low it was of you just now to bring up what happened way back then. *Believe me,* if I had to go back I'd do things a lot differently.'

His humour disappeared instantaneously. 'Including what happened with me?'

The answer to that was swift, borne from the gaping wound she still carried buried way, way deep inside.

'*Especially* what happened with you. That was the biggest mistake of my life. And if I could go back in time it would never happen!' She looked him down and back up, her next words enunciated with distinct iciness. 'Never in a million years.'

The air in the foyer went chilly. Arctic, in fact.

'Well, then, I've just had any questions I had about the way you left answered, haven't I?' This time when he smiled there was no hint of his earlier humour, his voice deadly calm. 'You'll get written confirmation of the sale in the next few days along with a list of alternative buildings. Choose one.'

'Don't bother sending anything. *I'm* not moving.'

Nodding, he glanced down at his watch again. 'Fine, then. Have it your way.'

Even after the doors had creaked shut behind him, Shannon still stood in the one spot, hands on her hips, head tilted back, as she took long deep breaths to try and calm herself.

Connor Flanaghan.

But as the deep breathing gradually brought her rapidly beating heart under control, the bare facts of their confrontation rose to the fore.

She had to stop him.

But could she, Shannon Hennessey—who had never once fought to stay somewhere before—stand up and fight for the place she now called home?

Yes, she could and she would. With whatever weapons she had in her mature arsenal.

Connor Flanaghan had a heap of trouble headed his way!

CHAPTER TWO

WHY WAS IT that, on top of everything else, he had thought it would be a good idea to go see Shannon Hennessey again?

Connor was still asking himself that question long after he'd left her. After he had been to three different meetings and looked over five buildings and was finally hauling off his tie in his suite in Galway's top hotel.

Pacing around the large, perfectly ordered room, he went over it in his mind.

Her name on the lease had been the last thing he'd expected to see. And, yes, curiosity had probably had a hand in him visiting her personally rather than sending an agent as he normally did.

But there'd been a time in his life when Shannon had almost been a part of the furniture. Always there, always in the background, so shy at the beginning, but then funny and cute and bright—the stereotypical girl next door. Swiftly followed by the time when he had noticed she was growing up, 'debating' everything with him, challenging him, flirting with him—treading closer and closer to that fine line between friendship and something more.

Until the one night he had let her play her somewhat dangerous game through to its logical conclusion.

But she was something altogether different now, wasn't she? Oh, yeah, now she was all grown-up. It had been no teenager or naïve virgin that had looked at him the way she had that afternoon. It took a fully grown woman to look at a man that way, with heavy-lidded eyes that had darkened in colour to a deep emerald-green, heating his blood faster than standing in front of an open flame ever would have. With just that look, a swipe of her full mouth with the pink end of her tongue, and he'd had a dozen memories from that one night with her bounce straight into the front of his mind.

Through every one of his afternoon appointments he'd still been able to see her face, hear her voice, mentally visualize that damn lock of hair of hers that constantly worked loose.

Yep, she'd left him angry and sullen for the rest of the day, because, if nothing else, his ego didn't appreciate her bitterness about that one night.

He paced up and down in the room, restless in the same soul-deep way he had been for weeks now. The root cause of it was easy to pin down, but the added complication of seeing Shannon again and the associated long ago memories that came with that…

Well, that had been an added complication he could have done without.

And yet practically the first thing he had done was go see her and bring up the subject of that one night. Maybe it had been crass of him, poorly handled. Okay, he would possibly have to admit to that. Shannon then throwing at him the fact that she wished it had never happened had maybe only been what he deserved as a result.

But it didn't make him any the less resentful of her reaction. And, little did she know it, she'd picked the wrong time to make him resentful.

The shrill sound of a mobile phone drew him out of his dark brooding, forcing him to take a moment to search the pocket of the jacket he had thrown to one side. But a quick glance at the screen simply made him scowl all the harder while he sighed and let it ring out.

He didn't want to talk to Rory. Not yet.

What he *wanted* was a drink someplace noisy with a crowd of people who wouldn't know him and enough pretty women to take his mind off the one woman.

What he *didn't want* in the first place he found was to see Shannon again. Was someone, somewhere, just hell-bent on keeping him in a foul mood? If they were then they were doing a very good job.

She was dancing on a small wooden dance floor to one side of the room, with a man way too 'pretty' in Connor's mind. That was her type now, was it? Somehow she'd never seemed the kind of girl to be easily swayed by someone so fashion-conscious.

But if Connor had been remembering only a half hour ago the girl next door she used to be, then the sight of her matching her lusciously curved body's moves with the tall man's only confirmed his thoughts of her being all grown-up now. And then some.

Leaning an elbow on the long polished bar, he nodded to the barman and placed his order, flashing a smile at the woman who was turning with her own drinks in hand, before he leaned back, one foot resting on the brass rail raised slightly off the floor, and continued watching Shannon through hooded eyes.

If she kept dancing like that then every red-blooded man in the room would soon be doing the same thing, wouldn't they?

And she'd have no one to blame but herself for the swarm of attention that might bring her as the night went on and alcohol clouded the judgement of those males' good manners. Would 'pretty boy' step up and fend them off—defending his territory, seeing off the competition?

Somehow Connor didn't think he looked the type.

All right, so there had been a time in Connor's life when he'd have had an avid appreciation for the kind of blatant sexual confidence in a woman that would bring that kind of trouble to his door. But this was *Shannon.*

And he found he didn't appreciate the exhibitionist in her quite the same way as he had with other women. If anything, it was like a red rag to a bull. He might just have to see for himself if 'pretty boy' was up to the task of some healthy competition...

As if in challenge, the man wrapped an arm around her waist, his fingers splaying against the skin revealed between her short black top and the waistband of her tight jeans, while he tilted his chin to watch as she brought her pelvis in against his hip, moving in a way that only had one point of reference off a dance floor that Connor could think of.

But he couldn't stop watching. He was a red-blooded male after all. The only thing that set him apart from all the other red-blooded males was that he had experience of what it felt like to have her body wrapped around his, to be buried deep inside her while her body clamped around his hard length as she fell over the edge.

On that one night she was so damn keen to forget.

With a quick flick of her head, her long blonde hair cascaded over one bare shoulder, the errant corkscrew curl immediately coming back to rest against her cheek. Then, with a smile on her lips, she glanced up. And her sparkling green eyes found his across the room.

Connor nodded his head once in acknowledgement. He didn't look away, didn't smile. He just continued to watch as she moved her hips again, her arms hanging back a little behind her body as her shoulders moved from side to side— the movement pushing her breasts up and forwards.

Two minutes.

Yep. That was all he was giving her. And then he was gonna walk right on over there and tap her partner on the shoulder. To see, just out of curiosity, how she might react to that. If she would fight him off before he could remind her of why singling him out as her first lover shouldn't be something she regretted doing. Or to see if she would remember how well their bodies had fitted, a little reminder of how they had moved and *could* move together.

After all, it wasn't as if she had complained at the time, not that Connor recalled…

Oh, yeah, he'd dance with her all right, he'd let her move her hips in against his side while he waited to see if her emerald eyes would darken the way they had when she'd looked at him that afternoon.

Only this time round they'd play the game *his* way.

But before he counted down the minutes she leaned up to speak into her partner's ear as the music changed, kissing him briefly on the cheek before she extricated herself from his hold and walked towards Connor with a tantalizingly confident sway of her hips.

She flashed him a brief look from the corner of her eye before standing on tiptoes beside him, her hand rising to run through the long curls of hair so they were off her forehead, leaning across the bar with a killer smile to order a drink, the barman smiling in blatant appreciation at her.

Connor tossed money onto the polished surface in front of her—taking care of her drink—then leaned back again to survey the crowd. Silently waiting to see what she would do next. Telling himself he'd take an apology for the way she'd been earlier, any time she felt ready to hand it out. He could still be a good guy when he put his mind to it…

He smiled at another passing female who smiled appreciatively at him on her way past with a friend, lifting his beer to take a long drink, while, glass in hand, Shannon turned round and mimicked his stance, surveying the crowd with her back against the bar.

Eventually he couldn't resist asking, 'Come here often?'

'It's one of our favourite places, actually, within staggering distance of home. Why, are you planning on selling *here* too?'

'I don't own it.' Ignoring her sugary-sweet tone, Connor lifted his bottle to his mouth again. 'You and your boyfriend can dance here to your heart's content.'

'Not that it's any of your business, but he's not my boyfriend. I'm not his type.'

He glanced at her from the corner of his eye, a small smile on his mouth. 'Prefers brunettes, does he? Man after my own heart, then.'

'Nope.' She quirked an arched brow in challenge as she turned her body towards him, her head tilting forwards a little so he could hear her lowered voice above the music. 'I'm not quite *man* enough for him, if you get my drift. He'd like *you* though, if you want an introduction?'

Connor couldn't help it; he laughed. Shaking his head as

he turned towards her, his elbow on the bar, he said, 'Oh, I think we both know that won't be necessary.'

Shannon shrugged off the innuendo, literally, eyeing him again from beneath long lashes. 'Well, I wouldn't know what else might have changed about you lately, would I?'

'Many, *many* things may have changed but that isn't one of them.' He leaned his face a little closer, watching triumphantly as her lashes flickered, her gaze on his mouth as he spoke. 'Trust me.'

There was a long silence while her eyes slowly rose until her gaze locked with his. The emerald-green taking on the darker shade he had planned on seeing when he danced with her.

She wasn't as immune to him as she'd like to think she was, was she? And that, coupled with the recent evidence of her dance moves, was more than enough encouragement. So he grinned widely, and winked at her.

Shannon laughed. 'No, some things obviously haven't changed.'

He continued grinning, even after she turned to face the bar again. And it felt good. Better than good. In fact he couldn't remember the last time when the mess of his life had been put to the back of his mind long enough for him to play a little with a woman. Even briefly. And with someone who less than a few hours ago had been so obviously determined they didn't want to play. Not with him, anyway.

Which made her *a challenge*.

Maybe persuading her to change her mind about regretting him might be exactly the kind of welcome distraction he needed after all, for a while anyway.

His phone vibrated in the pocket of his jeans and he reached in to retrieve it, the screen lighting up as he checked the number, briefly illuminating his face while Shannon turned to watch him.

He wasn't grinning by the time he turned it off.

Shannon was still watching as he pushed it back into a pocket. 'Avoiding some poor lovelorn woman?'

'Not this time. It's just Rory.'

The tension in his voice was obvious, causing Shannon to frown in confusion as she asked, 'As in Rory your big brother Rory?'

'That would be the one.'

'How is he?'

The beer bottle froze an inch from his mouth. 'I wouldn't know.'

Which only seemed to confuse Shannon all the more. 'Well, I could be wrong. But answering the phone might help with that, don't you think?'

When he looked at her face his eyes were dark, his expression grim and Shannon immediately knew it was meant as a 'butt out'.

Even before he added the firmly voiced, 'Leave it be, Shannon.'

She lifted her chin in response.

'So, no Senior Citizens Aerobics tonight?'

'I don't take the aerobics sessions.' With a shake of her head, tossing her hair over one shoulder, she took the lifeline afforded with his swift change of subject. It wasn't as if it were really any of her business anyway, so why should she care?

'I run a Tumblin' Tinies franchise for kids from eighteen months to ten years old, if you must know. And I do the reading group we have so the mothers can do their yoga classes in the mornings.'

'The *Yummy* Mummies? I have to say there's a certain element of fascination in the idea of good-looking women who can...*flex*...'

Shannon ignored the return of that silently teasing light in his dark eyes. 'I'll just bet there is in a mind like yours. But, yes, that's the ones. If they know the kids are happy they're more likely to enjoy some time of their own. So I do story time with the kids.'

'I don't remember that from the notice-board.'

'Well, that's a shame, 'cos we run a quiz on what's on the notice-board once a week. Winner gets a free yoga session.'

'You just made that up, didn't you?'

Shannon nodded. 'Yes, I did.'

Silence descended between them again until Connor took a breath and dived in on a bigger issue.

'You know, there was a time when we used to be able to get along without this much effort, if I recall. And I know we may possibly have gotten off to a bad start today—'

She shrugged. 'I liked you better when I knew you before—that's all. But then, in fairness, you'd never tried to make me homeless back then. And, anyway, this isn't us not getting along, not yet. You'll know when it is.'

Connor's eyes were still studying her as she looked around the rapidly filling bar. She didn't have to look up at his face to confirm it. She could feel it, as surely as she could probably have calculated to the very millimetre the distance between their two bodies. It was a senses thing, she supposed. But it was also a very basic-awareness-on-a-very-sensual-level thing, which both excited and frustrated her, in equal measure. He was temptation on legs, not a doubt about it.

Even so, she really *didn't* want to like him again if she could at all avoid it. She'd have to keep her wits about her if she was going to take him on to save her precious building…

And liking him might lead to her getting sidetracked.

But she hadn't come out tonight to play games with him, or have another argument with him. She hadn't come out with the intention of seeing him at all. She'd come out to enjoy herself with her friends, to *forget* about meeting the all new, not-necessarily-improved Connor.

The best laid plans…

'So, how was America?' he asked nonchalantly.

Her stomach flipped over and felt distinctly as if it hit the floor. *Hard.*

All right, so it was a logical question. The last time Connor had known her that was where she'd been headed. There was no way on God's green earth he could know what had happened when she was there.

So she took a breath, forcing a calm tone into her voice. 'It was great. I learnt a lot on the courses I did.'

'How long have you been home?'

'A year—after eighteen months in London—but I like Galway; we're a good fit for each other.'

When he went quiet she risked another sidewards glance to confirm that he wasn't questioning her because he knew something. Even when she knew he couldn't. Not without being psychic.

And there he was, large as life and twice as damn sexy without even trying, lounging laconically against the bar in the more familiar jeans-and-dark-shirt ensemble that had always had her drooling from a distance when she was old enough to know what it was she appreciated about him. Still studying her with his dark eyes, which unnerved her even more than his knowing anything could have.

'What?'

Connor shook his head. 'Nothing. I was just thinking.'

'Well don't make any effort on my behalf.'

With a smirk he reached over to leave his empty bottle on the bar, his arm accidentally brushing briefly against the side of her breast. And it took every ounce of self-control in her possession for Shannon not to flinch as her eyes locked with his.

He knew he had done it.

It was as clear as day to her that he knew what he had done, from the flash of awareness that crossed his dark eyes and the lazy smile that followed. He was silently challenging her to call him on it too! Thing was, what he maybe didn't realize was that that accidental touch had awakened a hundred memories in her mind and in her body, and allowed her to recognize that flash of awareness in his eyes for what it was: *sexual awareness*.

Maybe she wasn't the only one hearing Barry White. And *that* had to be something she could work with…

Shannon had seen that look in his eyes before. She'd even played up to it. In the past the way he had touched her hadn't been at all unintentional or accidental, it had been slow and deliberate, an awakening for Shannon—a long lesson in physical pleasure that she had never forgotten.

She would never have wanted there to be someone else her first time. Not then. She just hadn't known there would be consequences—if she *had*…

Connor smiled for another moment, but when she refused to rise to the bait he took a different approach. 'Tess was worried about you, you know. That time when you were ill in the States.'

Shannon's stomach somersaulted again. 'Ill?'

'Yes, she said you collapsed and had to go into hospital for a while.'

'Oh, that.' She damped her tongue along her dry lips and smiled through the lie. 'I had heatstroke. You know us blonde Irish girls and the sun.'

'Still, it was a long way from home to be sick and on your own.'

'I didn't have a home any more, Connor. Not after my nan died. And, anyway, everyone has something they have to get through on their own at some time or other. That's life.'

'Yes, it is.' He turned and looked out over the crowd.

A thought occurred to her. 'Is that why you're avoiding Rory? Because you have something you have to deal with alone? Or did you get in another one of those dumb ass fights with him?'

The Fighting Flanaghans they'd all been known as growing up. Four brothers completely devoted to each other who'd nevertheless spent half their adolescence arguing with each other over the most ridiculous things. And even now the memory made her smile a small smile.

But Connor merely shot her another warning glance in response.

So Shannon sighed. 'Right, I get it, you don't want to talk about it. Well, maybe I should just go get my good friend Mario to keep you company, then. He'd love that.'

'Uh-uh. I'm just fine with you to keep me company.'

Flattering and all as that was, Shannon was rapidly running out of safe topics to talk to him about. So, she ran a quick summary through her mind: he obviously didn't want to discuss whatever his problem was with his brother, she didn't want to start a row with him in public about the building issue until she had all her facts, and her being ill in America was a definite no-go zone.

Which left Shannon surrounded by choices between: a) a web of half-truths, b) dangerous topics of conversation or c) just standing still allowing the air to crackle between them while she played with the idea of using some of that sexual awareness in the here and now to her advantage.

Decisions, decisions.

'It's been unusually warm this summer, hasn't it?'

Connor smiled down at her with the kind of smile that reminded her of a time when they'd been friends without so much effort. 'And there we are—reduced to talking about the weather.'

'Well, you don't want to talk about Rory and I'm in no mood to talk about the building we're going to go to war over, so that doesn't leave us with much, does it?'

'So, dance with me.'

'What if I don't want to dance with you?'

'Tough.'

It was too late, already he was taking control, removing the glass from her hand, setting it on the bar behind her before he tangled his long fingers with hers and tugged, hard, forcing her forwards. He then looked over his shoulder as their feet hit the wooden floor, to inform her with gleaming eyes, 'Now that I've seen you have some moves it seems only fair you try them out on someone who *does* like women.'

O-h-h no. The only reason she let loose with Mario was because she knew he wouldn't read anything into it. He was 'safe'. She didn't go around dancing that freely with *every* man she met—not unless she actually planned on…

Well—with Mario she could lose her inhibitions, could

close her eyes and succumb to the sheer sexuality of a throbbing beat and a sensual rhythm. It was liberating, exhilarating, a small chance to be completely free for a few minutes.

With Connor it would be foreplay.

In fact the very thought of moving her pelvis in against him the way she had with Mario had her body heating up in ways and places it hadn't done in what felt like a long, *long* time!

This was a bad idea.

She needed a game plan before she stepped in the ring with Connor Flanaghan. A damned detailed one too!

She tried to shake her hand free. But Connor had always been stronger than her physically, and with another tug he had her hauled forwards against his body, his free hand snaking around her waist, fingers splaying against her skin to add just enough pressure so that she was held tight all along the hard length of him from thigh to chest as he began to move them in time to the music.

Shannon almost moaned aloud. Oh, Barry White had been right all along. This was *good.*

Her traitorous curves automatically fitted in against lean male muscle. And the joint movement of their bodies created friction on the most basic sexual level, pebbling her nipples harder against the lace of her bra, building a slowly widening knot of tension in her abdomen, sending a wash of moisture to her core.

Her breathing increased.

And then her eyes rose, slowly, moving from button to button on his shirt, lingering briefly on the column of his neck before she studied his mouth. His sculpted mouth with its wider lower lip—the mouth that had once kissed her lips, her neck, her breasts, the soft skin of her inner thigh…

She had to swallow down another low moan before she protested again. 'Connor—'

He held her firm when she struggled against him. 'Shush. You don't want to cause a big scene in this crowd, now, do you?'

When she looked into his eyes he had that same dark gaze that sparkled with knowing—he *knew* what he was doing to her. He knew and he was positively triumphant about it, *goddamn it!*

Tearing her gaze away, she pursed her lips together as she tried to think of another way of getting out of her predicament. She was actually fairly sure, if she did cause a big scene, she could get him kicked out. After all, she'd been coming to this place for a long time. It was her local haunt.

And one glance over his shoulder told her what she already knew—that her friends were more than aware that she was dancing with someone they had never seen before, which meant they would automatically keep an eye on her. And not *just* out of curiosity. It was something they all did for each other.

Though, in fairness, the sight of three thumbs being pointed upwards didn't give her much confidence in them as potential rescuers.

She chanced another look into his eyes. And her brain suddenly started to function.

Wait a minute. Why was she looking for a way out? Surely this was her chance to up the ante? If she was gonna go to battle with him then she couldn't go into it with him, knowing he already had an advantage over her physically. She couldn't let him think he could bend her to his will because she apparently still *wanted him.* What she needed to do was show him she was no naïve teenager any more. Hell, no. She was all grown-up now. Maybe it was about time he understood that.

So she tossed her hair back over her shoulder again, leaning back a little against his arms as she damped her lips, caught her lower lip between her teeth, smiled seductively as he watched the movement.

And for good measure she moved her pelvis across his, sliding back and forth until she heard his sharp intake of breath and felt his body go rigid.

Touché, Connor Flanaghan. Your move.

Her eyebrows quirked in challenge.

Connor's head descended slowly, until his clean shaven cheek was close to hers, musky male scent filling her nostrils as he grumbled into her ear, 'You know, they say when a couple can dance together like this it means they're compatible in other areas.'

Shannon leaned back, her voice low. 'Are you serious? That line gets you laid? *Really?*'

He angled his face above hers, his warm breath washing over her cheeks as he looked at her with hooded eyes, 'You'd be surprised.'

'Well—' she angled her face the opposite way, so that when she rocked forward a little and stood on her toes her mouth was inches from his, her eyes focused on the small distance between control and giving in to temptation '—on behalf of womankind everywhere, I am officially embarrassed that line worked for you.'

Connor smiled a lazy smile. 'Ah, but it's not really a line; it makes perfect sense. Both have to do with natural rhythm, working with the way your partner moves, adjusting the give—and the take—to make things better for each other. If you can synchronize on a dance floor then it makes sense that things are much better when—'

Whoa—and he could stop right there! She'd got it! And she needed to stay in equal control here, didn't she? So, with a cooling deep breath she leaned her head back again. 'I get the picture.'

Vividly and in Technicolor as it just so happened. Even accompanied with some bright sparks of multicoloured light when she closed her eyes as her lower abdomen came into contact with the beginnings of a rather impressive erection, and her body immediately flooded in readiness.

O-h-h—if she was going to play this game she really needed to get her responses under control, didn't she?

Instead of picturing hot, sweaty sex while her eyes were still closed.

'But then we already know we're compatible in that area, don't we, *Sunshine?*'

Her eyes flew open. He had used her nickname from the 'good old days' when she had been head over heels about him—when the very sound of that word had been interpreted as an endearment rolling off his silver tongue. And it immediately reminded her of a time when she'd had no control at all around him.

He played dirty!

His smile grew when her eyes narrowed in warning. 'I know you remember as much as I do, even if you want to try so desperately to forget it—which I really don't think you do, deep down. Not really. Maybe what we should do is try it again, just to see if it's as good a second time. You've obviously picked up some moves.' He leaned a little closer. 'I even have some new ones myself. And when you're crying out my name this time, you might find you don't regret crying it out the first time round either.'

Shannon gasped. 'Oh, well, you can just be a complete bastard when you put your mind to it, can't you?'

The arm around her waist became a steel band, his expression went dark, even his mouth twisted as he answered in a dangerously low tone, 'You have no idea how right you are.'

Shannon struggled to get free, then froze and decided instead to go on the offensive. 'You know what really got to me the most all afternoon, thinking about you knowing it was me that time? It's that you played along. The whole way through you never once felt the need to say you knew. Now just why might that be, do you think?'

He laughed. He damn well laughed out loud!

'Aw, c'mon, Shannon! You knew I knew. Pretending I didn't was all part of the game.'

He might as well have slapped her; the sense of humiliation was just *that* strong. Because he really *had* known it was her all along, hadn't he? Not only that—but he had thought it was all some big sexual game to her! He had played along for the sake of an opportunity for some hot sex! Despite her complete belief that she had seduced him into a fantasy night of memorable romance.

Which it had been. *For her*.

She'd been *so* naïve back then! So wrapped up in a romance and a happily ever after that hadn't existed. It had taken real life to teach her that one, hadn't it?

And now, thanks to Connor, she got to feel a little of that pain all over again. Slicing through her now as agonizingly as it had when she'd been alone and dealing with the aftermath of her *naïveté*.

What a bastard!

Connor leaned back in, his cheek against her cheek as his deep voice tickled against her ear. 'It was the most amazing night—don't you remember? I used to have seriously hot dreams about it after you left. I never knew that being seduced by a woman in a fantasy outfit could be so...*erotic.*'

Then his head turned a fraction, his lips brushing oh-so briefly against the sensitive skin below her ear as he spoke in a stage whisper. 'You were beautiful. A little nervous at first maybe, but then you just let yourself get lost in the moment, didn't you? And you were sexy as hell. I've never forgotten. The way you moved, the sounds you made, how you cried out when you came. *Any* of it.'

Shannon closed her eyes. It was just the absolute worst form of torture she'd ever been subjected to—laced with a bitter sweetness that tore her in two.

'It wasn't a game! You were never supposed to know it was me.'

He chuckled again. 'A mask and a cheap wig weren't gonna stop me from knowing it was you. I knew your scent. It was unmistakably you. Still is, as it happens; it's on you now. A combination of flowers and a hint of something fresh that always said Shannon Hennessey was nearby. You *chose* to make it a fantasy night—I just followed your lead.'

Perfume had given her away?

'Let go of me.'

Standing statue still in his hold, she refused to allow him to continue swaying their bodies, her eyes open and fixed on the open door across the busy bar. 'Let me go, right this minute. Or—I swear—I'll yell so loud my good friends the bouncers will knock you into next week. And I'll grin as it happens.'

Connor's large body went rigid for a moment before he took a step back, releasing her at a torturously slow pace along the way.

While Shannon stared up at his hooded eyes, her cheeks burning as her pulse continued beating erratically with a combination of arousal and anger. 'You don't know who I am now, any more than I know who you are. And quite frankly, I'm not sure I *want* to know the new you or experience any of your *new moves*. I may have been crazy enough about you seven years ago to want you to be my first time, but right this minute I dislike who you are just enough to never want to set eyes on you ever again.'

Connor's dark eyes flared as he stepped forwards, his wide chest an inch away from the rapid rise and fall of her breasts. 'Let's just take a second here and look back at who it was set up that little seduction scene all those years ago, shall we?'

'And then let's look at who played along with it right up to the end and never once let on he knew! But then maybe no-strings-attached sex was your thing? It suited you just fine to pretend you didn't know who it was underneath you!'

His mouth pursed briefly into a sharp line. 'It was what *you* wanted or it would never have happened! *Trust me.*'

The hissed words washed over her flushed cheeks as she fought to hold back angry tears. 'No. All I wanted at the time was *you!* I was just too young and too damn stupid to know any better, *obviously.* There were probably a half-dozen others who would have been a better choice!'

After a cursory flicker of his eyes over her face, he took a breath and leaned his face closer still, his mouth a mere whisper above hers while he locked eyes with her.

'If it was me you wanted, then you got your wish, didn't

you? No matter what kind of a person I was underneath. Well, you know what they say about being careful about what you wish for.'

While she stood gaping, he angled his head and added, 'What you should maybe remember for future reference is that no one is what they might like to think they are. Under that girl-next-door image of yours was an incredibly sexual woman, waiting to test out what she was capable of. It was just fortunate for you that you picked me. It could have been *much* worse.'

'Not from where I'm standing right this minute it couldn't.'

His thick dark lashes lowered as he looked down to where his mouth almost touched hers, then rose as he searched her eyes. 'Go ahead and forget it ever happened, if you can. I don't intend ever forgetting. You'll just have to learn to deal with knowing that every time you look at me, won't you? Because every time I look at you it'll be what I'm thinking of.'

'Well, it won't be what I'm thinking of when I look at you—' she almost spat the lie up at him '—so you'll just have to learn to deal with that. Because I'm no naïve little virgin any more, Connor. I'm a fully grown woman. If you thought last time was amazing—well, you just go ahead and have a little think about how much more amazing it could be with someone who actually knows what she's doing. *Then* remind yourself that the only reason you'll never get a chance to find out what it would be like is because you've turned into a complete and utter ass!'

And with that she turned, her head held high, and her hips swaying purposefully as she walked away from him.

CHAPTER THREE

THE LITTLE COMMUNITY that had built up within the walls of the building Shannon leased from Devenish wasn't long in gathering a head of steam and forming a committee.

It was what peaceful people did in times of trouble. They got together in a room to argue about what they should do next...

'I say we should get a petition together.'

'A petition isn't going to make a blind bit of difference to a company like Devenish. I say we do a sit-in protest.'

'A naked sit-in, like in the sixties? *I'm in.*' Mario winked across at Shannon.

A tiny grey-haired woman tapped her walking stick on the old wooden floor. 'We should chain ourselves to the railings outside!'

'Brieda, there aren't any railings outside.'

'Well, we have to do *something.*'

Silently, all eyes in the room swung in Shannon's direction. And she sighed in resignation. She really didn't want to do this right now. Not since she had read her e-mails that morning and found a reply from Tess, Connor's sister.

But since she had put a note on the notice-board about the sale of the building there had been a constant stream of people wanting to know what they could do to help and she knew she had no choice but to deal with it.

Even though she now had other things running rings round her mind.

'Well, in the meantime we have the lease agreement. That should buy us some time. But we'll need a solicitor to fight our case and that won't be cheap.'

'We could run some fund-raisers—get everyone who uses the building involved?'

'A sponsored walk maybe?'

'We could run a fête, bake cakes and have a tombola.'

Shannon raised her fingers to rub against her throbbing temples. They all meant well, she knew that, and she loved every one of them for loving the place as much as she did, really she did. That was the real problem for her, you see; she had fallen in love with the building the day she had set eyes on it—it had called to her. Within its walls she had made a place to call home for the first time in years. But, more importantly, in return it had supplied her with the makeshift family that now surrounded her; a family that would rely on her to find a way out of this current dilemma—regardless of just who that put her up against.

Shannon had a responsibility to do right by them. To make an effort to keep the place they all loved. And somehow, having others to fight for instead of just herself almost made it easier for her to stand her ground against Connor.

If it just didn't feel like such a very personal battle. If it just wasn't against someone she had once loved. But the very fact she knew him meant she should be able to do more, didn't it? And they needed her to think of *something*.

'I'm not sure that that'll be enough. Solicitors cost a lot of money these days,' Shannon said.

Her unguarded remark led to several crestfallen faces, and guilt immediately racked her in waves. 'But it would certainly be a start,' she added.

When she smiled encouragingly the room became a hum of voices again, until she had to clear her throat to be heard. 'What we need to do is find something about the history of this place that might get it listed as being of historical interest. Then at least it can't be torn down.'

It was a shot in the dark, she knew that. But immediately there was another flurry of loud conversation, and while her eyes fixed on Mario's proud expression as he walked towards her she didn't notice the door to the room opening.

Until Mario hissed down at her, 'Isn't that the hottie from the bar?'

Her gaze flew to the door where Connor was studying the crowd with a somewhat bemused expression. And her breath caught in her chest at the sight of him.

Because he had been right. Every damn time she looked at him she would *know*. And she hated him for it.

Large frame dominating the low doorway, he searched the room with a flickering gaze and Shannon, mimicking his search, was stunned to realize that no one seemed to have noticed his arrival. How could they miss him?

Because much as she hated him—he looked *sensational*. Dressed in another expensive, gorgeously cut dark suit with a crisp white shirt unbuttoned at the neck, his hair spiking in all directions and a hint of dark shadowed stubble on his chin—he had that 'I'd be great in bed' look that had caught her imagination so long ago.

And even more recently than that.

Only now she resented him for looking that way. Because

she didn't want to still be so aware of how he looked or to remember just how great he was in bed. And since they had danced and he had lightly suggested they try repeating the experience for some kind of comparison, despite her best efforts she'd been able to think of little else. Regardless of what she had said to him in the heat of the moment.

And it was a lie that had led to a distinct lack of sleep after she left him—which had led to even more thinking.

One of those thoughts being that their confrontation had killed every romantic notion she'd ever possessed about him. He had taken that one fantasy night and scrumpled it up like waste paper.

During the endlessly silent hours when she hadn't been able to sleep, she had steadily built a burning hatred for him for the constant, never-ending ripple of retribution that seemed to be foisted on her for what had once been, to her, a magical night.

But even while she hated him for the way he had been with her since he'd come back into her life, she now also understood a little better why he might possibly be acting the way he was—or, at the very least, maybe, *a part* of the reason why.

'You know him?'

Shannon laughed a bitter little laugh. 'Yeah, you could say that.'

'Who is he? Is he gay? Tell me he's gay and single and I'll love you for ever and ever.'

Connor's head turned again, his eyes searching until they eventually locked with hers. While her heart thundered in response as he then walked purposefully towards her, confidently, with determination, his dark eyes lacking in their usual hint of silent amusement.

Shannon frowned hard as she felt her body immediately react to his approach, her eyes looking down over his broad shoulders, his wide chest, all the way down his long legs. And she felt her breasts grow heavy, felt the knot forming in her abdomen.

Goddamn him! How could she hate him so much and still want him inside her so badly?

She wasn't ready to go through another confrontation. Not yet. Not while the sight of him kept on invoking such a powerful response of conflicting emotions in her. What she needed was a few more minutes to gather herself together before she spoke to him. *Just a few minutes.*

All she had to do was find a way of getting them…

'Erm, guys?' She held up her hand for silence. 'Ladies and gentlemen!'

The room fell silent and Connor hesitated, a frown darkening his face even more, if that was possible.

Shannon swept an arm in his direction. 'Mr Flanaghan is here to talk to you all. He's the new owner of Devenish Enterprises. I'm sure he won't mind answering all of your questions about the sale of the building.'

As the small crowd descended on him Mario leaned down to hiss in her ear. 'Mr Gorgeous-Hunk-O-Male is the new owner? The guy who tried to cop off with you on the dance floor before you had your big tiff?'

'He didn't try to cop off with me.' Which was an out-and-out lie, wasn't it? Would she ever stop lying?

But this one her friend wasn't buying. 'Honey, it looked like he did from where *we* were sitting. I can't begin to tell you how jealous I was of you. So, what's going on?'

'Why don't you ask *him?* He's the man of the moment.'

And with that she sneaked out of the room. The rest of the group could deal with him and vice versa while she got herself gathered together.

It took nearly a full hour before he negotiated an escape and found her upstairs.

Leaning against the doorframe, he watched in silence as she loaded dishes into cupboards, her lithe body moving fluidly as she worked her way back and forth, occasional upward stretching affording him a glimpse of smooth skin between her sweatpants and vest-top.

She had an amazing body, didn't she? Long, seemingly endless legs that ended at the perfect rounded curve of her ass, that deliciously feminine inward dip at the small of back, and as she turned a little to get to the top cupboard again he got a brief view of the flat, creamy smooth skin of her stomach and the upward lift of her pert breasts as she reached upwards.

The other night she had curved that sweet body in against his, he had felt her nipples against his chest, had had the torture of her hips moving in against his. Even while he stood in her doorway, remembering, he could feel the blood rush from his head, his groin tightening in anticipation.

He'd never wanted a woman so badly before.

And the fact that she'd said it would never happen made it an even hotter prospect in his mind—the erotic temptation of forbidden fruit.

Getting her would be a goal he could set his mind to achieving. It was something he could control at a time in his life when he needed some semblance of control. Unwittingly she had made him even more determined to get her, to torture her long and slow until she was begging him for the same kind of satisfaction he knew she'd experienced once before.

It had been a bad move in her latest game.

The reception she'd given him downstairs had been pretty much what he'd expected, barring the barrage of questions she'd forced him to face while she'd sneaked off. And in a small way he had found her method of avoidance ingenious, forcing him to smile a genuine smile of amusement on the way upstairs to see her.

Once she knew the method he'd used to get *away* from her little trap he knew he'd be smiling even more. It served her right for taking him on.

But he knew instinctively, while he stood watching her from the doorway, that she wouldn't appreciate it if he smiled a triumphant smile at her. Even if he managed not to add to his trouble with a sharp comment of some kind, many of which he had rehearsed before he'd fallen asleep the night before.

'Leaving me to the wolves was a bit sneaky, don't you think?'

The sound of his voice stiffened her spine. But, to her credit in the self-control department, she merely took a breath and continued clearing up, not even bothering to turn round to look at him.

'Nope. You're the big guy around here now. And they have a right to know why you're taking this place from them. On your head be it, Mr Big-Shot.'

'It's just an old building like plenty of other old buildings in this city—it's outlived its usefulness to the company. It's nothing personal. I believe I've mentioned that a time or two already.'

'Well, I'm willing to bet they didn't see it that way when you talked to them downstairs.'

She was right, they hadn't. Truthfully, Connor had been made to feel like the devil incarnate. But it *wasn't* personal, either to Shannon or the eclectic bunch of people downstairs. *And* he had promised them he would find an alternative building, same as he had with Shannon. Not that that had gone down any better with them than it had with Shannon on the day he'd arrived.

Connor just didn't get what the problem was himself. From the outside the place looked like a setting for a truly awful cheesy horror movie. And it wasn't a whole heap better inside, barring the miracles that Shannon had obviously managed with the floor she used as an apartment.

'It makes more sense to sell it when it's a saleable proposition. It's falling apart in places as it is.'

She sighed impatiently. 'Only because no one has ever bothered their backside spending any money on it.'

Connor's eyes narrowed as she slammed a cupboard door shut and turned to lean against the counter, arms crossed over her breasts as she attempted staring him out.

It was a nice try, he'd give her that. But she should know better. 'Well, do you think that could possibly be because to repair it would cost more than it would to tear it down?'

'And everything in this world comes down to money in the end, does it?'

Connor took a deep breath, glancing briefly around her apartment while he searched for patience. It wasn't by any means opulent, but she'd obviously made an attempt to make a home for herself. There was even a certain quirky charm to the place that reminded him of the Shannon he used to know. Not that he particularly wanted to be reminded of that version of her when he was intent on battling with her all the way into bed.

'I brought you brochures of new buildings to look at.'

'I already told you I don't want another building. I want this one.' Her voice remained low and calm.

Which drew his gaze back to her face—because he hadn't expected low and calm from her, not after last time. When they had both said things that couldn't be taken back.

He had been fully prepared for sarcasm and anger. And to give as good as he got.

'I told you it's already sold. It's a done deal.'

Shannon nodded. 'Because you're narrowing down the amount of properties on the company's books.'

'Exactly.'

There was a long pause while she studied his face, her long lashes blinking slowly, flickering slightly as she looked from one of his eyes to the other. Then she unfolded her arms, stretching them out to her sides and resting her hands against the wooden counter top, which allowed him to read the lettering across her breasts: '4 out of 3 people have trouble with fractions.'

And Connor felt a smile tug at the corners of his mouth again. One that grew when he noticed the rise and fall of her breasts increasing as her breathing sped up. Oh, she wasn't as cool and calm as she was pretending to be, was she?

If she was so determined not to end up horizontal with him again, then she shouldn't have such visceral reactions to him looking at her. But then if she didn't want anyone looking at her breasts she shouldn't keep wearing tops with varying different amusing sayings on them either.

She was bringing all this on herself.

When he looked up, her eyes were darker, more irritation evident in her tone when she spoke. 'So, it's not because you're trying to dismantle Devenish piece by piece?'

His smile faded. 'And why exactly would I do that?'

'You tell me.'

Shannon watched as he shook his head, his eyes narrowing a barely perceptible amount as he walked over to set the brochures he was holding onto the counter beside her. 'Let your agent know which building you're interested in and we'll get the ball rolling.'

Shannon frowned at him. 'I keep telling you I don't *want* another building, Connor. Not that you ever bother listening. But this isn't just about narrowing down properties, is it? There's more to this than that.'

'You can think what you want…' he leaned his head a little closer, his voice dropping to a low grumble '…but don't go looking for some deep psychological reason to justify why I'm selling. It's good business, that's all.'

How was she supposed to concentrate when he was so close again? He was overwhelming up close. She could see tiny paler flecks of gold in his dark eyes, could notice the small creases at the outside edges of his eyes and mouth that hinted at the constant smile he usually had close by, she could smell the scent of his expensive aftershave.

And she could hear Barry White in her head again suggesting they 'get it on'. Which was tempting—and it wouldn't take much either when he was standing so close already. In fact a tilt of her head would probably do it.

When she swiped the end of her tongue over her mouth, his intense gaze dropped, then rose, locking with hers. And for the life of her she couldn't find anything witty or sarcastic to say to him.

When he tilted his head a little past her face, she sucked in a gasp of air, holding it inside her chest while his gaze focused on the spiral of hair against her cheek. And while her heart thundered in her chest while she tried to keep her mind focused on how much she disliked him and not on how desperately she was physically attracted to him, his hand rose, trapping the end of the strand between his thumb and forefinger. But he didn't tuck it back into place, he twisted it a little so that the curl was tighter, then he let go, so that the curl bobbed briefly against her skin as his gaze went back to her mouth.

And the part of her that ached, low down inside, ignored her better judgement, so that the only thing she knew was that if he didn't kiss her soon or leave, she was going to scream.

The smile that slowly formed on his sensual mouth told her he knew what she wanted.

Shannon wanted to kill him.

She pushed her hands off the counter, attempting to move away from him, but Connor stepped in closer, pinning her in place just by standing there. Not touching, oh, no, not touching her *anywhere*, merely dominating her with his presence and the sexual static between them.

Shannon's head tilted back and she looked into his eyes with a quirk of her eyebrows.

It was apparently all the invitation he needed.

Because in a split second his hands rose, his thumbs tilting her chin up as his fingers slid back into her hair, caressing the nape of her neck as his head lowered and he grumbled above her mouth, 'You're right, though. There is more to it than that. There's this.'

Then his firm mouth settled on hers.

And it was as if a ticking time bomb went off inside her. Her hands rose, her fingers grasping the lapels of his jacket into tight fists as she vented all of her anger and frustration into the kiss. There was no tenderness to it, no gentle sense of longing. All there was was the release of the sexual tension that had been building since the day he'd walked through the foyer doors. And any need to discuss the damn building, or anything else off the long, *long* list of issues they had standing between them, left the room—at speed.

Connor's hands dropped from her face as he increased the pressure of his mouth, meeting her demands with some of his own as he plundered her lips from one edge to the other. And those hands then grasped hold of either side of her waist, pulling her forwards, grinding her pelvis in tighter against his hard body while he inhaled, drawing in the air she exhaled as she opened her mouth to give access to his tongue.

Shannon's hands rose, sliding up past his shoulders to tangle in the short, coarse hair behind his neck while she stood on her toes to demand an equal amount from the kiss. It was frantic, it was hot—everything she had fantasized about of late and so much more.

And it still damn well wasn't enough!

She gasped when he lifted her, as if she weighed nothing, depositing her on the counter so that she was slightly above him. So she was looking down at him when he wrenched his mouth free and looked up at her.

And she still couldn't speak.

He moved his hands down to her hips, down the outside of her thighs, ran his fingers under her knees and spread her legs a little wider to step between them.

And Shannon just let him.

Until his eyes searched hers, his head tilted again, and his warm breath washed over her swollen lips. 'I knew you'd be like this.'

Never in her life had there been anyone else who could wind her this tight, make her this hot this fast or force all rational thought to leave her head until there was only one thought left there.

'I've never kissed someone I didn't like before.'

He smiled, his hands moving slowly up her legs again. And the erotic suggestion of their position sent waves of moisture to Shannon's core. They could do it like this, just exactly where they were, a few less clothes, a little more kissing. It wouldn't take much.

Not when they'd been dancing around this for days.

And maybe if they just got it out of the way they could actually hold a conversation long enough to sort out a few other things.

'You liked me once. You'll learn to like me again. You've just got to allow yourself to.'

Damn it. And he'd said the words with just enough softness in his voice for her to believe him, hadn't he? While his hands stilled on her upper leg, fingers splaying so that his thumbs rested on the edge of the sensitive skin of her inner thigh.

'We were friends before we were lovers, remember, Shannon? I remember that.'

Shannon swallowed hard to shift the lump forming in her throat. Yes, they had been friends. They had laughed together, teased each other, spent time in each other's company without all this bickering and tension.

But that had been then. 'You're different now.'

He straightened a little.

But Shannon kept looking him in the eye, searching for a sign that the Connor she had known was still in there some- where. 'And why is it you're so different, Connor?'

His hands lifted from her legs, eyes narrowing again. 'I told you not to look for some deep psychological reason behind this sale.'

'And I told you that it wasn't about the sale this time. It's not even about *this*.' She waved a hand back and forth between them.

Connor stepped back from her, his brow furrowing into a frown, his voice clipped. 'Oh, really? Then what is it about?'

It would be so much easier just to leave it, to say some- thing to push him away and then to try her damndest never to see him again before everything got even more complicated with sex. Shannon knew that.

But she couldn't leave it be. When it came to the subject of Connor that had always been her problem, hadn't it?

So, she finally asked him in a husky voice, 'How long have you known?'

Connor's jaw tensed as he forced the question from between tight lips. 'Known what?'

'That Frank McMahon was your father.'

He stepped forwards again, his face dark with anger. *'What?'*

Shannon shimmied down off the counter so that he couldn't pin her into the same compromising situation as before, where she might get distracted from what she needed to know. 'I know, Connor. That's why you own Devenish now; he left it to you because you're his son.'

'Been doing a little investigating since the other night, haven't we?'

Shannon felt the heat build on her cheeks, 'I needed to know what I was dealing with.'

'Well, now you know.' The smile he aimed her way was anything but friendly. 'Congratulations.'

But before she could answer his sarcasm, he turned, and marched straight out of her apartment.

Leaving her standing in front of the counter with her mouth gaping open in surprise. *What?* He was just going to *leave?* He'd just wound her tight as a drum, softly reminded her of the time they used to be friends, told her she would get to like him again if she just allowed herself to—and then, when she'd given him the opening to explain why he'd been such an ass of late, he'd just *walked?*

Oh, Shannon didn't think so!

CHAPTER FOUR

SHE WAS IN THE foyer in less than a minute. From behind the reception desk, Mario glanced up, smiling knowingly before he waved a hand towards the door.

'He went that way.'

Out in the street she glanced left, then right, not noticing passing cars or anybody who wasn't Connor, until she spotted his tall frame as he held up an arm, the lights on a car slightly ahead of him flickering to signal he had opened it.

'Connor—wait a minute!'

He turned round and watched her jog down the street towards him, cautious eyes blinking slowly at her when she was standing right in front of him. While Shannon plucked the loose curl from her cheek to tuck it behind one ear before she tilted her head back.

'You're just gonna walk? You're not going to take a second to maybe talk about this?'

'There's nothing to talk about.'

Shannon laughed sarcastically. 'The hell there's not!'

She knew the anger in her voice was laced with her frustration, but she didn't try to disguise it. And for the first time since he had reappeared, she saw surprise on his face. But before she could figure out why he was surprised by it, it was swiftly replaced with yet another frown.

'Well, that's where you're wrong.'

When he turned she instinctively reached out for him, her fingers closing around the muscles of his upper arm, 'Wait damn it!'

He didn't turn to face her full on, instead glancing over his shoulder with narrowed eyes. 'Who did you speak to?'

'Tess told me.' Her hand dropped from his arm as she made the confession. 'I e-mailed her the day you got here.'

With a shake of his head, he slowly turned on his heel, towering over her as he asked, 'And you couldn't have tried something off the wall, like, I don't know, just speaking to *me* about it, like a grown-up would?'

Despite the stinging derision, Shannon laughed again. 'Oh, yeah, 'cos we've been getting on *so great,* haven't we?'

'And yet the first thing you did when I left was e-mail my sister to ask all about me.' He lowered his head a little, his dark brows rising in question. 'Where was the reasoning in that exactly?'

'What the hell else was I supposed to do?' She swung an arm out to her side. 'You just waltzed in after seven years and informed me that, not only were you some kind of millionaire, but that you're going to pull the rug out from under me as well! What did you *expect* me to do? Nothing made any sense—I needed some answers. You weren't the Connor I knew when I left and I wanted to know *why.*'

'Because the Connor you used to know couldn't possibly have made something of himself unless he won the lottery or got it handed to him on a plate?'

Shannon was astounded by his logic. '*No!* Don't be ridiculous, of course I didn't think that!'

'Why wouldn't you? It wasn't like I grew up surrounded by money, was it?'

They both knew that the Flanaghan family hadn't been wealthy growing up. Far from it. But even though Shannon had been glaringly lacking in more recent news, there were some things she had known.

'And yet you still managed to build a thriving business with Rory. One that helped support the rest of the family after your dad died. That wasn't handed to you on a platter, was it, Connor?'

It was one of the things that had made her feel the most proud of him, even after she'd left. Connor had always been so free and easy, so reluctant to take on any kind of long-term commitment, including one with a woman. Yet together with Rory he had knuckled down, shouldering real responsibility at an age when most guys were still running around acting like kids.

Connor stood tall again, his eyes searching hers for a long moment. 'Well, as it turns out, he wasn't my dad. So there you go—life's just full of surprises.' He smirked. 'Spot on with the bastard analogy, though, weren't you?'

Shannon gasped. *That* was what he had meant when he had told her she had no idea how right she was? It hadn't at all occurred to him that she had called him that because of the way he had been *behaving* at the time?

Connor's mouth twitched in response to what she knew had to be a stunned expression on her face. To a passer-by he might even have looked momentarily amused. But a passer-by wouldn't have known to search the dark depths of his eyes for that familiar silent amusement that was so often there—and noticeably absent this time. No matter how hard Shannon looked for it.

And now she was getting mad at him again. '*I* didn't *know.*

And that *wasn't* what I meant when I called you that. In case you missed it, I was *angry* at you at the time. You were being a *complete ass,* pretty much like you are now, as a matter of fact!'

He merely shrugged in answer. 'Apt, though, wasn't it?'

She watched as he took a deep breath, his gaze leaving her face and focusing at a point above her head before he nodded. 'Well. Now you know. Not that it makes any difference. I'm still selling your damn building.'

She didn't reach for him when he turned away a second time, but when he walked away she was on his heel. 'Is that why you won't take Rory's phone calls now? Why you haven't spoken to Tess? Have you spoken to *any* of them? Or are you being this much of a moron to everyone?'

'I'll speak to them when I'm ready to speak to them.'

'They're your *family.*'

Stopping at the side of his sleek car, he yanked the door open so that it acted as a barrier between them while he scowled down at her. 'Leave it alone, Shannon. It's got nothing to do with you.'

He was right. In the greater scheme of things it *didn't* have anything to do with her. It was none of her business. But apparently that didn't mean she didn't care. Because she knew how much he had to be hurting to break all contact with his family. He *had* to be.

And maybe, just maybe, that was part of the reason he was so different. She could just have a sit-down later to think about why she was still so physically attracted to him when he was so different. It certainly wasn't because she still felt anything for him.

But the part of her heart that *had* felt something once wanted to believe that that was the reason he had changed—

it didn't want to believe he had turned into someone she could hate as much as she had the last few days.

After all, the Flanaghans were the closest family she had ever known. Where one ended the other began. And Shannon knew how precious something like that was, never having had it herself. To suddenly discover that he was someone else's son must have crushed Connor. How could it not have?

When she found words again, her voice came out softer with perceived understanding. 'How long have you known?'

Dark eyes rose to the heavens for a brief second, as if searching for patience, before he sighed. 'Six weeks.'

That made it an all-too-recent wound—which gave her a glimmer of hope.

'There's no doubt about it? You spoke to your mother?'

'We had a little chat, yes.' Dark eyes locked with green. 'You done now?'

'No.' She shook her head, ignoring the curl that worked loose again to brush against her cheek. 'I don't think I am. Not if you're so keen I should allow myself to like you again.'

A heavy silence hung in the air between them while Connor's eyes studied the strand of hair against her flushed cheek. Then, just when Shannon honestly believed she would have to push yet again, his mouth curled into what looked like a half-smile, half-grimace, before he announced, 'All right, then, you want another confession, then I'll give you one. To a certain extent, you were right. When you said I was taking Devenish apart piece by piece you were pretty close to the mark. Property by property, I'm going to dump out all the original old buildings that Frank McMahon built his damn company on. I'm going to remove every hint of him from what's left and make money as I do it. Every pet project he had, every building that held sentimental value to him. I'll pull them down and build on them if I have to. So there's no way you're going to stop me from selling that place, Shannon. You need to just accept that and let it go.'

Shannon watched, wide eyed, as he lifted a hand from the top of the open door to brush the strand of hair off her cheek again, his gaze following his fingers as, this time, he tucked it neatly behind her ear.

So simple a movement, and yet there was a tenderness that hadn't been there before. A warmth in his eyes that reminded her of the Connor she had known before. And Shannon's heart twisted agonizingly inside her chest.

While his deep voice remained deathly calm as he continued carefully speaking each word with a slow, icy deliberation. 'That ugly building you care so much about is just a little part of it. No one will stop me or change my mind. Not even you, Shannon.'

Splayed fingertips resting on the sensitive skin below her ear, and on the line of her jaw, he slowly studied her face. 'But I can help you, if you'll let me. I'm an extremely rich man now. You just tell me where it is you want to move to and I'll make it happen. Then maybe we can get past this and deal with this thing that's still here between us. Because what happened in your apartment is just the beginning and you know that as well as I do.'

Shannon shook her head, the movement brushing his fingers a little deeper into her hair. 'This isn't you.'

A low grumble of laughter sounded. 'Oh, this is me, all right. Just a newer version than you're used to.'

'It's not the version of you I used to care about.'

He used his thumb to tilt her chin up. 'The version of me that you're so determined you regretted sleeping with seven years ago—is that the one you mean?'

Despite her best efforts, she felt her lower lip tremble and was forced to take a moment to bite down on it to hide the telltale sign from him. His words reminded her of the reason she had regretted it happening so much. But it was too late, and his eyes narrowed as he slipped his hand from her face, withdrawing his arm to his side.

'I guarantee you won't regret it this time. Because this time there won't be any games played. We're two adults who just happen to be extremely sexually attracted to each other. And there's only one logical conclusion to that.'

'Connor—'

'No.' He shook his head, his face an impassive mask. 'I'm not going to get into another argument with you, we're done for now.'

When she opened her mouth to protest he leaned in and silenced her with another firm, lingering kiss—taking his time with it so that she was left in no doubt that he meant what he said. Because even if he hadn't just made everything as plain as day to her with his words, the fact that her pulse jumped erratically, her breath caught, and her body immediately heated up again confirmed it.

There *could* only be the one logical conclusion.

His face mere inches from hers, he looked down into her eyes, his voice edged with calm determination.

'I have to go to a planners meeting. But I'll be back. And I'll keep coming back. You just need to get used to that. 'Cos we're not done.'

* * *

There was somewhat of a pattern forming when it came to seeing Connor when she least expected it. So, she wasn't overly surprised when he appeared during her reading of an outlandish fairy story to the small group of fascinated children two days later.

Though she *was* surprised—and possibly a tad on the miffed side—that it had taken him so long to return this time. So she frowned at him when he stopped smiling from the doorway and sat down cross-legged at the back of the room.

How was a girl supposed to do fairy and monster voices while he was sitting there?

'So you're stalking me now—is that the plan?'

It was a logical question as the last of the Yummy Mummies arrived to collect their offspring. ''Cos I should maybe warn you that there are laws against that kind of thing these days.'

'Actually, I'm not just here to see you. Even if the different voices you did were too good to have missed.' He nodded, a thoughtful expression on his face. 'I think I liked angry Mrs Bear the best.'

Shannon scowled at him. 'Why *are* you here, then?'

'Because I said I'd take some time to see what actually happens here on a day-to-day basis.'

'And *when* exactly did you say that?'

Leaning past her to lift a beanbag, he smirked at her profile. 'When you left me to the wolves that day.'

Tossing the two large cushions she had lifted onto the pile forming in one corner of the room, she took the time to wait for Connor to do the same with his beanbag, damping down the now familiar bounce of her pulse at the sight of him by concentrating on the topic of conversation.

'They talked you into spending time *here,* away from your busy, busy schedule? How did they manage that?'

It wasn't as if he'd spared time from his schedule to make good on the 'promises' he'd made to *her* the other day, when he'd left her standing in the street, more sexually frustrated than she'd ever been in her entire life. And with an ache in her chest that was refusing to go away. Even now that he was back.

'They were very persuasive. Particularly the little one— Brieda, was it? She had a walking stick?'

'Well, seeing as she was fully prepared to hit you with that very walking stick not twenty minutes before you got here, I'd say you got off lightly.' She watched with suspicion as he continued walking back and forth with her, ignoring the fact that she should be grateful it took less than half the time to clean up the room it normally did. The words 'Thank you' would have to be dragged from her lifeless body. 'What did you do to win her over, exactly?'

Connor's eyes gleamed across at her. 'I can be very persuasive myself, when I put my mind to it.'

As well she knew.

But hang on. 'You let them think that you spending some time seeing what we do here might change your mind? Wasn't that just a teeny-weeny bit of a lie?'

'I didn't say I'd change my mind, I said I'd see what you do here.' He raised his arm, throwing the last of the cushions into the corner as if he were making a basketball shot into a net. 'And the opportunity to watch some Yummy Mummy Yoga seemed too good an opportunity to miss.'

'And yet you ended up listening to a fairy story with a bunch of under fives instead.' She shook her head, avoiding looking at him while she looked round the room for something else to tidy away. 'The best-laid plans. But they do say karma will eventually come and get you one way or another. So whatever comes your way today will serve you right for getting their hopes up. You really have *no idea* what this place means to them.'

'Well, maybe I'll find out while I'm here.'

Shannon made a small snort of derision. 'No, you won't. You're on a mission. You're the man in black.' She nodded at his T-shirt, which *was* black, as it happened. 'And they're the little people you intend stomping over to get what you want. You're the baddie.'

He quirked an eyebrow at her, the silent laughter back in his eyes. 'How many of those stories have you read today?'

She rolled her eyes.

And Connor went silent while she made a meal out of putting away the last few dress-up clothes and pictures that would normally have been ignored until the next session. Still watching her, though, she could feel it, as if he were touching her. The way it always felt when he looked at her.

Shannon really hated that.

What she needed to do was find some common ground, or something they could talk about without it turning into another argument—in front of an audience. At least that way she would stand a bat's chance of getting through the day with him nearby, right?

Because if he said he was spending a day then he'd spend a day. He was too stubborn not to. Plus he got the added bonus of irritating her along the way, watching her to see if she'd accepted the fact that they were going to end up sleeping together again—which she pretty much had. It was inevitable if he kept coming back as he did.

Shannon might have known how pigheaded she could be herself, but she also knew herself well enough to know that the way things were going she would cave in to the temptation. And she'd even told herself that she could handle that. They were both adults now. They were both attracted to each other. It wasn't as if they lived in the eighteenth century. So why shouldn't she have sex with him if she wanted to?

It wasn't as if she would make the same mistake she had last time. And maybe, just maybe, it was what she needed to do to put the demons to rest…

When he spoke again, it was almost as if he read her mind. 'It'll do us good to spend some time with a crowd around us anyway—we're less likely to argue. And it might help if you spend some time around me, in company, without touching or kissing, so you get a chance to remember why it was you used to like me.'

The words raised a wry smile, even if it was a reflection of the sarcasm in her voice. 'Oh, really, and just how are we going to manage the not-arguing part? Are you gonna promise to keep your mouth shut all day? 'Cos every time either of us tries speaking it ends up in an argument of some kind, doesn't it?'

'Or doing something else we can't do in front of a crowd.' He chuckled when she glared at him. 'Maybe we just need to try and remember the time when we were friends. Pretend to be the way we used to be.'

The soft rumble of his voice in the quiet room was temptingly persuasive. But could trying to be the way they had been before really be any less dangerous than the way they were with each other in the here and now?

Shannon doubted it.

But Connor once again seemed innately able to understand

the root cause of her hesitation, even if, once again, he worded it badly. 'What's wrong—you too chicken to try? Or is it that you don't trust yourself to keep your hands off me for that long? 'Cos we could just go up to your apartment for the day and pick up where we left off if you like. You'll not hear any complaints from me. I've done nothing but think about the possibilities of that kitchen counter for two days now.'

Spinning on her heel, she glared at him across the room. 'Do you ever actually think before you open your mouth any more? Or are you just determined to torture me every chance you get?'

He smiled a very slow smile. 'You've been thinking about the possibilities too, huh?'

Her eyes narrowed in warning.

So he dropped his chin, forcing the smile off his face with some considerable effort before his brow furrowed as he looked at her from beneath thick dark lashes. 'I'm making an effort here. Doesn't that get me any Brownie points with you?'

'Oh, it takes more than that to make up for you being such an ass since you walked through those front doors.'

'You weren't exactly rolling out the welcome mat either. Sniping at each other is a two-way thing.'

With a defiant tilt of her chin, she picked up and hugged the large story book tight against her breasts. 'I didn't invite you here.'

'And when I came to Galway this time I didn't expect you to *be* here. That kind of makes us even, don't you think?'

So they stood there in the silent room for a long while, both of them staring across at the other, until Shannon honestly thought she would have been able to hear that pro-verbial pin drop.

Eventually she sighed in defeat. 'I give up.'

To her surprise he didn't pounce on her with another arrogant comment in answer. Instead a warm smile lit up his face, transforming him into a hypnotically charming image of the young man he used to be as he walked towards her.

'Don't ever give up, Shannon. I like the fact that you're no quitter.' He leaned in and pressed his warm mouth to her soft lips. It was a gentle kiss, an almost tender kiss, and it left her wanting so much more.

Because she didn't want gentle and tender from him. She wanted the anger and the arrogance and the sexual frustration. They were the things she could deal with.

'I thought you said no kissing?'

He grinned. 'I said not in front of a crowd.'

She shook her head in frustration.

While his grin was reined back into a smaller smile. 'In order to get through today we're *both* going to have to make a concerted effort to be nice to each other. I can do it if you can.'

She stared up at him with a look of disbelief. 'And you can still remember how to be nice?'

Still smiling, he quirked his dark brows in challenge.

So Shannon took a moment to calm herself and grumbled out, 'All right, so maybe that didn't exactly help with the making an effort to be nice.'

'Not so much.'

A forefinger waggled in his direction. 'Patronizing me won't help either.'

'Well, maybe being defensive about every single thing I say might stop you from interpreting honesty as me patronizing you. I was agreeing with you. If I bug you when I disagree with you and still manage to bug you when I agree with you, then that doesn't leave us much to work with, does it?'

Hell. He was right, wasn't he? It was just that hating him and wanting him and the conflict of the two emotions were so much safer for her. If she started to *like* him again…

Frowning at the thought, she watched with cautious eyes as he reached for her face, his smile still in place as he cupped her cheek. And every part of her instinctively wanted to either turn tail and run or to stand and fight. It was a basic animal instinct, she supposed. When confronted by something considered to be predatory, or just plain old dangerous to one's well-being.

At least Barry White had stopped singing in her head. Though that was probably because she'd started to *listen* to what he was saying.

Clearing her throat, she looked Connor straight in the eye. 'If any single one of those people out there asks me directly if I think you'll change your mind about this place, I won't lie. You need to know that. They're relying on me to find a solution to this. You're the enemy. I shouldn't even be fraternizing with you as far as they're concerned. And I'm not entirely sure I disagree with them on that one.'

And then she went silent.

Connor studied her face for a while. 'You're still trying to weigh up whether or not it's worth the effort being nice to me, aren't you? It better not be because you're toying with the idea somewhere inside that head of yours that you'll manage to change my mind by *being* nice?'

Damn it! How could he *know* that? It was something that had only just crossed her mind! Though, realistically, it would be a much more difficult plan to follow through on…

'Much as I love this place, and the people in it, there's a limit to just how "nice" I'd be to get you to change your mind. If that's what you're asking me.'

The low rumble of deep male laughter caught her completely off guard. So that she was once again temporarily mesmerized, this time by the sound as it echoed around the high ceilinged room.

Before he answered in a husky tone, 'If I was the kind of man that felt he had to blackmail a woman into being "nice" to him, I might take that offer a little further…'

Shannon's mouth opened in outrage.

But Connor held a hand up, palm towards her, before she could rise to the bait. 'But I'm not. Nothing you do would change my mind.'

'Well, then, there's not much point in—'

He leaned his head down towards her face. '*But*—I thought about it some and it seemed understanding this place was the right thing to do—and not just because the place means so much to you. It obviously means something to the wolves as well.'

'It might have made more sense to understand *before* you made your decision in the first place.'

'Maybe.'

Really? Shannon's eyes widened in surprise. *Wow.* He'd just backed down an inch there, hadn't he?

She swallowed before asking, forcing down another sarcastic reply, 'What is it you really want Connor?'

He smiled again.

While she quirked an arched brow in question.

Which gained her a smile that made it all the way up into his eyes, 'I take it you're not looking at me to give you the obvious answer to that?'

She quirked her eyebrow again.

And he chuckled. 'That's what I thought. All right, then,

maybe the idea of a day off appealed to me too—two birds and one stone and all that.'

Shannon suddenly thought about what his life must be like in the here and now. It was funny it had never occurred to her before. Any time he had 'popped by' it had been a fleeting visit between meetings, he'd always been dressed in a suit, apart from that one night in the bar, when he'd been drinking alone and more than likely seeking 'company'.

And he'd broken all contact with his family, maybe even his friends as well…

Didn't he ever get lonely while he was on his 'mission'? Not that she doubted for a second he'd ever be short of female company—she'd seen firsthand the way women had reacted to him in the bar that night…

But had he gotten so obsessed with what he was doing that he hadn't taken the time to remember what it was like to be around people, *real* people, who laughed and talked and forgot their troubles for a while?

And suddenly the idea of him spending time in the building, surrounded by the eclectic family she loved, didn't seem so bad an idea. If he had anything resembling a heart left, then surely he would soften to them as the day went on? And then Shannon could maybe butter him up a little bit more later on…

'Pulling the world apart at the seams taking it out of you is it?'

The lack of sarcasm in her tone, accompanied with a teasing light in her eyes, was enough to keep the smile on his face. 'It *can* be a little draining, as it happens.'

'I'd imagine so—' she tried an answering smile on for size '—but then they do say life's what we make it…'

'Not always. Sometimes life is what someone else made for us and we don't get a big choice in it.'

It was the first real insight into how he was really feeling that Shannon had been given. And was the first thing to allow her to let go a little, to be more relaxed—and to say what she thought.

'Do you really think he left you Devenish to make you miserable? I doubt that was what he had in mind at the time.'

The warmth in Connor's eyes faded. 'You knew him that well, did you?'

'No, I never met him.'

'Then you can't know what he was thinking. From where I stand it would have been much better if he'd left it the hell alone.'

Any warmth in his voice that had been there before was rapidly disappearing, and Shannon sensed that she was in danger of losing her window of opportunity.

Think, woman, think!

A surprisingly big part of her wasn't willing to let go of the small chance to do some good—make him realize there was a life beyond his vendetta, show him the damage he would do with the sale of the building, maybe even in some small way compensate for what she had done so many years ago by giving him a chance to get a life for himself again.

So, she took a breath and allowed her thoughts to stray into an area that she had tried to avoid as much as humanly possible.

'Would you have been able to leave it alone if you'd had a son out there somewhere?'

For the longest while he studied her eyes so intently that she feared he might see into her mind again.

But then he simply took a breath, his deep voice firm and determined. 'I'd not have waited until I was dead to do something for him. I'd search to the end of the earth for a child of mine. And he'd grow up knowing his father and where he came from.'

The words were like a knife in Shannon's heart.

When she didn't speak, Connor continued to stare deep into her eyes. 'I can't forgive him for not doing that, any more than I can forgive my mother for not telling me sooner. It just goes to prove that a lie on top of a lie doesn't ever have a good outcome.'

And still she couldn't find words.

Which brought a smile back to the sensual curve of his mouth. 'And now that you've pried that out, can we agree to try and be nice for the day? Because that happens to be the most discussion I've had on the subject.'

Shannon knew that, without even having to search his eyes for confirmation. Connor had shut himself off while he took revenge on the father he had never known. It was his way of working through it. Maybe not the right way, or the way she would have chosen herself, but it was the path he had taken.

Did that mean that the Connor she had known was still in there? Did it mean that he hadn't actually changed into someone she could hate as much as she had once loved him?

Shannon swiped the end of her tongue over her dry lips, pursing them together while she avoided his searching gaze. 'Maybe you needed to talk about this more than you thought you did.'

'Maybe.' He nodded in agreement. 'And maybe we didn't stand a chance at any kind of a temporary peace treaty until I told you even that much. I'm told trust is a two-way street.'

'I'd heard that.'

Mimicking her earlier move, he tilted his head to bring his face back into her line of vision, waiting until her long lashes rose and she was looking him in the eye again. 'So, what do you do after the story-telling, then? You're gonna have to keep me busy if I'm going to stick to the no kissing or touching rule.'

The silence was suddenly broken by the echo of music from the next room.

Connor's brows rose in surprise, his head turning to seek out the source of the sound. 'What's that?'

'They run a dance class here on a Friday. Jive, ballroom, that kind of thing.' She listened for a moment until the track was familiar to her. 'Sixties today, by the sound of it, so it'll be jive. All age groups can do that in varying degrees.'

When he looked back at her his dark eyes were lit up with what she immediately recognized as devilment. 'Excellent.'

'What are you doing?'

He had hold of her hand again. 'You want to show me what goes on here—then let's go. Dancing is close enough to the touching thing to keep me happy.'

'O-h-h no.' Her laughter was a little more genuine this time. 'I think we've established that when we dance together it isn't just dancing—it's foreplay.'

The tugging stopped while he smiled down at her with the kind of gorgeously sexy smile that set her alight every single time. 'I can behave if you can. And anyway—' he leaned closer to whisper in her ear '—play your cards right and the whole day will be like foreplay.'

Shannon shook her head. 'If your ego gets any bigger you'll have to give it a name of its own.'

Connor chuckled. 'It's either dancing or we go re-enact that scene from the movie in the Potty about Pottery class later. Your choice. I'm here to experience it all.'

A very vivid image of them sitting at a pottery wheel while

wet clay slid between their joined fingers did things to Shannon's pulse rate that she was quite sure shouldn't happen without her needing a heart monitor—and suddenly dancing seemed the safer option. So, setting the large book on a small chair beside them, she took a deep breath and tightened her fingers around his.

'You're just gonna love the embroidery class.' With her hand still holding tightly to his, she pulled him towards the door. 'Of course, then there's Tumblin' Tinies at six on this floor, a meditation class at seven, and—'

Connor squeezed her hand as they walked into the foyer and made the turn into the next room. 'Persuading me this place is so damn great might go better if you didn't make it all sound like some kind of endurance test.'

With her hand pushing the door open, she looked back at him with gleaming eyes, a bubble of mischief forming in her chest. Well, it was either that or nervous energy.

'I remember you having more of a sense of adventure, Connor Flanaghan.'

Connor merely grinned in response, raising his other hand to the small of her back to guide her forwards. 'Attempting to jive with a woman dressed as a fairy-tale princess is adventurous enough for me for one day.'

Shannon's chin dropped, her mouth an 'o' of surprise as she suddenly remembered what she was wearing. In a way she should have been thankful that he hadn't visited last week when she'd been dressed as a leprechaun, but even so...

'I can't jive in this!'

'Sure you can. If you can dance dressed as an Egyptian dancing girl then this should be a cinch.' He ignored the look of shocked outrage on her face at the mention of her seduction apparel from back in the day. 'Though I sincerely hope you kept that all these years. I wasn't done with it when you left in the middle of the night.'

Before Shannon could make a comment, he looked over her head and smiled in greeting—so she had to make do with smiling at the class as they joined it while swallowing down another sharp shard of pain in her chest.

Then she sent up a silent plea that she hadn't just got in over her head…

Again.

CHAPTER FIVE

'ALL RIGHT, WHAT'S next?'

Connor leaned across the counter in an attempt to read Shannon's diary upside down, glancing up at her face to see what he could see in her eyes while silently hoping there wasn't anything else in the damn diary. He knew what activity he wanted to spend the rest of the evening doing.

And it didn't involve a crowd.

The day had certainly brought a great deal more enjoyment than he had thought it would, even if he did now have more information on embroidery and pottery than he would ever be likely to use in everyday life. He'd obviously needed a break more than he had realized if playing around with bunches of kids, unemployed teenagers and old-age pensioners had brought a smile to his face.

But he knew it had more to do with being with Shannon. Because he'd been right—the day *had* turned into a kind of slow foreplay. Surrounded by people the entire time, each brief touch or sideways glance had felt as if it were stolen, forbidden somehow, which made it unbelievably erotic.

So that he had ended up having to focus on each new

activity with increasing degrees of attention in order to keep his mind off whisking her away for more adult activities.

It had been hard. *Literally.*

But there was something new between them too, something invisible that started as a niggle and became a nagging voice in his mind as the day progressed. And the fact that he couldn't put a finger on what it was was becoming more and more of a source of irritation to him.

It distracted him from the crackling sensual awareness that had been there all day, which at times had probably been useful, but Connor wasn't sure he wanted to be distracted from that *now.*

Which meant he was going to have to risk life and limb by trying to find out what it was, didn't it?

But it was bugging him.

She glanced up at him with a small smile, then back down at the diary. 'Oh, I think what you've done already could be deemed going above and beyond the call of duty. I was kidding when I said you had to do everything.'

Above and beyond the call of duty, maybe, but at least now he understood what happened there every day. They ran an eclectic group of activities to go with the equally eclectic group of people that came through the doors. But he still didn't get why it was the location made that big a difference…

'You wouldn't be trying to get rid of me, would you, Sunshine?'

She tried to hide it, but he caught sight of another small smile twitching at the edges of her mouth before she forced it away. It was something she'd been doing a lot of in the last hour or so. Almost as if she was giving away too much ground by showing she was having fun.

Though she hadn't managed to hide those smiles any better than she had the heated gazes they had exchanged.

Her long lashes flickered as she glanced up at his face again, green eyes studying him for a long moment while he smiled back at her.

Then she sighed, closing the diary. 'There's only film night left. And it's not for another half hour.'

'What's film night?'

Her head tilted, arched eyebrows rising in amused disbelief.

And Connor chuckled in response. 'What *kind* of film? 'Cos I don't do chick flicks. And why don't they just go to a cinema like other people do?'

'A lot of them like to come to somewhere close to home 'cos they find getting around tough as they've gotten older. And it's not a *chick flick;* it's a black and white movie night. We do all the classics—anything I can get on DVD anyway. You'll hate it. No blowing up things, no naked women, no fast cars.'

'You don't know I won't like it.'

'You'll be happy watching some period melodrama from the forties with a bunch of over seventies?'

He blinked at her. 'You said it *wasn't* a chick flick.'

'Not the way *you'd* think of one. But it's still hardly going to be anywhere near butch enough for you.'

Well, flattering and all as it was she thought him butch, she was right. A black and white movie wouldn't be his usual choice of activity for a Friday night. But after the twenty minutes he'd managed in the meditation class before laughing he reckoned he could pretty much endure anything she threw his way. It had become some kind of test in her eyes and he knew it. Which only made him want to succeed all the more at the things she'd decided he would fail at—so he shrugged.

'Depends on how good the film is, and whether you can manage to rustle us up some popcorn and a seat on the back row.'

Shannon studied him in silence.

'You don't *want* me to stay is the truth. You didn't think I'd last this long, even when you should know me better. And it kills you to admit you've had fun with me being here.'

'This wasn't supposed to be about me having fun, it was supposed to be about you understanding what we have going here.'

What they had 'going' remained to be seen in Connor's eyes. Occasionally, just very occasionally during the day, there would be small flashes of the way they used to be when they were together. Honest to goodness laughter, silly teasing comments, mutual understanding of a wisecrack that others around them might not necessarily have got.

It was exactly what he'd been missing of late. Just spending time in someone's company doing things that weren't a constant reminder of how complicated his life had become or the associated permanent bad mood that accompanied it was like taking a holiday.

But there was more simmering beneath the surface too—an anticipation of what was to come. He'd known it from the moment he had mentioned the 'disguise' she'd worn that one time, and the green of her eyes had darkened a shade. And he had felt it when they had danced again, when her body had moved with his and she would quietly catch her breath, or when he would spin her away and back and her breathing would speed up as she'd looked at him with languid eyes.

Every move, all day, had been a precursor.

He took a breath, his gaze still locked on hers as he smiled. 'You're not getting rid of me, you know. You're stuck with me.'

And there was the something again.

His smile remained. 'There's that look again. Do you want to tell me exactly what it is I've inadvertently done to bug you *this* time?'

'I don't know what you mean.' She made a show of straightening some of the papers laid out on the wide counter top, her hand moving up briefly to brush the corkscrew curl back into place.

Which made him smile again. She'd always done that thing with her hair when she was nervous, from way back when she was young. The mass of soft curls had been tough to control at the best of times, and Shannon had been so damn determined to tame it. As if she had to be in control of everything, or that it working loose from whatever band she had it in was a sign of her quirky personality trying to escape from the restraints she had on it.

A quirkiness she had no problem exhibiting these days. *Oh, no*. Her latest T-shirt announced: 'My imaginary friend thinks you have serious mental problems.'

'You do that when you're nervous, you know.' He nodded his head at the curl, which bobbed loose the minute she looked up at him. 'You always did.'

Her hand rose, stilled, and went back down to the counter while she mumbled back, 'Yes, well, I keep thinking I should just get it cut. But I never do.'

'I'm glad.'

She cleared her throat. 'Look, I normally don't stay down here for the film nights anyway—'

The gregarious, over-the-top Mario chose that moment to bound down the stairs beside the reception area with a large box of buttered popcorn in bags. 'I have the chairs all in place and the DVD wired up to the screen. Just the popcorn to put out and the tea urn to fill and that's me. I've saved your usual place near the back so that no one tries to steal it this time.'

He winked at Connor on the way past, 'Can't have some wrinkly taking her place, now, can we? She loves these things. Never misses a weepy, does our Shannon.'

Connor smiled, nodding at Shannon as Mario disappeared into the room that had been used earlier for the kids' story time session. 'Normally don't stay down for these, huh?'

A pink tinge was working its way up her neck. 'I don't go to every single one.'

'Yeah, I got that from the words "never misses".'

She sighed, her shoulders dropping. 'Look, Connor, I've been watching you today and it's pretty plain you think it's all some big joke here. Watching an old film with a room full of pensioners is hardly going to change your opinion, so why don't you just go do whatever it is you normally do on a Friday night while I try and find a way of breaking it to them all that there's nothing they can do to change your mind?'

When she turned to walk out from behind the counter, Connor pushed up off his elbows and stepped around, blocking her exit. 'Actually, you're wrong—I do understand a bit better what goes on here. It'll help me to find a replacement building that's right for everyone.' He dipped his head down to look up into her eyes. 'You're sure there's not something else bugging you? I thought as the day went on, if nothing else, we were making some headway towards remembering how to get along again.'

'There's not much point in us getting along.'

'I disagree.'

'There's a surprise.'

He stepped a step closer. 'There were plenty of times today when you looked happy I was here. And plenty of times when you looked at me with the same thing on your mind that I had.'

Shannon tried a sidestep and was blocked. 'Well, there were times when watching you trying to join in with some of the activities was amusing to watch, I'll give you that.'

Another forward step. 'I had fun, surprisingly—though I doubt I'll be taking up any of the activities in the near future. Go on, now you try—"I had fun too Connor. I'm glad you were here." You can even tell me how impressed you were with that gorgeous pot I made in the pottery class.'

She flashed him a brief smile. They both knew the pot had been horrifically sad. Then she stilled, her mouth pursed into a thin line while she studied the collar of his shirt. 'All right, I will admit there may have been *moments* of fun in there that reminded me of how you used to be.'

'For me too.'

The soft words brought her gaze up again, her throat convulsing as she swallowed, and Connor's eyes were inexorably drawn down to the rise and fall of her breasts, the movement speeding up the longer he looked, until eventually he forced his gaze upwards to lock with hers.

She glanced around the room, then back into his eyes, a smile teasing her full mouth again. 'Stop that.'

He smiled at the slightly breathless demand. 'Stop what?'

'You know rightly what.' The tone of her voice took on a huskier edge. 'You have a way of looking at a woman when you want her that leaves her in no doubt about what you're thinking. And that's a tad inappropriate in company. You'll give me a bad name.'

'Is that why your mood changed during the Tumblin'
Tinies session?'

'My mood didn't change.'

'Yeah, it did. You looked at me at one point like I'd just
taken the thing you loved the most from you and tossed it over
my shoulder.'

The *something* was there again as her hand rose to fiddle
the curl back into place, her eyes avoiding his. 'Which, believe
it or not, you *are* by selling this place. I guess I just foolishly
allowed myself to believe for a while that being here might
help you understand that.'

Connor's smile faded, because his gut was telling him
there was more to it than that, even if her answer did make
sense *to her*. And he hated that she felt the need to lie to him.
There'd been more than enough of that in his life lately. But,
frankly, despite the warm atmosphere within the crumbling
walls, he still didn't get what the attachment was.

'I've made it plain from the start I wouldn't change my mind,
Shannon. So how come it only hit you while I helped with
those kids? 'Cos that was when you first had that look you're
wearing now. Is there something else you want to tell me?'

'No, there's nothing else I want to tell you!' Her eyes
flashed when she looked back into his. 'Maybe for a little
while I *did* manage to convince myself that you being around
these people might change your mind. The more time you've
spent here smiling and having fun, the more I've seen the hope
come back onto people's faces—and that has *killed me*.
Because today isn't about fun or friendship, it's just business
to you—a deal you made to get out of any explanations the
other day. This is "nothing personal"—isn't that the phrase
you like the most?'

Ignoring the sneer that accompanied her words, Connor stepped closer again, so that his body was almost touching hers, the minute distance between them seeming to spark with tension again. Then he waited, studying her flashing green eyes, the slight flare of her nostrils as she took shuddering breaths, and he knew, deep down in his gut, that she was still lying to him.

'I think you know why I spent an entire day here—and it had nothing to do with business and everything to do with something personal. It's not about the building. This is about you and me.'

'It's not just about you and me, Connor. How can you not know that? How can I have sex—'

Connor silenced her with a single long finger against her lips, smiling when she froze and looked up at him with wide, angry eyes. 'Shush a minute.'

The eyes narrowed.

'We've done pretty damn well to go nearly a whole day without yet another big bust up, so let's try a little longer, shall we?'

Her head tilted to one side.

Connor nodded. 'Yes, I know you don't think that you're the only one causing the argument, but this time I can say with a good measure of "smug" thrown in that *I* didn't start this one.'

The lips beneath his finger parted slightly.

'You're only trying to argue with me because there's something else that you don't want to talk about. And I get that. Because that's the kind of thing *I* normally do.'

There was a small puff of air against his finger as she exhaled.

'We're not all that different, you and me. And if you remember, we used to argue a lot back in the day—only you liked to call them "debates." This is nothing new with us; it's just a new topic.'

In the brief silence, her eyes softened a shade and Connor knew he was making progress.

'The only difference between then and now, Shannon, is we don't know each other as well as we used to. You've probably got as much baggage from the last seven years as I have.'

And there was that 'something' again. Briefer this time, but there long enough for him to see it while he was studying her so up close. What was it? *He'd* be lying if he told himself he didn't want to know.

But, truth be told, Connor was getting tired of arguing over the damn building. It was getting in the way.

'I'll have a think about what it is that makes this building so important, all right? I still mightn't change my mind, but I'll think about it.'

This time her quirked eyebrows told him she didn't believe him.

So he smiled. 'Don't push your luck. That's a concession and you know it is.'

'Maybe I do.' The softly spoken, reluctant words moved her lips against his finger almost like a kiss.

He turned his hand so that he was cupping her chin and still had a finger brushing against her bottom lip, back and forth, back and forth; the softness of her mouth fascinating him out of speech while he suddenly became more aware of the familiar flowery scent that had only drifted occasionally by him during the day.

'Connor—'

She said his name softly. In a way that could be interpreted as a plea for him to stop or a need for him to take what he was doing a step further. And considering how she had looked at him for a good portion of the day he decided to believe it was the latter.

And there wasn't anyone around to make it a break in the rules…

So, with his gaze still fixed on her mouth, he lowered his head and pressed an almost exploratory kiss there. Which she didn't fight him on, so he took it as an invitation to continue, his mouth becoming firmer on hers, searching from edge to edge.

But just when it was occurring to him that, unlike any of the other times he had kissed her, this time *he* was the only one doing the kissing—there was the creak of the door behind them and a stunned gasp of outrage.

Lifting his mouth from hers he looked down into her wide eyes just before she tilted her head to look over his shoulder.

'Hello, Brieda, Connie. Early as usual, I see. Mario has pretty much everything ready.'

Connor stifled his laughter before turning round to face the twin looks of disapproval on the older women's faces. 'Ladies.'

The smaller of the two made remarkably quick progress across the foyer to them, leaning heavily on her walking stick. '*Mr* Flanaghan. When we said you should see what was on offer here we weren't referring to Shannon.'

'Brieda—'

Connor smiled down at her. 'No, now we can't have Brieda thinking I go around kissing women all over the place, can we?'

The little woman harrumphed at him. 'And don't you?'

All right, she maybe had a point there. He was no angel, after all. But this was different. 'I've known Shannon a long time. From way before I owned this place.'

The announcement seemed to knock some of the wind

out of her sails, momentarily. 'Well, then, why are you selling her home?'

When he glanced sideways at Shannon she had her arms folded across her chest and a look of challenge on her face. He wasn't getting any help from there.

'We're still discussing that one, as it happens.'

'Are you indeed?'

There was just something about being 'told off' by a woman of Brieda's age that made a man remember being scolded as a child, and the thought made Connor smile all the more. But it didn't have quite the same effect on Brieda that it normally had on the female gender.

She simply scowled even harder at him.

So he tried some charm instead, wrapping an arm around Shannon's shoulders to draw her close to his side as he tilted his head and announced with a nod of his head. 'We were sweethearts.'

Shannon gasped beside him, her head leaning back a little so she could stare up at him in shock. 'Oh, we *so* were not, you big liar!'

With deliberate slowness, he lowered his chin to ask in a low voice, 'And how exactly would you like to describe to the nice lady the way we were?'

The flush on her cheeks was immediate, the flash of anger in her eyes swift to follow. And Connor felt his mouth twitch with amusement even though he knew that laughing would put him straight back into hot water again. '*Well?* Please feel free to put it into your own words.'

After another brief narrowing of her eyes, she returned her gaze to Brieda. 'It was a long time ago.'

'Did he break your heart?'

Connor shook his head, still silently amused that no matter what was said he was still the 'baddie.' 'No, actually, *she* left *me.*'

'I did not *leave you!*'

'You didn't speak to me before you got on a plane and disappeared for seven years—it *sounds* like you leaving to me. What do you think, Brieda?'

The answer was mulled over for a while. 'Well, it certainly sounds like she left. But you must have done something. Did he do something?'

Connor turned to watch the play of emotions over Shannon's face, the colour in her cheeks increasing while she tried to think of an answer. 'Well, it was kind of…complicated. And I had already planned to leave before—'

Connor grinned when her gaze flew to meet his.

Which she answered with a glare before focusing back on Brieda. 'Before we…' she tilted her head sideways in emphasis '…*got together.*'

Connor dropped his chin, shaking his head as he spoke. 'And she never wrote me a letter or left a forwarding address or an e-mail…'

When he glanced at her from the corner of his eye, another glare headed his way. 'Your sister had my e-mail address if you wanted to talk to me so bad—which you obviously *didn't.*'

'Well, you see, that's the difference between being twenty-four and thirty-one. At twenty-four I hadn't been given any encouragement to go after what I wanted. At thirty-one I know enough about what I do and don't want to pursue what I do until I get it.'

Shannon gaped at him. And when he looked at Brieda she was staring at him through narrowed eyes. So he decided to quit while he was ahead.

'Well, I have to say, I'm really looking forward to this film, ladies. How long 'til it starts?'

Shannon shook her head, as if she was clearing her thoughts to think about the answer. 'Erm, half an hour give or take.'

'Okay, then. I'll be right back.' With what he meant as a winning smile aimed at the older women, he winked at Shannon before coming out from behind the counter. 'Save a seat for me.'

CHAPTER SIX

THE FILM TITLES were rolling by the time Connor came back.

And sitting in her usual place at the back of the room, Shannon had been glad of the break so that she had some time to think. In order to make sense of all the things he had said, all the looks he had given her during the day, and all of the varying emotions she was currently experiencing that went with them.

She didn't need this again. Really she didn't.

There had been times during the day when he had been exactly the Connor she had once been head over heels over. And that was just plain old playing *dirty!*

The creak of the door heralded his arrival and was swiftly followed by a set of reproving tuts and sighs while he found his way to her side. Where there was a space on the large worn sofa against the back wall.

And she had *tried* to quietly get rid of that space, had even threatened Mario that she would fire him if *he* didn't sit there. But all her 'friend' had done was grin, inform her he was *a volunteer* and therefore couldn't be fired, wink, and then add that if he were her he'd have paid him to stay away.

So she sighed in resignation as the sofa dipped under

Connor's weight while he leaned close to hiss, 'Did I miss anything exciting?'

'The titles.'

'So what's it called?'

'*Brief Encounter.*'

She glanced at his profile as he looked at the large screen the film was playing on. 'I thought you said this *wasn't* a chick flick.'

'It's a *classic.*'

'A classic *chick flick?*'

'Seriously—don't you have *anything* better to do on a Friday night but bug me?'

'Not this Friday night, I don't.'

Shannon sighed again. It was just too damn exhausting to keep up with this constant game they were playing. For ever trying to stay one step ahead, to play it by her own rules instead of his while trying to ignore the constant physical ache for him and trying to be patient and give him a chance to redeem himself on the building issue. She needed a rest from it, even if it was just for the length of a film.

There was a rustling sound from next to her, 'Hold out your hand.'

'What for?'

'Just hold out your hand.'

'I'm not closing my eyes for a *surprise.*'

His tone remained calm, but Shannon was sure she could detect the familiar note of humour laced through it. 'I didn't ask you to close your eyes. *Yet.*'

The rustling came again, so Shannon leaned forwards a little to see if she could find out what it was. Only to have Connor warn, 'No peeking. *Hand.*'

She pursed her lips together while she considered disobeying him. Because it had damn well *been* an order, hadn't it? But for the sake of a quiet life she held out her hand, palm upwards.

Warm fingers cupped in underneath it—more rustling, and then something was set onto her palm with his other hand.

She squinted to see what it was. 'What is it?'

'Put it in your mouth and see.'

'I bet you say that to all the girls.'

His bark of laughter earned several turning heads and a 'shh' from near the front, so he leaned closer to her to whisper, 'Just try it.'

With caution she lifted it from her hand, sniffing it for good measure before she popped it in her mouth, her eyes widening as the flavour spread out to tickle her taste buds into response. And she immediately turned her face towards his to whisper, 'You brought *Dolly Mixtures?*'

'Mmm-hmm.'

There was more rustling and Shannon watched in wonder as he popped a sweet into his mouth, the scent of candy immediately invading the air between them. It also meant that, when he whispered again, it was while still chewing. 'I'll pick out the jelly ones for you. You can thank me later.'

Shannon couldn't help but smile at him. Even the fact that he had remembered what she liked from back in the day warming a part of her heart that she had forgotten.

'How can you possibly remember to do that you moron?' She never had been able to stand the coconut taste of the other sweets.

'I have the memory of an elephant.' He leaned in close again. 'Another one?'

A nod of her head accompanied with an outstretched palm earned her a glint of white teeth in the dim light. After another rustle of the paper bag, his fingertips grazed against her palm and she smiled all the more.

Connor settled back deeper into the sofa with a deep sigh. 'I've decided to win you over with charm. My good looks and bulging wallet aren't having the usual effect.'

Shannon laughed quietly. 'Charm, huh?'

'Yup.' He leaned in a little closer. 'How am I doing?'

Not too shabby, as it happened. *Damn it.*

When she didn't answer he announced in a slightly louder whisper, 'Anyway, you can't watch a film without Dolly Mixtures. It's illegal.'

'You're a five-year-old in disguise, aren't you?'

'Nah.' The answer was whispered intentionally slowly. 'I'm a big boy now.'

The innuendo made her laugh again. The combination of being too tired to keep taking umbrage at everything he said, accompanied by a sudden sense of less complicated times between them, served to lull her into what was most likely a false sense of momentary security.

But he was truly incorrigible.

'How big a bag did you get?' She tried again to peer over his large frame only to have him lift both hands to her shoulders to pull her back beside him as he leaned deeper into the cushions, so she ended up shoulder to shoulder, arm to arm, hip to hip and thigh to thigh with him.

And she almost moaned aloud with the immediate reactions in her body. How in hell had she come to be such a walking set of raging hormones of late?

Connor turned a little so that her shoulder was against his chest, one long arm arcing upwards, then curling around her shoulders so that she was held close.

'What are you doing?'

'Another film tradition when sitting on the back row. And if you don't stay put and stop chattering in my ear there'll be no more sweets—I'll eat them all. I haven't been fed dinner yet.'

After a brief inner debate, she softened a little, settling against him as he handed her another sweet. But she couldn't relax, couldn't turn off her mind any easier than she could stop herself from being aware of everywhere he touched, or aching everywhere he *wasn't* touching.

He was making her insane. Okay, that ship had probably sailed—*more* insane would be more accurate.

But already she was beginning to wonder if she could cope with sex for sex's sake with him. All day he had been reminding her of the past, when he had been the young man she had silently loved. He'd been warm and funny and attentive and charming and hot as hell to look at all day long—and now he'd popped out and bought her favourite sweets.

It really wasn't fair. *Damn him!*

By sitting watching a film and being handed her favourite jelly sweets from her teenage years she wasn't forgetting any of the bigger issues, no way. Because she had told the truth when she'd said it had killed her to see hope on the faces of the people she cared about.

And now she was just so conflicted!

The movie continued, the palm of her hand brushed by Connor's fingertips at regular intervals. And her mind meandered to when he had said that she had 'left him,' suggesting there had been more to their relationship than friendship and a one-night stand—which there hadn't been.

No matter how much she had wished there had been at the time…

Right now, a big part of her really just wished he'd go away—far away from her sight and her physical proximity—so that she could *think* clearly.

'So, what is this movie about exactly?'

Shannon rolled her eyes. 'You are such a Neanderthal. It's *Brief Encounter*—it's famous.'

She felt his shoulder shrug beside her. 'Still don't get what it's about and I've been watching ten minutes now. You'll have to enlighten me.'

'You are really going to suck as a millionaire, you know, if you can't appreciate the finer things in life like all-time classic movies, fine wine, the opera…'

'Nah, I'm perfect millionaire material. I was training to be a playboy before I even had money.'

Shannon squirmed round a little to look at his profile in the dim light. 'You see, that's another one of those statements that keeps reminding me that I don't know you any more. Give me one good reason why I should bother getting involved with you again.'

Connor shrugged. ''Cos you already are.'

Damn again. He had her on that one.

'And do you like who you are now? Won't you worry that people will only be nice to you *because* you're a millionaire and they think they'll have something to gain?'

She raised her palm again, waiting patiently while the rustling signalled Connor's search for another sweet. When he found it and leaned forward to set it into her hand, his fingers lingered there, brushing softly against her skin.

'Shannon Hennessey, are you trying to pick a fight with me again?'

'No, I'm trying to hold a conversation with you.'

His face turned towards hers, hidden in shadows as his fingertips stilled, his voice so low she had to lean forwards to hear him. 'It just kills you that you're still attracted to me, doesn't it?'

She scowled at him. But it was pointless. No matter how she tried, she couldn't see his face properly in the dark, so there was no way he could see hers.

But apparently he could see better than she thought he could, because when his fingers left her palm he reached up and tucked her lock of hair in place without faltering, the scent of the sweets stronger again as his breath washed over her face. One finger traced down the side of her face, along the fine line of her jaw—hand turning, his knuckles brushing her cheek, finding her mouth, moving back and forth in gentle strokes.

Dear Lord. Would this sweet agony never end?

'In answer to your question—' his whispered words sounded close to her ear '—no, I don't worry that people will just be nice to me because I have money. Money gets respect, that's all.'

Hypnotized by his warm touch against her face, Shannon had to take a moment to concentrate on what he was saying. If nothing else to try and stop from ending up kissing him on the sofa at the back of a room full of pensioners—ones that wouldn't approve of who she was kissing.

'It doesn't buy happiness, though.'

'No. It doesn't.' And the deep tone of his voice told Shannon that he knew that only too well.

How many people would sell their souls for the kind of money Connor had had handed to him? But it really *hadn't* brought him happiness, had it? In fact, if anything, it had so far probably brought him the exact opposite.

She just couldn't believe that had been Frank McMahon's intention. He'd probably been trying to right a wrong somehow.

While she mulled that over, Connor's fingers sliding down the column of her neck, her gaze moved around the room to see who might be watching, settling on an elderly couple near the front just as the man reached his arm over the woman's shoulder.

And she smiled at the sight, reaching up to tangle her fingers with Connor's before setting their joined hands in her lap. Then she turned a little towards him, her chin tilting up as she sought his eyes in the dim light. 'Can you see the couple in the front on the right?'

Connor turned his face to look, leaving Shannon focusing on his profile just as the room lit up a little more with reflected light from the screen.

And she remembered how, back in the day, he had seemed so inaccessible to her somehow. It was why making a play for him had been such a big deal. He'd had charm by the bucketload, looks to turn any female head no matter what age, confidence to burn, a strong family bond behind him no matter what. He'd had everything while she'd had nothing from the moment her nan had got ill.

But knowing he had some tough stuff to work through in the here and now—that he maybe wasn't finding easy to deal with—somehow made him *more human.*

'The lovebirds?' He turned to look down at her, their heads close together as they continued to whisper conspiratorially.

Shannon smiled up at him. 'Yes, that's them. They've been married forty years, barely have a penny—and they're two of the happiest people I've ever met. They look forward to this every week—it's their only night out. Come rain, hail, or sleet they make their way from their little house just up the road to see the film. It's only ever ice or snow that keeps them at home and when that happens someone from here goes to visit them.'

Connor was smiling back at her.

But she couldn't quite manage to keep looking at him when he was doing that, even in the dim, sometimes briefly flashing light. So she looked forwards again.

'When the film's over they have a cup of tea and then they walk home arm in arm. They don't need money to be happy. They value what they have and they make the effort to hang onto it.'

'So now you think I should just give all the money away so I can be happier than I am now?'

The room went dark for a second, so that it took a moment for his face to come into focus when she looked his way. 'I'm not saying that either. It's not up to me to tell you what you should or shouldn't do. Not that you'd let me. I'm just pointing out that being happy isn't necessarily linked to being stupidly rich. Something I think you probably know round about now.'

Connor shook his head.

'And you disagree. That's a nice change.'

He leaned to whisper back, 'Are you still trying to persuade me not to sell this building, perchance?'

If he hadn't said it in such a soft tone then she might have risen to the bait. But, 'Maybe I am. I can't help it, Connor. This place means something.'

'And you're finding it hard to reconcile being attracted to me while technically I'm now the enemy, right?'

'Yes.' Well, it was part of it. So it wasn't a complete lie…

He turned away, his head facing the direction of the older couple again, and Shannon heard him take a deep breath. It was only when his fingers flexed around hers that she remembered she was still holding his hand.

But he didn't answer. And that left Shannon torn for the rest of the film. How could she get involved with him again, even in a purely sexual way, when he was taking something so precious from the people she loved?

CHAPTER SEVEN

'AND THEN THERE were two…'

'Nope, then there was one—I'm gonna have to kick you out. I'm tired and hungry.'

And Shannon needed more time before she slept with him—which was what would happen if he stayed.

Connor shook his head. 'You're not the only one who's hungry. We'll order pizza.'

Shannon mulled that over for a moment or two. Not that she couldn't have done with something to eat, but it would be too dangerous to have him stay. All it would take would be more touching, some kissing, then there would be the removal of clothing, more intimate kissing…

She took a deep breath and blew it out.

'I don't think that's a good idea.'

'You used to like pizza.'

'It has nothing to do with the choice of food.'

Connor's face changed, his dark eyes searching her eyes for a long moment. 'Are you going to try telling me you have a date lined up?'

She could feel yet another flush creep over her cheeks, so she turned away and headed towards the front doors—hoping he would take the hint and follow her. 'No, I don't have a date lined up. I'm just tired. One full day here wasn't enough for you?'

When she turned round he was still standing in the middle of the foyer, his large hands shoved deep into the pockets of his jeans. And he smiled a stunningly sexy smile across at her. 'Maybe I'm just trying to establish where you stand on the whole dating issue.'

'You don't need to know that.'

'Ah, now, you see, that's where you'd be wrong.' Freeing his hands, he walked towards her with slow, measured steps, his gaze still locked on her face. 'I definitely need to know that before I spend another day here.'

The sight of him working his way across the room to her with such a purposeful look on his face sent Shannon's pulse fluttering all over again.

But what she wouldn't and couldn't do was let him see it. It gave him the advantage again. So, she stood her ground— pulling open the door as he got closer.

'Whether or not I have dates lined up has nothing to do with you spending time here to see what this place is all about like you did today. This was a business thing, remember?'

'It may have started out as a business thing. But before we head where we're heading I should at least know whether or not I have to look over my shoulder for rabid boyfriends, don't you think? When we were kissing before the film, that could have been a seven-foot gorilla interrupting us to claim his woman.'

'That wasn't *us* kissing.' She frowned at him as he got closer. 'That was you kissing me to shut me up. I didn't do anything.'

Connor nodded solemnly. 'Only because we were inter-rupted—we'd have done more than that otherwise. And we're still going to, whether it happens right now or you kick me out and I come back for it to happen next time. So, tell me, have you been seeing someone?'

Shannon stared at him in stark amazement.

While his foot hit the first step up to her. 'I need to know before I kiss you again. Practice makes perfect, they say.'

Folding her arms across her breast to stop her heart from thundering its way out of her chest cavity, she leaned a shoulder against the edge of the open door. 'There'll be no practising going on here, trust me. I'm too tired to play with you. I think we should just quit while we're ahead. We've managed a whole day without arguing—and that's an achievement in itself.'

'It is…' the gleam in his eyes said he wasn't giving up that easily, while he made it onto the second step '—but we can't leave a half a kiss as the last kiss 'til next time. I have standards to uphold. This time you'll kiss me back. And then I'll think about leaving.'

'Honestly, Connor, I don't think us kissing again, or doing anything more than kissing, is such a good idea. Not while we have the issue of this place hanging between us.'

His eyes narrowed as he froze halfway between the second and third step. 'Why are we suddenly back to this again?'

'We're not back to it. It never went away. The fact that we got on better today doesn't change that.'

'So you *did* think that making an effort with me today would change my mind—is that what you're saying? Were you referring to yourself when you asked me if I worried about people being nice to me in order to gain something now that I have money?' The bitterness was all too evident in his voice. 'Maybe you should just tell me exactly how far you were prepared to go to keep this place?'

Son-of-a—

That was *not* what she'd meant! Immediately leaning away from the door, she began to unfold her arms, glaring across at him, 'Why, you—'

Connor shrugged. 'Well, tell me what this is, then.'

'I've just told you what this is! I can't sleep with you and still look those people in the face tomorrow!'

Moving onto the third step, he snapped an arm out to stop the door from swinging shut without Shannon's body to hold it open. 'It wasn't an issue in your kitchen a couple of days ago. It wasn't an issue when you looked at me the way you did all day today. It wasn't even an issue all the way through that stupid film we just watched about people in a train station.'

And all *that* statement did was convince her she was making the right decision in sending him away. How he had managed to watch even a small part of that film and not have got that there was so much more to it than trains just proved to her that, when it came to sleeping with her, from his point of view, there wasn't even a hint of emotion involved.

Shannon might have told herself that she could cope with sex for sex's sake. But having been reminded of the Connor she used to know so many times during the day, she wasn't just so sure any more.

'Well, I'm telling you it's an issue now.'

Connor let go of the door and it swung shut.

'So, let's just say for a minute the building issue didn't exist—'

'But it does.'

'Let's pretend it doesn't.'

'I'm too old for let's pretend.'

His eyes gleamed dangerously. 'Oh, I don't know. I think that let's pretend still has a place between consenting adults.'

She reached over to pull the door open. 'And on that note—'

Connor reached out his palm to close the door again, leaning on it so that he was distinctly inside her personal space, his deep voice low and seductive. 'With the building issue to one side, then.'

Shannon found herself mesmerized by the very male lump in his throat, watching it move as he swallowed. 'We can't put it to one side; we're *inside* it as we speak. It's not going away.'

'Well, let's say I made it go away.'

Her gaze shot upwards in surprise. 'Are you saying you'll back out of the sale?'

'No. I told you I wouldn't change my mind that easily. I don't want it. And I still don't get why you won't jump at the chance of a modern building more suited to the things you do here. But maybe, if it's that big a deal to you, you should just *have* the damn thing. And then you won't hide behind it any more.'

Despite the fact that she knew she was doing a really good impersonation of a fish out of water, Shannon continued to stand completely still and stare up at him. He could *not* be serious. People didn't just go around handing entire buildings to other people to settle an argument so the road to sex was clear. Was he *insane?*

'I can't afford to buy this place.'

'I'm a reasonable man, despite what you may think of me.' He smirked. 'I said you could have it. We'll find a nice, long payment plan for you—how does that sound? Because realistically they're like Monopoly houses to me—they don't mean anything beyond one hell of a retirement.'

'How can you *say* something like that? You can't tell me that the business end of that company doesn't mean something to you or you wouldn't be spending so much time working on it. Everything is worth something to somebody. You just don't see places like this as anything beyond their monetary value! And that has to make for a real big empty feeling when you *do* retire, if you don't already feel that way! How can you live your life like that, Connor?'

His expression darkened. 'Well, it's obviously worth something *to you.* Right now, as far as I'm concerned, it's getting in the way, so if handing it to you solves the problem then you can have it. And then we can just stop with the game-playing this time round so we don't make the same mistake we did last time.'

To some people she would have seemed as insane as him for not taking the offer in both hands and running like hell before he changed his mind. But it wasn't that simple, not to Shannon. Or for Connor, no matter what he thought. And that was before she even *thought* about visiting the subject of the game *he thought* she had played last time!

'Is your life really that unsatisfying now that you have to bargain a building to me for sex?'

'What kind of question is that?'

She folded her arms again. 'I don't think this whole—' then unfolded them to make invisible speech marks in the air '—"destroy Frank's legacy" mission you claim to be on is your real problem, is it?'

'I already told you I don't want any part of what mattered to him.'

'You might not want it, Connor, but you've got it. And believe it or not—in this world—with the company he left you comes responsibility. Or at least that's the way it should be. Responsibility to your own soul's well-being if not to the people whose lives and livelihoods rely heavily on the decisions you make every day! And you should know that coming from the background you came from—where it was people and family and caring that made the real difference—so this new attitude of yours doesn't make any sense, which means that the money and the company and the buildings aren't the real problem. The problem is inside you!'

Pushing back off the door, he nodded once towards her feet. 'Do you want a soapbox to stand on to continue this or should I just pull up a chair?'

O-h-h, that was *it!* Using all of her body weight, she reached her hands out to his broad chest and shoved—hard. And it was so unexpected a move that she did actually manage to rock him back a step before he grabbed hold of her hands and pushed upright again—in time for her to stand on tiptoe to get 'in his face' properly.

'No matter what mistakes Frank McMahon made in his life, he at least made something of it! And whether or not you care about that doesn't matter—because the man is *dead!* The only person you're letting down by being such a moron is yourself!'

Connor swore. 'And I'm getting yelled at for giving you the one thing you've argued with me most over ever since I've got here! How does *that* make any sense?'

'Maybe—*unlike you*—I get more satisfaction out of building something good and decent and worthwhile. Something that makes a difference to people's lives! Because when I wake up each day I have to look at myself in the mirror. Can you do that, Connor? Can you look yourself in the mirror and like what you see there? What happened to the man who built a business from the ground with his brother—the one who helped support an entire family when they needed it—the one who must have worked night and day to make sure it worked? Who cared that much! Where is *he?*'

'And your life is so perfect, is it? Hiding away here in this wreck of a place with a load of pensioners, a gay best friend, and other people's kids? I wouldn't go throwing any stones if I were you!'

Shannon's heart cracked open a little inside of her. 'When a single bit of my life is any concern of yours then you can go right on ahead and make judgements!'

'That goes both ways, don't you think?'

'Well, now that we both know exactly where we stand, why don't you just leave, Connor? Go away. Go make someone else's life difficult—I'm sure there are thousands of people living in Devenish buildings who'll be ecstatic to see you coming!'

But he leaned in closer, his expression dangerously dark, hands holding hers in a viselike grip as he told her in a strained voice, 'You know your problem, Shannon? It bugs you that you want me as much as you do, that's what this is really about. If that kiss hadn't been interrupted earlier we could have been upstairs using all this energy a *much* better way. You know that whatever was between us before is still here— in all its varying forms of complication. And it *kills* you that that might mean stepping outside of this safe little world you've made for yourself!'

The loud sound of their ragged breathing filled the short pause before he swore again, throwing her hands back from his chest, opening his mouth to say more—and then completely stunning Shannon by yanking open the door and stalking out through it.

Leaving her alone in the sudden silence.

After a moment she sagged back against the wall, staring into space, trying to figure out what had just happened.

She had just said things to him that had to have been very hurtful to him if his life really did feel at all empty. Of all people, *she* should know that—because he'd been right about her fear of stepping outside the safe little world she'd found. Not that she could ever begin to explain to him why. And yet she had thrown the words in his face to hit back at him regardless—leaving him little choice but to throw equally angry words back at her.

Every cruel, hurtful truth he had said in return had only been what she deserved. She'd made this mess, had probably laid the foundations for it seven years ago.

Why? Why couldn't she just leave him be to make his own mistakes? To learn on his own? How could it still matter to her so much?

It *was* the physical attraction addling her brain, wasn't it? It had to be. It couldn't be anything else.

If she had to find one thing she could blame her erratic mood swings on, then surely that would be it? Because from that first dance, hell, from the first day he had walked in looking so disgustingly sexy in his expensive suit, she had had to deal with her reaction on the most basic of physical levels. And having spent all evening with her body pressed alongside his, well—

But now she was left feeling so overwhelmingly alone and empty—and frustrated. It was almost as if, in the space of one full day in his company, he had become a part of her life again in all the ways that had made her want him so badly before.

Would she ever be able to just reach out and grab hold of something when she wanted it without worrying about the repercussions? Maybe if the repercussion hadn't been so life changing the last time…

But surely the one time would have done it? Sex for sex's sake, for mutual satisfaction and the removal of tension, maybe even to eradicate some of the haunting memories from before—at least for Shannon.

But any chance of that had just walked out the door, along with any chance of saving her building.

All those people that relied on her—all those people that she would now have to sit down to explain how she had lost them the one lifeline they had in their cash-strapped community—they'd be devastated.

Lifting her hands, she pressed the fleshy part of her palms tight in against her eyes, leaning over while she tried to even out her breathing. On top of everything else she really couldn't allow herself to have a panic attack, or—worse still—to cry…

After a few breaths she pushed up and off the wall, yanking open the inner door to step into the small vestibule so that she could lock the outer door. She reached into the pocket of her sweats to find the key, looked up—and gasped when she found Connor looking back at her through the glass.

The last of a glorious summer's day was dying in the sky behind him while he stared at her, his jaw line clenching while he thought. And on the other side of the door Shannon stood transfixed, holding her breath, waiting to see what he was going to do next.

'Open the door.'

Shannon shook her head and he scowled in response.

'Open the door, Shannon.'

She shook her head again. 'It's not locked.'

Stating the obvious tore a small smile from him, before he glanced away, looked heavenwards, and then pulled open the door, stepping into the small space she made for him when she stepped back.

Towering over her again, he searched her wide eyes for a long moment, watching as she pursed her lips together to stop saying something that might start another argument.

Then he took a breath. 'I wasn't trying to give you what you wanted to make things worse.'

'I kn—'

He held up a hand. 'No—don't say a word. Let's not do any more damage, okay?'

Shannon pursed her lips again.

While the hand in front of her curled until he had a forefinger to point at her. '*You*—are capable of making me angrier—' his hand uncurled again as he held both hands out in a sweeping movement '—than *any other* woman on this planet. I have *no idea* why that is you can do that.'

She pursed her lips even tighter together. Because that statement was just *begging* for an answer.

'But what beats me even more is that I keep coming back, every time.' He took a deep, steadying breath, glancing briefly upwards again. 'All right, so I'm not perfect, but you've known me a long time, so you've always known that. And, frankly, I have no interest in being perfect 'cos that's a lot of pressure to put on yourself. So, yeah, occasionally I *am* going to mess up—like I *apparently* did five minutes ago when I tried to remove this great pink elephant that always seems to be standing between us communicating.'

Shannon swallowed hard and allowed her mouth to relax. Because she genuinely didn't want another argument with him, and when he was making this big a gesture by staying to talk it through with her there was just no way she was going to do anything to spoil it. She even tried a small smile of encouragement on for size.

Which brought his gaze to her mouth for a long, long while before he swallowed hard, locked eyes with her again, and his voice became huskier. 'The thing about being a crusader, Shannon, is that you have to have a "She who casts the first stone" quality to you. I could say plenty about you building some kind of stand-in family for yourself here rather than making one of your own with someone—'

Oh, and that *had* to be answered!

But he raised a hand again as her mouth opened. 'No, now you *know* that's true. Don't bother denying it. Many things I may be, but blind isn't one of them.'

She resorted to scowling up at him instead.

'It's like this. Neither of us are necessarily doing a good job with our lives right now this second. But you can't make me find my path—that I'll do on my own—which, right now, leaves me with just the *one* problem to deal with…'

Her eyebrows rose in question.

And finally he smiled a small smile in return. 'Aren't you going to ask me what that problem might be?'

'Oh, I'm allowed to speak now am I?'

'Yes, you are.'

'That's gracious of you.' She smiled to negate the sarcasm in her words. 'So, what *is* your problem?'

'You. *You're* my problem.'

The answer took her breath away, said with such intensity

in his voice and his eyes that she was left in no doubt that his inner struggle was as torturous as her own.

Placing them on equal ground for the first time.

'You see—' he took a step closer '—while I seem to have this inability to stay away from you for long and together we seem to have this ability for ending up in an argument of some kind or another every damn time—I'm left with a real problem deciding whether to strangle you or kiss you senseless. Because you have to know as well as I do that most of this arguing comes down to one thing.'

'And that is?' She knew the answer before he said it.

'It's sexual tension. What we ended on last time is exactly what we've started with this time. We're not done. We're nowhere near done.'

Shannon damped her lips with the end of her tongue, watching him watch the movement with heavy eyes and without taking the time to think about the repercussions—she dived right in with the one choice that her pulse rate would be happy with. Her chin rose in challenge.

'Well, I don't want to be strangled.'

Connor's hands reached up to frame her face, his long fingers threading deep into the thick hair at her nape while his head lowered until his warm breath was fanning her lips. 'Good choice.'

CHAPTER EIGHT

THIS TIME THERE was no question about Shannon not joining in. No question at all—regardless of where it would take her. She'd deal with the damn consequences later.

The door key she had been holding made a loud jangle as it hit the tiled floor. But Shannon couldn't hear anything beyond the roaring in her ears, couldn't feel anything but the pressure of Connor's mouth on hers. She barely even noticed the taste of Dolly Mixtures in his mouth.

He was right. They weren't done. Nowhere near it.

That one unmatched night of sheer passion had never left her memory. But the experience had been overshadowed by so much sadness afterwards that she now wanted nothing more than to overshadow the shadows with more of that same passion. She'd just been kidding herself she didn't want that from the very second he'd walked in the door, hadn't she?

It *was* why she couldn't leave things be, why she argued with him so much. She'd been fighting against something she had no control over—she'd never had control of it.

Her hands bunched into tight fistfuls of shirt against his chest while she moved her head to keep her mouth constantly on his. And she felt dizzy for a second as the memory of his kisses invaded her mind, tangling the past and present together so that it was tough to know what was then and what was now.

The moment he ran his tongue over her bottom lip she sighed, opening up to him. Kissing him was *good!*

But it wasn't enough. Not when her body already knew what could follow.

Instinctively her hands flattened, smoothing over the broad expanse of muscled chest, then lower—where she felt his stomach muscles contract. And when he dragged his mouth briefly from hers, she smiled as he grumbled down at her. 'Slowly.'

Standing up on tiptoe, she continued smiling against his mouth. 'We did slowly last time.'

'And slowly worked if I recall.' He pushed her back against the cool plaster wall, his head descending to the sensitive skin below her ear where his tongue flickered out to taste her and tease her even more.

Shannon raised her arms, frantically tangling her fingers in his short hair to draw his head up to see his face. When his eyebrows rose in question she told him firmly, 'When we last did this I was a twenty-year-old virgin—slow was exactly what I needed. I'm a fully grown twenty-seven-year-old woman now who has just had a massive row with you. What we're about to do is make-up sex. Make-up sex isn't slow.'

Connor grinned wickedly. 'And I thought we were just kissing…'

'We've never *just* kissed.'

At some point, while they'd been 'just kissing', he had let go of her face, his hands dropping to her hips to hold her in place. And while she had her arms raised he took advantage of the unrestricted access to her body, smoothing up her sides until his thumbs were underneath her breasts.

'Make-up sex, huh?' He looked down at his thumbs as they rose, tracing the lace of her bra through the thin material of her T-shirt. 'You might have to show me how that goes, because I've never actually stayed in a relationship long enough for that.'

Shannon was looking at him in disbelief when he glanced up, a wicked gleam in his eyes. 'But then, like I said, I've never actually argued with someone the way I end up arguing with you.'

His mouth stole the gasp from her lips when he cupped her breasts, kneading through the soft material, gently at first, then with more pressure, until Shannon thought her knees would buckle underneath her. She moaned in protest when he stopped, twisting her head back and forth when he began to tug the T-shirt upwards, freeing it from the waistband of her sweats.

Eventually he tore his mouth free to grumble, 'Where did you drop the key?'

'What key?' There was a key?

'The key to the door—we really need to move away from here. 'Cos I'm fairly sure that we can be seen from the street.'

Shannon swore softly. You'd have thought that, as the one who lived there, that thought might have occurred to her. If they stayed where they were for much longer, doing what they were doing, then any passer-by was in for one hell of a show.

But it gave her a moment to pause for thought—to seek some sense of rationale. She could stop this if she wanted to.

To hell with that!

When he kissed her again, this time harder and with more un-bridled raw passion than before, she knew she was already lost.

She wrenched her mouth free when she couldn't get enough air into her lungs. 'I dropped it. It must be on the floor.'

They pulled apart long enough to find the key, lock the door, and push back through the inner door to the foyer. And by then they were already wrapped around each other again, lips tangled while they fumbled frantically to remove layers of clothing.

'Are you sure everyone has gone home? No Yummy Mummies or Briedas to appear from behind one of those doors?'

Shannon's answer was as breathless as Connor's question had been while she kicked off her shoes and hauled his shirt down over his elbows. 'Positive.'

She disappeared briefly underneath her T-shirt as Connor pulled it over her head. Then he took a long moment to kiss her senseless again while he deftly unhooked her bra and slid the scrap of material off her shoulders.

It was only then, as he stood back a little from her and watched his hands on her naked breasts, that everything slowed down a little.

And in the silence of the room their ragged breathing and the thundering of his heart in his chest made Connor feel as if it was a moment he would never forget.

Just as the last time had been.

He splayed his fingers, studying the contrast between his tanned skin and her pale breasts. When he held his fingers wide that way he could hold each breast completely within his palm—which was sexy as hell—and the sense of urgency came back in a single heartbeat.

He needed desperately to be inside her. He'd waited long enough.

She moved her hands up his arms, grasping hold of his

shoulders to rock back a little on her heels, pushing her breasts tighter into his hands. And the sight of her arched towards him like that was as much as he could take, his erection straining agonizingly against the buttons of his jeans.

He sought her lips again, plunging his tongue into the sweet-tasting recesses of her mouth in a way that could leave her in no doubt of what he wanted. And she met him kiss for kiss, touch for touch, her hands frantic on his back, grasping hold of his shoulders, nails digging into his skin as she moaned into his mouth.

'We're never going to make it up four flights of stairs.' He looked around the foyer.

Reluctantly he freed her breasts, wrapping his arms around her narrow waist to lift her off the ground and march them behind the large counter, while Shannon's hair brushed against his chin as she looked to see where he was taking her.

Using his forearm to clear a space on the lower shelf, he hoisted her higher, groaning at the delicious sensation of her soft breasts crushing against his hard chest, before he unceremoniously plunked her down, smiling at her as she grinned up at him.

'Right here?'

'We've gone past the window of opportunity for slow. And I told you that kitchen counter has been on my mind for days now. So, yes, *right here.*'

Leaning down, he kissed her again, plunging his tongue deep into her mouth while one hand reached for her breast again, the other snaking lower, turning over, so that his knuckles grazed over her flat stomach and along the edge of her white lace panties.

Drawing another low moan from her throat to echo around the cavernous room. But when she reached out for the button on the band of his jeans he stepped back out of her reach, wrenching his mouth free to rest his forehead against hers for a moment.

'You do that and you really are going to end up with the hard and fast version of this.'

Almost panting, she looked up into his eyes. 'I want hard and fast. We just had a fight, remember?'

'I remember. But we both need to be at the same place. I want you to come when I'm inside you.'

He watched in amazement as she smiled a purely sexual smile up at him, her eyes gazing into his up close and personal as she whispered, 'Who says I'm not at the same place you are? I want you inside me. *Now.*'

Connor didn't need much more of an invitation, but he needed to be sure she was ready for him, so he slipped an investigative finger beneath the lace—and found liquid, molten heat. With his eyes still focused on hers, he watched her eyelids grow heavy, saw her arching her head back from him as she moaned again.

He'd known it would be like this with them, hadn't he? Had known it from the moment he had seen her on the dance floor of that small bar his first night in Galway. The first time had been unforgettable, but this was unforgettable on a whole new level. Who wouldn't want a woman like this?

'I remember this.'

He stepped in closer again, his finger sliding back and forth inside her as she arched into his touch. 'I remember what it felt like to have you naked against me.'

Shannon's head dropped back further, her body bowing up from the counter as she made small sighs and gasps of pleasure.

'I remember those noises you're making right now.'

Using his knuckles to stretch the lace a little more, he ran his fingertip up and circled her—the touch eliciting an upward buck of her hips towards him.

She rocked forwards, her forehead against his chest as she gasped out, 'Please tell me you have a condom with you.'

'In my wallet—back pocket. Lift your hips for me.'

It seemed to take for ever for her to find the condom in his wallet, while he took an equal amount of for ever slowly removing the last scrap of lace from her body. And all the while Shannon had her head tilted back enough for her glorious curls of long blonde hair to cascade over her shoulders while she smiled up at him.

And Connor suddenly realized that that wasn't an echo of an image from his memory. This one was new. Last time she had had that sultry outfit on so that he hadn't been looking at Shannon, not really, just glimpses of her. This time he could see the corkscrew curl he was so fond of plastered against her damp cheek, he could see the smile on her swollen lips, the slow blinking of her stunning green eyes. He wasn't looking at a fantasy version of Shannon. This time she was trusting herself to him completely.

And he felt ridiculously humbled by that.

Smiling down at her, he reached forward to take the foil packet from her fingers. But Shannon shook her head, her hair moving in waves as she damped her lips again.

'I'll do it.'

'That's not a good idea. I'm hanging by a thread here as it is.'

She shook her head again.

Shedding his jeans and boxers he grasped hold of the counter on either side of her, his arms flexing as he gritted his teeth to fight for control while she rolled the condom onto him, her eyes focused completely on the task. 'It's always going to be a battle of wills with us, even over the little things, isn't it?'

She tilted her head forwards, her lips against the taut column of his neck as her small hand encircled his raging erection. 'Nothing little about it.'

Sidling forwards on the counter, her heels brushing up the back of his calves, she shook her hair back and looked up at him, her eyes studying his for the longest time. And she held the simple unspoken contact with him as he lifted his arms, placing one hand in the small of her back and one in her hair, as he slowly slid into her slick warmth.

Shannon drew in a long, slow gasp of air as she took in every inch of him, until he was buried as deep as he could go.

And Connor closed his eyes for a moment, lost in the sensation of her body sheathing his. There was no barrier this time; her gasp wasn't an indication of the brief pain she had experienced losing her virginity before. When he opened his eyes she was staring up at him, her hands whispering against his skin.

For that brief moment Connor's heart stopped. She was truly, truly amazing. It was true that no other woman had ever made him angrier. But it was also true that no other woman had ever had him so hot so fast.

She was *amazing*.

'I remember this too.' He flexed his hips, drawing back until he had almost left her, then sliding back until his pelvis hit hers, tilting his head to look down as he repeated the movement, watching the way her stomach was sucked inwards every time he slid home.

Lifting a hand from his side, she cupped the side of his face, biting down on her bottom lip as he slid back and forwards again, damping her lips before she angled his face up and drew him down for another searing kiss. 'I remember too—all of it—this most of all.'

Already he could feel her beginning to clamp around him, her inner muscles tightening as she got closer to release. It was the sweetest kind of torture, the answering build of tension in his abdomen, the most basic of male responses. But with Shannon tearing her mouth from his to rest her forehead against his chin, breathing in sharp gasps, Connor felt something else build inside him. Something he didn't recognize; something almost painful.

But they were too far gone for him to take time out to think about it or to try and pin a name to it while he increased the pace, heard her moans growing louder as her damp body arched back from him. So close. He was so close.

'Shannon—'

'I know.' She silenced him with another kiss. 'I know. Don't stop.'

She kissed him again. And again. And when he reached a hand between their slick bodies to touch a fingertip to her sensitive nub, she cried out against his mouth, her body convulsing inside and out as her release pulled him over the edge.

And she kissed him again. And on and on until they both had to stop for breath, foreheads touching, eyes fixed on each other's. Then, as the rippling sensations ebbed, Connor smiled again, slower this time, wrapping his arms around her slender frame to draw her closer against him.

'Oh, yeah, definitely a fan of make-up sex.'

Shannon laughed, her sweet breath washing cool air over his heated skin. 'That's just as well considering the way we argue.'

'We could have been doing this for the last seven years, you know.'

'No, we couldn't.' Her hands smoothed up his back while she tilted her head back to look up at him, wearing a more serious expression on her face. 'But you were right; we weren't done with this.'

Connor frowned at her reasoning, more irritated by her swift dismissal of a potential relationship than he could ever remember being with any woman before. In fact, he'd dated women before who, if they'd even mentioned the 'R' word, would have had him on the run pretty damn fast. But this was Shannon, and even if he hadn't found his way in other portions of his life or even decided what in hell he was going to do with it in the long term—he knew he wanted her in it in the here and now.

In the meantime he picked on the one thing she had said that he agreed with. 'No, and we're still not done.'

When he kissed her this time it was slow and deliberate, placing a seal on his words, because he had meant them. Figuring out how to make everything work could come some-where along the line, he reckoned.

'Do you have to go or are you staying?'

He smiled softly at the question. 'I have to go meet some of the guys from the gym at six to go hang-gliding.'

Shannon rolled her eyes. 'Course you do.'

'No, really, I do. We have a gym here in the city and when I visited the other day we arranged to do a team-building trip. It's not an excuse to not stay the night.'

She frowned in confusion. 'You have a gym in Galway?'

'Yep. And technically I still own half the business so I dropped in to see how they were doing.'

'How long has it been open?'

'Nearly a year.'

'Did you set it up or do you hire people to do that?'

His fingers absentmindedly played with his favourite curl while he answered. 'I do all the set-ups for the new places. When Rory was overseas I did General Manager between the three we had but since he came home we've split it between us and expanded.'

She was still frowning.

'What?'

'You were here when I arrived in Galway.'

'Was I?'

She nodded, then leaned forwards and kissed him again. 'Small world. And now I'm starting to get cold.'

'Maybe we should try and find all our clothes before anyone else does?'

The idea made her laugh. And Connor laughed with her—he could just imagine how that would go down with the Briedas of her world!

'It would certainly be less embarrassing than coming down here in the morning to explain, yes.'

After another loud smacking kiss, Connor pulled away from her, bending to lift his jeans and pull on his boxers. Then together they searched around to find all the items they had discarded along the way, rewarding each rediscovered item with another kiss.

Another thought occurred to him. 'What are you doing on Monday night?'

'We're quiet on Monday. Why?' Her eyes sparkled with mischief from across the room as she hauled her T-shirt over her head, her voice muffled for a second. 'Do you have something for us to argue about so we can make up?'

He didn't answer for a second while he watched her breasts lift upwards as she raised her arms. Though she'd obviously lost weight at some point, judging by the almost invisible fine lines he could see on her stomach, all the varying sports and activities she had studied in America had left her more toned than she'd been before she'd left. But she still had more than enough curves to fill his eye and he looked upwards for a second to thank whoever was responsible for that.

He assumed a straight face before she reappeared from behind her mussed hair. 'If we get to make up after then I'll think of something we can *debate*. But I have a do to go to— so come with me.'

'What sort of a do?'

He shrugged. 'Just a do. I'd tell you more but it would take away the mystery of it. When two people have known each other as long as we have it's important to keep working on that, I feel.' He discovered his last shoe and pushed it on before stepping across and kissing her one last time, smiling down at her when he lifted his head. 'So I'll see you Monday. It'll be a date. We never tried one of those before.'

Shannon stared at him for a long while, the 'something' that had been so elusive earlier in the day briefly making a reappearance before she answered him, 'All right. What should I wear?'

'My preference will always be nothing. So I'm not the right person to ask that question.'

CHAPTER NINE

THE PARCEL ARRIVED Monday morning, causing quite a stir. Mainly because Shannon hadn't been there to sign for it and it had become the focus of much debate in her absence—so that by the time she returned it had a small guard of honour.

'Delivery for you, sugar lump!' Mario beckoned her over with a rapidly gesturing hand. 'And you have to open it here so we can all see what it is. The curiosity has been killing us!'

Shannon scowled at the flat box when there was enough of a gap for her to see it. 'I didn't order anything.'

'Honey, if this came from the shop named on the delivery docket you couldn't *afford* to order anything.'

His flare for the dramatic was almost legendary, so Shannon ignored the glee on her friend's face and studied the box. She was almost afraid to touch it. Especially if it had come from where she thought it had come from.

Not that he had bothered his backside picking up a phone in two days.

Which had left her feeling more than a tad annoyed— well, furious would be more accurate. She'd been in a foul mood for most of the weekend because of it, and it hadn't gone unnoticed either. So much for dealing with the consequences of her actions!

'C'mon and open it. It might cheer you up!'

Yep. And it was Mario who had been *pointing out* her mood all weekend. He'd tried to pry the gory details out of her. But she wasn't ready to talk about Connor to *anyone*. Where would she begin?

'Well, actually we had a row after the film and then great make-up sex.'

Not that 'great' was the right description. Yes, the sex itself had been great there was no arguing that—it had been better than great. What had caused her almost obsessive angst ever since had been what *hadn't* been so great about it. For starters she had the old sex-versus-making-love debate going on in her head…

Two people who cared about each other didn't just have sex. That was what it said in all the women's magazines, right? And there was no doubt in Shannon's mind that what they had had was great, hot, mutually satisfying sex. The tension that had been building between them from argument to argument had been based in the sexual relationship they had that obviously wasn't over and done with yet. Just as Connor had said. It had been there ever since he'd come back— bubbling under the surface—simmering away until it had to have a natural release of some kind or another, right?

But it wasn't the same as the first time. When they *had* made love. And it hadn't taken away the magical quality of that night, or any of the agony that had followed it.

If anything, it had made things worse.

Her eyes still on the box, she began to tug off her coat, walking around the counter to put it away while Mario practically danced from foot to foot with excitement.

'If you don't open that thing in the next two seconds I swear *I* will!'

'He's been like a child at Christmas since it arrived.'

Shannon glanced up at the sound of a familiar voice, smiling a genuine smile when she saw the young woman's face. 'Hello, Mary. It's good to see you again. How's the baby? Did you bring her with you?'

'Yes, she's asleep in her pushchair—'

'And you can see her *after* you open the box…' Mario tapped it with his index finger. '*Box*—remember?'

All eyes refocused on it while Shannon sent a silent prayer upwards that there was nothing too personal in it. Especially if it *was* from Connor, double especially after the make-up sex. Who knew what he might have put in there?

With a flex of her fingers, she leaned forwards and undid the straps, lifting the lid to discover layers of tissue underneath—with an envelope on top.

Shannon stared at it as if touching it might burn her.

'Oh, for goodness' sake!' It was unceremoniously pushed into her hand. 'Just read it!'

She stepped back while she opened it. To find a familiar scrawl on a piece of white card.

'For tonight Sunshine. Will be there 7.30.'

'It's from *him,* isn't it?'

'From who?' Mary grinned at Mario's beaming face. 'Has Shannon met a man? I knew I'd miss something good while I was in hospital—it's always the way.'

With a deep breath, and her heart beating erratically in her chest, she stepped forwards again to push back the layer of tissue paper.

'Oh, what a gorgeous dress!' Mary and her friend oohed

and ahhed before Shannon even had it out of the box, 'It looks really expensive.'

'When you have a millionaire for a boyfriend, then money's not a problem.' Mario peered down at the label. 'Oh, dear, another Dior. You have a wardrobe stuffed with those already. *Not.*'

As he lifted it with a flourish from the box Shannon continued to stare in silence. It was the most beautiful thing she had ever seen, even held up in front of a six-foot lunatic wearing a Gay Pride T-shirt.

A deep emerald green, the material shimmered in the light, so soft that even the minuscule airflow in the foyer made it shift back and forth like a whisper. And it would feel like that against her skin too, wouldn't it? Wearing that dress for the evening would be foreplay again when she was in Connor's company.

'He must be taking you somewhere nice.'

She finally managed to mumble back an answer. 'I have no idea. All he said was it was a "do".'

'If this dress is anything to go by, then I bet I know what "do" he was referring to.'

Her gaze shifted to the smug expression above the dress. 'What is it?'

'Hottest ticket in town if you move in the right circles.' The glare she gave him was apparently enough for him to continue. 'It's the launch of the new wing at the museum—part of the celebration for Galway's bid for European City of Culture. Your gorgeous man won't be the only millionaire there, I bet. And with you in this dress he'll have a job keeping them away from you.'

Shannon shook her head, reaching out to touch the material of the dress. It was beautiful. The most beautiful thing anyone had ever given her. And it was from *Connor.*

He had looked at this dress and thought of her in it. And that thought made her smile.

Dolly Mixtures and Dior. It was a potent combination.

'I don't know that I can do this dress justice.' She reluctantly folded it back into the box, stroking her palm over it lovingly. *Connor* had bought her a *Dior dress*. It was surreal. 'I've never worn something this beautiful.'

Somewhere in her furtive imagination, it briefly felt like payment for Friday night. But that was ridiculous, and she knew it was a callous thing for her to think, even for a second.

She just felt so empty inside.

She could pinpoint the beginning of her awareness of that emptiness to when he had told her he had been in Galway when she'd arrived there. He had probably been there for months while she'd looked for a place to live, while she'd tentatively begun to open her heart to a brand-new group of friends, while she'd tried for once to allow herself to fill the void she'd had inside ever since America.

He'd been here in Galway, living his life without her—had maybe even passed her in the street or on a sunny day in Eyre Square and not even noticed she was there.

When she'd purposefully picked Galway to make sure she would never have to bump into him again.

Knowing he had been there had made her ache and that was when she had first felt the emptiness. Even when he had been inside her, filling her body and sending her spiralling off the edge, there had still been something missing—something that might have helped fill that emptiness.

Mario's hands were on her shoulders, shaking her, 'That is the daftest thing I've ever heard you say! When I'm done with your makeover everyone will think you do the gardening in Dior—you just wait and see.'

Shannon smiled a small smile. '*No one* gardens in Dior. I'm sure you can be shot for that kind of sacrilege.'

'Someone somewhere probably does.' He shook her again. 'You just listen, my girl. Cinders will go to the ball with Prince Charming whether she likes it or not. And when Cinders has the prince wrapped around her little finger she can just persuade him to hand back the nice derelict wreck we all love and adore. And then all the hair-straightening, eyebrow plucking, leg waxing agony I'm about to put you through will all seem worthwhile.'

The smile became a grimace, but not for the reasons Mario probably assumed. Because Prince Charming had already tried to hand back the building, hadn't he? And Cinders had basically told him to *stick it!*

It didn't really matter if she got to the end of the evening feeling even emptier than she already did. If nothing else came out of what was going on between her and Connor, she had to somehow try and make sure the people she loved weren't caught in the fallout. Even if accepting the building meant she might feel that, somehow, she had paid for it with sex.

One night in a Dior given to her by the man she had once loved couldn't make things any worse than they already were, right?

C'mon! After all—it was Dior. What was a girl *supposed* to do?

Shannon's transformation became a group effort as the day progressed. So that by the time she was standing outside the front door looking down at Connor, she did feel a bit like Cinderella.

And if she was, then Connor sure filled the other role to

perfection. He was *sensational* in a tux! Even with his short hair spiking and a bad-boy gleam in his eyes. Rock star chic—that was what it was. And he wore it *so* well! He could have been born in one of those things…

Lifting one side of her long skirt, she tilted her chin down to make sure she didn't fall on her way down the steps. It felt like years since she'd last worn heels so ridiculous and impractical to walk in. And shoes were normally her one foray into the ridiculous and the impractical. When she could afford them.

As she finally stood in front of him he grinned broadly at her. 'Nice dress.'

Shannon lifted her nose and blinked disdainfully at him to cover any sense of discomfort she felt as he looked her down and then back up—with torturous deliberation. 'It's Dior as it happens.'

'Is it now?' He nodded at her, his grin still in place. 'Just something you had hanging around from all those other millionaires you know in Galway?'

She smiled at the memory from their first conversation. How had he remembered that?

'My other designer dresses are in the dry-cleaner's.' She stared at him for a moment and then turned on her heel to give him the full effect of his purchase. 'Will I do?'

'You'll more than do. You look *stunning*.' His dark eyes swept upwards, the grin fading as he examined her hair. 'What have you done to your hair?'

One hand automatically rose to the back of her head to make sure it hadn't fallen out of the chignon 'masterpiece'. 'Mario spent two hours straightening it and putting it up, so I'm under strict instructions to tell you that if so much as one drop of rain touches my head I will "poof up" into the frizz I normally live with.'

'Well, then, let's give him a fright shall we?' He stepped in closer. 'Cos he's watching, isn't he?'

Her green eyes widened. 'Oh, you *cannot* touch the hair.'

'Well, that's a given, but it doesn't mean I can't kiss you and make him think I *might* touch the hair.'

When he leaned closer she leaned back, avoiding his mouth. But it had nothing to do with not wanting to frighten her hairstylist. 'You'll ruin my make-up.'

Connor's eyes narrowed at her excuse. Then he nodded, just the once, before stepping back to open the car door for her. 'Just so you know, that "Get Out Of Jail" card is only valid for use once—at the *start* of the night.'

There was silence for a while as Connor pulled the car out, focusing all his attention on getting them off the cobbled street and onto a wider road. But once they were moving properly he glanced across at her.

And she managed only half a smile.

Which made him frown briefly. 'Is something wrong?'

'No. Why would there be anything wrong?'

'Now, you see, I know you well enough to know that's a lie. So what did I manage to do to make you mad when I wasn't even here?'

She glanced across at his profile as he made a turn. 'Maybe I'm just nervous about going to the "do" of the year. It's not like I make a habit of wearing designer dresses and mixing with the rich and famous.'

Connor's mouth twitched as he glanced at her from the corner of his eye. 'How do you know that's where I'm taking you? It's supposed to be a surprise.'

'Are you telling me that's *not* where we're going?'

The twitch became a smile. 'I don't believe you're nervous. Nothing fazes you.'

'Well, then, maybe you don't know me as well as you think you do. Lots of things faze me, *every day*. It's a fact of life for most people.'

'Like what, for instance?'

'You need a *list?*'

'An example would do.'

The temptation to cross her arms was agonizing. But there was no way she was going to crease her dress. She even missed the stupid curl she was always pushing away—at least it gave her something to do with her hands.

'One little one. Go on, give it a go. It's called sharing. People do that when they get involved, I'm told.'

Involved? She blinked at him. But when it was met with another smile she gave up and stared out of the dark-tinted windscreen, searching her mind for a non-Connor-related-faze-her topic to share as an example. 'Large families faze me.'

So much for the non-Connor part. It was getting to the stage where nigh on everything kept coming back to him, didn't it?

'That's not true. I come from a large family and they never fazed you—it was like you'd always been there from the first day Tess brought you home from school.'

It was a tad close to the bone to discuss anything related to their past. From the time when everything in her life had been so wrapped up in him. As it was getting to be in the here and now.

'No, they fazed me. For years.' She took a deep breath and let it out. 'To someone like me, a family like yours—the way you all are together—well… Let's put it like this—it's like going into a room where everyone is laughing at a joke and

I'm the only one that doesn't get what's funny. Only all of you all knew the joke from birth so when you try to explain it to me, you only say the punchline, expecting I'll get it—so there's no way I'll *ever* understand. Even after years of going in and out of your house I still didn't completely get it, no matter how much I wanted to or how many times I tried asking someone to explain it to me. Eventually I understood *most* of it. But I never laughed the way you guys all did. And I felt left out. *That* fazed me.'

Connor went silent for a long while as Shannon hid the expanding emptiness inside her with another smile. 'You see, I knew you wouldn't get that. Why would you? You knew the joke.'

'It's not that I don't understand. It's just you put it into a very clever, if rambling, analogy and it's going to take me a minute to think up one as smart.' He glanced her way again as he made another turn, smiling at her in a way that almost looked affectionate. 'You do know that you babble when you're nervous too, right?'

Shannon frowned. He knew her better than she liked to think he did.

His deep voice dropped an octave as he reached across to wrap his fingers around her cold hand. 'What you're saying is that you always felt like an outsider? Right?'

'Probably. A little.'

'Well, let me just put something straight, Sunshine—you were never an outsider. Everyone loved you.'

Everyone except the one person she had wanted to love her. But she couldn't say that, could she? And as they pulled up outside the museum the emptiness inside her almost doubled her over.

Connor parked the car, turning in his seat to look at her with a thoughtful expression—until she could take no more. 'What now?'

'Look at me.'

Forcing strength into her spine, she turned to face him, her eyelashes slowly rising until her gaze locked with his. And the air tingled between them as it always did, his sensual mouth curving up into a smile that sent hundreds of lights flickering through the dark depths of his eyes. It wasn't fair. Men like him weren't supposed to exist outside female sexual fantasies—they really weren't. It wasn't that he was perfect, she knew that. But he was Connor. And there was just something about him that had always fascinated her—drawn her in—made her want *more*.

So much more than he had ever been able to give her.

She watched in silence as a large hand rose to her face as it had so often of late, his fingertips stroking tenderly against her cheek, his hand turning—knuckles grazing along her jaw and down the column of her neck.

And when he spoke his voice was husky. 'You look very beautiful tonight. And there isn't a single person that won't turn to look when you walk through those doors—'

'Not helping with the nervous thing.'

Connor chuckled. 'You meet people every day, Shannon. You talk to them, listen to them. It's what you do—so just be yourself.' He leaned closer. 'And trust me—if I hadn't already said I would be here, then we would be heading to my hotel right now and we wouldn't be leaving the room for the next twenty-four hours.'

Truth was, any nervousness she had probably had less to do with where they were or who they might meet than it had to do with the prospect of another night in his arms. Having sex—not making love.

But it wasn't as if she could tell him *that*.

He leaned further across the centre console, a wicked smile in place. 'Sooner we go inside, the sooner we can leave.'

Shannon's eyes narrowed, despite the smile she could feel growing on her face. It was just so difficult to focus when he was like this—so charming and persuasive and damned tempting and with that silent amusement in his eyes.

Yeah, he had her and he knew it, didn't he?

She should hate his guts for that ability to draw her in every single time. But she didn't hate him.

And as he leaned in to mess up her make-up a little Shannon had a sudden realization.

Not hating him any more was the biggest problem of all, wasn't it?

CHAPTER TEN

CONNOR COULDN'T TAKE his eyes off Shannon. And he couldn't remember ever being so proud of the way that one person could manage to look so confident, so beautiful and yet so unaware of how beautiful she was. She was truly amazing.

Her small hand had been cold inside his warm grasp when they had first walked in, and she had clung to him through the first introductions and conversations. Selfishly he had liked that she had clung to him that way, relying on him being beside her. Even if he knew without a shadow of a doubt that the independent Shannon he knew would soon step up.

Fairly soon her smile and her wit had people stealing her from his side to introduce her to other beautiful people or to talk to like-minded supporters of community projects.

She was a hit.

Connor wouldn't have expected anything less.

Finally extricating himself from a group who had been most eager to bend the ear of the new owner of Devenish Enterprises, he stood to one side of the room to watch her.

She really was beautiful. The dress had caught his eye in a shop window when he had been stuck in traffic going to an early meeting. The exact green of her eyes when she was aroused, he had known instinctively it would look stunning on her. But it took her to be wearing it for the dress to take on a whole new dimension.

With her back to him, the halter neck afforded him a mesmerizing view of creamy skin from her shoulders to the slight inward curve above the base of her spine and with her hair up he couldn't help watching the way her long elegant neck turned, how the movement of her head as she talked would frequently offer up that sensitive section of skin below her ear that he loved so much.

And his body tightened in response to the thought of running his tongue along that skin, just so she would make those little sighs she made.

Her head turned, her large glittering eyes searching the room until she found him. And when she smiled, for the first time in his life Connor understood what people meant when they talked about someone being the only one they could see in a crowded room.

Someone sought her attention again, drawing her down the room so that Connor got to watch the long skirt shimmer around her legs as she moved. He wondered how it felt against her skin, how she felt with it against her skin. He even took a deep breath as he debated what she was wearing underneath it that was so invisible to the naked eye—and decided there and then that they had stayed as long as they needed to.

But before he could stalk over to reclaim her he noticed the group she was being introduced to—some of their faces *very* familiar to him. And he smiled a knowing smile. All right, he could wait. Once she'd finished talking to them, *she'd* come to him.

'Connor.'

'What the hell are you doing here?'

His younger brother walked straight over and embraced him in a manly, back-slapping, brief hug, before standing back and grinning at him. 'Hottest ticket in town? Where else would I be?'

Connor laughed. 'You might have mentioned you were coming when I saw you at the weekend.'

'You never asked.'

Connor shook his head, a broad grin on his face. 'I take it there's a woman involved in your decision to be here.'

And Mal laughed in return. 'You know me.'

'How did I guess?' Connor smiled.

Then Mal's expression changed and he took a deep breath before lowering his voice. 'Mum rang today.'

Connor sighed impatiently. 'I thought we agreed to leave me be on this. *Remember?* Just about ten minutes before we went jumping off a mountain at the crack of dawn on Saturday?'

'She really wants to see you.'

Feeling the familiar dark cloud descending above his head, Connor automatically sought Shannon across the room, watching as she laughed, her hand lifting to brush an invisible lock of hair behind her ear. And he could almost hear her voice in his ear telling him in no uncertain terms just what she thought of him not talking to his mother—which made him smile wryly.

'I'll go see her next week.'

'You will?' His brother's expression of disbelief told the tale of how unexpected Connor's answer was. 'Just like that? When half the family has been trying to speak to you for weeks and you haven't been answering their calls?'

Connor shot him a warning glance. 'And I told each and

every one of them that if they'd had the same bombshell dropped on them I did then they'd have needed some space too. Remember that bit?'

'Well, yeah, but this is the family we're chatting about here. They were never going to leave it be, you know that. You'd have been the same if it had been one of us.'

Yes, he would. But he doubted any of the rest of them would have taken the news the same way he had. If he hadn't already been so unsettled, so jealous of his older brother's happiness, so desperate to get away from the responsibility he had unwillingly shouldered for years, then maybe he wouldn't have felt that discovering he wasn't a full member of the family was some kind of retribution for not appreciating what he'd already had.

Blaming his mother for something that had happened before he was born wasn't going to fix what had already been wrong with him, was it?

Mal wasn't done. 'You need to speak to Rory too.'

Connor could feel any semblance of the good mood he'd had trickling away like water through his fingers. 'Rory knows where to find me.'

'I don't think he thinks it's his job to come to you.'

'Well, he can think what he wants.'

'You two are too alike, that's the problem. If you'd just both—'

Connor fixed him with a steely stare, his mouth a thin line. 'Well, you see, that's where you'd be wrong. We're nothing alike.'

'*Mal?*'

Connor frowned hard as he watched Shannon smile broadly at the younger man—who gaped at her in return. 'Shannon? No way! Wow, girl—you look fantastic!'

She leaned in closer to inform him, 'That's your brother's doing—he bought the dress.'

He gaped all the more at Connor. *'Did he now?'*

There was no way Connor was going to stand there and let his brother look at him with that knowing look. Hell, no. Already a grin was growing that, if he knew Mal, would be followed by at least an hour's worth of ribbing…

'We're leaving now. Good to see you, Mal.'

Shannon frowned up at him. 'What if I don't want to leave?'

'You didn't want to come in not two hours ago.'

She tilted her head to the side, which left the exposed part of neck Connor had been appreciating not five minutes ago exposed to Mal's sweeping gaze. 'Maybe I changed my mind. Women do that.'

Connor scowled hard as Mal looked down past her neck. *'Mal—'* the warning tone was enough to get his attention '—has a date of his own somewhere to attend to.'

'Maybe I'd like to meet her.'

Oh, he knew that edge to her voice. Only too well. When she said the words so calmly and so carefully, it meant they were two steps away from yet another argument. And there was no way he was letting that happen where they were. Or in front of his kid brother.

Which left him the option of standing there to make nice long enough for Mal to tell her all about the bust-up he'd had with Rory or dragging her back home where he could deal with the fallout the way he knew worked best.

He chose the latter. 'You don't want to keep Mal away from enjoying the rest of the kind of evening he no doubt has planned with her any more than he would want to keep us from the same, do you?'

Mal made a grimace, stepping back a little as they faced off against each other. 'Well, good to see that you two picked up exactly where you left off in the whole battle-of-wills thing. Let me know who survives.'

Shannon smiled sweetly at him. 'It was nice to see you Mal.'

'You too, Shannon. We've missed you.' He grinned over at Connor as he stepped away. 'We used to talk about you a lot after you left.'

Next time Connor saw his kid brother he would pay for that.

But he had another storm to weather first as Shannon stepped closer to him, smiling through gritted teeth at someone she must have met earlier as they passed by, before she turned her head to tell him, 'And now we really are leaving. Before I ruin any good impression I may have made on anyone I met tonight by telling you exactly what I think of you right this very second.'

When they were in the car she gave him the silent treatment while she tried to get her anger under control enough to speak.

And he seemed content to let the silence continue, which probably meant he thought he could find a way out of this one. Well, he could think again!

Because there was no way he could be such a complete ass and then think that sex would solve everything.

'You spoke to McIlwaine and Murphy, I saw.'

Shannon shook her head, her tongue shoved firmly into the corner of her cheek as she stared ahead. 'Who?'

'The men who want to build the shopping mall where your building sits.'

She turned her head so fast that she almost put her neck out. 'You're going to try and get round what you just did by playing the "I done good" card? Oh, you're a piece of work!'

'They told you about your building.'

'Well, as a matter of fact, yes, they did.' She forgot about her dress and folded her arms firmly across her breasts. 'They even asked me to try and persuade you to reconsider. Seems it has put quite a spanner in their plan, you backing out of the sale.'

'Picked the wrong woman to persuade, didn't they?'

'Well, why *wouldn't* they think I could persuade you? I mean, that's how it's done in some places, isn't it? Business deals done over the pillow, so to speak.'

He slammed on the brakes so hard at the junction that they were both thrown forward a little in their seats, Connor's face livid with anger when he looked at her. 'They *said* that to you?'

'No—' her mouth curved into a smirk '—but if they had it wouldn't have been any worse than what you just said to your brother about leaving to have sex. That doesn't make me seem at all *easy* to you?'

'I didn't say that to Mal!'

'You may as well have done!' She was really getting into her stride now. 'What else was he going to think you meant? You just threw that out there to get to leave—so you could stop me from talking to him—because if *you're* not talking to your family, then *I* shouldn't either, right?'

'It didn't occur to you that maybe I might not want you dragged into that?'

'O-h-h.' She laughed incredulously, 'I more than get where I stand in the great scheme of things with you—don't you worry.'

'And what does *that* mean?'

'It doesn't matter what it means.' The truth of that hit her like a slap in the face. Because it was true, wasn't it? No matter how many times she argued with Connor, he always seemed to manage to take control. Whether that was done by bully tactics, doing something amazingly nice to try and negate it, or just simply by trying to make it all better for a while by having sex. He was controlling her life. And he could do it because a part of her still probably loved him. She'd known that the minute McIlwaine and Murphy had told her he'd backed out of the sale. When, for a brief second, she had wanted to run across and kiss him silly because she'd been so happy.

Only to have him tell his brother they were off to have sex.

In *his* mind he probably saw it as his reward for doing the right thing—when he could have done the right thing to begin with, and she wouldn't have been left feeling as if it was just another move in whatever game he was playing with her.

'So long as you get to do everything on your terms then everything is fine, isn't it?' she said.

She turned her face away, looking out of the side window as they got close to home. Because she'd be damned before he would see the angry tears that were forming in the backs of her eyes.

Behind her, she heard the hiss as he forced out a swear word, the gear stick being yanked violently into place. 'I have *no* idea how your mind works sometimes.'

'You don't want to know.' The words were flat, emotionless, but that was what she did when she was hurting most, wasn't it? She shut herself off. Closed down inside. It was a survival tactic she had learnt the hard way.

Connor didn't say anything in reply for a long while, the tension inside the car palpable until, as they made the last turn onto the cobbled street, he took a breath and answered her in a similarly flat tone.

'You see, that's where you're wrong. I do want to know. I want to know every thought you have, I want to hear your opinions—even when I don't agree with them. I want you to yell at me when you're mad and laugh when you're happy. Because when you shut yourself off—that's when we have the most trouble. And if this is going to stand any chance of working, then we need to find a way around that.'

The car came to a halt in the same space it had occupied when he'd first arrived. But when Shannon reached for her seat-belt release, he captured her hand and held it tight, stopping her from escaping while she fought hard against the tears that were so determined to break free.

'We need to talk whatever this is through.'

She swallowed hard. 'I don't want to talk.'

'Than how are we supposed to fix this?'

'We're not.'

He let go of her hand. 'So what, then? Now that you know you have your building safe you don't have to make an effort any more? Or is it that now you've not got that to hide behind you might actually have to open up?'

That got her to look at him—her glare scathing.

'Because that's what the real problem is, isn't it?'

'Well, you're obviously the expert here. So well done. Congratulations. Whatever game you're playing, you win.'

When she got out of the car, slamming the door behind her, she let an angry sob out, fumbling in her small clutch bag to find her keys while she looked down at it through eyes threatening tears.

At the door she couldn't get the key in and as she sniffed loudly his hand appeared—taking the key from her. He didn't say a word, just leaned past her to fit it and turn it, while

Shannon stared downwards, the first tears balancing precariously on her lashes.

He pushed the door open. Stood back.

And Shannon walked through, opened the second door, leaning in to flick the light switch. Then, swallowing down the knot sitting at the base of her throat, she looked over her shoulder.

'I'm sorry, Connor. I can't do this with you any more. I thought I could, but I can't.'

'Can't do what?' He stepped in through the outer door, his dark eyes focused completely on her.

She swallowed again. 'This. Us. Whatever *this is*—I can't do it any more.'

'Because it hurts too much to try?'

Her breath caught, but when she tried she couldn't get the words out. So she nodded, just the once. Before looking away, and walking further into the foyer—turning around when she was in the centre, her hands on her hips, head tilted back to look up at the peeling paint on the cornice while she fought for some semblance of control.

She should never, *ever*, have conned herself into believing she could do this again.

What was she? Masochistic? So desperately in need of punishment for something she had long since paid for?

Connor walked to her with silent steps, stopping a 'safe' distance from her, as if he knew to come closer would only make things worse. He even seemed to understand that she needed a minute, that once she had that minute she might maybe tell him more to help him understand.

She took a breath, shaking her head with fresh determination. 'It's not enough.'

His deep voice remained low. 'What isn't?'

'*This*—' She exhaled the word, her arm swinging out to her side as she finally looked at him again. 'This fighting and then trying to fix it with sex.'

'And you think that's all we do?'

'It's what we *did!*'

His dark brows quirked. 'Wow.'

Shannon watched as his hand rose to run back through his hair. Then he looked her in the eye again, his voice still low.

'I don't think that was all we did.'

His calm response made her even angrier. 'Well, it was how it felt.'

'During or after?'

The question made her avoid his steady gaze, because even telling him as much as she had was costing her.

'I'm not saying that the act itself wasn't—'

'Well, at least we agree on that—that's a start. But in some way I've left you feeling used? Is that what you're saying?'

'No!' She frowned hard at his interpretation. 'It's not that either. What we did—we did together. And I wanted it—I did. But it just felt—'

'Like a one-night stand—sex for sex's sake—like there was nothing there except the release of sexual tension?' He shrugged his shoulders. 'Help me out here.'

Although a part of her understood that the change of tone in his voice was more to do with frustration and confusion than with any anger on his behalf—the very fact that he had worded it the way he had was enough to put her back up again. As if it confirmed to her that he had known that was exactly what it had been. Which made her right, didn't it?

And maybe that was what she needed. Maybe she needed

him to confirm it for her to get her to hate him again. To make her angry enough to finally send him away.

'It *was* sex, Connor. *That's all.* And I'm sorry, but that's just not enough for me. I need more than that.' She shrugged her shoulders, feigning nonchalance. 'And the truth is, I just don't think you have it in you to give me more. So, we're done.'

It was a low blow. And it was the first time in her life she had ever seen Connor look lost for words. But his recovery was quick, any hint of confusion or frustration—or even the patience he had shown so far—immediately replaced with out and out anger. So that she was left in no doubt she had just hit the mark.

'Is that the game we're playing now? Do I even *know* you?' He shook his head. 'Any wonder you're still on your own if this is how you deal with the beginning of a relationship! All of this is nothing but sex to you? You think we do this constant battle of wills for no reason? You seem to forget that we had years of history before we even got started this time round! But then walking away is your thing, isn't it? It's what you do best.' He laughed cruelly. '*Man,* and you think *I'm* messed up inside!'

Rather than backing down in the face of such raw anger she met fire with fire, her voice rising to echo around the large space.

'And you seem to forget that we spent seven years *apart!* You think that you're the only one who went through some kind of emotional upheaval in that time, Connor? You think that just because I argue with you and challenge the things you do that that means I'm the one with all the great answers to life's problems? Well, I'm *not!*' She jerked a pointed finger at the ground. 'I have just as much to deal with from those seven years as you do! *Probably more.* Because you always breezed through life and nothing was difficult for you until the day you found out you had a different father from the man who raised you. You have *no* idea what *I* might have gone through!'

'And just how am I *supposed to* when you keep fighting me off?'

Stunned into silence by how much she had just let out, she stood frozen to the spot, her breathing as rapid as the erratic beating of her heart. She stared at Connor with wide eyes, watching as he waged the same inner battle with himself to gain control.

It would have been so very easy to close the distance between them and give in to a raging passion to dissipate the tension again. But that was what had started this in the first place, wasn't it?

And she just couldn't keep on doing it.

Connor moved before she did, both hands lifting to rub up and down his face while he started pacing up and down in front of her. Then, side on, he nodded, as if he'd made some kind of decision, before he turned his head to look at her, one long finger waggling briefly in her direction.

'At least we're getting down to the crux of it now, aren't we?' The pointing stopped and the pacing continued. 'I knew there was *something*. It's been there since the first day. Don't get me wrong.' He glanced at her again with a wry smile. 'You're *good* at trying to cover it up behind the guts and quirkiness I'm used to. But I knew there was something different. Something that happened that changed you and left you hiding away in this place.'

The air in her lungs stilled on an inward gasp that she held onto. *Dear Lord.* What had she just done? Connor had never been dumb. And now she'd just given him some of the pieces of the puzzle, hadn't she?

He stopped pacing again while he thought, and then—
so suddenly it made her jump—he stepped in front of her,
less than a few feet separating them. 'You're right. Neither
of us knows what the other went through in those seven
years. There's no way we could. But you're wrong about
me breezing through life, Shannon—I wish you weren't,
but you are.'

She exhaled, took a deep, shaky breath. It had never in a
million years occurred to her that he had been unhappy before
he had found out about Frank McMahon. And it stunned her
beyond belief.

Connor stepped another step closer, his voice husky. 'The
only difference between us is that I'm not the one trying to
turn tail and run away from this, *whatever it is.* So, fine, we
both have stuff. Who doesn't? Big deal. What this needs is
time. You've just got to decide that you're prepared to put in
that time. And a good dose of old-fashioned trust.'

Could she really do that? How could she begin to tell him
about the pain she carried when he was so tied up in that pain?
By making it a mutual sharing he was inviting her to help him
work through whatever it was he was carrying around—which
made it a shared therapy, didn't it? And that made it so much
harder for her not to at least give it a try.

Could she manage to get through it without falling for him
twice as hard as she had the first time round? That would be
the gamble she'd be taking.

But what if helping him work through all the things he was
having difficulty dealing with now was her only way of
making up for what she had held back from him?

While her heart demanded she try, her head kept
weighing up the odds of an outcome that wouldn't cause

both of them pain—and in the meantime Connor had stepped another step closer.

'Now with that out there in the open, let's move on to the sex issue. I'm assuming that we're looking at the age-old debate of sex versus making love are we?'

There were times when he really could read her mind, weren't there?

'Yes, I think we are.'

He nodded. 'Yeah, I thought so. C'mon, then—'

Shannon's eyes widened as he grasped her hand in his and tugged her towards the stairs, her voice rising again. 'Oh, no, you can't keep trying to solve it like *that!*'

Still tugging her, he threw the words over his shoulder. 'Well, it's getting solved somehow. And I, for one, am getting sick of pacing.'

'Connor, let go of me!' She practically careered into his back when he stopped suddenly, releasing her hand at the same time to turn round and hold his hands up in surrender.

'Fine—look—no hands. I'm serious, Shannon—I'm not leaving 'til this is resolved one way or another. Don't make me carry you up three flights.'

And Shannon knew he meant it. 'We're just talking.'

'I'll leave that decision to you. We'll talk it through, then, if it's what you want, I'll go.'

'You'll leave?'

Another nod. 'For tonight.'

When he held his hand out in silent invitation she stared at it for a long time. But who was she kidding? She knew she was going to go upstairs with him and talk it through. She'd already dug a deep enough hole.

But she'd feel better if she managed not to touch him just

yet, so she reached out and set her clutch bag in his open hand, glancing up into his eyes as he smiled in amusement. 'I hate you.'

'No, you don't. And that's the biggest problem you've got, if you bother being honest with yourself.'

CHAPTER ELEVEN

UP IN SHANNON'S apartment, Connor set the small bag she had handed him on the kitchen counter while he watched her move around the room, switching on table lamps that cast a soft glow around them.

She had said that she wanted more and that she didn't think he had more to give her.

That had grated on him more than anything ever had.

She sat down on one of the large sofas that dominated the living area, smoothing her hands down over the soft material of her long skirt as she took a breath and looked up at him.

'All right, then.'

The determined upward lift of her chin brought another smile to his mouth as he walked across to sit on the other sofa, facing her. But for a long while he didn't speak, he just smiled at her, until eventually she sighed and shook her head.

'I'm glad you find all this so amusing.'

'I don't.' He shrugged his shoulders, reaching up to undo his bow-tie and loosen the top button of his shirt. 'I just can't remember ever being on a first date when I ended up sitting down to have a conversation about the vagaries of sex. It's not exactly what I had planned for the evening.'

Her arched brows rose in challenge. 'Which pretty much brings us onto the subject of sex anyway, doesn't it?'

'And there you go differentiating between sex and making love again. When what you need to realize is that, with us, there isn't a difference.'

'Spoken like a man.'

'That's a whole other argument for another day, that one.'

'And that's what we do, isn't it? We argue. About pretty much everything.'

He leaned forwards, resting his elbows on his thighs, 'Yes. It's what we do. Lots of couples argue.'

There was a flicker of surprise in the green of her eyes. 'We're *a couple* now?'

'If we're not, then what are we?'

'And when did that happen in your mind? 'Cos I must have missed that memo.'

'Shannon, we've always been a couple—one way or another. This is just the first time we've had to deal with it, that's all.' He smiled again when she looked distinctly as if he'd just told her something that had never occurred to her before. 'Tell me this—when we slept together the first time, did that feel like just sex between two people seeking a cheap release to you?'

The direct question brought her gaze up to lock with his, her eyes softening briefly as she played the memory in her mind, so that he knew the answer before she said it.

'No. Now that I know you knew it was me I know that was us making love. But for your information, I wasn't playing a game. It was something I wanted and I figured if I made it an anonymous fantasy it might be something you'd want too.'

Connor's eyes widened slightly. 'Nice to know your low

opinion of me goes so far back. All right, then, so, what was different this time?'

And her brows quirked again, this time in disbelief. 'The fact that you have to even ask me tells me you're not going to understand the problem.'

'I was giving you the opportunity to tell me how you saw it. That's all. But if you want me to say what I think, then, fine—I'll tell you.' He looked to the side, away from her face, while he put the words together in his head first. It was getting to be a necessity around Shannon. 'I think the reason it has blown up out of all proportion in your mind is the word "sex." But you need to remember that the phrase "make-up sex" was yours, not mine.'

She opened her mouth to protest.

'No. I gave you the opportunity to go first and you didn't take it, so now I'm just telling you what I think. And then you can say what you think.'

The simple order did what any order or demand he dished out normally did with her. It put her back up. But he loved that she fought him on those issues. He was a strong-minded male, after all; it was the very fact that she was equally strong-willed that made them such a combustible combination.

So, while she straightened her spine, folded her arms across her breasts and lifted her chin another distinct notch, he kept right on going. 'It was a phrase, nothing more and I understood that—I thought you did too—'

The terse interruption surprised him. 'Yes, fine, you're right—I gave it that label and that label has stuck in my head ever since.'

Connor jumped on the opportunity. 'And can you tell me why?'

The fact that she struggled so long to find the words to answer him told him how difficult she was finding it to talk it through. 'Probably because you left so fast and didn't bother calling for three days. It made it feel like a one-night stand— which made it feel like sex for sex's sake. And that left me feeling…'

Connor leaned forward when her words tailed off. 'Feeling what?'

She swallowed hard, her gaze dropping down to study the toe of her shoe as she moved her foot from side to side. 'Empty, if you must know. Like I should never have let it happen again.'

The thought of her feeling that way almost floored him. Empty was such a huge feeling. He knew that. And never in a million years would he have wanted to leave her feeling like that. He'd always prided himself on the fact that any partner he had felt as fulfilled by the act as he did. It was the man's job. But somehow he had left her feeling used, tawdry, and that hadn't been what he'd been aiming for—not with Shannon, of all people.

She was worth so much more than that.

'I never meant for you to feel like that.'

Her lashes rose enough for her to look at him. 'I know. I guess I just stupidly thought I would get to hear your voice at some point over the weekend, that, I dunno—you might maybe have bothered to call to say hi or at least talk about the weather.'

'I thought you understood what I was doing this weekend.' He frowned a little. 'I told you I was away.'

She nodded. 'You said you were hang-gliding on Saturday with some of the staff from the gym.'

'No, well, yes. But it was a bit more than that. It was a

team-building weekend. They take us to the middle of nowhere and we camp out. And then we spend the weekend doing a mixture of challenges that make us work together—bridge-building, rock-climbing, hang-gliding. Every gym does it once a year to help them work together better.' He sighed, taking a moment as he tried to remember how much he had told her at the time. He had been sure he'd explained all that. 'And I'd signed up for this one a long time ago. I really thought I'd explained that. But what I maybe didn't explain is it's a wilderness type idea—so that means no laptops, no iPods—definitely no phones. They're very specific on that. And I didn't think you'd appreciate a call at one in the morning when I was driving back home, after leaving the last of the team who travelled with me.'

Shannon stared at him from beneath her lashes. 'You didn't tell me all of that.'

'I should have.'

'Yes, you should. It might have helped.'

He nodded, smiling a small smile when she didn't call him on it. Was he finally making some headway? Well, if forthright was what it took…. 'But I need to carry that through to today for you too, don't I?'

A smile twitched at the edges of her mouth.

'This morning I had company meetings—this afternoon too. Some of them put back from Friday so I could spend the day here.' He grimaced. 'I've had nothing but meetings for weeks now, as it happens, and I'm sick to death of them. But, yes, I could have called.'

Her eyes sparkled across at him. Oh, she knew she had him on this, didn't she? He'd messed up. His arrogance had let him assume that she'd have no problem with him disappearing for a few days because she'd known he was coming back. He'd assumed she'd known that meant he wasn't bailing on her and that there wasn't a problem with him *wanting* to come back. But that was what assuming got him. Some consideration would have worked a lot better.

'That was obviously a mistake too. But now that I know it's a problem I can make damn sure it's not a problem again. If I have an early meeting I'll call you at six when I get up— and if I'm coming back from somewhere, even if it's three in the morning, I'll call. And that'll fix it, will it?'

He knew she'd never go for that either. She wasn't the type to try keeping someone on a leash…

And, right enough, her smile grew. 'Let's just not go to the opposite extreme either. There's bound to be a compromise in there somewhere.'

If she was open to discussing compromises, then he was making ground, wasn't he? That left him with just the one hurdle to get past so he could breathe again.

'All right. That leaves us with the sex versus making love again.'

Her smile faded. Lifting her chin again, she frowned as she glanced around the room—giving the distinct impression of someone seeking an escape, which brought an affectionate smile to Connor's face that he didn't try to hide from her.

She chanced a glance at him from the corner of her eye. Saw the smile.

And Connor waited while she battled with herself over whether to listen or to argue again and try to run. She could *try* the latter. But she wouldn't get far.

Shannon sighed.

Well, she'd asked for this, hadn't she?

Thing was, piece by piece and subject by subject, Connor was taking the time to ease her through all of the things that worried her. And surely he wouldn't do that if it didn't matter to him a little?

If she'd had the courage downstairs to tell him that the 'not enough' she had been referring to had more to do with the lack of real emotion then she could probably have avoided all of this. Because that was the real truth behind her emptiness, wasn't it? She had wanted the whole package from him once before and hadn't got it. It was what she had meant when she had said she didn't think he had it in him to give. She had prior experience.

Not that she thought he was incapable of love. She just didn't believe he was capable of loving her the way she would want him to. But she had always known that. Right from the start. Both times.

When she turned her face fully towards him, she studied him for a long while—searching his eyes for some sign that this wasn't just damage control for him. That it could really matter.

And there was such a fierce warmth in his dark eyes that she was almost rocked back by the force of it.

It was genuine affection she could see, affection for *her*. And when he spoke, his voice wasn't just low and deep. There was an edge to it that went straight from her ears to her heart, and, almost as if her heart hoped for its meaning before her mind could accept there was even a chance of it, it leapt, and sped up in response.

'The only difference I can see between the first time we were together and this time is that the first time was the slow and torturous kind of love-making and this time was the hot and fast kind. And I think it's maybe the slow and torturous that works best for you.'

Shannon swallowed hard.

'For a while, anyway, until you trust me enough to play a little.' His smile took on a purely sexual edge. 'You need to remove the word "sex" from your mind when it refers to what we do, Shannon. We don't just have sex. We know each other too well for that.'

Even listening to him talking about it—while he looked at her with that warmth in his eyes, and that wicked smile on his face—it *felt* as if he were already beginning to make love to her, all over again.

'Mal said that we had picked up where we left off—and he was right. That's exactly what we've done. The only difference is we've had more baggage in the way this time round. So, yes, we've fought more—but the outcome has been exactly the same, hasn't it? Whether we've approached it from a friendship angle or from an antagonistic angle, we always end up back at the same place.'

Did that mean that he knew how much she had loved him before? Did it mean that he knew a part of her had never stopped loving him? It was certainly the reason why she'd been having so much difficulty with all of it lately, wasn't it?

'This…chemistry…we have—it's always been there. I don't think that something on so basic a level is something that anyone has any control over. It's here now. You can feel it just as much as I can.'

Yes, she could. Connor had once talked about the building being a pink elephant constantly between them—if that was the case then between them now was an open fire, the heat from the flames fanning out to wash over her skin.

Thick dark lashes blinked slowly as he studied her with an intensity that took her breath away all over again. 'And I know you can feel it. Because I *know* you. Right now it's in your eyes—they go a darker shade of green when you're turned on. Did you know that?'

Shannon slowly shook her head.

Connor nodded in reply. 'They do. It's why I knew that dress would look so spectacular on you. It's the same shade your eyes are right now.'

She ran her tongue over her lips.

And his smile grew as he looked at her mouth. 'You do that too. You wet your lips just like that—which, whether you know it or not, is an invitation for me to kiss you. It's like you're getting your mouth ready for me. And for the record, it's one of the things I find sexiest about you. *One* of the things…'

Shannon was slowly reaching boiling point, her lips parted as she drew in deeper, faster breaths of the heated, heavy air that hung between them. He hadn't even touched her and she was so aroused that she dearly wanted to squirm on the soft cushions beneath her to relieve some of the ache between her legs.

His smouldering gaze dropped lower, following the line of her neck to the deep vee at the front of her dress, his voice taking on a husky edge that left her in no doubt that he was as turned on as she was.

'Though the way your breathing changes is damn sexy too. Deeper breaths, like you're taking now—that get faster and shorter when you're close to the point where you can't take any more.'

'Connor—' His name came out on a hoarse, agonized whisper—because she really *couldn't* take any more.

The sound brought his gaze back to her eyes. 'I know you

want me. And you know me well enough to look at me right now and know that I want you too. This is always here with us—it's when we fight it that we end up arguing the most. But never, ever, for one second, think that it hasn't always been here. This isn't just sex, Shannon—it's much, much more than that.'

Shannon knew he was right. For the first time in a long time she had no desire to argue with him over it—because there was really no point in trying to deny any of it. Everything he had said about the signals she sent out was true. Looking at him, she could see the signals in him too—the intense heat of his gaze, the slight part of his sensual mouth, the exaggerated rise and fall of his chest beneath his crisp white shirt, and—when her gaze dared to drop lower to his wide-spread legs—the ridge of his erection pressed against his stretched trousers.

'Shannon—' Her name was spoken on a warning tone, bringing her gaze back up to his face.

And the set of his jaw, the tight line of his mouth, the hooded eyes told her volumes about his state of arousal. Yes, she could read the signs too. Because she knew him every bit as well as he knew her in that department.

She tilted her head, looking at him with the kind of confidently slow, seductive smile a woman gave when she knew she had equal powers of attraction to her man as he did to her. Then, purposefully, she licked her lips to show him what she wanted him to do while she leaned forwards, perched on the edge of the sofa.

'You said I could decide whether you stayed or left.'

He leaned forwards, balancing on the edge of the sofa he was on. 'Yes, I did. But I also said I would be back. I'm not going away, Shannon, no matter how many times you try to push me away. Get that clear. So, whether we clear this up today, tomorrow, or next week, it's getting cleared up. Make no mistake about that.'

And Shannon knew, even now, when they were both so aroused that if she said go, he would. He was a man of his word. And he would see it as another way to earn her trust. But she didn't need him to leave and keep coming back to earn her trust. It had never been a trust issue.

She didn't need him to prove himself to her. What she needed was to take a chance—to meet him halfway, to work through the pain that seven years apart from him had brought her way, and to hope and pray that they could build something strong enough to survive when she told him the truth.

'Stay.'

The slow exhalation was immediately followed by an expression that almost looked like relief. Then he smiled at her with that oh-so-sexy smile she loved so much while he told her, 'Just so you know—this time is the slow and torturous version of the love-making we do. And I'm talking *very* slow. And *extremely* torturous.'

Shannon's eyes closed briefly as the ecstasy of anticipation caused her body to flood all over again. 'It's already torturous.'

But he didn't move, not yet—almost as if he was loath to stop her from suffering. And just when she was about to take matters into her own hands—literally—his dark brows quirked in question. 'Do we have a bedroom this time?'

She lifted her arm to point to her left.

And it was then that he stood up, his hand offered to her, palm upwards, the same way it had been at the foot of the stairs.

So Shannon reached her hand out and placed it in his, her fingers tangling with his while she watched. Such a small gesture, so much meaning. With her paler, smaller hand framed by his larger, tanned hand she was telling him that she trusted him, that, in a small way, she was surrendering herself to what came next.

Her eyes rose, head tilting right back so she could look into his eyes as he drew her to her feet. And with their gazes locked, he lifted the back of her hand to his mouth, his lips warm against her skin, his breath fanning over the back of her wrist.

And Shannon had *thought* she had loved him before…

CHAPTER TWELVE

'DON'T MOVE.'

The soft demand was made as Connor stood Shannon at the side of the bed, her back close to the dressing table. So she stood still while he found the nearest lamp and stepped past her to close the bedroom door. Then he was back in front of her, his gaze once again fixed on hers.

It slid to the side, his head tilting closer to her face, forwards to look behind her ear, so that his warm breath was on the side of her neck and the scent of his aftershave filled her nostrils

Large hands slowly rose to the droplet earring brushing the skin below her earlobe and he focused on removing the clasp at the back to free it from her ear, his gaze returning briefly to hers as he completed the task and set the earring down on the dresser.

And Shannon's heart twisted at the simple tenderness of it, her neck tilting to the other side, eyelids heavy, as his attention moved to her other ear—repeating the action.

And his gaze locked with hers again while she stared back up at him.

Then his fingertips brushed from her bare shoulders, down

each of her arms, until he touched the bracelet on one wrist and lifted the arm to carefully remove it. Setting it silently onto the dresser before his gaze came back to lock with hers.

And still he didn't speak. He didn't have to. Because, as his attention went to the pendant lying at the base of her throat, his gaze following the line of the chain until he had to tilt his head over one bare shoulder to unhook the tiny clasp, he was saying more *without* words—his gentleness and careful focus on each task touching her deep inside her soul in the same way that he had when he had first made love to her.

He let the pendant slide down a little between her breasts, watching the reaction in her eyes before it too joined the other items on the dresser. Then his hands lifted again, fingertips brushing along each side of her neck, teasing the sensitive nerve endings awake as he searched up into the intricate knot of her hair for the clips that held it in place.

Shannon closed her eyes as he drew each one free, her weight swaying forwards off her high heels as she tried to compensate for her wobbling knees. As the last clip was placed on the dresser, she opened her eyes, knowing before she did that he would be looking at her as his fingers drew her hair down around her face and over her shoulders.

'Shake it loose for me.' He stepped back a little to watch as she tossed her head from side to side.

Confidence growing exponentially by the second, she smiled as her hair fell around her face, Connor seeming to revel simply in watching her.

Using his hands on her shoulders to turn her around, so that she could see the two of them reflected in the mirror above the dresser, he continued smiling as he watched her expression change, her eyes wide with wonder at the sight of her hair cas-

cading in unfamiliar soft waves around her face, rising to look
at the flush on her cheeks, before they rose further and locked
with his.

'I don't think you know how beautiful you are.' He
smoothed her hair back, running his fingers down through the
long silky length until he was tracing the rise and fall of the
ridges of her spine, which made Shannon arch her back, her
head falling back against his shoulder. 'You always were.'

Not that it wasn't what she wanted to hear, but, 'No, I
wasn't. Don't you remember? I had braces for years.'

'No, I don't remember that. And you're trying to ruin a
compliment that I'm not taking back.'

She nodded her head up and down against his jacket. 'I did,
though—from fifteen to seventeen.'

'Ah.' He nodded, turning his head to press a kiss against
her hair. 'The shy and quiet years. You see, you weren't a pain
in the ass until you turned eighteen.'

Shannon nudged him with her elbow.

But even though he chuckled, he was already moving his
hands up her spine, turning his fingers to brush the backs of his
hands over her shoulder blades, pushing her forwards an inch
or two so he could tilt her head forwards, smooth the hair from
her neck and undo the tiny hooks of the dress's halter-neck.

The soft material slid down over her breasts in a whisper,
leaving her staring at her reflection as his hands smoothed
round to flatten over her ribcage, fingers splaying, his eyes
fixed on hers in the mirror.

Shannon laid her head back again, tearing her gaze from
his, so that they were both watching as his hands rose, cupping
her breasts with such tenderness.

How could anyone blame her for wanting this?

But as his fingers moved, teasing her nipples into hard buds, she moaned, her lips parting to gasp in air—because it was almost *too* slow, too torturous to stand.

And Connor knew what he was doing to her, his head turning so that he had access to her neck—his lips leaving a string of butterfly-soft kisses on her skin before he whispered in her ear, 'And just think, we haven't even got started yet.'

She moaned in frustration. Then in annoyance as he freed her breasts and set her away from him again. But she should have known he wasn't stopping. So when she felt his fingers against the skin of her lower back and heard the soft hiss of the zip being lowered, she pursed her lips together, her gaze rising to watch his reaction as the dress slid to the floor and she stepped out of it, turning to face him.

Connor's face changed, a look of the same torture she had been feeling written all over him. When she tilted her head, her hair falling over one side of her face, one hip tilted towards him, he frowned, stifling a low groan as he looked up into her eyes.

'I've spent half of the night wondering what you were wearing under that dress that was so invisible.'

'I have a thing about nice underwear.' She glanced down at the sheer lace thong, stay-up stockings with their equally lacy top, and her ridiculously impractical strappy heels. 'And shoes. Shoes are my weakness.'

When she looked up, Connor was swallowing hard, his eyes a midnight black. 'Don't ever, *ever* lose either of those weaknesses. In fact. The stockings and the shoes can stay on. *Seriously.*'

No one had ever told her that to have a man like Connor so very visibly weak at the knees was such a huge turn-on. Someone so strong in body and in character hanging by a thread because he wanted her that badly—and she could see that in his eyes, in the clench of his jaw, the single, tiny bead of sweat that trailed down along the side of his gorgeous face.

She'd never felt so close to him before. They were truly equal in their weakness for each other.

'So, this torturous thing—that's supposed to be a one-way deal, is it?'

His dark eyes widened briefly at the question, his voice a low grumble. 'Sweetheart, if you don't think I'm tortured over here then you have no idea of how you look right now wearing what you're wearing.'

'Well, then…' she stepped closer, looking up at him from beneath long lashes '…shouldn't you be wearing less?'

Connor held his arms out to his sides. 'Be my guest.'

With another smile, she focused on pushing his jacket off his broad shoulders, Connor lowering his arms to help her out. Then she turned her attention to the small pearl buttons on his shirt, purposefully taking her time slipping each one free.

'Not that there isn't something incredibly sexy about a man in a dress shirt with a bow-tie loose around his neck. Many a fantasy has been launched on that image.'

'You just let me know what your fantasies are and I promise to do my very best to oblige…'

Her fingers still working on the buttons, she looked upwards, biting down on her lip as she thought. 'Mmm…'

Connor groaned again, the sound a low rumble in the base of his throat. 'Don't do that.'

Shannon blinked innocently at him. 'Do what?'

'Make that noise while you bite down on your lip.'

'Why?' She smiled mischievously. 'What's that a sign of? You're the one that knows me so well.'

'It's not a sign of anything,' He leaned in and suckled on the side of her neck again, his voice muffled against her skin. 'It's what you do when you come. Remind me and I'll let you know when you're doing it again, which incidentally…' his head rose as she undid the final button, her knuckles grazing against the flat skin above his trousers '…I intend making you do again and again tonight.'

Shannon's hands flattened out against his abdomen, smoothing up, fingers tracing over each of his ribs, while she revelled in the sensation of warm skin over tight muscle. 'All those years in the gym business stood you in good stead, didn't they?'

He grinned proudly as she slid the shirt off him, 'Very important to create the right impression for the clients, I feel.'

'Very.' She nodded in agreement, her hands already on the button of his trousers as she smiled again. 'I'm not the only beautiful one in the room.'

A look of chagrin was aimed her way. 'Men aren't beautiful.'

'This one is.' With the zip undone she slid the palms of her hands under the waistband and the edge of his underwear, bending her knees as she slid them both down his legs, her eyes full of what was hers to take. She could torture him to a whole other level if she—

'Shannon, don't even think about it.' He reached down, hands under her arms to pull her back upright. 'I meant it when I said I was tortured already. You do that and it'll take me at least a half hour to recover enough to do what I plan on doing.'

She chuckled. And he chuckled back in return, crushing her to him as he spun them in a circle to the edge of the bed. 'You're a witch.'

'Not with anyone else, I'm not.'

They stopped with the back of her knees against the mattress, Connor's expression and tone fierce as she swiped her hair out of her eyes.

'*Never* with anyone else. Ever again.'

'Connor—'

It was too much. And the fear of a promise made that might not be kept must have sounded in her voice, because he silenced her with a, 'Shh…'

And finally, for the first time in what felt like for ever, his mouth came down on hers in a heated kiss, placing a seal on his possessive words. He stole the air from her lungs, traced the parting of her lips with his tongue, until her mouth opened on a moaning sigh and she met him touch for touch, taste for taste, her hands rising to frame the strong lines of his face, her fingers threading back into his hair to draw him even closer.

But it still wasn't close enough. She wanted him as close as a man could be to a woman. She wanted him to fill her body, to take away any semblance of the emptiness she had felt without him for the last three days.

With his strong arms wrapped around her slender frame, he lowered her to the bed with a reverence that belied the ravage of his tongue inside her mouth.

He encouraged her without words to move further up the mattress, by using his arms to lift her a little, by then moving his hands down to the backs of her knees to lift her legs one by one as he removed her thong—her high heels pressed against the edge of the bed when he threw it over his shoulder. Then, with a long groan, he tore his mouth from hers.

'Back in a minute.'

Shannon rose onto her elbows to watch with amusement as he sought out his discarded jacket, retrieving the small box that he then ripped open—tossing it on the bed near her when he had what he sought. And Shannon turned to find it, lifting it to look up at him in challenge while she waved it back and forth.

'You only brought *three?*'

'A bumper pack would have been seen under my jacket.' He grinned at her. 'Don't worry, I can be creative.'

Then he was over her again, balancing on his elbows as he framed her face, his thumbs teasing the corners of her mouth. 'Now, where were we?'

Shannon framed his face in return, her eyes gleaming up at him as she ran her tongue over her lips and drew his head down. 'Right here.'

The kiss was slower, softer, warming her heart in places that had been so badly hurt in the past that she had closed them off so she wouldn't feel anything there ever again.

She bent her knees more, making a cradle for him to rest in as she wrapped her calves around his, creating static where her stockings brushed against the hair on his legs. And still they kissed, Connor's head lifting only long enough for him to kiss her from another angle while he pressed the tip of his erection against her slick heat.

Shannon writhed beneath him, her breathing rapid and shallow, her hips rising to meet him, inviting him deeper, pleading silently for him to end the torture.

When he slid his full length into her she wrenched her mouth from his, her head arched back into the covers as she gasped his name, his mouth on her jaw, on her neck, his teeth nipping against her collarbone. And all the while he was starting a slow rocking of his hips, building the knot of tension inside Shannon until she thought she might die if she didn't find a release soon.

'Connor—' She gasped his name again, looking up into his face as he rose above her on arms that shook as he tried to hold himself in check—his chest grazing back and forth so that her over-sensitized breasts were teased by coarse chest hair, creating a delicious friction that sent her closer and closer to the edge. *'Connor!'*

The constant gasping of his name and the little sighs and moans that she made seemed to drive him equally close to the edge, the struggle evident on his face and beneath her hands as she grasped at the taut muscles of his upper arms while he increased the rhythm, pushing into her a little harder with each stroke.

And when she began to buck beneath him in the throes of pleasure, her teeth biting down firmly on her bottom lip, he smiled briefly, then his body went rigid and a long, low groan of satisfaction pierced the air as he rested his forehead against hers.

Shannon looked up at his closed eyes, her body still trembling as the last ripples of intense pleasure spread out from her abdomen into every nerve ending of her body. She listened to their matched heavy breathing, felt the hard beat of his heart pressed against her own. And the overwhelming sense of love she felt for him was so complete that she just wanted to stay where they were for ever. To freeze the moment, to never have to visit a place where they weren't this close.

But there would be a day of reckoning, wouldn't there?

No matter if they managed to work everything else out, no matter how happy they were together—the day would come. It was just the way it was.

When he opened his eyes, he did it slowly, so that she had time to force the telltale pain from her eyes, instead smiling

up at him with the smile of a woman who had just been taken
to heaven and back.

'Well, hello, there. How you doin'?'

He grinned down at her. 'Not too shabby, as it happens.
And I don't need to ask you—you're pretty vocal. Not that
I'm complaining about that.'

Shannon giggled—an amazing sound to both of them—as
she remembered how long it had been since she had last giggled
that way and Connor pulled her on it by scowling ridiculously.

'Oh, there's something amusing is there?'

'Only that I'm still wearing my stockings and shoes.'

'And rightly so too.' He took a long moment to kiss her,
his mouth then peppering small kisses over her cheeks, her
eyelids, her forehead, then back to her mouth. 'So, which side
of the bed do you want?'

The thought of spending a night wrapped in his arms
almost brought tears to her eyes. This time she wasn't going
to sneak away while he slept and he wasn't going to leave her
on her own. *Bliss.*

'I want whatever side of it you're on.'

'I tend to sprawl in the middle—' he wriggled their still-
joined bodies further up the bed '—and hog the duvet.'

'I believe that. But with a little training we might make you
more considerate; given the time.'

When he looked down at her, his gaze was intense, his
words deeply sincere. 'We have time.'

But no matter how she tried to convince herself that could
be true, as Connor moved to remove her shoes and stockings
before drawing her into his side she just knew that it wasn't.
She was already on borrowed time.

CHAPTER THIRTEEN

MARIO BOUNDED INTO the end of the reading session as the last child was leaving. 'I tell ya. You can wait all day for a bus in this town and then two just roll in at the same time. It's always the way, isn't it?'

Shannon laughed at him. 'Have we had one too many coffees this morning, precious?'

He leaned in against her side. 'What is it with you and tall, dark and handsome men at the minute? Did you change your deodorant? 'Cos if you did, I might need to know what brand you're using…'

'What *are* you talking about you loon?'

Mario lowered his voice to a stage whisper. '*Well,* there's another *very* beautiful man in the foyer looking to talk to you. I told him you were spoken for but he still wants to see you…'

Shannon played along. 'Did he happen to say who he was?'

'He did. Just his first name, though…'

She smiled encouragingly. 'And do I get to know what that name is?'

'Rory. Suits him actually. Though I should warn you, this one is wearing a wedding ring.' He held his left hand up and tapped his ring finger. 'So even though you *are* spoken for, be careful. Don't get suckered in by a "my wife doesn't understand me" story…'

Connor smiled in satisfaction as he pushed open the inner door to find scaffolding half dismantled in the foyer. The work was almost done—which was just as well with the big party planned for that weekend.

It had taken nearly a solid twenty-four hours in bed to persuade Shannon that she should help him set up a community-owned trust to manage the place, even after he had tried playing the 'tax exempt to a charity' card. Not that he had in any way, shape, or form had a problem with the persuasion part. And it had been worth it to see her come alive with the project, her astute gaze never missing a trick with the building contractors who had worked wonders inside a few short weeks.

She even demonstrated her enthusiasm and rewarded him with another twenty-four hours. Connor officially loved Sundays now.

'Well, hello, lover.'

He grimaced at Mario's greeting. He wasn't sure he would ever adjust to a six-foot male who wore pink. No matter how much respect he had for the way Mario looked out for Shannon's welfare like some kind of loyal Great Dane.

'Hello, Mario. Where is she?'

'Who?'

Connor shook his head, smiling in resignation.

'Oh, you mean Shannon. She's upstairs. I'll lock up down here before I leave. Though I should warn you—I think she's ticked off at you. Just so you have a heads up.'

'Any idea what the builders did this time?'

'Don't think it was the builders.'

Well, it wasn't something *he'd* done, not this time. In fact, life had been fairly harmonious of late. He'd even been the perfect guy and looked after Shannon when she'd taken a stomach bug. Connor felt he was even more of a helluva guy than he'd been before he'd discovered her again.

So he held his hands up as he walked past the counter. 'Not me this time. I'm a guilt-free zone. Night, Mario.'

Mario laughed. 'G'night, Connor.'

Two steps away, a thought occurred to Connor, and he stepped backwards again. 'I have to ask you. Is your name really Mario?'

Mario rolled his eyes, leaning forwards to answer in a stage whisper, 'No telling.'

Connor answered with some trepidation. 'O-okay.'

Mario looked from side to side. 'It's Patrick. But Mario sounds much more interesting, don't you think?'

'Does Shannon know that?'

'No. So it's our secret.'

Connor laughed, taking the stairs two at a time to get to Shannon. Not pausing on any of the three flights, until he was standing in her doorway again, his eyes immediately searching the large room for her.

Norah Jones was singing in soft tones in the background, low light warming the room from an assortment of lamps and candles. And there, legs curled up beside her and a blanket over her knees, was Shannon.

Connor exhaled.

As if she had heard the sound, even over the music, her eyes rose and she blinked slowly as she studied him. And Connor could see the momentary caution there.

Uh-oh.

'Hello.'

He stepped into the room, his eyes still locked on her face as he got closer. 'Feeling better?'

'Yes, thanks.'

Stopping a few feet away from her, he narrowed his eyes as he searched the familiar green of hers. And there it was—the ever-elusive *something*. Only this time it was tinged with a something he knew only too well.

'What's wrong?'

Swinging the blanket back, she blinked up at him. 'Now, why would there be something wrong?'

'You see, that's why I'm asking. I have *no* idea. But Mario said I should be prepared before I came up here.' He leaned in for a brief kiss as she got close to him. Which she responded to the way she usually did, so he couldn't be in *that* much trouble.

But when he leaned back she was more blatant about blinking, her lashes fluttering as she accompanied it with an innocent pout. 'That's sweet that you two are such good friends now.' Then her head tilted and she smiled. 'Remind me to fire him again tomorrow…'

'You already fired him three times this week. I don't think he's going anywhere.'

'He *is* right, though. We do need to have another little one of our *talks*.'

'About what? 'Cos I know I haven't sold a building you love today, kicked any kittens or informed any small children that fairies don't exist. So it can't be me on your hit list.'

Shannon stepped round him and walked into the kitchen area of the large room, refilling her glass with water at the counter before she looked him directly in the eye again. 'Rory came to see me.'

Connor wouldn't have been any more surprised if she'd told him that Santa had been there. 'My brother came to see you to get *you* to talk to me? Oh, that's rich. Not like him to get a woman to do his dirty work.'

Shannon laughed sarcastically. 'From what I hear, you're damn lucky his wife didn't find you first.'

The thought of that raised the first open smile he'd smiled in a while when he thought about his elder brother. 'Well, I'll grant you, Cara can be scary when she gets on a roll. But it's not like Rory not to pick his own fights.'

'Oh, I think if he'd found you he'd have picked a fight all right. From what he tells me you two still have the odd wrestling match.' She shook her head. 'You'd think two grown men would have more sense.'

'It takes two to make a wrestling match. And he threw the first punch this time.' Connor scowled hard as he replayed that day in his mind. It had been ugly. 'Anyway, he shouldn't have to hide behind his wife, or you.'

When he folded his arms across his chest Shannon shook her head again. 'You're both pathetic.'

'So what did he want you to do exactly? Send me home to apologize to him with my tail between my legs?'

She ignored his sarcasm, sipping her water before she pursed her lips together in thought, her gaze focusing on the glass as she ran her forefinger around the rim. 'Don't you want to know why he didn't want his wife traipsing up here even when she was determined she could get you to listen to her before you'd listen to him?'

'I get the feeling you're about to enlighten me.'

'Yes, indeed I am.' She walked back towards the sofa, waving a hand as she went past him. 'Help yourself to beer, wine, coffee, whatever. You know where everything is.'

Tempting as a drink was, Connor decided against it.

Somehow he had a feeling that he was going to have to keep his wits about him. So he turned around and sat opposite her, his elbows on his knees while his errant eyes made an intensive study of her legs as she folded them back up on the sofa again.

He was definitely a legs man. And Shannon had *great* legs. Long, shapely, soft-skinned legs. And, as always, the sight of them reminded him of those legs wrapped around his while he pushed deep inside her body. Which would lead to the memory of her crying out his name, her sighs, her body tightening round his and pulling him over the edge.

Like last night, and every night since the night they had sorted through those few things.

When he smiled, her hand appeared in his line of vision, drawing the blanket back over her knees. And when his gaze rose to her face he saw a flush on her cheeks and a frown between her eyes. She knew what he was thinking. But she wasn't happy he was thinking it.

And Connor wondered if it was because she was annoyed at his sense of timing, his one-track mind, or just bugged by whatever his darling brother had said.

Any thought he might have had about finding out which one it was was abruptly interrupted by the frustrated edge to her voice.

'You know, if you stopped being such a moron for five minutes and answered the phone when he called you I wouldn't even have to have this damn conversation with you. I hate that there's still one of them that you haven't spoken to.'

'You don't have to have this conversation. Rory should never have asked you to get involved. And frankly I'd be much happier if you didn't get stuck in the middle.'

She shook her head in annoyance. 'He didn't ask me to get

involved. He came looking for you 'cos Mal told him where to find you. And since you weren't answering the phone—'

'I'm not ready to talk to him.' He frowned hard at the confession. 'I've already built plenty of bridges this last while. I'll get round to him. And if he didn't ask you to get involved, then why—?'

The outburst caught him unawares. '*Someone* had to tell you what an idiot you're being!'

And there was the *something* again. Way more obvious than it had been in a long time—and laced with a raw anguish that startled him.

'Shannon—'

'Do you know *why* he's been calling you more this last couple of weeks? No, of course you don't, because *you* don't answer the phone. Well, I'll just tell you why he's been calling—'

'I know—'

'No, *you don't!*' She leaned forwards, her eyes flashing in the soft light. 'Because you think he wants to try and force some kind of mutual admission of guilt on you that you're not up for. When all he wants to do is tell you that you're going to be an uncle!'

The statement momentarily silenced him. Because he knew what it would mean to his brother and his wife, hell, what it would mean to the whole family. It was a major event, the first of a new generation of Flanaghans.

When he didn't answer her straight away, Shannon made her own interpretation of his scowl and unfolded her legs again, to lean forward and ask him in a voice laced with emotion, 'How can that not matter to you? *How,* can you be this stupidly stubborn?'

The tears forming in her flashing eyes held all of Connor's attention. She looked as if he had somehow deeply hurt *her* by not talking to Rory. But that couldn't be right. So what in hell was wrong?

He felt an angry bubble of frustration building in his chest. Was she ever going to completely trust him? Hadn't they already proved how great they were together—how their lives had slotted so neatly around each other's? It all made perfect sense to *him.*

In the silence, the calm edge she forced into her voice was all the more noticeable to him. She was drawing back again, shutting herself off, forcing whatever pained her down inside as she always did. Where he supposedly wouldn't see it. 'You have such an amazing family and you've always been so close—even with Rory, who was away so much. How can you not know how very lucky that makes you, Connor?'

Suddenly part of her motivation in being so upset about the fight he'd had with his brother, even the earlier rift that he had had with the rest of his family until he'd started making amends of late, made more sense to him. And he mentally kicked himself for not piecing it together earlier. It wasn't as if she hadn't hinted at it before.

'I know you didn't have a big family growing up—' he took a deep breath before he continued '—and maybe I do need to talk with Rory, especially now—'

'*Maybe?*'

Keeping calm and avoiding another of their famous arguments was the least he could do this time, considering he knew her history, her way of building a substitute family within the walls of this building that she loved so much and considering that he knew she was only interfering because she cared.

He could give a little under those circumstances. 'All right. I do need to talk to him.'

Her green eyes widened marginally in surprise at his back-down. Then they narrowed in suspicion. 'Sooner rather than later.'

Connor smiled a half-smile. 'You're pushing it now. I'd suggest you quit while you're ahead.'

The very visible rise of her chin made him smile all the more. Until she eventually announced, 'You needn't try turning on the charm either. Because I know on top of everything else, you lied to me way back at the start.'

His smile left, at speed. 'Did I now?'

'Yes, you did. And you know you did.' When he simply stared at her with the same implacable gaze he had worn that first day, she shook her head and rose from the sofa again. 'I don't know why you feel the need to pretend to be someone you're not, Connor, especially with me.'

As she stepped near to his chair he reached a hand out and grasped her wrist, his long fingers tight against her beating pulse. And she froze. Nothing more than the skipping beat against his fingertips betraying the fact that she was affected by his touch. But it was enough.

Enough to encourage him to lean back in the over-stuffed chair a little while his fingers relaxed, his thumb brushing back and forth against that beating pulse. And his eyes watched the movement, still fascinated by the velvety smooth softness of her skin, even after being able to touch it and kiss it so often. He remembered seeing his hand on the pale skin of her shoulders, on her flat stomach, cupping her beautiful breasts; most of all he remembered it framing her face, when she closed her eyes and kissed his palm. So many new memories now.

When he spoke his voice came out a little huskier than he'd planned. 'What did I lie about?'

'Did you tell so many that you don't remember which one it might be?'

The question forced him to think about that while his thumb continued to rub back and forth, his eyes still fixed on the movement. 'I didn't lie about the building, or owning Devenish or never forgetting that one night we had. I didn't lie about not knowing sometimes whether to strangle you or kiss you—though I do think I have a preference firmer in my mind on that one now…'

Her pulse fluttered again.

'You told me when you were angry and bitter that you were on that mission of yours to have all that money to retire with.'

The soft background music came to an end, and Connor could hear her breathing, the small, shallow breaths she was taking that told him she was still annoyed enough to try to resist the effect of his touch.

'Yes, but you know I've bought more properties than I've sold lately—'

And he had, *surprisingly*. He was even getting a kick out of it. Once he'd finally come to the conclusion that he couldn't change the past and that he had to try and find a way to deal with what had been handed to him. Though Devenish Enterprises was a very different company in his hands than it had been in Frank's—it had moved into the twenty-first century, to begin with.

Connor was quite proud of that achievement.

'But you lied about the money.'

'No.' He smiled laconically at her wrist. 'I definitely have the money. You've stuck with a bone fide multimillionaire. In all his glory.'

She paused, took a deeper breath. 'You were using great chunks of that money to set up trust funds for your younger brothers and sisters. And paying off the entire families mortgages, even when you refused to speak to a single one of them.'

'Yes. Though, in fairness, Rory wasn't best pleased when I tried to pay *his* off. He was, shall we say, *rude* to the agent I sent…' He flashed a grin up at her.

When she didn't speak, he tilted his head to look up into her eyes, while she looked down at him from beneath long lashes, a myriad of emotions crossing her expressive emerald-green eyes. And then she smiled.

She was beautiful.

'Were you trying to get me to hate you on purpose?'

He felt his gut tighten in response, his hand automatically mirroring the sensation on her wrist as he tugged her round to the front of the sofa and down onto his lap, easing back into the cushions as he wrapped his arms around her. 'I was possibly a tad irritated by you at the time. We've come a long way since then, don't you think?'

Her throat convulsed, her tongue swiping across her bottom lip before she answered him with another half-hidden tremor in her voice. 'I really hated your guts for a while.'

He'd probably hated himself a little at the time.

'I know you did.' He pulled her closer to him and she lifted her knees, her head tilted back against his arm so she could look up at him.

'You can be such a pain when you set your mind to it.' She found one of the gaps between the buttons on his shirt and threaded her fingers in to touch his skin. 'But you looked like the weight of the world had been lifted off your shoulders when you came back from seeing your mum—think how you'd feel if you sorted things out with Rory.'

'Maybe.' He leaned down, resting his chin on top of her head, his fingertips smoothing from her knee to the edge of her loose shorts while he took a deep breath. He guessed if she was ever going to trust him with that something she still hid from him, then he had to show that sharing was something he could do too. 'But there's a longer history in my dispute with Rory. It's part and parcel of why I was a man on a mission when I came here.'

The surprise sounded in her voice, her fingers already beginning to undo buttons. 'I thought this was just about the fight you had at your mother's. Rory said you were angry at the time, said a few things he didn't appreciate you saying to your mum, and that he hit you for it. I'd probably have done the same thing.'

Connor smiled a very small smile. 'Yes, well, that's certainly a very condensed version of what happened. I got the solicitor's letter that morning bringing me the glad tidings and Rory was there when I confronted her. She felt that I hadn't had any need to know because my dad had loved me like all of his kids. I said that every child had a right to know where he came from and that every father should know he had a child—which she obviously *partially* agreed on 'cos Frank had known about *me*. She then had to confess to both of us that, after Rory was born, she and Dad were so young that they couldn't deal with a baby and keep their marriage afloat, so they split up—and then when they got together again she was already pregnant with me. And I made a few snide remarks about secrets and why Dad had forgiven her. And what kind of a guy Frank must have been for never wanting to see me.

And Rory stepped in when Mum got upset. He hit me when I wouldn't stop asking questions—I hit him back. And then when he wrestled me out the door, we had—*words*.'

Shannon went still against him.

He glanced down at the top of her head. 'And none of that's anything either of us can do anything about. It happened.'

'It must have been awful.'

He considered lying so she wouldn't think less of him for his behaviour, but decided he'd rather be honest and have her mad at him for a while. 'It wasn't pretty. But then you know how I can be in an argument—I have a tendency to fight fire with fire.'

Shannon seemed to be undoing the buttons on his shirt absent-mindedly, while her thoughts remained elsewhere. 'Maybe standing on the outside looking in on a family like yours is what it takes for me to see how important it is to hang onto something that rare—with both hands—no matter what. You know you need to sort it out with Rory. You won't be happy 'til you do; I *know* you.'

The familiar, telltale scent of flowers that would always be Shannon surrounded him, filling his senses and clouding his thoughts as she slid her hand inside his open shirt, her finger-tips tracing over his skin before she reached her other hand up to his face, tilting her head back as she drew him into a slow, tender kiss that didn't last anywhere near long enough as far as Connor was concerned. Then, her nose close to his, she stared him in the eye while she told him in a determined voice, 'You're very dumb sometimes for someone so smart. You were never any less a brother or a son. One mistake before you were born was never going to take that away. *Idiot*.'

It had just taken him a while to remember that.

'I was smart enough to keep coming back to fight with you. I happen to think that redeems some of my other mistakes.'

She smiled with a familiar glint of mischief in her eyes. 'Mmm, you're still a work in progress, though.'

'You'll just have to fight to keep me, then.' He angled his head and kissed her again. This time with the kind of hunger that never seemed sated with her. No matter how many times he kissed her or made love to her. Which was *plenty*. He took winning her over *very seriously*.

But when he lifted his head and her lashes flickered upwards, revealing her familiar eyes, she seemed to momentarily forget she had to keep covering the something and the green shadowed over, even while she smiled at him.

Connor had been through a dozen scenarios for what was behind that something, some of them too horrible for him to even consider. If someone had *physically* hurt her, he would kill him.

'You hungry?'

Connor smiled back. 'Not for food.'

'I give up—you're officially insatiable.'

'You love that I'm insatiable, you know you do.'

Another long, hot kissing session, and they both scrambled to their feet, bedroom bound. And Connor's mind wandered along the way. If somewhere there *was* a man who had broken her heart to the extent that it held her back from loving again—then Connor was determined to make love to her again and again and again. Until that memory was erased from her mind and her heart. Then maybe she would tell him what had happened, and he would hold her and tell her that it would never happen again. He wouldn't let it. It was as simple as that.

Then his phone rang.

CHAPTER FOURTEEN

'How is she?'

Connor's voice sounded tired on the other end of the line. 'She's fine. Doctor's looked at her again this morning and she's home now, surrounded by people fussing over her—which she hates.'

Shannon smiled. 'I bet. You'd hate it too, so that must be where you get it from. And they reckon it was just an angina attack?'

'Yeah, a warning, they say. But that's the second warning in three years so she has to start and behave. I think the excitement of being a grandmother was maybe too much. Cara says she has been running herself ragged buying baby things already. She'll have kittens when it gets here at this rate.'

And there it was again—the twisting agony inside her. She wanted so badly to be able to deal better with someone else's good news—but it had taken every ounce of strength she had in her to smile when Rory had beamed down at her as he'd told her about his baby.

By the time Connor had come home to her, she had managed to get herself calmer. But she had still had to fight to keep the pain of old from him—and it had been getting tougher to do every day as it was. Each day she spent with him, every night that she spent in his arms, made it more and more difficult to face the prospect of losing him.

'Where'd you go?'

She smiled, even though she knew she didn't have to force a smile when he couldn't see her. 'I'm here. So you're at the house now?'

'Nope—I'm on my way back. Should be there in just over an hour.'

'You're not staying?'

'She's kicking us all out, one by one. I didn't get a choice. And anyway—maybe I missed you.'

Her breath caught. Hell, but she had missed him too—big style. All night long she had tossed and turned, caught between horrible nightmares and periods of staring into the darkness. She couldn't hold it back from him any longer. Already she had stolen more time from him than she had a right to. And he didn't need her to remind him of how he used to be any more. He was already the man she had loved ten times over—slipping into the role of property developer with an enthusiasm that had made her so very proud of him.

But she couldn't stop herself from digging herself a little deeper in. 'Well, maybe I missed you too. There was no one here to make coffee first thing.'

Connor chuckled. 'Good thing too. No one makes coffee the way I do or wakes you up the way I do.'

Shannon smiled affectionately. 'Don't go over the speed limit, you idiot.'

'Too late.' He chuckled in return. 'I can't miss the lead-up to the big party tomorrow night, now, can I?'

'Not when you're the guest of honour—no.'

'Well, there you go, then. I'll see you soon.'

Shannon stood in the empty pottery room for a long while, listening to the bustle of people in the foyer. The party was the official opening night of the brand-new revamped community centre, but, while she was filled with joy and immense pride for all that Connor had done to make it happen, she also felt physically sick, mentally drained, as if she were carrying the weight of the world on her shoulders at the prospect of finally telling him what she had been holding back.

That was what someone got for holding back the truth for so long, she supposed. And the truth was she had probably used up all the strength she had trying not to love Connor any more than she already did. Not that that had worked. Because either side of the short bouts of depression she'd been suffering the last couple of weeks she had been ridiculously happy.

She was still trying to think of when would be the right time to tell him what was long overdue as she got ready for the party, rehearsing the words in her head and trying to keep busy to hide how much even thinking of saying them was hurting her. She was lugging away the last of the boxes and running up and down ladders to put streamers up—hauling one particularly heavy box when she cramped up.

The pain was sharp, taking her breath away.

'You'll pull a muscle like that.' Mario grasped hold of the other end of the box. 'After three. One, two, *three*—'

The second cramp doubled her, her arm automatically circling her stomach as she looked up at Mario's concerned face. 'No—'

He was at her side in a split second, his arm around her shoulders. 'I told you you'd pull something. You're a strapping lass, my precious, but you're no weightlifter.'

But Shannon could already feel tears welling in the backs of her eyes. Suddenly the way she had been feeling lately couldn't be put down entirely to her guilt, could it?

'I need you to take me to the hospital.'

'Does it feel that bad?' He laughed down at her. 'Everything still looks attached to me—'

'Please!' She grasped hold of his arm, looking up at him as the tears blurred her vision, her voice an anguished whisper. 'I think I might be having a miscarriage.'

Connor stood in the open doorway looking in on Shannon sitting on the edge of the bed, her eyes wide and unblinking, her nose and cheeks red—from crying? And he was torn between wanting to sweep her into his arms or turning round to go for another long walk up and down the disinfectant-scented corridors to get his own emotions under control.

Instead he stayed frozen to the spot until she took a shuddering breath, reaching up to wipe her eyes again, and she caught sight of him from her peripheral vision.

When she didn't speak he walked in and sat down on the bed beside her. 'Mario rang me. I let him go on—said I'd bring you home.'

'Okay.' She didn't manage to look him in the eye when he turned his face towards her. 'What did he tell you?'

'He told me.' Connor had never felt so inadequate, each word taking more effort than he had ever put into talking before, especially with Shannon, and especially after their last few weeks together.

'I wasn't pregnant.'

She said the words on that flat tone that he knew meant she had closed off again. And the swift shard of pain in his chest snapped him out of his own thoughts and into action, drawing her into his arms and kissing her hair before he asked in a husky voice, 'Are you upset you weren't?'

A part of him really needed to know whether having his child was something she would want too. It would have been fine with him—she'd have been bound to him then. And he wanted that. He wanted her inexorably tied to him. With no more doubts.

But he was glad she hadn't lost their child. It would have hurt unbearably if she'd miscarried and he'd have had to hide that from her while she needed him to be strong. That was another part of the man's job, after all, wasn't it? Through thick and thin—for better or for worse…

The thought surprised him. But it shouldn't have, not really. He'd known for a while.

With his head turned, his chin resting on the soft curls of her hair, he listened to her choked answer.

'The timing probably isn't right.'

'Maybe not. It's something we've not talked about either. After this, maybe we should…'

He let the suggestion hang in the air between them, giving her time to figure out that he was open to the idea of them having a family in the future.

But she went stiff in his arms.

'Yes, we should. It's a long overdue talk.' When she pulled out of his hold and stood up—reaching for her sweater in a room that already felt like a sauna to Connor—he frowned, watching her push each arm into a sleeve, pulling her head through, reaching up to free the long hair she had trapped.

Was she going to tell him that she didn't want to have kids with him some day? But Shannon loved kids. She worked with kids every damn day. And if she loved kids and still didn't want them with him, then did that mean she didn't love him? Or that she simply didn't love him enough yet to even think about it?

And if that was the case then what would it take to get her to feel that way?

Her eyes rose and locked with his across the narrow space between them. And with a jolt so strong it almost knocked him into next week—*Connor suddenly knew.*

He had no reason to know, but he knew—because the *something* was written on her face as clear as day. Not hidden. Not even an attempt made at hiding it from him.

He swore. 'You lost a baby before, didn't you?'

Shannon stared at him for a long while, her arms wrapping around her waist as if she was still cold—in a hot room with a sweater on.

Then she looked over his shoulder. And nodded.

Connor thrust himself upright, his words coming out on a wave of frustration. 'What about the baby's father—wasn't he there for you? Tell me you didn't go through that alone!'

Shannon visibly baulked, stepping back from him so that her back was pressed against the wall, her eyes wide with what Connor immediately recognized as—fear. She tilted her head, pursing her lips together as she stared at him with tears brimming over her bottom lashes.

This wasn't the Shannon he knew—the one who had fought him off for so long, the one who had taken on the woes of a building full of people, the one who met him halfway in everything, and then some. *Why* would she be afraid to tell him? Unless.

His heart stopped. *No.*

But before he could ask the question a nurse appeared

through the open doorway, staring at both of their faces with a curious expression before she smiled at Shannon and handed her a slip of paper.

'That's your prescription, Miss Hennessey. Plenty of fluids as well and you should shift the end of that bug you have.' She turned her attention to Connor. 'And make sure she doesn't go trying to lift something that heavy again too, won't you?'

Connor nodded dumbly.

So Shannon stepped in, filling the silent void with the obvious question. 'I can go now?'

'Yes, just make sure you visit your GP.'

'I will.'

Connor stepped back, allowing her to go through the door ahead of him, neither of them speaking until the lift doors swished shut.

Where he finally asked the question that was burning like acid in the pit of his stomach. 'You didn't have heatstroke when you were in hospital in the States, did you?'

He didn't look at her as the doors opened on another floor, an elderly man stepping in to join them as Shannon managed a small-voiced, 'No, I didn't.'

The elderly man got out a floor before them, where they were joined by two nurses. And Connor frowned at the intrusion. But he didn't want to hear what Shannon had to say in a lift or in the car park. Taking her back home wasn't an option either—not with the last of the party preparations ensuring there would be a crowd to hear what they were talking about.

It was entirely too personal for that.

So when they stepped out of the lift he grasped her elbow in a firm hold, his calm tone not even hinting at the myriad of conflicting emotions he currently felt.

'We'll go to my hotel.'

Shannon nodded in silence, her chin rising so that he knew she was preparing herself for confrontation.

So, to make sure she was in no doubt whatsoever, he leaned in closer to add, 'And no more lies—nothing held back. I *mean* it.'

Shannon endured the awful silence between them in the car as Connor guided them through Friday-night traffic to the hotel. Her eyes fixed on her reflection in the side window and beyond to the faces of all the smiling, laughing people in the streets heading out for a night of fun in bars and nightclubs. Their lives looked so simple in comparison to where hers was now. Smiling, laughing, happy—the polar opposites of everything she was feeling.

But she had known this day would come. Hadn't she?

'No more lies,' Connor had said.

The hotel was way too expensive for her to have ever visited before, but she didn't even glance at the marbled columns or the beautiful bouquets of flowers that scented the air around them. She didn't even look at Connor as he strode purposefully through the giant foyer, nodding to the concierge who greeted him by name.

But she was so very conscious of the fact that this was Connor's new world. It was almost representative of the vast distance between them.

She, who had been happy, she'd thought, building a simple life, surrounded by warm people who had welcomed her into their lives without any questions or explanations of what had happened before she'd met them. Connor, who, although he was still finding his feet in his new life, had only taken a temporary break in that world, until he found out what had happened before, when he would leave and step straight back into this new world, wouldn't he?

She'd been a rabbit in the headlights since he'd come back, hadn't she?

Still hugging her arms tightly around her waist, she glanced briefly around the pristinely clean room with its perfectly co-ordinated soft furnishings. Then down at her loose sweater, worn jeans, and tattered trainers.

'Were you *ever* planning on telling me?'

She straightened as Connor's voice sounded close behind her, the strain in his voice clear.

'Yes.' It was the truth, whether he chose to believe it or not. Finding the right time had been the biggest problem of all even when it had happened—finding the right time in the here and now to right the wrong that had been done so long ago, twice as hard. And letting him go the main reason she couldn't bring herself to do it since she had had him back again and discovered that how she felt about him was stronger than it had been before.

So much for the theory she'd had on seven-year cycles!

'What about back then, Shannon? Did it occur to you that I might have wanted to know I was going to be a father?'

'Yes.' It had more than occurred to her. But the simple fact was, she hadn't told him, and then it had been too late. Their baby had been dead and she had been alone.

Connor appeared in front of her, grasping her elbow in a similar hard hold to the one he had used when they had come out of the lift at the hospital. And he looked so angry, so dis-appointed in her—

It opened the dam inside her as he swore viciously beneath his breath.

But what had she expected? It was an echo of the pain he'd felt when he'd found out about his own father. And he'd been so very angry about that.

'Then why didn't you? Did you think I wouldn't care—that I wouldn't want to know—that I wouldn't *be there?*'

She snatched her elbow free. 'You think I didn't want you there? As far as I knew, you didn't even know it was me that night! How was I supposed to call you out of the blue and announce you were going to be a father?'

'By picking up the phone! I *knew* it was you!'

'*I* didn't know that!' Her voice cracked as tears spilled over her lashes, any semblance of control she had left evaporating. 'And if you think that I didn't want you there then you have no idea how much I used to love you! I loved you so much that leaving you almost killed me—but I only *thought* I knew what it felt like to die inside. I only *thought* I knew how much one person could hurt to lose someone until—until—the second that—until—'

She turned away in frustration as words failed her. Because she needed him to understand. And in order to do that she needed to be as clear and lucid as possible.

Connor was staring at her with what looked like horror on his face when she finally looked at him again. Then he scowled hard, shaking his head as he began to pace in front of her, which gave her time to take deep, shaking breaths while she swiped the tears off her face with her palms.

When she spoke again, she had almost managed to put the flat tone back into her voice—almost. Only the odd word shook when she spoke.

'I was so miserable when I got there. I don't think I had dealt with my nan's death, and then there was leaving you—

even though I knew I had to leave you—winning the scholarship for that course was my only chance to try and make a life for myself. I just wanted that one night. I wanted to be with you—because I didn't want someone else the first time. I didn't want it to be someone I didn't love.' She took another long breath. 'And it was, it was—'

'Yes, *it was*. And yet the first thing you said when I saw you again was how much you'd regretted it. How it had been the worst mistake you ever made.'

The fact that his tone had changed from frustrated to husky tore her in two inside, so that her attempt at control started to slip again. 'Because I knew what the outcome of it was. I can never, ever think about that night without thinking of all the pain that came after it.'

Connor's jaw clenched hard, so that he spoke from between gritted teeth. 'I want to know all of it. Every single bit. When did you miscarry?'

The sob came from low inside her, from the dark place where the agony still lived. 'I didn't miscarry.'

The pacing stopped immediately, all the colour draining from his gorgeous face.

Shannon turned her head so that she couldn't see the torment in his eyes, her gaze focusing on the empty middle distance as she rhymed off the details with a series of shuddering breaths, sobs, and occasional wiping of her cheeks with the end of one sleeve of her sweater.

'I did have heatstroke when I got there. I was sick for weeks one way or another. And I thought it was because I was so tired and so miserable. They kept us on the go all the time at the activity centre—swimming, hiking, trampolining, abseiling. It never once occurred to me—I mean—I just thought

I'd messed up my cycle—I never thought. And then—when I knew—it was like I'd been given this amazing gift. I had a part of you inside me. I could have a family again—someone I could love without trying to hide how I felt. I rehearsed a dozen different ways of telling you—I wrote letters—'

'I never got any letters.'

'I didn't send them.'

'Why not?'

She blinked away the fat tears on her lower lashes, risking a quick glance at him while wiping her cheeks again. 'I'd been talking to Tess and she told me you were seeing someone.'

Connor frowned hard. 'Who was I seeing?'

'I don't know—Sharon someone.'

He swore again.

'I tore the letters up. I told myself that I couldn't tell you if you were already seeing someone else. It wouldn't be fair. It would be like I was trapping you.'

He swore again.

And Shannon grimaced at the sound of each sharp expletive. 'When I heard you weren't seeing her any more I wanted to tell you then but—'

When she fought to hold back an uncontrollable bout of savage sobbing, Connor stepped in closer. *'But?'*

It took several moments before she could speak, her arms wrapped firmly round her waist as she gave up on wiping her cheeks and instead tried to hold the debilitating cramping agony inside where she had locked it all this time.

'He stopped moving. He stopped moving and for days I didn't think there was anything wrong. But he had stopped moving—and when I went—when I saw the doctor—he said…'

She took a massively large breath and choked out the rest. 'He told me that it was too late. The baby, he had—well, his heart—you see, it had stopped beating. And I had to go all the way through labour knowing that I wouldn't have a baby—our baby—at the end of it. Because he was already dead.'

CHAPTER FIFTEEN

IT WAS TOO MUCH to watch Shannon's pain, take it all in, and deal with his own emotions as he processed it all. Connor had promised himself that he would kill whoever it was had hurt her so badly, when all along it had been him.

He had caused her this pain because he hadn't fought to keep her when he should have.

In the midst of the conflicted emotions he felt, he found only one question to force out. '*He?* The baby was a "he"?'

She nodded.

And Connor badly wanted to throw something. To shout and yell at the unfairness of never having been told so that he'd have had a chance to be there.

But just how much Shannon had already suffered was written all over her—in her glistening eyes; in the almost translucent paleness of her face; in the hunch of her shoulders, and the stance she had adopted hugging her arms around herself. She was trying to hold the something inside the way she had all along.

Since the day she had watched him with the kids in her group. When she must have looked at him with them and thought of the child she had lost.

The something had to be agonizing. It was hell for him and he hadn't lived through it.

For better or for worse.

That was the decision he'd already made, wasn't it? And this definitely fell into *worse*. Connor couldn't think of anything worse.

Enough was enough. So, with a low groan, he stepped forwards and hauled her into his arms, crushing her to him. When she struggled, he held tighter, when she finally succumbed and sobbed against his shirt, he looked to the heavens for strength to be the man she needed him to be.

She should never have had to go through it alone, 'I should have been there.'

Her head shook back and forth against him, lifting back a little so he could hear her words. 'I never gave you the choice. It was my fault, Connor—all of it. And if we hadn't ended up together again I don't know that I could ever have searched you out to tell you. And that makes me as much of a liar as everyone else who has hurt you this last while by keeping secrets. I should never have let this happen with us again. But I couldn't stop it.'

'I didn't give you a big choice this time round. It's what I should have done the first time. But you sneaked out in the middle of the night and I never got a chance to talk to you again. I let my pride get in the way.'

'I couldn't take a chance on you figuring out it was me—'

'That didn't go so well.'

'I know that now. But I didn't then.' She sniffed, and he could hear in her voice that she was getting back some of her control—though her voice was lacking that deathly calm, emotionless edge that he had learned to hate so much lately. 'But it wouldn't have stopped me I don't think—from leaving, I mean. I thought about it from so many different angles after I'd left. And it didn't matter what had happened—you didn't feel the way I did. I'd have told you if—I'd have let you know if—'

Connor tightened his arms around her, reassuring her that he understood without her having to say the words. 'I wish you had told me. I won't say that I don't. But it was seven years ago, Shannon. It can't be changed.'

Finally her arms reached up to circle his waist, wrapping around and holding on equally tight as he held her while she pressed her cheek against his shirt, directly above his heart. 'I wanted you there. So much. I can't tell you how much. After it happened, when I was alone—'

'*Stop.*' He squeezed his arms again.

'No.' Her head rose and she looked up at him with her large green eyes filling with tears again. 'I want you to know everything Connor. All of it.'

And as difficult as it would be to hear, he wanted to know all of it. So that there wouldn't be any more secrets between them. Without a doubt, as far as he was concerned, this was the beginning for them. It had to be done right. So he nodded.

After a moment, focusing on the hollow at the base of his throat, she took a breath and told him the rest. 'When it was all over, there was a long time when I didn't think I would ever get out of bed again. I wanted to die. But eventually I found a way to get through the day.' She glanced upwards from below lashes still thick with the diamond bright sparkles of her tears. 'It never goes away—the pain of it—it never does. And I don't think I remembered what it felt like to be really happy again until I came to Galway.'

Connor saw the tiny wistful smile when she looked up at

him again. 'When you found a family inside that run-down old building.'

'Yes.' The smile remained. 'I'd forgotten about the ability of the Irish to laugh and smile, no matter what life throws their way. And some of those people have had a much worse time than I had—have lost loved ones, fought through illness, had days when they had to scrape together enough money to feed their kids that night. And they still get together and laugh and tell jokes. They taught me that one person can get through more than they think they can. They're my family—every single one of them. And in that building I had my first real home in a very long time.'

'Until I came to take it away from you.'

A nod. 'Until you came to take it away from me.'

Now he knew why she had fought him so hard at the beginning. It had taken him a long time to understand even half of it, but now that he had the whole story...

'It makes sense now.'

Her hands smoothed up his back as she loosened her hold on him a little. 'At first I felt like it was some kind of punishment. I don't expect that you'll understand that, but it was how it felt. And I fought that—especially when you were so—'

'Disagreeable?' He raised an eyebrow.

'Well, yes. I just thought, no, I've paid for my mistakes for so long. I can't keep paying for them.'

'And I don't want you to either—let's just get that clear. You went through all that on your own—that's more than enough punishment. But you're not the only one who made mistakes.'

Oh, no, because Connor could see everything clearly now. Suddenly everything made sense. Like the pieces of a puzzle slotting into place. *Finally.*

But his words seemed to stir up more pain, her voice cracking again. 'But it *was* my fault. No matter what way you look at it—what happened to our baby was my fault. If I'd known sooner—if I'd taken better care of myself—if I'd noticed he'd stopped moving sooner—'

'Stop.' He hauled her in tight again. 'Stop doing that, Shannon. I mean it. Sometimes things are just beyond our control. It's the way it is and nothing we can do now can change it. You can't live your whole life torturing yourself over it any more than I can change things and go back to stop you from leaving in the first place. What happened, happened. All we can do is try and make things right from here on in.'

Yes, he'd learnt a lot this last few months, hadn't he? And most of it due to her.

Her head tilted back, green eyes wide with stark astonishment. 'How can you say that? How can you forgive me for keeping all this from you, especially after everything you've been going through this last while? What I did—by not telling you—is just as bad as the secret your mother kept from you. You were so very angry with her. And even knowing that I still allowed myself to get involved with you—because when it comes to you I just can't seem to stop myself. It's always been that way. *Always*. And the number of times when you made love to me and held me and I still couldn't find the words to tell you…'

As her words tickled away into silence he saw how all he had said and done recently had to have added to her sense of guilt and her pain. She had been holding back from him since they'd got back together because he had given her no choice. He had walked into her life, threatened to take away the one place that meant something to her after years of being unhappy and alone, and then he had gone on and on about being lied to, his sense of betrayal, his anger at his family—no matter how much he loved them.

Yet even while he had been unwittingly making things worse, she had still fought the bit out with him to make him see sense, to yell at him about the way he was behaving, to allow him—despite what she thought—with *considerable* persuasion back into her life, and to then encourage him to build bridges with the people that loved him.

She had done all of that—*for him.* Did she think he would push her away after all that? Didn't she know what it had been like for him without her?

'There's something you need to know about that time when I was so angry at the world. We need everything from those missing seven years out in the open. And now that you've bared your soul to me I want to tell you. Because I do know about that sense of being punished for something. It was how I felt when the letter came from Frank's solicitors.'

A small vertical line appeared between her shining eyes, confusion written all over her face. 'What did you feel you had to be punished for?'

He managed to tear his gaze from hers, looking around the large suite he had barely spent any time in for weeks now before he unwrapped his arms from her slender frame to take her hand and lead her to a sofa. 'Over here.'

And she followed without any resistance—trusting him enough to sit down at his side, to allow her hands to be folded in his where they lay on her lap.

Damn, but he loved this woman. And all of the strength it had taken her to get where they were now.

'When we had that big row the night of the museum do,

we both threw at each other the fact that there were things that had happened when we were apart, remember?'

'I remember. That was the sex-versus-making-love issue night.'

'Yes.' He smiled slowly. 'Now that you've told me about your missing seven years, I'm going to do the same. And when I'm done you'll realize that I've been just as miserable without you as you've been without me. The reason all this happened was because we weren't honest with each other back then—that's not going to happen this time.'

Two more silent tears dropped slowly off the end of her lashes, trickling down her cheeks, mesmerizing him. And in that moment he vowed to himself that those would be the last. Tonight would be the last time she would have to cry about anything wrapped up in their relationship. Past, present, or future.

'I don't think I understood what had been wrong with me until I saw you again. Being with you has made sense of it.' He took a breath to give himself time to get it all straight. 'I was angry for a long time before that letter even came. You left—and I spent years being angry and resentful about that. I thought you had played me. And I swore that would never happen again. I would never get sucked into something that wasn't solely on my terms. Rory was always the responsible one—he took that kind of thing on for everyone, it was just in him. I think he flourished under it. But he also got to go away and do what he wanted to do, which left the responsibilities at home on my shoulders. And I did it. But I resented him for it. I thought that he got to breeze back and forth playing some kind of hero while I got to sit at home and keep everything ticking along in his absence. He forced a life on me I didn't want.'

'I thought you enjoyed running the gyms? You did such a good job of them. Tess was never done singing your praises.'

'I did enjoy it. But I was restless. Rory was out in the Middle East doing something he believed in and I felt trapped by the responsibility he left behind. We even argued about it when he got sent home the time he was injured and met Cara. And I even felt jealous of him for that—everything seemed so easy for him. He got to join the army when he wanted to, live a well-paid adventure when he wanted to, meet someone he could spend the rest of his life with at just the right time for him to come home and settle down. And I resented the hell out of him for that. So, when the letter came and we argued—a lot of that came spilling out while I was so angry. Suffice to say—it wasn't as easy for him as I'd always thought it was. I was wrong. I had to apologize to him for that when I saw him last night.'

Shannon turned her small hands inside his, her fingers weaving with his before she gave them a squeeze of encouragement. 'Go on.'

He took another breath, looking up into her eyes, 'To me, finding out I wasn't a part of the family the way I'd thought I was was like some kind of punishment for not realizing what I had. I'd been so resentful of how restless I'd felt for so long that I needed a kick in the ass to make me think straight. And then, when I saw you, I think I knew. It just took me a while to figure it out. I guess at the end of the day I have Frank McMahon to thank, ironically. If he hadn't left me that building I might never have met you again. And then I might never have known the truth.'

Her breath caught, her voice a whisper. 'Which is?'

'That I'd spent all that time missing you. I should never

have let you go—I should have followed you over there and dragged you back. And now that I know what you went through without me, I'm all the more certain that that's what I should have done. Then we could have spent those seven years together and not had to put each other through all this, this time round.'

Untangling one hand, he lifted it to the side of her face, smiling when she leaned into his palm as his fingers threaded into her hair. 'You were wrong about how I felt. I loved you then, Shannon, I should have told you that but I always assumed you knew. And the fact that you knew and still left killed me. I walked around for months angry at you. Then I dated Sharon for a while to try and forget you. But it was too soon. So I buried myself in the work I resented and became a serial dater for a while. But none of them were you. I never loved anyone else the same way.'

Shannon's answer was anguished. 'I didn't know Connor, I swear. If I'd known I wouldn't have left.'

'And if I'd known then that *you* loved *me* I wouldn't have given you a choice. We both got it wrong. And we've both paid a price for getting it that wrong. Now we've got a chance to put it right again.'

More tears fell down her cheeks, some of them into his palm where her cheek was nestled, so he brushed them away with his thumb, leaning in closer to her to continue in a low voice.

'You still love me, Shannon Hennessey. I know you do. Because ever since I found you again you've done nothing but force me to think about the kind of person I'd become. To make me open my eyes and see what was really worth hanging onto. And you did that even though every day with me reminded you of what you went through on your own. You love me. And, like you said, I'm still a work in progress, so there's no way I'm letting you go again. I need you.'

Her answering smile was as bright as her nickname of old. 'Yes, I still love you. I never stopped, even when loving you hurt, even when I hated you—I never stopped. All this while I've been convinced that when I told you everything I would lose you. And I would have understood that. But I wanted to hold onto you for as long as I could. Because I love you more now than I did then. I was young then. Now I'm all grown up and I know better how hard it is to find something like this.'

Releasing his other hand, he framed her face, leaning in closer to inform her in no uncertain terms, 'You won't lose me. Get that straight. You've got me. You had me again at that first dumb T-shirt. And as to you being scared—*nah.*' He shook his head. 'You're the bravest woman I know. You went through all of that on your own when you didn't have to and you came out the other side and still took a chance on us again.'

'Well, I did try for a while to keep you at arm's length but you wouldn't let me, remember?'

'And why do you think that might be?'

The way that her gorgeous eyes shimmered at him told him that she knew the answer now.

So he leaned in further and claimed her mouth, tasting the saltiness on her lips from her tears as he kissed the last of them away.

And the familiar heat between them fired immediately; as if all of the confessions had somehow seeded a deep need in them to finally let out in one go all the emotion that they had been holding back.

Connor kissed the corners of her mouth, her cheeks, her eyes, her forehead, down the side of her face to the neck she automatically tilted his way, while she told him again, 'I love you, Connor Flanaghan.'

He leaned back long enough to pull her sweater over her head, before he kissed her again, the words husky against her mouth.

'And I love you. I've been trying to show you how much this last while by making love to you every chance I got. I don't know how you didn't know that.'

Shannon lifted her hands and framed his face, her eyes filled with emotion. 'Show me again and I promise I'll listen this time.' She took a breath. 'But I don't want anything between us again. I want a baby with you, Connor. Not to replace the one we lost, 'cos that'll never happen. But I want children with you. I want us to have a family. I know that's not maybe what a lot of people our ages want, but I don't care.'

'Then we'll just stay in bed until we make one.' He leaned his forehead against hers. 'All that time when I knew there was something you were holding back from me I thought that it was that you'd fallen in love with someone else and he had broken your heart. So I decided I would spend as long as it took getting you to trust me and love me. Even earlier on, when I was being such a pain, I kept coming back to argue with you and listen to everything you threw at me—even when I didn't realize why I kept coming back. But somewhere inside I knew why I was doing it. I wasn't letting you go again. I'm never letting you go again. We're going to get married and have dozens of kids and we'll find a house and live happily ever after. It's just that simple.'

Her hands rose to rest on his against her face, her voice back to the confident tone that he loved. 'Yes, to all of those things. I want to spend the rest of my life with you—making love and arguing and making up and laughing and doing all the things that other couples who love each other do. I want you to bring bags of Dolly Mixtures for us to eat on film nights—like the boiled sweets that old man in front us that night does every week for his wife, and has done every Friday night for forty years.'

Connor's smile grew. 'You didn't tell me that.'

'I thought you'd read something into it at the time—having just done the same thing for me. When you remembered them that night I think I knew then that I wasn't going to be able to resist you this time round. It frightened the life out of me. So I tried pushing you away again. But you wouldn't go. And I couldn't resist when you wouldn't go.'

'I'm irresistible. That's basically what you're saying?'

'Heaven help me—yes it is.'

'Good.' He kissed her again, long and slow, feeling her lean into him as his body started to tighten with need. So he lifted his mouth an inch from hers to tell her, 'Then let's start right now with making that family. As one of six I have a tradition to uphold.'

'And then we can go to the party tomorrow night and tell Mario he's going to get his wish to be a bridesmaid…'

'The hell we will.'

Shannon laughed, the sound warming his heart in a way it hadn't been warmed in seven years. She was his. For better or worse. Together they could get through anything. Apart they were both giant big train wrecks.

Maybe that was part of what that dumb film he'd watched with her had been about? Who knew?

As he stood and tugged her to her feet, his eyes dropped to the message on her T-shirt. And when he looked at her face, she was lifting her chin, obviously having read it herself.

She grinned at him. 'It's my favourite one.'

Connor read it again: 'Here I am. Now what are your other two wishes?'

He laughed, leaning in to kiss her soundly again as he led her to the huge bed on the other side of the room. 'I need one that says "Marry me and make love every day for the rest of our lives."'

Shannon was already reaching for the buttons on his shirt. 'Then I'll need one that says "Yes to all of the above."'

And Connor proceeded to show her he was very happy with that answer.

The slow and torturous way.

Look out for
Mills & Boon® TEMPTED™ 2-in-1s,
from September

*Fresh, contemporary romances
to tempt all lovers of
great stories*

Special Offers

Every month we put together collections and longer reads written by your favourite authors.

Here are some of next month's highlights— and don't miss our fabulous discount online!

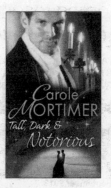

On sale 6th September   On sale 6th September   On sale 16th August

Save 20%
on all Special Releases